JAMES CALBRAITH

THE YEAR OF THE DRAGON

Published by Flying Squid, May 2013

eISBN: 978-83-936713-0-4

ISBN: 978-83-936713-1-1

Visit James Calbraith's official website at

jamescalbraith.com

for the latest news, book details, and other information

Map Illustration: Jared Blando (Eurasia, Chinzei)

and Flying Squid (Orient, Gwynedd)

Inside illustrations: Victoria Shaad and hanyasatu

Cover Art: Collette J Ellis

Cover Design: Flying Squid

E-Book formatting: Flying Squid

TABLE OF CONTENTS

GOTO
ISLANDS
DETAIL

CHINZEI
IN THE BEGINNING OF THE
ANSEI ERA

BLANDO 12

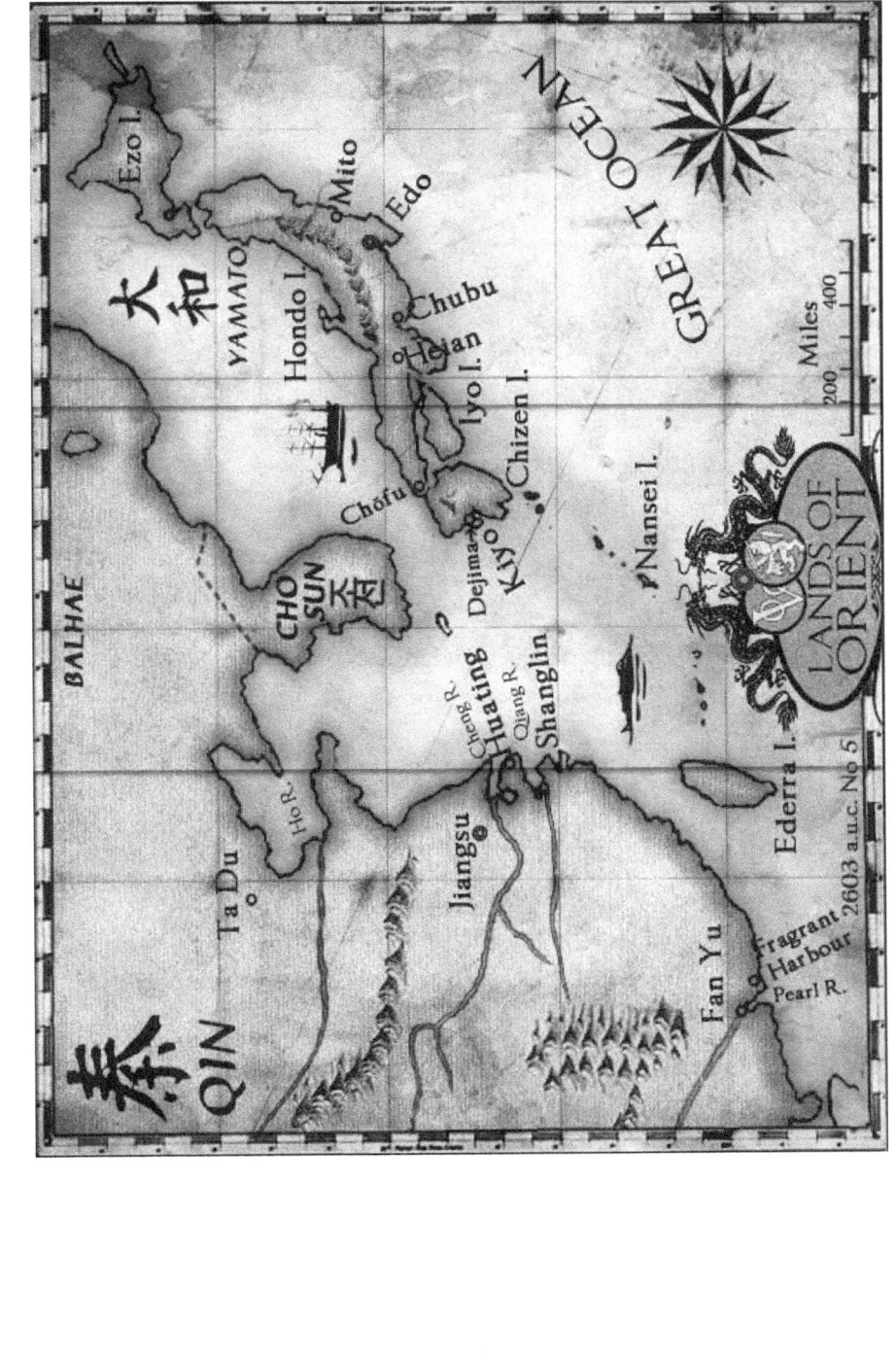

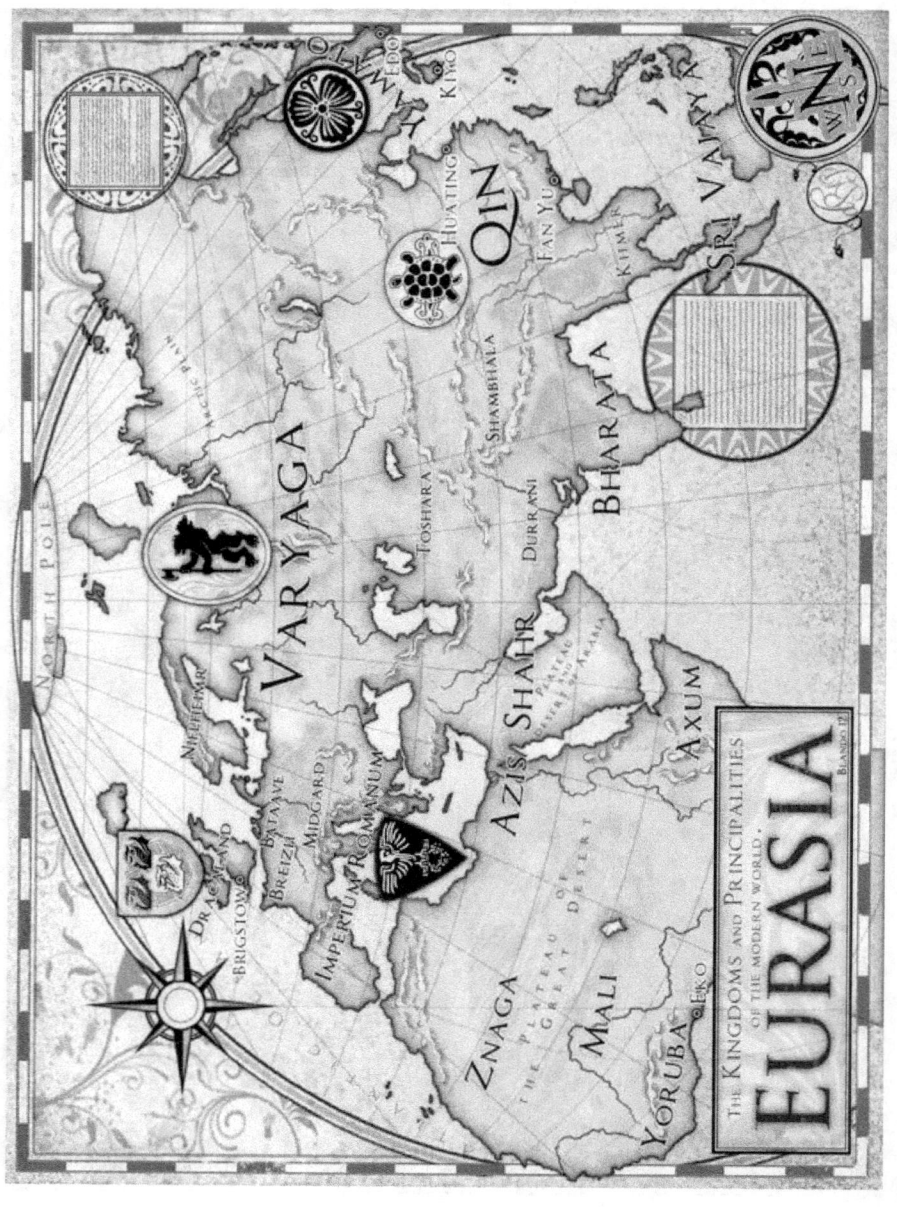

THE BIRKENHEAD DRILL

It came out of the fog.

An old, ghostly, Bataavian man-o-war, glowing crimson, its tattered black sails full even though the sea was silent for miles. Gunports open wide along the broadside; cannons primed and ready to fire. And not a soul on board.

The look-out was the first to cry the words everyone knew and dreaded in these seas south of the Cape: "The Flying Bataavian! Straight ahead!"

Prone to superstition, the sailors fell into disarray. The captain and the officers tried to stem the chaos, but it was too late. Panic spread like wildfire. The helmsman, deaf to the orders, turned the Birkenhead to the starboard to evade the wraith ship coming towards them.

A terrible sound of iron plating searing and the wooden hull cracking, splintering and tearing came from the bottom of the Birkenhead as it struck an unseen reef. The frigate shook and stalled.

"Astern! Astern!" cried the captain, and the crew obliged — backwards seemed the only possible way to go. The ghostly Bataavian was now almost upon them. The paddle-wheels turned with effort and the frigate started sliding off the rock. That was a deadly mistake. The sea rushed into the hole, the plates buckled, the bulkheads ripped open. Whoever was still under the deck drowned in an instant. The flooded engines hissed and stopped. The Birkenhead began to break in two.

"Drop the anchor!" the captain cried. "Lower the quarter boats! Women and children first!"

The thick oaken door of his cabin muffled the sounds of alarm whistles and bugles. With no sense of urgency, the old Bataavian physician was packing his meagre belongings into the black leather bag.

"Master von Siebold," the cabin boy pleaded, glancing anxiously at the porthole. He could see nothing through it but raging seawater.

"You go, boy, if you are in such a hurry," the old man said, nodding, "I have witnessed my share of sinkings. It will be hours before the entire ship is submerged."

He hesitated for a moment, picking up the small black lacquer figurine of a dragon. "My dear Ine," he smiled sadly, "I wonder if you found a husband yet?"

The cabin boy could take it no longer and dashed for the door. At the same time, it burst open. Several soldiers grabbed the physician by his black coat, dragging him out onto the deck, their eyes mad with fear and anger. "It's all your fault, Bataavian! Look, your people are coming to get you!" they cried and hissed, pointing towards the ghostly ship. They pulled the old man, still clutching desperately to his black leather bag, over to the side of the quickly sinking frigate, ready to throw him overboard to pacify the angry spirits of the sea.

"Seventy-Fourth! Halt! Are you men or beasts? Stand to attention when an officer speaks!"

A voice demanding immediate respect barked out behind them. The soldiers turned around and stood rigid at once as they faced their regimental commander in full Highland dress, impeccably neat and absurdly out of place in the middle of the southern ocean.

"Release this poor man and get on the poop deck. I will deal with this insubordination later."

The chaos on board was by now mostly under control. Discipline and sense of duty prevailed at last over fear and superstition.

"Doctor," the commander said, reaching out his hand, "if you could please go to the boats. I believe there is still a place."

"Thank you, Colonel Seton, but I'm sure there are younger and more useful men among your crew. I am old, and all my family is lost."

The Colonel looked at the physician for a moment, and then nodded sharply, with respect.

"In that case, I will be honoured to accompany you to the poop deck. All my men are there, awaiting salvation — or death."

Only the stern section of the frigate was still above the water. Soldiers of the Seventy-Fourth and Ninety-First Foot stood, silently, as the ship sank slowly and surely. All the women and children were safely away on the ship's surviving quarter-boats; all the horses driven into the sea so that they might try to swim ashore.

Calm and composed now, the soldiers and the officers observed the Flying Bataavian in its full glory as it passed them by without a single sound, and without firing a single shot.

"What do you think, Doctor?" the Colonel asked, pointing at the ghostly ship disappearing back into the fog.

"An illusion of the Xhosa shamans, no doubt," replied Von Siebold, "they are very crafty with shaping mists and clouds."

"Very crafty indeed," the Colonel said, nodding, "I wonder if we'll ever win this war."

The ship's Captain approached them. "Colonel, we are done for here. Perhaps you should release your men to make for the boats, if they can?"

"Nonsense, Captain. The boats would be swamped. Stand fast, men! We will die like gentlemen!"

"Aye, Sir!"

And so they stood there, valiant, as the water came creeping up to the poop deck, then to their feet, ankles, knees... some of the soldiers started climbing onto the rigging, a few hurled themselves into the abyss, but others remained unmoved, even as another piece of bulwark broke off with a tremendous crash.

"Ho! In the skies!" somebody pointed up.

"Another illusion," spat another.

"No, it looks like... it's dragons!"

The men started cheering as the two brightly-shining dots dived towards them like a couple of bullets, soon growing into mighty silver-scaled dragons. They hovered several feet above the sinking remnants of the Birkenhead, beating their great leathery wings and shaking their horned heads. One was ridden by a man seven feet tall, slim, silver-haired, with vertical pupils in amber eyes like a cat — a Faer Folk. The other rider, black-haired and green eyed, wore the scarlet uniform of a Royal Marines Ardian. He cried out in a firm calm voice.

"Ahoy, there! I'm Ardian Dylan ab Ifor of the Second Dragoons. Is the commanding officer still among you?"

"Lieutenant Colonel Seton, of the Seventy-Fourth Foot, Twelfth Light. Damn nice to see you, Ardian."

"We noticed your signal flares. The Lioness is steaming at full speed and should be here in an hour. Can you hold out that long?"

"We will do our best."

"My dragons can pick up some of the weak and wounded in the meantime," the Ardian said, scratching a scar on his face in thought, "select the first ten, Colonel, we'll be back in no time. Edern, you stay and keep an eye on the sharks."

"Aye, Ardian," the Faer Folk said, saluting.

"Well, Doctor," Colonel Seton turned to the Bataavian, "this time I must insist. You will go with the first sortie. Somebody must take care of the wounded."

"I yield to that," the physician agreed and reached out his hand, "it was an honour to meet you, Colonel."

"Likewise, Doctor," the soldier said and shook the old man's hand with vigour.

Book One

The Shadow Of Black Wings

Unchanging the river flows, and yet the water is never the same.

In the still pools the foam now gathers, now vanishes, never staying for long.

So in the world are men and their dwellings.

Hōjōki

PROLOGUE

A single gear whirred and clicked into place. A valve opened, letting out a thin plume of grey steam with a quiet hiss. A gold-plated dial moved by a notch. A tiny mallet sprang from its compartment, striking the brass gong - one, two, three, four, five, six times.

Master Tanaka looked up in surprise - an hour of the Hare already? He turned towards the window and the pink light of dawn illuminated his face. The temple bell only now started to ring out the time. He sighed then yawned, rubbing tired eyes. Another night had passed without him noticing.

The elementals inside the clock awoke with a soft purr and the automatic brush began to move swiftly inside the glass cloche. A slot opened in the mahogany pedestal and spat out a piece of paper upon which was written the day's divination. Hisashige reached for it absentmindedly, his attention focused on the piece of complex clockwork on which he had been working. He glanced briefly at the calligraphy - *Oku*, "a gift". He smiled to himself and nodded knowingly.

A higher-pitched chime rang eight times – counting out the hours of the Western reckoning. The door slid open noiselessly and a small boy entered the workshop. With his long and angular face, puffed lips and wide straight nose, he bore no resemblance to Master Tanaka.

"It came from Kiyō this morning, Father," the boy said, presenting Hisashige with a large, ornately packed wooden box.

"Excellent!" the old master exclaimed.

He put the box on the workbench beside the clockwork and began to unwrap it eagerly.

"Shūhan-*sama* was supposed to send me some Walcheren glass."

He stopped abruptly and his shoulders sank when he saw the crest on the box, in golden leaf – three lines in a circle. He lifted the lid without enthusiasm. Inside was what seemed like a small human head, completely bald.

"Some *gift*." Hisashige looked at the clock with reproach. "It's just another of Zōzan's broken dolls."

He took out a small paper envelope containing his fee, and gave it to the boy.

"Put it in the treasure box later."

The old master opened a hatch in the top of the doll's head and studied the complex web of gears, cranks and pulleys for a moment. With one swift twist of his fingers, he snapped a rubber band back onto the hooked lever.

"Hardly worth the effort," he murmured, closing the head and the box. "I really need those divinations to be more precise in the new clock."

"Is that the new year-plate?"

The boy craned his neck to see over Hisashige's shoulder to view the mechanism sprawled all over the workbench.

"Yes. You have a good eye, Daikichi," the old master said with a gentle smile.

"Still can't get it to work?"

Hisashige shook his white head.

"Come, I will show you."

He put the loose screws and gears back into place and lifted the plate gingerly. He moved across the workshop to a tall sculpted cabinet of Western make, and opened the oaken door.

There was another clock inside, similar to the one standing in the corner of the room, but larger and with even more dials, switches and levers.

Hisashige inserted the clockwork plate precisely into its slot and turned the key. The gentle warm hum of the elemental engine filled the cabinet. Steam hissed from the valves.

"I don't understand. Everything seems perfect," the old master commented as the dials turned to their desired positions, showing exactly the same time and date as was visible on the old clock. "I can't find any fault within the mechanism. The minute hand is even more precise than before. All the Major Trigrams match. But look at that zodiac dial..."

A round ivory plate turned slowly. Pictures of animals, encrusted in black lacquer, appeared in the glass lens one by one – monkey, rooster, dog, boar, mouse, ox...

"It should stop now," said Hisashige, and the boy nodded.

It had been the Year of the Ox for a few months now – water ox, to be precise. But the plate continued to turn inexplicably past the tiger and hare until, at last, it halted.

The black lacquer silhouette of a coiled sleeping dragon glinted mockingly from the lens.

CHAPTER I

Gwynedd, May, 2606 ab urbe condita

The distance from Llambed to Dinas Bran is computed at seventy miles, as the crow flies. The prevailing wind is north-westerly, steady at fifteen knots along the entire distance. Given an average velocity of an unladen Purple Swift equal to forty knots, and allowing for the pressure pocket of Berwyn Hills – oof!

Bran bumped into someone and dropped the exercise book to the ground, his notes scattering all over the freshly cut grass. He knew who it was just from looking at the thick leather boots. Only the Seaxe wore shoes on the sacred meadow of the Scholars' Grove.

"Honestly, Toadboy, it's as if you wanted to be beaten up," a familiar vile voice mocked.

Bran looked up and sighed. Wulfhere of Warwick towered above him in his impeccable blue uniform. His sky-blue eyes stared at Bran from under a neat flaxen-yellow fringe with disgust.

"Sorry, Wulf." Bran stooped to pick up his papers. "I'm in a hurry for the Octagonometry exam…"

"Pah!" snorted the Seaxe. "What's the point? You and your Toad will never pass the Aerobatics."

"Its name is Emrys," Bran said coldly, "and it can outfly any dragon in this school, including your fat thoroughbred."

Wulfhere narrowed his eyes and tightened his fists. Tiny sparks crackled around his knuckles and Bran prepared himself for a blow. The Seaxe glanced towards the red brick arches of the Southern cloister where the house prefect stood, watchful.

"Out of my way, serf, you're lucky I'm not in the mood today," he scoffed and pushed Bran aside.

The papers scattered again. Gathering his notes, Bran mumbled a Prydain slur, loud enough only for Wulfhere to hear. The Seaxe stopped and turned back slowly.

"What did you just say?"

Bran looked around helplessly. Nobody was coming to his aid, of course; this wasn't a fight worth joining in. Somebody was paying attention though. The red-haired Pictish lass, Eithne, stood under a large oak tree with several giggling friends. Their eyes met. He saw pity and embarrassment in hers, and something inside him sank.

She wore the robes of the Geomancers, although Bran knew her dream was to one day become one of the *Derwydd* – Druids, guarding Gwynedd from their fortress at Mon Island since ancient times. The brown-green, plaid cloak suited her auburn hair and green eyes, framed in a delicate spiral tattoo. They liked each other but never went any further than a few walks under the oak trees and an occasional awkward teenage kiss. In the end their relationship had simply fizzled out, to Bran's sporadic regret.

He repeated the slur, suddenly feeling brave. Now everyone heard him. Several people stopped curiously, waiting to see what would happen. But with only a few days left until the final tests, Bran no longer cared. After the exams none of it would matter, anyway.

"You've done it now, Taffy. You'll have to take your tests in the infirmary!"

The Seaxe grabbed Bran's neck and the boy tensed. With an electric crackle and sizzle, a cloud of painful sparks appeared around Wulfhere's hand. Paralysed, Bran made no sound, though his eyes welled up when he felt his nerve endings scorched. His neck was on fire, but he knew too well the electricity would leave no marks on the skin. The ability to tap into the lightning power of his mount, Eohlsand – a Highland Azure – made Wulfhere's punishments both immensely painful and perfectly undetectable.

Just as Bran felt he could no longer take the pain and would have to cry out for mercy, the provost finally appeared, heading towards them. Wulfhere let go of his victim. Bran fell to the ground, gasping.

"I'll get you next time, Taffy," the Seaxe hissed and shuffled off, unhurriedly.

"Are you alright?" the provost asked, reaching his hand out to Bran. "Did he hurt you?"

"I'm fine," Bran murmured with embarrassment and raised himself slowly, wincing as he massaged his aching neck. He glanced towards the large oak tree. The girl was nowhere to be seen. Sighing, he retrieved his papers from the grass for the third time and headed towards the dormitory cloister.

He tugged both sets of reins sharply and leaned back. The dragon pulled up and rolled on its back in a tight half-loop. Ground whizzed past the top of Bran's head. He jerked the top leeward rein. A leather strap fastened to the base of one of the dragon's horns tightened, and the mount turned upright. With one beat of its leathery wings it caught a strong waft of the Ninth Wind and its flight stabilised. The boy breathed out.

The series of manoeuvres finished, Bran brushed an unruly fringe of black hair out of his flying goggles and bade his mount swoop fast down towards the target range. The dragon needed no guidance here. They had been practising on the range for two years and both knew exactly what to do. The beast turned confidently towards the first objective: a large bale of straw. The dragon's neck stretched in a straight line. Its jaws opened but it coughed to no effect as the target dashed past. Shaking its head, the beast turned around to try again. Again it merely coughed and spluttered with great effort and a thin plume of smoke puffed from the dragon's nostrils.

"What's wrong, Emrys?" Bran asked, distraught.

The dragon whimpered. It could not breathe fire. The boy recognised the acrid smell in the dragon's breath: Iceberry water!

Only one person was capable of such a cruel prank on the day of the exam; but there was no time to think of vengeance and Bran was starting to panic. Seconds were running out, the teachers below were no doubt already frowning at his lack of performance. Not one of the targets had, as yet, been set on fire.

Fire. He didn't need Emrys' breath. He could channel the power of flame himself. It would have a far shorter range and energy, but it could still work. He focused on the Farlink, the mental connection giving him far greater control over the dragon than just reins and knees. The beast, following his unspoken orders, dived once more towards the bale of straw. He only had a split second as the mount sped past the target, whooshing a few feet above the grass at a dazzling speed. He reached out with his fingers.

"*Rhew!*" he cried in Old Prydain spell-tongue.

A blazing bluish spark of dragon fire shot from his fingers. Its tip reached the straw and the bale burst into flames. Elated, he repeated the exercise with the next target, a wooden horse, then with yet another and another, five more times in total. With each objective destroyed his exhaustion grew. Channelling the dragon flame drained his energy immensely, and reduced his control over the magic. His hands began to shake and his fingers grew covered with swollen blisters from the heat. With bleary eyes he searched for the next target, but couldn't find it.

At last, he realized there was none. The exercise was over. He managed to land before the teachers' observation tower, panting, sweating, too tired to even dismount. Struggling to keep his eyes open, he listened to the Master of Aerobatics assessing his trial.

"That was certainly... unorthodox," the teacher said, coughing nervously, "but I appreciate the initiative. You *did* hit all your targets in time, so I have no choice but to pass you."

Initiative? This was not the kind of school that encouraged initiative... Bran sighed deeply and closed his eyes. All thought of revenge disappeared from his mind. It didn't matter anymore. He had passed his final exam and was out of the wretched place at last.

Bran's fingers played with a fiery-coloured tassel on the grip of his heavy cavalry backsword, a proud, solid three feet long single-edged blade, a pattern tested in the Mad King George's wars. The quillon was curved in the shape of a rampant dragon, the brass mountings and circular guard ornamented in the form of claws, flames and leathery wings. The wyvern-hide grip culminated in a pommel sculpted into a dragon's head. Anyone looking at the sword would have little doubt as to its owner's profession.

He sat among thirty other similarly armed boys and girls, all excited and relieved at the same time, all wearing the uniforms of the dragon cadet corps, steel blue with golden stripes. They hailed from all over the Dracaland Empire. Most of them were Prydain, like Bran, with black hair, Roman noses and olive complexion, or the golden-haired, blue-eyed Seaxe from beyond the Dyke. A few dark-eyed Cruthin from Ériu across the sea and tattooed Picts from the northern realm of Alba were keeping to themselves at the back.

The headmaster was nearing the end of his speech. Short and impish, he had to use an ornate mahogany step to reach over the pulpit. His long red beard was forked neatly and tucked under a gem-studded belt. Wind tore on the bushy tufts of his hair – there was no roof above the ruined keep inside which they had all gathered. The headmaster was a Corrie, a member of an ageless race of wrinkly-faced, pointy-eared and red-haired dwarves living among the dales and lakes of Rheged in the North.

The headmaster finished the main part of his speech, waited until the din of whispers quietened and then held up a sword in a trembling hand. The straight, broad blade was rusted and notched in a few places, although the hilt was new, gleaming gold and encrusted with gems.

"It was seven hundred and ten years ago that Owain the Wyrmslayer established this illustrious Academy for the purpose of studying the ways and lore of the mighty Beast, after defeating the Norse dragons at Crug Mawr with this very sword," the headmaster shook the old blade.

He gestured around and Bran's eyes inadvertently followed towards the familiar thick walls of the Great Auditorium, rising towards the sky like the crooked teeth of a long dead giant. Tapestries of red and white dragons had been brought to adorn the cold stones of this vast ancient ruin for the duration of the ceremony. The heavy oaken chairs upon which the teachers were sitting recalled the time of the War of Three Thorns and the realm of Harri Two Crowns. Leaves rustled and sparrows chirped on the branches of ancient oak and elm trees growing in a dense circle around the keep. Far in the distance a booming sound of a siren announced lunch break at the local elemental mine.

"The graduates of the Sixteenth Year of Victoria Alexandrina, the Queen on Dragon Throne! Today you finish your first four years at the Academy. The bards will now take my place on this stage to tell tales of past glory much better than I can. Let me just put a final touch on all of you before I release you into this dangerous ever-changing world."

This was the moment Bran had waited for the whole day. The headmaster straightened himself, full of youthful vigour. He raised Owain's Sword towards the blue sky and whirled it around in a complex pattern. The air sparkled and buzzed with powerful magic, and the fresh scent of ozone spread throughout the auditorium. A flash of dazzling light flared above the heads of the gathered, taking the form of a great white eagle hovering in the blue sky. The raptor shrieked and a shower of stars rained down from under its spread wings, each dazzling star landing upon a shoulder of an astonished student.

"You have all been marked with the Seal of Llambed," explained the headmaster after the spell dissipated. "Those who know how to look will always see it upon you. Bear it proudly. It is not only a sign of education - it is your talisman, a precious gift. Three times in your life you will be able to call upon its power - and it will deliver you from any danger."

A murmur spread throughout the keep. For some of the students this was the first time they had heard of the magic mark and its power, but not so for Bran.

"You will use up your Seal before you know it," his father, Dylan, had told him. "It's only there to help you through the first years of life as a dragon rider outside the school walls."

"When did you use yours for the first time?" the boy had asked. "Was it in a battle?"

He had been only eleven then, just about to enter the Academy, as was expected of the son of a Prydain officer.

"No, nothing as glamorous as that," Dylan replied, chuckling. "I was still in the Academy, getting my baccalaureate. I was racing another boy, one of the Warwicks, along the Dyfrdwy Valley and I broke my dragon's wing under the Pontcysyllte Aqueduct. A hundred feet drop, that is. I had no choice but to call on the White Eagle."

"And what happened?"

"It brought me straight into the Dean's office!" Dylan laughed. "I got a right telling off for wasting a charge so recklessly. But that's how the Seal works – unexpectedly. You never know where it will take you. Other schools have similar charms, but none are that fidgety – or that powerful. It will save your life, always, one way or another."

"*Mages of Llambed! Arise!*" the headmaster's voice boomed.

The school bard entered the podium to lead the choir, and the crowd erupted into the Academy's anthem enthusiastically, startling a flock of sparrows hiding in the branches of an oak tree.

Men of Llambed, on to glory

Victory is hovering o'er ye,

Pride of Prydain stands before ye,

Hear ye not her call?

Rend the skies asunder,

Let the wyrm roar thunder!

Owain's knights fill world with wonder,

Courage conquers all!

Dean Magnusdottir, head of Dracology, a gentle-faced, mousey-haired woman, browsed the piece of paper unhappily.

"Bran ap Dylan gan Gwaelod. I can't say I'm not disappointed," she said, tutting and shaking her head, "your father was – "

"The best student this Academy ever had," muttered Bran, rolling his eyes. "I know, ma'am, but aren't you being a bit unfair? I did quite well where it matters."

"Where it matters, boy? Where it *matters*? Every single subject in this school matters. You have barely passed the athletics, your history knowledge is non-existent and your alchemy score was the worst in your class."

Bran looked down, feigning embarrassment, but he couldn't bring himself to care. He had graduated, and nothing else was important right now. He did not wish to spend anymore unnecessary minutes within the college walls.

"You are a good rider, certainly," continued Madam Magnusdottir, calming down. "One of our best. Your Farlink quotient is frankly astonishing. That much of Dylan's blood shows, and you have his magic talent, of course. You could easily take up wizardry as the second faculty – we could help you develop the necessary skills. But it takes much more to achieve real success in a dragon rider's career. In truth, I would rather you stayed in school for four more years. Catch up a bit on the old *scientia vulgaris*."

Bran looked up, startled.

What?

Stay in school for four more years? That seemed like such a nightmare right now. Besides, usually remaining for a baccalaureate was considered a reward, not punishment for bad grades.

"Think about it, my boy," the dean insisted when Bran did not reply, "you have time until October, hmm? Will you consider?"

"Er... I will, ma'am." Bran hesitated. "Will there be anything else, ma'am?" he asked, reaching for his diploma.

The teacher stalled, still holding the paper.

"Son," she said, looking earnest, "I don't mean it in a bad way, but - we could get you a better dragon if you remained with us."

Bran stood up, barely concealing his anger.

"There is nothing wrong with Emrys!" he exclaimed. "How many more times do I have to prove it to you all?" He grabbed the diploma from the teacher's grasp, tearing off a bit in the corner. "This is all my father's doing, isn't it?"

"I assure you, your father had nothing – "

"I've heard quite enough, ma'am." Bran raised his hand. "I bid you farewell."

He turned around and stormed outside, heading straight toward the stables.

CHAPTER II

Yamato, Spring, 6th year of Kaei era

Hendrik Curzius sweated profusely.

A servant brought him another silk handkerchief and took away the previous one, damp and smelly. The wizard put the cold wet cloth to his bald forehead. *And it's only May*, he thought. *What an accursed place.*

The Nansei Islands lay far to the south of Yamato. Even in the deepest winter it never got really cold around there. In spring the weather became fickle, alternating between gusts of cold northerly winds, bringing showers of freezing rain, penetrating to the bone, and waves of heat coming from beyond the southern horizon, foreshadowing the unbearable tropical summer - like today.

"I wish there was somewhere else we could meet," said Curzius, quaffing cold spring water from a clay cup.

"You know very well it's impossible, Overwizard-*dono*. We can never be seen together. Only this island is truly free of the *Taikun*'s spies."

The man speaking these words was broad-shouldered, balding, had a long oval face and close-set eyes. He wore the flowing silk robe of a Yamato aristocrat. His name was Nariakira Shimazu.

The small cosy villa they were in belonged to this man, as did the garden around it, filled with the fresh scent of azaleas exploding everywhere in bursts of maddening pink. In fact, the entire island and the surrounding archipelago was Nariakira's property. This was one of the most powerful men in the country, a daimyo – lord of a province. Curzius recalled what little he had learned about the complex feudal power structure of the Yamato from a small booklet given to him before he had left Bataave to take over the post of the Overwizard of the trading factory at Dejima. Below the daimyo were their many retainers, forming the samurai warrior class. Above them – the Tokugawa *Taikuns*, a dynasty of generals ruling from the eastern capital of Edo. And watching over all of this, at least nominally, was the half-divine *Mikado,* an emperor-like figure whose true name could never be spoken without first ritually purifying one's lips.

But the *Mikado* had no real power over Yamato, and even the *Taikun* had no power over the Nansei Islands. This was the Shimazu clan's sole domain, by right of conquest and cunning. Never officially recognised as part of the greater Yamato archipelago, the islands were suspended in a kind of diplomatic limbo. They had their own laws, own customs, even own language. The government's edicts did not reach the islands and the foreigners could come and go as they pleased – as long as they knew how to reach them, of course, and for the last two hundred years this had limited the number of visitors to just the Bataavians.

He waved a paper fan, desperately trying to cool himself enough to think clearly. What he had come to discuss with Lord Nariakira required his utmost concentration. Curzius may have been a newcomer to Yamato, but he was an experienced diplomat and had been thoroughly briefed by his predecessor. He could only hope it was enough to deal with the deceptively gentle-faced man before him.

"Three hundred years ago, when the Westerners first arrived in Yamato, we were all awestruck and terrified of your power and wealth," he started. They were conversing in his own language which the daimyo knew fluently. "It was the same with Qin and Bharata, and Sri Vajaya, and everywhere else in the Orient. There were just so many people in the world, so many riches, so many warriors! We could only hope to gain some profit by subterfuge and cunning, never by force. Yamato itself had more men than Rome's entire Imperium, Qin, ten times of that, and in those days of sword and musket, sheer numbers mattered most. Now the Bharata jungles are overrun with mercenary armies led by Dracalish generals. The Qin is thrown to its knees by the West, and everyone is looking for the next conquest. There are not many left here in the East."

Lord Nariakira nodded. Curzius guessed the daimyo must have been well aware of the recent events in Qin - the Cursed Weed trade, the Emperor's futile edicts, the countless rebellions and the war so badly lost by the imperial army.

If mighty Qin fell so quickly, what hope was there for Yamato?

"When you first arrived, you were but children and we were like your ancient ancestors," the daimyo said, pausing often. "Your priests like beggar monks at the *Mikado*'s court, your merchants like village peddlers trying to hawk their wares on the festival market. Now the children have far outgrown the parents. The teachers have fallen asleep, their *dōjō* overgrown with moss, while the world outside turns faster and faster. How many people live in your greatest cities now?"

"More than a million in Ker Ys, twice as many in Lundenburgh," answered Curzius.

And only two hundred thousand in Noviomagus, he thought, *but you don't need to know that.*

"*Pah!*" The daimyo clapped his knee in an expression of helplessness. "That's already more than Edo, and I bet it won't stop at that. How is it that you can spawn so fast?"

"It is not that we bear more children than you; our medicine and science help us keep more people alive. You may have your shrine healers, but we have conquered the pox and cholera, and those kill thousands more than battle injuries. Our crops are more plentiful, our storage and transportation systems more efficient, so we keep famine at bay. There are also many other improvements that allow us to combat death and disease. You know it as well as I do - we finally caught up with the East."

Nariakira nodded again.

"Yes, the world outside seems to spin much faster than in Yamato. It's as if every year passing on the Sacred Islands is merely a day in the lands of the West. The Divine *Mikado* in his everlasting palace and the illustrious *Taikun* behind the impregnable walls of his castle are barely aware of what's happening just outside their shores."

"The winds of history blow fast and strong, Shimazu-*dono*."

"I know what you're after, Curzius-*sama*. Don't think that your reports to the *Taikun* are the only source of my knowledge of the West."

The Overwizards of Dejima were responsible for providing news of events overseas to the court in Edo. They had abused this monopoly to produce reports that were increasingly further from the truth, as Bataave was losing its significance as a major Western power. The *Taikun* had no knowledge of the revolutions rolling through the continent, or of how close the Kyrnosian Imperator and his invincible legions had come to vanquishing the tiny merchant republic sixty years before. How the small nation had been split even further by wars and rebellions and economic crises, how they were slowly losing their hold on all colonies, until only the precious trade monopoly of Dejima remained as the main source of income. All this was omitted from the annual report on "Western matters".

"You are as frightened of other Westerners as the *Taikun* himself, aren't you?" Nariakira continued. "That is why you came to me so eagerly, because, unlike the old Tokugawa, I understand your plight and can assist you - *if* you assist me. What is that funny saying in your country? You scratch my back…"

"…I'll scratch yours," Curzius said, nodding.

"I hope there can be a mutual understanding between the two of us. I have great respect for the men of your talent."

Curzius sensed a hanging "but". Respect did not mean leniency.

"I know of the little network of friends and allies to your cause that your predecessor has been building around the Southern provinces," Nariakira pressed.

"It is well known that your web of spies is second only to that of the *Taikun* himself," Curzius said, having no choice but to admit the truth.

"There was barely need for spying; you Westerners are too clumsy. I also know why you asked to see me today, but be warned - a daimyo's price is far greater than that of some grey-haired scholar or masterless samurai."

"Of course, I am prepared to make many concessions."

"Ah, concessions. Is a warship an acceptable concession?"

The Overwizard's eyes narrowed.

"What kind of a warship?"

"A mistfire engine," said the daimyo, and started counting on his fingers. "Hull clad in iron plate, armed with repeating cannons, lightning throwers and rockets, and with a small dirigible for long-range observation."

"I'm surprised you know of these things," Curzius said, raising his eyebrows.

The mistfire ironclads had been around for some time, but the armaments the daimyo mentioned belonged to the latest trends in the fashion of war. He himself had only seen a few such ships so far.

"You shouldn't be. Has not the previous Overwizard told you what kind of a man I am? What kind of people live in Satsuma province?"

"He has, but I did not believe it. I now see he has even underestimated you."

The daimyo dismissed the pleasantries with a wave.

"Never mind the flattery. Can you give me such a ship?"

"Would you be able to keep it a secret from the eyes of Edo?"

"The eyes of Edo cannot see over the mountains. It would be safe and hidden until the time would come to use it."

"And when would that be?"

"Perhaps never..." Nariakira shrugged. "*Butsu-sama* knows war is the last thing on my mind. But it's always shrewd to be prepared."

"If we were certain the *Taikun* would never learn about the ship and where it came from, and if you could afford it, then yes, I believe we could provide you with one."

"Don't worry about the gold. I cannot spend it fast enough. How long would it take?"

"It would leave our shipyards in less than a year. Before next summer it could reach Kagoshima, or wherever you would wish it to sail."

"Excellent."

"Then you would join us?"

"No," Nariakira said unexpectedly.

Curzius was taken aback.

"No, but I would let you join me."

"I'm not sure I understand."

"Do you think you're the only one conspiring and conniving?" The daimyo laughed heartily. "The Shimazu have been plotting for centuries. It's in our blood. Our influence is vast, our allies powerful. Your little network of scholars and *rōnin* would make a fine and valuable addition to it, but that is all it would ever be – a single cell in the sprawling network."

"I… I see."

The little man wiped more sweat from his forehead. The tropical sun did not suit his pale skin.

"Good. I had hoped you would. Yes, if you promised me a warship, I would consider letting *you* join *my* conspiracy. My resources would be yours, and vice versa. Of course, the ship would only be the beginning, you understand - a token of friendship."

"There must be no war in Yamato," Curzius warned, wondering what exactly he was getting himself into. He was only beginning to perceive the undercurrents of ancient vendettas and grudges these people must have been holding for centuries. *Of course, the Shimazu hated the Tokugawas with a burning passion,* he remembered. *Perhaps it had been a mistake to come here after all.*

"We can provide you with defensive weapons only."

"I have no need for anything more," the daimyo replied, smiling sweetly and falsely. "It is just a precaution, you understand. Also I need to satisfy my urge to study your magical sciences and technologies, and a modern ironclad is the finest example of both, wouldn't you agree?"

"That is true," the wizard replied with a nod.

"A year is a long time. I will need another token of friendship before that."

What else would this old fox ask for now? Curzius thought with a shudder. *A squadron of dragons?*

Those he could not grant him. Bataave had no more dragon riders.

"Send me the plans for a smaller vessel. A mistfire ship good enough for me, and a few men. Just a little something to pass the time before the real prize arrives."

The Overwizard sighed with relief. Just that? That was easily arranged.

"I will have the plans sent as soon as I get back to Dejima."

"We can do better than that. Sign this document and they will be delivered to my men on the morrow."

The daimyo pushed a sheet of paper towards the Overwizard. Curzius picked it up and neared it to his face. It was a letter to the quartermaster of Dejima – written in his own handwriting, sealed with his own seal. He looked up. Lord Nariakira smiled gently, but his eyes mocked the Bataavian. Curzius swallowed.

"Why not forge my signature as well?"

"That would be dishonest of me. I'm not trying to cheat you, I only wish to hurry things up. We are still allies."

"I hope we can become more than that, Shimazu-*dono*. I hope we can become friends."

"Signing this letter would greatly improve the chances of that happening," the daimyo said with a grin.

The Overwizard reached for the pen. Despite the heat his hand was shivering as he wrote his name on the paper.

The rain poured incessantly with the noise of gravel beating on a tin plate, with the force of a great waterfall, with the coldness of a mountain stream. A million cascades gushed from the blue clay roof tiles and gutters of the narrow wooden townhouses. The packed dirt roads turned to treacherous swamp paths. All the late blooming trees had lost their flowers, their petals washed off by the rain like make-up that had gone out of fashion.

A shallow brook, which in good weather trickled quietly along the town's southern limits, now swelled to a roaring river. An old heron stood on the edge of the thundering waters, unmoved, enjoying a feast of eels and sweetfish, battered dumb on the cobbles by the swift current. The rolling billows licked the brink of the causeway dangerously, the last of the late farmers hurrying across it with their belongings.

Nagomi stared at the raging waters, trembling. A straw cloak and a wind-tattered umbrella did a poor job of protecting her sodden clothes from the elements. Water dripped from the strands of her long, luscious amber hair sneaking out from under the indigo-striped hood of the raincoat.

She was rarely so far from the comforts of her home city of Kiyō, so exposed to the raw elements. The swollen river carried tonnes of yellow mud, debris and flotsam, gathered along its way from the hills, but there was something else in the water, something Nagomi knew only she could see. Streaks of blackness, threads of un-light flashed among the waves. She knew at once what it was – somewhere upstream the river had disturbed a cemetery shrine, and released the troubled Spirits into the world. She shivered, only partly from the cold.

"I thought as much," her mother, Lady Itō, said, observing the chaos before them. She straightened her silk *yukata* robe, once dazzlingly colourful and light as a feather, now grey and heavy with water and dirt. "We cannot cross today."

"It's still safe!" said Satō, a ponytail of black hair bobbing up and down with her every agitated move. Nagomi's best friend cut her hair and wore her clothes like a samurai; down to the long katana sword in a red lacquer scabbard dangling from her silk sash.

"Look, if we hurry…"

"It's too risky," Lady Itō said, shaking her head.

"Can't we just go back to the inn, Mother?" Nagomi asked quietly. "Drink some hot *cha*…"

"I don't like their *cha*," muttered Satō, "it's bland and dead. They boil it too hot, and serve it too cold. If we go back now, we'll have to wait for days until this calms down."

Lady Itō looked at the river doubtfully.

"All right, but be very careful. Let the porter through first."

She waved at the servant, who entered the causeway with trembling legs, the heavy bundle of their belongings bending his back. They followed him across. A small group of men and women in simple linen clothes, tattered and mud-stained, waited on the other side – the causeway was already only wide enough for single file.

"Almost there," said Satō.

They now waded through shallow mud as the swollen waters started breaching the crest of the causeway. The other side was now closer than the one from which they had started.

Nagomi said nothing. She clutched her cloak tight. It was neither the water she feared nor the cold, but the dark Spirits in the water, now floating around her legs. It was like wading through sewage. The souls of the dead whispered and buzzed with an incessant droning hum and, worst of all, they seemed to be gathering around her, sensing a holy presence. She was almost certain she could hear her name repeated in their humming.

"*Nagomi*," they whispered. "*Nagominagominagomi…*"

A horseman appeared on the road ahead, a governmental courier speeding on a white stallion, crying for them to make way. The peasants on the shore dispersed before the horse, and the three travellers managed to wade to the side, but their porter lost his balance and stumbled into the water. The courier did not stop, bound by duty to deliver his urgent message, splashing the yellow muck all around. The commoners rushed to the servant's aid. With Satō's help, they managed to pull him out of the raging current, but the man was already unconscious, his head cracked, bleeding.

Without thinking, Nagomi dropped to her knees beside the porter, straight into the brown-yellow sludge. The black Spirits still swirled about her, repeating their monotonous mantra:

"*Minagominagominagomi…*"

"Nagomi, dear," Lady Itō tried to admonish her in exasperation, "it's just a hired servant, not worth your attention…"

The girl didn't listen. She examined the porter's wound. It was not as severe as she had feared. She threw back the hood of her cloak and the people around gasped at the sight of her copper-coloured hair. Some pulled back, crooking their fingers against bad luck.

The girl ignored them. She was used to this reaction whenever she showed herself outside her hometown, and understood the cause. Nobody in all of Yamato had hair of the same colour. Some – a few close friends and family – regarded it as a blessing from the Gods. Most, however, treated it as a curse, an abomination. Luckily it did not affect her healing powers.

She drew a tasselled paper wand from her sash and started waving it vigorously, chanting a prayer. She could feel the holy energy filling her body with warmth. It was the warmth of a fireplace in winter, of the summer sun, of a mother's arms. She forgot all about the other-worldly coldness of the dark Spirits in the water below. At last, when she was almost at the point of bursting, she released it into the unconscious man's body. It blazed with a blue light for a moment and the wound started sealing up almost immediately. The man stirred and moaned. She staggered as blood rushed from her head. It was an exhausting exercise.

The villagers eyed her suspiciously, as if she was a demon in disguise.

"Take him somewhere warm. He should be back up in a few days," she said, trying not to let their hostility get to her. The response was silence and accusing glares, as if the villagers were telling her "you healed him, you take care of him."

"Are you deaf?" Satō glowered at them, putting her hand on the hilt of her sword. This made them move. A couple of men carried the injured porter across the sinking causeway, and the remaining peasants followed, throwing fearful glances over their shoulders.

"You did well," Satō said, helping Nagomi up with a smile, "and see, we've crossed to the other side."

She turned to Lady Itō with a beaming grin.

"Yes, but *all* our luggage is lost in the river," her mother replied, shaking her head with disappointment.

"So we'll travel faster." Satō said with a shrug. "We'll be back at Kiyō in no time."

The girl hurried onwards. Nagomi stuck her wand back into her sash, sighed, recited a quick prayer of gratitude and followed her friend into the rain.

It was a busy day, a happy day, the Day of the Ship. A new Bataavian merchantman had arrived at Dejima with news and visitors from the mysterious exotic world beyond Yamato's shores. The streets of Nishihama-machi, the old merchant district of Kiyō, bustled with handcarts and porters carrying wares from all over Chinzei – the southernmost island of the Yamato archipelago, of which Kiyō was by far the largest and richest port – to storehouses and shops. Pottery from Arima in the east, knives and blades from Matsubara in the north, silver from the mines of Ginya, malted rice from nearby Kojiya, dyed cloth from Bungo on the north-eastern coast; anything the Bataavian representatives could be persuaded to spend their gold and silver bullion on. To serve the crowds, food and drink stands sprouted along the main streets. Summer fruit and pickles were brought in from the countryside. Fishmongers hawked their morning wares; marinated eel from inland waters, and freshest mackerel and skipjack from the sea. There were boiled sweets and rice crackers for the children. There was saké and strong shōchū for adults.

Any other time, Satō would have been the first to venture among the stalls, looking for bargains on Western accessories and magical ingredients; lenses and copper tubes from Bataave, dried herbs and powdered bones from Qin, elemental essences and black iron from Chosen. All these things were always much cheaper and more abundant on the Day of the Ship, but this time she was simply too tired to care. All she wanted was a bath and a hot meal.

"Do come with me," she said to the others, "I'm sure Father will love it if you stay for dinner."

"That is most kind," replied Lady Itō politely. "Nagomi, you go with Satō. I will come later."

Nagomi agreed eagerly. The Itō house was farther up the hill, beyond the Sōfukuji Temple, and Satō's family residence was much more luxurious, commanding a beautiful view over the city.

The Takashima household was a massive compound, built on the very top of Maruyama Hill, dominating the neighbourhood with its thick stone walls. Two spearmen stood by the main gate, vigilant. The younger of the guards lowered his weapon threateningly as the girls approached, but his older companion shook his head.

"It's all right - that's the young *tono*."

Satō stopped by the younger guard. To him she was a samurai boy, son and prospective heir to her father's school of *Rangaku* – the study Western magic.

"You're new here, aren't you?"

The man nodded. He couldn't have been more than five years older her.

"What do they call you?"

"Kaiten, Takashima-*dono*."

"You're supposed to be keeping people *in* that house, Kaiten, not out of it."

"Yes, Takashima-*dono*," he replied pursing his lips, uncomfortable and irritated.

Satō didn't worry about his discomfort. She enjoyed mocking the guards, playing pranks on them and being generally obnoxious towards the frequently changing spearmen. The soldiers did not belong to her household – they were employed by the city magistrate, who, in turn, took their orders straight from the *Taikun*'s court in far-away Edo. Her father was under house arrest ever since he had tried to convince the magistrate to put the masters of Western magic, like himself, to work on the city's defences. The idea proved too radical and deemed a treason: even in Kiyō, a city more open and diverse than any other place in Yamato, nobody trusted the wizards enough to give them access to military secrets.

"It feels more empty than usual," remarked Nagomi, entering the residence.

"Everyone's either helping their families in the stores or has just wandered off to see the Ship," explained Satō, "besides, we don't get that many students these days. It's been six years since my father lost favour with the *Taikun*, people are starting to lose faith he will ever regain it."

A white-haired figure lurked in the hallway. The old servant cried out in joy and disappeared to summon the master of the household. Shūhan hurried down from the library wing. He was a short man, long-faced and small-eyed, clad in a short, black pleated skirt, a kimono of the same vermillion silk as Satō's garment – the colour signifying he was a scholar of *Rangaku* – and a black vest bearing the Takashima clan crest, four diamonds in a triangle, embroidered on the shoulders. His head was shaven in front, with a small bun of tied greying hair at the back. He hugged Satō, who flushed with embarrassment, and greeted Nagomi warmly.

"Do you have it?" he asked. "Show me the blade!"

Satō drew the sword and presented it proudly. The blade was magnificent; long, slender, perfectly balanced, with distinct temper lines forming a small circle at the tip, the signature of the Matsubara swordsmiths. The hilt and hand guard were decorated with the cherry blossom seal of the Ōmura clan and the *tsuba* handguard carved with the butterfly insignia of the Heike clan.

Satō smirked every time she saw the butterfly crest. The Heike clan had been vanquished eight hundred years earlier, and still the Matsubaras, their once-sworn vassals, clung to the ancient allegiance. This unwillingness to change was exactly what her father had always warned her about. "The elements are always mutating, always transforming, and so must a wizard", he had taught her. "That's why the *Rangakusha* are so feared and hated in Yamato. We are the harbingers of revolution".

"Splendid, *splendid!*" exclaimed Shūhan, admiring the weapon in the sunlight. "Shigehide-*sama* has truly outdone himself this time. I dare say it's even finer than my own. It was worth the trip, eh? You know, the old fools say a sword is the warrior's soul – but I can see how this one truly fits you. You must tell me all about your journey... but you are dying for a bath and change of clothes, right? We'll talk at dinner. I've ordered eel from Yorozuya today!"

The girls bowed and hurried to the bathroom. Nagomi threw her travel uniform into the washing basket, while Satō removed the *Rangakusha* garments and began to unwind a bandage that flattened her breasts.

"Phew! Finally," she groaned, "you've no idea how uncomfortable this is."

"Believe me, I do," replied the younger girl, "you've been complaining about it every night since this trip started. I thought you'd got used to wearing boys' clothes. Weren't you always trying to sneak into kendo trainings in this disguise?"

"I was an urchin then, and didn't need those." Satō threw the bandages into the laundry basket. "Still, it's a small price to pay for being able to walk around the city with a sword."

When they came out of the bath, relaxed and refreshed, clean summer *yukatas* waited for them folded neatly on the straw mat. Nagomi changed into a pink floral robe, while Satō dried herself with a fragrant towel.   "I like this blue dye," said Nagomi, picking up the other *yukata*, "I haven't seen it before."

"Father must have bought it as a surprise. I don't think it's local."

"Looks like Arimatsu cloth. It must have cost a fortune!"

"Sometimes I think he doesn't really know how much things are worth... Since Mother died, he's been useless with money. Like this sword he got me – it's marvellous, but was it really necessary to buy a *Matsubara* blade? He always says the blade is only a tool..."

Satō shook her head and stood up to put on the *yukata*.

"What about your father and sister? Will they be coming tonight?"

"I believe so," answered Nagomi. "I just hope Father doesn't have any patients booked for the evening."

The girls tied their sashes and Nagomi finished braiding her long auburn hair. The sound of the kitchen gong and the smell of broiling eel coming from downstairs announced it was time for dinner. Satō felt her stomach rumble with the thought of a good meal. She had forgotten how hungry she was.

CHAPTER III

Gwynedd, June, 2606 ab urbe condita

The buxom barmaid glanced at Bran sipping his half pint of Llanfairfechan Black and passed the table without stopping. The Red Dragon *tafarn* was overflowing with guests. Tonight, the graduates of Llambed came in great numbers to celebrate.

Bran was alone at a small table in the corner, trying to listen to the old harper over the din of the lively crowd. The bearded bard was just finishing the last of the Royal Triad, three epic poems recalling the deeds of the most famous kings of Gwynedd: Owain the Wyrmslayer, vanquisher of the Norsemen; Llywellyn ap Gruffud, the Hammer of Rheged and Harri Two Crowns, the first to sit on two thrones.

The triad finished, Bran saw the bard look hesitantly around. Failing to spot anyone still paying any attention to his poetry, he bowed to nobody in particular and removed himself and his bulky instrument from the open space by the fireplace. Three other musicians moved to replace the lofty tones of the harp with a coarser tune of fiddle, drum and pipes, more suited to the playful mood of the patrons.

"What about you, Bran?"

The dragon rider looked up, surprised. Two boys slammed their pint tankards, filled to the brim with dark foaming *cwrw*, onto his table. Hywel and Madoc came from Llyn, north of Cantre'r Gwaelod. Like Bran, their families lived by and from the sea and, like Bran, they were commoners. They were the closest Bran had to friends at the Academy.

"Sorry...?"

"What are your plans for after the summer?"

"Oh, I haven't decided yet..."

"I'm off to join the dragoons in September," said Hywel loudly, taking a great gulp from his mug. His face was flushed red, his brown eyes bloodshot. "Father's already arranged everything."

"The Third or the Fifth?" asked Madoc, wiping froth from his proud Prydain moustache, dyed with lime for the Graddio in the ancient fashion. It was the envy of all other boys in the Academy.

"The Twelfth," Hywel said ruefully, "they don't take the likes of us into the Guards."

"My folks want me to stay for the baccalaureate," said Madoc. "I've got no real prospects in the army."

Hywel nodded. "Yeah, I figured you would stay. You always had the best grades of the three of us."

"Surely your *tad* prepared a spot for you in the navy?" questioned Madoc, turning to Bran, "with his connections…"

"I haven't talked to him about it yet," Bran replied, "in fact, I haven't even seen him yet since last summer."

"Ah, well, that's the navy for yous," Hywel said, his speech starting to slur. "You'll have to tell him about your areo… aero… flying exam! That was something!"

Bran shrugged. He was certain all his father would get from the tale was that Emrys had failed as a mount – just as he had always predicted.

"I see you have your trinket out," Hywel continued, pointing to a ring upon Bran's left hand, a simple twisted band of gold with a single blue gem, an irregular, jagged shard, semi-translucent like a pearl. "Trying to get the girls' attention with jewellery?" he guffawed.

He was wearing two golden bracelets upon his left wrist and a bronze torc around his sinewy neck.

"It's a family heirloom," explained Bran. "I figured it's time I started wearing it."

"I see, I see," said the other boy nodding absentmindedly, his attention already turned to the musicians.

The band was playing "The Trouble at the Tavern", an old bawdy jig, and Madoc and Hywel joined in with the loud singing, leaving Bran again to himself.

As he brooded over the half-empty glass, the boy noticed another student sitting alone at a table across the room: Wulfhere of Warwick. The other sons of Seaxe noblemen, his usual entourage, were for some reason sitting together at another table, in another part of the room.

What's going on?

Wulfhere of Warwick noticed Bran's curious stare, stood up and, slightly swaying, crossed the hall in quick steps.

"What are you looking at, *Taffy?*"

Bran blinked, surprised.

"What's it to you, *Sais?*" he replied. Now that they were on equal footing he was no longer frightened. Blue sparks appeared around Wulfhere's tightened knuckles, but dissipated when a heavy hand fell on his shoulder.

"Go back to your ale, Wulf." Hywel said threateningly. The Seaxe's uniform under his fingers started smouldering faintly – Hywel's mount was an Eryni Ruby, a firedrake. "You shouldn't even be here."

He was one of the few Gwynedd-born boys who could stand up to the tall burly Seaxe. The Warwick stared at him for a moment then grunted something and staggered away towards the *tafarn* door.

"What's up with him?" asked Bran. "What did you mean, he shouldn't be here?"

"Didn't you know? Look at his Seal."

Bran looked after the Seaxe. Among the many enchantments woven into Wulfhere's aura his True Sight could not spot the mark of the white eagle.

"It's not there… He failed to pass!" he whispered, astonished.

"Aye," nodded Madoc, taking another gulp of ale, "for all his *Sais* boasting and bullying, he turned out to be one big failure. I wouldn't like to be in his skin now!"

"Serves him right," Bran replied, remembering the Iceberry water and all beatings he had to endure over the years.

The song was finished, and so was Bran's glass. The musicians started another dance tune, and the other two boys moved into the crowd to find themselves partners for the jig. Bran rose and headed for the door to get some fresh air.

Once outside, looking at the starry sky above the empty cobbled street leading towards the faer iron gates of the Academy, he decided it was time to go home. Having sat at the table for an hour and drank a glass of ale, he felt his social duty fulfilled. His head was beginning to hurt from the noise of the crowd, banging of the drum and screeching of the fiddle.

I will not be missed.

He headed for the dragon stables, a wide, high-roofed building of sandstone, with long, slate-tiled eaves. Somebody emerged out of the shadows and walked towards him.

"Hullo, Wulf."

Bran tried to walk around the Seaxe, but the flaxen-haired boy moved to the side, blocking his passage again.

"So you've passed, Toadboy," the Seaxe snarled.

"And you haven't," Bran said, unable to stop himself gloating.

Wulfhere pointed his finger at him accusingly.

"You've had your *faeder* pull the strings, haven't you? You'd never pass otherwise. Not with that flying frog of yours."

"No, Wulfhere. I simply practiced for the exams instead of wasting my time beating up others and playing with poisons. Besides, your father knows plenty more 'strings' to pull."

"*Pah-!*" the blond-haired boy scoffed. "I should have known not to go to a *waelisc* school. You guys always stick together."

"If you choose to believe this, so be it. Now, please let me through," Bran said and made a step forward.

"No." Wulfhere stood firm. "Not before I see whether you really deserved to pass."

"What?"

The Seaxe crooked the fingers of his left hand, summoning a *bucler,* semi-translucent shield protecting his forearm, and tightened his right hand into a sparking fist.

"Don't be absurd, Wulfhere." Bran raised his hands. "It's over. I'm tired and just want to go home."

"Oh, but that won't do at all! I need to see what it is that a peasant's boy can do better than one with royal blood."

Three hundred years earlier, at the end of a long civil war, the first of the Warwicks, Richard the Kingmaker, had reached for the Dragon Throne. His triumph was brief; Harri Two Crowns had crossed over from Gwynedd and destroyed him at Bosworth a mere two years later. The Kingmaker's blood ran thinly in Wulfhere's veins, but all the Warwicks still harboured deep resentment towards the people west of the Dyke.

"I'm not a peasant," protested Bran, raising a weak single-layer *tarian* shield just in case Wulfhere was seriously intending to hurt him. "I'm townsfolk, and I don't need to prove anything to you. You can see I have the Seal."

"Then I will have to make sure you're dead three times to make it disappear!"

Bran reeled back. Dead? Had the Seaxe gone mad?

Is he drunk?

There was desperation in his voice that worried Bran more than the smell of liquor in the boy's breath.

A blue electric spark struck from Wulfhere's outstretched fingers, piercing Bran's shield with ease and hitting his chest painfully. Bran waved his hand defensively, summoning a plume of bluish flame. Wulfhere covered his nose.

"You're trying to scare me away with your swamp stink?"

He punched Bran again, this time simply with a fist. Bran gasped, grabbed Wulfhere's hand instinctively and cast a Strike of Repel.

"*Gwrthyrru!*"

He was still determined not to let himself be dragged into a senseless fight. The Seaxe slid away a few feet across the slippery cobbles. He regained his balance and shook his head.

"Oh, *come on*, you're not even trying!"

His blue eyes glinted. He raised his hand again and this time Bran ducked, barely dodging a shot of lightning. Another bolt deflected off Bran's *tarian* and hit an iron lamp post, showering the street with sparks.

"You can't win a *gornestau* like that!" Wulfhere laughed. "Show me what you're really made of, swabbie. *Draca Hiw!*"

He roared and leapt towards Bran, shape-shifting midflight into a blue were-drake. He was now six feet tall, covered in scales and hovering above the Prydain boy, his great azure wings spreading, his bright eyes blazing.

In a reflex, Bran jumped backwards and crouched, compressing his *tarian* into a stronger thrice-layered shield. He clapped his hands then spread them apart. A Soul Lance shimmered between his palms and solidified. He hoped the sight of it would bring the Seaxe to his senses. The Soul Lance was a deadly weapon when used against dragons and Dragonforms, the only blade certain to pierce through any dragon scale. Wulfhere pressed on though, with claws and lightning, pounding relentlessly against Bran's *tarian*. The lightning strikes bounced off the shield in all directions, throwing tiles off the stable roof and scorching the wooden beams. The dragons inside the building woke up and started snorting and screeching in agitation.

The magic duels, *gornestau*, never lasted long. No man could keep casting spells or sustain shields for long. The victory was usually a matter of who ran out of energy faster, or first made a mistake...

Bran's shield fizzled and vanished. He raised his lance in both hands. Wulfhere grabbed it with his talons and they wrestled for a while, lightning crackling around them, scorching the hair on Bran's head.

"*Rhew!*" cried the Prydain boy, summoning a little dragon flame.

The lance burst with bright blue fire, blasting the opponent's clawed hands and the Seaxe pulled away briefly. A scream of pain turned into a roar of rage.

Bran darted inside the stables and tried to slam the gate shut, but the thick fireproof door burst open, and the impact of the explosion threw him back. Wulfhere leapt inside. It was difficult for him to move in the confined space, but he still pressed on towards the hapless Gwynedd boy, who stood up on shaky legs and continued his retreat.

The dragons around them went mad with excitement, filling Bran's head with a buzz of Farlink messages and emotions. He swayed and almost fell down again. His skull throbbed with pain. He hit something with his back: a ladder leading to the stable roof. He grabbed a rung and hoisted himself upwards in a flip. Wulfhere's claws smashed the ladder underneath him, but Bran managed to grab onto a ledge and climb outside.

A slight breeze cooled his aching head. The slate covering was damp and slick. He only managed to tread a few steps away from the ladder chute before the roof exploded. The dragon-formed Seaxe flapped his vestigial wings and landed clumsily on the tiles.

"Wulf..." Bran pleaded. "Stop this, *please*. I don't want to fight you..."

But the Seaxe was too far gone to be reasoned with. He opened his mouth and let out a mindless bellow. His clawed hand scratched at Bran and the boy leaned backwards in a reflex. His feet slipped on the edge of the roof. He had been learning how to take falls for four years and the training kicked in instantly. He imagined his legs and torso following the perfect curve of spiral rotation. He had a split second to calculate the optimal trajectory for the manoeuvre. The air around him heated up as the dragon magic enveloped his body...

A memory flashed in his mind: a student in the second year who, failing to perform a proper rolling leap, had lost focus and fallen to the ground from a dragon's back, a hundred feet down. The medics had carried him off the training field and nobody had ever seen him again. The enchanted acrobatics had always made Bran uneasy since. He wasn't built for physical prowess and found it difficult to grasp the complicated calculations necessary for merging his own body with a stream of mystic force...

Landing, his feet slipped and he fell face first into the mud. He hissed with pain and cursed aloud. He tried to scramble to his feet clumsily, but slid on the wet cobbles whenthe Seaxe landed before him with a massive thud, instantly reached out a clawed hand and lifted Bran by the collar of his blue uniform. The Gwynedd boy grasped powerful talons, trying to wrestle himself free, in vain; the Dragonform was unstable and a risk to the caster but for a moment provided him with almost unlimited strength.

There was a whoosh of wings and the sound of claws scratching against the cobbles and Bran was thrown aside by an impact of a large warm body. He looked up and saw a large grey dragon standing before him, pinning transformed Wulfhere to the ground with its fore talons like a hawk holding a mouse. Bran turned his gaze away; it hurt to look straight at the beast for too long. The glamour cast on its scales caused them to shimmer and shift, making the dragon seem transparent, half-invisible. It was easy to forget it was there at all.

The Highland Greys were bred exclusively on the Isle of Scathach in the north-western Alba, to be used by spies and scouts. Only one person in the Academy rode one. Madam Magnusdottir, the Dean of Dracology, sat calmly in the saddle. She nodded at Bran to stand up.

"Thank you ma'am," he said, half-relieved and half-embarrassed.

"You're lucky. I was flying close enough to see everything! This is very serious."

"It was just a *gornestau*, ma'am."

She eyed him suspiciously. The Dragonform had to be fed on a very strong emotion and was too powerful and intense enchantment to be used on a whim. Even soldiers on the battlefields were reluctant to transform unless their life depended on it.

"Transformation is forbidden in magical duels."

"We're not at the Academy anymore, ma'am."

She laughed briefly, clicked her tongue and the shimmering dragon raised its talons. Wulfhere, back in his human form, cast Bran a furious look, scrambled to his feet and ran away into the night without saying a word. Madam Magnusdottir looked after him pursing her lips in thought, then turned back to Bran.

"Is your leg all right? You're limping."

"Yes, it's just a bruise."

"That was a particularly shoddy performance, young man. Enchanted acrobatics is an essential skill to the dragon rider!"

"I'm sorry."

He scratched his head, not knowing what else to say.

"That's all right," she smiled, her features softening. "You've passed the exam, after all – barely, if I recall. I suppose all that ale does hamper one's abilities a little. Give my regards to your father when you see him," she added before launching into the air. A moment later the dragon shimmered and disappeared in the darkness.

Just then several boys and girls had run out of the *tafarn*, intrigued by the noises of combat and their dragons' distress calls.

"What's going on?" asked Madoc.

"Wulfhere Warwick transformed. I think he had too much to drink tonight," replied Bran, rubbing the bruises on his face.

A red-haired girl tugged Madoc back towards the *tafarn*.

"They're playing 'Farmer's Fancy'! I want tae dance!" she said, rolling her "r's". She noticed Bran and lowered her head, bashful. It was Eithne.

"You coming back, Bran?" Madoc smiled, wrapping a muscular arm around the girl. "The night is young."

"Thanks, but I think I'll fly home." Bran sighed heavily. He knew, no matter what his own decision after the summer, he would not see her ever again – she was moving to the Mon Island in October. This was his last chance to say goodbye – the *Derwydd* lived in monastic fortresses where none but them could enter.

"I don't feel so good. I think I've bruised my ankle," he said instead.

"As you wish."

The other boy shrugged and returned to the Red Dragon with Eithne in tow. She looked back once, briefly.

Bran limped towards the stables. The dragons were slowly calming down. He patted his mount on the neck soothingly.

"Let's get out of here, Emrys," he said quietly.

The beast grunted in response.

The unmistakable whoosh of a landing dragon came from the front yard. Dylan ab Ifor put away *The Cambrian* and stood up from the black wood armchair to welcome his son. The boy entered the living room straight from the door, staining the carpet with dirt. The white mice Bran's mother employed as household imps scurried to clean away the mud. Dylan cast him a quick glance.

He's really grown.

"I see you didn't even bother to come to my Graddio."

Dylan scratched the scar running across his cheek with discomfort.

"I only just got here from Brigstow, son. We had to pick up survivors from the *Birkenhead* and then our Weatherman came down with jungle fever," he explained. "I really hoped we'd get here much sooner."

Bran shrugged dismissively. Dylan moved to an awkward embrace when his wife entered the room, wiping muddy hands on a linen cloth. The sweet smell of vervain and betony followed her from the garden. Certain herbs had to be picked at night.

"Oh, back you are!" she exclaimed with a smile. Dylan always wondered why Rhian still spoke with the gentle southern valley lilt, even after all the years of living on the coast. "How was it? Did you get the Seal? Dylan, did he get the Seal?"

"Do you not see it?" Dylan raised his eyebrows. "Ah, right, I forgot." Rhian had some magical talent, but she had never pursued the scholarly path, preferring the ways of the Cunning Folk – making potions and casting small mending charms. She had never developed the True Sight necessary to perceive the Academy's secrets.

"It's just above his right shoulder, as bright and beautiful as any I've seen."

"What did the dean say?" Rhian asked.

"She... asked me if I wanted to stay for baccalaureate," said Bran.

"See, I told you they'd want him back!" She beamed to Dylan. He smiled knowingly.

So the old Magnusdottir had received my letter.

"You seem tired... Your face is dirty and your hair is singed. Did something happen?" Rhian continued her investigation.

"Nothing, I was just playing with Emrys," Bran replied.

Dylan knew this was not the case – he could still detect the faint lingering traces of battle magic. He chose not to say anything; there was no point in worrying Rhian. Boys would always be boys, but something else in Bran's response made him frown.

"Do you still have that toy drake?" he asked, sharply. "You know I could get you any breed you wanted."

Bran scowled.

"I have Emrys. He's my friend."

"Bran," Dylan looked his son straight in the eyes, "you can't get attached to a dragon. They are the most egotistic of creatures. Sooner or later it will betray you, no matter how kind you are to it."

"Emrys is more loyal to me than any human."

"There's no such thing as a loyal dragon. I have scars to prove it."

"Well, maybe you just don't know how to handle them! What have you told Magnusdottir?"

Before Dylan could answer, Rhian intervened.

"Can't you stop quarrelling even for a moment? Let him have his pet *dab* for a while yet, Dylan. The lad's just graduated. Starting his holidays, he is. He won't need a new *draigg* for some time."

She went on to put the kettle on the stove and the two men sat down in front of each other, uneasy.

"You've been away for almost a year," said Bran, interrupting the silence.

Dylan looked vacantly around. The room, with its white-washed walls, heavy oaken furnishings and a roaring fireplace, seemed at once familiar and unreal. Had it really been just a few months since he had been sitting in the tent in the middle of the savannah, negotiating with the Bataavian commander?

"I was overseeing the Transvaal agreement," he said, more to himself than to Bran. "The negotiations were very difficult."

The herd of wildebeest the only witness to our quarrels.

"How did it go then?"

"Her Majesty finally granted sovereignty to the Bataavian settlers. Our borders in the South are secure and our friendship with the Bataave strengthened."

"You sound like a royal pronouncement."

Dylan chuckled. "I had to talk like this for a year."

"What about the *Birkenhead*? There was something in the papers, but I didn't have time to read before the exams."

"She was brought upon the reefs by Xhosa illusions, off the Cape. We had to run twelve sorties to bring everyone safe."

"Then the war with Xhosa is still on?"

"More than ever…"

"It must have kept you busy."

"Rest is a rare privilege in a war zone."

That was as much as he could say. Most of his work had to be kept secret even from his closest family. In the silence that followed Dylan decided to change the subject.

"So, have you been thinking of what you will choose for your baccalaureate?"

"I'm… I'm not sure. I don't really like that place," Bran replied with a shrug.

"I know, son, but believe me, things change later. As an alderman you're too highly ranked for – "

"It's not just that… I want to…" Bran paused. "I don't want to go back."

Dylan glowered.

"Look, boy, you can't just decide your future on a whim. What else would you do? Work down the pit, herding fire elementals?"

"I could join the navy…"

"You don't know what you're talking about."

"Most of my… friends will be enrolling in October."

"Most of your friends didn't get a choice. By Owain's Sword, you're not some farmer's son!"

Rhian entered the room with a tea tray. Dylan leaned back, putting a smile on his face. He relaxed the grip of his fingers on the leather armrest.

"Are you two still arguing?"

"No, dear. Oh, I just remembered. I brought some tinned fruit from the South. Why don't I go get them?"

CHAPTER IV

Yamato, Summer, 6ᵗʰ year of Kaei era

From the window of her room on the top floor, overlooking the quiet suburb
sprawling along the hillside, Satō first saw the herald bearing the orange standard
of the Merchant Republic of Bataave. A retinue of servants and guards followed
and then, at the end, an ornate palanquin climbed up the steep hill road, carried
by six porters. The guards halted the procession at the gates of the residence.
"His Excellency, *Oppertovenaar* of the Dejima domain, Hendrik Curzius, here to
see the master of the household, Takashima Shūhan," the herald announced in a
loud shrieking voice then presented a rolled up paper to the elder of the guards.
The spearman checked the seals and nodded at his companion. The two bowed
and stepped aside.

She leaned further; she had not seen the new Overwizard before. A
short portly Westerner stepped down from the carriage, straightened his long
vermillion tailcoat and put on a wide-brimmed green top hat.

"*Welkom, Oppertovenaar,*" a voice spoke in nigh impeccable Bataavian.
Satō's father was proud of his ability to speak the language without a strong
accent. He claimed it made his spells work that bit more precisely. "I'm grateful
for your visit."

"I'm grateful for your welcome, Takashima-*sama*," the guest replied in
the language of the Yamato, in a correct, but rather coarse, manner.

She ran down to the main hall just in time for the two men to enter the
building.

"My heir, Satō," Shūhan introduced the girl and sat down beside her by
the low table. The Westerner bowed and joined them, his legs crossed casually.

"Aah, my limbs are not what they used to be," he explained.

Shūhan laughed politely, poured saké into three shallow cups and raised
a toast.

"To the eternal friendship of Bataave and Yamato! *Kanpai!*"

"*Proost!*"

Satō swallowed the warming liquid and felt immediately relaxed. She
reached for another portion, but her father discreetly moved the cup away.

"I'm so happy I can finally meet you, Takashima-*sama*," said Curzius,
sipping saké. "It's so difficult to be granted the permit. The Magistrate finally
agreed when I threatened to delay my visit to the *Taikun*'s court."

"I'm honoured," bowed Takashima.

"No, no," protested the guest, "the honour is all mine. I've heard so
much about you from previous Overwizards. The great Takashima Shūhan, one

of the finest *Rangaku* scholars in all of Yamato! The airgun, by the way –
marvellous, one of my marksmen shot a pheasant from two hundred yards last
week! I'll be sending it to the *Stadtholder's* court in Bataave; he enjoys game
hunting."

"That pleases me greatly."

"But let's get down to business!" The wizard looked around, watchful.
"Are we in a safe place?"

"There are only the three of us here."

"I'm not sure if it's a conversation for a young... boy," Curzius said.

He knows, she realised. *Of course he does. He's the chief wizard of Dejima. He must
have spotted through my disguise the moment he entered.*

"Satō is my heir," Shūhan replied, "whatever is said or done in this house,
he is part of it."

"I'll get straight to the point, then. I come not of my own accord, but
on a mission from my master, the *Stadtholder* - a very special mission."

"You intrigue me."

"There is something... *new* in the air. Our soothsayers are anxious.
They say the threads of Fate are tangled, disordered, and they all seem to focus
here, on Yamato."

"Surely, your soothsayers are mistaken," protested Shūhan. "We are an
isolated and peaceful nation, far from the events of the outside world."

"And yet the world seems to be reaching out towards you. The
Westerners are encroaching on the lands of the East. The realms of Bharata
have fallen. The Qin barrier is breaking."

"I'm familiar with all this," said Shūhan, "but I would think the spoils
of Bharata and Qin are quite enough to entertain the Westerners for generations
to come."

"You underestimate our greed, Master Shūhan," Curzius said, "and the
soothsayers of Dejima are rarely wrong – after all, they have learned their skill
from your priests. The Empire of Yamato is on the brink of a major change – a
change that may have repercussions far beyond your borders. The *Stadtholder*
wants me to be more than just aware of it happening. I am required to take an
active part in the events, however should they unfold, and for that, I need
trusted men on my side."

"You want me to stand with you against the *Taikun?*"

The Overwizard puffed his cheeks and looked sharply at Shūhan – as
did Satō.

"I... I did not say that."

"But that is what you meant."

"I only wish to know what you will do when the time comes to choose
sides."

"There can only ever be two sides in Yamato: those with the *Taikun* and
those against him. I've learnt it the hard way – this is why you found it so
difficult to come here. Tell me, have you spoken to anyone else about it yet?"

"I have," the Overwizard replied, nodding. "I cannot give you the names, of course, but there is a... network of likeminded people, growing slowly."

"A *conspiracy*, you mean."

"I would not call it that."

"Call it what you will, you're still talking about sedition and treason."

"This is not just for our benefit, you must understand. We care about the good of your people. You make decent trade, and are an honourable and trustworthy race. We are happy with our agreements. The others, however... they will not care for deals, they will come to steal and conquer. We need to work together against this new threat."

Shūhan pondered this for a while, scratching his greying beard.

"Will you speak to the *Taikun* openly about these - signs?" he asked

"As much as I am allowed to divulge, yes, but from what I've heard of His Excellency, he is unlikely to be interested in what I have to say."

"Yes, the *Taikun* can be a stubborn man," said Shūhan, "and tough to deal with. There was a time when I desired nothing more than to serve His Excellency, but he chose to surround himself with advisers who cared for little but themselves. The 'reforms' they've introduced have only served to keep people like me away from the court."

There was bitterness in his voice Satō was familiar with; he sounded like this every time he spoke of the Edo government.

"What about the *Mikado*?" she blurted. "If the news are as grave as you say, shouldn't he be notified as well?"

The two older men looked at her in great surprise. She realised immediately how ridiculous she sounded. She might have as well proposed to discuss current affairs with the Gods.

"The *Mikado* has even less freedom than I do," said Shūhan, "you know that. Only the *Taikun* matters."

"Are we in agreement, then?" Curzius pushed, ignoring Satō's question.

"It is yet too early to decide, Overwizard-*dono*," Shūhan replied. "As your soothsayers say, the threads of Fate are tangled, but I can promise I will always do what I believe is best for my people and country, not just for *Taikun*'s courtiers."

"That is as much as I wanted to hear."

Curzius extended his hand and Shūhan shook it awkwardly. They both rose and headed for the exit. Shūhan held the Westerner back just before they were about to cross the doorway.

"This 'network' of yours..." he said in a low voice that Satō could barely hear from where she was sitting, "would they be in a position, should anything happen to me, to take care of my heir?"

"Is this your price?"

"It's my condition."

"Then I will see to it that they would. Farewell friend."

She watched her father return to the table, sit heavily on the straw mat with a sigh and pour himself yet another cup. The room was deadly quiet, even the cicadas in the garden fell silent.

"Well," he said at last. "What did you think of that? Not my noblest moment. To stand against my ruler and master, betray him in the hour of trouble… is that the way of a true samurai?"

"And is it the way of a true master to give ear to false accusations and imprison those who only wished to serve him? Kōshi the Philosopher said a faithful servant must – "

Shūhan smiled bitterly and raised a hand to stop her. "Quoting Kōshi is not as popular as it once was. Make sure not to repeat such words outside this house."

"Of course, Father. I'm not a child anymore."

"No. You're not."

He swallowed his saké in one gulp and stared grimly at the bottom of the empty cup. A lone raven cawed in the distance.

The great Suwa, chief of Kiyo's shrines, lay to the north-east of the city on the steep slopes of Tamazono Mountain. Beyond the long stairs and many gates, beyond the souvenir stalls and main worship halls of the shrine, beyond the cemetery, lay the forested inner grounds where only the priests could enter.

There were many sand and gravel paths climbing among the camphor trees, connecting the separate wooden buildings. Some led to lesser shrines dedicated to the worship of various local *kami*, others to warehouses or storage sheds, or, farther up the mountain, huts of hermit priests who chose a life of separation. A few disappeared into the underbrush, their original destinations long forgotten.

Nagomi scaled one of those white gravel paths, wearing her finest ceremonial gown of pale green silk embroidered with red thread, a wreath of flowers and ribbons of paper in her braided copper hair. On her wrists and ankles she wore bracelets of tiny brass bells. She was following Lady Kazuko, the wrinkle-faced, bright-eyed High Priestess of the entire Shrine. Despite the woman's drab plain garments, she displayed an aura of authority and wisdom.

The gravel path led past a persimmon orchard then along a grove of tall green bamboo swaying gently in the wind. Nagomi and the High Priestess reached a square building with walls of cedar logs, curved tiled roof and a narrow entrance without a door. Nagomi hesitated a moment before passing under the thick straw rope tied across the entrance to mark sacred ground.

The inside was dark and musty, a faint smell of sulphur and brimstone permeating the air. The High Priestess pulled out a small clay vessel and blew on it – a tiny Spirit of light living in the pot awoke and an orange flickering flame burst forth, casting disturbing shadows on the wooden walls. The building had no floor or foundations. Its walls were sunk deep into the forest soil around a flat rocky outcrop. A narrow jagged crack ran through the rock, venting dizzying fumes from the depths of the Earth. A large bronze bowl stood on a tripod above the crack, steeped in smoke, filled with dark motionless water.

The source of the foul-smelling exhausts and vapours was hidden somewhere deep inside the Tamazono Mountain. They leaked through cracks in the ground in many places throughout the shrine grounds. The savage deadly movements of the Earth that produced these cracks were both a curse and a blessing. They provided fertile soil and the relaxing hot springs, but once in a while the *kami* of the Earth would show their terrible wrath and bring fire and death upon common and noble folk alike. Such was the lot of Yamato: what the Gods gave with one hand, they took with the other.

Atop certain holy mountains, like Tamazono, the sulphuric vapours had yet another valuable property. They enabled a suitably attuned soothsayer to see into the future. It would take years of practice for a priest to read the Waters of Scrying properly, to not be overwhelmed by the Spirits of the mountain's heart and understand the secret signs. But Lady Kazuko, as if in anticipation of this day, had brought Nagomi to the Waters when the girl was only thirteen and had done so for a year now, getting her accustomed to the fumes surrounding the rock fissure.

The High Priestess nodded and Nagomi, as instructed so many times, approached the tripod and inhaled the pale yellow vapours until her head started spinning. She leaned over the bowl, stared into the cold surface and softly chanted the prayer. Lady Kazuko joined her encouragingly. In the stuffy darkness Nagomi recalled the dark dreams she kept having since returning from the excursion to get Satō's sword. The Spirits in the flood waters, calling her name... A house of red stone by the sea... a black ship that moved without sail... a winged shadow in the night sky. It were these dreams that caused the High Priestess to take her to the Waters today, to peer into the bowl on her own for the first time.

She sang a droning chant and clapped her hands in a slow deliberate rhythm, the tiny brass bells around her wrists ringing in unison. As she became entranced, the mists grew thicker, almost tangible, like wisps of pearly sea foam engulfing her, the tripod and the bowl. A rip in the air opened and a waft of the cold wind blew from the depths of the Otherworld. Nagomi sensed the presence of the Spirits before she saw them, little faces in the smoke, studying her curiously, attracted by the sound and movement. The surface of the water stirred and muddied. One of the faces spoke unexpectedly, startling the apprentice.

"What do you seek from the Waters of Scrying?" enquired the Spirit.

"That which lays ahead," she answered, as taught.

The Spirit giggled and disappeared, replaced by another.

"Look into the Water," demanded the new spectre, "if you can see, of course!"

It laughed and swept aside.

"Can she see? She's so young!" whispered another.

"We know her. Yes, we do," replied yet another, "we called her and she came."

Nagomi focused on the bowl and the dark water within, ignoring the giggling, prattling Spirits around her. A red spark suddenly appeared in the bowl then a blue one followed by a green one. Three round jewels in a triangle glistened in the water. They twirled for a moment, and one of the giggly voices whispered in her ear:

Turning, turning, jewels three,
What through blood stone can you see?

The ruby came to the fore of the vision. The other two jewels vanished.

Nagomi peered deeper into the dark mist and saw that the ruby orb was lying upon an altar in some ancient shrine, calm and timeless, shining with soft inner light. A hand appeared over it and grasped it firmly. The hand belonged to a long-haired man wearing a red flowing robe. The apprentice looked up from the jewel, but could only see a black oval where the man's face should be, a shadow darker than night itself. The man leaned closer as if sensing Nagomi's presence, and the shadow that was his face grew and grew until it engulfed the entire bowl in the darkness.

The other two gems appeared, and the whispering voice returned.

Turning, turning, jewels three,
What through tide stone can you see?

It was the turn of the blue jewel, the sapphire. This one started growing fast, encompassing the entire surface of the bowl within seconds. The water turned a stormy dark blue, dotted with tiny white streaks. Nagomi realised she was looking at the sea from high above, and the white streaks were billowing waves.

Something was stirring beneath the waves. The water bubbled as if a volcano was waking up at the bottom of the ocean. An enormous dark shadow appeared, rising fast, greater than any beast, a sea monster with broad, black wings. Just as the creature was about to break through the surface of the sea, the vision shattered into a myriad of tiny blue shards of sapphire glass.

The water was calm again, and dark. All three stones came into view one last time.

Turning, turning, jewels three,
One stone left, what can it be?

The third jewel, the jade, shone with a warm, hopeful life-giving glow. Nagomi sighed with relief and joy, her heart warmed by the gem's radiance, but her sigh broke the spell before the last jewel could fully unveil its vision. The mists scattered, the portal to the Otherworld closed and the water in the bowl turned to its usual, no longer ominous, murkiness. The apprentice swayed and staggered away from the bowl.

"What did you see?" the High Priestess asked.

The vision was only ever given to one soothsayer. Exhausted, with a weak voice, Nagomi described what had been revealed to her in the water. Lady Kazuko's eyes narrowed.

"Are you *sure* this is exactly what you have seen?"

"Yes, High Priestess. What did it mean?"

"Come with me, child."

They trudged down the gravel paths towards the living quarters, past the narrow corridors into Lady Kazuko's private chambers and library.

"Wait here," she said.

She walked up to an octagonal rotating bookcase, wherein sacred musty scrolls lay on many shelves and turned it until she found the right compartment and took out an incredibly ancient-looking document. The priestess blew off the thick layer of dust and unrolled the paper.

Nagomi gasped at the beautiful illumination, a detailed image of dragons drawn in black ink, flying over the brightly red rising sun, the colours still vivid after uncountable ages. Below and alongside the dragons were calligraphic letters in the script so old and elaborate that Nagomi barely recognised it as ancient Yamato writing. She squinted, trying to decipher it, but the High Priestess started reading the squiggly words aloud.

"Ruby, the blood of the Dead,

Sapphire, the jewel of Awakening,

Jade, the bringer of Life,

Black, the wings of Despair.

The monsters come from without,

But the foe lurks within.

The Eight-Headed Serpent rises,

But the Storm God's sword is sheathed.

At the breaking of the world

The Mightiest will fall"

Here the scroll ended abruptly, the edge torn off and scorched.

"What is it?"

"This is one of the oldest prophecies given to us by the Spirits of the Cave of Scrying," explained Lady Kazuko, "older than the shrine itself, passed through untold generations of first shamans and later, the priests. That it survived for so long is a miracle in itself – as you can see, part of it was lost in one of the fires. No living person remembers the rest. Most of the divinations in these scrolls have already come to fulfilment," she continued, carefully rolling up the paper and putting it away onto a shelf. "This is one of the few still remaining unrealised. It is said that when all prophecies of Suwa come to fruition, Yamato will no longer require the Gods and the priests to guide it. I wonder…"

"But what does it mean? Why has it been shown to me? Who else saw it?

"I know of nobody else witnessing the prophecy since it was first recorded, and very few even know of its existence," the High Priestess said. "The *Taikun*s were always very keen to keep it secret – as I'm sure you understand."

"I… I don't think I do."

"*The Mightiest falls*, child. There is only one man in Yamato who fits this description. This is most portentous. I must meditate on the meaning of what has occurred today, and you…" she neared the young apprentice with great seriousness in her eyes, "*you* must be very careful. Do not tell anyone what you have seen today. Not your family, not even your friends. Can you do that for me, child?"

"Y-yes, High Priestess," Nagomi stuttered, frightened. The priestess had never before asked of her anything of the sort. *A secret of the* Taikuns…?

"Good." Lady Kazuko's face wrinkled in a relieved smile. "Now you should rest. It must have been a tiring experience."

Satō wiped the sweat from her brow, grasped firmer the sharkskin-covered hilt of the Matsubara sword and raised the weapon to chest level, aiming straight at the unseen enemy.

"Once again! *Ei!*"

She made a sudden thrust. Half a dozen boys repeated her movements, their swords glistening in the late summer sun, feet slipping on the gravel.

"From the stomach!" She pointed at her abdomen. Her own muscles tightened as her concentration grew. "*Ei!*" – the blade went sideways in a perfectly straight motion.

"*Ei!*" cried the boys, more or less in unison.

"Good, Shōin," she praised the only boy who managed to repeat the cut precisely. "Now, gather the energy. *Ie!*" She raised the blade over her head. A chill went through her arms, her skin was covered with goosebumps. She could feel the sword grow icy cold. "And release - *tō!*"

Satō struck down powerfully, finishing drawing the rune. Even without pronouncing the spell word, a wave of cold air spread from the tip of the sword. The boys repeated after her, but their movements were imprecise and had no effect.

"Listen to the cicadas," she explained, "that's the rhythm we use in this exercise. One, two, three and *four!*" She accented the fourth prolonged cry. "No pause. Focus on that final strike, put your entire soul into it. Come on. *Ei! Ei! Ie - Toooh!*"

The boys tried again, and again they fell out of rhythm by the last strike. Satō sighed. She had never imagined teaching others would be so difficult. As a prospective heir to the Takashima *Dōjō* she had to take over some of the training duties. She was given the youngest pupils, six thirteen year olds, sons of samurai and wealthy merchants at a cusp of puberty, to teach them the very basics of the Takashima method and assess their innate abilities.

"Don't think of the sword as a weapon," she explained one more time, "it is just a tool. This," she said, pointing to her heart, "and this," to her head, "are your weapons."

The boys looked at her blankly. To them a sword was both a symbol of prestige and the power of their parents, and a toy they could play with pretending to be grown-up samurai. They had only recently been given real metal blades. Normally boys of their age would still train with wooden ones, but the Takashima method required affinity with steel from an early stage. Satō struggled to keep discipline among her unruly pupils, but as a girl she could hold no authority over them whatsoever.

As they tried the exercise again one of the boys, supposedly by accident, bumped into another and a quarrel quickly turned into a bout. The cheap blunt blades soon broke and Satō's pupils started punching each other with fists.

"*Stop it!* Oh, I can't stand it," the girl despaired. "*Bevries!*" she cried and drew an ice-shackle rune with her sword. A simple holding spell froze all six boys in a chain of ice, binding their wrists and ankles together.

"Calm down and think of what I have taught you today. I'll be back before dusk to release you – maybe…"

She grinned mischievously, enjoying the look of panic in their eyes. She knew the ice would quickly melt in the scorching summer sun. One of the boys cried in protest, but the rest accepted the painful punishment in silence as was proper. The cicadas laughed.

The wizardess walked up the hill near Sōfukuji Temple, and entered the small house of the Itō family, where Nagomi lived with her mother Otakusa, father Keisuke and elder sister Ine. It was empty and quiet, only the wind bells chimed in the breeze.

"Hello, anybody here? Nagomi? Itō-*sama*?"

She heard light steps on the wooden floor. Nagomi ran out to meet her, tying a red ribbon around her copper-coloured ponytail.

"Sacchan! Finished the class already?"

"I can't do it anymore today, it's too hot. Where is everybody?"

"Daddy was called off to Nagoya. There's an outburst of smallpox there. Mother went to see him off at the harbour. Ine is on a house visit, so I'm left to look after the home."

"Nagoya? But that's on Hondo!"

The main island of the Yamato archipelago lay days of journey away from Kiyō, and the city of Nagoya was right in the middle of it. One needed to have a really good reason to embark on such a journey.

"Daddy was born there, actually," Nagomi explained. "He only came here to study."

"I always forget your family is not originally from Kiyō."

"It was so long ago… He was just a herbalist's apprentice then. Now the lord of the domain himself requested his presence."

"You must be proud."

"I am," Nagomi answered, "but I wish he'd come back soon."

"Do you want to go to the bathhouse?"

"I was going to prepare some talismans for the shrine shop, but I guess I could do it later…"

Soon they lay naked on the stone bottom of a shallow steaming pool, only their heads bobbing above the surface. The spring water was steaming hot and crystal clear, with only a slight scent of sulphur. It was early in the day, so they had the bath all to themselves.

"Aah," sighed Satō, "that's just what I needed. These kids make my head ache. They can't even hold the sword straight!"

"They are only thirteen."

"I could cut down a straw pole at their age!" protested Satō, "and shoot an ice lance through a wooden plank one sun thick!" She spread two fingers to show the thickness of the imaginary piece of wood. "But, of course, boys are so useless." She sighed and lay back onto the stones. "All they care about is fighting. They just can't focus. No wonder none of them could ever beat me."

"My parents say Takashima-*sama* should officially name you his heir already. No one in Kiyō would be better suited to the position – and he's not getting any younger."

"That's very kind of them, but there is no law for a daughter to inherit a *dōjō*. It wouldn't be very wise for us to draw attention to ourselves."

"He's not planning to marry you off to some snotty-nosed son of a samurai, is he?"

"Gods, I hope not!" Satō laughed briefly. "I doubt if he even thinks about these things. He's not interested in anything apart from his experiments."

At least that's what I must believe, she thought, *that he's just forgetful, or waiting for the right moment.* Why else would he wait for so long? Nagomi's parents were right – she was the best pupil her father could ever dream of having.

"I hear there's a new resident wizard on Dejima." Nagomi reached for a face towel to wipe droplets of steam from her brow. "Have you met him yet?"

"I have," Satō replied with a nod, "he came to talk with my father before leaving for Edo. He's… different. Small and round, but very clever."

And frightening.

"Did he bring any gifts?"

"Just another sparkleball," she scoffed. "As if I was a child."

"I love sparkleballs! I need to come over and see it! What colour is it?"

"It's red, yellow and blue, a bit bigger and flashier than the last one. Father and I had really hoped for a new spell scroll or a blueprint, but I guess they're not allowed that anymore."

The apprentice lifted herself up and sat on a cypress board lining the edge of the spring, with only her legs still in the water. She ran her hand through her long hair, sparkling fiery red now that her locks were wet. Sometimes they seemed to change their hue according to Nagomi's mood.

"It's so hot today," she complained, "I can't sit still for more than ten minutes."

"It's better to come here in the winter," Satō agreed.

"I won't be able to do it as often when the summer ends."

"Why not?"

"After the Kunchi Festival I'm moving into the shrine permanently. I'm becoming a full-time apprentice."

"That's..." Satō hesitated. "That's great!" she said without conviction.

"Oh, you are always welcome to come up and see me." Nagomi smiled. "I'll just have to pay more attention to my duties, that's all. Besides, I'm sure you will be busy too, with all the training and teaching..."

"I guess so." Satō nodded solemnly. The lazy, relaxed mood perished. She became keenly aware of the passing of time.

Even in Yamato nothing ever remains unchanged, she thought.

She stood up abruptly. The hot water rippled before splashing onto the cold stone floor.

CHAPTER V

Gwynedd, July, 2606 ab urbe condita

Bran sipped on his ale and winced. It was too warm; everything was too warm this summer. The eldest of the yeomen gathered at the Red Dragon *tafarn* could barely remember a July as hot as that of Victoria Alexandrina's Sixteenth Year. The south-easterly wind bringing rain and fog from over the bay was gone. The air was stale and dry.

"I'm telling you, it's all the damned navy's fault," said a tall stout fellow wearing a blue felt cap crooked over one ear. "They've taken all our best Weathermen and left us only the shoddy ones, who messed everything up instead of fixing it."

"My well is running dry," another yeoman added to the complaints.

"What if there is famine, Huw?" a younger lad said. "I don't want to have to leave my land and sail to Gorllewin."

"Gorllewin? Those merchant folk across the sea?"

"That's what they did in Ériu. My cousin said the entire villages packed and left overnight. Swathes of land left abandoned…"

"They say nobody ever came back from Gorllewin," the man called Huw said grimly.

"And who would?" scoffed the third of the farmers, stroking his greying beard. "I've heard that anyone who sails there gets a piece of their own land the size of a village."

"A piece of wild forest you have to fell yourself, or a piece of stony grassland you have to till yourself," said Huw, shaking his head.

"And they're all Grey Hoods there. Sun worshippers," added the youngest, spitting, "as devoted as the Romans. You'd have to convert back to the Old Faith."

"It's better than seeing all your crops wither," the third man snorted, "and all your livestock perish with famine."

"Don't worry, Rhys, the Llambed boys won't let us starve. Right son?"

Huw raised a tankard towards Bran. He smiled weakly, knowing too well that if the crops *would* fail, the villagers would soon find somebody to blame, even though there never were any Weathermen at Llambed. Even his father showed some concern about the weather. There had already been recruiters from Gorllewin sneaking around the town – shifty, grey-hooded men, speaking an oddly twisted version of the Seaxe tongue, offering land and untold riches across the ocean.

"Why, I can feel the rain coming already."

The man in the felt cap winced and rubbed his elbow emphatically.

The weather was beginning to take its toll on Emrys. The dragon was of the race the scholars called Draco Palustris, a Swamp or Marsh Wyrm, said to be descended from the great Tarasques of the Rodanus delta. Its domain was the wet mud pits, peat moors and shallow brackish pools. Now the swamps along the Teifi river, which flowed through Gwaelod, were scorched dry and the beast's parched body demanded moisture. Bran did what he could to accommodate the beast's needs, but bathing in seawater brought only a little respite to the land-born creature. When Bran had to help with something at home he would have Emrys sleep by the well and, from time to time, pour buckets of cold water over the dragon's jade scales.

Sometimes when he glanced at the windows of their house, with its old walls painted bright red, he saw his mother observing these efforts with concern. The dragon was a constant source of problems – and mockery from neighbours, family and other pupils at Llambed. It was a child's toy, the first dragon Bran had ever ridden. By the time of the Graddio most dragon riders would already have moved on to one of the large races, Belerion Crimsons, Forest Viridians or Highland Azures, but Bran grew attached to his mount and had never considered replacing it.

The jade green drake looked particularly wretched next to Afreolus, Bran's father's mighty mount. Reserved for the noblemen and soldiers of the Royal Dragoons, the Mountain Silvers or Wyrmkings, as they were more commonly known, were rare and expensive. Larger than any other race, bred exclusively on the royal pastures of the Pictish Highlands in the far north or imported from overseas, these were the dragons with the most strength and stamina of all the known Western races, and Afreolus was a prime specimen.

Dylan was spending most of the summer away from home, always finding something with which to busy himself. Between shopping excursions to Penfro, hunting trips with army colleagues and helping with research at the Llambed Academy, he was almost as rarely seen in the small, slate-roofed house as when he'd been sailing. They rarely talked. Most of their conversations turned to quarrels.

Bran was restless as well. The days of reckless adolescence may have been over, but he did not care much for the duties of a grown-up yet. He wasted away the days swimming in the cold sea, wandering the hills, and picking berries and nuts in the forest. In the afternoons, when it was cool enough, he and Emrys flew around, training acrobatics over the green tops of the five-peaked Pumlumon, or chasing red kites over the Elenydd uplands, enjoying the solitude of the blue sky.

On calm warm evenings they glided over the shaded hazel groves and slate-walled sheep pastures. Rising currents of the Ninth Wind carried the dragon effortlessly along the elm-lined brooks and across the green marshes, all the way towards the tall brick chimneys and iron towers of the Enchanted Mines along the southern coast, where the wizards cut deep into the Earth's crust to reach the realms of the fire elementals. Sometimes the air got so hot and stagnant Emrys refused to fly. Then Bran wandered alone about the wilderness of Eryri, far to the north, until he reached the summit of the mighty Yr Wyddfa and looked down over the misty crags, ridges and peaks towards the northern sea and the dreaded Ynys Mon, the foreboding island fortress of the Druids, Guardians of Prydain, in a foolish hope of catching a glimpse of Eithne's red hair among the oak trees.

These were the limits of his world. Here, unbound at last from the walls of the Academy, he could go wherever he wanted. From Mon in the north to Ynys Dewi in the south, from the sunset-facing beaches of Gwyddno to the peaks of Brycheinniog where the dawn rose and the silver-haired Tylwyth Teg, the Fair Folk, danced around the ruined gate to their long lost homeland.

He could just wander these wild lands forever, chasing deer and falcon, growing old, watching Emrys grow and mature. He could live the life of a small town mage, settle down somewhere near Penfro, meet a nice girl... but of course his father would *never* have that. He had to come up with a better idea for his future and his time was running short.

Old Huw's rains neither came in July nor August. It was now September and while the evenings got somewhat cooler, the clouds were still scarce in the azure skies.

The earthy scent of fresh peat and dew on wet heather rose on the breeze. Bran stooped as he neared the pond in the middle of the dried-up moor, hiding in the brambles and thorn. He brushed the sun-scorched yellow fern aside and sniffed. There it was; the unmistakable smell of sulphur and methane. It was very faint - a less experienced tracker would have dismissed it as the natural aroma of the swamp. The beast was very careful not to let itself be detected.

The young stalker sneaked through the hazels and rowans around the pond, to stay downwind. He was now entering a shallow treacherous bog – the river flowed freely here in spring, but now it was all but dried out. It was harder to move quietly and smoothly. Soon Bran had to half-creep, half-swim in the brackish mire, his jacket now blackened with mud. He suppressed a sneeze.

He could see it now, almost submerged in the shallow water, larger than a fully grown bull, horned head covered under a leathery wing, long tail coiled neatly around the scaled body, sleeping - or feigning sleep. Bran unsheathed his sword, pointed it in the direction of the creature and murmured the Binding Words. The spell was not powerful enough to fully chain its target, but it should make its movements sluggish and restricted.

The dragon stirred as it detected magic. This was the moment to strike. Bran raised his sword and jumped ahead with a battle cry but his boot got trapped and he fell face-first into the water with a loud splash.

By the time he got up, cursing, the dragon was fully awake. It bared its teeth, hissing at short intervals.

"Oh sure, laugh", muttered Bran, trying to wipe the mud from his leather tunic and squinting his bright green eyes, full of brackish stinging water. "I almost had you this time, you know."

The dragon yawned and stretched to its full six feet, still sluggish from the effects of the spell. Bran licked the blood trickling from his knuckles, grazed against something hard in the water.

"What the *Duw* did I trip on? There shouldn't have been any roots here…"

He stooped to investigate by the light of a conjured flamespark and saw what looked like bones of some great ancient animal submerged in the mud. As the riverbed dried out in the heat, the falling water levels had revealed the ageless fossil. Bran touched the remains gingerly.

"I wonder what it was. Something big – an elk maybe, or a wyvern – "

The blue gem on his left hand suddenly burned up with a bright, warm azure light. Bran stared at the jewel in disbelief for a moment, before something else drew his attention.

"By Owain's Sword…"

The fossilised bones stirred and started moving, crackling, slithering in the mud like ivory snakes. Bran jumped backwards, frightened. Emrys whinnied anxiously as the shattered parts of the massive skeleton combined into one and the creature slowly started rising from the moor.

There was now no doubt as to what manner of a beast had died and left its remains in the peat. What had once been a great dragon – easily twice the size of Emrys – towered over the boy menacingly, swaying and staggering as it tried to find its balance after waking from aeons of sleep.

"W-we'd better go, Emrys," Bran stuttered, retreating onto the higher ground, searching for the wind goggles in his pocket.

The ring was now almost burning his finger. The jade-scaled dragon crouched towards its master, whimpering. Through their Farlink connection, Bran felt primeval fear growing in his mount's heart as the skeletal creature began stumbling out of the mud pool. The bone dragon spread its wings – or what remained of them. Names from the anatomy manual popped into Bran's head - *humerus, radius, phalanges*… It felt surreal to see the skeleton in reality, in full scale, dried-up joints grinding against each other.

Can it fly? Impossible, there is no membrane to give it lift…

The jaws, still full of teeth, opened as if the beast wanted to roar. There was no roar – there couldn't have been, the monster had no throat, but, disturbingly, there came a sound, a stifled, echoing humming rumble, as if from the depths of the Otherworld.

Bran managed to mount Emrys, his hands shaking with terror. He was trying to spur the terrified dragon to flight, when the bone monster flapped its wings and pounced onwards.

"*Duck!*" Bran cried out loud and in his head.

Emrys flattened itself in the marsh as the skeletal dragon, capturing the Ninth Wind in its phantom wings, soared above their heads. The monster circled in the sky once before swooping straight back at Bran, its jaws open, the unearthly noise rising again within the non-existent throat.

The boy tugged on the upper reins and pushed his heels into the dragon's sides. Emrys stood on its hind legs and spewed bluish methane fire. The skeletal monster reeled in its dive and ascended again, gaining altitude for another swoop. With a single beat of wings, Emrys leapt over the tops of the trees, and farther up. Alone, it would stand little chance against the dragon twice its size, but Bran had been trained to fight exactly this kind of aerial battle, and now it seemed his life depended on his skill.

A summoned Soul Lance hardened in his hands into an unbreakable crystal. The bone dragon plunged forwards in a mad head-on charge, like a raging stag. Bracing himself for attack, Bran adjusted his goggles and raised the lance in an outstretched arm as he had trained so many times, although his hand was shaking with dread and excitement. He could not guess whether the weapon would work against a living skeleton – there were no internal organs to penetrate after all, no scales to pierce. He could only hope.

He waited until he could feel the buffeting of the Ninth Wind coming from the skeletal wings. He tugged on the reins, banking Emrys to the left and pushed his right arm forwards. He missed – the lance hit the air. The bone dragon flew past, the stench of death around it so nauseating it almost caused Bran to fall off his mount.

The bone dragon turned back and roared again. The tops of the trees beneath turned black and withered; the monster was spewing *something* from its maw, not fire or lightning, but some invisible veil of death.

I won't get another chance, Bran realised, spurring Emrys to a charge. The two dragons sped towards each other, air whistling around them. Bran closed his eyes and focused on the Farlink connection he had with Emrys. Only this gave Bran the precise control he needed.

Down!

Emrys's wings folded and the beast dropped down, underneath the belly of the bone monster. Bran opened his eyes, breaking the Farlink, and struck upwards with all his strength. He felt the lance smash through the monster's ribs and penetrate further, piercing through something that was as unlike a real chest and heart, as the unworldly rumbling was different from a real dragon's dying roar.

He let go of the lance – the weapon disappeared in an instant – a fraction of a second before the impetus would've broken his arm. He watched as the monstrosity tumbled downwards and crashed into the marsh below, bones scattering into pieces again.

Emrys snorted and flew up higher and higher, until it deemed it was at a safe distance from the cursed pool. Bran was too exhausted and confused to command the beast, so he let his dragon do as it pleased for a moment.

The blue gem on his finger was as calm and dark as it had always been. Bran welcomed the sight of the familiar, tall sandstone towers and oak tree groves of the Llambed Academy with relief. Usually he went go out of his way not to pass it, but this time he wanted to see something real, something certain, and he needed some answers.

A flag with the four lions of Aberffraw flew proudly over the pile of grey stones. A remnant of a Norse castle, at the confluence of the Rivers Teifi and Dulas, only a few months ago had served as the Great Auditorium for the Graddio ceremony. The ruin had been left standing as a reminder of Owain the Wyrmslayer's great campaigns against the Norsemen of Niflheimr and their Frost Armies. It was here, on the shores of Teifi, that the freedom of Gwynedd had been won once and for all, and the alliance with the oppressed Seaxe on the other side of Offa's Dyke forged for the first time of many.

The grapevine leaves clung to the cracked walls, lush green when the summer had begun then scorched yellow by August heat, growing scarlet now. The oak trees in the sacred groves turned golden-bronze. The college grounds, sprawling to the north and east of the castle ruins, were eerily quiet during the summer holidays, with only the gardeners and janitors remaining. Gone was the daily hubbub of hundreds of boys and girls, learning, training and playing around. Gone was the noise of dozens of dragons stationed in the Great Stables, the flapping of wings, roar of wyrm flame and crackle of lightning, but there were always lights and fires coming from the Research Tower, and there Bran landed his dragon.

"I don't see anything peculiar about the ring, I'm afraid," said Doctor Campion upon finishing a long examination of the jewel. "The band is a local work, of that I am sure. The gem seems valuable – a sapphire, I believe, although we would need to do an analysis to make certain. Interesting shape. Where did you say you got it?"

"My grandfather."

"And he...?"

"I... don't know."

I never really asked about it.

"Mm, mm."

The doctor nodded distractedly, playing with knobs on his telescope. They were sitting in the astrological observatory on top of the Research Tower. Doctor Campion was the only scholar who had time to meet with Bran at such short notice, as during the day he had little to do other than browsing through old horoscopes and solar tables in the library.

"What about the bone dragon, Sir?"

"This is an ancient land, boy, full of mysteries. You would not have heard of such things – it's deep in the archives... Old, forbidden magic."

"You mean - raising the dead? It's just a legend, isn't it...?"

"Nay, son." The doctor leaned forwards and lowered his voice. "It's more than that. The dead walked the land when the wars with the Sun Priests ravaged the world. It was almost the doom of us all..."

The clergy of the Bull-slayer God, the Old Faithers of Rome, had once been sworn enemies of all magic users, so much Bran knew. It had taken two centuries of war to settle their mutual differences at last. Many gruesome tales were told of the terrible Wizardry Wars, but this one Bran had not heard before.

"I'm not surprised," the doctor said. "We have kept it secret – us, magic users and the priests alike... I'm only telling you this because you've already met one of those creatures, and because I know your father."

He leaned closer to Bran, his eyes narrow and focused.

"It started with the Grey Hoods, the elite of the Sun Priests. They have discovered some ancient scrolls in the monasteries of Illyria, in the East. They were appalled at first, but when faced with defeat from the wizards they began to turn to anything that could give them advantage."

"Necromancy..." whispered Bran. The word had a dark taste on his tongue.

The doctor nodded.

"They were using it to raise fallen soldiers at first, but soon discovered that by using blood magic curses they could imbue the walking dead with great power, and keep them under control. They started raising *our* dead and send them against us. Then the wizards stole the secret and began doing the same. Not only with humans, but as you have also seen, dragons and other beasts. It was a travesty of a war; lifeless armies that could not be killed. Ere long the abominations learned to disguise themselves as if they were still alive. Bonds of trust have been broken – anyone could be killed at night and wake as an undead. Soldiers returning from the battles were no longer welcome home. And worst of all, some of the Abominations started to work together, turn against their masters..."

"But we've prevailed in the end."

"At a great cost. We signed a truce with the Sun Priests, a temporary alliance against what we had created. Both sides had to agree to abandon such pursuits, destroy the Abominations, unravel the magic, erase the very memory of the evil power. You must have stumbled upon some remnant from just before the Truce, some bone golem cast in the river when the war was over."

Bran scratched his forehead, trying to absorb all he had just heard.

"But what does my ring have to do with it?"

"Oh, I don't think it does, to be honest." The scholar leaned backwards. "It must have merely resonated to the magical energies abundant in the marsh. Some minerals do that, nothing mysterious about it. It's a neat trick, certainly, but that is all."

"I see..."

"Mars is in Sagittarius," the doctor added, raising a finger, "which means people and beasts awake, stir, become restless. The heat doesn't help – there hasn't been a summer this hot for decades. The water reveals what it had once taken. I would advise you to stay away from dried up riverbeds, landslides, ancient ruins... All these places may be dangerous right now."

"Yes Sir."

"You did well." The doctor smiled and patted Bran on the shoulder. "To have faced such a creature and defeated it takes skill and courage, especially when riding such a weak dragon. I would expect no less from the son of Dylan ab Ifor."

Bran let the insult towards Emrys go.

"Thank you, Sir."

"By the by, would you like to see your father?"

"He's here?"

"I believe so, I've seen him heading for the Chambers of Precision."

Bran hesitated.

"I… I'm sure he wouldn't like to be disturbed at work."

"As you wish. Now, you must excuse me." The doctor sighed, reaching for a pile of densely scribbled documents. "I do have a few divinations to prepare for tonight…"

CHAPTER VI

Gwynedd, August, 2606 ab urbe condita

Bran raised his ring to the light, straining his True Sight to the limits. There wasn't even a trace of magic to it.

"Something wrong with it, is it?" Rhian asked.

"Nothing," he lied. "Where did *tadcu* get this ring?"

Dylan had given it to him on his eleventh birthday, just before Bran's entrance to the Academy; he had worn it on a cord around his neck then, his little hands much too small for the piece of jewellery.

"Oh, Ifor brought it from one of his travels," Rhian answered vaguely, "he kept bringing us trinkets like this all the time, he did."

"So why was I given *this* one?"

"Before he left, he insisted you be given this ring. I don't really like it myself – a Prydain boy should wear a torc. "

"What was he like, grandfather?"

"Shouldn't you ask your *taid* about that?"

Bran shrugged.

"Father never tells me anything. You know what he's like."

Rhian smiled and pulled up a chair.

"You know, you're beginning to look a bit like young Ifor on the True Images, you are," she said, "soon you'll start growing a tidy moustache then you'll be the same *dap* exactly."

"Father's not wearing a moustache."

"Ah, well, he's in the Lloegr Navy now, he is. They like 'em clean-shaven." She laughed briefly, but then turned serious. "Ifor was… a funny old man, as we call them down south. He never was much of a family man. You could tell he was a sailor through and through. I don't know why he decided to settle here in Gwynedd after Dylan went to school – it was obvious he wasn't in his oils on land."

"Is that why he ran away?"

Rhian brushed a dark lock from her brow.

"Well, he did *not* run away – he promised us that he would return, one day, but he wasn't all there at the end."

"What did he think of Father going to Llambed?"

"Oh, tamping mad, he was! At least that's what Dylan told me. He hated wizards - superstitious, like all sailors. He wanted Dylan to be a Sun Priest."

Bran's eyes widened.

"*A Sun Priest?*"

There was still a *mithraeum* in Caer Wyddno, serving the small community of Old Faithers, but Bran had never seen his father as much as go near the cavernous building.

"Aye. *Only the Unconquered Sun will save us when the Abomination returns*, he used to say. I don't know what he meant. He had the house painted red, to ward off *evil*. I told you - funny old man."

Abomination?

"I had no idea about that."

"You'll find there are many reasons why Dylan is not eager to talk about his family. Now see, it's getting late - I'll run the bath, shall I?"

"Yes, please!" Bran agreed.

Rhian stood up and thought for a second.

"If you really want to find out more about your *tadcu*, have a tidy in the attic. There's bound to be something interesting up there. I don't think even Dylan has ever looked through everything that's in those chests."

"I'll do that."

"Will you come to watch the Ellylldani dance?"

Bran smiled. When he was little, he loved to observe the tiny Fire Fairies – *Salamandrae Inferiores,* as the biology teacher called them – frolic under the bathtub as the water boiled above their heads.

"I think I'm a little too old for that, *Mam.*"

"Yes, of course, son."

Rhian smiled, but Bran could see sadness in her eyes.

A couple of old navy trunks of thick leather hidden away in the corner of the attic contained a treasure trove of books, scrolls and old papers, printed long before Bran's birth. Most of them were accounts of trade negotiations and maritime treaties, but there was among them a collection of fascinating reports on mysterious lands of the Far East, including a volume on Eastern dragons, long-bodied, wingless creatures that very few Western Dracologists had a chance to see and research. Bran searched through the books, trying to discover any clues on Ifor from notes on the margins, but they were all written in strange scribbly markings of some unknown Oriental script.

One early September evening, hot and muggy, he dug down all the way to the bottom of the largest trunk, hoping to find some more forgotten mementos. There was usually something interesting at the very bottom of a chest like this, some artefact from Ifor's journeys, either deliberately hidden or sunken through the papers over the years. A pile of documents and books grew on the floor as Bran dived farther and farther in. At last, he reached one final bunch of yellowed, densely written pieces of paper. Apart from those, the trunk was empty. Slightly disappointed, he picked up the sheets and found a small box of strange material lay underneath.

It was neither wood nor metal, smooth to the touch, but strong like ivory, raven black with a reddish glint. On the top was a golden emblem, a diamond shape split in four.

He lifted the box carefully and stared at it for a while, hesitant to open.

Why had it been hidden in this chest?

It certainly seemed more precious than any of the useless souvenirs forgotten in the attic, the unknown material glistening mysteriously in the light of the setting sun like polished onyx. The emblem, as far as he could tell, was made of real gold leaf.

He opened it carefully. Inside, the box was split into two compartments. One of them held a golden brooch of an unusual sort, or rather a buckle tied to a slender ribbon of silk, in the shape of an Eastern dragon coiled around an irregular jagged hole, where a stone was missing. Bran pressed his ring to it – the blue stone fit snugly.

In the other compartment lay a round silver medallion with the True Image of a young woman. The woman, gazing sadly at Bran from the thaumaturgic illustration, was unlike any the boy had ever seen. Her skin was pale and without blemish, her eyes child-like, almond-shaped beneath thin straight eyebrows, her nose small and flat, her hair black and glistening, coiffured into a tall bun intertwined with flowers and elaborate leaf-shaped ornaments.

When he touched the surface of the image, the scribbled hieroglyphs from the margin notes appeared vertically along the side of the medallion. A translation in Prydain materialised below.

BELOVED ŌMON. IFOR, 51 GEO. III

Whoever the woman was, she was not Bran's grandmother. The boy remembered *mamgu* Branwen well as a decent Gwynedd woman with nothing remotely exotic about her.

The yellowed crumbling papers covering the box appeared to be the pages from Ifor's diary. Bran had found a few scattered fragments of the memoirs earlier, but these sheets had been set apart, tied together with black cord and stamped with a red ink seal of the same split diamond shape as the markings on the box.

With racing heart Bran took them to the window, where the last rays of the setting sun cast a crimson tint on the paper.

HMS Phaeton, Temasek, 48 Geo. III – he deciphered. Year Forty-Eight of the Mad King's reign.

Forty-five years ago.

It was too dark to read the rest of it, so Bran snapped his fingers and a hovering flamespark appeared over his head. In its flickering bright light, the boy continued.

HMS Phaeton, *Temasek, 48 Geo. Iii (2561 A.U.C.), July 14*

We got a new captain today. Broughton Reynolds, a brash young fellow. He's barely nineteen and has already made a name for himself with dauntless attacks on Bataavian ships. Looks like our two years' holiday is over.

HMS Phaeton, *East of Bashi Channel, 48 Geo. III (2561 a.u.c.), September 23*

We are chasing a stubborn Bataavian merchantman across the South Qin Sea, and have now entered, on good wind, the uncharted waters east of Ederra. The captain refuses to give up the chase. Where is the Bataavian going, anyway? There are no ports here other than the Qin beyond their tarian, and if he wished to cross the Ocean then we've already missed the currents.

HMS Phaeton, *Unknown Waters, 48 Geo. III (2561 a.u.c.), September 30*

The sea is like nothing I have ever seen. It's calm where we sail, but mists and storm clouds are all around us. The Weatherman stands on the prow and says nothing. The navigator hasn't left his room for days. Men say his mind is going. At least the Bataavian seems to know where he's headed, and we're still able to follow him.

HMS Phaeton, *Unknown Port, 48 Geo. III (2561 a.u.c.), October 4*

We have entered a pleasant warm bay surrounded by green hills. A great city sprawls on all sides, with all dwellings made of dark wood and whitewashed stone. The Bataavian anchored at a fan-shaped island in the middle of the bay, connected with the mainland only through a narrow bridge and a gate. There is a multitude of Qin and other ships in the harbour, all very primitive.

Both the island and the city are within range of our guns. There seem to be no proper cannons defending the bay whatsoever. We are flying Bataavian colours.

HMS Phaeton, *Keeyo, 48 Geo. III (2561 a.u.c.), October 5*

The Bataavian officials entered the ship to inspect it. The captain ordered them captured for hostages and to fly the Imperial Jack.

We've learned from our prisoners that the island is called "Dejeema", the city is "Keeyo" and the country is that of "Yamato". I have sailed these oceans for the best part of my life, but I've never heard of this port. Where in Annwn are we?

The merchantman was running empty, so to gain anything from the adventure, the captain demanded the Bataavians to provide us with supplies and some silver bullion, of which we know the red-heads always keep plenty. Our Carron guns gave a warning shot and, judging from the reaction of the locals, this was the first time they had ever seen or heard such devices. The authorities of this Keeyo seem unable to stage any sort of effective defence, so it looks like the matter will be resolved only between us and the Bataavians.

HMS Phaeton, *Keeyo, 48 Geo. III (2561 a.u.c.), October 6*

A most unexpected development. Today a boat approached our ship and a local woman — very pretty, I must add, and wearing the finest of silks — begged to be let on board. She spoke good Bataavian. The captain took pity on her. He is now discoursing with her in his cabin. What can all this mean?

Later today another boat arrived and a local official, through an interpreter, demanded the release of the woman in a very haughty tone. We've "released" a musketful of lead shot instead, and he turned tail.

HMS Phaeton, *Keeyo, 48 Geo. III (2561 a.u.c.), October 7*
Out of the blue, the captain ordered us to set sail in the morning, even before we received all the supplies we asked for.

As we were about to lift the anchor, there was an explosion on the island and a raging fire spread quickly throughout the wooden buildings. The Bataavians and locals alike fled from the flames to the boats. Soon there was only one man left standing on the shore. I looked at him through the spyglass to see what manner of fool he was.

It felt like he was looking straight at me, even though the ship was by now a good half a league away from the island. He wore a flowing crimson robe, his hair was long, dark, flowing in the wind and his eyes – I swear – gleamed like nuggets of pure gold. He raised his hand and pointed accusingly at the Phaeton.

I shiver even now writing about this queer incident. I am glad we've left the wretched place behind.

HMS Phaeton, *South Qin Sea, 48 Geo. III (2561 a.u.c.), October 10*
As soon as we had left Keeyo harbour, a strong north-easterly carried us towards charted waters. We should be back in Temasek much sooner than we hoped.

Saw the Yamato girl promenading the deck with the captain. She really is the most striking beauty. Like all her kin, she seems to belong to the same race as the people of Qin or Siam, but her skin is very smooth and pale, almost glowing. We exchanged glances and she smiled.

There is sadness in her brown eyes, and she is looking sickly, as if she was carrying some heavy burden on her heart. I hope we can get her to a safe harbour soon.

That was the last page. There was no mention of the pendant or the medallion. Bran could only guess what happened next, but the inscription on the locket proved Ifor and the mysterious woman at some point had grown closer. Their happiness, however, could not last long. Dylan had been born two years after the True Image's creation, and he was definitely the son of Branwen, Ifor's first and only wife. Something must have separated Ifor from his beloved Ōmon... Perhaps she had at last succumbed to the sickness mentioned in the diary. On the other side was a rough sketch of a map. He studied it carefully, read aloud the names he had barely recognised. Where the easternmost verge of the vast Varyaga Empire met the mysterious land of Qin out in the ocean, on the other side of the globe from Dracaland, there was a red question mark signed *YAMATO*.

His heart pounded madly. He looked out through the attic window, where the Sun traced scarlet the edge of a long line of dunes. Beyond the dunes lay the endless sea, the slow humming of its waves clearly audible in the twilight. He imagined himself on that sea, on a ship bound for uncharted shores, sailing to Bharata, Temasek or even Qin. The low hills and forests of his homeland appeared too familiar, boring, suffocating. Now he knew why his father - and his father's father – had abandoned the friendly plains of Prydain and sailed the wide oceans; the wanderlust stirred within him and there was no escaping its call.

Sweat streamed down Dylan's furrowed forehead in thick rivulets, even though the Chamber of Precision was always cooled to exactly sixteen point four degrees centigrade. He stared at the floating needle intently, without blinking.

The silver needle entered a tiny hole in the side of a bronze cylinder, alongside a hundred other identical needles.

The last one.

As it settled in with a barely audible click, Dylan sighed and fell back onto his leather chair.

"Fantastic work, Master Dylan." The assistant, wearing the white and blue mantle of a thaumaturgist, clapped his hands. "Without your help, assembling this lightning capacitor would have taken us a month!"

"It's nothing. I'm glad to be useful."

"There is always a use for one with such talent. If I may be so bold, why didn't you stay at the Academy, Sir?"

Dylan looked at the boy and smiled.

"How old are you, son?"

"Nineteen this year, Sir."

"Ah, you've got your baccalaureate then?"

"Just this June."

"I can see by the way you wear your coat that you are used to wielding a sword. Second faculty in Dracology?"

"My first, actually. I've only taken up thaumaturgy as an alderman, but I much prefer it here in the Tower of Research."

"Yet you still fly sometimes?"

"Oh, yes, Sir, once in a while," the boy said with a nod, "I don't have a dragon, but I borrow one from the Academy stables."

"Are you a good rider?"

"So I've been told, Sir."

"Then you understand what it's like to have a passion for one thing and ability for another. I won't give up the feeling of hot wind on my face, or the smell of the sea any less than you would give up your experiments."

The assistant's face lightened.

"To take pleasure from what you do for a living is a great gift, boy," Dylan added. "You and I are both very lucky to have it this way."

"I can't disagree with that, Sir."

Dylan nodded to himself. The boy seemed happy enough where he was. Why Bran couldn't be more like him? Dylan wished to give Bran the same simple happiness, the joy of living his life doing what he was best at but his son's lingering uncertainty irritated him.

He must grow up.

The heavy faer iron door to the Chamber of Precision hissed open and Doctor Campion entered with a bundle of notes.

"Here are the divinations you asked for, Dylan."

"Ah, excellent, give them to the gentleman here," he said, pointing to the assistant. "You know what to do with it, boy?"

"Of course, Sir, the calculations of Solar and Jovian tides are of the utmost importance to our work."

"By the by," the astrologer said, turning from the door, "I keep forgetting to tell you – about week ago I've seen your son."

"What, here?"

"Well, yes. He stumbled upon some lich dragon in the marshes and wanted to know what it was."

Dylan frowned.

"A lich dragon?"

He never said anything...

"The swamps up here are full of those remains, you know – all the monsters escaped from the Ruin of Aberteifi."

"And have you... told him?"

"About the Abominations? As much as we are allowed to divulge, yes."

Dylan scratched his scar in thought.

"Was he all right?"

"He was unscathed as far as I could tell. He is a very brave lad, Dylan. I told him not to worry."

"Did he know I was here?"

"He said he didn't wish to disturb you. That sounded like a sensible idea."

Dylan stood up abruptly and glanced first at the lightning capacitor then at the assistant.

"You'll be all right with that on your own?"

"Of course, Sir, but – "

"I'm going home. I think I need to talk to my son."

Dylan wanted to talk about the bone dragon, but Bran would hear nothing of it.

"I want to sail with you on your next voyage, Father," Bran said with a firm, unwavering voice.

Rhian put down her cup of afternoon tea noisily and looked at her two men with concern.

Out of the question! Dylan wanted to say, but only sat down and started at his son, dumbfounded. He suspected Bran's primary motive was a trip overseas and back, giving him at least a year to decide about his future.

"You've told me so many stories about your youth out at sea," argued Bran, as the silence prolonged, "but I've never been anywhere. My idea of a 'faraway land' is Glowancestre!"

"I only joined the corps after eight years in the Academy," Dylan reminded him, but there was no conviction in his voice.

He had sailed around most of the Dracaland's colonial dominion before the age of twelve, accompanying Ifor on various merchant and warships. He had witnessed all the perils and dangers of life on the open sea and hoped to shelter his son from them, but it seemed the call of blood could no longer be ignored.

"And you are certain this is what you want?"

He raised his green eyes and looked straight into Bran's to try to discern the truth.

"On my dragon's wings," the boy replied with an oath understood by every dragon rider.

"Let me talk to your mother in private."

Dylan stood up and nodded at Rhian. They disappeared into the kitchen.

"I knew it would end like this. He kept asking me about your father, he did."

"It was bound to happen. He's got the Sea in his blood. Like me."

"You're not thinking of letting him go with you?"

Dylan bit his lips nervously and took her by a hand.

"Is that such a bad idea? A trip like this would be a perfect opportunity for us to bond."

"He's your only son, Dylan. He should be at school. You could force this decision on him if needed be."

"Then he will despise me even more."

"Isn't it dangerous out there?" she asked.

It's not exactly safe here, either, thought Dylan, remembering the bone dragon.

"I have been sailing for almost thirty years now and no harm has ever come to me. Besides, this is just a simple diplomatic mission."

"He is not you," she said.

"He's not a *dwt* anymore – he'll be sixteen next year. His friends are already joining the army."

Rhian sat down on a stool and gazed outside the kitchen window.

"You Gwaelod folk just can't stay in one place for too long. It's that damned sea at your doorstep. I should have gotten used to it by now."

Dylan embraced her tenderly.

"Look at the boy, Rhian. I can sense his dislike. He thinks *I* dislike him! I've never taken him anywhere; I'm always late for everything. We'd be back before summer."

She gave him the look of silent, resigned disapproval he had known so well.

"I will consider it," he told Bran when they returned to the room. "I'm to sail to the land of Qin in October, so I'd suggest you learn whatever there is to learn about it. At any rate, a little knowledge never hurt anybody."

"Yes, Father," Bran said, bowing respectfully, barely containing his excitement.

He walked slowly out of the living room, but as soon as he was out through the doorway, he sprinted to the stables.

Dylan looked after him and shook his head.

"I do hope he's not planning on taking that *thing* with him..."

CHAPTER VII

Gwynedd, October, 2606 ab urbe condita

"What's that on the coast, Father?" Bran shouted over the wind.

Emrys was slowly growing tired, barely keeping up with Dylan's silver dragon. They had travelled over a hundred miles since leaving Cantre'r Gwaelod early in the morning, and were flying over the mighty Severn Barrage construction grounds – an imposing wall of faer iron and silksteel, stretching for over ten miles across the estuary, that was to provide the Dracalish mages with an inexhaustible supply of Water Elementals – when an even more unusual sight on the horizon caught the boy's attention.

"That's a city, boy!" laughed Dylan. "That's Brigstow!"

The city surpassed his boldest expectations. Neither Aberdaugleddau, a port town in southern Gwynedd he had often travelled to, nor Caerlion, the largest settlement west of the Dyke, could even compare to this immense expanse of stone, timber and tile.

Before reaching Brigstow itself, they first had to pass over a deep gorge, carved where the river raced towards the sea. A tremendous tower of gleaming white marble spiralled upwards some three hundred feet, parts of it still under construction, cranes and scaffolding climbing around crenelated walls, peaked arches and buttresses. On the other side of the gorge another smaller tower grew over a golden dome and a grandiose sandstone building. A broad bridge thrown over the gorge, suspended on silver silksteel ropes, connected the two structures.

"That's Clistane, the Tower of High Magic," explained Dylan as they circled the taller spire, "and the Brigstow Academy on the other side. Designed by the arch-thaumaturgist Brunel, himself."

Dylan's voice, used to shouting orders in the midst of battle, carried loud over the buffeting of wind above and the din of harbour below.

"And that one?" Bran mouthed, pointing to another tall ornate spire of red brick and white limestone.

It towered over a vast vaulted structure, with copper roof supported by a forest of wrought iron columns, hidden behind a turreted facade of black granite. A huge tube of imbued glass emerged from the eastern side of the building and disappeared into a nearby hillside.

"That's a terminus of the Atmospheric to Lundenburgh," his father replied. "A two-hour journey takes you straight into the heart of the capital. That's also one of Brunel's."

The city spread out for at least three miles each way, street after street of tall, massive stone houses, palaces, towers, warehouses and wharves. Bran felt as if they had travelled not only in space, but in time. A few hours before they had left their little slate house where Rhian was baking cakes for breakfast using an old iron griddle and a single fire faery. The house and the little town of Caer Wyddno – with its grey stone walls, fishermen coming from their morning catch, farmers departing to till the barley fields – seemed like something out of the Age of Unbridled Flame now as they circled over the naval harbour, a marvel of engineering and thaumaturgy, floating above the river in a series of terraced cascading docks supported on arches of wrought faer iron.

Modern, sleek, mistfire-powered ironclads prepared for their long journeys, spreading the power of the Dracalish Empire over the high seas. There were battleships and frigates, infantry transports and dragon carriers. A few airships hovered above it all, ever watchful. One of them, a streamlined chaser, approached Bran and his father menacingly, to ward them off, away from the docks. The Dracaland was always at war somewhere with somebody; it was its way and purpose.

They ascended to avoid a large glowing orb, travelling slowly in a perfectly straight line – a carrier wisp, delivering some important message to one of the ironclads. Another long line of warships piqued the boy's interest, steaming out of the harbour at full speed.

"Where are they all going?"

"There is some trouble brewing in the Scythian Sea," said Dylan. "The Varyaga and the Shahr are at each other's throats again, and Rome will not stand by idly either, when there's fighting so close to Taurica."

Bran was barely familiar with the names his father dropped so effortlessly. He knew only that the Scythian Sea was somewhere east, far beyond Midgard.

"Taurica?"

"A province of Rome on the northern coast of the Sea, stuck like a thorn in Varyaga's side. Remind me to show you the map later, if you're curious. The *koenigs* of Varyaga have been eyeing it for a long time."

"And why is our fleet involved in this?"

"The balance of power must be sustained. Rome, Varyaga and the Shahr are the most powerful nations on the continent – we can't let any of them grow any stronger."

"We will stand against all three?"

"By Owain's Sword, no!" Dylan said, laughing. "That would be our doom. Diplomacy, trade, spying - that's the great game the Dracaland plays, son. The navy will be just one of our assets."

They banked to avoid another airship emerging from beyond a steep tower. It was black and threatening, armoured with iron spiked plates.

"A Midgard delegation," said Dylan, pointing to the Fafnir insignia painted on the side of the ship, an emerald dragon over two crossed swords, volant, which served as the symbol of this militant northern nation. "I wonder what their official business is, apart from spying on our fleet. You know, I'm glad we're leaving now. Your mother worried needlessly - the East should be a much more peaceful place than here."

Bran looked down to the bustle of the streets below, overwhelmed by the immense splendour of the city. He could not believe the crowds moving along the broad pavements and boardwalks. They seemed like living creatures, giant, thousand-headed serpents slithering their way in every direction.

"How many people live in this place?"

"More than in all of Gwynedd combined!" his father yelled back over the noise of the
factories, mills and mistfire plants they passed as they circled the eastern industrial district. One of the multitude of chimneys belched out a great cloud of thick, black sooty smoke. Dylan's dragon swerved right immediately, but Emrys was too slow and rushed straight through it.

Bran and his dragon hovered over the factory, both covered in soot, coughing and spluttering. The boy futilely tried to wipe the black dust from his goggles. The silver drake looked at them with scorn. Dylan stifled a laugh and sighed.

"All right, that's the end of sightseeing. I can see your dragon is too exhausted, let's get you to the hotel. There's only one in Brigstow, but it's quite decent."

"What's a hotel?"

"An inn! Of sorts."

The Brigstow Grand looked like no inn Bran had ever seen. The ground floor was shot through with giant panes of crystal glass, and there were three more rows of windows above it, dividing the yellow facade with straight stylish lines. A balcony with intricate iron balustrades spanned the length of the second floor. The roof was surrounded with a line of sculpted plaster supported by heavy stone brackets.

The valets reached for the dragons to take them away to the stables. Emrys was anxious at first, but Bran managed to placate the beast and it shuffled off, still snorting and sneezing from the dust. The boy followed his father through the entrance, a portal of crystal and wormfire-wrought steel, braided and spliced together in floral ornaments worthy of a nobleman's palace. The lobby was as big as the Great Auditorium at Llambed and lavishly decorated. Bran felt dizzy from all the excitement - and the black smoke he'd inhaled.

"See that dining hall, son?" Dylan said and pointed to another crystal and steel entrance. "Get yourself cleaned up and come down here for supper. I have to deal with a few formalities and make sure all our bags have arrived. The bellboy will take you to our room."

The "room" was an apartment, almost as big as their slate-roofed house in Caer Wyddno, with a palatial bathroom, blue-tiled, with a huge enamelled bath. The water was kept hot constantly by a couple elementals trapped in the fire-stone piping.

Soaking himself in the luxurious bath, he wondered why Dylan had never taken him to a place like this before. Brigstow did not lie beyond impassable mountains and oceans, it was easily reachable by dragon or mistfire omnibus. Why had they never moved to a city? Life here seemed much more convenient than in Gwaelod - and much more interesting.

Half an hour later they were sitting by a large oak table, waiting for the main course. Dylan wore a knee-length black frock coat embroidered with golden thread, with silk-faced lapels and a grey waistcoat. His face, furrowed by age and experience like a bark of an old fir tree, was smooth-shaven and freshly powdered to conceal the scar on the left cheek and his eyes, glinting the same green as his son, shone brightly. Bran had never seen his father look so dapper before.

A human-shaped, turbaned and bearded creature of smoke and fire whooshed out of thin air by their table, with a carafe of rose wine and a bread basket.

"Who... or what... was that?" whispered Bran when the creature had disappeared in a puff of scentless smoke.

"That's a Djinni. They come from the deserts of Durrani," explained Dylan. "A few of them served as porters and interpreters in the Dracalish army and when we moved out, they chose to come with us rather than remain and be branded traitors."

"I don't know these names. We weren't taught anything about this history."

"I'm not surprised. These were Dracaland's wars, not Prydain, and not something to boast about. The Queen's armies tried to conquer the Durrani some three years after you were born, but they were decimated. They say only one dragon survived the retreat from Gandhara."

"I thought the Dracalish soldiers were invincible."

"Mm, so did they."

"Were you taking part in this war?"

"No." Dylan shook his head. "I was never in that part of the world. Durrani is inland, between Varyaga and Bharata." The tip of Dylan's finger lit up and he traced a simple map in the air. The drawing hovered for a moment before Dylan dispersed it with a wave. "Maybe one day. We will return to Durrani, eventually, it's too precious to leave it alone. The Dragon Throne always hungers for more riches."

He keeps saying we, thought Bran. He didn't like it. Although both sides of the Dyke were formally united under one crown, most of the freemen of Gwynedd prided themselves in their independence from the White Dragon Throne in Lundenburgh.

The Djinni appeared again, this time with platters of fancily prepared meats and salads. Dylan chose the dishes, as the names on the menu, all in Latin, meant nothing to Bran.

"This is duck, I believe," explained Dylan.

"How... how is this duck?"

The bits his father pointed to on the platter resembled no food he had ever seen.

"It's foamed and pressed through a cold steel tube."

"Why?"

"This is a restaurant for spoiled city folk who are bored with normal food. But that's still tasty."

"And this?"

Bran pointed to a small golden cube.

"Try it."

The boy gingerly put the cube into his mouth. At first it tasted of seared beef, but then it exploded in his mouth with a rainbow of tastes and aromas, which he barely recognised. Bran opened his eyes wide. Dylan laughed.

"The cook here is also a wizard. I'm sure there are many other surprises like this. But now, tell me, what have you managed to learn about Qin?" Dylan asked, putting a spoonful of foamed duck onto his plate.

"Not a lot," Bran admitted. "I read of the silk trade, of their wars with the Horse Khans and Toshara, and their dragons... I studied this *Boym's Travelogue* you gave me. But it looks so old! Are you sure it's up to date?"

Dylan chuckled. "I'm sure it's not. But we don't have much else. You'll find the Qin are a notoriously elusive race."

Two centuries had passed since the Venedian named Boym had travelled the length of the old Silk Route, across the great plains of southern Varyaga, the steppes of the Horse Lords and the deserts of Toshara before reaching Ta Du, the capital of the mighty Qin. In the West, the Wizardry Wars had been at their most terrible. Millions perished in battle, poverty and famine but Qin was populous, rich, peaceful and technologically advanced beyond imagining. Boym had spent a great part of the book describing the marvels of the Emperor's palace, as big as a Western city, clockwork humans that raced down the corridors with messages, walls that moved aside on their own as the guest approached, mechanical servants pouring tea and war machines that marched on legs of metal.

"I learned about the Qin dragons, *long*, at the Academy. They say you don't feel dragon fear around them but rather a dragon awe."

Dylan nodded.

"Not long after Boym's travels the Qin sealed themselves off behind a giant shield, like a country-sized *tarian,* impenetrable to outsiders. *Haijin,* they called it, the Sea Ban."

"Why would they do that?"

"You've read the books. Back then the Qin was an island of wonder in the sea of despair. There was nothing the outside world could offer them except refugees and disease."

Bran pondered the news briefly.

"You said we're sailing *to* Qin..."

Dylan smiled.

"Ten years ago we've managed to penetrate their shield by force and establish a factory. There is now decent trade flourishing between Dracaland and Qin."

"Then what are we going to do when we get there?"

"You, boy, will be mostly sightseeing and learning." Dylan pointed his fork at Bran's pouting face. "I have my mission, and that is an actual state secret, so I'm not telling you anything else. You'll read about it when the state archives open in fifty years.

"Be Sires caring for appraisal of our dessert course?" interrupted the Djinni, hovering over the table with a silver bowl. "We having offering of sherbet of hibiscus and sandalwood, or offering of pistachio halva, garnished with saffron."

"I'll have the halva," Dylan said, "the boy will have sherbet. You'll love it," he added, smiling at his son.

Bran only nodded, too busy trying to tell apart the changing flavours in his mouth.

The airships passing overhead whirred their propellers monotonously. The mistfire carriages – Bran had only seen one of the contraptions before, driven by the richest merchant in Caer Gwyddno – clinked and clanked about the broad cobbled avenues with a whistle like a boiling kettle. The omnibuses, crammed full of people, hurried between their destinations with the great roar of their elemental-powered engines, ringing of bells, screeching of geared wheels upon grooved iron tracks. The horses whinnied, the wyverns bellowed, the paperboys and greengrocers tried their best to shout over the constant din.

The streets reeked of sulphur, soot, smoke and the acrid stench of wyvern droppings flowing down the open gutters. The *tafarns* and restaurants spread the smell of burnt meat and spilt ale, the bakeries overpowered Bran's nostrils with the sweet, mouth-watering scent of freshly baked bread and moist aroma of yeast. The river, split into several canals running through the city centre, stank of silt, seaweed and something else Bran could not easily identify - an oily chemical stench. The water in the river ran brown, with rainbow stains of grease.

The people of Brigstow liked to build high. Tall towers rose on every corner, delicate spires of steel or stocky turrets of white stone. The topmost levels of the merchant residences and aristocrat mansions appeared to float in the air, supported by a thin latticework of miststeel. The rooftops peaked in a series of narrow conical turrets, almost piercing the clouds. Bran wondered how the inhabitants could enjoy climbing so high up every day, until he saw the lifts – stone platforms rising and falling noiselessly on pillars of compressed Ninth Wind. At night, the city streets were as bright as day, illuminated with blazing evertorches and glistening sparklespheres.

This place never sleeps.

Hosts of people he had never imagined could exist in one place filled out vast market squares and broad thoroughfares. The men all wore dark frocks and tall top hats, the ladies donned flounced skirts, capes and bonnets. This was a far cry from the simple country garments he was used to back in Gwynedd, or the practical uniforms of the Academy. There were more different kinds of clothes, shoes and hats to buy at the market stalls and in shops lining the main streets of the city than he had ever thought necessary. Bran's clothes all came from the same tailor in Caer Wyddno, and he only had two pairs of shoes, one for flying, one for walking.

In time, Bran began noticing other, more subtle, things. There were very few dragons. He had become used to their presence at the Academy, their smells, their sounds, the constant buzz of Farlink feeds passing through the air that his sensitive mind would inadvertently pick up on. Here only the town guards travelled regularly on dragonback, mounting purple hawk drakes, a small swift and agile race fit for chasing ruffians along the narrow alleyways. Sometimes a nobleman or army officer would soar past on an expensive thoroughbred. Ordinarily, however, even Emrys was bound to make a sensation when it landed in the middle of the market square, startling the much smaller, two-legged wyverns of the common townsfolk.

"A dragon is an expensive creature to keep in a city," explained Dylan.

They were sitting on a bench in the Empress's Square, watching the well-to-do citizens of Brigstow walking their pets. This was the only quiet part of town, although even here the honking, whistling, clacking, roaring and shouting carried over from the surrounding streets, drowning the singing of birds and wind rustling in the oaks and limes. On one side of the square the buildings were strangely ruined, abandoned, staring at the garden with black empty windows.

"You need stables, pastures… Land is too precious," Dylan continued. "You can get anywhere by omnibus or automated carriage, really, which don't need feed and freedom to roam."

"And what about mages? I haven't seen any since we arrived."

"You won't see them just wandering the streets, they're always busy." Dylan smiled. "The Brigstow wizards don't like to cause a fuss. They're just holed up in the Tower of Grand Magic and get everything they need delivered there... Brunel's the only one who regularly comes down to the city on one of his contraptions, to look after the ships and trains."

"I'm glad I didn't go for wizardry, then."

Dylan laughed loudly, startling a passing lindworm, which let out a puff of sulphuric steam. The creature's owner gave him a scornful look.

"It certainly is not as glorious a job as they present it in the Academy, but think of the advances we've made thanks to the wizards and thaumaturgists. Imagine what this place would look like without airships, mistfire, automatons…"

Bran nodded, without conviction. In the countryside where he had grown up there was little use for these novel inventions. Spark oven and Faerie laundry was all the modern magic his mother used on a regular basis. He realised how remote his father's life had become to that of his family. They were almost strangers.

"Yes, imagine if the Sun Priests got their way," Dylan added to himself, gazing vacantly at Brigstow's spiralling towers, "this place would look like Rome…"

"Have you ever been to Rome?"

The ancient Imperium was no friend to the Dracaland and travel between the two empires was rare and restricted except to the open ports of Vasconian coast.

"Only once, on a spying mission," Dylan replied without much enthusiasm. "All the palaces, temples and circuses of the top tier are still there and they're a magnificent sight, no doubt, but the squalor, the filth, the poverty… I have been the lower levels and I would never want to see it again."

He shook his head.

"Lower levels?"

"The entire city is built in seven tiers, like a giant cake. You know how obsessed the Old Faithers are about the number seven. The richer and more powerful you are, the higher you live. The Imperator's court and the Mithraeum Maximum are on the seventh tier, but the first floor is a slum bathed in perpetual darkness. Six million people in one place. Can you imagine?"

Bran couldn't. Until they came to Brigstow he didn't even know what a few hundred thousand people gathered in one place would look like. The world was far bigger and scarier than he had ever envisioned.

"Is it true they still have gladiator fights?"

"Oh, yes." Dylan nodded. "The circus for the games is perhaps the greatest building in the world, and sits right in the middle of the second tier, beneath the Imperator's palace. But they no longer fight to the death. The Romans are not barbarians, even though they are so backward. They still have the old gravity plumbing, and only the richest can afford spark ducts."

And we're still using a well for water and Faerie fire for heating, Bran thought.

A drop of water fell on Dylan's nose and he looked sharply to the clouds.

"Oh, look, I do believe it's going to rain. Finally! Let's go to the old Trow before the skies open."

By the morning a message had come from the harbour; their ship was ready to depart. Bran and Dylan packed their belongings and sent them via pneumatic courier to the harbour. Dylan insisted they took a leisurely stroll along the streets of Brigstow towards the seaport, one last time.

They walked down the canyons of tall yellow brick warehouses; sloping bridges, down which the porters rolled barrels of oil and wine, joined the two sides of the street. Iron cranes squeaked, lifting heavy crates to the top floor windows. At length they arrived at the river and moved along the bank, past the sleek yachts and copper-clad barges, until Dylan turned into an alley between another row of warehouses to their left and a great wall of black iron and steel to their right.

"When do we get to the ship?" Bran asked, by now completely lost. "I thought the quays would be somewhere around here."

Dylan smiled mysteriously, but said nothing. They reached a flight of metal steps leading to the top of the wall of steel, some fifty feet up. He silently gestured Bran to climb it.

The roof of the strange edifice was completely flat, covered with wooden planks and surrounded by silksteel railing. Brass coils, glass pipes and a row of four, tall black funnels running through the middle and six tall wooden masts protruded from the rooftop, with a white mansion-like building between the third and fourth. Dockers and seamen busied themselves around the structures, hauling goods and making some hasty repairs. The whole construction filled out a wide canal joining the main docks of the Brigstow harbour with the Afon.

"You're standing on the deck of MFS *Ladon*," Dylan announced proudly, "the largest ship ever built!"

"This can't be..."

"See for yourself!"

Dylan guided him around the deck. One of the structures on the bow hid a giant capstan, with an anchor chain the links of which were the size of an adult man. The quarterdeck boats attached to the sides of the ship were as large as the canal barges. The staircases leading to the lower decks were as deep and wide as those in the towers of Llambed.

"Can it even move? Where are the paddle wheels?" Bran asked, full of doubt, and Dylan smiled.

"Fifteen knots against a gale-force wind, son! It's another feat of Master Brunel. Come, I will show you the engines."

The engine room was built like a basilica, vast, tall, vaulted, running through the entire length of the colossal ship. The engine itself was three storeys tall, surrounded by a maintenance gallery on every level. Four giant cylinders of crystal and copper lined the floor in a row, joined by a network of pipes, valves and flanges. In the massive boiler, forming the core of the engine, hundreds of the purest Jorvik elementals rested dormant, waiting for the command from the ship's captain. A double row of piston rods, tall as tree trunks, lay in the back of the engine room around a crankshaft.

"This turns the screw which propels the ship," Dylan said, patting the massive crankshaft, "the largest piece of wrought faer iron in the world. We are now twenty feet under the waterline. Impressive, isn't she?"

Bran nodded, staring agape at the tangle of metal around him. The buzz of magic needed to keep the elementals in peace, the smell of grease and oil made his head hurt. He wanted to ask about something else, but was finding it difficult to speak.

"You're pale," Dylan noted. "Let's get you some fresh air. Come, I have something else to show you."

Bran followed his father outside up the winding metal staircase and onto the raised part of the upper deck, a large platform of reinforced wood with a broad ramp leading down into the bowels of the ship.

"This is the landing deck. And ho, they're bringing in the dragons!" cried Dylan, pointing to the sky, his eyes laughing.

Bran looked at him in surprise. Once on board a ship his father became a different man - tall, strong, bright-eyed and somehow younger and more handsome than he had ever seemed at home. Unwittingly, Bran smiled.

A squadron of Silvers and Azures landed around them. The soldiers climbed down from their beasts, unbuckling the saddlebags. Bran ran up to them. The heat of the dragon breaths made the air around the beasts shimmer.

"What unit are you?" Bran asked one of the soldiers, not recognising the winged anchor insignia on their navy blue uniforms.

The man was lanky, slim and silver-haired. When he turned to answer, his cat-like eyes glistened bright amber in the sun.

"You're *Faer Folk*!"

"And you're a rude little boy," the soldier said with a grin. "Why so surprised? Haven't you seen a Tylwyth before?"

"I didn't know you served in the army."

"Why not?" The soldier shrugged. "Even Faer Folk need money these days. You can't spend all your life hunting and singing. Not when there's no more game in the forests."

"I've seen your people... Dancing in Brycheiniog."

The Tylwyth nodded thoughtfully.

"That's where my mother comes from. They are the last to keep to the old ways."

There was among the dragons one very different from the others, a sleek, smooth-scaled bronze beast, with large, wise eyes and long, slim neck.

"Who's flying *that*?" Bran asked, admiring the beautiful creature.

"You are, son."

His father approached. The soldiers stood to attention.

"At ease, men. Soldiers, this is my son, Bran. Bran, this is the Second Dragoon Regiment of the Royal Marines. We'll be travelling together."

The soldiers saluted the boy, but Bran's attention was elsewhere.

"What did you say?"

"It's your new dragon, Bran. A bronze thoroughbred – fast, elegant and presentable as befits my son. It's the latest fashion among young riders these days, I hear."

The joyous mood perished in an instant. Bran narrowed his eyes and leaned his head forwards.

"This is *not* my dragon. Where's Emrys?"

"That old thing? I left it at the hotel. But look at this one, son! Isn't it a beauty?"

"I don't care, father. I'm going to get Emrys."

He pushed through the soldiers, passing his father by. Dylan reached out to him.

"Son, wait." There was pleading breaking through his commanding voice that made Bran stop and turn. Dylan nodded at him to step aside, away from the unloading soldiers.

"I know this is not easy for you, but it's better to do it now, before we leave."

Bran relaxed his fists and unclenched his teeth.

"I'm sorry, father. It's a beautiful mount, and I'm sure it was expensive, but I can't leave without Emrys."

"But you're too old! It's as if you'd insisted on bringing a pony! It's a danger for you – *and* for the others in the open sea. It's bound to go feral soon."

"It will stay calm as long as I'm with it."

"You can't promise that and I can't take that risk. If you want to sail with us, you must leave the dragon behind."

"Very well. I'm going back home. Maybe I can still make it to the inauguration, just like you wanted."

"It's you who wanted to come with me in the first place!" he heard as he stormed towards the metal stair.

"What happened? I've seen the boy leave the ship in a great huff."

Dylan was pretending to study the maps, too distraught to focus, when Reeve Gwenlian found him on the bridge.

"I've decided my son is not mature enough for this journey," he said, turning to her.

It'd been months since he had last seen her soft features, surrounded by a storm of jet-black hair. He almost forgot about the quarrel.

"You're letting him go back home?"

Dylan's fingers rattled on the table.

"Tell me, Gwen - at what age does a young dragon rider obtain his second mount?"

"I got mine when I was thirteen."

"And the third?"

"Ooh… seventeen I think. What is this about?"

"Bran's had his beast since he was ten. It's a Marsh Wyrm!"

"So?"

"He refuses to leave it on shore."

"Is that it?" She almost laughed. "I'm sorry, Dylan – I mean, Ardian ab Ifor – "

"It's alright, we're alone here."

"Dylan – I know you're used to tough negotiations, but the lad's your son. It was to be your first trip together. Let him be."

"You sound like the boy's mother," he scoffed, "but you're a rider yourself, you should know better. By Owain's Sword, how can I make a man of my son if I let him keep his childhood toys?"

"Looks like you've been doing a great job so far. You know what will make him even more manly? A whole another year without seeing his father."

He took a deep breath. This whole affair was taking too much of his time and nerves. The ship was about to take off and he hadn't even talked to its captain yet.

"How do you know so much about me and Bran? I don't remember telling you about my family."

"I have brothers – and I know *you*," she replied, touching his face gently. Her face lit up in one of her famous smiles.

From dragonback, Bran could appreciate the full size of the MFS *Ladon*. It was aptly named after the legendary Broodfather of the volcanic dragons, Ladon of the Hesperides. Other vessels, even the great ocean-going warships, seemed like mere toys compared to this black floating monster. The four enormous funnels of the ship were already spewing white steam as the elementals inside the engine cauldron awoke in preparation for the voyage.

Feeling the warm Ninth Wind on his face calmed him down. He still wanted to sail – even more now that he had finally seen the ship – and the thought of coming back to school filled him with dread. But there was nothing Bran could think of that would convince Dylan to take Emrys. His reasons made sense, but Bran wished Dylan acted more like a father than a soldier. And for as long as Bran remembered, in Dylan's mind the navy had always taken precedence over the family.

If I start flying now, I should be at Abertawe before nightfall – and back home for tomorrow's lunch... Mother will be surprised.

He saw a silver shape launching from the *Ladon*'s deck. *Father?* No, the dragon was smaller and nimbler than Afreolus; but it was heading unmistakably towards him and as the beast got closer he saw an astonishingly beautiful and strong faced black-haired woman riding it.

"You must be Bran," she cried over the sound of her dragon's beating wings, "I'm your father's Reeve, Gwenlian. Ardian ab Ifor asked me to take you back to the ship."

"I'm not leaving my dragon!" he cried back.

"It's alright. You can keep it. Come, the ship is about to steam off."

As he landed, Bran could feel the entire deck humming and trembling with the tremendous power of the engine. Emrys snorted uneasily; this was unlike any surface it had landed on before.

"I will take you to your quarters," the Reeve said and smiled warmly at Bran, removing her goggles. Her eyes were dark as night. He felt his cheeks redden.

"What did you call my father? Ard..."

"Ardian - that's his rank in the Royal Marines, commander of the regiment. You may have noticed our titles are different from the other units. I'm a Reeve – equivalent of a Sergeant."

Commander of the regiment?

This meant all the riders on the ship were under his command. Bran knew Dylan must have been a high-ranking officer, but he had never suspected just quite how high.

I know nothing about him, really, he realised.

"Can I talk to him now?"

"He'll be busy at the bridge, with the ship's captain and all the steersmen. We're sailing any minute now and there are still some preparations to take care of."

"Any minute now?"

His stomach turned. He didn't feel ready yet. He looked towards the spiral towers of Brigstow. He was about to leave it behind together with Gwynedd, Dracaland, all that was familiar and safe. White smoke puffing from the ship's funnels changed to grey. Water on the aft-side boiled as the massive propeller started turning.

A couple of soldiers were standing by the railings, singing.

Ffarwel fo i Langyfelach lon,

A'r merched ieuainc i gyd o'r bron;

'Rwy'n mynd i dreio pa un sydd well,

Ai'm wlad fy hun, neu'r gwledydd pell.

Farewell to gay Llangyfelach,

And all the young girls;

I'm going to see which is better,

The faraway lands or my own country.

"What's that song?" he asked the Reeve.

"Farewell Langyfelach," she answered, her black eyes glinting. "It's a song of those who sail away from the shores of Gwynedd into the unknown."

CHAPTER VIII

Yamato, Winter, 6th year of Kaei era

The training at the *dōjō* continued throughout the winter. Six months in, only the two most talented and persevering students remained in Satō's little class of *Rangaku*.

Shōin was a son of a family of tailors and cloth merchants from Nagato, tall for his age, but thin, with his ear-long black hair always messed up and uncombed, and simple unkempt townsman clothes. Keinosuke was his opposite, an heir to a rich samurai family from Chūbu, always impeccably dressed in a black and white kimono with the crest of his clan, Sakuma, on the shoulders and back. The boy usually kept to himself unless asked directly, silently observing the world from under thick eyebrows.

In the winter months the class moved from practising in the courtyard to studying the theory of magic in a small six-mat room on the upper floor of the main hall of the Takashima mansion.

"Remind me, what did we start on after the runic alphabet?" Satō asked, checking her notes.

The boys sat at a low table covered with small scrolls of paper written over in the scribbly Yamato letters and runes of the West.

"Potentials," answered Shōin eagerly, rising slightly from his knees.

The other student just nodded.

"Ah, that's right. Answer me this, then: which is easier, encasing a boy's hand in a block of ice, or freezing a cupful of water?"

The tailor's son looked to the ground, sheepishly.

"Freezing a boy, *sensei*," he said quietly.

"And why is that?"

"Because... freezing water is True Magic not a mind trick?"

Satō shook her head.

"That's not quite it, Shōin. When you're frozen, you not only think you're frozen - that would be an Illusion. The ice is real, it melts and leaves puddles on the ground. Keinosuke, do you know why?"

The other boy raised his eyes as if surprised that somebody would mention his name.

"Water... is not alive. It is fixed in form, unchangeable. It has no, er... potential," the boy replied, struggling.

Satō smiled and nodded.

"Every living thing, from a tree to a samurai, has the potential to change itself and its nearest environment. The Bataavians call it *mogelijkheid*.

That's how it's written." She presented them with a piece of paper with the new word inscribed in decorative runes, and waited for a minute until the boys scribbled it clumsily to their notepads. "This is what makes living things grow and transform, from a single bean to a beanstalk, from an egg to a sea-hawk – and that's what a magic user taps into if he wants to enchant something that is alive."

"So our nature is actually making it easier for you to enchant us?" asked Shōin. "That doesn't seem fair."

"It may seem unfair," Satō agreed, "and if there was no power other than *mogelijkheid* involved, wizards would be truly terrifying people, once they'd reach their full power. However, as you grow up, your resistance to enchantments grows also. Without realising it, you become more and more resilient to magic, even if it's beneficial to you. That's why it's so hard to heal adult men, compared with children."

"Is this why the Spirit healers have to use *sakaki* wands and boiled rice to heal old men, but prayer and touch is enough for us?" Shōin guessed.

She nodded. "Eventually, even the power of *kami* cannot heal the injuries or extend life for infinity. Some say if it wasn't for this natural resistance, we could be immortal."

"Is it also something we have no influence over, like *mogelijkheid*?"

"You can train it, to some extent. Your resilience will grow as you become more attuned to your magic talent."

"Can you train yourself to become completely immune to magic?" Keinosuke asked softly and unexpectedly.

"There... there are legends of such feats, usually achieved by powerful priests or demi-Gods in ancient time. They were called *Hanryū*, Half-Dragons. Can you guess why?"

"Because the *ryū* are immune to magic?"

"The *ryū* were said to be immune to magic. But it may just be a legend - nobody has seen one in Yamato for hundreds of years. Anyway, going back to the lesson... Now, to easily freeze a cup of water, which is, as you said, fixed in state and has no *mogelijkheid* of its own, you need to use one of the two methods. The first one the Bataavians call *thaumaturgie*, or wonderwork. That's the most difficult and complicated school of *Rangaku*, and I doubt you'll ever need to concern yourself with it. It's the art of transforming lifeless matter. Look at this sparkleball."

Satō produced a round object the size of a large orange, which glittered and sparkled in all colours of the rainbow. Colourful flames travelled over the surface of the ball, sparkles formed random flowery patterns. It was impossible to tell what the ball was made of. It was cold and firm to touch, its edges blurred by all the glittering points of light.

"This is what young thaumaturgists practise on," said Satō. "They take a round polished stone and change it into this - it's called *twinkelbal* in Bataavian - forever. It will never cease to sparkle, it is Truly transformed."

"Does Takashima-*sama* know any thau... wonderwork?" Shōin asked.

Satō shook her head.

"Only very little. It's most difficult to perform in Yamato. From what I understand, when many people start using magic in one place, a field of *mogelijkheid* grows into which one can tap. The Bataavians call it *morfisch veld*. However, since we have so few wizards in Yamato, our field is very weak. Do you understand?"

The boys nodded, but their expressions were blank.

"Still..." Satō continued, "that's thaumaturgy, but there is another way to freeze water, and that's to use the elemental magic - wizardry. This is something not only the *Rangaku* use - the shamans of the Northern Tribes know it, and priests of the mountain temples use it in their purification rituals, even if they don't understand how it works. It may well be the oldest magic known to men. Through it, we use the potential of the Earth itself, the *mogelijkheid* of Nature, of elements. This is the power of water drilling through the rock, of wind eroding a mountain. Now, our scholars recognise five basic elements, but the Westerners only concern themselves with four – Are you writing this down, Shōin?" she interrupted.

"Of course, h-here it is!" the tailor's boy stammered, and presented his notepad.

There were several words written on it in the runic alphabet, full of spelling mistakes, and a doodle of a sparkleball.

Satō sighed. After a few months of performing teacher's duties she had learned she couldn't really expect thirteen-year-old boys to absorb that much knowledge all in one go. Even Nagomi often got bored when Satō became too involved in describing some peculiar aspect of an enchantment.

The wizardess looked out through the window, the black frame cutting a serene painting out of the city landscape. A thin blanket of pure snow covered the roof of a nearby house and the boardwalk of the street visible beyond. It was a rare occasion in Kiyō. The snow fell in soft gentle flakes and the world outside was silent and calm. Only a lone hotpot vendor praised the qualities of his dishes into the empty streets.

She knew it was her duty as an heir to teach the boys – but she wasn't an heir yet. Until her father officially passed the inheritance, was she truly obliged to do anything for the *dōjō*?

Of course you are. Heir or no heir, you're still a Takashima.

"Just remember about the four Great Elements - earth, fire, air and water," she told the boys, "you can write it down in normal characters, not runes - *Chi, ka, fuu, sui.*" She paused and waited as they struggled with their calligraphy. "Like our *Butsu* scholars, the *Rangakusha* don't count the Void, *ku*, as a Great Element."

The boys stared at her blankly. *They have no idea what I'm talking about.* She cleared her throat.

"We'll get back to that next week. You don't have to remember it all yet. It's too nice outside to stay indoors," she concluded, "that's it for today."

Shōin jumped up immediately. He bowed fast, picked up his notebook and brush, and ran off before the other boy had even managed to reach for his bundle.

Keinosuke bowed slowly and deliberately.

Satō finished rolling up her scrolls and noticed the boy was still in the room.

"What is it?"

"Takashima-*sensei*, do you have any books or writings about dragons - or *hanryū*?"

"Keinosuke... this knowledge is forbidden. I'm not even sure I should have told you about those legends."

"I see."

The boy seemed dejected.

"I'm sorry, but my family is in trouble as it is. Even the Bataavians aren't keen to mention these matters openly. Maybe one day you'll get to talk to one of them about the dragons… but you're way too young for it now."

"Yes, *sensei*, but..."

"What else?"

"You didn't say you don't have the books."

How does he …?

"The class is over," she said abruptly, and slid the door open, "see you next week."

The samurai son bowed again, unsuccessfully concealing a satisfied smirk, and left without a word. Satō followed him down the stairs, made sure he put on his winter sandals and watched him walk past the guards at the gates. Returning to the upper floor, she entered her father's library. She knew Shūhan would still be in the elemental laboratory he had set up on the other side of the residence, across the courtyard, far away from his precious books. A tall, Bataavian-made bookcase stood in the corner. Satō rose on her toes and reached to the top-most shelf with an effort. From among many identical leather-bound tomes she chose one without hesitation, wiped the dust and spoke a magic word. Crimson fiery letters appeared, burning upon the leather cover.

She did not know the language of the book - it was some Western tongue, but not Bataavian - but she knew what the letters said, for the smuggler who had brought it from Dejima had told her father as she listened through a hole in the floor, hiding upstairs while the men talked in hushed, rasping voices one moonless night.

The fiery letters spelled the long, mystic title: *Applied Dracology, Student's Handbook, Year One. Property of Llambed Academy, Ceredigion, Gwynedd.*

Satō did not open the book, just gazed at it admiringly. She did not understand many of the foreign words of the title, but still it invoked in her mind an image of a great hall filled with books of lore and magic scrolls, a tall tower of stone - as she had seen in a Bataavian painting once - around which dragons of all shapes and colours soared, and a crowd of wizards practising their powerful spells on wide bright courtyards. This image appeared in her dreams ever since she had first heard of the "Llambed Academy", dreams full of mysterious words like "Ceredigion" and "Gwynedd" and of majestic winged, serpentine creatures, spewing fire and lightning.

Keinosuke's words made her uneasy. How could the boy possibly have known the secrets of the Takashima library? Had he been spying on her? But how? The residence was guarded, surrounded by tall walls... she shook her head. He was just a kid! It must have been something else. Maybe she had blabbed something unwise in improper company... Or maybe he had overheard Shūhan talk about the book with his father. Master Sakuma was a renowned *Rangaku* scholar in his own right, and as frequent visitor to the Takashima mansion as the conditions of Shūhan's house arrest allowed. Yes, that must have been it.

I hope the kid knows how to keep his mouth shut. His family would also get in trouble if they were caught dabbling in dragon lore.

She heard familiar steps on the squeaking stairs. Quickly, she slid the book back among the others and sneaked out of the library.

CHAPTER IX

Off the coast of Yoruba, West Africa, December, 2606 ab urbe condita

A deafening broadside roared over the beach, startling a flock of parakeets that fluttered away in a green cloud. The shower of cannonballs brushed the tops of the palms and disappeared into the jungle beyond.

As soon as the ringing in his ears quietened, Bran heard his father speak in the commanding tone he had always assumed when talking to other soldiers.

"Still no reaction, Banneret?"

Dylan, wearing the gallant uniform of a Royal Marines Ardian, scarlet with golden Aberffraw lions on cuffs and buttons, turned to the Tylwyth standing beside him. Edern lowered the brass telescope and shook his silver-haired head.

"Nothing, Sir."

"I told you, Ardian, Tinubu will not give up easily," a third man spoke, rubbing the back of his neck. His dark bronze skin stood out against the white linen of his navy shirt.

"Don't worry, *Oba* Akintoye," replied Dylan, "we'll get you back on the throne today. The navy always keeps its promise."

It was not the first time the ship had to turn from its course towards Qin to play a part in some local skirmish or influence a diplomatic stalemate one way or another. The *Ladon's* course had been plotted deliberately so that the ship would pass near as many of the empire's troubled colonies as possible. A month had passed since the *Ladon* had set sail from Brigstow and they had been barely half-way to the Cape.

The bronze-skinned man was, as Bran had learned, some native pretender whose claim to the throne the Dracaland had decided to support. The reason did not matter; the orders from Lundenburgh rarely divulged more than the details necessary for a particular mission.

"Banneret, aim at the fort, and load the wall-breakers," ordered Dylan.

"Aye-aye, Sir."

Edern's cat-like eyes glinted in anticipation. The smooth-bores lowered in preparation for another salvo. The striped banner of the incumbent ruler Tinubu flew proudly over the fort's stone ramparts.

Bran noticed something on the horizon, a square of white in the sea of azure.

"Another ship, father?" he asked. Dylan looked to where he was pointing.

"Well spotted, son. Edern, what is it?"

The Banneret did not even need to raise the spyglass. The Tylwyth were famed for their keen eyesight.

"They're flying Napolion's Eagle, sir. That's a Vasconian man-o'-war if I've ever seen one."

Romans!

Bran had never seen a Roman ship before. Of all the many nations inhabiting the Imperium only Vasconians, from the northern coast of Iberia, were an ocean-going race – although their sail-driven ships could not dream of matching the mistfire ironclads of the northern nations.

"They dare not intervene," Dylan said. "They're just here to observe. Fire at will, Banneret!"

The guns bellowed again and this time the shells struck the limestone walls with a terrifying force. The rolling thunder of repeated explosions shook the small island, and a thick pall of black smoke hid the beach from sight.

"The wall's been breached, sir," the Banneret reported, when the echoing rumble had passed and the smoke rose in the wind, revealing the scene of destruction. The officer's words were something of an understatement: the fort's sea-side ramparts were reduced to a smouldering pile of rubble. Still the striped banner flapped defiantly in the wind over the tall sandstone turret, in the middle of the stronghold.

"Right," said Dylan with a sigh. "I don't have time for this. Scramble up, we're coming in."

"Careful, Master Dylan!" Akintoye said, "Tinubu knows many tricks!"

"So do we, *Oba* Akintoye," Dylan said, laughing.

"Father, *look*!"

Bran pointed at the sea between the island and the ship. The waters bubbled and frothed, and the rolling waves parted, revealing the head of a giant hissing serpent. Its emerald-scaled body, most of its coils still hidden in the water, was easily as big as a frigate. The snake rose from the sea and sped towards the ship.

The Royal Marines dragons, which were waiting impatiently for their turn to take part in the battle on the landing deck, were now shaking their neck frills and snorting boiling steam from their nostrils. Their metallic silver scales glinted blindingly in the tropical sun.

"*Damballah*! I told you, Ardian! I warned you!" cried Akintoye.

For a brief moment Dylan gazed at the creature unfazed.

"Shall we launch the torpedoes, Sir?" Edern asked, glancing nervously at the approaching serpent. It was not big enough to threaten the *Ladon*, but it could still do some costly damage on deck.

"No, Edern," Dylan replied, "the time for trinkets is over."

He turned to his son.

"You'd better step away from the railings. This may get nasty."

As the dragons flew past the bridge of the *Ladon* like two silver bullets, Bran shouted and waved. He was certain his father did not see him, but at the last moment Dylan turned in the saddle and waved back – seconds before his dragon and the giant serpent struck against each other with tooth, flame and claw.

The parade processed down the main broad street of the town, rising clouds of yellow sand billowing into the sky so bright and pale blue it seemed almost white. Crowds of natives lined both sides of the road cheering and dancing, throwing wreaths of flowers, beads and bird feathers under the feet of the marching soldiers.

Ekō. That's the name of this hovel, Dylan remembered. He had lost count of how many towns like this he had helped conquer, liberate or destroy. For a moment he pondered why the Dracaland's complex interests required the previous ruler toppled – *Tinubu, was it?* – but he quickly decided he didn't really care. He did not expect this new *Oba* to last any longer than the Dragon Throne's interest required.

Dylan was riding Afreolus in front of the marching Marines. The silver dragon ambled onwards awkwardly, grunting unhappily, unused to walking for such long distances. Bran was sitting behind him on the dragon's back. One dragon was more than enough for the small parade.

"Are people always so glad to see us?" asked Bran.

Dylan let out a short laugh.

"They have no idea why they're here, or who we are. The local king ordered them to cheer. See how well dressed they all are? This is all just for show."

The locals forming the crowd were all wearing their finest clothes, loose-fitting, wide-sleeved robes of purple, crimson or white silk, embroidered with golden thread, and long colourful headscarves. Many wore jewellery, silver chains and small gem-studded rings, pearls and glass beads.

The cavalcade reached the steps of the palace of the *Oba*. It was not a grand building by any measure, a single storey high, with yellow thatch and white-washed walls covered in black ink paintings and bas-relief, damaged in places by the recent battle, but it stood out from the mud-brick houses around it enough to give its owner sufficient prestige. A hastily sewn standard of the old reinstated clan replaced that of the abolished one over a single square turret. A fountain in the courtyard provided a little respite from the overwhelming heat, even if not from the stifling humidity. Several remarkably life-like bronze statues of previous kings and queens decorated the square. Miraculously, they all seemed to have survived the fighting unscathed.

Those bronzes would have been worth thousands at an auction in Lundenburgh, Dylan thought briefly.

The marines positioned themselves in a half-circle around the courtyard, Bran among them in the first row. Local soldiers, armed with ceremonial spears and antique muskets, stood in front of the main entrance. Dylan, along with two other men – the Captain of the *Ladon* and the representative of Dracaland trade companies – moved forwards, to be greeted personally by the *Oba* Akintoye himself.

The reinstated ruler of Ekō stepped out of his throne room almost unrecognisable in his dazzling coronation robes. He walked magnanimously, the tails of his kaftan supported by two squires in silk loincloths. In his right hand he held a bronze spear tied with beaded string. He raised his left hand and Dylan bowed before this gesture. Others followed his example.

The *Oba* gave a short speech in his native language – although he spoke perfect Seaxe – thanking the Dracalish Empress for assisting him in regaining his rightful place on the throne.

He speaks as if he was Victoria's equal, Dylan thought. *His entire kingdom would fit into* Ladon*'s holds with room to spare.*

The three men were each given a large heavy necklace of gold and jewels. Dylan knew that the trade representative valued ink and paper over gold, but the treaties had to wait. Once the rewards were given out, Dylan stepped back, making way for others – local allies of the *Oba*, spies and traitors. Every one of them demanded praise and reward.

How many will live to see tomorrow?

The ceremony was coming to an end. One last ritual remained – the blessing of the ancestors over the new king, a renewal of contract with the Spirits.

The low droning of drums started, slowly at first, and the dancing shaman, *Egungun,* wearing a loose kaftan stitched of a thousand different patches of cloth, emerged onto the courtyard. White heron feathers, lining his mask and scarf, shook with every movement. He was already in a trance, spinning, jumping and howling. The drums picked up the pace and the dancer moved faster still, always a step ahead of the rhythm, as if anticipating the musicians' strokes.

The dancer neared the *Oba* and performed a series of complicated gestures and leaps. He took out a bunch of parrot feathers from the pocket of his kaftan and threw it over the king's head. They perished in a flash. The king bowed, smiling. The Spirits were approving.

This should have been the end of the ritual, but the *Egungun* dance did not stop. He looked around the courtyard from under the heron mask, as if searching for something. Dylan frowned when he noticed the direction in which the dancer headed. The shaman whirled towards the row of marines, where Bran stood. For everyone else it must have seemed a harmless extension of the ceremony. The dancer stopped in front of his son, screeching wildly. Suddenly something long and metallic glistened in his hand. Dylan launched forwards, but even as he started moving he knew he would be too late. The dancer dropped his arms down on Bran's head. Gwenlian, standing beside the boy, raised her hand at the last moment…

By the time Dylan reached the place where Bran stood, everything was settled. The dancer was lying on the courtyard floor clutching a broken arm, the piece of metal beside him. Bran was breathing hard, but was otherwise unharmed.

"Take him away," Dylan commanded sharply. "Hide him in a safe place."

Gwenlian grabbed Bran and pulled him towards the harbour. Dylan crouched by the injured shaman to examine the item with which he believed his son had been threatened.

I promised Rhian there would be no risk, he thought. *I should have left him on the ship.*

The bit of metal was shaped like a long chisel with a short handle, it was blunt and rather harmless-looking - a mere ceremonial weapon. The shaman started explaining something in an agitated voice. Dylan stood up and looked at the *Oba* quizzically.

"What is he saying?"

"This is a Spirit dagger," explained Akintoye, "it destroys all evil."

"Why did he attack my son?" Dylan enquired, allowing himself to sound angry.

"Not the boy, but the evil that is to befall him. It is a great honour."

Dylan frowned.

"Great honour? How so?"

"The *Egungun* deemed the boy worthy of their blessing. Rarely does one of no royal blood deserve the power of the daggers. I assure you the shaman meant no harm to your son."

Dylan nodded and helped the dancer to stand up.

A blessing dagger. Of course.

He remembered he had seen this sort of harmless "weapon" before.

"Tell the shaman I'm sorry for what happened. I'll send the ship's doctor to treat his arm."

According to the ship's calendar it was the middle of the winter, but Bran had never been so hot and sweaty. He was finding it very difficult to concentrate, and he needed all the attention he could spare. He was playing *tafl*, the King's Table, with Samuel, the ship's doctor. He had never played the game before boarding the *Ladon*, although the Seaxe boys at the Academy had been spending hours at a time pondering the movements of the black and white figures. After a few weeks of Samuel's tuition it had quickly become his favourite pastime.

"This is like a dream," he said, trying to turn the doctor's attention from a particularly bad move he made with his Archwizard. "I never imagined the world was so vast and beautiful."

Samuel nodded, moving one of the Priests along the diagonal.

"And you've only seen a fragment of it."

"I think I understand now why father so rarely comes home. There's just so much to see. I can hardly remember Gwynedd now."

"Believe me, you will always remember your home. Now watch your Wizards, boy. You've completely exposed yourself with that move."

"It's this damn heat. Will it never end?"

"The weather rarely changes in these parts, so close to the equator," Samuel explained. "Only the wind can grow weaker or stronger."

As if in confirmation of his words, a gust of wind bent the palms on the beach low to the ground - a finger of a winter storm they were holding out in

Goa, a Vasconian outpost on the coast of Bharata. The proud golden eagle of Rome spun on its mast like a weathervane.

By the evening the wind lessened and a small black ship steamed into the harbour, adding its grey banner with a strange black sigil of a horned circle to a multitude of colours already gathered in what was the only neutral port for days. Not long after its arrival, shouts of joy and gun salutes roared all along the *Ladon*. The agitated dragons buzzed with excitement in their holds under the deck.

Bran wanted to ask his father about the sudden celebration, but he was nowhere to be found. This was not unusual; Dylan rarely kept himself idle. There was always some errand he could run for the Empire, even without direct orders. Instead, the boy stumbled onto Edern.

"What's going on? Who sails that ship?"

"The ship is Gorllewin – don't you recognise their crest? It doesn't matter. What matters is the news they bring: the war with Arakan is over!"

"What's Arakan?"

"A kingdom on the other side of Bharata. We had some nasty border dispute with them."

"But why so much celebration?" Bran said as another of *Ladon's* guns thundered joyously.

"Had the war continued, we would have to join the fighting. And Arakan is a terrible place to do battle: hot, wet, fever-ridden jungles full of monsters and hostile natives. It would also have meant at least another month of delay. Now we can sail straight past Temasek, the shortest route possible."

The soldiers of the Second Dragoons prepared a great feast on board the *Ladon*. Dylan, having at last returned to the ship, ordered signal flags thrown from the masts inviting everyone in the harbour to celebrate the victory. The Breizh and Bataavian sailors came first, with song and wine. Their nations may have had their differences with Dracaland, but here in the colonies all Northerners were allies. The Vasconian rulers of the outpost were at first reluctant to bask in the glory of a competing imperial power, but then they saw barrels of prime grog being rolled out onto the deck and quickly changed their minds.

As dusk fell, a group of silent men in grey hooded robes entered the ship: the Gorllewin delegation. They stood on the side, in shadows, everyone giving them a wide berth.

"Come, Bran," said Edern, winking. He held a jug of grog in one hand and a chunk of cheese in the other. "I bet you haven't talked to a Grey Hood yet."

The two of them came up to the grim figures. One of the silent men came forward and cast down his hood. He was bald shaven, and had a horned, crossed circle tattooed on his forehead. His eyes were black as night, but his face lit up with a gentle smile.

"You have brought us joyous tidings, friends," said Edern, presenting him with the jug, "you should come closer, join the festivities."

The man nodded. "Thank you for the invitation, Arthur's Kin, but we are tired with the journey. We came here hoping we might speak with your Commander."

"Oh, Ardian ab Ifor? He's over there, on the bridge," Edern said, waving his cheese-arm.

"Why did he call you Arthur's Kin?" Bran asked when the hooded men shuffled off.

"Because that's what we are. Your king Arthur was of our people. Who's been teaching you history?"

"Miss Farnham," Bran said. Edern chuckled.

"Yes, I remember her. She wasn't too keen on the history of the Faer Folk."

A firework shot up from a Congreve rocket launcher and lit the sky up with red, white and blue, the colours of Dracaland Empire. At this signal, several dragon riders took to the air in a show of acrobatics. Chasing after them a bright green shape emerged from the holds..

"Emrys!" Bran cried. He focused on the Farlink connection to command his dragon back, but the distance and excitement coming from the beast were too big.

"Who let it out?" he asked, angrily.

"We thought your pet could use some fresh air," said Edern. "Look at it fly!"

The celadon-scaled dragon fumbled comically in an attempt to match the silvers and azures aerial prowess. It tumbled over itself chasing after the larger dragons.

Edern laughed.

"I can see why you like it so much. That's just priceless!"

"It's really a good beast," Bran said quietly. "It's just... not used to the life at sea, that's all."

"I'm sure it will grow up into a decent dragon."

"It is grown up!" the boy blurted, "I've had it for six years now."

"*Duw!* A six-year-old Swamper that's not gone feral yet?"

"Is that so strange?"

Despite Dylan's warnings, Bran had not seriously considered the likelihood of his mount turning against him. It was the eventual fate of every dragon rider and Bran knew how to deal with it, but unlike Afroleus and many other military dragons he had known, Emrys had never yet shown any signs of rebellion. In time, Bran had all but forgotten about the risk.

"Aye. Our silvers can last ten years, but they've been bred for loyalty. I've never heard of one of the lesser races take more than five years to turn wild. I take everything back, that's a fine specimen you've got there!"

"Father doesn't seem to think so," Bran looked at the bridge, where Dylan turned for a moment from his conversation with the Grey Hoods to look at his son. Bran could not see his face clearly but was certain it was filled with disdain as always when Emrys was around. Edern coughed.

"I'm sure Ardian ap Ifor does whatever he thinks is in your best interest."

"It's what's in *his* interest that concerns him most."

"I believe you're being unfair. He sounds worried whenever he talks about you…"

"I wish he talked less *about* me and more *with* me."

To that the lieutenant found no answer.

Whatever was left of the grog after the feast at Goa was now shared among small party of the crew and the soldiers in Bran's honour. It was the boy's sixteenth birthday. The Ardian's son was sitting at the top of a long table in the officers' mess, in a neatly ironed blue uniform. After the squadron's piper finished his celebratory ditty, Samuel stood up and rubbed the back of his bald head. Everyone looked at him expectantly. He presented the boy with a set of ivory-carved Staunton *tafl* pieces, where the blacks were Sun Priests and whites, the Wizards and a small spyglass, richly ornamented with brass lions and copper elephants he had picked up at a market in Temasek.

"It is a most precise instrument," he explained, "and I trust you will take good care of it. The barrel was wrought on the island of Kilwa in Zangibar, the iron came from the secret mines of Motapa. The glass is Bataavian, of Walcheren, enchanted at Delft. The case is made of grey selkie skin from Brendan's Island, so that it never sinks when dropped into the sea."

Samuel was delighted to see sparks of recognition light up in the boy's eyes as he listed the exotic place names. Over the last six months he had witnessed Bran's transformation from a country bumpkin, a landlubber, into a true traveller.

It reminded Samuel of his own humble beginnings in the navy. Son of a *mohel* from Bethnal, he had known nothing of the world outside the dark, narrow stinking streets of eastern Lundenburgh until he had boarded his first ship as a surgeon's apprentice. That very first voyage had taken him through lands of myth and legend, through oceans and continents he had only ever read or dreamt of. He had seen monsters and Gods, and ancient magic hidden in the jungles and deserts - and he never wished to go back home again.

It must have been the same for Bran. Any journey with Ardian Dylan and his dragoons was bound to be filled with adventures and excitement. On Brendan's Island they had flown over active volcanoes, assisting a group of Dracologists in their research. At Oyo they went with the embassy to the Yoruban King, who had treated them to a show of horsemanship and archery. Past the Skeleton Coast they'd sailed through mist so thick one could not see the end of an outstretched arm. On a south-westerly gale they'd passed the whitewashed, many-pillared walls of Zangibar and tall-spired fire-temples of Pemba, past the islands of sea coconuts until they reached the jungles of Bharata. From Goa the *Ladon* hurried across the Bangla Sea, past Temasek, due east, towards Qin.

Along the way Bran had become acquainted with most of the crew and the marines on board. The soldiers let him join their training in fencing and lancing. Samuel watched these bouts with slight concern at first. The army issue swords and cutlasses were larger and heavier than what Bran was used to, and their Soul Lances were solid flexible shafts of energy, a full nine feet of length, as befitted trained soldiers. The boy had to build up some muscle before he could think of matching their skill. The physical effort made wonders for his mood. Even Emrys eventually earned the crew's sympathy as the ship's informal mascot.

Among all the new friends and in all the excitement of the journey, Bran must have felt even more acutely the neglect with which his father seemed to have been treating him throughout the journey. The first few weeks of the voyage had been exemplary. Dylan was showing his son around the ship, introducing him to the crew, spending as much time with the boy as he could, trying to rectify the years of abandonment. The two had spent an entire day together on Brendan's Island and then another on the Rock; but the idyll had ended once the *Ladon* moved into the colonial waters. The commander of a Royal Dragoons regiment was rarely at rest. The dragons were too precious to idle for several months at sea.

Dylan was noticeably absent at his birthday party. At last, when the brief celebration was almost over and there was no fruitcake left, the Ardian appeared in the mess with an apologetic look on his face and a small bundle in his hands.

"Happy Birthday, son," Dylan said sheepishly, "I'm sorry I'm late."

"It's all right - work. I understand."

Bran waved his hand generously, although his voice was cold.

"It's only a little something…" Dylan presented the parcel. "I got it from a Bataavian physician we picked up on Birkenhead and thought of you. I hope it's to your liking."

"Thank you," Bran said quietly, unwrapping the gift.

Father and son shook hands. Every show of affection between the two always seemed awkward, as if they weren't sure how to go about it, but Samuel could see sincere concern in Dylan's eyes. Bran, on the other hand, seemed much more interested in the present, a small dragon figurine, its red surface glistening with a reddish tint in the lamplight.

"Thank you, Father," the boy repeated, and gently placed the statuette into his satchel, along with Samuel's spyglass.

Samuel smiled to himself. The night before the Ardian had arrived at his cabin, visibly distressed.

"I don't have a gift for my son. I never had the time to go to the market at Temasek. I know you spend a lot of time with Bran – I need your help, Samuel."

The doctor nodded and thought for a moment.

"I have just the thing."

He reached into a drawer of his desk and took out a small figurine of a dragon, intricately carved in red oriental resin. The serpentine creature resembled those of the Qin race, but was longer, more slender and sported two large leathery wings not unlike those of the Western beasts. The wide open mouth was surrounded by long whiskers and beard, two sharp horns split into antlers protruded from its head and the tail was on fire. In one of its three-clawed paws it held an orb. On the base were carved initials, in Roman alphabet: "P.F.V.S.".

"Bran is obsessed with the Eastern dragons, he should like it."

On the morning after his birthday Bran stood by the starboard railings, wrapped in a storm cloak of thick oily krakenhide. A cold eastern wind blew across the deck. The *Ladon* was passing a small harbour town clumped around a steep mountain. Through his new spyglass he observed a cluster of off-white buildings disappearing behind a rocky outcrop, warehouses, trade factories, merchant houses and the rising spire of a wizard tower. Some of the buildings had odd roofs that resembled peaked hats with up-curved brims, but most of them would not have been out of place in any town in the west. Dracaland Jacks fluttered in the breeze above the docks and on the masts of many merchant ships moving to and fro among large gaff-sailed junks of the Qin. The same imperial flag – red, white and blue dragon heads on green - was hoisted on a tall mast atop the summit of the mountain.

"Ah, Fragrant Harbour!"

A sudden voice jerked Bran out of his pensive observations. Dylan came up to his side, looking wistfully at the town.

"Ten years have passed since I last saw its piers and storehouses. How it has grown!" He sighed like a proud parent observing his child. "It was barely a fishing village when we got it from the Qin. It may well become the greatest merchant port these seas have seen, one day."

"And what's that over there?" Bran pointed to the west, where, farther away, a similar cluster of houses clung to a tiny island. He couldn't see the design on the flag through the spyglass.

"Vasconians."

"They seem to be everywhere."

"They've been here for much longer than us. Still, now the Qin prefer to make trade with the Dracaland. I suppose we're more reliable than Sun worshippers," Dylan scoffed.

"We're not coming to port here?" enquired Bran as the ship made no indication of changing its course.

"No, our duty is elsewhere this time. We go farther up the river."

"Why, what's up the river?"

"Fan Yu, the Great Harbour! A Southern trade centre for all of the empire. Now brace yourself, we are passing through to Qin territory!"

Dylan pointed to the blue sky in front of the great ship. Squinting, Bran noticed a slight shimmering in the air some two miles ahead. As they moved closer, the shimmering grew to a visible distortion, a pinkish hue added to the blue of the sky, like misty dawn. The air around the ship turned noticeably colder and the waters of the delta, still and calm until now, rose in a windless storm. The *Ladon* started to heave fore and aft over the waves.

Lightning cracked from a cloudless sky and, in its light, Bran saw the full size of the magical barrier. It stretched endlessly from east to west, separating the islands of the delta from the mainland, and rose straight up for at least a mile before starting to gently curve inland.

"How do we get around *that*?" Bran cried out in disbelief.

Dylan smiled.

"That, my son, is what we fought a war for."

Just as the ship's bow was about to hit the barrier, Dylan raised his arms and bellowed in a deep voice, an incantation in a language Bran had never heard before. His hands flared up with golden light. More lightning streaked right above the deck and a round portal, bound in blue and green dazzle, opened before them. On that signal the engines of the *Ladon* pushed one last time and the ship surged forwards, passing the barrier. With a loud whoosh and a pop, the magic door closed behind them. The sea became calm and quiet again and the ship chugged along merrily like a packet steamer on a summer morning.

CHAPTER X

Fan Yu, Qin, March, 2607 ab urbe condita

The ship passed the whitewashed watchtowers guarding the entrance to the harbour, and Bran saw, spreading before him, the vast imperial metropolis of Fan Yu. It was almost a country of its own, sprawling over hills, terraces and islands of the delta for miles. Boats of all shapes and sizes, coal barges, tea junks, fishing sampans, dinghies, ketches and yawls passed in all directions, like grain carts on the busiest of market days. The *Ladon* had to move slowly in this maze of vessels, careful not to crush the boats beneath its powerful iron-plated bow. The riverside was lined with facades of the many-roofed, clay-tiled houses of the townsfolk, suspended on wooden pillars over the water. Further upstream the dwellings of the rich and powerful encroached on the rising banks. Tall, tiered temple towers, the red and yellow walls of monasteries, ancient gold-plated palaces of local magnates and new, Western-styled marble facades of trade princes' houses.

It was all designed to awe the passengers of the vessels passing towards the harbour, but all this magnificence, all this splendour was marred by signs of destruction and misery. Walls were pocked with shot marks, wooden pillars splintered, shutters broken to pieces. Paint was peeling off in patches, and of the gold leaf on the sculptures and carvings only sad remnants remained. A layer of dust covered the rooftops and gutters. The damage seemed old, as if the city was in a constant state of disrepair, slowly eaten by some creeping war with no beginning and no end in sight.

It took *Ladon* half a day to navigate from the shanty outskirts of the town to its centre, where Thirteen Factories stamped their heavy colonial mark on the oriental surface of the city centre: a collection of western-style buildings, two and three storeys tall, fresh, new and magnificent. The colonnaded facades of purest white marble shone brightly in the sun like polished ivory, as did the zinc-covered roofs. Flags of the colonial powers and trade corporations flapped in the wind on tall masts of cedar wood, the Dracaland Jack flying between the banners of Midgard and Bataave. A small aerostat floated in the air, moored to a landing mast, which also served as a receiver for carrier wisps.

There was no pier big enough for the *Ladon*, so the ship was forced to stand at anchor a little off the harbour. A few of the crew, Bran and his father among them, boarded a cutter and made landing near the mouth of a small creek, by the customs station.

The Imperial Factory was the greatest of all, a three-storey edifice, with a row of blue-shuttered windows above a sculpted architrave showing the greatest triumphs of the Dracalish and Prydain might. Bran strained his memory trying to recall all the wars and battles he had always paid little attention to. He easily identified Arthur's march into Rome and the defeat of Norsemen at Crug Mawr, for that was part of Gwynedd's history too. It took him considerably more effort to name the siege of Ar Roc'hell during the Wizardry Wars and a more recent sea battle of Cape Spartel, where the dreaded Kyrnosian Imperator's invasion fleet was vanquished. The conquest of the northern Bharata he recognised from the stories told by some of the elder soldiers. But the last scene he could not remember at all: an ironclad battleship sailing into a walled harbour with all guns blazing.

There was a warehouse on the lower level of the factory, full of tea bricks and bales of fresh golden silk piled in pyramids on one side, and large unmarked crates of red wood on the other. A group of Qin workers emerged with another cartload of tea, and it was the first time Bran had seen these mysterious people in the flesh, with their narrow eyes, flat noses and long braided ponytails under round cloth caps. They moved about silently, like automatons, their emotionless faces grey with fatigue. Their vacant eyes glanced through Bran as if he was invisible, as they proceeded to unload the cart onto the warehouse floor.

The meal they were served was, somewhat disappointingly, what one would expect to eat in any dining room of the Dracaland. Only the surroundings made it feel exotic. There was white fish with roast vegetables, imported all the way from the West but, not having survived the journey well, everything was withered and bland.

Bran wondered why anyone would go through so much effort when the land around the city seemed fertile and plentiful. He chewed the badly seasoned fish in silence, sitting at one end of a long table, his father at the opposite end already discussing some important local matters with a gentleman in a black magisterial robe. They talked in hushed voices, sometimes slipping into some sort of code, and Bran could not make much sense of the conversation. Prices of rice and silk were mentioned, and army movements, weather forecasts and geomantic divinations. Bran wiped his lips with a serviette, coughed and excused himself to leave the dining room.

Dylan paused the conversation and turned to his son.

"Yes?"

"I thought I might do some sightseeing in the harbour."

Dylan thought for a brief moment then nodded.

"Yes, I suppose."

He snapped his fingers, whispering a spell. Bran felt a tinge of protective magic field surrounding him.

"Just don't go out too far. There's not much to see outside the Factories anyway, and you won't be allowed past the walls of the city proper on your own." Dylan lowered his voice. "The locals..."

"What about them?"

"Well, they rarely speak our language, that's all." He smiled and patted Bran on the shoulder. "Off you go. There's a boat dwellers' village to the west - that might be of some interest. Be back by supper. Don't get into trouble."

"Yes, father."

"Good lad," said Dylan and turned back to the man in black robe. "I'm sorry, *tai-pan*, you mentioned Xiuquan's new policies..."

Bran walked the long narrow lane at the back of the factories. There were no magnificent facades here, clean white plaster replaced by plain practical wood and low-fired brick, but it was still a neat and well-kept area. He passed dozens of natives, construction workers, dockers and porters, carrying their goods on bamboo poles. There were very few Westerners here, mostly foremen or guards. A few loud drunk sailors stumbled from a tavern on Hogs Lane, noticed they were in the wrong part of the city and swayed back. Among themselves, the Qin walked straight, talked and laughed, but when Bran or any other Westerner approached they all fell quiet, turned their eyes away and dispersed, skulking. All except one man, resting under the eaves of a tea house, looking the passing men straight in the face in silence. His hair was uncut, his eyes bright and on his forearm was carved a tattoo of a black lotus flower. Bran nodded at him lightly and the man's lips curved in a wry, mocking smile.

The dragon rider turned left towards the riverside, past the anchorages of long narrow boats covered with thick canvas, and noticed an opening in the fence surrounding the Factories, through which some workers sneaked with sacks of rice and construction materials. Curious, he decided to follow them.

Past the fence lay a different, more native area. The houses here were low, but densely packed, with blue-tiled overhanging roofs. The wooden and clay walls were painted in bright colours, the windows and doors opened out onto the loosely cobbled streets and narrow canals filled with stale smelly water. People lived here, not only worked. Old women sat outside spinning yarn or milling grain, children played with their funny little dogs. That much was the same as in every village in every part of the world. Here the women and children looked at him curiously and without apprehension. He saw a few girls who resembled the image in Ifor's medallion but their faces were grimy and their teeth had fallen out.

But there was something else, odd, disturbing. On the constricted alleyways, along the canal shores and gutters lay half-naked emaciated men with blank eyes, smoking long wooden pipes attached to some copper contraptions. The men looked straight at him and through him as if in a daydream. The whole district was filled with the sweet and sickly scent of the strange smoke.

The farther into the village Bran went, the more of these strange people he saw, gathered around their copper pots and clay pipes, huddling together, shivering despite the heat. He noticed some of them sitting on top of red unmarked crates, the same as the ones he had seen in the factory warehouse. These were darker, more sinister alleyways. The houses here were poor, dirty, half ruined, in disrepair, just like the ones along the river. Again he found markings of some past war, never fixed, and there were people wounded or maimed by sword and bullet, in rags, hauling buckets of water or pots of rice to their desperate households. The children were running naked amongst the rubbish and rubble strewn on the streets and, what somehow seemed the most ominous about the area, there were no dogs here. Bran instinctively touched his shoulder where the unseen Seal of Llambed buzzed patiently, and hoped his father's protection spell worked.

Some of the younger children approached him with outstretched hands, begging. He had nothing of value to give and tried to wave them away, but they saw his rich clothes and his pink skin and followed him. More came like scared goats to a shepherd, all crying:

"*Tai-pan, tai-pan!*"

He started to feel uneasy. The men paid no attention to him, deep in their narcotic daydream, and the women passed him by too busy with their ceaseless chores to notice. But the children were now coming from all the nooks and alleyways, demanding gifts now, not begging.

He raised his hand and they shushed. He fluttered his fingers and cast a simple illusion, a kid's toy spell, one of the first any student of magic would learn.

"*Pili-pala!*"

A dozen rainbow-coloured butterflies flew from his palm.

The children gasped in delight.

"*Blodeuyn!*"

The flowers followed, whole and petals, falling from the sky. The little ones tried to grab them, disappointed when they proved no more solid than soap bubbles. Bran continued his show with some fireworks and little birds, but by now he had caught the attention of the grown-ups. A few of the less drug-addled men were looking at him now, their brows furrowed over narrow eyes. One of them stood up heavily, swaying, raising his hand and shouting something.

Bran felt strangely tired. The simple spells were much more exhausting than they should have been. He wondered if it was the effect of the Barrier. It was time to return to the Factories. He bowed to his audience, spread some more bubbles from his fingers as an encore, then turned around and froze. A small mob of tall burly men was standing across the narrow bridge, looking angry. They were dressed in rags and loincloths, but they stood straight and their eyes were not as milky and blurry as of those lying in the gutters about the village. The men murmured at him in their strange tongue.

"I... I don't understand," he answered, trying to sound apologetic.

Still they approached, waving their hands and talking with loud voices, agitated. A small stone thrown by an unseen hand buzzed off the shield surrounding Bran and fell at his feet. He stepped backwards, but behind him there was a crowd of children, still eagerly waiting for more entertainment and to his sides – only the murky waters of the canal. He drew the sword by few inches to show he meant to defend himself. The runes on the blade and the eyes of the dragon on the hilt lit up with a bluish glow. Somewhere in the *Ladon*'s stables his mount raised a scaly head and Bran felt a familiar surge of power.

"I don't want to hurt you," he said, now with a threat in his voice.

The men in front of the group halted and let a few others pass from behind. These new adversaries carried wooden clubs and some broken farming tools. A couple more stones whizzed past Bran's head.

Suddenly one of the men reeled back in terror, pointing at something in the sky above Bran. He felt his energy coming back. The boy looked up and saw a great silver dragon hovering above the bridge, its wings rising clouds of yellow dust, dispersing the sweetly scented smoke. The men who threatened him disappeared in an instant, scurrying into the shadowy alleyways.

"*Bran!* What are you doing here?" Reeve Gwenlian cried, her long black hair billowing in the wind. "This is not a place for a Western boy. Hop on, I'll take you back to the Factory."

Bran did not see much of his father for the next few days. Dylan scarcely left the confines of the Imperial Factory's boardrooms, where he discussed matters of national importance with the *tai-pans* – chiefs of trading companies – and other officials.

After his misadventure beyond the fence, he was cautious not to venture beyond the walls of the Western settlement again. Bran could fly his dragon along the length of the Pearl River, from the harbour to the sea, as long as he took care not to land on or fly over the riverbank. Whenever he got too close to the city walls, Qin aerial patrols, flying on hand-crank whirligigs, scrambled to frighten him off with flares and fireworks. Although Emrys could blow the fragile bamboo vehicles out of the sky with one breath, Bran was not too keen on starting a war on his account, and dutifully obeyed the warnings.

Bran sensed that Emrys disliked the whole experience, dizzy and uncomfortable whenever they flew too high or too far from the Factories. There were powerful enchantments, remnants of old spells and forgotten curses woven across this ancient land for generations after generations, which the creature felt with its entire self. The currents and updrafts of the Ninth Wind, which gave the dragon wings their lift, were treacherous and unstable. At least the river, being so close to the great sea and used by foreign traders and travellers for millennia, was more or less clear of these dense influences.

The boy soon found that the people of the boat anchorages, the Tanka, were much friendlier and more hospitable than the town dwellers. They were not afraid of his magic, minor illusions he cast as thanks for small gifts and snacks they gave him as he hopped from one canvas-covered boat to another. A few of their tradesmen, who delivered fresh fish and mussels to the dining rooms of the Thirteen Factories, even spoke a little Seaxe. Bran befriended one of them, Bou, a small happy man with a bald head, which he usually covered with a garishly-coloured scarf. Bou volunteered to be his guide around the anchorages, gaining visible satisfaction from the fact he could be seen accompanying a rich child of the foreigners.

Bou was equally curious and asked a lot of questions, and the boy obliged him with all the information, glad to have somebody eager to talk to. In exchange, Bou tried to respond to all Bran's enquiries in a mixture of broken Seaxe and mime.

"What are they singing about?" asked Bran one evening as they sat on Bou's merchant boat, watching the sun set over the mountains.

They were munching on some sticky rice balls covered in sesame. Bran loved these new unknown tastes, and often snuck out to the Tanka anchorage at dinner time, to avoid the bland "Genuine Dracaland" canned food served at the factories.

The boatmen sang a long-vowelled, wailing, trilling melody without any recognisable words.

"Fish... and women. Most important in man's life," said a grinning Bou.

"I suppose the women sing about fish and men then," Bran guessed, nodding towards a group of fishermen's wives cleaning oysters on a nearby boat.

"No." Bou shook his head. "Women sing about *you*."

"*Me*?" Bran almost dropped his rice ball, his ears reddening. "Why me?"

"You're a new, curious thing - Western boy with power - not often among the boat people. Worth singing about."

"I don't understand. Why is my magic so curious? I can sense the power running through the bones of this country. The Barrier is like nothing I have seen before – you must have had tremendously powerful wizards... and yet, wherever I cast the simplest of tricks, a crowd gathers."

"The boat people - never much trade in Words of Power." Bou shrugged. "We are simple folk, fresh fish and peace from typhoons are all we need, but the town-dwellers, they many-many witch, long time ago, before the Cursed Weed."

"The Cursed Weed?"

Bou nodded again.

"It muddles thoughts... makes one forget what's real. It... eats your power and your pride."

"Is that what they smoke, the sweet scent? But... why? I can't imagine anything I would wish to give up my Power for..."

"The Cursed Weed asks no questions. It just is. It gives all he wants and takes all he cares. This not a happy land, only the Weed makes happy."

The sad expression did not fit Bou's round wrinkled face.

"Where did it come from? What is the Cursed Weed?"

Bou turned to Bran and looked him straight in the eyes, which was rare even among the Tanka.

"Ask your father, boy with Power. Not my tale to tell."

Bran opened his mouth to answer, but something else caught his attention. A white dot appeared over the hills to the west, approaching quickly.

"What's that?"

"*Long*," Bou answered piously, standing up, "the Heavenly One."

It took Bran a moment to realise what the man had said. A Qin dragon! At last!

"Run to your people, boy," said Bou, pointing towards Reeve Gwenlian, who was heading for Bran with concern on her face.

The silver dot turned towards the Factories.

"The war is near."

"*War*? What war?"

"There always war in Qin," the little merchant said sadly.

The dragon came fast like the hurricane, its alabaster scales glowing crimson in the setting sun. The elongated serpentine body coiled among the clouds as it soared on the Ninth Wind without the aid of wings. The silver antlers on its head glistened brightly, and the tip of the long tail blazed with a red flame. The rider, a tiny black figure, could barely be seen on the dragon's jagged back.

One of the town guard whirligigs tried to get near the splendid creature, shooting its usual red and blue flares to frighten it away. The dragon opened its wide mouth and a powerful stream of water gushed from it like from a fountain. In an instant, the thin bamboo and paper structure of the flying vehicle shattered into splinters and the hapless guard plummeted to his death with a bloodcurdling cry.

The soldiers of the Second Dragoons observed the dragon in silence at first, admiring its beauty, but when it attacked the guard, they immediately sprang into action. A wing of three Silvers scrambled off the deck of the *Ladon*. They were smaller than the graceful flying serpent, but more muscular and aggressive. The Qin dragon was almost within range of the dragoons' lances when its rider decided to turn tail. The beast spat a dense puff of protective mist and disappeared into the thick grey clouds above.

Dylan watched the skirmish from the balcony of the Imperial Factory, stern-faced. As soon as the white dragon vanished he ran down to the stables and mounted Afreolus.

He came back two days later and, without even changing his clothes or washing himself, called a meeting in the dining hall between himself, the *tai-pans*, superintendent of the port and captains of the royal troops. Before long, a decision was made.

Dylan paced the deck of the *Ladon* observing the ceaseless commotion around him. The carrier wisps travelling back and forth between the ship, the Factory and Fragrant Harbour. The soldiers armed with pneumatic rifles, glass air tanks strapped to their backs, standing watchful as the Qin porters filled the hauls to the brim with rice, grain, dragon fodder, dried fruit and Bangla rum. Weapons hauled up from their hidden compartments onto the gun deck. The armament was all state-of-the-art, as modern as the ship itself. Four huge mistfire-powered autoguns of Brezhon design, each with four rotating barrels, were winched onto the top deck, aft and fore; smaller smooth-bore cannons firing explosive shells lined the broadside. A battery of Congreve's rocket launchers was mounted on the foredeck. A lightning thrower, complicated coiled apparatus capable of hurling electric bolts over vast distances, was assembled in the machine hold and connected to the copper-gilded rods of the main mast with rubber cables. Magic amplifiers hummed in glass canopies along the sides.

He climbed onto the landing deck, where Gwenllian was briefing the stable masters. Even with all the magical arsenal the dragons were the ship's main weapon, and their comfort on the journey was of utmost importance.

"Have you seen my son somewhere?" he asked her after they exchanged greetings.

"He went to see the Gorllewin steamer. Do you want me to bring him?"

"No, no, you're busy. I need to talk to him myself."

He flew back over the Fan Yu harbour. He easily guessed what had intrigued Bran about the ship of the Grey Hoods. Many vessels were arming themselves with guns, canons and other machines of war in expectation of conflict, but only one was carrying dragons: a broad black steamer with four of the snow white beasts on the landing deck.

He found Bran observing the ship from the end of the pier.

"Surprised? I know I was."

"You didn't know the Grey Hoods keep dragons?"

Dylan shook his head. "Not until recently. We still know little about what they're up to. The Gorllewin have appeared in these waters only a few years ago, keeping themselves neutral from all the conflicts."

"These dragons were not bred for fighting," said Bran. The white beasts were squat, heavy and slow. They paid little attention to their surroundings, dozing off on the landing deck in the afternoon sun.

"Oh, a *Snaellander* can be fierce if it is roused. But you're right, they're not much of a threat. Not sure why bring them all the way here..."

One of the dragons raised its head and yawned lazily.

"We're moving out tomorrow," said Dylan.

"Where to?"

"We sail north, to Huating and then Jiankang. It's the southern capital of Qin, and it's about to be besieged. The viceroy requested our help."

"Besieged? By whom?"

"There was a major rebellion not far from here. That's what's causing all this... ruckus."

Dylan waved his hand around the harbour.

"You feared the rebels would march on Fan Yu?"

"Yes, but we managed to... *convince* them we're not worth the trouble."

A year's worth of unmarked crates it cost us, he remembered.

"The court at Ta Du is their target and enemy."

"And now we go to help that court against the rebels, even though they left us in peace?"

"The Dragon Throne's interests are diverse," said Dylan, the corner of his lips raised in a faint smile.

We need to recoup our losses after all.

"I'll go get myself ready."

"*You* are staying in Fan Yu."

The boy stared at his father in silence.

"I promised your mother you would stay safe. The ship is moving to a war zone, that's no place for you."

"Father, don't you even – "

"I'm serious. Fan Yu is safe. In Jiankang there will be a real battle, real death. I will not dare losing you to a stray bullet or arrow."

"Or do you think that I will not manage, that I will shame you with my toy dragon?"

"By Owain's sword, don't be ridiculous!"

"Do you think I have not noticed the way you kept shunning me, the way you've always looked at Emrys with contempt? Would you have let me go if I rode that bronze you wanted to give me? Is that it?"

Bronze – ? Ohh, that thing. He still remembers.

Dylan scratched his forehead, sighed deeply, sat down on a bollard and loosened a button in the collar of his uniform.

"Look, Bran, I had no idea... I didn't even remember – "

"Why not just send me back on the first ship to Dracaland? I'm obviously of no use to you here."

"What would you have me do? You're my only son. You're just a boy..."

"I know you've almost managed to forget it, but I just had my *sixteenth* birthday," Bran reminded his father dryly. "I could just go to the quartermaster and volunteer myself to join the regiment."

Bran was right - past sixteen, he was free to sign up to the army if he so wished. Of course as the regimental commander, Dylan had a final say in who got accepted but he knew the refusal would only further antagonise his son.

He closed his eyes and clasped his furrowed forehead in his fingers.

"Right," said Bran, turning around, "I'm off to enlist."

"*Wait!*" Dylan grabbed him by the arm and sighed deeply. "Promise me... promise me you won't be doing anything foolish," he said at last.

"Father!"

"Promise!" Dylan cried impatiently. Bran pulled back in fright.

What am I doing?

"If you want to be treated like an adult, behave like one," he said, calming down. "In the army you have to listen to your superior's orders. Well, on board the *Ladon* you will listen to me. This is my order."

"I promise, Father."

"And not a word about this to your mother. She would skin me alive."

CHAPTER XI

Fan Yu, Qin, April, 2607 ab urbe condita

The large dining hall on the top floor of the Imperial Factory had been turned into a war room. A great geomantic map of Qin was spread out on a surface made of several dinner tables. The map did not show the physical or administrative layout of the country, but was a diagram of ley lines, hot spots and power points that were known or detected by the map makers. Sacred and Cursed Grounds were painted white and black, while crucial nexii were marked with red wax seals. The entire land was divided into sixteen regions, each signed with one of the geomantic tetragrams. Dozens of tokens and markers were spread throughout the map. Some obvious, like miniature cinnabar pagodas where temples and monasteries were known to exist, others obscure, like a small turtle of black clay, which moved a little bit every evening on its journey from north to south towards the centre of the map, where a large yellow Qin dragon was painted, sleeping.

Dylan stood over the map, observing intently the changing colourful lines and flickering flaming dots lighting and extinguishing, seemingly at random. He scratched his scar in distress. Once the rebel army had passed through the province, his precious network of spies and scouts became dispersed, communications broken. He had to rely on divinations and geomancy to track the movement of enemy armies, and it troubled him. One could never depend fully on magic in this ancient, tormented land.

"The ship is ready, Father."

Dylan turned around, surprised. Bran was standing in the doorway looking at the map curiously. He was wearing his blue cadet's uniform.

"And they've sent you to tell me this?"

"I... volunteered, Father. Is that the map of Qin?"

"Yes. See, we are here." He pointed at a bright dot on the Southern coast and the runes *Fan Yu* lit up. "We sail north-west – Ederra Strait is still out of bounds for our ships – to here, the port of Huating. I've never seen it before – that's a new one for me," he said, smiling.

Bran studied the map for a while, trying to make sense of the moving lines, lights and symbols.

"There's always war in Qin," he murmured.

"What did you say?"

"It's something the Tanka people said."

"Mhm. Yes, I suppose some of these townsfolk can't even remember a time before all the wars and rebellions..."

"The Qin I read about was a mighty, rich, beautiful empire, a land of fairy tale. But all this… is nothing but a shadow. What's happened to this place?"

Dylan scratched his beard, covered with a three-day stubble. Lately he was so busy it was getting difficult to maintain the regulation clean shave.

"Stagnation," he replied after a while. "Inability to deal with new threats."

"What new threats?"

"Us."

"You mean the Cursed Weed?"

Dylan glanced at the boy sharply.

"I see you haven't been spending time idly. What do you know about it?"

Bran shrugged.

"I have seen what it does to people. The boat people told me to seek answers from you. Did we bring the Weed to Qin?"

"It's not quite like that. The Qin have always grown and consumed the plant, and so have we, for medicine. You may have heard of laudanum?"

"Some sort of an analgesic," Bran recalled.

"The same plant. The Emperor of Qin had the Weed banned over a hundred years ago and it has become much more desirable and expensive since, as with all things forbidden. This is where we – rather, the Dracaland trade companies - came in. They have flooded the land with the cheap product grown in the plantations of Bharata."

"The unmarked crates?" Bran guessed.

"Yes. We bribe the authorities to overlook them in our warehouses."

"It's shameful."

"It's good business," said Dylan, shrugging, "and what our Empire is built upon. Without the Cursed Weed money you would have no tea for breakfast."

"*Our* Empire? This is the Dracalish way, not Gwynedd."

"There is one crown on both sides of the Dyke," reminded Dylan, feeling increasingly uneasy about the way the conversation was progressing.

"But you're still a freeman of Gwynedd. You don't have to be doing this."

"I don't deal with the Weed trade. I just... know about it."

"So you just close your eyes and let things happen around you."

Dylan sighed.

Yes, sometimes I have to close my eyes to stay sane, he thought.

He remembered himself, on his first assignment in the Imperial Navy, sent to fight in the Cursed Weed war. Corruption, smuggling, assassinations, blackmails... There was nothing decent or just about the way Dracaland waged its wars. But, that was a long time ago and he had since learned to accept the harsh realities of the war and diplomacy. He knew Bran would too, one day.

"Why aren't the rebels attacking us?" Bran asked.

"We manage to funnel their wrath at the Emperor."

"We then get paid for helping him to deal with the rebels?"

"You grasp it quickly."

"We're behaving no better than Warwick," his son said through clenched teeth.

"*Warwick?*"

Dylan frowned at the sound of a familiar name. The old Warwick was his persecutor at the Academy. Did he have a son?

So that's why you didn't want to go back.

He put his hand on Bran's shoulder and looked him in the eyes.

"You're no longer at school, Bran. Adults don't live in a fairy tale. The Qin are not innocent themselves. They have also conquered nations in the past, and they did it with might and subterfuge, not morals and good deeds. They were a brutal, atrocious race while they were yet strong. Who knows, they still might be, one day..."

"And now we are the strong ones? Is that your lesson, Father? Power prevails?"

"No, Bran..." Dylan grew exasperated. "Listen –"

"What would Grandpa say to all this?"

"Ifor?" Dylan blinked.

What is he on about?

"He was a decent, straight-forward man. I'm sure he would disagree with all this subterfuge and deception."

Dylan almost burst out laughing.

"Who told you that? I'm sorry, but there was nothing straight-forward about that man. Your grandfather left my mother, left all of us when we most needed him, chasing after some long lost dream, disappearing into Sun knows where. If *he* dared to talk to *me* about morals, I'd laugh in his face. Look, you don't know – "

"I know enough. Leave me alone."

The boy shrugged his father's hand off his shoulder.

"Your soldiers are waiting," Bran said, then turned around and stormed out of the room.

It had taken the *Ladon* a full week to navigate around the island of Ederra and along the eastern shore of Qin towards the Chang River delta.

Bran's excitement grew as the ship sailed north. They were now in the waters mentioned in Ifor's diary, sailing past the Tagalogs out onto the open ocean where the big red question mark had been scribbled on his grandfather's map. Plenty had changed since HMS *Phaeton* ventured through these straits. The sea was now properly charted, the Qin coast accessible to Western shipping in several places. None of the crew, however, made any mention of the mysterious land of Yamato as if Bran was the only person on board aware of its existence. It wasn't even on any of the navigational charts at the bridge.

The *Ladon* was to wait about a hundred miles offshore for the Qin official guide-ship that would lead them past the small, but swiftly growing, port of Huating deeper into the delta where Jiankang lay.

Dylan walked the length of the ship back and forth, checking the equipment and weaponry in preparation for another Barrier crossing. There was now a great deal of delicate and precise equipment on board, so everything had to be carefully taken care of. Bran followed, trying to learn as much as he could from observing his father's meticulous craftsmanship. They may have had their differences, but Dylan's skill was next to none and it would be unwise – and childish, Bran reminded himself – to ignore the opportunity to study.

By evening they reached the foredeck, where Dylan hunched over the launching pad for Congreve's rockets. He examined it and grimaced.

"What the...? This has not been properly locked. Help me with that wrench."

"Why do you have to do it yourself? This ship has got an army of technicians."

"I need to know the position of every screw and bolt on this vessel if I want to weave them all into the Passing Spell."

Despite himself, Bran glanced at his father with admiration. He could hardly imagine the mental strain caused by such a complex enchantment. He tightened a few bolts in the base of the machinery as instructed. His father, with some effort, pulled out a coiled copper wire from inside the launch pad, held it in a clenched fist and murmured a few words of a Binding Spell.

"That should do it." He pushed the wire back, closed the hatch and stood up, stretching his back and arms. "That was the last thing. I'd say we're good to go." He stood for a while, looking longingly over the bow at the waves below. He spoke at last. "I remember sailing these seas with my father – before he settled down - the best years of my life. I should've brought you here earlier, son, when the world was much safer."

"To show me how you help enslave some other people?"

Dylan shook his head.

"There's more to the world than Dracaland's wars, son. I can show you so many beautiful things..."

"Can you show me *Dejeema*?" asked Bran.

Dylan stared at the boy.

"Where have you heard this name?"

"I... overheard Bataavian merchants in the harbour. I haven't seen it on any maps."

"They must have been most careless." Dylan licked his lips. "The very existence of this place is one of their best kept secrets."

"What is it, then?"

"Some four hundred miles that way," Dylan said, pointing to the east, "lie the islands of Yamato. Dejeema is where their main harbour is – so I've heard."

"So you've never been there?"

"No. No Western ship can sail there, except Bataavians." Dylan shook his head. "Who knows how they've managed to do it."

"*Can't* sail? With all this power?" Bran asked, waving his hand around the *Ladon*.

"There are powerful storms and currents along the way, like an ocean maze. The navigation tools become useless. Even the clocks run in a strange way. In a way it's even more effective than the Qin Barrier. I've heard rumours of a Dracalish captain once forcing his way into Dejeema, but that was long before you or I were born."

There was some shouting coming from the port side of the ship. Dylan broke his tale and turned in the direction of the noise.

"That will be the Qin boat. I must welcome it."

He walked off leaving Bran alone. So Dylan didn't know his own father had been to Yamato… The boy stared towards the eastern horizon, trying futilely to see the distant harbour of *Keeyo*, but there was nothing but grey clouds.

He took his grandfather's box and the dragon figurine from the satchel. Bran wondered if the dragon, too, had come from Yamato; both things were made of the same smooth, glistening material. The medallion lay inside peacefully, but there seemed to be a faint azure glow within the blue stone of the ring, which Bran had been keeping inside throughout the journey, near the golden brooch from which the stone was taken. He raised the jewel to the sun. The gem was no longer translucent, but slightly cloudy, as if it had begun stirring back to life.

The Qin pilot arrived in a small junk with three square red sails, tiger eyes painted on the bow and a band of gold and enamel running along the broadside. Two bronze cannons adorned the foredeck, more decorations than real weapons.

The pilot and his entourage, all dressed in rich dark yellow robes, were shown around the *Ladon*. Their faces showed no sign of emotion as they examined the advanced weaponry and technology of the ship. They listened to the interpreter's explanations and nodded in unison. Eventually they were led to the mess hall where dinner awaited.

As soon as the second course was served, Bran slipped outside. As he would most nights when the ship was in the open sea and he didn't play *tafl* with Samuel, he went to the stables on the second deck, untied his dragon and led it outside via a large ramp leading astern.

Emrys would only want to fly for a few minutes each night, just enough to straighten its wings. It was still afraid of the open ocean, even after so many months at sea. If the weather was less than clement, the dragon loathed even to leave the stable for too long, but it enjoyed strolling the width and breadth of the top deck, breathing the salty air while Bran looked at the stars through the spyglass, marking subtle changes in their positions in his notepad as the ship moved through latitudes.

The dragon fell asleep on the foredeck, and Bran put the spyglass back into the satchel and took out a book on *tafl* rules he had borrowed from Samuel. These were his favourite moments; the dark silent nights. There was nobody outside except for a couple of watchmen on extreme points of the ship, each far away from where he sat. Some noise was coming from the mess hall where the Qin pilot and the crew still banqueted, but it was muffled and easily ignored. Apart from that, only the soft lapping of the waves and gentle ringing of the rigging in the breeze disrupted the quietness. With a snap of his fingers, Bran conjured a floating flamespark and settled himself among the coiled ropes with the book.

The lookout on the bow cried out. The portside searchlights lit up, their beams setting the sky ablaze, and all the bells and sirens rang out in alarm. Three long whistles meant they were being attacked from the air.

Emrys stirred and woke up uneasily. The boy jumped up, but could not yet see anything in the night sky. Unlike the lookouts, he did not have the naval Farfinder device that could spot danger for miles, at night, in storm or in fog.

Within seconds the soldiers and crew started appearing on deck. Bran had seen them train the battle alarm countless times before, but now, at last, it was the real thing. The great hatch opened, the ramps lowered and the dragons were led by the stable hands out onto the landing deck, one by one. Their riders poured from the forecastle cabins, strapping swords to their belts and donning flight hauberks and wind goggles. The gunners ran to the fore and aft turrets. Smaller rapid guns, six of them clustered on the aft side, were the first to howl. The operators, always on watch, appeared inside the glass turrets moments after the alert rang, propelled from their cabins under the aftercastle by mistfire lifts. The smooth-bore broadsides were useless against an aerial attack, but the quadruple barrels of the great self-repeating cannons could be winched to a high enough angle to wreak havoc in the sky above the ship.

Dylan was already on deck, shouting orders and peering into the darkness, paying no attention to Bran. At last the enemy was in plain sight. A whole skein of Qin *Long*, twelve at least. They were glorious to behold; long coiling bodies surrounded by a haze of mist and lightning, scales glinting with all colours of the rainbow in the beams of the searchlights.

"*Mount up!*" cried one of the marines. Bran recognised Banneret Edern by his silver hair, eyes burning brightly as they always did when he was agitated. "*Scramble the Silvers!*"

"Gunners, protect the pilot boat," ordered Dylan, "and prepare Afreolus, I will lead the first squadron mys – *Bran!*" He noticed the boy at last, somewhat surprised. "What are you doing?"

Bran had finished preparing the saddle by now and was ready to mount Emrys and join *Ladon's* defenders.

"What are your orders, Ardian?" the boy asked solemnly, putting on his flying goggles.

"I order you to stay here where it's safe. You are not a soldier yet."

"Father, I'm more than capable —"

"We're in a war zone now. Do me a favour and just keep quiet," Dylan snapped. The Qin dragons were almost upon them. "You'd only get in the way."

"So that's what you really think of me?"

"Boy, I have no time for your quarrels now!"

"Then just let me —"

"*By the Red Dragon's Breath*, just stay here and wait!"

Dylan pointed at Bran and spoke Binding Words. The boy felt himself freeze, his entire body paralysed by the powerful enchantment. Amazingly, the spell was strong enough to even to stun his dragon. Bran could only speak — barely more than a whisper — but his father would not listen anymore.

Dylan spread the palm of his right hand and summoned his Soul Lance. This was the first time Bran had seen his father's weapon. It was unique; as bright as the sun, a twelve foot long shaft of solidified golden light, slightly curved and broadened at the end, like the blade of a cavalry sword. Dylan grabbed the lance firmly, mounted his great silver dragon and launched into the air, followed by other soldiers of the Second Dragoons.

With his fists still clenched the way they were when he was Bound by the spell, and heart burning with rage, Bran could only observe the battle in the night sky, illuminated by searchlights, flares and blasts of the guns. The Qin dragons were swift and agile, and there was a whole flock of them now swarming over the ship. They were blue, red and yellow, spewing dense mist, spouting streams of boiling water from their maws and shooting lightning from their antlers.

Ridden by skilled men, these would be formidable opponents, but their riders were nowhere near as well trained or experienced as the Dracalish soldiers and were soon overwhelmed by the *Ladon*'s squadron. Dragonflame of the Silvers proved a terrible weapon against the beasts of Qin. Even before the marines closed in for a melee with their brightly shining lances, the first of the Qin *Longs* fell, burning, spilling golden blood as it tumbled towards the dark sea, still coiling like a silk ribbon in the wind. Seconds later another followed. At last the others started breaking off. The marines followed them in hot pursuit, swiftly disappearing beyond the range of *Ladon*'s lights.

Silence fell upon the ship as the fighting dragons departed towards the western horizon. Bran could only wait for them to return, still paralysed by his father's spell as if he was a child.

He felt a presence. Somebody was sneaking along the line of coiled ropes and toolboxes. A man crept out from the shadows and looked the boy straight in the eyes. It was a Qin man. Bran recognised him by the black lotus tattoo on the forearm: one of the gaffers from the Fan Yu harbour; the quiet one.

He was holding a large tube of soft iron. Bran felt cold sweat trickling down his forehead as he realised what it was — the warhead of Congreve's rocket, a hollow chamber filled with potent explosives.

Bran struggled to speak.

"What… what are you doing?"

The man grinned.

"What do you *think* I'm doing, boy?" the Qinese answered in surprisingly fluent Seaxe.

"You're going to b-blow us up!" Bran stuttered.

Big though the ship was, there was enough ordnance, magical and otherwise, in the munitions hold to split the *Ladon* in two, and a lot of it was now brought up to the upper decks in preparation for the battle.

"So the dragons were just a ruse! You are a rebel saboteur!"

"I don't care one way or the other for the rebels - or the court. My cause is older than any of them."

"What do you mean?"

The Qinese looked sharply at the boy.

"What's it to you? You don't know me, I don't know you, and I'm certain it's the last time we will see each other. You better make ready to meet your ancestors."

The man grinned again. It seemed to Bran that his eyes glinted gold for a moment, but it had to be a trick of the light, a reflection of an evertorch. He bowed mockingly and sneaked away, clutching the piece of rocket in his hands.

Bran remained where he was, still unable to move. One long terrible minute passed then another. Emrys struggled against the Binding Words. Groggy and dazed, the beast tried to shrug the enchantment off its wings, lift its head and open its jaws. It managed to nudge Bran's shoulder with its snout and sniffed around, sensing danger.

The dragon rider dared not think he would die there and then, but, unwittingly, his thoughts went back to the red walls of his home, his favourite beach on the shore of Cantre'r Gwaelod, his mother's dark eyes. For a brief moment he evoked the tattooed, sad-eyed face of Eithne and recalled the day of the Graddio ceremony... Then, he remembered. Llambed's Seal! Of course, he only had to...

A low, loud rumble went through the ship spreading from the centre to the edges. A long second later a tremendous explosion burst through the hull from deep in the cargo hold with a deafening blast, showering the main deck with rubble and shrapnel. The blast did not simply make a hole in the ship – it broke it apart. The middle section, with the bridge, vaporised in an instant. The stern and the bow rose to the sky and the two parts started sinking within moments.

The eruption swept Bran several feet into the air and he was struck dumb. When he came to, the foredeck he and Emrys were on was already sinking into the water at a sharp angle. With a deafening creak, shatter and hiss, the massive boiler came loose from its bolts and smashed into the dark ocean. The released elementals turned the water into white steaming foam. The men in the water screamed in terrible agony. Others still held on to various bits and pieces on the bow as it sank fast into the deep.

By a stroke of luck, the force of the explosion broke Bran free from the Binding. He managed to grab onto some hatch handle firmly attached to the deck. His dragon was shrieking in panic, beating wings and jumping chaotically in place. It still could not fly away. Sliding towards the water, Emrys scratched the deck boards in desperation as the foaming and hissing surface of the boiling sea got ever nearer. Bran, his consciousness slowly slipping away from him, tried to dispel Dylan's enchantment on the dragon. It wasn't easy. With his True Sight he could see the individual strands forming the magical net. In the surrounding chaos, Bran had to focus on the one crucial strand and either dissolve it or snap it in two.

"Hounds of *Annwn*, I'm not a wizard!" he cursed in despair, as the dragon continued to flail about. Bran could feel its fear and confusion through the Farlink and it did not make things any easier for him. At last he found it, a single thread glowing bright gold, Dylan's signature colour. He reached towards it with his free hand and made a pulling gesture as if he tugged on an invisible rope.

"*Chwalu!*" he cried at the top of his lungs.

The Binding Spell unravelled in an instant. Suddenly released, Emrys leapt forwards with a single beat of wings into the starry darkness and disappeared out of Bran's sight.

With an effort, the boy turned his head and looked to the western sky – he could faintly see the first dragons of the Second Dragoons speeding back towards the sinking ship. They were flying fast, but it was too late. Below, the waters fumed and boiled as the ship slipped inexorably into the scalding deep. Bran felt his grip on the hatch handle slip.

With the last glimpse of awareness, he invoked the Seal of Llambed. At first nothing happened and the boy gave in to despair. So this was how it would all end, his short uneventful life. At least he had managed to see a little of the world before he died...

He then felt a burning sensation on his right shoulder and saw a pillar of blinding bright light envelop him. The raging sea, the sinking ship, the dragon regiment, all disappeared in the radiance. The last thing he saw was a silhouette of a great white eagle, swooping towards him from the sky.

CHAPTER XII

Yamato, Spring, 7th year of Kaei era

The shrine gardens overflowed with sweetly-scented blossom bursting from the branches in waterfalls of white, overhanging the gravelled pathways, showering the lawns and ponds with heart-shaped petals.

Watching the cherry trees bloom was something best done in company.

Nagomi wore the plain clothes of a shrine maiden, a white *haori* jacket and red split *hakama* skirt. Her long hair was pale strawberry blonde, as if the whiteness of the cherry blossom reflected in its gleam had weakened the mysterious hue. She stood at the top of the three hundred steps leading to the main entrance of the Suwa Shrine and watched her friend run up from the riverside, past a pair of stone-carved lion-dog guardians, by granite lanterns and under a row of stone *torii* gates. The wizardess clutched a bamboo leaf box in her hand.

"I brought pink sea bream," she said, catching her breath, "and pumpkin *mochi*."

"My favourite!" said Nagomi, smiling. "Let's go to the turtle pond, you can see the whole harbour from there."

"Is your father still away?" Satō asked, sipping from a cup of a salty, but refreshing, drink of pickled cherry petals.

"Yes," Nagomi replied, "and now Mom decided to pay him a visit. The house is all on Ine's head."

"He's not coming back soon then?"

"Doesn't look like it. The pox is still very bad in Ōwari and my father can only produce so much vaccine. It's difficult to obtain all the equipment he needs in Nagoya."

"If only the *Taikun* would let my father travel," said Satō with a sigh. "The Bataavians have been filling our house with all sorts of glass and copper apparatus that I'm sure Keisuke-*sama* could use in his laboratory."

"Have the rules of arrest been relaxed then?"

"Yes but only a little. The Overwizard is keen to have as close a relationship with my father as possible without attracting too much attention, so we are now being showered with more gifts than we know what to do with." Satō laughed. "Blueprints, equipment, exotic ingredients... My old man rarely ever steps out of the laboratory these days."

"And how are the boys?"

"The students? Not as annoying as they used to be, that's for certain. Keinosuke can still be scary when he sits silently for an entire lesson and then comes up with some random question... but I think he knows now I'm not going to tell him anything really important or secret. He's much too young for that!"

"Must be his father's influence - you said Sakuma-*dono* is a great scholar."

"He is," Satō replied, nodding, "perhaps the greatest alive, or so my father says. He also says it will all end badly for him and his family one day."

"That may be. The times are dangerous." Nagomi bit her lip. "That's what Kazuko-*hime* told me. The Waters of Scrying are shrouded in shadow – " she stopped abruptly.

Not even your friends...

It was difficult to keep secrets from Satō, even more than it had been from her family. They had been the closest of friends for as long as she remembered. Satō was the only kid in the neighbourhood who hadn't mocked the colour of her hair, and their friendship had grown ever closer since then. This was the first time she couldn't tell the wizardess about something important.

"*Not until we know more,*" the High Priestess had told her, "*not until we're certain you're safe.*"

A sudden breeze from the sea shook the branches and the white flowers fell like fresh snow. The girls were both silent and solemn for a while, but then Nagomi giggled.

"What is it?" Satō asked.

"I just imagined... You're the only daughter of the finest teacher of *Rangaku*, and Keinosuke is the only son of the greatest scholar in Kiyō... Isn't that a perfect match?"

"Don't be absurd!" Satō was genuinely flabbergasted. "He's three years younger than me – *and* a precocious little brat!"

"But you have to admit, he does come from a great family, and your father's *dōjō* –"

"*I* will inherit the *dōjō*, not some arrogant idiot. Just because he's a boy, doesn't mean... *Ugh*, I can't even think about it!"

"I was only joking..."

"It's easy for *you* to joke, you don't have to worry about getting married to some random fool."

"I won't be a maiden forever, you know. Priests can marry too."

"Yes, but only if they want to."

"I'm sorry, I didn't mean to upset you."

"It's all right," Satō said, calming down, "I should not have lashed out like that. It does not behove a samurai to lose temper so easily."

"Have you gotten any further with the book?" Nagomi asked, quickly changing the subject.

There could only have been one book she meant. Ever since Satō had discovered the Dragon Book in her father's library, she spent every free moment trying to decipher as much of it as she could.

"I'm barely past the first few pages. The language is somewhat similar to Bataavian, but not enough. I'm not even sure I'm doing it right." She shook her head. "I'm getting an odd word here and there, but really, I could be wrong all the time. Oh, but the drawings! They come alive on touch, the scales start to glint in the lamplight, the wings flap, the flames burst from the page, scarlet and golden…" Satō's eyes burned with passion. "I have never seen anything like it. The drawings made by our chroniclers, when the Vasconians first brought the *dorako* – they might as well have been lizards and dried up newts. Oh, I'd give anything to see a real *dorako*…"

"Can't you get one from Dejima?" asked Nagomi.

She did not share the wizardess's fascination with the strange Western creatures. In truth, she was barely aware what they looked like. For all she knew, they were just big lizards.

"Do you think these are chickens?" Satō was taken aback by her friend's ignorance. "A grown-up *dorako* is as big as a merchant's ship, and Bataavians would never dare to bring one to Yamato. They would be banned from Kiyō in an instant if they so much as mentioned the beasts."

"I didn't know…"

"No, of course, all this is secret knowledge. There are only a few scholars in the country who claim to know anything about these creatures."

"And none of them has a book like yours," added Nagomi.

"No, I don't think they do," Satō said with a grin. "That's what makes the whole thing so great; this feeling of exploring a whole new uncharted land, a journey into the unknown."

"I'm happy for you."

The apprentice felt a pang of guilt. Satō had no qualms about divulging forbidden knowledge, yet Nagomi could share none of her secrets in exchange.

"And how about your apprenticeship?" asked the wizardess, biting off a piece of chewy, rubbery *mochi* cake.

"Kazuko-*hime* said I'm making good progress," said Nagomi. "I have already tried some Scrying under supervision."

Should I have said even that much?

"That's great, that's really great." Satō smiled brightly. "I've always known you'd make a great priestess."

Nagomi turned her eyes to the horizon, her cheeks suddenly hot.

"It's nothing."

"What are you talking about?" Satō protested. "You're fifteen and already a skilled healer. You can commune with the Spirits, and that's something I could never do. I can only banish them to the Otherworld."

"Any other girl in the shrine can do what I can do," Nagomi said, shaking her head.

"You're better than any of them, I'm sure. Here, have another drink – to the two best girls in all of Kiyō!"

Satō raised the cup with blossom water in a toast. Nagomi joined her, but turned her face towards the harbour to hide the tears welling up in her eyes.

The wind picked up, once more showering them with the rain of white petals. The sun drifted beyond the mountain tops. The lunch box was empty. Satō rose and cast one last look at the sea.

"I need to go back; I bet the old man forgot to eat his supper again."

A streak of bright white light appeared high over the horizon for a brief moment, like distant lightning. A shooting star crossed the sky, but it was unlike any shooting star Nagomi had ever seen. It fell straight down, silently, towards the city, eventually disappearing somewhere in the harbour area, beyond the warehouses lining the bay north of Dejima's fan-shaped island.

"*Did you see that?*" Satō exclaimed.

"Yes..." whispered Nagomi piously. "It fell from Heavens..."

"Let's go see what it is."

"But–"

"We won't be long. It's just by the beach. *Come on!*"

"What now?" asked Nagomi, catching her breath after the long run.

They were at the open beach near the fishermen huts, having just run down the streets of the magistrate quarter, through the harbour, and past the quays and wharves full of foreign goods, fishing nets and crab pots. The sailors and workers watched them in surprise.

What a sight we must be, she thought. *A shrine maiden and a samurai among the filthy warehouses and muddy alleyways. And my hair...*

Some superstitious fishermen crooked their fingers and clapped their hands to repel evil, but none dared approach them.

The tide was coming in, but the beach was yet wide - and empty.

"Look! Near the mackerel pier."

Satō pointed at something in the water beside bundles of old fishing nets. There was a faint glow, receding fast, barely discernible now, like the fluorescence in a boat's wake.

Before they reached it the glow was gone, but now they could easily see a shape lying at the edge of the water, half-submerged and tangled in the nets. Satō stumbled across the wet sand towards the puzzling object, dark now in the quickly falling twilight, and knelt down to examine it.

"It's a *person!*"

It was indeed a human being, face down in the sand, wearing odd foreign clothes, blue jacket and a shirt that was once white, all tattered and singed, and a buckled leather bag was slung over the shoulder. A strap with two round pieces of glass hung around his neck.

The girls turned the castaway onto his back.

"*Gaikokujin!*" Nagomi gasped. "A Westerner!"

"A soldier," said Satō, frowning. "Look at that sword!"

Attached to the leather belt was a sword in a broad scabbard, with a sculpted hilt in the shape of a winged golden *dorako*. The foreigner seemed to be about their age. He had a gently hooked nose and deeply set eyes under thin brows. His short black hair was clumped with mud, his square face pale and bruised. Up close, his skin was still radiating a faint glow.

"I thought they all had yellow or red hair like you," remarked Satō, "or maybe he's a Vasconian…"

The apprentice put her head to the boy's chest.

"He's alive," she whispered, "what do we do?"

"We need to take him away from here first. He'll drown in the tide."

Nagomi waddled into the water and picked up the boy's legs, clad in thick cloth trousers. Satō did the same with his arms. The sword dragged a deep line through the wet sand. Heaving, they carried their load into the shadow of the willow trees by the fishing pier.

"I have to get my father, or, or Ine." Satō stood up and paced about in confused excitement. "We need to hide him from the authorities. You stay here, I'll get help."

"You are leaving me alone with him?"

Satō handed Nagomi a dagger.

"Use this if he tries anything."

"I didn't mean that…Go now, but be quick."

The wizardess' feet thumped on the sand as she disappeared into the darkness.

Nagomi leaned over the boy, studying his face in the light of the Spirit flame she always carried in a small clay beaker. There were some cuts and bruises on his skin, which she cleaned up with water from a nearby stream, but there were no major injuries visible. The boy didn't seem to need her healing. Where did he come from, and why? The sword by his side showed he was a soldier, but of what army?

A will-o'-the-wisp of a lantern appeared on the beach. Nagomi stood up at first, thinking it was Satō returning with help, but the light moved towards the waterline then hopped along the waves. Nagomi hid farther into the shadow of the pier, blowing out the Spirit light. She could now see two men searching the beach. They wore brown vests with the city crest on their shoulders.

The magistrate officials!

The girls obviously weren't the only ones who had seen the falling star…

The boy stirred and moaned.

No! Not now!

Nagomi knelt down by the stranger. It would be a disaster if they were found out. The law was clear – no foreigners were allowed on the sacred soil of Yamato without permission. The punishment for trespassing was death by beheading. Even the castaways were not exempt.

In desperation, she cradled the boy's head in her arms, trying to muffle his groans with the sleeve of her kimono. The magistrate men were now very close. One stray sound and they would notice the apprentice and her secret. Nagomi prayed silently to all the Gods she could remember. The boy's breath was distractingly warm against her hand.

The men passed her by and the light of their lantern bobbed away. She sighed with relief. The boy stirred more strongly and Nagomi had to let go of his head. He opened his eyes slowly and painfully, squinting with effort. At that moment, the moon came out from behind the clouds and lit up the boy's face. In a reflex, he reached out his hand trying to touch her hair, glistening red gold in the moonlight.

"Eithne," the boy whispered, and the strain caused him to lose consciousness again.

His hand fell to the sand limply. Nagomi sat silent, awestruck. The boy's eyes were as green as jade — as green as the jewel she had seen in the Waters of Scrying.

CHAPTER XIII

Yamato, Spring, 7ᵗʰ year of Kaei era

Old Yoshō, the white-haired servant of the Takashimas, arrived at the Itō's house in the middle of the night, requesting a palanquin. Doctor Itō Keisuke had sometimes been using one to bring in the sick from outside the city.

"Did something happen to Shūhan-*dono*?" Ine enquired, looking worried, "or Satō-*sama*?"

"The master and yun' missus are in no danger," the old servant mumbled a reply through toothless lips. "They ax'd me to fetch the palanquin to the beach."

Ine dispatched the old man with two of her porters and waited anxiously.

"Who's that?" she asked when, half an hour later, the porters brought out an unconscious boy with a face wrapped in bandages made of what Ine identified as cotton torn off the under-kimono.

"I dun' know nothing", Ine-*shiama*," the old servant mumbled. "Nagomi-*shiama* tol'me to bring the boy and not touch the bandages."

"And where *is* my dear little sister?"

"She's gon' back to the shrine, Ine-*shiama*, she said she'll come in the mornin'."

Ine frowned. Of all the annoyances her sister's overt benevolence caused, this one was the most peculiar. Nagomi was like a misguidedly generous cat, constantly bringing dead mice and birds to the house as unwanted gifts – only *her* gifts were sick children, poor cripples, dying old men she kept finding on the streets of the deprived outer districts of Kiyō.

"What do you expect me to do with all these people?" their father despaired. "We have no means to help everyone in need, and they are scaring away the paying customers."

But it was enough for the girl to look at Keisuke with her eyes of a doe and the doctor's heart melted. He had dedicated a separate room in the attic for the treatment of Nagomi's "strays", and – to prevent them from mingling with the richer clientele – had a separate entrance and stairway built at the back of the house. Despite Keisuke and Ine's best efforts, most of them never survived, and had to be carried away through the same entrance, preferably out of Nagomi's sight.

It was to this entrance that the porters now brought the mysterious boy. He seemed like none of the usual foundlings. The briny smell of seawater permeated his thick clothes. Underneath a blue jacket she noticed the bulge in the shape of a sword. In an instant Ine realised whom he was.

"Bring him up, quick. *Hurry.*"

She could only hope the porters failed to recognise the obvious. The boy was a castaway, a foreigner, a *Gaikokujin* soldier. This was too much.

Damn that girl! What was Nagomi thinking? Why bring him here? If the authorities found out they were harbouring a castaway, their family would be finished. They would be happy to get away with exile.

It was too late to do anything now. If Yoshō was sent to bring the foreigner, it meant that Master Takashima himself was aware of the situation. Ine had to trust the old wizard's judgement. Perhaps it was only for one night. Perhaps tomorrow somebody from Dejima would appear and take the dangerous guest away.

The boy moaned as the servants put him on the floor. Ine waved them away and unwound the bandages from around his face. Cleaned up, he even looked quite handsome, for a Westerner, with symmetrical well-defined features and prominent cheekbones. He smelled faintly of butter and meat, like all of his kind, but not as much as most Ine had met. He had a sharp-edged, olive-coloured face, not a pale round one like those of the Bataavians, which always reminded Ine of a full moon. His chin was strong and slightly jutting, his lips wide and thin. His skin was covered with tiny splinter wounds, as if he had head-butted through a wooden plank, though they were all sealed up. His breath was regular and blood had returned to his face.

She took his dirty clothes – the shirt and trousers almost fell apart in her hands, soaked and tattered – and covered him with a warm blanket.

Bran opened his eyes slowly, achingly. For a moment he couldn't see anything as his sight adjusted to the darkness. He was strangely weary. His bones ached, his head thumped and his entire skin burned with a myriad of tiny pinpricks.

What an odd dream, he thought. The enormous mistfire ship, a long journey, the city of the narrow-eyed people...

I must tell Mother about it in the morning.

He turned on his side. A thin mattress filled with some hard husks or chaff rustled when he moved. There was no bed underneath, just soft floor. He realised he was naked, wrapped in a warm blanket.

This is not my bed. This is not my house. How did I get here? What's going on?

He remembered. The ship was real. It was called MFS *Ladon*, and Bran had spent the last few months aboard it, sailing across half the world towards the land of Qin. Now they were on their way to some city to... He struggled to recall – fight the rebels, that's it.

I must've bumped myself on the head, he guessed, massaging his throbbing temples, *and they put me in the infirmary.*

The room smelled strongly of medicaments and rubbing alcohol, but there was also another odour, a strange, nauseatingly sweet scent, like damp straw in the barn after the rain.

He was hungry and thirsty. How long had he been out? His lips were parched, his eyelids glued together with sleep. He blinked repeatedly and lifted himself up onto one elbow, his head spinning. He was starting to see shadows and edges in the darkness, in the faint moonlight seeping through a window. Something was odd.

It couldn't have been the ship. The floor was solid, unmoving, there was no trace of the familiar swaying he had become accustomed to over the months. No room on the *Ladon* was this big, not even the captain's cabin. Certainly not that empty. He was in a house, on land, but where? Why? He closed his eyes, trying to recall the last thing he could remember before waking up.

The visit of the Qin pilot... The attack of the dragons... The rebel spy lurking in the shadows... The explosion...

Bran opened his eyes wide in terror. The *Ladon* was no more, obliterated in the blast, sunk with everyone on board - Doctor Samuel, the old Weatherman, the cooks, the mechanics, all his new found friends in the crew. All dead, except those men and women of the Second Dragoons who were in the air at the time.

He was still alive, seemingly unharmed, not counting the headache and overall state of exhaustion. The magic of the Seal must have saved him and bring him here, wherever *here* was. He had no idea how powerful the Seal was, or how it chose its destination. Most likely he was somewhere in Qin. If so, his father would no doubt...

Father...

It had all been Dylan's fault, Bran remembered, gritting his teeth at the memory. If he hadn't pointlessly Bound the boy like a spoiled brat, Bran could've stopped the Qin rebel. Everyone would be alive now. Everything would have been all right.

Bran punched the floor in anger. Somewhere in the corner of the room something clanked metallically. He stared in the direction of the sound, trying to penetrate the gloom. There was a little moonlight in the room, but it was strangely dimmed, as if filtered through gauze. Under the wall he made out a bundle on the floor. Slowly, Bran unwrapped himself from the blanket and crept across the soft floor towards the bundle. His bones and joints pained with every movement, but it was no more than how he would have felt on the morning after a tough training session.

He touched the bundle with his fingers – it was a neatly folded pack of clothes, but not his old ones. They were alien, made of very fine smooth cotton, almost silk-like. He felt farther and his fingers found the cold touch of a scabbard and a dragon-shaped hilt.

My sword!

Probing on, he found his flying goggles and a leather satchel lying beside it. He tried to unbuckle the bag to see if all his treasure was inside, but sudden weakness overwhelmed him.

Bran realised he was shivering with cold, his teeth chattering. It was an early spring night, he was naked and a chilly draught was blowing in through some crack in the wall. He crawled back to the blanket and managed to wrap himself back up before succumbing to deep dreamless sleep...

When he awoke again it was already light. He lay still with his eyes open, trying to get his bearings. The room was not as big as he had first thought in the darkness, but very neat, impeccably clean, with walls of light wood covered with grey paper on one side of the room and a lattice of black slats and white translucent paper on the other. The bundle of clothes still lay in the corner, as did his sword and the bag. Everything in the was divided with straight lines – the floor made of large mats of packed straw, lined with dark material, the walls and windows segmented by planks and slates into asymmetrical rectangles. There was a small cupboard in the corner with what looked like medical instruments, but no other furniture – no chair, no table, no bed. The room was made to look like a prison cell or a hospital ward.

The latticed wall slid apart and a Qin woman came in, carrying some towels and a porcelain bowl filled with steaming hot water. She was wearing a white flowing robe with wide sleeves, as clean and sterile as the room, tied with a wide grey sash at the waist. Her hair was tamed in a threefold bun, with an ivory comb stuck through, a hairstyle that seemed oddly familiar. Her feet moved in tiny measured steps. She knelt by his bedding and noticed Bran was awake. She let out a quiet gasp, but composed herself momentarily and put the bowl and towels by his bedding. Then bowed, rose and left, sliding the latticed door behind her.

Bran raised himself up on his elbows and waited until the spinning in his head subsided. He was about to move towards the water bowl when the door slid open again. The woman had a clay cup in her left hand and a small bowl of rice and a pair of chopsticks in her right.

She knelt down again and watched him intently. The cup was filled with some greenish brew. He took a sip, but it was yet too hot for his parched lips. He looked at the rice. He had seen locals using chopsticks in Fan Yu, but never got around to learning how to use them. He didn't want to seem barbarian, but was too hungry to pretend, so started eating the sticky rice with his fingers. The woman smiled approvingly, as if she was familiar with dealing with strangers. By the time he had emptied the bowl, the brew in the cup was cold enough. He drank it in one gulp, it was bitter and savoury.

"Thank you," he said, trying to convey the feeling of gratitude in his words as best as he could. "*Xiexie*," he added in Qin.

The woman smiled again and nodded. She brought in a large clay pot and a lidded black box then disappeared again, this time for good. Bran investigated the contents of the vessels - more rice and more of the green brew. The rice was bland, unseasoned, but it filled his stomach pleasantly and there was enough liquid to quench his most immediate thirst. He felt the energy and warmth slowly returning to his body.

He managed to carefully wash himself with a wet towel, hissing with the pain radiating from taut muscles. He tried to stand and, after a few attempts, managed not to tumble back down onto the bedding. He picked up the clothes. There was a long strip of linen cloth the purpose of which he could not identify, but after not finding anything else resembling an undergarment he decided it had to be the kind of loincloth the porters wore in Fan Yu. He wrapped it clumsily around his waist and between his legs then put on a loose indigo-dyed gown and tied it over with a broad sash made of thickly spun silk. The clothes were comfortable and pleasant to touch, almost luxurious. The fine cloth felt cool against his skin.

He sat down, leaning against the wall, and opened the satchel. All the contents were there. The spyglass lay untouched in its selkie skin case, beside the small notepad and the precious Keswick pencil. The tip of his lucky *tafl* wizard was broken off, but the dragon figurine had survived unscathed, as had the black box. He held the spyglass in his hand, remembering poor Doctor Samuel, his sallow gentle face and wise dark brown eyes. Did he have a family of his own? Bran had never heard him mention anything about it; all he knew was that the Doctor's ancestors had arrived in Dracaland at the end of the Wizardry Wars. And now he was buried at sea, along with so many others.

Bran reached for the sword, and the warmth of its wyvern-hide grip reassured him. He shook off despair and suppressed the tears welling up in his eyes. There would be a better time to mourn. For now, he had to gather his racing thoughts and assess the situation.

He was alive and healthy, but alone in a strange, possibly hostile place, maybe even imprisoned. He was now certain the Seal had brought him back to the land of Qin. The locals looked like Qin, ate rice like them and drank a hot brew with their meals, although slightly different in taste to what he had become used to in Fan Yu.

He could still feel a faint delicate link to Emrys, which meant that his dragon was also still alive, somewhere. He remembered the beast desperately flying away into the starry night sky. This thought relaxed him. Things weren't as bleak as they might have been, all things considered. The house he was in was probably somewhere near the coast... His father would be searching for him, others too, and the local authorities were no doubt already alarmed to the presence of a Western boy. It was surely only a matter of days before he'd be rescued.

The moment he stood up supporting himself on the sword, the door slid open once more. The woman aided him back to the bed. He could smell the faint scent of flowers on her hair and clothes as she laid him back onto the floor. She brought incense, a cone of pressed powder sitting on a pile of ash in a clay bowl. The room quickly filled with the aroma of plum blossom.

The woman offered him some more rice with an encouraging smile, but he declined as politely as he could, already feeling full and warm. He found the blanket snug and cosy, and suddenly felt very tired again. He laid his head on the thin mattress.

The Seal's magic must have drained my energy, was his last conscious thought as a quiet dreamless sleep enveloped him.

The girls came at noon, their faces beaming with excitement. Ine led them hurriedly to a room at the back where she was certain nobody could hear them.

"Perhaps you wish to explain what exactly were you planning to do with this... *stray*," she asked Nagomi.

"We couldn't have just let him drown in the tide, could we?"

"When he's alright, we'll just send word to Dejima," said Satō.

"*When he's alright?* How long do you think I can keep him here?"

"I don't think he comes from Dejima... He fell from Heavens, not from a ship," said Nagomi.

"Fell from Heavens?" Ine raised an eyebrow.

"He was cast down to the beach on a beam of white light," Nagomi said.

"Some kind of Western magic," Satō added. "Father already used his contacts to ask around. There were no boys of his age on Dejima this year. And he doesn't look like one of the Red Hairs."

"Whoever he is, the Bataavians need to take him away," said Ine.

"Won't they report him to the authorities, though? You know how concerned they are with observing our laws," said Nagomi, worried.

"Not if my father asks them not to," replied Satō, "they owe him too many favours."

"Good," Ine said with a nod, "he's awake now, so he can be moved somewhere more suitable. This is a respectable infirmary, not a smugglers' den."

"*Eeh*! He's *awake*? Why didn't you tell us sooner?"

Nagomi and Satō started down the corridor to the infirmary room, but Ine stopped them with a single sharp word. She had learned this assertiveness the hard way, running the infirmary single-handedly whenever Keisuke was away. The patients rarely believed a woman could, or indeed should, know enough to be a scholar of medicine. They often objected to the treatments they deemed too bizarre or expensive, but Ine did not care for their protests. Once inside her infirmary, regardless of class or wealth, they were hers to command. Illness made everyone equal, this much she had learned from her father. For the treatment to be effective, all her patients had to be obedient, peasant and samurai alike.

"He needs rest. He's still disoriented and weak."

"Is he saying anything?" Satō asked, her fingers tapping on the hilt of her sword.

"No, he's mostly asleep. Whatever happened to him must have been exhausting. He did eat some rice, though. You can come in, but be quiet."

Ine slid the door a bit to see if the stranger was still sleeping. He was sitting cross-legged on the floor, examining the many straps of his new clothes. She had explained to him before, in mime, how to put on the paper-lined *kosode* robe and tie it with a broad sash. Ine nodded to the girls, and stepped into the room.

The door slid open and a girl and a boy entered, along with the woman who took care of him. He faintly remembered seeing the girl when he awoke for the very first time, but the boy was a new guest. His haircut was odd, neatly and close cut all over except a ponytail at the back. His face was smoothly shaven, soft and handsome. The girl's shiny copper hair was tied in a long braid falling down her back, almost reaching her waist. They were both rather short and Bran found it difficult to tell what age they were, although the girl seemed younger.

The pair sat down under the wall, staring at him curiously. Bran gazed back at them, especially the fiery-haired girl. He had no idea the Qin could have hair like this, glinting almost like dragonflame in the light of the sun seeping through the paper-covered window. Her locks were redder even than Eithne's, almost orange, like fox hide. He remembered a student at Llambed with similar hair, a wizard named Willem, from Bataave.

The girl wore a billowing, pleated vermillion skirt and jacket of thick white cloth, pure and immaculate like freshly fallen snow, as was everything Bran had seen in this place so far. She was quite pretty, he assessed, in an innocent childish way. Why were these two youngsters here at all?

The elder woman sat down in front of him and looked intently in his eyes.

Biting her lower lip, Ine managed to recall the first words of Bataavian she had ever learned.

"*Spreekt u Bataafs?*"

The foreigner thought for a moment then shook his head.

"Seaxe? *Latina?* Brezhoneg," he replied instead. "Umm... *Ne Hao?*"

"No, not Qin," she replied, but the boy didn't understand her.

As almost anyone of importance in Kiyō, Ine knew some Bataavian, but she was only vaguely aware of other Western nations, much less of how they spoke. They had to revert to more primitive means of communication. She pointed at herself.

"I-ne. Ine."

"Ine," repeated the boy. "Bran," he added.

She struggled.

"Bu-ran?"

He smiled and nodded.

"What is *Bu-ran*? Is that his name, nationality or profession?" Satō asked from the back.

"His name, I think," Ine answered. "Be quiet. I need to teach him a few basic words, we can't communicate with signs all the time. Luckily it seems he's got his wits about him."

"*Go-han. Gohan,*" she said, continuing the lesson, pointing to the bowl of rice.

He nodded, uncertain.

"*Ha-shi. Hashi,*" Ine said, picking up the bamboo chopsticks, still clean and unused.

"He's not a Bataavian." Nagomi whispered.

"I know!" replied Satō. "Isn't this exciting?"

"Where could he be from?"

"Well, he's definitely not from Dejima. They wouldn't let in anyone who doesn't speak their language. He's looking at you again. Maybe he fancies you," said Satō and giggled.

Ine noticed the boy's gaze and turned around to see Nagomi look away in embarrassment, her cheeks flushing red. Her little sister wasn't used to men paying attention to her. Of the two sisters, Ine was always the pretty one. She had the same black braids, dark eyes and flat nose as any other girl in Kiyō. She did have a hint of something eccentrically exotic in her features, but it made her seem only more attractive to the Yamato men. In contrast, they looked at Nagomi with barely hidden disgust. This was unfair; both girls knew there was little difference in looks between them other than the colour of their hair.

But there was no repulsion in this boy's eyes.

Of course, Ine reminded herself, *in the West people's hair and eye colours varied.*

They could have hair of copper, bronze or gold, their eyes could be brown, green, grey or blue. He did not see anything out of the ordinary in Nagomi's auburn tresses.

Satō interrupted her thoughts.

"What's he saying now?"

The boy raised his hand as if to ask about something important.

"Qin?" he asked again, making a wide gesture.

Ine sighed and shook her head. She spoke slowly and precisely.

"*Dat is niet* Qin. Ya-ma-to."

"Yama…"

The boy collapsed, his head hitting the pillow with a thud.

"Yamato…" he repeated.

Ine was disturbed by his sudden weakness. Obviously this was not the answer he had expected. She wiped his forehead with a damp cloth.

"What is it?" Nagomi asked, "what's wrong?"

"Our conversation must have tired him," Ine replied, "it's best we leave. Satō, please open that window before you go. He needs fresh air. This attic gets stuffy in the evenings."

CHAPTER XIV

Yamato, April, 2607 ab urbe condita

"Dat is niet Qin."

He didn't know Bataavian, but this sentence was easy to understand. His head started spinning again, and he had to lie back on the floor.

This is not Qin.

This was Yamato; a strange uncharted country, the land of his grandfather's mysterious adventure, the land of the black box. There would be no Westerners here, except a few cunning Bataavian merchants. Nobody else knew how to get here. His father would not be coming to his rescue. He was all alone, far away from home and from anyone who could save him.

The woman and the two younglings left the room. Bran's thoughts raced. Why did the magic of the Seal bring him to this strange land? The last thing he remembered thinking about, on the deck of the disappearing *Ladon*, was his family and friends. Mother, father, the Academy... The spell must have brought him to the closest place that had some ties to his home in Gwynedd, or maybe one of the items in his satchel resonated with the Seal's magic?

Yamato...

The large wooden orb covered with blue paper, darkened black with age, was affixed to a brass stand at the poles. The golden stains of continents had turned grey, and very few symbols could still be deciphered.

Satō strained her eyes by the light of the oil lamp. Biting the tip of her tongue, she traced the lines of islands and continents with black ink on a sheet of rice paper. She could only hope the boy – *Bran*, she remembered – would understand what she had copied from the old Vasconian globe. She tried her best to replicate as many distinctive features as she could – the few meandering rivers, a couple of cities marked with clusters of houses – she could only name two of them, Rome and Noviomagus, and she wasn't very certain which was which. There were also animal symbols, the meaning of which she was not aware – a two-headed bear drawn on the northern wastes of Varyaga, a man with an elephant's head in what must have been Bharata, in the south, and three dragon heads on the westernmost tip of the great continent. She copied them all, just in case.

There was some noise outside in the corridor, and loud voices. Satō hid the paper in her kimono and slid the door panel just enough to peek out.

Two magistrate officials stood before her father, angry and suspicious.

"You know the rules, Takashima-*sama*," said one of them. "You have to let us do the search otherwise we'll have reasons to suspect you of harbouring fugitives."

Satō stifled a curse.

"Of course, I have nothing to hide," replied Shūhan, "but you must allow me to welcome you as befits your position. Won't you sit down for a couple of cups first? I just got a flask of saké from Fushimi."

"You can afford such treats?" The official eyed the old wizard suspiciously. "We may have to look into the conditions of your arrest."

"It's a gift from an old friend that I will gladly share with you. Please, have a seat in the main room. You must be tired; it's a long way here from the magistrate office."

"Well…" the official grumbled, "I don't see how it can hurt. You men," he turned to his guards, "stay here, keep a lookout."

Guiding the men to the main hall, Shūhan cast a glance towards Satō's room. Their eyes met. She nodded reassuringly, letting him know he had nothing to worry about. She knew the routine. While the officials drank their saké, she would quickly run around the house and hide anything that could be deemed strange, suspicious, or simply too extravagant, starting with the old Vasconian globe.

When he woke up, the woman called Ine was sitting beside his bedding, waiting. From the amount of light falling through the paper windows he guessed it was evening or dawn. It had become cold again, but he was now getting used to it.

She bowed and gestured him to rise, helping him to put on the indigo gown. When she had made sure he could stand straight, she went out of the room, nodding at him. Hesitantly, the boy followed. She was just like any Western doctor he knew: her commands simply had to be obeyed.

She led him down a narrow corridor, its floor lined with dark squeaking planks and walls built of the already familiar wood and paper lattice, down the stairs, creaking with every step, until they reached another small room smelling of soap, steam and cleanliness.

"*Oyuu*," she said, motioning him inside.

There was a square wooden tub in the corner of the room, small but deep, with steam rising from under the board cover, several low stools and a shallow bucket. Bran rejoiced. Although he had washed himself several times already with a wet towel and bowl of water, the sterility of the house made him shamefully aware of his own dishevelled state. He welcomed the chance of having a hot bath with great enthusiasm.

The boy looked at the woman, but she had no intention of leaving him alone. She indicated him to take off the gown. After a moment's hesitation, he did what was asked.

She's just a nurse, he told himself, *she must have seen naked men before*. She *had* seen him naked, he remembered, when she had put him to bed for the first time.

The nurse gestured him to sit on the stool.

"No bath?" he asked, jokingly, but the woman did not reply.

She disappeared from his sight for a moment, he heard the wooden cover pulled back, something splashed and, with no warning, a stream of hot water poured onto his back from a bucket. He yowled and jumped up from the stool, but her strong arm pushed him back down. For a moment a startling thought raced through his head: he was going to be tortured with boiling water! But then he felt a sponge rubbing lye soap into his back and shoulders with care, and he felt his tense muscles relax.

It was a pleasant feeling, not unlike being washed by his mother when he had been a child. Just as he started to unwind and drift off, another bucket of scalding water woke him up violently. The nurse started massaging his scalp, rubbing a lather smelling of raw egg and ash into his hair. Another splash of hot water made him shudder. He forgot all about the cold evening breeze - his skin was now turning a healthy shade of pink.

His head and back clean, the woman laid the sponge and soap container before him on the stones. He scrubbed the rest of his body then poured water from the bucket over his head. It felt great to finally wash. Unlike some of their neighbours, the Prydain prided themselves on their cleanliness. Were it not the Prydain who had invented soap? On *Ladon* there was always a dearth of clean fresh water. He lived in fear of getting lice in his hair or fleas on his body, like most sailors. Luckily, as the son of an officer, he had priority access to the scarce bathing water. The Factory in Fan Yu was run primarily by the Seaxe who did not pay much attention to matters of hygiene, so he had to make do with bathing in the Pearl River. He was glad to find the Yamato appeared as concerned with the purity of their bodies as his own people.

As his ablutions finished, she removed the cover from the tub completely and helped him climb inside. The water was pleasantly hot and crystal clear.

How clever to wash oneself before coming in, he thought.

Soaking himself in silence, Bran saw the woman's perpetual smile disappear as she drifted off into her thoughts. He wondered what she was thinking. He needed to know more about his situation. That he was not yet dead was good news, but what was his status here? A prisoner of war? The house did not seem like a military establishment and there were youths here, but he knew nothing of the strange customs of these people. Perhaps they were trained to watch the prisoners die, or perhaps he was simply kept here until he was well enough to stand before a court...

There had to be a way to communicate. He knew of only one place in Yamato. It was a long shot, but worth a try.

"De... Dejima?" he ventured.

The woman blinked and nodded enthusiastically. She motioned him to get up. After he had dried and clothed himself, she led him up the stairs to the top floor and up a rickety ladder-like steep staircase to the roof. She opened a hatch leading outside and a waft of fresh cold air almost made him fall over. He looked out and saw a sprawling city of wooden, clay-tiled, white-walled homes. The house he was in had to be on the slope of a hill, for he could see far ahead. The city was vast, neatly organised, spreading in straight lines of streets along a narrow river towards a thin blue line of the sea on the horizon. The bay was attractive, wide, surrounded by tall green hills, sheltered from winds and storms, a perfect harbour. Just like in his grandfather's diary.

She climbed after him and they sat together on the tiled roof, looking at the city and the harbour below. The setting sun was shining straight at them, and the air was surprisingly warm for the time of day – warmer than inside the house. The woman stretched out her hand, pointing at some area of the shoreline, and said:

"*Dejima!*"

Bran squinted, wishing he remembered to bring the spyglass from his bag, and saw two islands in the middle of the bay, one square, one fan-shaped, connected by a single bridge to the rest of the land. An unmistakably spiralling tower of wizardry rose above the fan-shaped one, topped with a minuscule dot of an orange flag fluttering in the breeze. So he had guessed correctly. Of all the places in Yamato the Seal brought him almost directly to the only one he knew about. Looking to the horizon it was easy to imagine a ship of the line standing at anchor, its cannons aimed menacingly at the wooden buildings of the city. The vessels he could make out in the harbour were all, as far as he could tell, small and insignificant compared to a full size Western frigate. The arrival of HMS *Phaeton* must have been a shock to these people.

The island was closer than he had hoped, and so were the Bataavians. He only needed to reach them and explain his situation.

They heard shouting from below, and the woman gestured him to come down. When they reached Bran's room, the red-haired girl and her friend were already waiting for them, impatient and anxious.

"Sister, what are you doing?" Nagomi asked with a raised voice. "Somebody could see him! *We* saw him! Do you forget what would happen if he was reported to the authorities?"

"Quieten down, Nagomi." Ine raised her hand. "Your yelling will raise more alarm than us sitting on the roof. From a distance, nobody can tell him from a Yamato boy when he's wearing these clothes."

"What were you doing there, anyway?" asked Satō. "Is he all right to go outside like that?"

"He's perfectly fine now. He mentioned Dejima, so I wanted to show it to him. Now at least he knows where he is."

"He knows of Dejima? So maybe he is from there after all." Satō sulked.

Ine noticed a rolled-up piece of paper the wizardess held in her left hand.

"What do you have there?"

"I drew the map of the West from my father's globe. We want to see where Bran-*sama* is from."

"All right, you can come in, just don't be noisy. He still needs to rest."

"Of course we won't be *noisy*, we're not kids, sister." Nagomi pouted. "Can we give him some rice balls?"

Satō pulled out a bamboo box.

"He's a boy, not a monkey! Besides, I'm not sure if he'll like them. You know how Westerners are about our food. You'd do better to fetch something from the Qin quarter next time, or one of the bakers at the harbour."

"Nagomi," the apprentice introduced herself. "Satō," she said, pointing at her friend.

"Saato," he repeated.

She corrected his accent. He repeated again and she nodded approvingly.

They presented him with a small box made of dark red lacquer. Inside were three balls of sticky rice wrapped in dried seaweed. The boy gobbled them up, nodded and smiled. They smiled back.

Satō unrolled her map. The boy's eyes lit up with recognition. He studied the drawing for a while, his brow furrowed in deep thought, before pointing to an amorphous blob near where she had tried her best to duplicate the three dragon heads. Satō's eyes widened.

"*Dorako?*" she asked to make sure.

"Draigg, *hai*," the boy answered, pointing at himself.

Satō's sat back for a moment, not saying anything, her heart racing. Then, on an impulse, she reached into her sash, producing another bundle of crumbled papers - her notes from the Dragon Book.

The boy looked through them, perplexed. Suddenly he cried something out and started speaking fast, waving the pieces of paper. Satō looked at him not understanding anything he said. He pointed to the paper at the runes and then to himself.

"*Dragon Rider*," he read the letters aloud and stretched out his arms imitating a dragon in flight.

"*Doragon Raidaa…*" the wizardess repeated. It sounded just like the Bataavian word "*rijder*".

"What does it mean?" asked Nagomi, silent until now.

"I… I think he means he rides dragons, like in the book. That would certainly explain the sword."

"But he's so young!"

"Maybe he's only training to… wait, he's saying something else."

The boy raised his finger. The girls fell silent in anticipation. He reached for his satchel and unbuckled it. Satō watched him take out a small lacquer figurine of a serpentine dragon. There followed a black lacquer box with a crest of four diamonds on the top. The boy opened it and took out a small flat medallion, a golden buckle on a silk ribbon and a golden ring with a strangely cut jagged stone, blue and translucent. Once out of the box, the jewel suddenly sparked with bluish light within, surprising even the boy, who almost dropped it.

"What are all these things?" Nagomi asked quietly.

"I don't know... That one's definitely a *ryū*," Satō said, giving the figurine a cursory glance, "something you would buy at a souvenir stall in the harbour... The box is from Yamato, too – I wonder what family's crest this is. And this – this is an *obi* buckle, isn't it?"

She traced the scaled coils of the golden dragon with her finger.

"I think so. I've never seen one that elaborate before."

"A very rich lady must have worn it once... That ring looks Western, I'm sure. My father might know more. What's this?"

The wizardess picked up the medallion. As she touched its dark surface it glowed, showing a picture of a noblewoman in a red kimono, more vivid and truthful than any painting. A thaumaturgic True Image! She knew about these things – a piece of imbued glass transformed to hold the image forever – but had never held one. A string of characters showed along the side of the image.

Nagomi let out a gasp. "She's beautiful!"

"My love, Ōmon. Bunka year five," deciphered Satō. "Hold on, I know that date. That's the year of the foreign ship incident."

"What does all this mean?" Nagomi asked. "He is from Dejima after all, or a spy?"

"If he is a spy, he would at least know Bataavian. There is something more going on here..."

Nagomi noticed the boy's uncomprehending expression. She turned to him, pointing to the figurine.

"Um... Bataave?" she asked.

He nodded. She then picked up the medallion.

"You wouldn't remember the name of that ship from years ago?" she asked Satō.

"Of course I do, it's my father's favourite story. It was *Feeton*."

"*Feeton?*" Nagomi repeated.

The boy thought for a moment then confirmed her guess enthusiastically and spoke a few more words in his strange language.

"What about the ring?" Satō asked, touching the glowing gem.

The boy understood the question, but they could not understand his answer.

"*Phaeton,*" he repeated at last, shrugging.

The door opened. Ine looked sternly at the girls.

"Are you still interrogating my patient? You're worse than the magistrate officers!" she scolded them. "He's still tired. Leave him be."

"Of course, sister."

Nagomi stood up, bowed and bid the boy farewell. He tried to repeat her gesture and words – a clumsy effort, but it made her smile.

"We need to find a way to communicate with him," said Satō. They were walking the cherry tree lined street back to Takashima mansion. "We have to know what all those items in his bag mean."

"Isn't there anyone in Kiyō who would understand his speech? What about Bataavians?"

"There aren't that many of them on Dejima at the moment. All the merchant ships have gone for the winter and won't be back for at least a month. I asked Father, but he said it would be very difficult. You know the Bataavians can't just go around visiting random houses as they wish. The gates to the island are shut when there's no trade. There will be papers to fill out, questions to answer... and the magistrate is already snooping around our house."

"But we do have to do something about him. I can tell Ine is growing inpatient." They reached a crossroads. "I need to go to the shrine now. See you tomorrow."

Nagomi turned towards the shrine mountain. Satō headed home along the wide empty street then she started to run. She stretched out her arms and roared. Tonight, she was a dragon rider.

CHAPTER XV

Yamato, April, 2607 ab urbe condita

He sat leaning against the wall of the infirmary room, eyes closed, meditating. On his left hand he was wearing his ring; the stone radiated a warm blue light. It had been glowing like this ever since Bran had taken it out of the black box. He wondered what unseen currents of magic it was picking up on. He was trying to clear his mind, to establish contact with his dragon, to learn where it was and what had been happening to it. It wasn't an easy task.

Questions raced through his head. The notes he had been shown were from a book he knew all too well – the Llambed *Dracology* textbook, first year. Where did they get it, halfway across the globe? That map was badly copied, but definitely from an accurate enough source. From the little he had known about them, he had imagined the Yamato as a backward people, secretive, hiding away, cut off from any civilisation beyond their sea maze. It seemed they were anything but...

The jewel heated up and Bran's mind was transported away from the small room. He was inside the dragon's head now. The beast was very tired and hungry. Bran could feel the dragon's exhaustion overwhelm his own body. Emrys was resting, lying on some rocks, dormant after a great effort. It could not gather its bearings, having flown over nothing but empty featureless ocean. It was unhurt, as far as Bran could tell, just weak, confused and weary, too weary to respond to the Farlink beacon. Slowly the vision faded as the blue gem cooled down.

Bran was troubled. They had never been so far apart. What if they were separated for so long that the dragon turned feral? He could not bear the thought. He had to leave the strange house and try to get to Dejima on his own. From the roof it did not seem far at all. Days had passed and he still wasn't contacted by anyone of authority, only those two kids and the nurse woman. There had to be someone else who could help him.

He woke up screaming.

His body was covered in cold sweat. The traces of the nightmare were vanishing fast from his mind, but the feeling of terror still lingered. The cries of the *Ladon*'s crewmen, dying in the burning ocean, ringed in his ears. He shook his head and took a couple of deep breaths.

He waited for a while to see if anyone would come to check on him but the house was sound asleep. He stood up and snapped his fingers. A flamespark appeared in the air. The familiar flickering light comforted him.

He grabbed his bag and the sword and reached for the door. It was unlocked - in fact, he couldn't find any lock on it at all. It slid open noiselessly. Encouraged, he walked down the narrow musty corridor. The floorboards creaked with his every step. It was hard to be stealthy in this old wooden house.

He reached the small vestibule before the front door. The wooden floor descended in two steps onto a stone pavement. There was an umbrella stand here and many shoes of various types, mostly sandals and straw slippers, all quite small. Bran hesitated for a moment. There was no guard, nobody rushed to stop him from going outside. It felt like he was betraying someone's trust by running away.

The stones radiated coldness. He looked down at his bare feet. They seemed big compared with the tiny sandals on the floor. He stepped down and gasped. The pavement was slick and icy. Dew froze on it after sunset. He dared make one more step then another, and reached the door, a dense weave of reed on a wooden frame. He found a shallow indentation in the frame where a doorknob would normally be, and slid the door wide open. A tiny bell hanging from the beam tinkled in the wind, startling the boy for a moment. Still nobody came. He stepped outside underneath a rectangle of cloth hanging across the doorway and found himself on the street under the broad eaves of the house.

The city was utterly quiet. A single cat meowed in the distance and then he could hear no other noise except the wind blowing under the eaves and a faint rush of the sea somewhere far away. The narrow street, running steeply downhill, smelled of wet wood and stone, and rainwater. None of the usual city smells were present, none of the sounds. It felt as if the town had been deserted for a long time.

Bran walked down the hill for a bit. The main street mingled into a myriad crossroads below, all lined with the same rows of low, dainty wooden houses, one barely distinguishable from another in the moonlight, walls washed white or covered with vertical wooden slats. The air was fresh and crisp. Bran shivered and the cold sobered him. He was alone in an unfamiliar city, trying to get to a place of which he was barely aware. The streets and houses seemed identical, featureless in the darkness. If he became lost he would wander around the same district for hours. For all he knew, he may have been safer inside than out. Perhaps the only friendly people in the city were in the house he had just left. He had already learned that the people of the Orient did not necessarily take kindly to users of Power. What if the Yamato were as hostile as the people of Fan Yu?

He climbed back up, but did not enter the house. He let the tranquillity of the night soothe him. He extinguished the flamespark and was instantly wrapped in complete darkness. The moon hid behind a thick cloud and the city was now just sounds and smells. He listened to the calming distant rush of the waves, to the whistling of the wind dancing over the roof tiles. He breathed in the gentle aroma of fresh moist wood and cold slate. Deep within he could faintly feel Emrys. The dragon was bewildered, confused, alone. Bran tried to placate it through the Farlink, but it was futile.

He heard a shuffle. Somewhere near, somebody or something was trying to sneak past him. Bran slid out his sword from the sheath as quietly as he could and crept in the direction of the sound. Barefooted, he made as little noise as a cat. As a faint ray of moonlight pierced the clouds he saw a shadow, a silhouette against the wooden wall. Bran leapt, lighting the flamespark again with a blinding flash, his sword pointing towards the shadow. He saw a little boy huddling, pinned against the wall. The boy was covering his eyes from the flash, looking for a getaway. Bran instinctively raised his sword threateningly and grabbed the boy by the coat.

The boy twisted his fingers into a rune and cried out:

"*Bevries!*"

The freezing spell fizzled out without effect, but Bran was thrown off guard by what he recognised, without a shade of doubt, as Western magic. The boy slipped out of his grasp, leaving only the outer coat in Bran's hand, and disappeared into the darkness.

The commotion finally awakened the household. A servant ran out with a lit lantern and was now staring at Bran with a puzzled expression. Ine appeared a moment later, hastily tying up her kimono. She grunted something to the servant and took his lantern away. She looked carefully around and motioned Bran to come back inside.

She took the captured piece of clothing from him and frowned at the large round crest on the back then she looked outside once again and closed the door shut. This time she put a heavy crossbar against it from the inside. She followed Bran as he went back up to his room then showed him how to lock his door too. It wasn't much of a fortress - the walls of the infirmary looked as if they could easily be kicked through - but the house was filled with a sense of insecurity, as if some pact with the outside world had just been broken.

The wizardess burst into her father's study, beaming.

"Father! Guess what?"

Shūhan lifted tired eyes from a piece of paper he held in his hand.

"What is it, dear?"

"The *Gaikokujin* – he's a *dorako* rider!"

"He started speaking then?"

"No. Well, sort of. We don't know what language he speaks, but I showed him the map and he – " She paused, not wishing to admit to her knowledge about the Dragon Book. "He's from Dracaland, and showed us the rest in mime... What's wrong?"

"Nothing, dear, that's... interesting."

Shūhan pretended to smile, but Satō could tell he was scowling underneath.

"You are worried."

The wizard sighed deeply.

"There have been too many of these 'accidental visits' lately. First the Varyaga castaways then that foreigner who looked like one of us –" he hung his voice trying to remember the name.

"Black Raven," she said. She was too young to have met the mysterious stranger before his sudden disappearance, but the story of how he had been brought to Kiyō from the far north and kept in a cage for the amusement of the Magistrate, like a monkey, was as famous as it was shameful.

"That's right. I wonder what happened to him. And now this... It's as Curzius-*sama* said – the Westerners are encroaching on Yamato on all sides. Soon they will find a way across the Divine Winds, like they broke the Qin Barrier..."

"Father, I don't understand... Why are you concerned about this? Isn't opening Yamato what we've always wanted? Isn't it good that Dejima's monopoly is broken, and other Westerners are forcing their way in, at last? You've always said we're only being fed scraps from the Bataavian table..."

Shūhan scratched his neck, as he always did when he was uncertain of something.

"It is always better to control than to be controlled. Yes, I would love nothing more than if the *Taikun* relaxed his anti-foreign laws and established more trading posts, but I wouldn't want him to do it at sword-point. It's what the Dracalish have done in Qin, and we have heard of nothing but calamities and disaster since."

"Bran-*sama* is not like them. Besides, he's just a boy..."

"He's a soldier. You told me he carries a sword, and now we learn he rides dragons. Who knows where he's coming from? Perhaps there's a Dracalish fleet waiting for a message from him beyond the horizon..."

"He would make a rubbish spy – he doesn't even know Bataavian!" protested Satō.

Shūhan chuckled and nodded.

"Maybe you're right. I'm being too mistrustful. Sometimes I forget the outside world is not full of spies and traitors, like Yamato. It's because of this letter here," he waved the piece of paper in his hand, "it's a message from Curzius-*sama*, from Edo."

"Bad news?" asked Satō.

She was acutely aware of the distrust with which her father treated the conservative officials at the Edo court. The feeling was mutual.

"The government is fractured. The courtiers are quarrelling and bickering with each other. The *Taikun* barely had time to see him between one meeting and another. It's as if a stone's been thrown into the hornets' nest. They can all sense the oncoming storm, and there are always people who want to profit from chaos."

"Do you think there will be a war?" Satō asked with a grave face.

There had been peace in Yamato for over two hundred years. The threat of war seemed as distant and mythical as the tales of Gods, demons and dragons, but it had always loomed somewhere on the horizon, like a storm brewing slowly in the distance or a quietly rumbling volcano.

"War?" Shūhan looked at her with surprise. "No, I don't think so. There would have to be armies for there to be a war, and only the *Taikun* has an army. No, a war is out of the question, but a coup would not surprise me... One minister is replaced by another, one daimyo is exalted while the other is humbled, that sort of thing."

Stricken by a sudden thought, the old wizard stood up, put his hand on Satō's shoulder and looked into her eyes with concern. It frightened her.

"The courtly intrigues, the rumours of war, the treaties and spies," he said, "in the long run, all this is not important. What matters most in life are good health and a happy family. Do you understand this?"

"I do," she replied, nodding obediently.

"Remember this, then: should anything happen to me because of all we've talked about today – you *must* keep yourself safe."

"Father, I'm sure – "

"No, listen." He raised his hand to silence her protests. "We have friends who will not abandon us. Our family is well known, our name will always open certain doors even in times of trouble. If you ever have to look for help, go south, always south - Kumamoto, Kagoshima... The farther you are from Edo, the safer. If I could, I would take you away from Yamato altogether."

It's my fault Father is worried. I brought the danger to our house.

"South, I understand," she said, trying to sound as reassuring as possible.

Shūhan's face wrinkled with a relieved smile.

"Forgive an old man's talk," he said dismissively. "I'm sure this will all blow over in a few months and everything will be back to normal. It is normal, as far as we're concerned. We mustn't let some distant gossip change our way of life. We still have students to train, a household to run. Nothing changes."

"Yes, Father."

"Now, if you could boil some water for me, dear. I need to go back to my experiments, and let's forget all about this conversation for now."

"Yes, Father."

She met Nagomi in front of the Itō house.

"Did Ine send for you too?" the red-haired apprentice asked. She was out of breath, having run all the way from Tamazono Mountain.

"Yes, she said it's urgent. I hope Bran-*sama* is fine..."

Nagomi's older sister awaited them in their father's office. The longest wall was lined with rows of small wooden drawers filled with Qin herbs and Bataavian medicinal ingredients. The room smelled sweetly of crushed spices and molasses, as Ine was in the middle of preparing some mixture in a large mortar. She put away the pestle when the girls entered.

"Good, you're both here. Sit down. Things have taken a rather nasty turn." She opened a drawer and took out the cloak. "Do either of you recognise this crest?"

Satō drew a sharp breath when she saw three horizontal stripes, the symbol of the Sakuma clan.

"It's Keinosuke's, one of my students," she explained, "where did you find it?"

"Bran-*sama* caught him spying around the house at night."

"What was he doing outside?"

"He walked out," Ine said dismissively. "I told you before, this house is a hospital not a prison. I cannot close the door for the night; everyone in the neighbourhood knows they can visit me at any hour if there is an emergency. What worries me most," she pointed at the cloak, "the boy saw the *Gaikokujin* and ran away. If I know little boys, half the town will know of our secret by dinner."

"You don't know this boy." Satō grimaced. "He's... peculiar. I would expect him to bargain something from us for the knowledge."

"The Book?" Nagomi guessed.

Satō nodded.

"He's been more and more persistent about it lately. I'm sure your house was not the only one he's been spying around."

"There is one more thing," Ine added, "not that it makes the situation much worse, but I believe the boy is a wizard."

"*What?*"

"I saw him use magic - in the middle of the street, no less."

"We had no idea…"

"This place is not safe anymore," said Ine authoritatively. "I've brought the boy back to health because it was my duty as a physician, but now he must leave."

"I understand," said Satō, "he will be gone before nightfall."

The two girls descended to the small square garden at the back of the house, separated from the street by a high clay wall. The bamboo rocker was silenced in the rainless weather. Cherry blossom petals floated on top of the stone basin, naked cherry tree branches reflected in the water. The short blooming season was almost over, so now green leaves were sprouting from the black twigs and spring proper would start. A single hydrangea bush in the corner was also turning green.

They sat on the edge of the veranda. Nagomi dangled her short legs over the edge, not quite reaching the ground. Satō started contemplating the day's news. A wizard – of course! It made sense. Dragons were no ordinary creatures, and to ride one would require extraordinary skills.

At least now it's definite he was brought by magic, not by divine intervention, she thought with surprising satisfaction.

The fact that the boy was a wizard changed everything. Even if Satō might have considered giving him away to the authorities this was out of the question now. Nobody would believe Shūhan had nothing to do with the sudden appearance of a fellow magic user. It was now even more imperative to keep Bran-*sama's* presence a secret. They were making a very shoddy job of it. Keinosuke she might hope to deal with – he was just a kid, after all, nobody would believe his word against hers and that of the entire Itō household, but if anyone else caught wind of the foreigner… She had found and saved the boy, so it was up to her to make the decision.

"What should I do? I can't bring him to our house," Satō said, moping. She did not wish to involve her father any more. "And without the Overwizard present, nobody at Dejima wants to take any responsibility for the castaway."

"We might transport Bran-*sama* to the Shrine," replied Nagomi.

Satō looked up at her.

"Kazuko-*hime* mentioned she'd like to see him."

What part of "keeping a secret" does she fail to understand? thought the wizardess angrily, but then calmed down. With Nagomi's parents constantly away, Lady Kazuko had become a surrogate parent to the girl. If Satō told her father about the boy, there was no reason for the apprentice to not discuss it with the High Priestess. Still, the speed at which the news was spreading throughout the city was worrying.

"I suppose it's the best idea we have," Satō said at last. "It's not far from here, and he could go all the way in a palanquin… but how safe would he be in the shrine?"

"Safer than anywhere else," Nagomi reassured her. "We'd put him in the private quarters, where even the Magistrate's men can't reach without a permit. The Suwa Shrine is under *Taikun's* direct protection."

"Good. I will yet consult my father, but I'm sure he will accept this plan," decided Satō.

Maybe the Gods of Suwa will help us where men can't, she thought.

These were the greatest trees he had ever seen. Ancient and primeval, they rose into the clouds like mountains of timber, their trunks straight, broad as houses, their roots interconnected into an imperceptibly vast network of gnarled, moss-covered limbs. The forest was shrouded in a thick mist, filled with sounds of the jungle – screeching of monkeys, whistling of birds, deafening buzz of cicadas.

He was starving and worn out, growing drowsy and irritated with hunger. He hadn't eaten for days, flying from one rocky outcrop to another over a vast featureless ocean. At last he had reached this island covered with dense vegetation. He found water, roaring waterfalls and calm mountain springs, but where was food? It'd been so long since he last ate… The fires in his belly were nearly extinguished.

Something stirred in the undergrowth. A scared tiny deer, no bigger than a dog, jumped out of the ferns. With a snap of powerful jaws he swallowed it in one gulp. Sustenance at last. But he needed more if he wanted to fly any further. Much more.

There was a knock on the door and Bran snapped out of his meditation. The jewel on his finger darkened, the Farlink vanished.

"Yes?" he said, before remembering where he was. "*Hai?*" he repeated in the language of the locals.

The door slid open and a familiar face appeared in the gap – the boy in the black and orange clothes. Bran bowed and greeted him in his own tongue.

The boy said something and gestured him to follow outside. Bran struggled for a moment with the straps of his clothes, and started to move towards the door, but his guide pointed to the bundle of his meagre belongings under the wall. Apparently they were going outside.

"Another lesson in geography?" he joked, though the boy would not understand, "or maybe history?"

He strapped on the sword belt, put on a blue short-sleeved cotton jacket, slung the satchel over his shoulder and the two walked out along the dark corridor, down the steps, through what Bran recognised as the kitchen, to a back exit. It led onto a small paved courtyard hidden away from the street, with a narrow gateway leading outside. Straw sandals, a few sizes too small, waited for him on the stone pedestal. In the middle of the courtyard stood a kind of a litter, or a covered sedan chair, a black and red ornate box. A heavy cloth embroidered with a clover-like insignia covered its entrance, the same crest that was moulded onto the roof tiles around the courtyard and painted on the cloth rectangles over the doors.

The Yamato boy looked nervously around before leading Bran into the litter. The dragon rider climbed in, bending his legs and back in a most uncomfortable position. The cloth cover fell down and he became enveloped in stuffy darkness, his legs cramped in the tight space. For a fleeting moment the curtain parted and the boy looked inside. He covered his mouth, then disappeared and it was blackness again.

The litter rocked, heaved and rose up into the air. Bran found a horizontal slit in the curtain through which he could peep outside. He saw the bare back of one of the porters. It was the first time he had been in a vehicle not powered by magic, mechanics or animal muscles, but by a human being. The box hobbled out through the gate, out onto the cobbled streets of the city. He could see it for the first time in daylight, up close. He hoped they were taking him to Dejima at last, but he could not tell – by day, all the streets looked the same as well.

The litter was – deliberately, he guessed – carried along the less attended alleyways at the backs of long wooden townhouses, shops and inns. There were mostly porters here, unloading their wares, store workers in blue jackets with large white Qin characters on their backs, merchants counting their stock, servants cleaning up the cobblestones and sweeping pavements. Some wore straw sandals or wooden clogs, but most walked around barefoot. The servants wore only loincloths, and scarves wrapped around their heads. It was a warm day and they did not seem at all uncomfortable.

Bran quickly learned to recognise which of the people on the street were of a lower rank; they stood with their heads bowed down, or even prostrated themselves on the ground when the palanquin passed them by. Others paid no attention to him. There were nobles and commoners in his homeland, of course, and the divisions were stronger east of the Dyke, but even the Seaxe peasants were not obliged to kneel or fall face down in the dirt whenever a nobleman's carriage passed by.

There were no unpleasant odours, even in the back alleys. The streets were immaculately clean. Brigstow, he recalled, had stunk mostly of mistfire fumes and wyvern dung; Goa, the Vasconian outpost in Bharata, was filled with humid vapours from a nearby jungle and the salty odour of the open ocean. The aroma of Fan Yu was that of food, fried, dried, cooked in a myriad of ways, meat, fish and cabbage, mixed with the brackish smell of the waters of Pearl River, but Kiyō smelled only of the wood and stone of which it had been built.

Sometimes, when a servant woman poured cold water onto the pavement before her store, a waft of fresh moistness entered the palanquin. Other times they passed a cherry tree still in bloom, sweetly fragrant. The whole neighbourhood around a tea store, before which the porters paused for a short rest, was infused with the bitter scent of the brew, but these were only brief accidental occurrences, pleasantly accentuating the freshness and spotlessness of the city. There was a bluish tint of sea mist and dew about everything, and the air was humid, although not as unpleasantly as in Goa or Éko. Seen from the roof, Kiyō sprawled vastly in all directions, an area as large as any city Bran had seen so far. On the street level the houses were all small and inexpensively built. They were delicate, thin-walled, more garden gazebos or elaborate sheds than sturdy homes of stone or bales. This was a city built to a human scale, with convenience rather than boastfulness in mind. There were no excessive noises, no vehicles or mounts - everyone moved about on foot. People passed each other in polite silence, only the street vendors cried out advertising their colourful stands.

The palanquin stopped abruptly. Bran peeped through the slit carefully. They were on a broader street now, leading uphill. The aroma of alcohol and tobacco lingered faintly in the air. Two men were standing in the middle of the road shouting and pointing at each other, their faces fierce and flushed red. They were both wearing dark, sleeveless vest-like tunics with prominent shoulders, embroidered with circular crests, and the pleated skirts with which Bran was already familiar. They wore tight topknots on top of neatly combed heads. Each had two, long straight swords in plain black scabbards stuck into their sashes. The passers-by stopped, observing the scene from a safe distance.

In the blink of an eye, one of the men drew his sword and cut across the other's chest. Blood spurted in a wide crimson stream. The victim staggered back, trying yet to draw his own sword for a second then fell, thrashing briefly in death throes.

The first warrior grunted, satisfied with the result, put the sword back into the sheath and drunkenly swayed back into the establishment from which he had emerged. The crowd moved on, unperturbed. A pool of blood blossomed on the clean sand. Bran's palanquin carriers also lifted the vehicle and passed by the body as if nothing had happened.

Bran's fingers let go of the slit in the curtain and he stared into the darkness of the palanquin blankly. This was not just another drunken brawl – having spent time in harbours all over the world by now, Bran had seen what sailors and soldiers would get up to when they had consumed too much rum. *This was a murder* – no, an execution, swift, cold death...

The vehicle left the shadows of the backstreets and emerged onto a broad avenue lined with weeping cherries no longer in bloom. The crowds were thicker here. He spotted a few palanquins, but mostly men on foot, wearing the same style clothes as the two drunken brawlers, all carrying swords, sometimes with a second shorter one beside them. Women accompanied them in long flowery robes, bound with wide sashes. Some covered their heads under hoods, walking slowly and majestically behind the men, always silent; others showed off intricate hairstyles and gaudy make-up, and accompanied the men side by side, laughing and flirting. A multitude of children and babies, half-naked or naked, raced all over the thoroughfare undisturbed. Commoners mingled among the crowds wearing straw, mushroom-shaped hats, simple cotton coats and knee-length pantaloons.

The carriers paused and, encouraging themselves with a shout, heaved the litter higher above their shoulders. They started to climb a large set of stone stairs lined with lanterns and trees. Two great slim pillars of granite, connected with a double crossbeam slab, formed an entrance to this stairway. This was not the way to Dejima, Bran guessed – he remembered no hill between the infirmary and the sea.

After a long climb, the palanquin passed through a richly decorated gateway onto a lush garden courtyard surrounded by low wooden buildings, the roofs tiled grey, gables undulating softly like sea waves. The trees here were sprouting fresh green buds. The grass was the colour of rich spring. Bran's palanquin carriers moved deftly through the crowd of visitors, across a long and narrow pond, down a gravel path flanked by rose bushes, under another smaller gateway and onto another, empty courtyard. The litter stopped in front of a latticed doorway.

Bran heard the porters dismissed by a familiar voice - the red-haired girl. When they had gone she unveiled the palanquin and helped him alight. Quickly, not giving him time to stretch his cramped limbs, she gestured him to take the sandals off and led him, barefoot, inside the wooden building. He walked through the labyrinth of narrow corridors, squeaking wooden floors and sliding doors. Finally they reached a small square room. She pointed to the door at the far end of the corridor.

"*Oyuu.*"

He nodded, already more than familiar with the Yamato word for bath. The girl waved her hands around the room. This was where he was supposed to live from now on. He nodded again and she smiled.

He stepped inside and began to undo his sword belt. When he turned around, she had already gone.

The room had a window overlooking the gardens and other buildings of the complex. He gathered he was either in some palace or a temple, as the layout and architecture were somewhat similar to the temples he had seen at Fan Yu. Round wooden pillars supported the roofs covered with long tiles of bluish stone, the eaves were richly carved and gilded or painted with floral decorations. Perhaps at last he would speak to someone of authority.

He breathed in the fresh air with a still lingering aroma of cherry blossom, so delightful and easy on his lungs after an hour spent in the stuffy interior of the palanquin. A stream trickled across the meadow lined with white-blooming magnolias, and birds chirped in the trees. The sun was some three-quarters down on its way towards the western horizon.

Bran stretched, yawned and looked around his room. There was a small cupboard under one of the walls, with a clay pot and a cup. One of the walls slid away to reveal a wardrobe with a rolled-up mattress and bed linen. A narrow strip of paper hung on the opposite side, with a sublime painting of a kingfisher perched on a branch, in black ink. This was all the furniture in the room, yet somehow it seemed just right, as if adding anything, another table, another cupboard, another pillow, would break the invisible harmony. Bran realised the lack of furnishings was not a result of austerity, but a deliberate choice. Like the city below, this room was built with nothing but the convenience and inner peace of the guests in mind.

There was a knock on the door. He opened it and saw a girl he hadn't seen before, in the same white and vermillion outfit he had seen the red-head wearing.

"Dōzo."

She gestured towards the end of the corridor. He smiled and nodded, but she did not smile back. Her eyes were milky-white.

CHAPTER XVI

Yamato, Spring, 7ᵗʰ year of Kaei era

Tokojiro poured himself another cup of shōchū and gulped it down in one go. The warmth spread through his body. The liquor was poor, but cheap and strong, and this was all he needed.

He picked up a thin brush, held it over a stained piece of paper then put it back onto the table. His mind was empty, unfocused, as it had been every day for the last few weeks. His work on the Seaxe grammar progressed ever more slowly until it halted. He could see no point in struggling with it anymore.

Nobody in Kiyō needed a Seaxe interpreter. All the books and reports from abroad were written in or already translated into Bataavian. Study of other languages was forbidden. Tokojiro's work was nothing but an expensive and exhausting hobby. He could not hope to ever sell his book, not as long as Yamato's only contact with the outside world was through the narrow bridge to Dejima.

Why had he allowed himself to be convinced by that strange barbarian to study the wretched language instead of Qinese or Bataavian like everyone else? What good was his knowledge now?

He could curse at the owner of the inn in perfect Seaxe.

"*Damn you man, bring me more ale!*" he yelled. "Don't you understand? Of course you don't. Nobody does. The nearest people who would understand me live three thousand *ri* across the Great Sea. Black Raven, where have you gone, eh?"

He stood up and swayed. The innkeeper approached him cautiously.

"What do you want?" Tokojiro reached for his sword. "You want to throw me out?"

"Perhaps guest-*sama* would like to cool his head," the innkeeper replied, bowing and pointing to the open door.

"*Cur! Knave! Rascal!*"

Tokojiro spewed more Seaxe obscenities. He wasn't drunk enough not to see his presence at the inn was no longer welcome – not least because he had not paid yet for anything he had drunk since morning.

The interpreter headed outside, but in the doorway bumped into a young bald priest.

"Ah! A *shaved head!*" he exclaimed. "*I'm sorry.* Excuse me."

He tried to walk around the priest, but the youth stopped him and dragged him gently aside.

"You must be Tokojiro-*sama*," he whispered, "I was told I could find you here."

"You're looking for me?" the interpreter cried out, but the priest's hand on his mouth silenced him. "Looking for *me*?" he repeated, quietly. "I don't recall borrowing anything from the shaved heads. Well, maybe that one time…"

"Your talents and services are required at the Suwa Shrine. The High Priestess herself requests it."

"My services…?"

It took Tokojiro a while to realise what the priest meant.

"A Seaxe interpreter is needed urgently, although I suppose we can wait until you bathe yourself."

The priest sniffed in disgust.

"Why are we whispering?"

"The High Priestess counts on your loyalty and discretion. Remember how we helped you after Black Raven's disappearance?"

"You don't need to remind me." Tokojiro straightened himself, trying to recover some of his dignity. "I will come at once."

"The High Priestess awaits you in her quarters. Make sure you look… presentable."

Lady Kazuko's audience chamber was known as the "Crane Room" and it was easy to see why. Its walls were covered with white paper and adorned with paintings of cranes, in black and red ink, standing amidst a winter garden. A low table made from a heavy slab of dark wood, carved intricately with serpentine coils of Qin dragons, stood in the middle. Lady Kazuko was sitting at one end in an official robe of yellow and emerald, with a chain of gold and jade around her neck and a flower ornament in her greying hair tied in a bun.

Tokojiro wore the best clothes he could find; a long, tan pleated *hakama* skirt and brown cloak embroidered with white flower crests on the shoulders. He had his two swords at his side. It was important to him to show that he still had both of them, that he did not yet fall low enough to pawn his weapons for saké. His long narrow face was shaven smoothly for the first time in weeks, and his hair tied neatly.

This was his moment.

"The boy is a castaway," Lady Kazuko explained, after swearing Tokojiro to secrecy at the shrine's altar, "and speaks no Bataavian or Qin. I believe he speaks the language of your *sensei*, although I can't be certain."

"Why hasn't he been reported to the authorities yet?"

"It is my decision and responsibility to conceal his presence. I hope that is answer enough."

"Of course," he answered, although it was far from enough.

"*Let him in*," the priestess commanded loudly.

The door to the Crane Room slid open, and in came a boy, black-haired and green-eyed, slightly scared, wearing a dark purple kimono.

"Good morning, Sir," the interpreter said as he stood up and bowed. "I am Namikoshi Tokojiro, and I will attempt to translate your words to Yamato, and Lady Kazuko's to Seaxe. Please excuse any faults in my speech."

He looked at the boy expectantly. What if he got it wrong? It had been so long since he had practised the language with a native speaker... The boy let out a sigh of relief and bowed back stiffly.

"A pleasure to meet you, Sir, my name is Bran ap Dylan."

It worked. Black Raven, wherever you are, I hope you're proud.

He could still speak good Seaxe.

"I am the High Priestess of this shrine, the Suwa," Lady Kazuko said, and waited for Tokojiro to translate. "First of all, are you well? Do you need anything urgently?"

"I am fine, Lady," the boy replied swiftly, "I have been well taken care of."

"No doubt you have many questions. I shall try to answer them for you and then ask a few of my own. How does that sound to you?"

The boy agreed. Lady Kazuko smiled at him invitingly.

"I... um," he stumbled falteringly, before continuing. "That first house, with the infirmary – how did I get there?"

"I only know what Nagomi – the copper-haired girl – told me. She said you were seen brought down to a beach near Dejima on a beam of light - take it as you will. She and Satō then transported you to the Itō residence."

"Itō?"

"Nagomi's family. The nurse, Ine-*sama*, is her older sister."

"Can't I simply go to Dejima now and find myself a boat home?"

"It's not that easy," Lady Kazuko said, shaking her head, "otherwise we'd have already arranged this. We really do not wish to keep you here against your will. There are no ocean-going ships at Dejima at this time of year, and even if there were... The island is surrounded by a high wall, with only one Gate leading through it. It's heavily guarded and everyone and everything coming in or out must be checked by the magistrate. Every foreigner on the island is listed and registered with the daimyo's office. If an unknown Westerner was to appear out of nowhere, on Yamato side of the gate... A wizard, no less...!"

"I'm not a wizard," the boy protested, "just a dragon rider."

"A... a dragon?" Tokojiro hesitated. "I'm sorry, Sir, do you mean *long* – a Qin dragon or *ryū* – a Yamato one?"

"I mean a Western dragon," replied Bran.

The interpreter paused, startled.

A wizard, dragons? What mess am I getting myself into...?

"I was told you can use magic," the priestess said, surprised. "The lights you summoned last night..."

"We are all taught a little of it and we can channel the power of our dragons... but a wizard is something completely different – they use elements to –"

She raised her hand, smiling.

"Forgive me, the intricacies of Western magic are beyond my understanding."

Tokojiro noticed she brushed over the mention of the dragon as if the boy said he was a cart driver.

A dragon. Where is it now...?

"The boy I've seen – he used magic…" the foreigner said.

"Oh, there are some wizards in Kiyō!" The High Priestess nodded. "Satō's father is one, for example. Because of our trade with the Bataavians and Qin we are not as wary of Westerners and their knowledge as the rest of the Empire."

He saw a frown pass the boy's face at the mention of "the Empire".

He has no idea what this place is like. For his sake, I hope he never learns.

"And yet I am not allowed to leave the walls of this precinct?"

"It is illegal for any foreigners to be in Yamato without a permit and a state-appointed guardian. It wasn't so bad a few years ago," the priestess explained, "but now you'd probably just be killed straightaway. The streets are full of armed men who would cut you on sight. Even castaways are not exempt."

The boy nodded slowly, more to himself, as if remembering something. "What is to become of me?"

"We are working on a solution, but it may take time. In the worst case scenario you'll have to wait until Minazuki…"

"That's two months from now," Tokojiro added an explanation to his translation.

"…when the Dejima magistrates make their annual report to the city masters," the priestess continued. "We could smuggle you into their entourage then."

"Can't you at least get the message out?"

"As soon as the Overwizard arrives back from Edo, we will let him know of your plight, of course."

The boy looked at Tokojiro quizzically.

"Edo is the capital city," the interpreter said, "far to the north of here."

"And what's an Overwizard?"

He really knows nothing!

"The Bataave commander at Dejima."

"Is there anything else you would like to ask?" Lady Kazuko interrupted their exchange.

"I just wanted to congratulate Sir Tokojiro. His Seaxe is very good."

The interpreter bowed, surprised at the praise.

"Thank you. I studied with Black Raven Somerled."

No reaction to the name.

Of course, why did I expect otherwise?

"Now, if you are willing to answer," the priestess interjected, "I would ask you my own questions."

"Naturally."

"Tell me, what happened to you before arriving in Yamato – on a beam of light, if Nagomi is to be believed."

The boy hesitated.

He does not want to reveal too much, thought Tokojiro. *Black Raven was just the same when we asked him how he got to Kiyō.*

"I… was on a ship sailing along the shores of Qin with my father," the boy finally said. "There was a disaster at sea. I invoked a… spell, which for some reason brought me here."

"Your father was a Dracalish sailor?"

"He is a free man of Gwynedd, as am I," the boy announced proudly. "An officer and a diplomat."

"I'm sorry, I don't understand," Tokojiro interrupted.

"Gwynedd lies to the west of Dracaland. There is no border between the two, and one monarch sits on both thrones, but we rule ourselves as a separate nation."

"I… I see."

The interpreter turned to Lady Kazuko trying to translate the complicated sentence as best as he could, but she silenced him, not interested in the foreign politics.

"Your father," she asked instead, "do you know his whereabouts?"

"We were separated in the disaster. I… don't know where he is now, but I believe he's alive."

The priestess gave the boy a long, inquisitive look.

"The items you have with you," she continued, "I was told about them. Can you tell me how they have come into your possession?"

"The dragon figurine was a gift from my father, he found it on one of his travels."

"And the black box?"

The foreigner paused again.

"My grandfather sailed these seas, and he once came to this very city," he divulged at last.

"Your grandfather was a Bataavian, then?"

"No, a man of Gwynedd as well. He was on board a Dracalish ship called *Phaeton.*"

Lady Kazuko's eyes widened. Tokojiro remained professionally calm, even though he also recognised the ship's name.

"I remember. I was Nagomi's age then. It was a famous incident. The commander of our fleet committed suicide because he was unable to stop the warship leaving the harbour."

"Suicide…?"

"Such is the law of this land. There can only be one punishment for failure. It was after the *Phaeton* incident and the great fire of Dejima that the law against foreigners was strengthened, but the sailors from that ship never landed in the city, as far as I know – so how did your grandfather come to have a Kutsuki lady's jewellery box?"

"Is that what it is? What's a Kutsuki?"

"The markings on the box, that's the crest of the Kutsuki clan of Fukuchiyama Castle, far to the north, beyond the Imperial Capital."

"I don't know anything about the clan or the castle," the boy said, shaking his head, "but the box was brought to the ship by a woman who fled from the city. It seems she and my grandfather had… been friends for some time."

"How curious," the priestess said, "I don't think I ever heard that part of the story. You wouldn't know who the woman was, or why she was fleeing from Kiyō?"

"All I know is that her name was Ōmon. Her picture is in the box, and I can only guess that golden buckle also belonged to her. I think she died not long after meeting my grandfather. In his diary he mentions a man clad in a crimson robe, who was chasing after her, but I don't know anything else."

"A man in a crimson robe?"

"*A flowing crimson robe, his hair was long, dark, flowing in the wind and his eyes gleamed like nuggets of pure gold,*" the boy recited, obviously having learned the diary off by heart.

"I see."

The priestess's brow furrowed in deep thought. They were both silent now. A single grey starling chirped outside as the sun slowly climbed up the morning sky. Tokojiro looked from the priestess to the boy, waiting to continue the translation. He hoped it would not last long; his throat was parched and his head throbbed after the night at the inn. Lady Kazuko stood up.

"I must now proceed to my duties. Your conversation has given me much to think about," she said.

The boy stood as well. The High Priestess rang a small porcelain bell.

"The girl who brought you here will take you back to your room. She is sworn to secrecy, but not everyone is, so be careful. I want to assure you we are doing what we can to help. The streets outside may be dangerous, but you are in the care of the shrine now. You are safe here."

"I am grateful for your help," the boy said, bowing.

"We could do no less."

You could have sent him to the magistrate, thought Tokojiro, *and saved us all a beheading.*

By the evening Bran began to grow hungry. The sunlight was fading outside, and the twilight choir of birds hiding in the rose and magnolia bushes started in earnest. Little shy wrens and chatty redstarts, noisy finches, blackbirds and thrushes with their artisan melodies, all erupted into song, a concert punctuated by the regular staccato of a lone cuckoo somewhere in the distance.

The entire part of the building seemed cut off from any visitors. There were faint noises and voices all around the compound and in the garden, but never near his room. Through the window he saw some women pass from one pavilion to another and once he thought he caught a glimpse of the red-haired girl. As the night drew in the garden fell quiet, and only a few women remained - priestesses or shrine attendants, he guessed. The atmosphere was calm and focused, monastic, the people moving purposefully and in peace.

The place was having a strange effect on him. He felt acutely alone, melancholic. He realised he had been feeling like this not just since waking up in the Itō's household, but for much longer... since leaving Brigstow at least. Perhaps, he thought, he had been alone all his life, but only now with his mind so clear in this meditative atmosphere had he began to notice it.

He wished there was somebody he could tell about all his adventures, but there was nobody waiting for his stories back at Llambed. Of the people whom he could have counted among his friends, Eithne was lost beyond the Hawthorn Wall at Mon, Hywel had joined the dragoons and was probably already seeing his share of the world, and Madoc had never been interested in what lay outside Gwynedd. Would any of them even remember him when he returned – *if* he returned? Bran had no knack for making his friendships last.

He sighed, looking out through the window. The moon peered between the branches of the gingko tree as in a beautiful painting. So much wonder, lost in his own head... If he died now it would perish, like the memories of those poor souls gone down with the *Ladon*. Perhaps he should start writing a memoir, like his grandfather? He opened his satchel and took out the Keswick pencil and what remained of the notepad, but his hand hovered with no purpose over the oiled-paper sheet. He didn't know what to write. He didn't even know what date it was.

His stomach rumbled and he remembered he hadn't eaten anything since breakfast. He was resigned to going to sleep hungry when a female voice called him from outside the room. He slid the door away cautiously and saw the elderly woman who questioned him earlier, her long, greying hair let loose down the flowing light green robe. She was holding a tray with several bowls of food and a lit oil lamp. It was already getting dark outside. The woman observed him intently with wise gleaming eyes set deeply within a wrinkled face.

The interpreter had called her "Lady Kazuko", he remembered - the High Priestess. She had been very inquisitive in their morning conversation. Bran was uncertain how much of his story he should have revealed to her. In practice, MFS *Ladon* was, at the moment of the disaster, a navy ship at war, and its expedition to Jiankang was a military matter. Bran knew enough of army protocol to be wary of mentioning too many details. Why did she care so much about the contents of his satchel? What use was it to her or to anyone? Eventually, though, he'd had little choice but to answer her questions. The woman most probably held the key to his release. Certainly she had good connections – after all, she had managed to procure a Seaxe interpreter at short notice. He was surprised they even had one in a city so cut off from the outside world. It seemed prudent to stay on her good side.

He took the tray from her and bowed as best he could.

"Thank you, Lady Kazuko," he said in Prydain.

The woman smiled silently, turned away and disappeared into the darkness of the corridor without a sound.

Bran was nonplussed.

What was all that about?

The exquisite smell of food reached his nostrils and he remembered how famished he was. An entire mackerel grilled to perfect crispiness and an aromatic broth with thick noodles accompanied the usual bowl of rice and cup of *cha*, the hot bitter drink. He put the tray on the straw mat and waited for the meal to cool down – he could still only eat it with his fingers, the way to use the wooden sticks remaining a mystery. The mackerel was large and fat, oil dribbled down his chin and stained the purple kimono as he sank his teeth into the soft moist flesh.

I must seem like a barbarians to them, he realised. *It's a good thing nobody's here to see my clumsiness.*

Bran was writing down some of the new Yamato words he had just learned from Nagomi. "*Phoodë*" - brush, he started, "*soomeë*" - ink, and so on, adding words he had learned earlier until he reached the end of the page. The red-haired girl had provided him with writing utensils the locals used and explained in mime how to create the thick ink from black stone and water, but the thin brush was too unwieldy for Bran and he reverted to a pencil.

The next sheet was invitingly blank, but so was Bran's mind. He glanced out the window and tried to draw a sketch of the scene outside, branches of a tall gingko tree strikingly black against the blue, cloudless sky and the rooftops of the shrine compound, grey and black in the sun.

He looked down at his piece of paper and sighed. The sketch was just a poor jumble of shoddily drawn lines. To top it off, the paper itself was full of smudges where his hand clumsily smeared over soft graphite. The Academy had taught him to draw maps from dragonback – a necessity for a future soldier – but that was the limit of his artistic abilities. Bran reached for his satchel's front pocket and took out a small sharpening knife. He had to be careful – now that he had no idea how long it would take him to get out of this place, every sliver of pencil was precious. The knife's blade was dull and beginning to rust– he had forgotten to take proper care of it since his arrival in Yamato. It snapped and cut him on the index finger.

Clenching his fist to stop the blood trickling from the small wound, he leaned against the wall and closed his eyes, listening to the soft wafts of the wind whistling gently through the gutters and roof tiles, the rushing of the flat, fan-shaped leaves of the tree outside and the incessant tweeting of a family of swallows building an early nest in the eaves of one of the buildings.

Did she really mean they'd keep me here for two months? There must be another way…

He hadn't told anyone about where the dragon was yet. He could tell Emrys was getting near. What if it would find its way to Kiyō? Bran could only imagine the chaos the city would be thrown into by the appearance of the jade green beast. He wondered where the dragons of Yamato were kept – he had not seen any yet, although they seemed omnipresent in the carved ornaments and painted ceilings throughout the shrine. Perhaps they were all kept on the other island the interpreter had mentioned. How big was this country, anyway? Tokojiro called it an "Empire" – was it just a case of mistranslation, or could there really have been enough ocean to hide a land the size of Qin or Rome? Not for the first time Bran wished he had paid more attention to geography...

The ring on his finger lit up like a flare. He was overwhelmed by a flood of images and emotions. He could barely gather his bearings, but he was on a beach somewhere – in the waves – on a rocky reef – in the trees – back on the sand. Panic and anger swept through him, danger and pain. A group of people - short stocky men with spears, nets, bows and arrows – approached him, creeping. He tried to get away, but a net entangled his arms, his legs and his... wings?

Bran opened his eyes, the images perished. He immediately realised what he had just seen – Emrys had been captured. Its abductors looked like the Yamato, but he couldn't be sure, as everything had happened too quickly. The boy did not know if what he had just experienced happened now or was an echo of some earlier events. He tried to focus again, but there was no more response.

The dragon rider fell back against the wall, his heart racing. He could not wait any longer until whenever his hosts deemed him ready to sneak to the Bataavians. He had to do something, but what? Leaving alone was out of the question. He had tried this once already, and it had only brought trouble. Besides, now he had even less idea in which part of the city he was and how to get from here to Dejima. No, to save Emrys he needed to get help from the few Yamato people he already knew.

CHAPTER XVII

Yamato, Spring, 7ᵗʰ year of Kaei era

Keinosuke arrived late. He sat down by the table beside Shōin, unpacked his bag and prepared for the lesson, while the others waited.

Satō glanced at him with irritation, but said nothing.

He dares to come? What's he playing at?

"We're talking about Elemental Affiliation today," she explained, and continued from where Keinosuke's arrival interrupted her, "can you guess what element is your teacher's preferred one?"

"*Sui* – water," moaned Shōin, rubbing his arm in remembrance of the freezing punishment then laughing.

Satō laughed too. Keinosuke was silent and distant, obviously thinking about something other than the lesson. The wizardess bit her lips, but decided to ignore the boy's behaviour.

"You will choose your element, eventually, or rather, it will choose you. You will find some of the transformations are easier to perform, some invocations don't require as much effort, some enchantments come more naturally. Through practise and understanding of the nature of your Power, you will learn more of this special communion with elements."

"Do all wizards suffer from this limitation?" Keinosuke asked, suddenly breaking his broody silence.

"We don't regard this as a limitation, it's just a way the Power manifests itself..."

"It *is* a limitation if you confine yourself to just one aspect over others."

"It's only as much of a limitation as becoming a samurai confines you to not being a farmer or a merchant," Satō argued.

She preferred him when he was simply sitting quietly and listening to the lecture. The boy was barely capable as a wizard, in fact, Shōin, for all his giddiness and goofing off, had much greater innate talent and showed much more progress, but was boastful and arrogant, and interested only in self-aggrandisement.

"Nonetheless, are there wizards able to wield all elements with the same ease?"

Satō rolled her eyes.

"Yes, they are called Prismatics and they only appear once every few generations. They reach great fame and power – then they die young," she added grimly.

"Why is that?" Keinosuke pressed her, undeterred.

"Their life energy is spent too fast. They accomplish wondrous feats of magic, but the conflicting elements within eventually tear them apart."

The lesson continued in peace and quiet. The boys wrote down a long list of historic wizards and their biographical notes then tried to freeze a cup of water. Shōin managed to cover the surface of the liquid with a thin layer of frost remarkably quickly. At the same time, Keinosuke's cup barely cooled down. Frustrated, the boy decided to heat it up instead. He clutched the thin-walled clay cup in his hand. Suddenly it broke apart. A potsherd scratched his palm and he started bleeding.

Satō quickly wrapped the wound in a piece of cloth. Keinosuke was beaming.

"Did you see it? I only wanted to heat it up, but it exploded! Does that mean I am a fire wizard?"

"You squeezed it too hard and it snapped, that's all."

Stupid boy.

The training mugs were quite expensive, having been imbued with four elemental runes at the bottom to make the exercise easier. The shards of the cup she picked up weren't even warm.

"*You lie!*" the boy shouted.

Satō looked at him sternly. Even Shōin turned serious.

"You shouldn't say that to the *sensei*," the merchant's son said.

"Or what?" Keinosuke stood up, clutching his bleeding hand. "I know your lies and secrets, *sensei*, and you can't do anything about it!"

Here we go.

"Be quiet, boy."

"I won't! You can't make me! I'm a samurai and you're just a girl!"

"You're not a samurai yet. You're just a spoiled brat."

"I could cut your head off for this!"

I'd like to see you try.

"Shōin, the lesson is over," she said, standing up, "please leave us."

The boy swiftly picked up his belongings and made for the door. He turned around before leaving.

"Same time next week, *sensei?*" he asked.

"Yes, of course," Satō said, not looking in his direction, as she was concentrating on Keinosuke's arrogant burning eyes.

Shōin stepped outside and slid the door behind him.

"You have something to say, apart from insults, Keinosuke?" she asked when they were alone.

"I lost a coat two nights ago. I would like to have it back, *sensei*."

"I don't know anything about it."

"It was black and white with the crest of my clan. I lost it near the Sōfukuji Temple. I thought you might have seen it, it wasn't far from the Itō house."

"Little boys should not wander around the town at night."

"Daughters of disfavoured samurai should not become acquainted with criminals."

How does he even know so much about politics? What has his father been telling him?

"Mind your words, boy. I don't know anything about your coat or any criminals hiding in the night. What is it exactly that you want from me?"

Keinosuke smiled mischievously.

"I would like to read about dragons. If you were bring me a book I could forget all about the coat, or how I came to lose it."

This was too much for Satō to bear. She would not let herself be blackmailed by anyone, especially this boy. She drew her sword and invoked the Power of flame. This wasn't her affiliated element, but she felt ice or water would not be dramatic enough to make a lasting impression. She wrote a Bataavian fire rune in the air. A barrier of flames rose around the boy, who had lost all his smugness.

"I am the heir of the Takashima *Dōjō*, I wield the power of *Rangaku*, I command the elements!" she cried in her best theatrical voice - she adored the theatre and often sneaked herself into the performances. "I will not be threatened by little boys!"

Keinosuke turned pale and instinctively reached for the dagger at his belt. Satō flicked her sword, and a tongue of flame licked the tip of the dagger's hilt. Keinosuke yowled as his hand got burned.

"You're heir of nothing! You're a girl! You'll never be allowed to inherit anything!"

Satō's eyes narrowed. The wall of flame tightened around the boy, singeing his hair.

"You mad sow, that hurts!"

"It will hurt more if you don't apologise."

"What? I'll never... *Ow!*"

"Apologise to your teacher!"

"I'm sorry, I'm sorry!" cried the boy with tears in his eyes.

Satō's forehead trickled with sweat. This show of power was exhausting her.

"If you ever talk about this to anyone, these fires will devour your flesh. Even your old man can't save you from the Curse of the Flames."

There was no such spell, but she hoped the boy would never dared to check. She dispersed the fiery circles with a wave of her hand.

"Do not ever come here again, boy. Your lessons are over."

Keinosuke picked up his books, his burned hand still trembling, tears of rage and fear trickling down his cheeks. As he reached the door he turned his head and seethed.

"You'll regret this, Takashima Satō. One day I will gain power far greater than you or your father."

When he had left, the girl sat down on the floor, breathing heavily. She reached for the remaining cup of ice-cold water and drank it in one gulp. She recalled all the inauspicious prophecies, omens and forebodings of the past months, and her father's strange words. She was naïve to think she could handle this situation. With one word whispered to a willing ear, Keinosuke could easily bring doom upon the Takashima household, already in a precarious situation.

Oh, why did the Gaikokujin have to wander outside in the dark! How thoughtless of that Ine to leave the door of her house unlocked!

Shūhan already had enough trouble on his shoulders. They were running out of money and the *Taikun*'s officials were coming to the end of their patience with his increasing connection to the Bataavians. There was already a faint rumour circulating about the conspiracy her father was a member of, not enough to act upon, but enough to grow suspicious. He was already in the court's great disfavour – Satō dared not think what would have been the next step taken against the family if the rumour had grown any further.

She could almost see the thick dark clouds envelop her and her home.

The door to Satō's room slid open noiselessly. Shūhan's bare feet stepped quietly onto the straw mat. He looked at his daughter in the light of a small paper lantern. Satō had rolled off her futon onto the floor, arms and legs spread apart, her blanket kicked off in the corner.

Shūhan picked the blanket up and covered the girl. She stirred, but did not wake. He started to softly sing a lullaby.

"Nen, nen kororiyo, okororiyo…"

He couldn't remember the rest of the words, so he put his hand on her head and gently ran his fingers through the girl's short hair.

It could be as beautiful as your mother's, he thought, *if only you'd let it grow…*

The old wizard slid the door close and headed back to his room. He cast a guilty glance at a pot of cold *chazuke* – rice with tea broth and pickled plums. Satō worked hard to prepare his meals and he kept forgetting to eat them, too busy with his experiments and research.

A family shrine stood in the corner of the room. Shūhan opened the little black lacquer doors and lit a couple of incenses. The light of the lantern flickered playfully on the brass and golden ornaments, but the tiny figurine of the *Butsu* god seemed stern, serious. He began praying to the Spirits of his ancestors, silently, careful not to wake anyone.

By night the house seemed even more empty. Only his daughter and a few old servants remained in the great residence. The Takashimas had once been a rich and powerful family. Shūhan's father had been a master of defences of the Kiyō harbour, dismissed after the *Phaeton* incident – getting into trouble with the government was becoming a family tradition... Now Satō was the last of the line - an heir to everything and nothing in particular; an empty house and a school without students.

"It's a good thing you gave me no sons, dear." He smiled bitterly as he prayed before the Spirit tablet representing his wife. "What kind of legacy would I give to a son?"

He was aware that several neighbouring families still hoped their sons would inherit the prestigious school through marriage to the master's daughter, but that was different. Without the tainted Takashima name, the school could start again. Ever since Satō had turned twelve and was of engagement age, various relatives, friends and matchmakers had started to appear at the house with talk of marriage, suitors and courtship, but she would hear none of it. His daughter was satisfied with her life as it was. She was getting used to walking around the streets of Kiyō in male clothes, with her head held high, hair combed straight and simple. She had often told him -she could not bear the thought of having to follow some fool of a husband, with small steps enforced by her kimono tied just that little bit too tight as noble ladies did. Shūhan was willing to indulge her for a few more years. She would have to conform to what was expected of a Yamato woman eventually, but he was too soft-hearted to command her. Without his wife, he had no idea how to raise a daughter properly.

He would not yet consider adoption either, another common and obvious solution to the problem of inheritance.

"What is wrong with my son, Takashima-*sama*?" a proud parent would enquire when another supplicant for the legacy was refused. "Is he not the best of your pupils? You're not getting any younger. It would be a shame if the school was to perish when you're no longer with us."

"If he defeats my daughter, he will be worthy," had been Shūhan's only response, and it was enough. None of his students matched Satō's skill, raw talent, power and dedication.

"She has a rare gift, our girl," the old wizard said, still kneeling before the family altar.

The Yamato people often lacked the innate talent needed to perform western magic with
ease, but Satō showed a remarkable natural aptitude.

"She will be far greater than me one day."

If she's ever given a chance, he thought.

"I did everything a mortal could to protect her," he told the Spirit of his wife, "now it's up to you. Please, keep an eye on our daughter."

Shūhan bowed then closed the altar. One last time, he made sure all the traps and magic barriers he had set up throughout the house were in good order then went to sleep.

Satō entered the lecture hall and slipped past the small crowd of *Rangaku* scholars. In her usual black-vermillion *Rangakusha* attire, with the Matsubara sword stuck proudly in the sash, she could easily pass as one of them. They were all too focused on Grand Master Tanaka Hisashige's speech to pay attention to her, anyway. Only one man cast her a curious glance. *A Taikun spy*, she thought, *here to note who comes to the lecture.*

Master Tanaka was a renowned expert on mistfire and enhanced hydraulics. He had come to Kiyō all the way from Saga to give the lecture, and

Satō was happy her father had managed to obtain an entrance permit. The scientist read from a Bataavian book on engines and presented his famous masterpiece, the Myriad Year Clock.

The mechanism was a miraculous feat of engineering and magic, combining western technology and thaumaturgy with eastern geomancy and astrology. The mistfire-powered dials showed not only the precise time and date, days of the week, months and years, phases of the moon, times of sunrise and sunset, signs of the zodiac - both the yearly of the Qin and monthly of the Western Magi - but also the predicted elemental alignments for the day, geomantic measurements and a brief divination chart for the start of each week. Master Tanaka claimed he was planning on having the prophecies match in accuracy those produced by the shrine Scryers themselves.

"It is made of one thousand mechanical parts, bound by two hundred Words of Power. Eight elementals are trapped inside, and the mistfire engine inside is of my own design. It's taken me three years to reach its current form, and I am now working on a second, even more precise, prototype."

Eight elementals! Shūhan's precious airguns contained only one Wind Spirit each. This was fantastically impressive machinery and Master Tanaka's efforts were loudly fêted by the gathered *Rangakusha*. Satō sneaked forwards to touch the clock. She could feel the trapped elementals buzzing inside a case of brass and teak wood, the power of *thaumaturgie* binding the iron springs and copper tubes together – Grand Master Tanaka was one of only a few scholars in Yamato powerful enough and sufficiently familiar with this magic to use it. She could hear the tiny engine puffing away quietly in the middle of the clockwork, beyond the panels of glass and copper.

"Ah, you must be Shūhan's heir," the old scholar said, having noticed her among the other scholars.

"Yes Sir."

"Too bad your father couldn't make it. I really wanted to see him. Ah, but I *do* have something, will you give it to him from me?"

"Of course!"

The old mechanician reached deep into the wooden chest and took out a small bundle no bigger than a grown man's hand. He unwrapped it carefully and showed the artefact to Satō.

It was a fingerless glove of thick brown leather, with a couple of gears, cranks and clockworks attached to it, a large dial on the outside and an oblong bulge on the inside. Satō could feel the binding enchantment buzzing throughout the mechanism.

"What... What is it?"

"Something I worked on with your father. This should help combining swordsmanship with *Rangaku*. I'm not a glover, so it may be a bit unwieldy..."

"But what does it do?"

"Oh, I'm sorry. It does all sorts of things. This dial shows the life energy quotient, and into these gears below you compose a spell pattern... Your father will know what to do with it."

"He will be very grateful."

"Oh, and look out for this spring," he added, pointing to the oblong bulge, "it pops out a needle conduit."

Satō was appalled.

"Blood magic?"

"Your father's request; I copied the design from an old Vasconian book."

"I see. Thank you, Tanaka-*sama*."

Satō bowed and pulled back into the crowd of scholars, each of whom wanted to have a chance at conversation with the celebrated mechanician.

"Fafnir the Green of Osning Forest was the Broodfather of the Forest races: the Viridians, the Celadons, the Verts and the Emeralds. These are robust practical races, beneficial for civilian labour, known for their reliability and stamina."

A detailed ink drawing of a large green *dorako* in flight, hauling a huge load of stone on a platform tied under its belly, filled out a third of the page. The dragon's wings moved slowly, and a man sitting on the stones waved to the reader merrily. Underneath, the black runes on a yellowed parchment spelled mysterious words with no apparent meaning. Even though Shūhan, unlike his daughter, had a cursory knowledge of Seaxe, the particular jargon in which the *Dracology, Student's Handbook* had been written was hermetic and complicated.

Some fifteen years ago, Shūhan had bought a copy of an incomplete Seaxe wordbook from a Bataavian merchant for a hefty sum. The dictionary, written by someone called Medhurst, had lain unused on the upper shelf of the library until another smuggler had brought the enigmatic *Dracology Handbook*. It had taken the old wizard a while to recognise the language of the book and remember where he had hidden Medhurst's piece. The dictionary itself was difficult to work with; its author seemed not to be aware the Yamato wrote in a vertical fashion, used only one of the three writing systems and was completely unfamiliar with the consonant markers or long vowels. Still, without the dictionary, the Handbook would have remained just an undecipherable set of runed pages bound in thick leather.

Always a regular person, Shūhan devoted every third day's afternoon to his attempts at decoding the book. He knew Satō was also sometimes sneaking into the library to take a peek at the pages, but he didn't mind as long as she put it back safely every time. It did spoil the surprise a little, as he planned the book as a gift for the girl's eighteenth birthday next year, but he wanted to provide her with as complete a translation as he could manage.

It was the day of Grand Master Tanaka's visit to Kiyō, and the wizard was all alone in the residence, apart from servants and guards. All his students and friends, including his daughter, had gone to see the great engineer's famous Myriad Year Clock. Days like this were when the house arrest felt most inconvenient. Shūhan really wanted to see the wondrous machine for himself. On the other hand, he had an entire afternoon to work on the translation in peace and quiet.

He was stuck on a long, many-vowelled word that he could not find anywhere in the dictionary, when he heard a cracking and shattering noise coming from downstairs, as if somebody had broken through one of the thin paper walls. At first he thought one of his old servants was being particularly clumsy, but the sound repeated, accompanied by brief, but bloodcurdling, shrieks of pain. Shūhan stood up, alert, and reached for his sword. The house was under attack.

Too soon. She's not ready yet.

The enemy, whoever it was, managed to scale the staircase in two great leaps. With a third leap, the assailant appeared in the doorway, sliding the delicate panel away with a force that made it break out from the grooves and fall to the floor with a loud crack.

"The barbarian," seethed the man in the crimson robe, "where is he?"

She almost skipped along the way, like a child at play. The sun was shining brightly, warming her face in spite of the crispy, cold mid-spring air. Just a few white clouds were hanging over the horizon. Black kites and sea hawks screeched resolutely over the harbour as fishermen were returning with the first haul of the afternoon. The day couldn't get any more perfect. Everything would work out, she told herself, she was sure of it.

She stopped by the Fukusaya bakery to buy a piece of moist castella cake then she remembered she was supposed to get some rubbing alcohol for the laboratory. She headed for the Itō house – the family of physicians held ample supplies of the medicinal preparation.

Satō turned in front of the Sōfukuji Temple onto a narrower lane leading up the hill to the Itō residence. The entrance door was wide open, but there was nobody in the vestibule. This was unusual. Satō immediately remembered her worries. Warily she went inside the house. A servant was lying in the entryway, his skull cracked on the wooden floor, bleeding. Satō knelt by his side.

"Save... Ine-*sama*..." the old man moaned.

Satō ran up to the first floor. All the thin sliding panel walls were shattered, all the rooms exposed. There was debris everywhere. Ine was lying against the wall, bruised but conscious.
Satō helped her to sit up. The woman looked at the girl with blurry eyes.

"What's happened here?"

"There was a man here – a strange man. He was looking for the boy – the *Gaikokujin*."

"Bran-*sama*?"

"Yes, who else!" Ine coughed. "He tore through the walls and when he had found nothing, he – he leapt through the window."

He will go to my house next, Satō thought.

"Will you be all right here? I must see if my house is safe."

"Yes, I'll be fine. You'd better run to your father!"

The guards at the gates of the Takashima residence house had already been gruesomely disposed of by the time she arrived. They were not slain by a sword or spear, rather their throats seemed to have been torn apart by a wild animal. One of them – Satō recognised young Kaiten – was sprawled across the threshold, slain in a brave, but futile, attempt to defend the residence.

Foolish boy, Satō thought briefly. *I told you - keep people in, not out.*

The gate had been crashed open. Satō dashed across the courtyard to the main hall and up the stairs straight for her father's study. She could hear the sounds of a fierce battle inside. Her father fought against the invader with all his power.

She entered the room, stepping over a discarded lightning trap, its deadly energies spent. The study was ravaged by flame, ice, wind and lightning thrown from Shūhan's sword and other focus artefacts scattered all over the floor, as the energies within the room soared to a point of oversaturation. All the hair on Satō's body stood on end, electrified, and the air smelled of ozone and burnt plums.

This magical onslaught was not enough to stop the enemy, who slowly inched towards the *Rangakusha* holding a long bronze knife. Another blade of the same kind was lying at Shūhan's feet, its tip bloodied. A great two-handed sword was slung over the stranger's back. A loose flowing robe of crimson fluttered in the hurricane of energies.

Satō shuddered, recognising a demonic presence in the room. Having trained partially in the arts of the *onmyōji* magic she was sensitive to evil Spirits, and could tell that whoever stood before her was no mere human. The smell of blood and death filled her nostrils. She drew her sword and released the most powerful enchantments she knew, adding to the already magically permeated atmosphere. A cascade of energy enveloped the assailant, vapour in the air crystallising into chains and shards of ice. Icy spikes and icicles threatened to pierce and crush the crimson-clad man.

The mysterious enemy simply shrugged off the chains of frost, dispelled the icicles and turned towards the girl with deliberate slowness. There was a strange hypnotising beauty in his long gaunt face, pale like the moon. The almond-shaped, predacious eyes gleamed pure gold and when he opened his mouth in a scowl, sharp blackened fangs glistened behind bloodless lips. Transfixed, Satō observed how in one smooth, dance-like move, the man threw his bronze dagger towards her. She moved, but not fast enough. The long bronze blade dug deep into her left shoulder up to the hilt.

At that moment, Shūhan yelled and leaped at the enemy, pinning him to the floor.

"Satō, run! Hide yourself!" he screamed as the creature held him in a lethal embrace.

Their bodies became enveloped in the crackling black and purple energy of fierce raw magic, overcoming each other's defences.

Satō felt her strength seeping out of the wound. She tried to launch another barrage of spells, but the enchantments fizzled out and all the ice melted. The creature's willpower was too strong.

"On your mother's name, girl," Shūhan cried again, "*save yourself.*"

Satō swore through gritted teeth. She could not disobey this command, and she could do nothing else to help Shūhan. The mysterious blade seemed to be sapping all her magic away. The black and purple vortices swelled, filling the room, threatening to envelop the wizardess. She was well aware of the dangers of finding herself within uncontrolled currents of raw magic.

"Be brave, Father," she said, her voice shaking, "I'm going to get help."

She ran away, tears rolling down her cheeks, her father's dying screams ringing in her ears, the bronze dagger tearing through her skin and muscle with every step. At last she pulled it out and threw it away, screaming with pain. Leaving a trail of blood on the dirt of the street, she ran north towards the Suwa Shrine, the only place she knew was safe in this time of darkness. The last thing she saw were people running towards her to assist, their hands stretched out helpfully as she fell down.

"Suwa Shrine… Help – my father…" she managed to whisper before the world around her was enveloped in a thick, black impenetrable shadow.

Jōtarō passed under a stone torii gate, over a bridge spanning the moat and onto the artificial island in the middle of a large pond. He moved slowly, bent, supporting himself on a sturdy bamboo stick, holding a long bundle of black silk under his arm.

Struggling through the overgrown beech grove, he located a low earthen wall and, hidden under a massive tangle of wisteria, a large round boulder. With strength defying his fragile form he ripped away the thick dense mass of purple-blooming vine, grabbed the massive rock and rolled it away, revealing a dark round entrance. He picked up a bronze lantern from a niche in the wall, cleaned it up, filled with fuel and lit it with a Qin firestick.

He descended down the corridor leading deep into the earthen mound. As he walked the light flickered, reflecting on lime-plastered slabs of fine granite, dancing on immeasurably old frescoes, paintings of zodiacal beasts, phoenixes, turtles, tigers and dragons. Jōtarō passed under fading images of courtiers and court ladies whose names and titles had long been forgotten, of princes and emperors never mentioned in the chronicles. He moved on, paying no attention to any of these wonders. He had seen them so many times…

The passage narrowed slightly and ended with a large bronze door. Jōtarō grabbed the round handle, turned it and - this time with considerable effort - pushed the great bronze slab in. It moved with a dreadful creak, disrupting the age-long silence of the vast cavern beyond. A plume of dust whirled from the floor as fresh air whooshed inside.

The walls of the perfectly round chamber were painted with pleasant scenes of courtly life - hunting, playing, lovemaking. Once it had been filled with treasure, bronze mirrors, spearheads, swords, clay figurines of Gods and ancestors, pots of coins and rice. All that had been long gone, save a few broken potsherds and unrecognisable bits of metal scattered in the thick layer of dust, unworthy of the attention of generations of grave robbers.

In the very centre of the chamber, on a square pedestal, stood a large richly carved chair made of cryptomeria wood. Sitting on it was a statue of a tall samurai clad in a purple cloak thrown over rich, extravagant, garishly coloured clothes. A shallow saké cup rested in the samurai's hand.

The statue wore an unmarked black helmet and a moustached face mask with fierce demonic eye slits. The helmet and the mask were the only pieces of clothing on the sculpture that seemed truly ancient. They were cracked and stained in places, the pigments faded.

Jōtarō hung the lantern on a hook on the wall, climbed the two steps of the pedestal and started dusting the sculpture, removing cobwebs and stains of moisture that seeped through cracks in the ceiling. He was in no hurry. Nearly an hour passed before he was satisfied with the outcome. The statue shined like new in the flickering light of the lantern.

The old man then drew a sharp dagger from a sheath hidden in the folds of his robe. Without flinching, he cut a long deep wound into his forearm. Blood dripped into the saké cup in the statue's hand. When it was full, Jōtarō put the cup to the open lips of the demonic mask.

As the liquid dripped into the opening he spoke in a trembling, but loud, voice.

"Bennosuke-*sama*! I call upon you with the name your father chose for you on the day you were born. It is time!"

This had no effect, so Jōtarō spoke again, louder.

"Shinmen-*sama*! I call upon you with the name you chose for yourself on the day you killed your first man. It is time!"

Still nothing happened, so the old man straightened himself and cried at the top of his lungs.

"Niten-*sama*! I call upon you with the name the Great *Butsu-sama* himself chose for you on the day you started your new life. *It is time! The Shard has returned!*"

There was a cracking sound. The statue stirred, its arms moved. A grunt came from beneath the demonic mask. Eyes flickered opened in the slits. The statue's hand reached for the helmet and cast it away.

The face that appeared from beneath the mask was that of a man in his early thirties. The top of his head was shaven bald, with fringes on the sides and a thick, straight shaggy ponytail sticking out at the back. His lower face sported a thin whisker and the pointed beard of Vasconian fashion.

The man grimaced and stretched his jaw, trying out muscles he had not used for a very long time. He flexed the fingers of his right hand then the left and wiped the blood stain from his lips. The skin on his hands, and on his face, was yellowy pale and paper-thin. His almond-shaped eyes, slightly bulging from under bushy eyebrows, glistened with cunning, intelligence and cruelty. They were the colour of pure gold.

When the man spoke, his voice was hoarse and broken.

"Is this true, Jōtarō? Has the Shard really returned?"

"Yes, *tono*, just as had been foretold."

On hearing these words, the samurai slowly stood up to full height and stepped forwards from the pedestal.

"How long has it been?"

"Almost fifty years."

"And what of the Seven?"

"They have already made their first move, *tono*. I am ashamed. I was unable to stop the Crimson One."

"No, you wouldn't have been. I never gave you enough power. Very well, give me my swords."

Jōtarō untied the silk bundle and unwrapped two swords of nearly equal length, sheathed in plain, featureless black scabbards. His master stuck them both into his sash then pulled out one of the blades and examined it carefully.

"You have taken good care of them, Jōtarō. There is not a spot or blemish."

The old man only bowed, but said nothing.

"Is everything ready for my return?"

"Just as you have ordered, *tono*."

"Excellent. This makes me very glad. What reward do you wish for your efforts?"

Jōtarō raised his head, and his sad wrinkled eyes met those of his master.

"My *tono* knows my desire."

"You have not changed your mind then?"

"Never."

"Very well, you have served me faithfully, and the time has come. You deserve nothing less. Assist me outside, please."

Jōtarō raised the lantern and lit their way out of the mound. Once outside, his master stopped, gently touched the light pink flowers covering the tomb's entrance and looked at the sun. He breathed in the fresh crisp air of the morning and grinned. His eyes turned plain brown.

"On ceaseless breeze," he improvised, "sweetly lingers the scent of wisteria flowers."

"*Tono*," Jōtarō reminded patiently.

"Oh, forgive me. It's been so long…"

The samurai approached him and put a hand on the old man's shoulder.

"I release you from my service. You are free to join your ancestors."

A shudder came through Jōtarō and he felt his body start to painlessly scatter into ash. He raised his eyes up, tears streaming down his ancient, cracking face.

"Thank you, *tono*," he managed to speak one last time.

"Farewell, friend," the samurai said solemnly.

BOOK TWO

THE WARRIOR'S SOUL

The same attitude is needed to defeat one man and ten million men.

Go Rin No Sho

PROLOGUE

The majestic brilliant globe of the sun ascended slowly out of the waters of Kinkō Bay, beyond the slopes of the imposing cone of the Sakurajima Mountain. The first fishing boats of dawn were scattered on the pastel blue ocean like dots of silver thread embroidered on an indigo-dyed kimono. From where Atsuko was sitting the entire scene – the great mountain, the sea and the boats, the rising sun – formed a living backdrop to the lush green garden, gentle hills covered with fresh grass and tall dark trees cut to form a frame for the moving picture.

"This is my favourite season in the garden," said Shimazu Nariakira, sitting beside her on the veranda of a small, perfectly proportioned teahouse.

"Surely the time of blooming azaleas or flowering hydrangeas is much more beautiful, Father?" she said, referring to the bushes lining a narrow pond winding at their feet. Atsuko knew her adoptive parent enough to know the answer to this riddle, but she also knew he enjoyed telling it. The great *daimyo* of Satsuma rose a little and leaned to her side.

"I have designed this garden to show the spirit of the Satsuma clan – for those who know how to look. Right now, gazing at the pond, we see the present. The azaleas are already past their prime, a reminder of glories gone by. But the hydrangeas are yet to sprout flowers – "

"A promise for the future," she said, finishing his thought. He smiled and nodded.

Once, at the height of their power, when the civil wars ravaged Yamato, the Shimazu had gambled to conquer all of Chinzei Island. They failed, but, unlike other defeated clans, were not destroyed. Allowed to live, but not flourish, like the early spring hydrangeas, the clan bided their time for revenge. Time and patience was what the Shimazu had in excess. Two and a half centuries had passed since their last unsuccessful gambit and it seemed like even more would have to pass before they could try again.

"All this beauty and refinement," said Nariakira, taking a long, sad look at the flowers, the maple trees and the framed landscape, "all this futile, fruitless effort is just a substitute for the power and action we are no longer allowed. Have you read of the eunuchs at the Qin emperor's palace?"

"I have, Father. An awful fate for a man."

"We are all like those eunuchs. The *daimyo*, the samurai... Castrated by the Tokugawas, rendered feeble and powerless by the system they've introduced. Like the eunuchs we concentrate our energy on the meaningless pursuits of art, philosophy and courtly intrigue. We concern ourselves more with the taste of tea and smell of cherry blossom than warfare."

Atsuko nodded politely. She was the only one Nariakira could discuss such matters with. He had no sons and he trusted none of his advisors enough to share the most secret plans with – except perhaps Torii Heishichi, his Chief Wizard.

"Appreciating fine art refines the swordsman's soul and skill," she said.

"What need is there for a swordsman's skill when he stands against a peasant armed with a thunder gun?"

She laughed. The thought was preposterous.

"That will never happen. No peasant could afford a thunder gun."

"It will happen sooner than you think. And the samurai, with all their elegance and comfort and refinement, will be caught completely unprepared – mark my words."

"The samurai are the world's greatest warriors."

"We were once – and we might be again... but under the Tokugawas we've become a mockery. All the neighbouring countries laugh behind our backs. All the Westerners are sharpening their teeth, ready to pound their ironclad fist on the gates of Edo. Even the commoners no longer respect their superiors."

"And do you plan to defeat them all with your smoking boat?"

Nariakira turned his gaze north, where the garden ended with a tall impenetrable hedge, and smiled. There, beyond the hedge and the cliff side, lay his secret wharf and in it his beloved ship – a black yacht with no sails.

"That's just a toy. A little more than a model."

"An expensive toy."

She knew he could afford it. After Nariakira's father's reforms, the Satsuma fiefdom was the richest in the country. The Bataavian machines had opened new lands for farming, the overseas trade – through 'smugglers' based on Nansei Islands, which Nariakira only pretended to fight – was more profitable than ever. The *Taikun*'s tax collectors had no idea of Satsuma's real income. Here, far beyond the Southern mountains, his word meant little, his spy network was non-existent. The province was so remote and inaccessible it was almost like a separate country. No Tokugawa ever decided to risk an all-out war to bring the impudent Shimazu to heel, and no Shimazu would ever dare to dream of openly opposing the *Taikun* and his many vassals.

"I needed to know I can build it without having to rely on the Bataavians in case they change their minds."

"And can you?"

Nariakira grinned. "The blueprints came from Dejima, but everything else was made by my men. Satsuma's shipwrights built the hull, Satsuma's engineers created the engine, Heishichi provided the fire elementals from a pit inside Kitadake Mountain as good as the Bataavian ones. I could build ten more ships like it before the end of the year."

"Ten more toys."

He chuckled. "Put a gun on each and we would already have a mightier fleet than all of the other *daimyos* put together. And the ocean-going warship I have ordered will dwarf even that. But then what? Nobody ever won a war in Yamato by the strength of ships alone. I would need something else to change the balance of power… something radical, something new."

There was movement in the bushes and Nariakira froze, his hand reaching for the sword. Atsuko drew breath. There wasn't supposed to be anyone in the garden at that time.

"*An assassin?*" she whispered, but Nariakira shook his head.

The man emerged onto the path in a hurry, making no effort at secrecy. It was one of the *daimyo*'s personal messengers. Nariakira frowned.

"What message is so urgent that it has to be brought to my private garden at dawn?"

CHAPTER I

"So you're saying the neighbours saw nothing?"

"Nothing, *doshin* Koyata. The silk merchant from across the street heard some screams and noises, but that's all."

"What about the girl? We still can't reach her?"

"She's hiding in Suwa – outside our jurisdiction."

Koyata stood before the entrance to the Takashima Mansion's main building, squinting at the afternoon sun. This day was too long. The plain grey overcoat marked with the red pentacle badge of the Kiyō police lay heavily on his shoulders. His clues were as scarce as his resources – the precinct could only spare two men to help him. The bodies of the guards had disappeared before anyone could inspect them. The members of the household were all either dead or missing and, worst of all, nobody could investigate the scene of the crime.

"I will try again," declared Koyata, whose high rank of a *doshin* meant he was responsible for supervising all crime-fighting activities in the district.

"Be careful, Koyata-*sama*," Ishida, the shorter and fatter of his two subordinates warned him earnestly.

Dismissing their fears, he entered the building and climbed the narrow steps to the first floor. He stopped in front of the remnants of the broken sliding panel separating the ruined study from the corridor. He carefully reached into the room with the *jutte* truncheon. Nothing happened. Encouraged, he stepped forwards, crossing the threshold.

Lightning struck him in the chest, and he flew a few feet into the air before landing painfully on the other side of the corridor.

"Koyata-*sama!*"

The two policemen hurried to his assistance.

"I'm all right. *Kuso!* When is Sakuma-*dono* going to help us with this barrier?"

"He said he won't leave his son's bed as long as the kid is unconscious," explained Ishida.

"Such a tragic accident…" added the other.

"If it *was* an accident," Koyata said under his nose.

"You don't think – "

"I think it looks like somebody's targeting the *Rangaku* scholars, and I think that's why Sakuma-*dono* doesn't want to leave his house."

The only item found at the scene of the crime was an antique bronze dagger, covered with dried-up blood, discovered on the road a few yards away from the gate of the residence. Koyata recognised the pattern from his days in the forgery trade – he would not have progressed so high up in the hierarchy if he hadn't a keen eye for such detail. The dagger was at least two hundred years old, of the type used in the Yōkai War. The bronze blades were manufactured with a singular purpose – to vanquish magical creatures, or users of magic.

He rotated the bronze dagger in his fingers. He could feel the barely noticeable buzz coming from the blade, a confirmation of the latent magical ability he did his best to conceal from his colleagues and superiors. He had always admired real wizards, in secret. Takashima-*sama*, Sakuma-*dono*... Those names meant much to him. It worried him greatly that somebody would wish to hunt them down.

"Well, if you ask me, I won't be sorry if they all go to hell," said the taller policeman. "Just look at all this barbarian junk on the floor," he added, pointing to the books and magical artefacts scattered all over the study. "I bet he just killed himself with one of these contraptions."

"There would at least be a body," Koyata replied, dismissing the idea outright.

"Exploded, melted, eaten by a demon," the policeman said with a shrug.

The *doshin* looked sharply at his subordinate and clapped his thigh.

"Hirata, you're brilliant!"

"I am?"

"We'll just say the wizard did it to himself! That will save us all the work!"

And keep the superiors off my back, he thought. Already the magistrate officials had contacted him regarding the mysterious attack.

"We are certain you will find evidence incriminating the Bataavians." The city bureaucrat's fat jowls shook as he spoke.

"I'm not so sure, *tono*. You know as well as I do that the Bataavians regarded Takashima-*sama* with great esteem. What possible motive – "

"I don't think you understand, *doshin*. You *will* find the necessary evidence."

"I... I see."

An accident – due to mishandling Bataavian technology. *You'll have your evidence, but good luck incriminating anyone with it. What do you say to that, you fat brush-pusher?*

"It's a good idea," Ishida agreed. "It's just as believable as an abduction by rival mages, or a *shinobi* attack, or any other mad theory spun by the folks back at the precinct."

"Are they really talking about a *shinobi* attack?" the *doshin* asked, laughing.

"Old Jūzō does. He sees ninjas and demons everywhere."

"He's been watching too many *kabuki* plays. The *shinobi* are extinct. Let's go back and write this one off; there's nothing more for us to do here."

Koyata grinned. His mood improved. He would still try to solve the mystery of the Takashima Mansion, of course – but now he could do it in his own time, by his own rules.

He shook off the doziness and yawned discreetly. He retreated behind the frame of a ground floor sliding panel and observed the courtyard outside through a hole in the paper. The hours of waiting paid off – somebody *did* appear at the Takashima residence.

An unmarked palanquin stopped at the gates. The night was pitch-black, illuminated only by a single paper lantern carried by one of the priests accompanying the vehicle. A youth wearing a wide-brimmed, face-concealing hat stepped out of the palanquin and limped towards the main hall, supported by the priest with the lantern. This must have been Shūhan's heir, Satō, Koyata realised. He had heard rumours the wizard's daughter preferred to wear male clothes – and a sword. In any other city this would have been reason enough to arrest and disgrace her. In Kiyō this was merely an eccentricity.

Koyata sneaked after the heir and two priests. As she climbed the stairs, the girl dispelled all the protective spells with a wave of her hand. She entered her father's study without a hindrance.

The residence, like all aristocratic houses built in times of the assassins, was full of hidden corridors and hideouts, and the *doshin* had all day to discover most of them. With the magic barriers gone he could now reach a small concealed alcove from which he had a good view of the entire study.

The girl gingerly touched the floor. The air crackled with remnants of a powerful spell. She gasped with pain, touching her shoulder.

"We did warn you, Takashima-*sama*," the priest with the lantern said in a worried voice, "the wound has barely sealed. If you will not rest now, it may never be healed completely."

"It doesn't matter. I have to take care of my legacy. Help me clear these up."

The girl and the priests gathered all of wizard's belongings into a great pile in the library. Koyata watched it in horror. Was she planning to burn it all? So much knowledge, so much research... If she did, the *doshin* would have to come out of his hiding place and stop the girl, he decided, even if revealing his continued interest in the case brought the wrath of his superiors upon his head.

The girl reached for a large black book at the bottom of the pile and picked it up tenderly. The cover and the edges of the pages were burned. Several pieces of paper fell out from between the pages, scribbled with composed writing.

"It's difficult to carry such a bulky tome," remarked one of the priests.

"I know." The girl sighed and threw the book back onto the pile. "I don't need it anymore."

I need to find out what that book is.

She lifted one of the floorboards and picked up a roll of golden coins. A fortune in gold! Koyata gulped. He had only ever seen so much money in the treasure houses of the gambling dens he had raided.

"There is nothing else I want to take," the girl said. "All these things…" she pointed to the pile of magic contraptions, books and documents, "I can neither carry nor leave to the robbers or magistrate."

Right, that's it. Koyata grasped the handgrip of his truncheon, ready to pounce, but the girl turned to the accompanying priests and said something which made him stop and let out a quiet sigh of relief.

"Throw it all into the dry well by the cemetery. Bury it deep. My father and I will come and retrieve it once this is all over."

She arrived at the servants' quarters dressed in the simple common uniform of a shrine attendant; a grey cloth *monpe*, pantaloons that ended at half-knee, and a brown jute tunic. It was itchy and chafing compared to silk, but Satō found it remarkably easy to walk, even run in the narrow trousers.

It was Lady Kazuko's idea for her to hide in the servants' quarters. Even though the shrine was probably the safest place in the city, its walls still could not provide a complete guarantee of safety.

"This will be the last place anybody would look for a samurai's daughter, and it will help you to pick up some of the language and behaviour of the lower classes in case you need to disguise yourself."

"Why would I need to disguise myself as a serf?"

"Do you not intend to look for your father?"

"Of course I do!" the girl blurted out.

Finding Shūhan was the only thing on her mind right now. No body had been found at the mansion, and she had recognised the faint pattern of a transportation hex still lingering on the floor of the study. The thought of her father being still alive, somewhere, was the only thing keeping her from breaking down.

"Well then, you can hardly travel as Takashima Satō, as long as there's an unknown enemy waiting for you outside the shrine's gates."

"I suppose not," she agreed reluctantly, "but a *servant*? They are so uncouth and – and *smelly*!"

"Just try to see how they live," said the High Priestess, "they may surprise you yet."

The poor commoners were employed by the shrine to assist with the simplest menial tasks – carrying luggage for the guests, chopping firewood, transporting heavy goods. Satō entered the quarters with hesitation, holding her breath, expecting to find it in a state little better than the village of *eta*, the untouchables. But, though very poor and simple, the rooms were as clean as any and, to her surprise, everyone inside seemed rather cheerful.

Despite her being dressed like one of them, the servants immediately fell to their knees.

"I, uh… why are you kneeling? I'm just a commoner like you…"

One of the girls raised her face, smiling broadly.

"*Tono*, if you want to hide among us lowly serv'nts then by all means you can, but you ain't foolin' nobody 'ere just by wearing the garb of a common'r."

Satō winced on hearing the peasant's crude accent.

"Please stand up, all of you. I need to learn how to be more like one of you, and quickly."

The servants stood up slowly. The girl who spoke first approached the wizardess boldly.

"Please come, *tono*."

She led Satō to sit beside her on the bedding. Satō looked at the quilt reluctantly, expecting bedbugs and fleas to scurry off it the moment she sat down, but it too was clean and freshly washed.

"First off, you need to grime yerself. Ye'r not tanned 'nuff, yer skin's too pure. Any fool can see you come from a good 'ouse."

"What do you propose?"

"Lessee… Why don't you rub some walnut juice on yer skin? Not too much or ye'd look like an *oni*. There ain't that much sun now, so it needn't be much. An' maybe some lamp oil if yer don't mind t'smell."

"What else?" encouraged Satō, wondering how many other fugitive nobles before her had been through the same ordeal. The girl seemed experienced.

"Yer need to slouch, like this. See how every'un is bent, that's from carryin' all them heavy bags and such. Yer walk straight, proud. That's a samurai walk. Walk low, don't look at the high-up folk."

"I see."

"An' yer looking mighty grim, if you don't mind me sayin' so. You should always smile."

"How so?"

"If we don' smile, a samurai could think we don' like summat about'em, and that be trouble, so we smile. An' what's not to smile about? Our life's a good'un."

"*Eeh!* You call this a good life?" Satō cried out.

She looked around at the squalid dormitory full of people whose combined wealth was maybe less than a tenth of a golden coin, if that.

"Sure, *tono*, an' why not? As long as we do our duty well, we ain't got nuttin' to care about. T'shrine gives us food and a place to sleep. That's more than we'd'ave in our home village. We ain't be needin' no more than that and we're all in the same boat, so we don't fight or bicker with each other. Ye'll see if yer spend a day 'ere, this life's as good as it gets."

Satō pondered the girl's words for a while.

"What is your name?"

"They call me Ikō, *tono*," the girl answered, still with the same beaming innocent smile.

"And how did you come to live in the shrine?"

"I'm a *kambe*; a payment, like," she proceeded to explain. "When t'news of great famine came from up north, all villages in Saga ran to the priests like 'ens to a cock. Ours was a poor place and t'only thing we could promise to t'great shrines were t'first girl babies born after 'arvest. The famine never came after all, but a deal was a deal. On t'day after the 'arvest feast, me mom bore three daughters in one birth. When we were five, we each got sent to one of t'great shrines – 'ere, Karatsu and Kirishima."

"Have you ever seen your sisters?" asked Satō. The three shrines were quite a distance apart from each other, even for a wealthy traveller.

"Only once, we all came back to t'village for our brother's wedding five years back. But I know them's all taken care of well, just like me, and that makes me 'appy."

"And your parents?"

"Me mom's died a few years ago, but she lived a long and good life, bless her. Me dad perish'd with t'pox when I was but tiny. 'scuse me, *tono*, but I mustn't tarry no more, there's work to be done, always. Ye'll be alright 'ere, *neh?*"

The girl stood up, leaving Satō on the jute quilt alone with her thoughts. The wizardess found her gloominess had disappeared. If the girl managed to stay so merry despite the hardships of her life, what right did Satō have to stay depressed? She was healthy, well fed, a roll of golden coins she'd taken from her father's safe box – a real fortune by any account – tightly wrapped on her stomach. She had friends and allies. Her father was very likely alive, and even if not – such was the lot of a samurai. She would continue his legacy and rebuild the dōjō. Yes, she decided, there would be no more misery. Like Ikō, she would meet her fate with a smile.

There was some commotion outside and the few servants remaining in the room scrambled to the small window to see what was happening. Satō stepped up and they politely let her closer to the opening. She could see almost the entire main courtyard from here, as the servant quarters were built on a low prominence to the west of the main gate.

The High Priestess, accompanied by several other priests and attendants, was arguing loudly with a troop of samurai. The warriors carried themselves very pompously, their rich kimonos gaudily festooned with golden dragons and silver leaves, boasting wealth and prestige. A sign of mallow was embroidered on their collars, and their leader, wearing a wide-brimmed lacquered hat, frantically waved a narrow wooden paddle, the symbol of high status.

"It's *bugyō*, the *Taikun's* magistrate!" Satō whispered, recognising the markings of high office. The magistrate was the highest ranking official in Kiyō, equal to the provincial *daimyo*s.

The servants at the window, and Satō with them, gasped audibly as one of the magistrate's retainers pulled out his sword by an inch. Lady Kazuko halted her protestations for a moment, before renewing them with even more vigour.

At last the magistrate gestured his men to calm down, barked a few more words indignantly and turned away.

The High Priestess watched the officials march away down the stairs then turned her face towards the servants' quarters. Satō could not see her face clearly at that distance, but she could imagine the look of anxious concern in Lady Kazuko's eyes.

Even the Suwa Shrine was no longer a safe place.

Lady Kazuko had barely managed to confront the magistrate at the gate when Nagomi approached her with news that the Westerner suddenly grew very agitated.

"He keeps saying, "Kazuko-hime, Kazuko-hime"," reported the girl.

The priestess pursed her lips. What other unpleasant surprises would this day bring?

It took her priests an hour to find Tokojiro in some tavern by the harbour. By the time she finally called for the Westerner, he had managed to calm himself down.

"It's about my dragon. I didn't think there would be any need to mention this," the boy said apologetically. "We... I was separated from it in the disaster and I had little hope of seeing it ever again. However, I believe it has now been captured – somewhere in this land."

"How do you know this?"

"I have a... link, a mental connection with my dragon. I can tell it arrived on a beach somewhere – to the south of here, if I have my bearings right – and was captured by armed men."

The priestess closed her eyes and prayed for guidance. How could she have missed that? Of course a dragon rider would have a *dragon*. She was silent for a long while.

"This is all too much for me, especially considering the other events... I need to consult the Spirits."

"What other events?"

He does not know, the High Priestess reminded herself.

"Satō's house was attacked – by a man in a crimson robe," she said.

"Crimson robe... you mean – "

"With long black hair and eyes like nuggets of gold, apparently."

She let the news sink in as she observed the boy.

"I must leave this place." He stood up. "I am putting you all in danger."

The boy thinks, the priestess thought with satisfaction.

"Sit down, please," she said. "The shrine is still the safest place for you to be right now, if not for very long. The others are also under its protection. We can think of something together."

"But I need to find my dragon. It can't be kept in a cage for too long. It may even die if it's not taken care of properly. Besides, it... it's my friend."

A friend?

Lady Kazuko glanced at the interpreter. Tokojiro nodded and shrugged.

"Does your… *friend* pose any danger to others while in captivity?" she asked.

"I don't know." The boy shook his head. "It depends on how long it is kept imprisoned, and in what conditions… If it turns – "

There was a word that Tokojiro did not understand and had to have explained by the boy.

"Goes wild, breaks the link with me, its rider. A feral dragon will burn villages, slaughter livestock - kill people… Even a small one, like mine, can be terribly dangerous."

"I have heard enough," said the High Priestess, her hand raised. "We will help you, I promise," she told the boy, "we will find a way, we need just a little more time. Have faith. Make sure you stay out of sight – at all times. I predict further trouble coming our way."

And I don't need the Spirits to tell me that.

At the back of the shrine gardens, in the part most overgrown and unkempt, stood an old teahouse. Funded by one of the *Taikun*s of old, the small square building with walls of unpainted wood and bamboo was the quintessence of simplicity and aesthetics. These days, the High Priestess alone used it for her contemplations. Only she and a few gardeners even knew of its existence. The roof of dark straw badly needed repairing and the tea stove begged for replacement, but it was still the best place to meditate in the entire shrine.

A flock of blue-winged magpies darted, screeching, from among the pink azaleas growing wildly over the earthen walls of the pavilion as Lady Kazuko sat on the narrow veranda overlooking a small lotus pond with a cup of fragrant, frothy *cha* in her hand. She liked the cup. It was covered in a sky-blue glaze, spotted and cracked in a deliberate, yet seemingly random, pattern. She had bought it in Heian, a long time ago. The best potteries in the country were selling their wares on the approach to the great Kiyomizu Temple. An old frail woman had walked among the rich merchants trying to sell just this one bowl. She was blind, and this was the last vessel she had created before her eyes died.

"You have a gift of seeing," the old woman said, touching Lady Kazuko's hands.

"I do," the priestess agreed. There was no point in asking how the woman knew.

"I could tell you this cup is mystic and will aid you in your divinations, but all I can say is that it will hold the *cha* without spilling, and that the glaze will not peel or lose its shine for many years."

"That is as much as I expect from a teacup."

Despite the old woman's words, Lady Kazuko did enjoy making her divinations while drinking from the cup. Perhaps the gentle blue of the glaze helped to clear her mind, or perhaps the amount of *cha* it held was just right.

She reached for the small round bamboo box and shook it vigorously. A single stick fell out. She picked it up and smiled. Forty-four - life is a game of *shogi*. All success depends on cunning and strategy.

The sticks were just a toy, of course, a souvenir from the Qin district, but in the shrine, where the air itself was permeated with spiritual energy, even children's toys could tell the truth. The sticks simply confirmed what she had already learned from all the other divinations - the yarrow, the compass, the bones, the Four Pillars, the Six Planets, even the *omikuji* ribbons... She had spent the better part of the day trying to pierce the veils of fate and, of course, she had visited the Waters. The Spirits were most obliging, providing her with many detailed visions, but little guidance as to which of the futures was the most probable one. It was often a problem with the Waters of Scrying. Only very rarely were they as straightforward as when they had presented Nagomi with her first prophecy. And clear answers were what she needed most on this day of decisions.

She could still have given away the foreigner to the authorities. She could say he had been brought to the shrine against her will, that she knew nothing about it. None would dare question the word of a High Priestess, not over that of a drunken unemployed interpreter and two children. This would be the clever, rational solution. The shrine would be safe, her duty to the *Taikun* fulfilled; but she did not need the bamboo sticks or twigs of yarrow to see that the boy's arrival was no accident. One did not give away the gifts from the Gods.

She had had ample time to observe the foreigner, ever since she had requested his presence at the shrine. The circumstances of his arrival, as reported by Nagomi, piqued her curiosity. Then the blue ring on his finger caught her attention - a shard of sapphire stone, like the ones Nagomi saw in her vision. The boy said at first it was just a gift from his grandfather, but then admitted that it, too, had come from Yamato. A coincidence? The High Priestess knew there was no such thing when it came to divination. The other parts of the puzzle started falling into place. The crimson robed enemy assaulting Satō's and Nagomi's houses, and now the boy's *dorako*...

The mightiest will fall, remembered Lady Kazuko. She was bound to serve the Edo court with wisdom and advice. In exchange, the shrine was given protection from the domain lords and city magistrates. But the prophecy was older than the castle of Edo, and it concerned more than just the *Taikun*. The priestess had to consider the fate of all Yamato before making a decision. It was a heavy burden, but she was prepared to carry it.

Where did the foreigner come into all this? Would this boy bring the darkness upon Yamato, or deliverance? Was he just a harbinger of doom?

The situation required a decisive unorthodox solution.

"Cunning and strategy," reminded the bamboo sticks.

The High Priestess lifted her head and looked towards the top of the mountain, where the forest was the darkest and most dense. Sudden understanding dawned on her. For a moment she had gained a prophetic vision of the threads of Fate, all converging on Suwa, the Shrine in the middle of the tangled, glistening spider's web. Nagomi's apprenticeship and prophecies, Satō's escape, the boy's arrival - even Tokojiro's old, forgotten debt of gratitude, all played a part in the greater divine scheme.

The Suwa Shrine was not just a place where all these things had happened, she realised. The shrine itself was the solution.

I need to write a few letters.

CHAPTER II

The shrine bell struck nine times. The door to Bran's room slid away. The red-haired girl's slim, almond-eyed face was lit by a small flickering flame in her hand. He got up and straightened the creases on his new *kimono*, a deep, dark purple silk gown embroidered with the crest of a triangular mountain reflected in the water. The High Priestess had given it to him as a gift, and taught him how to wear it properly.

He pursed his lips and inhaled deeply in unsure anticipation.

"Kazuko-*hime*," the girl said, their limited mutually known vocabulary making it impossible to explain further what she wanted. "*Dōzo*," she added, giving him a rolled up piece of paper.

It was a letter from the High Priestess, written in the elegant, if oddly spiky and angular, handwriting that he guessed belonged to the interpreter, Tokojiro.

Please follow the girl.

Do not fear. Keep your mind clear.

I will help you find what you are looking for.

Trust us, we all want to help you.

This was all very cryptic and vague, and did not inspire trust in him at all. Why couldn't the priestess just send the interpreter to explain what was going on?

A whole day had passed since he had reported about the dragon and nobody had come to see him except the blind girl bringing him food and some strange moustached man who carefully studied his sword and then left without a word. What did they want from him now?

He looked at the girl, but she only stood, smiling shyly, in silence.

"*Dōzo*," she repeated, gesturing him to follow her outside.

They walked down the long winding corridors and then, after putting on uncomfortable wooden sandals, out of the building into the night. The moon was waning, but still bright. The garden was completely silent. They passed through a small gateway leading out of the main compound, walked across the bridge over a stream – here there was, at last, a sound, the trickling of a waterfall and the croaking of frogs – then the path started ascending steeply into a deep forest growing beyond the northern limits of the shrine.

The wood here was different from the cultivated orchard of the inner shrine. It was ancient, thick, not even a sliver of moonlight filtering through the dense canopy. There was something sinister in the darkness, giant gnarled trees brooded over the narrow path and invaded it with their black roots, covered with moss, vine and cobwebs.

"Where are you taking me?"

Bran was losing his patience. He had trusted the girl and the priestess so far, but his trust was running thin. Where was the translator? Why were they taking him deeper into the forest? Cold sweat trickled down his spine – what if they were going to sacrifice him to their Gods? He was, after all, in a temple, and he knew nothing of the religions of the locals...

"Kazuko-*hime*," the girl repeated, and from the helpless look in her worried eyes Bran guessed she knew as little of the purpose of their nightly escapade as he did.

At last they reached the end of the trail, the heart of the forest. By the light coming from the stone lantern standing between two enormous cedar trees, Bran saw a cross-beam gate of cinnabar wood and, beyond it, a little shrine, no bigger than a shed, made of round white stones under a thatched roof. The bargeboards of the roof crossed and formed a fork at the top of the gables. The structure was leaning a bit to the side, the stones covered with thick pillow moss, and the thatch was black with age.

The red-haired girl drew a sharp breath seeing the building. The inquisitive boy – Satō, the wizard's son, Bran remembered - and Lady Kazuko were also there, waiting for him. The boy's arm was bandaged. The High Priestess reached out her hand expectantly.

"What do you want from me? Where's Tokojiro?"

"Tokojiro-*sama dame*."

The priestess shook her head and crossed her arms.

"Forbidden?" Bran tried to guess, "Is the translator forbidden to come here?"

There was no answer. He looked at the red-haired girl. She tried to smile encouragingly, but the concern was still in her eyes.

Lady Kazuko said something and he sensed urgency in her voice. He took her by the hand at last and, lowering their heads under a thick straw rope hung across the entrance, the two entered the tiny shrine. There was barely enough room for them to stand here, slightly bending their backs. It was pitch black, cold and damp. He could hear water dripping somewhere far below. The air smelled faintly of sulphur.

When his eyes got used to the darkness, only faintly brightened by the stone lantern outside, he noticed a flight of steps carved into the rock, leading downwards, damp, slick and coated with lichen. Somehow he managed not to slip and tumble down, slowly following Lady Kazuko. Soon they reached a vast underground chamber filled with smoke and mist.

There was a wide lake at the bottom, its waters sparkling and shimmering with their own pale light as if the moon was trapped underneath the surface. The blue light dispersed on the whirling mist, carving fantastic shapes from the shadows. The smell of rotten eggs and ammonia was now almost unbearable. The rocks around the pool were coated in fine yellow powder.

Bran glanced at the priestess nervously.

"What now?"

She made a gesture he did not understand at first, but when she repeated it he realised she wanted him to disrobe and enter the water. This was not another hiding place. There was to be some kind of ritual performed on him, but the priestess was frail and unarmed, he couldn't imagine her wanting to harm him. There was something in the old woman's eyes that made him believe her good will. If only they could somehow communicate… There was only one way to learn exactly what it was she wanted to do with him on that mysterious night - obey the command and see the ritual through to the end.

Bran cast the dark robe to the floor and undid the loincloth. He was naked, but not cold. The warm mist surrounded and caressed his body, as if it had a mind of its own. He stepped forwards and touched the surface of the water with his toes. It was bubbling and hot, almost as hot as the water in the *Oyū* bath. He looked at the priestess and she nodded. He took another step. The stone bottom of the pool descended steeply and before long he was submerged up to the chest.

The experience was not altogether unpleasant. His muscles relaxed, his joints lost their stiffness. He could sense underwater flows and currents warming his thighs and calves, streams of heat emerging from cracks in the bottom of the lake. He stepped deeper and the water covered his shoulders. He inhaled deeply.

The mist around him became denser and thicker, now milky-white. The thicker it became the deeper breaths he had to take and the more of it he took into his lungs. He was starting to feel nauseous, and turned around to come out of the pool before it was too late. The priestess observed him intently, but made no move.

Suddenly the mist whirled around him again and some shapes appeared in the fumes, wisps of thicker yellowish smoke. For a second he thought he saw a human face looking at him curiously. Then another appeared, and now he was certain - there were eyes gazing at him from the steam, faces of all shapes and sizes, small, large, narrow and round, gentle female ones with sad eyes and fierce male ones frowning under bushy eyebrows - dozens of them, swirling around in silence, crowding and pushing each other to get nearer.

Some of the faces then grew necks, shoulders and arms. The hands of smoke started touching him, stroking and poking his flesh. He yowled as wandering fingers pinched him on the back, on the shoulder. He was surrounded by a crowd of hands, a forest of palms, now scratching and punching each other to get closer, and some of the scratches and punches would reach him by mistake. "Stop it!" he wanted to say, but the mist had enveloped his head and mouth, making it difficult to breathe or speak.

He was terrified. He could not get back to the shore. The ghosts were pushing and pulling him around in a whirlpool of limbs, fighting for the prize of a young body. He noticed the female faces had now gone from the immediate vicinity, as stronger, more virile Spirits of men took their places in the front. Some of the ghosts procured weapons of smoke and fog, swords of mist, spears of steam, and started fighting each other in a manner of warriors on a battlefield. Misplaced blows fell on Bran's arms and head. He raised his hands, defending himself from the strikes, and closed his eyes...

As suddenly as it had started, the chaos stopped. Bran opened his eyes. The ghosts were still there, a troop of grizzled warriors armed to their lucid teeth, but they were no longer fighting. The throng parted, making way for somebody coming in from the darkness - a Spirit of a huge man in full armour, wearing a masked helmet with a fan-shaped ornament. In his chest stuck an arrow, still trembling as if it had been shot mere seconds ago. The Spirit raised a great, narrow-bladed halberd and pointed it in Bran's direction. Other ghosts bowed in respect and pulled back.

The warrior Spirit roared and lunged towards the dragon rider. Bran's mouth and eyes were forced open by an unseen power. The Spirit transformed into several wisps of white smoke that entered Bran's body. The boy felt an exquisite pain, as if molten lead was poured down his mouth, nostrils and ears. He wanted to scream, but he couldn't.

After what seemed like an eternity, the High Priestess climbed up the stone stairs and out of the shrine carrying the Westerner's limp unconscious body on her back. Immediately, Nagomi jumped to her aid and, with Satō's help, took the burden off the woman's shoulders.

"Did it work?" she asked.

She didn't exactly know what was supposed to work, or how.

"We won't know until dawn," replied Lady Kazuko, catching her breath.

"Why, what happens at dawn?"

"Patience, child, you'll see for yourself. Until then, we must wait and pray. Let's take him back to the shrine then beg the *kami* for a happy outcome."

Nagomi helped carry the boy's body down the hill, through the dark forest and quiet garden. It seemed lighter than what she remembered from the beach.

"Take him to my quarters," the priestess commanded.

They laid the unconscious boy on the straw mat floor in the Crane Room and sat beside him. Lady Kazuko closed her eyes and started chanting a monotonous droning invocation to the *kami* of Suwa. Nagomi joined her quietly, still casting worried glances at the Westerner.

"What is going on, Kazuko-*hime*?" she asked at last, when the chant finished, "what happened in that cave?"

"I'll tell you in a moment, but let me start with what happened yesterday. This will help you understand why I had to do what I did."

"You mean the magistrate agents," said Satō.

"Yes. They came to search the shrine for a harboured fugitive. Luckily, the *bugyō* made a mistake – he came without a proper warrant, so I could refuse his request and buy us a little time. However, when he's back with the *Taikun's* seal I will have no choice but to let him in."

"The magistrate should be investigating my father's disappearance, not chasing after harmless Westerners," Satō said, clutching her fists.

"How did they know Bran-*sama* is here? Who betrayed us?" asked a worried Nagomi.

"I'm afraid they were not looking for the boy. They were looking for you, Satō. Your family has been outlawed. *You* are now a wanted fugitive."

"*What?*" Satō cried out.

The boy stirred on his bed and moaned.

"I'm sorry," she said, remembering her manners, "but... I don't understand..."

"I'm not exactly sure what is going on here, either," the High Priestess admitted. "Perhaps the magistrate decided to use this opportunity to finally get rid of the Takashima family... They claim that your father perished through his unlawful experiments and you, as his heir, are equally dangerous."

"At least the boy is still safe," Satō said, biting her lip.

"But you're not. I told them you have already left the shrine in search of your father. This is what you will do today, at any rate, before they return."

"Today...?" The wizardess looked outside. It was still dark, the sky in the east slowly turning grey. "But, I don't even know where to go – what to look for..."

"And you will take Bran-*sama* with you," continued Lady Kazuko, "he will help you and you will help him."

"How can he help me – he's just a lost boy," Satō scoffed, "and he'll be slain the moment he steps out of the shrine."

"He may be lost, but there is a reason why he became lost here, of all places. This is not the first time his kin has met with the man in the crimson robe. He told me his grandfather met a similar being once before."

"So he came here because of the crimson robed man?" Nagomi guessed, trying to make sense of the fast-changing events.

"That I don't know, but there is more. If it was only a matter of hiding from the man in the crimson robe, or the authorities, I believe I could manage this without going through today's ordeal. But the boy must leave the shrine and the city. There is something he must go looking for."

"What's out there that's so precious to him?"

"The boy's *dorako*."

"The beast? It's *here?*"

Satō could not contain herself again, rising from her knees, almost standing up with excitement.

"That's what the boy said. He can somehow sense the creature coming. He says it landed somewhere south of the city."

"*Monsters from without*," whispered Nagomi. Lady Kazuko gave her a sharp warning look.

"*Eeh?*"

Satō turned to her friend.

"Nothing," the apprentice replied quickly and shook her head.

"South… Father told me to go south if anything happened to him," said Satō, now remembering her own urgency. "Kumamoto, Kagoshima… If our family still has any friends left, that's where they would be."

"You have been brought together by Fate," declared Lady Kazuko prophetically. "I have meditated on this for long hours and I am now certain beyond any doubt. The boy, the dragon, your father, the Crimson Robe, the strange items in the boy's box… You must venture south together, to find out the solution to this puzzle."

"But how?" Satō still doubted. "Are we to wrap his face in bandages and pretend he's a leper? Are we to mime our way throughout Yamato?"

Before the High Priestess could respond, the first ray of dawn pierced through the latticed paper window. The Westerner stirred again, violently this time, agony twisting his face.

"It has begun," said Lady Kazuko. "Now you will have your answer. Observe!"

He dreamt of a battle, a siege of a great stone castle overlooking a raging sea, with walls smooth and curved, rising high towards the clouds. Horsemen charged against the sallying defenders with long swords and great bows and arrows. Footmen in black armour scaled the walls, rectangular banners flying on their backs. Bronze cannons roared, spewing cannonballs over the battlements.

A Bataavian man-o'-war of ancient design sailed up to the castle. A terrifying broadside from its guns shook the walls to their foundations. Still the defenders stood strong, jeering and mocking the hapless assailants for asking the barbarians' help.

The final charge, one last push against the keep was his last chance to prove himself as an apt commander before the *Taikun* relieved him of his duty. All men were ordered forwards, all guns screamed in unison. The assault was exhilarating in its totality, a formidable rush of battle fever. They climbed past the first rampart, the second, reached the third…

A stray arrow buried itself in his chest. He fell off his horse. His men rushed to him, but it was too late. A retainer leaned over to listen to his final words - the death poem of a dying samurai.

> *"Among the bullets,*
> *At the start of the year,*
> *The name of*
> *Scattered flowers remains*
> *The only certainty."*

Satō was the first to notice the transformation.

"Look at his face!" she whispered, astonished. "What – "

Lady Kazuko silenced her with a raised hand then leaned over the boy.

"Now is the crucial moment. Everything hangs in the balance."

The Westerner's face started melting and changing. His features rounded, his eyes narrowed, his nose became shorter and wider, his skin pale. There was a faint creaking of bones and strained ligaments. The boy squirmed in pain, but did not wake up. Nagomi turned her eyes away, unable to look at his suffering. At last the metamorphosis was complete, and on the bedding lay not a Western boy but a Yamato one, not unlike any of the boys she knew from the streets of her city.

"It's not over yet," the High Priestess remarked quickly. "We must pray that the Spirit who is in Bran-*sama*'s body does not overwhelm him and take over. The boy is strong and the power of his will is great but anything may yet happen at this point."

She chanted another invocation. Her hand resting on the boy's forehead glowed up with white light and the Westerner started grunting in his sleep.

"He's waking up," Lady Kazuko noted. "Satō, dear, would you call for Tokojiro-*sama*? He should be waiting in the common room."

"Yes, High Priestess."

The wizardess stood up, cast a confused glance at the boy's transformed face and disappeared outside.

"I'm sure you have noticed the significance of the events we spoke about today," the High Priestess said.

"The Prophecy," Nagomi answered, not looking at Lady Kazuko.

She was focused on the unconscious boy, trying to understand what had just happened. The transformation was like nothing she had ever heard about. She had no idea the High Priestess was in possession of such power.

"Things are happening much faster than I expected," continued Lady Kazuko. "Bran-*sama* and Satō must leave the shrine and the city - that much is clear. I will have Tokojiro-*sama* accompany and assist them, but what shall we do about you?"

"Me...?" she asked, looking back at the Priestess.

"You were there when the boy fell from Heavens and I believe your visions from last year portended his coming. It is obvious you too are greatly involved in this matter. But their quest is a dangerous one and I cannot put this burden upon you against your will."

"Oh, I understand." Nagomi lowered her head Her heart sank. When the High Priestess had spoken of Satō and the boy venturing upon a journey south, she naturally imagined herself accompanying them. Had she been expecting too much?

"Of course, if my duties to the shrine…"

The High Priestess scoffed.

"There are many ways to serve the *kami*, child. No, I don't mean you are to stay here when your friend embarks on a perilous mission, but it is something you must choose to do of your own accord."

"Oh, Kazuko-*hime*!" Nagomi said, lifting her eyes in renewed hope. "Need you ask? Of course I will go. Wherever Satō goes I will follow. If I am allowed, of course," she added hastily.

"You have my permission, child, and I'm glad you've agreed. The quest could prove impossible for just Satō and the boy. With you, it will be merely difficult. They will need your protection."

"*My* protection? But… they are the warriors, the wizards. They have swords and magic. I can only heal …"

"You can do much more than this. There are perils that cannot be subdued by steel or spell."

What does she mean?

"I will do what I can – if there is anything I can do."

"You can be yourself, for a start," the priestess said with a smile. "Satō will need your cheerfulness, and Bran-*sama*…" She turned her head towards the door.

"I can hear Tokojiro-*sama* coming. Could you leave us alone for a moment?"

CHAPTER III

He winced, opening his eyes. His face felt sore, tense, and there was something wrong with his vision, although he couldn't pinpoint what. He was lying in the Crane Room, the High Priestess and the interpreter, Tokojiro, sitting by his side staring at him intently.

"Why are you looking at me like that?" he asked the interpreter.

Tokojiro glanced at the High Priestess. Without a word she produced a small, round, mirror of polished bronze. He looked into it warily and then dropped it.

"*By Owain's Sword!* What... What trick is this...?"

The face in the mirror was not his - flat wide nose, narrow eyes, pale-yellow skin, high angular cheekbones. It was the face of a Yamato man. He knew now what was wrong with his vision. He was used to seeing the tip of his hooked Roman nose in the middle of his face. It was gone. He touched his skin. It felt alien, flabby, soft.

"What is this...?" he said, still in shock.

"You have asked me for help."

Tokojiro translated Lady Kazuko's words.

"If you want to seek your *dorako* throughout Yamato, you will need more than just a good disguise. Your current appearance is that of one of the Ancestors in the Cave of Scrying. I trust the ritual was not too painful for you."

"Seek my..."

This wasn't what he had in mind at all. When he had asked for help, he hoped the priestess would use her contacts to expedite his transfer to Dejima or at least let the Bataavians know of the danger posed by Emrys. He never considered actually *travelling* across the unknown alien land in search of the dragon. Certainly not looking like this...

"Can I – can I change back?"

Lady Kazuko smiled encouragingly. "Why don't you try?"

"How? I don't know..."

"Remember how you normally look. Focus your will. The change will come."

It wasn't easy to remember his own face. Bran did not yet shave, so he had little reason to be looking in mirrors. Even though he tried his best, nothing happened at first, but then several muscles in his jaw crackled and moved. He cried out with pain and surprise.

"It hurts," he moaned.

The transformation continued against his will, muscles and joints slithering underneath his skin like living creatures.

"It will get better in time," Lady Kazuko said, leaning over him and touching his face, "so I've read."

Her hand was warm and soothing, but her words were not.

"You've *read*? Then this was something you had never done before?"

"The ritual of the Caves had not been performed since the Civil Wars," the High Priestess admitted with slight embarrassment. "The Spirits in those days had turned... belligerent. It was getting difficult to conduct the ritual peacefully."

Spirits? he thought, trying to understand. *Ancestors? What kind of magic is this? What happened to me in that cave?*

"But you knew it would work for me?" he asked.

"I had prayed it would, but there was always a risk."

"Why didn't you warn me?"

"You told me the *dorako* was your friend. Would you not have faced the risk for a friend's sake?"

Bran thought carefully about the answer. Yes, the priestess was right. What good was notifying the Bataavians? Emrys was *his* dragon, *his* responsibility. He had to find it on his own.

"I would," he admitted at last.

The priestess's face wrinkled in a gentle smile.

"Remember about how you feel right now. Remember this conviction. It will help you go through the hardships of the journey."

Hardships?

"Your face has returned to normal."

The priestess presented him with the mirror again. It reflected his round, jade-green eyes in a Prydain, lightly olive-toned face.

"Try not to do that too often. If you forget to transform back and are seen in public, your life is forfeit," she warned him, and clapped her hands twice.

The door slid open and the two familiar youths came in.

"Now, I believe some introductions are in order." The High Priestess gestured to the two. "You will, after all, travel together."

"We will?"

Bran blinked. How much of this had the woman prepared beforehand? Was it really fine to trust her?

The boy approached first, looking at him slightly suspiciously. He bowed deeply and spoke in a bright tinkling voice. The interpreter tried his best to translate the formal noble manner of the boy's speech.

"I am Takashima Satō. My father is Takashima Shūhan, son of Takashima Shirobei. I am the heir to the Takashima-Ryū School of Western Magic. Pleased to make your acquaintance."

Bran nodded. School of Western Magic... Lady Kazuko had mentioned there were wizards in Yamato and Satō's father was one of them, but a whole *school?* Was Satō a wizard as well?

He looked at the red-haired girl.

"Itō Nagomi…" she said, shyly, "daughter of Itō Keisuke. I'm the apprentice here in Suwa, training to become a priestess. I was with Satō when we found you on the beach…"

Bran bowed back.

"I am Bran ap Dylan o Cantre'r Gwaelod." His name sounded strange to his own ears. "Graduate of Llambed College of Mystic Arts, dragon rider."

"You will all need new identities," declared Lady Kazuko, "and disguises – except Bran-*sama*, of course, he's already as disguised as is possible for a man…"

"Wait," Bran said, raising his hand, "this is all happening very fast, I need time to…"

"I'm afraid there is no time. You must leave today."

"*Today*! But…"

"We don't know when the magistrate will return with a search warrant, how long your *dorako* can stay in captivity. This all means our time is short – very short."

"*The magistrate*? I don't understand any of this."

With Lady Kazuko's permission, Tokojiro quickly explained to Bran the arrival of the magistrate officials at the shrine. The news shook him. Focusing on his own problems he had forgotten of the risk his presence was posing to the others. He glanced at Satō's arm injured arm; the boy was hurt because of him. And the High Priestess – what could happen to her if she was discovered disobeying the laws of the city? He still did not fully understand the situation, but he could clearly sense the overwhelming sense of danger.

"Now you see why we must hasten," the High Priestess said.

"Still – " he replied slowly, hesitating, "is it really safe for me to go outside? I may look like one of you, but I can't yet speak your language, don't know your customs…"

"You have sworn the vows of silence," declared Lady Kazuko, and Bran again wondered how much of this she had planned ahead. "Tokojiro-*sama* has agreed to come with you – as translator and guardian."

"Guardian?"

Bran looked at the young interpreter doubtfully. He noticed Satō doing the same.

"I have the reputation of being as skilled with the sword as with the tongue," Tokojiro said, bowing slightly and smiling. He then repeated it – Bran guessed - in Yamato, for the benefit of incredulous-looking Satō.

"Let us pray your reputation never needs to be tested," said the High Priestess. "If you should encounter on your journey anything you're not capable of dealing with, send word. As long as I'm alive, Suwa will assist you to the best of its abilities. Now, let's not dwell too long on this. Bran-*sama*, a bath is ready for you."

Bran agreed, still a little dazed. He was conscious of the smell of sulphur and sweat that his body emanated and for some reason he was growing increasingly ashamed of it. Nagomi and Satō bowed and left the room hurriedly. Bran stood up, his head spinning slightly, and headed for the door.

"You will need to tie your hair in the samurai manner," Tokojiro said after consulting with Lady Kazuko. "I will help you with that, and with the proper way to walk. Playing dumb will only get you so far if you don't learn a few basics."

What's wrong with the way I walk now?

"*Hai* – yes."

"I'm sorry everything's so sudden," the High Priestess said, pursing her lips. "I know it must be difficult for you."

"It's fine," he replied, though he wasn't certain it was. "I understand it is for the best."

"I'm glad somebody thinks so," she said.

He made sure all the elements of the dark kimono were properly adjusted, the mountain crest on his shoulders – he was now a member of an *Aoki clan*, he reminded himself, like the man whose kimono he was wearing – in plain view. He then felt to see if the newly tied knot of hair at the top of his head was in place, buckled the leather satchel tightly and thrust his Prydain sword into the silk sash. The metal scabbard was painted black and the shrine blacksmith – the moustached man from earlier – had prepared a rough replacement hilt, a long wooden handle wrapped in black cord, that made the cavalry blade look almost like the swords he had seen other Yamato men wear. The proudly sculpted dragon-shaped handgrip, far too elaborate for the simple local style, was hidden in the satchel.

He was trying to wrap his mind around what was happening to him. His face and body changed. He traced the still unfamiliar features with his fingers. The intricacies of the magic involved evaded him – maybe he would understand it better if he knew thaumaturgy. The transformation was perfect, seamless; after the initial odd sensation had passed the new face felt as if it had always been there.

His thoughts... There was something going on there too, something the priestess had not told him about. When he had been given a bowl of breakfast rice, after his bath, his fingers reached for and deftly grasped the quaint bamboo chopsticks. His hand brought morsels of food to his mouth without hesitation, without mistake.

The many-layered robe felt much more familiar than before. The bowing seemed more natural than handshaking. *Something* was happening to him, and he wasn't sure he liked it. The High Priestess didn't know all the details of the ritual. What if the Spirit within was slowly taking him over?

He looked out through the door at the pouring rain. There was no more time to linger. According to Lady Kazuko's plan, Satō, Nagomi and Bran were to leave the shrine one after another at intervals and meet inside an inn at the bottom of the long stairs. Bran was to go last, accompanied by Tokojiro. The interpreter waited impatiently outside under the grey-tiled eaves. It was their moment to leave.

The dragon rider gingerly touched the cold red scabbard of Satō's sword, lying on the straw mat floor. As the Yamato boy was disguising himself as a commoner, he could not bear a weapon – it was decided that Bran would carry it for him. Bran had already noticed that most noblemen in Kiyō walked around with two swords at their belts, so it made sense for him to do so as well. Curious, he pulled out the blade for a few inches. It was of damascene steel of great quality, razor sharp, with a rich hardening pattern and a blacksmith's signature carved near the circular guard.

His Prydain weapon, a sturdy heavy blade of ancient design, was more a mark of his graduation from the Academy than a martial tool. A proud sign of an age-old legacy going back ten centuries to the times when wild dragons roamed the land and brave warriors stood in their way, and later, when dragon riders flew to battle alongside regular horse cavalry against humans cast in steel and mail. A little more than a decorative piece of iron, although the edge was still sharp enough to cut through muscle and bone. Yes, it could maim and, in skilled hands, kill. The runes carved along the fuller shimmered with gentle magic at the touch. They enabled the sword to break through magical shields and armour. Bran was taught how to use it to hack and slash with great force, like a carving axe or, in a bind, thrust.

A sword was never the primary weapon of the dragon rider – Soul Lance against the scale, magic against the shield, dragon against everything else. This was what the Academy had taught him. Other than the symbol of prestige, the sword would only be used in self-defence, when all else failed. Some young riders even went as far as to forgo the sword and replace it with a lightning pistol or pneumatic rifle. They would certainly prove more useful in this age of mistfire and thaumaturgy.

Looking at Satō's sword Bran recognised a weapon designed with just one purpose in mind – to kill a man with a single, fast, precise strike. It was sharp enough to cut through a falling piece of paper. It was well balanced, swift and strong, flexible enough not to snap and hard enough not to bend. The steel was of fantastic quality, the craftsmanship involved incredible – but there were no ornaments on the hilt other than a butterfly crest on the handguard, no superfluous carvings on the scabbard. This was the product of a culture that still esteemed swords as the main armament of a warrior, and knew their value. The boy was certain the blade could easily slash off a man's arm, leg, or even, with enough skill and strength, a head. But there was no magic about it. A simple *bwcler* would hold the deadly edge back. This was the most interesting bit of information, and Bran made sure to remember it well.

He thought again of the two men duelling in the streets of Kiyō and wondered whether Satō had also been trained to so ruthlessly destroy a human life. He must have been. The Yamato boy was of a soldier's age and bore the sword effortlessly. Admiring the blade, Bran was glad to have its owner on his side.

I owned a blade like this once, he thought. *It's a Matsubara if ever I saw one.*

"No, I didn't," he corrected himself immediately, startled. "I have no idea what a Matsubara sword is."

He waited for a moment to see if the strange memory would return but there was nothing but silence inside his head now. He sheathed Satō's sword, stuck it in the sash beside the Prydain blade and went outside.

Dear Tokojiro

How have you been? Edo is cold and wet right now. How's the weather in Kiyō? Oh, how I miss the sun of Chinzei!

Did you like the salted beef I sent you? It's of the same cattle that feed the Taikun's army. I hope it was to your liking. Not as good as Kuma horsemeat, I bet!

Regarding your question — no, unfortunately the court is still not looking for an interpreter of the Seaxe tongue. I assure you, if there is any need I will recommend you for a position at once.

Please take care of yourself,
Einosuke.

Tokojiro crushed the letter in his hand and threw it into the corner of the room in anger. Damned Einosuke - always so nice, always so proper.

"*Did you like the salted beef?*" He mocked the letter aloud. "The pox on you and your beef! Why don't you give me your *job* instead?"

Eight years had passed since the fourteen of them had met for the first time in Black Raven's little class, sitting around the cage in which he had been imprisoned. The mysterious Barbarian, who looked and spoke like a Yamato man, was teaching them Seaxe, the language of Dracaland, a nation of which they had only heard sometimes in Bataavian reports.

"They will come," he had been telling them, "one day. They are already at your doorstep, in Qin, and their ships are big and fast. Not only the Dracalish — others will come too - the Midgardians and maybe even the Gorllewin, all of them understanding Seaxe much better than your Bataavian. Nobody speaks Bataavian except Bataavians. When they all come you will be sent out to greet them, trade with them and negotiate with them. Your ability will be priceless."

They believed him, why not? With his almost-Yamato narrow-eyed face and almost-Yamato speech, he seemed to them like a messenger from the Gods. As the Gods had brought humanity the skill of planting rice and casting iron, so did Black Raven bring new forbidden knowledge to the chosen few. They were his disciples, his apostles. They were young and full of dreams.

And then everything turned to ruin. Black Raven disappeared and his students were accused of aiding his escape — treason of the highest order. Ten of them were executed. Two managed to run away, to vanish without a trace.

Tokojiro fled to the Suwa Shrine, where the High Priestess agreed to hide him until the scandal quietened down. And Einosuke...

Einosuke was already safe in Edo by that time, as the official Seaxe interpreter to the *Taikun*'s court. And there had only ever been one interpreter needed. Despite Black Raven's warnings, the Dracalish never came. Tokojiro, his name blemished by the *bugyō's* accusations, equipped only with the knowledge of an unusable language, could find no employment. His samurai stipend was only enough to keep sobriety at bay. At the age of twenty six his life was as good as forfeit.

Now, though, it seemed the Gods took pity on him. With one stroke of luck, the hapless interpreter had gained a chance to prove his loyalty to the *Taikun* – which would no doubt be rewarded – and humiliate the *bugyō,* who had persecuted him so wrongfully.

He put a straw cloak on top of his brown kimono and walked out into the rain. It was time for him to accompany the Western boy on his strange adventure.

The gardens of Suwa Shrine exploded with mounds of purple, blue, pink and red. All the flowers opened to drink the most of the first strong rain of the season. Bran didn't know the names of most of them. A storm of lilac icicles hung from the eaves, frayed balls of crimson and mauve burst on the bushes below. Late magnolias still clung to the green branches, like great white and scarlet butterflies frozen in time in their finest hour. Spiral fireworks of icy white erupted along the walls and streams. Heaps of otherworldly pinks and reds exploded with a dizzying sweet smell. The air was so dense with fragrance that it turned almost tangible, edible; an air one wished to drink, or bathe in like perfume.

The lanes and avenues of the shrine were being decorated for some upcoming event. Along every path were strung ropes of colourful paper ribbons, fluttering in the wind in their hundreds. There were few people on the shrine grounds at this time of day, in this weather.

At first Bran was apprehensive – he had been hidden for so long, he was used to skulking and creeping along the eaves. Unnoticed, he passed towards the main gate, a great, heavily ornamented construction of gilded wood. He stopped for a moment, ostensibly to admire the intricacies of the carvings, the workmanship involved in the building. In truth, passing this threshold was a difficult decision. Outside was an unknown dangerous world, a world where the only protection he could trust would be his own wit and strength.

There were dragons carved upon the gate, winged and wingless ones, and horses and fish with dragon heads. The craftsmen who had built the shrine seemed obsessed with the creatures. Bran wondered again about the Yamato dragons. He had seen them painted and sculptured throughout the shrine, but no live ones. Then again, he had not seen much of Yamato outside the shrine and the nurse's house, either.

Tokojiro coughed, urging him to hurry. Taking the presence of dragons on the gate as a good omen, Bran stepped forwards. He looked down and his heart froze. Up the stairs marched a troop of armed and armoured men in rich clothes. The *samurai*, Bran remembered the interpreter's explanation, the knights of Yamato. He was to pretend to be one of them. They were led by a grim-faced official in a wide-brimmed lacquered hat, accompanied by a standard-bearer. There was nowhere to hide at the top of the long empty stairs. He had to pass them.

He tried to look inconspicuous, which seemed to work at first – but after a few steps one of the samurai turned towards the boy angrily, waving his little wooden paddle like a sword, and launched into a furious tirade. One of his men drew his weapon halfway out of the scabbard, threateningly.

Bran started panicking. He had no idea what he had done wrong, or how to appease the angry man. He looked at Tokojiro, pleadingly. The interpreter suddenly grabbed the boy by the shoulder and cast him forcefully to his knees. He spoke to the samurai, bowing deeply. Bran caught the word *Karasu* spoken several times – it was the name he had taken as part of his disguise, meaning "Crow", a name written on hastily forged identity papers he had been given by the High Priestess. The men laughed and sneered. One of them kicked Bran playfully then the group moved on upwards.

"Apologies, Bran-*sama*," said Tokojiro when they continued down the stairs.

"I don't understand, what happened?"

"The *bugyō* holds the highest office in the city. Above him is only the *Taikun* and the divine *Mikado*. You have insulted him greatly by not bowing first. Even if you did, you would probably still insult him."

"How come?"

"It's important how low to bow before whom. In this case, a long bow, bent in half, and you wait in this position until he responds."

"Why did they leave us alone?"

The interpreter smirked.

"I told them you were my cousin who was dumb and weak in the head. If I hadn't been with you, they would have cut you down on the spot."

"Cut me…" Bran remembered the two swordsmen, "for not bowing properly?"

"Of course," Tokojiro scoffed. "You must learn these things if you wish to survive. For now, just observe me and play dumb." Saying this, he bowed slightly in the direction of another samurai passing them by. Bran repeated the nod. "That was my equal, a mid-ranking samurai, so we only needed a little more than a nod, and it didn't matter who bowed first. Never bow first to one lower than you, and *never* bow to a commoner."

"How did you know what rank he is?"

"In this case, I knew the man personally, but you can tell by the way men dress, walk, speak, if you're observant. Now be quiet," Tokojiro warned him, as they reached the bottom of the stairs and found themselves at a crowded street running along a narrow canal, in front of what Bran guessed was an inn.

It was Nagomi who found them, as Bran was looking for her fruitlessly. He would not have recognised her easily with her jet-black hair tied in a bun and the simple travelling clothes she was wearing instead of the shrine uniform.

She exchanged a few questions with the interpreter then they went towards the stables.

"The hair..." Bran whispered, reaching out a pointing finger. Tokojiro translated.

"I dyed it with a mixture from Kazuko-*hime*. It would be too conspicuous otherwise."

"I... I liked your real hair better," he said with a honesty which surprised him.

The girl blushed slightly and looked away.

"Let's find Satō."

They could not find the boy anywhere.

"Where is he? The rain is getting stronger."

Bran was growing irritated. He still could not shake off the edginess brought on by the incident at the gate and the nagging feeling of something odd happening to his mind. There were too many people around, too many men, armed and scowling. They needed to move on.

A street boy, all bent in polite bows, clothed in the stained cotton jacket of a commoner, torn at the elbows, approached Bran trying to sell him a tattered paper umbrella. The dragon rider waved him away, but the boy insisted, pushing against Bran with his wares. Annoyed and frightened that he would be recognised, he tried to evade the peddler. At last he looked at the boy's face, dirty under the straw conical hat.

"Sa-!" he started, but the boy put a hand on his mouth.

His face beamed with a wide smile, showing milky-white teeth, contrasting with the colour of his skin, bronzed with soot.

"Good, we're all together now." Tokojiro appeared between them glancing around nervously. "Let's get out of here."

Bran followed the others into the criss-crossing network of narrow streets of the merchant district. They were slowly directing themselves towards the southern borders of the city.

An endless array of tiny shops, workshops and dining establishments lined the thoroughfares on both sides. It seemed almost every house had some kind of mercantile enterprise going on at the ground floor, with sliding doors opened wide invitingly under a piece of green or blue cotton. The whole district was one big market. Nobody here afforded a moment of idleness. Entire families of owners worked in these businesses, from pretty young girls inviting clients in, to shrivelled old grannies dusting the shelves.

The wide avenues lined with peach and plum trees soon gave way to the winding paths of the residential area sprawling over the low hills south-east of the city. The houses here were small and narrow, with open windows and doorways staring at each other across the street. As the hills rose and the buildings grew more scarce, all the roads eventually combined into one highway leading towards a mountain pass. Rows of meagre narrow houses, covered with thin thatch, lined the road.

"Who lives here?" Bran asked.

"Servants, cleaners and seasonal workers," answered Tokojiro. "Those who keep the city working."

Beyond the pass the road descended slowly into a narrow canyon, its banks covered with dark unkempt conifer forest. The landscape here, in the low mountains surrounding the city, was one to which Bran was more accustomed.

"These woods look just like the ones in Gwynedd, my homeland," he remarked.

They didn't speak much as they walked down the road, keen not to draw attention to themselves. There were crowds moving in both directions along the thoroughfare and he had to pause between sentences whenever a stranger was passing them by, waiting until Tokojiro translated his words. All the questions crowding in his head had to wait for when they were alone.

"It seems most of the world between here and Dracaland is covered by jungle or desert."

"You must have travelled a lot?" asked Satō.

"It was my first journey." Bran smiled, pleased to talk about something other than the urgency of his plight. "Six months sailing from the port of Brigstow to Fan Yu in Qin. Twenty thousand miles, over three oceans," he added, proudly.

"I have never even been out to sea," said Nagomi, chuckling at herself. "A Kiyō girl, can you believe it?"

"I have never been farther out than Naniwa," said Satō, "and that was a long time ago, before my father's arrest. I only remember waiting for the tides to change at Tomonoura…"

"I've only been a passenger on the ship," Bran said. "I didn't do any sailor's work. Walking is challenging enough for me. How far do we have to go today?"

There was no answer – the interpreter was silent. The boy looked up. Tokojiro was looking back towards the city, not paying him any attention.

"Sir?"

"Ah, yes, I'm sorry." Tokojiro turned back towards Bran. "You were saying?"

Bran repeated the question and this time it was promptly translated.

"Mogi is our first stop – a fishing harbour on the eastern coast," the Yamato boy replied. "We should reach it easily before sunset if nothing slows us down. Beyond this valley it's just one *ri* downhill, along the river. Lady Kazuko mentioned a *Butsu* temple that can accommodate us."

"I hope she's right," added the interpreter. "there are only few inns in Mogi and the harbour may be crowded today."

"Crowded? Why?" asked Bran.

"Tomorrow is the great festival of rice planting at Suwa," explained Tokojiro, "and there will be many pilgrims arriving to Mogi from the big cities on the other side of the bay."

"I see," Bran said, nodding.

He glanced back to see what Tokojiro was looking at, but could see nothing except the narrow road winding among the trees.

CHAPTER IV

When he awoke, Shūhan found himself lying on a cold stone floor in a straw-padded chamber. The setting sun's red light penetrated through a narrow window fortified with sturdy bamboo bars. He was gagged with a piece of cloth, his arms and legs tied tightly with a single length of rope, his fingers bound stiff to bamboo sticks so that he could not cast even the weakest of enchantments.

The burn wounds he had suffered from magical energies and the dagger cut in his side had been treated roughly to ensure he would not die, but not enough to diminish the pain. He was stripped to the loincloth and shivering from the cold.

A door opened and into the cell came his adversary in the long crimson robe, hair tied neatly in a ponytail. His face was gaunt and pale-yellow like old paper, once handsome but now twisted perpetually in a mocking scowl. A crest of a black eight-headed serpent adorned his chest. He crouched before Shūhan with a mocking smile. The wizard winced at the strong odour of blood and death surrounding the creature.

"That was quite a trick you pulled off there. I had to port us out of the city to break down your defences. Almost ruined my plans, that."

Shūhan closed his eyes, relieved. He had bought Satō enough time to reach safety.

"But I've got you, and that should be enough. I'm sure you can tell me everything I need to know. Don't look at me like that!" the man protested. "We are both noblemen. I won't dishonour you with torture. I don't need to torture people to learn their secrets," he continued, his smirk revealing sharp, blackened teeth. "At least not anymore, not since I have my Tetsu."

He rose and called out. A creature of nightmares stepped slowly and hesitantly into the cell. It was clad in the orange robes of a *Butsu* monk. Black, parchment-like skin barely covered the bones and joints. Its face was a skull covered with thin leather, with gaping holes where the eyes and nose would be and an eternal creepy smile of gumless lipless jaws. It moved slowly, feeling its way with a claw-like hand. The smell of forbidden alchemy and arsenic surrounding the monstrosity was overwhelmingly nauseating. Shūhan jerked back in horror, but the ropes held him in place.

"Isn't he remarkable?" chuckled the Crimson Robe, guiding the mummy to its place in front of Shūhan. "I found him twenty years ago at Yudono. I didn't even know anyone still practised the art of *sokukamibutsu*. Don't mind him, it will take him a few minutes to warm up," he remarked as the mummy settled uneasily on the floor.

"When alive, he was a celebrated monk at the Chūren Temple. I have observed him for three years. Do you know what they do there? It's really quite admirable. They starve themselves for years, living on nothing but berries and nuts. Then for a thousand days they only drink tea made from the sap of the lacquer tree. That mummifies them from the inside. Imagine the pain! After that, they seal themselves in airtight tombs until they finally die."

"The disciples wait for another thousand days before opening the coffin and venerating the mummy, but I did not wait that long. I opened the tomb after five hundred days, just enough for poor Tetsu to attain the Third Power, the Knowledge of Minds. That's when I turned him into my slave." He patted the mummy with a smile. "It was easy enough, as he was already dead anyway!" He chuckled, boastfully. "It looks like he's almost ready."

Shūhan looked at the creature before him with deep compassion. Here was a monk of such rare piety and devotion that he had managed to fully perform the deadly *sokukamibutsu* ritual. If left undisturbed, he would no doubt have become a living incarnation of *Butsu* and now be venerated in a temple of his own. Instead, the wretched creature was suspended halfway between mortal life and Enlightenment, a fate a hundred times worse than simply dying.

As he reflected on the sorry state of the monk, the wizard felt a probing presence in his mind. He could do nothing about it. The mummy stared at him with the gaping eyeholes, reading his every hidden thought with such ease as if his mind was an open book.

The Crimson Robe spoke again, this time addressing Tetsu.

"Where is the *Gaikokujin*?"

In his head, Shūhan saw a kaleidoscope of random scenes from the recent past as the mummy browsed through the memories searching for the ones that would best answer the question. Eventually the wretched monster opened its ever-smiling jaws and produced a croaking struggling sound that could hardly be recognised as speech.

"In a large shrine on the mountain top."

"Suwa. I thought so. What is he doing in Yamato?"

There was another quick browse through the wizard's memories and the creature croaked again.

"He is cast away on a beam of light. Lost. Alone."

"What do you mean *on a beam of light*?"

"It has been said so."

"How odd. Does he know anything more about the *Gaikokujin*?" the golden-eyed man asked, nodding at Shūhan. "Tell me all. What are his plans?"

"It is not known."

"What about the Shard?"

"It is not known."

The monk jolted back as if startled by something in the wizard's mind.

"What is it?"

"It has been said the boy flies on a *ryū*."

"A dragon rider? Now that *is* interesting, but where's the dragon?"

"It is not known. The boy is alone."

"You don't really know much, eh?" The Crimson One leaned over Shūhan. "All right, no point in torturing poor Tetsu anymore. You may go."

The mummy rose slowly and made its hobbling way to the exit.

"Now, that wasn't so bad, was it?" The Crimson One smirked at the wizard. "I think I'll keep you here. If you play nicely, I may even ungag you and we can have a proper conversation."

The wizard was left alone. He was satisfied with how the interrogation had gone. It had been wise of him not to let Satō babble too much about the Westerner. He didn't even know the boy's name. That the dragon rider was hiding in Suwa was obvious. This was where Nagomi lived – and if the enemy knew so much, he must have known about the young apprentice too – and this was where he hoped Satō had escaped. Something was telling him the Crimson Robe would not strike at the shrine. Not yet, at least.

The girl was safe. Nothing else was important.

The sun was almost set beyond the mountains when they finally reached Mogi, nestled between a line of low forested hills and a narrow inlet of the Amakusa Bay. Tokojiro halted for a moment, taking in the view. Even though Mogi was a mere half-day's walk from Kiyō, he had not visited it in years.

What have I been doing all this time?

"What is this blossom?" asked the Westerner, as the road led them down among palm-like trees, heaving under the weight of large, stacked white flowers. The orchard was filled with the low droning hum of thick hairy bumblebees and the intermittent buzz of honey bees, dizzy with the abundance of nectar.

When will his questions stop? It had been like this ever since they left the shrine. The boy was curious about everything he had seen in the city. Tofu curd, *cha*, fish, brooms, fans, even roof tiles and details of clothing. He kept asking, keen to learn new words, new things. Once Tokojiro would have found it endearing. He used to be such a curious boy too, a long time ago. There was no harm in trying to learn about the world, was there?

"*Biwa,*" he explained, sighing, "the town is famous for it. In summer it produces sweet yellow fruit. I believe it came from Qin."

She used to wear it in her hair.

The first two small inns in the village were both full, just as he had predicted.

"There's no point in looking any further," the Takashima girl decided, "it's going to be like this everywhere. Let's go and see that temple."

"I agree," said Tokojiro, absentmindedly. He looked back towards Kiyō again.

The Shiomisaki Temple of the Merciful Bodhisattva was built on a narrow peninsula jutting out into the bay on the south-eastern end of the village. A sandy path through the bamboo grove led to the top of a low rolling dune, overgrown with tall, wind-tattered pines, just as Tokojiro remembered.

The old wooden hall of the merciful Goddess Kannon emerged from among the black pines. One of the orange-robed monks was just finishing his evening prayers. He jumped off the veranda with agile keenness, bowed with hands put together and looked at the travellers curiously.

"We bring greetings from Kazuko-*hime* of Suwa, and humbly request a place to spend the night," said the apprentice girl, bowing.

"From Suwa? Of course, of course, follow me!" The monk led them to the white building. "I'm afraid we cannot offer you the comforts of a guesthouse, but there is a roof above and a straw mat below."

"That will be more than sufficient," replied the apprentice graciously.

Having eaten what small packed meals they had brought from the shrine, the travellers were accommodated in two neighbouring rooms separated by a thin paper wall – the girls in one, Tokojiro and Bran in the other.

"There is only one *futon*," said the interpreter, sliding open a cupboard sunken into the wall, "you can have it."

"You mean a mattress, don't you?" the Westerner guessed. "What do you call the blanket?"

'*Mōfu*," Tokojiro replied, sighing heavily. He was standing by the narrow shutterless window, peering outside discreetly. "*Kakebuton* if it's a winter one."

"So how did you learn Seaxe so well?" the boy asked, preparing his bedding. "Who is this Black Raven of whom you spoke?"

Tokojiro turned away from the window and stared at the boy. Now there was an interesting question at last. He sat down cross-legged.

"I was eighteen when I met him… He came from a distant land across the Great Sea – one we did not know from Bataavian maps. A castaway like you, except that he had been cast off a beach in the northern island, Ezo. He was eventually brought to Kiyō, but along the way he had learned our language well enough to teach us his own."

"Black Raven is an unusual name."

"He was not a usual man. In his land he was a great prince, or so he said. He looked like one of us… He believed his people had come from Yamato. That's why he had sailed here, to find the land of his ancestors. We greatly respected him for that – we, the Yamato, worship our ancestors like the Gods. He was imprisoned in Kiyō, near Sōfukuji, but allowed to have visitors. He would teach anyone who wanted to learn."

"What happened to him?"

"Black Raven's gone," Tokojiro said with a shrug.

"Executed?"

"No, he was too precious to be killed. He just… vanished from his cage one day."

"I could be precious…" the boy said quietly, thinking about something.

Tokojiro laughed, somewhat more bitterly than he intended. If only the boy knew how precious he really was… He stood up and glanced through the window again. "If you'll excuse me, I have to check something outside. You should probably go to sleep now. It would be good to move out as early as possible."

"We don't even know where exactly to go…" said the boy, yawning, "but I suppose you're right. You can have this… *mōfu*, it's a warm night."

Tokojiro accepted the blanket with an embarrassed bow.

He's not a bad boy. More's the pity…

The moon shone faintly from beyond the clouds, but Tokojiro did not need much light to find his way to the back of the white-washed building where they had been accommodated, down a sandy path among the black pines and up a low grassy mound overlooking the sea, where a few monoliths of black stone marked the graves of those who had died in the service of the temple.

He lay a twig of *biwa* flowers on the top of one of them and bowed, silently.

You would not approve of what I'm about to do, he thought. *You'd find a way to convince me I was wrong.*

But it was too late. The wheels had been set in motion. Turning back towards the temple he saw a faint shining dot of a lantern moving stealthily among the trees.

It was a night of unquiet slumber. Bran dreamt of ancient conflicts, of great, multi-tiered castles of whitewashed stone under siege. He dreamt of the samurai warriors charging against stone ramparts, brandishing long sharp blades under a hail of arrows. Of destruction and death, bodies filling up the moat, floating down a river red with blood.

He then dreamt of women in silk flowery robes, their faces painted with white lead and lips daubed with crimson, young and old, all beautiful and eager to please their lord with their dance and song – and their bodies, pale and soft to touch.

He dreamt of falconry and hunting, of drinking expensive *cha* and sniffing precious incense, of reading poetry and writing calligraphy, of tasting refined food and admiring meticulously arranged flowers.

Bran awoke in the middle of the night. For the most part the visions quickly perished from his memory, the details difficult to retain, but the overwhelming feeling of their *reality* remained. These weren't just dreams – these were somebody's memories. And now they became *his* memories.

As a boy of barely sixteen, he had seen only a few dead bodies at family wakes. He saw some soldiers of the Second Regiment wounded in fighting. He had kissed a couple of girls, he had *played* at war. But as the Spirit whose memories he shared in his sleep, he had lived and loved, killed and died – all within a span of one night. Who was the mysterious man from his dreams? A warrior – a leader of men, a general without a name…

His head hurt and he felt nauseous. He shuddered. The night was cold after all. He now wished he hadn't given the interpreter the blanket.

The boy's eyes tried to pierce the darkness to find sleeping Tokojiro, but he couldn't see him anywhere in the room. He was too sleepy and tired to wonder about it. He fell asleep again, and his dreams were again haunted by memories of another man. He was back in some courtly mansion among poets, warriors and philosophers.

It was the last night before the great battle. They all watched him dance a slow methodical dance. He sang a majestic measured chant, the words of which he – dreaming Bran – could not understand.

Saké wa nome nome, nomu naraba

Hi no moto ichi no kono yari wo

Nomitoru hodo ni, nomu naraba

Kore zo makoto no Kuroda-bushi

He finished and gulped a great cup of saké, given to him by an attendant. Everyone cheered. A woman came up to him, smiling, inviting, her brocade robes smelling of rosewood and cherry blossom.

"Shigemasa-*dono*," she said, bowing, before leading him to her bedchamber.

As she lay on a silk futon, he started to disrobe himself, but his arms became entangled in the sleeves of the kimono. He stumbled clumsily over his *hakama* skirt and fell onto the futon. The more he tried to wriggle out, the more the bed sheets and layers of clothes wrapped around him. He wanted to scream, but couldn't, his mouth refused to open. He struggled in panic, unable to make a sound. The woman disappeared somewhere in the darkness.

Bran woke up. He was still bound. He was lying on the straw mat with a rope tight around his hands and legs, a cloth gag in his mouth. Tokojiro was standing above him with a paper lantern, watching.

"Good, you're awake. The *Taikun*'s men should be here any minute."

"Mmrph?" Bran muttered through the cloth.

"Why?" the interpreter guessed. "I may be destitute and unemployed, but I'm still samurai. I'm loyal to my masters, and to the *Taikun*. You're a wanted fugitive; did you think I would let you go simply because some priestess told me to? I just did not wish the magistrate to lay their hands on you. The *bugyō* doesn't deserve such a prize." He glanced through the window. "They're coming. Don't try to transform back to your Yamato face," he advised.

Bran realised he had slipped back to his usual looks while he slept.

"I'm not sure how that will work with a gag in your mouth, and I need a way to prove it's really you."

Bran thought fast, desperately. Gagged and bound he could not invoke the power of dragonflame – even if his link with Emrys was strong enough. The

Soul Lance was also out of the question. He could maybe surround himself with a *tarian*, but what good would it do him?

That he was not yet dead meant he was worth something to his captors. Perhaps he could negotiate... Perhaps Nagomi and Satō could help him...

He had forgotten all about them! He turned his head towards the thin paper wall. Tokojiro noticed this.

"They can't help you. I took care of them in the same way. Don't worry, these men are only coming for you, they're not interested in your companions – although the magistrate might be, I suppose..."

Bran started wriggling desperately, trying to release himself from the bonds, but Tokojiro put his foot on the boy's stomach.

"Please stop. You're only hurting yourself. I know how to tie ropes; the more you struggle, the worse it will get."

"*He's bluffing*," a voice spoke suddenly in Bran's head.

"What... Who is that? Is that you – the Spirit?"

"*A child could get out of these knots.*"

"You – you are Lord Shigemasa, aren't you?" Bran remembered the name from his dreams. "I can understand you!"

"*I am Taishō Itakura Shigemasa of Mikawa*," the voice in his head grew louder and stronger, "*our souls are bound, it seems we can talk without words.*"

"Can you help me?"

"*Only if you let me. Open your mind, so I can reach you - your joints, muscles, limbs... then I can try to release us from this amateur's trap.*"

"How do I do that?"

"*I don't know, Barbarian. I've never done this before. Improvise, but be quick about it.*"

Not really sure what it was that he was supposed to do, Bran imagined himself floating away into the recesses of his consciousness. Immediately, the general's Spirit jumped forwards, pushing the boy's mind even farther back, giving Bran a glimpse of what it felt like to be a ghost attached to someone else's body.

Bran's muscles momentarily went limp, and the rope fell loose off his limbs. Before Tokojiro could react, Bran's body jumped upright, shaking the interpreter off. Tokojiro drew his sword and tried to strike the boy, but Shigemasa, in full control of Bran's movements, reached with his hand, grabbed Tokojiro by the wrist and twisted. Everything happened too fast for Bran to see clearly. Within moments, Tokojiro was lying on the floor, clutching his face. Blood spurted from between his fingers, from a cut dealt with his own blade, now in Bran's – the general's - hand.

"*Thou art no warrior.*" Shigemasa spat out the gag and scoffed through Bran's lips. "*Thou art naught but a craven coward.*"

The door slid open loudly and four other samurai rushed inside, all wearing a mallow crest on their clothes, brandishing long silver swords, ready to fight.

Bran could sense the general calculate his chances. Shigemasa decided to flee.

"*No!*" the boy cried into the void. "We mustn't leave the others alone!"

It was too late. The general kicked his way through the outer wall of thin bamboo and straw, and leapt outside into the darkness.

Something was very, very wrong.

The moment Satō awoke, sensing her wrists and ankles tied up, she understood what had happened. They had been betrayed. Dryness and a bitter taste in her mouth told her they had been given a sleeping herb in their evening *cha* – skullcap leaf, most likely. That's why she hadn't woken when the interpreter was tying her up.

She looked around. Nagomi was still sleeping. The light from a small lantern was seeping from the room on the other side of the paper wall. She could see the silhouette of a man leaning over something – she guessed it was Bran, no doubt bound like they were. The boy must have been Tokojiro's main target and the reason for betrayal, but why now? Why not give them up back in Kiyō?

There was no time to think about such things. She had to set herself and Nagomi free. Luckily Tokojiro was not only a traitor, but also a fool. He had forgotten to gag her. Did he not know that all a wizard needed to perform magic was his mouth?

Without a blade to focus or fingers to weave patterns, all she could do was cast the simplest of spells. She hoped it would be enough.

"*Ijslaag!*" she commanded the elements.

Her hands, the only conduit she could use, were covered with a layer of ice – thin at first then growing thicker as the spell sucked moisture out of the humid air. Her skin was freezing, but so was the rope. The jute fibre became brittle. Her training made her endure the horrific temperature long enough for the rope to reach snapping point.

"*Genoeg,*" she whispered with blue trembling lips.

The ice dissipated. The remains of the shattered broken rope fell from her wrists. She felt around the floor and found her dagger – another reckless omission on the part of the traitor. She cut the knots between her ankles and stood up.

There was a commotion in the room next door. She saw silhouettes of four men jump inside, swords in hand. She saw Bran steal the interpreter's weapon with an amazing agility and then disappear through the wall. The four men followed. Tokojiro screamed in a shrieking panicky voice.

Nagomi stirred awake. Satō cut her binds with the dagger.

"What's going on?"

The apprentice looked around her, numb and bewildered.

"*Get up,*" the wizardess commanded sharply, "we've been attacked."

"Bran-*sama?*"

"He ran away – I think. Stay here. I'll see what's going on."

Satō slid open the paper panel dividing the rooms. The first thing she saw was Tokojiro crawling on the floor, blood pouring from between his fingers smearing the straw mats. A hole was torn in the outer wall. All Bran's things were still there, including the Matsubara sword Satō had entrusted to his care.

She picked it up and pointed it at the interpreter. Tokojiro only now noticed her presence and the tip of the blade aimed at his head. He reached out his hand in feeble defence. An ugly bleeding scar ran right across his face through his left eye – now rendered useless – nose, corner of his mouth and chin.

"No, please... Don't kill me..." he begged, gurgling through blood.

"What have you done? Why? Who are these people?"

Satō spat out the questions in quick succession.

"*Taikun*'s men... I only wanted to... prove my loyalty..."

The wizardess lowered her sword. This was a sentiment to which she, daughter of a samurai, could relate. At that moment Tokojiro shrieked and leapt at her with surprising swiftness. She fell to the floor. The interpreter's one healthy eye looked at her with an odd combination of gratitude and hatred and he scrambled hastily on all fours outside.

Nagomi ran up to her.

"Are you all right?"

"Yes. Quick, he must not get away..."

"What about Bran-*sama*?"

Satō hesitated. They had barely left Kiyō and she already had to make a decision on her own. She glanced at the corridor where the interpreter had disappeared, then at the hole torn in the wall through which the Westerner fled, pursued by the swordsmen. She nodded to herself.

"Let's go."

They hurried through the pine forest, lighting their way with the paper lantern, Satō in front, trying to track the foreigner and the men who had attacked him.

It wasn't easy to follow the tracks in the darkness. Soon she lost all trace of the boy and could only spot the four sets of footprints left by his assailants in the sandy floor of the forest.

She kept thinking of Tokojiro's betrayal. How could they have made such a mistake? How could the High Priestess have trusted the interpreter so blindly? She should have guessed a true samurai would keep to his old loyalties.

It's a wonder we are still alive – but for how long? She shook her head. It was not the time to fall into despair. There was a clear task before her. One thing at a time.

"They separated here," she said, kneeling in the dirt. "I think they lost him as well. He was running really fast!"

Typical Barbarian, better at running than at fighting.

"Where did you learn to track?" asked Nagomi, catching her breath. "I can't see anything."

"My old man took me hunting on Mount Inasa a few times, testing the airguns. That was when mother was still alive and we would..." She stopped talking and raised her hand. *I can hear them*, she mouthed silently, and pointed to her right, from where the faint sound of conversation was coming. *Stay here*, she gestured, and started creeping through the undergrowth.

In the faint moonlight she saw three of the four *Taikun*'s samurai. One was lying dead, his blood staining the sand scarlet. Two others were standing over him, uncertain.

"Nobody told us the boy was good with a blade," said one, looking around warily.

"Don't be absurd, Tendō, he just got lucky," replied the other.

"Are you blind, Saotome? That's a masterly cut." The first one pointed to the dead body with the tip of his scabbard. "Where did he learn to fight with katana?"

"It doesn't matter. There are three of us with Hibiki, and one of him. We just need to stick together."

"And where is Hibiki?" The first samurai's voice was increasingly shaky. "He was supposed to be here by now."

"He'll come, don't worry, and the boy can't be far away. We'll catch him before dawn."

Satō listened to the conversation with increasing amazement. What were they talking about? Bran – master of the sword? It didn't make any sense. He had no samurai training. He may have been a soldier back in his homeland, but she had held his Western sword in her hands – it was a heavy, unwieldy, badly balanced hatchet, there was no way somebody familiar only with that blade could handle a katana with ease.

Suddenly the bushes parted and the fourth warrior appeared in the glade, clutching his stomach.

"*Hibiki!*"

The other two ran over. The samurai slipped to his knees, gasping for air.

Satō could not comprehend what she was witnessing. She considered Bran amusingly helpless, a nice boy who could tell her about dragons, but was generally useless, like most foreigners. It seemed she couldn't have been more wrong.

She slowly crept back to Nagomi who was crouching under a big larch, trying to hide herself as best she could.

"Bran-*sama* is here somewhere. He's alive and free," she told the apprentice, whose face lit up with joy and relief. "Let's try that way."

She had to find him. She had to learn his secret.

CHAPTER V

There was darkness at first, and emptiness. No sensations, nothing to touch, smell or see. He was *nowhere*. Cut off from the reality around him, from his own body, he found himself in a hollow featureless void.

Slowly some shapes began to emerge from the darkness all around him. A red light pulsed in the distance. As the veil lifted, he found himself lying on a vast barren plain of red-brown dust, with a tall spire of grey stone rising on the horizon. It was from the top of this spire that the red light was coming, like the beacon of a lighthouse.

He heard a voice booming, God-like throughout the strange domain - the sound of General Shigemasa's thoughts. Was this how the Spirits experienced the reality? Was this what Shigemasa's world was like ever since his soul fused with Bran's in the cave?

Or was he still dreaming...? There was no magic that could rip the consciousness straight out of one's body and cast it into this empty realm of nothingness. There couldn't have been. It was all a nightmare. Soon he would wake and everything would be back to normal.

Something appeared in the sky, coming from the direction of the tower. A speck at first, bright green against the auburn clouds, it grew into the familiar silhouette of a jade dragon.

"Emrys?"

The dragon landed gracefully on the dust and chirped welcomingly. It seemed real enough... Even the faint smell of brimstone and methane was there. Bran touched the beast carefully. In an instant, he was flooded with images and emotions, just as if he was using Farlink – but far stronger than ever before. The cage, the hunger, the bewilderment... he let go of the dragon and breathed out.

He was beginning to get the idea of what was happening to him. The world around him was, somehow, an image in his mind. The dragon represented the Farlink connection. The pulsating, beckoning red light remained a mystery, but there was no other feature in the landscape. Was this where he had to go to regain control over his body?

Bran looked doubtfully at the jade dragon beside him. Would it accept commands from him, just like the real Emrys? Was there such a thing as a Farlink to the Farlink? He climbed upon the dragon's body as he would normally. Emrys lowered its head and spread its wings ready to fly.

So far so good.

He could hear Shigemasa's loud euphoric thoughts. The general was overcome with joy at having a body of his own again. The red light projected images from the Taishō's eyes upon the auburn sky, the red clouds serving as an enormous screen – a samurai emerged from among the pine trees, sword lowered, unwary. The general cut him down with one stroke, without mercy. Blood stained the sand.

Emrys launched into flight. They were heading straight for the spire of grey stone. There was nothing but the featureless plain before him. If the general was at all able to notice him approach, he was too busy enjoying his newfound perceptions and senses to do so.

A great cry echoed throughout the realm of Bran's soul.

"*Life! How I've missed you!*"

"It's not *your* life!" cried Bran defiantly, surprised by the strength of his voice which echoed throughout the dust plain. "Give it back!"

This finally drew the general's attention. The red light turned straight on him. Shigemasa began to defend his dominion. First, a stone wall rose from the ground between Bran and the grey tower, but he managed to fly over it before it grew to tall. Next, some horrible demonic minion launched from the tower's balcony, a creature of nightmares, creation of a twisted mind, with shadowy body and wings of night clouds.

This was something Bran knew best – aerial combat. He swooped his Farlink dragon towards the creature. Claw clashed against claw and tooth against tooth, but the demon stood little chance against Emrys and its rider. With a thrust of its powerful limbs, the dragon shoved the creature tumbling towards the ground and then dived after it, spewing bluish fire until it made sure the demon perished, its shadowy body razed to ash.

"Is that all you've got?" Bran shouted.

"*No!*"

An invisible shockwave spread from the tower, casting Bran and his dragon away.

"*I have waited for two centuries for this, I am not letting go!*"

A deluge of images and sensations flooded Bran's mind as the general raged, waves of memories and pent-up emotions washing over the boy: painful death from a heretic's arrow; awakening to a ghostly existence in the Cave of Spirits; hopeful expectation that a spy, scholar or poet would descend into the misty sulphuric waters to merge its soul with Shigemasa's; centuries of pitiful existence, after the closure of the caves, shared with innumerable other Spirits trapped for eternity, with no chance of ever solving the riddle of their entrapment, and hesitation when the filthy barbarian had submerged his stinking body into the Waters. Had the general really sunk so low as to possess this long-nosed half-animal, this hateful, devious *Gaikokujin*? Finally an acceptance of fate and firm resolution. He had no trouble exerting his dominance over the other rivals. They were no match for him, the Taishō of the *Taikun*'s armies.

"*The old witch had no idea what she had unleashed,*" Shigemasa said, chuckling boastfully, '*say farewell to your body, Barbarian – I will find a much better use for it!*"

Bran spurred his spectre dragon back into flight. He was not giving up that easily. Suddenly he felt a burning sensation on his hand. The blue ring – it was also here, in this phantom world! But why…? It blazed brighter than ever before. The light grew stronger and soon it was brighter even than the red beam coming from the tower. Bran raised his hand and the ring shone like a little sun on his finger.

"*What – what is this?*"

Bran could sense Shigemasa's bewilderment and pain.

"I'm coming to get what's mine."

"*No… No! You cannot send me back into the darkness – you can't…*"

In the blue light of Bran's ring, the grey tower started to crumble like a melting candle. By the time Emrys had reached the stone bulwarks, it was all but reduced to rubble. Only a single floor around the gate remained standing. Bran bade his dragon land in front of the massive wooden door and banged his fist against it. The gate dissolved into dust.

"*I won't let you – I won't… Two hundred years…!*"

Before entering the gateway Bran turned around and touched the scaly neck of the dragon one last time. He linked through to the real Emrys – the beast was half-sleeping, dormant, imprisoned somewhere far away, but at least it was still alive.

He crossed the threshold of the tower of his mind and the dirty red world around him disappeared.

He panicked at first, fearing something had gone wrong. He was again surrounded by impenetrable darkness. And then he remembered to open his eyes.

The pines rustled above him in the morning breeze. It dawned. He stood up slowly, staggering, dizzy, his right hand still clutching the hilt of Tokojiro's sword.

The air in the forest was cool, fresh and aromatic, smelling of resin and sea salt. Bran's head was clear. He could sense the general very faintly somewhere far at the back of his mind, cursing and thrashing about helplessly. He could feel his shame and despair, but he did not care.

Something rustled in the undergrowth. Bran grasped the sword – it was a bit lighter than his cavalry blade, and oddly balanced. He tried to swing it like he would his own weapon. It almost flew out of his hand. The rustling in the bushes repeated. Bran retreated against a large tree trunk, holding out the sword before him defensively. He summoned a *bwcler* to shield his left hand. Whatever was coming, he was ready.

"Bran-*sama!*"

The apprentice girl ran out of the bushes crying with joy. She stopped a few steps short of hugging him and pulled back, embarrassed. Satō followed warily, looking at Bran with anxiety.

"Good, he's alive," the boy said, nodding with relief.

"W–what do we do now?" Nagomi said. "We have no way to communicate without Tokojiro-*sama…*"

"We'll have to think of something. For now let's try to go back to the temple, avoiding the *Taikun*'s men if possible."

Bran listened to their conversation with increasing bafflement. Was he still dreaming, or trapped within his mind? The youths seemed to speak perfect Prydain. He understood every single word.

"I – " he started.

They turned to him swiftly.

"I comprehend thee."

"How…?" Satō opened his eyes wide. "What magic is this?" he questioned, holding out his sword threateningly.

"I do not know." Bran shook his head. "'Twas the Spirit from the cave – somehow, the ritual must have…"

"Oh, who cares *how*? Isn't it brilliant?" Nagomi clapped her hands. "We don't need an interpreter now!"

"Are you *really* you, Bran-*sama*?" the boy was still suspicious. "Did you cut those samurai who were after you?"

"I understand thy trepidation," he said, suddenly aware there was something odd about the way he spoke. "It was not me who did the slayings, but the Spirit within me. I do not possess the skill with this blade."

He presented the sword to Satō.

"Leave it," the boy said, "I don't want anything that belonged to that traitor."

"We can discuss everything on our way back to the temple," said Nagomi.

"You're right." Satō nodded solemnly. "Let's move. It seems we have a lot to talk about. Oh, and Bran-*sama* – your face…"

"I understand."

Bran nodded and turned around reluctantly to focus on the agonising transformation back into his Yamato disguise.

The warmth with which the monks of Mogi Temple had greeted the travellers the previous day was gone. The head monk stared at them coldly as they emerged from the pine forest.

"You are wanted by the government," he announced, "you have brought violence under the roof of this temple. If it weren't for the debt we owe to the Suwa Shrine, we would not let you go free. As it is, we can only request that you leave promptly."

He nodded at one of the monks, who dropped their travel bags to the floor in silence.

"You will find the boats at the pier. Now go, before I change my mind and report you to the guards."

"Thank you, Sir," said Nagomi, bowing.

Bran also bowed. They picked up their belongings and departed towards the harbour.

"Shouldn't we go back to Suwa?" asked Nagomi as they stood on a low hill overlooking the harbour, trying to decide their next move. "We can't possibly go farther on our own…"

"Why not?" Satō shrugged. Going back was the last thing on her mind. The entire shrine may have been swarming with traitors like Tokojiro. "It's not like that interpreter would have done us any good. He was all talk. He said he was good with the sword, but Bran-*sama* disarmed him in one move."

"Th-that wasn't me," protested Bran.

She stared at him, still surprised that the boy could talk.

"It doesn't really matter," she said, waving her hand at last. "What matters is that we're just as fine without him, now that you can speak our language. The three of us will be less conspicuous anyway."

"Those samurai who pursued me," said Bran, 'shall they not return, with more men? Now they know who to look for…"

"This is why we must move on." Satō was adamant. "The roads back to Kiyō will be swarming with guards by now. We can only go forwards as far away from the city as we can."

"And as far south as we can," reminded Bran, "that is where my *dorako* is."

"You're right," she said, nodding, "let's go get that boat."

It was early morning and there was only one ferry ready to depart in the harbour, a narrow vessel with a single sail and a square of canvas stretched over the deck as the only protection from the elements. A single samurai in a dark purple hooded cloak had just disembarked, paid the fare and hurried into the village without giving the three travellers a glance.

"Can you take us to Kumamoto?" Nagomi asked the ferryman.

"Kumamoto? That's too far for this tiny thing. I can take you across the bay to Shimabara, where the big ferries are," said the helmsman. "In fact, that's just where I picked up that gentleman," he added, nodding towards the fast disappearing samurai.

Satō watched the shoreline fade away as the small boat, barely big enough to fit the three of them, travelled eastwards at full sail. The westerly wind blew strong. The clouds receded a little and the rain stopped.

Of the three travellers only the foreigner was used to sailing. Poor Nagomi, first time at sea, sat on the bottom with her eyes closed, praying, her face a delicate shade of green. Satō made a valiant effort of trying to stay on deck, but, as the little vessel entered the wide waters of the bay and started rising, falling, bobbing and rolling on the high waves, she also had to sit down near the edge of the boat. In the end, the Westerner joined the girls, settling on the wet bench under the canvas windbreak.

The sea calmed down after an hour, and Satō stopped leaning over the side of the boat. Her skin returned to a healthy colour and she could pick up a conversation with Bran. She still could not get her head around the fact that the boy was suddenly speaking fluent Yamato.

"Not even the Overwizard can talk our language so effortlessly."

"I wish I knew how it happened," the boy admitted, "it would be a most valuable secret to any scholar."

"Or a spy," added Satō, observing the boy carefully. The High Priestess had never mentioned he would gain such an ability after the ritual. What if he had understood them all along and only pretended not to?

She realised her stare was rude and turned her eyes towards the west, where the easternmost cape of the Mogi Peninsula, jutting out into the sea like the back of a great whale, was slowly disappearing beyond the horizon. It reminded her of the few sea journeys she had taken with her father and tears started welling up in her eyes. She focused on the more recent past.

"I wonder what he meant," she said.

"Who?" Bran asked.

"That monk, what did he mean when he said they owe the Suwa Shrine a great deal?"

"He means the Sun God rebellion." Nagomi spoke softly without opening her eyes, her lips trembling with nausea. Satō turned to her in surprise. "The priests at Suwa protected the monks and treasures of the Mogi Temple when it was attacked and razed to the ground by the rebels."

"Tell us more!"

Satō moved closer to her friend. She loved tales of old times, even more so if they were bloody and violent.

"That's all I know... I saw this written in the shrine chronicle. It was in the fourteenth year of the Kan'ei era."

"*I remember that year,*" said Bran unexpectedly. His eyes turned from green to black, gazing towards the western horizon. There was a melancholic sadness in his voice. "*The muskets of the heretics poured lead like rain on our heads; their arrows turned the day into night; their spears were like blades of rice in the field. From hamlet to hamlet they went, ravaging the shrines, plundering the altars and melting the sacred mirrors into weapons, saying their God had conquered our Sun Goddess, and all other Gods were just demons in disguise. They burned the temples and slew bald monks by the dozens. A youth of mere sixteen summers led them to their doom – Messenger from Heavens they called him. On these shores the mutineers clashed with the samurai army, overwhelmed them and chased the recreant cravens all the way back to Kiyō.*"

He finished and mused at the waves in silence. At last his eyes turned back to green. The boy snapped back to the present.

"What just happened?" Satō asked suspiciously. If it was just a performance, it was a very convincing one. Perhaps he was telling the truth after all...

"It's..." Bran hesitated. "The Spirit's memories o'erpowered me..."

"Is it dangerous?"

"I... don't think so," he replied.

She sensed he wasn't telling the whole truth.

"What was this vision?" he asked. "Who were the heretics?"

"Those who shared the religion of the Westerners," explained Nagomi.

"The Vasconians," added Satō. "The Bataavians were on our side."

"The Sun Priests!" the boy said. "They had reached even here?"

Nagomi only shrugged.

"I don't know much. The heretic beliefs were banned a long time ago. The rebellion you spoke of was their last stand."

"That Spirit inside you…" Satō looked into Bran's eyes, trying to discern a trace of the alien entity. "Do you know its name?"

"He calls himself Itakura Shigemasa."

The wizardess thought carefully. The name sounded vaguely familiar.

"What else do you know about him?"

"He styles himself *Taishō*. What does that mean?"

Satō opened her eyes wide and gasped.

"*Chief Commander!*"

"I dreamt of leading a great multitude of men to their deaths," Bran said, nodding solemnly. "I thought 'twas merely a nightmare…"

Now she remembered. Itakura was the name of a clan of famous warriors and *daimyo*s from the northern province of Mikawa.

"He must have fought at the Shimabara siege," she guessed.

"It may yet be a good thing that you have bonded with such a powerful and wise Spirit," said Nagomi.

Or very dangerous, Satō tought.

"I would gladly be rid of him," replied Bran.

"You would not be able to talk to us then," Nagomi said and smiled.

"However jarring your manner of speech sounds," added Satō.

"Be it truly so strange to thy ears?"

"It's… outdated, archaic. I suppose it's how Shigemasa spoke two hundred years ago."

Or how a Vasconian spy would know it.

"You can understand *everything* we say, can't you?" the wizardess asked.

"I do, although sometimes it sounds to me…" the boy hesitated, "rude, uncouth. Some words I even feel are… *obscene*."

Satō chuckled. She knew that, disregarding some boyish quirks, she spoke the most ornate style of the language, as befitted a daughter of an aristocrat. She had been taught that nothing ever changed in Yamato. The islands, as the poets, scholars and court historians told about them, were ageless, set in their ways forever. Any transformation, any progress was simply unthinkable. The system imposed by the *Taikun* was supposed to be as unalterable as the sky above and the earth below. This is what everyone had been telling her – everyone except her father.

"Our people have always changed and adjusted to the circumstances," he had once told his daughter, "Since the earliest days. We've learnt from the Qin how to plant rice and grow silk. We've learnt to build houses that withstand earthquakes and typhoons. When the Horse Lords invaded, we had to learn their strategies to beat them back. When the Westerners came, we learned from them anything they were willing to teach us and more – their magic, their technology, we've even tried their religion – but we saw it did not fit our needs… This is how Yamato grew to such greatness – through evolution, not through stagnation, no matter what the courtiers at Edo would want us to believe. The Yamato should be like water, and the *Taikun* had frozen us into ice – but ice can break."

"For now we can pretend it's an accent from Mikawa," she said. "I will try to teach you the modern manner, or you will draw too much attention."

"I shall endeavour."

"*I will try,*" she corrected him, and chuckled again as the boy winced hearing her "uncouth" words. "You can practise with the commoners, they won't know any better."

CHAPTER VI

The boat turned north around the tip of another peninsula, and entered a narrow inlet.

"Be this Shimabara already?" Bran asked the boat's steersman, looking at a rather disappointingly tiny village at the end of the inlet through his telescope.

The device drew the man's attention, and Bran had to explain he had bought it at the great market in Kiyō.

"No, kind *tono*, that's Kuchinotsu. It takes two days to sail to Shimabara and we're not likely to reach another port before the sun sets."

"I trust they have inns there."

"There's a guesthouse by the pier that a cousin of mine runs."

"I see. How very shrewd of thee," said Bran.

The old steersman grinned, exposing his toothless gums. His smile was contagious.

Satō looked jealously at the instrument, but was too polite to ask outright. Bran noticed the boy's stare and gave it to him.

"We don't get things like that at the market," he said, admiring the craftsmanship and power of the lenses. "Keep it safe," he added, reluctantly giving the spyglass back, "in the wrong hands something like this could start a war."

"It's just a small hand-held," Bran replied. "The case has more magic than the spyglass."

"Why, what's in the case?"

"It is made of a selkie skin, so it shall never sink."

He remembered Samuel saying these exact words at the birthday party. His face must have reflected his mood, for Satō asked immediately:

"What's wrong?"

"The man who gave it to me is now dead," Bran replied with a sigh.

"I'm sorry."

"It's all right." He shook his head slowly. "I had only known him a few months. He was one of the crew on *Ladon*."

"What was it like on the ship?" the boy enquired.

Bran rotated the barrel of the telescope in his hand and put it back into the selkie-skin case before answering, slowly and carefully rolling the words of the new language off his tongue.

"Crowded... Dirty... Noisy... Smelly. The food was bad, the water stale. Most of the time, nothing happened. For days and days the sea passed underneath and clouds above, and that was the only change, but then we would get an order and the ship would alter its course. There would be some sea battle or a landing, or just a diplomatic visit, and we would see another part of the world, completely different to what we had seen a few weeks before. My father told me no two harbours look the same."

"That sounds amazing…" Satō whispered.

Bran nodded in silent agreement.

The boat rocked, bumping into the wooden pier.

"*Kuchinotsu!*" announced the steersman.

Bran and Nagomi settled at the guesthouse for the night while Satō had to stay in the servants' room by the stable. At nightfall she smuggled herself into their quarters through the garden veranda.

The night was still young. They drank *cha*, sitting for a moment in silence. At last Satō found the courage to ask the question she had longed to pose ever since she had learned who the foreigner really was.

"Bran-*sama*," she started, "I'm sorry to keep asking you questions…"

"It is understandable," he replied, "I have many questions as well."

"What's it like to fly a *dorako*?"

Bran put down the half-empty teacup and pondered the answer with his eyes closed, remembering.

"Imagine thou… *you* are standing on the top of the highest mountain," he started carefully. "You canst – *can*, sorry, see all the way to the horizon, for a dozen *ri* or more. The fields, the pastures, the forests, a lonely village in the valley… the people and animals below are as tiny as ants. Rivers are as thin ribbons of blue, crossed by ribbons of brown dirt roads. A strong cold mountain wind is howling around you, tugging at your clothes, forcing tears into your eyes. Imagine now that the mountain beneath thy feet starts to move," Bran continued. "All the fields and pastures and forests become splashes of colours, blurred as thou fliest past. The wind grows stronger, but it's not cold anymore – the dragon's breath blows around thee, keeps thou warm. Thou holdst onto the reins as it goes ever higher and ever faster. The mountain is gone and there is nothing but the blue sky all around thee, the Earth a forgotten memory somewhere far below…"

"Can you reach the clouds?" Satō asked dreamily.

"Oh, aye, easily, if it's a day such as today, when they hang low o'er the land. The clouds are cold and wet, like a very thick mist. When the day is cold and overcast, thou could even fly through the clouds for a short while, where there is always sun, but it's difficult for a human to last long at that height; not enough air to breathe."

"How long did you have to learn before you could fly?"

"I was flying with my dragon before I joined the Academy, but that was because my father showed me how and looked after me – when he was not on one of his expeditions, that is. Otherwise thou needst to first learn some navigation and special spells that slow one's fall. One can easily lose one's head in the clouds. When we find my *dorako* I will take thee for a flight," Bran said unexpectedly, and Satō jumped in surprise and disbelief, her eyes growing large and round.

"*Eeh!* Really?"

"Verily," the Westerner said, nodding, "thou art light enough, there should be no trouble, and thou, of course, if thou wishest," he said turning to Nagomi, who also listened to his tale.

The girl smiled and waved her hands.

"Oh, there's no need to trouble yourself. Sacchan's the one who's crazy about *dorako*."

"I sure am! I'm going to dream about them again tonight… but it's getting late. I should go back to the servants' quarters," said Satō.

She forgot about her suspicions for the night. What did it matter if the boy was a spy, after all? Her father might have worried about the intruding foreigners, but she didn't care. All that she cared for was that, thanks to Bran, for the first time in days she dreamt of something else other than the man in crimson robe and her father's agonising screams.

The simple breakfast served at the guesthouse surprised Bran. He was growing used to the strange familiarity with which Yamato began to greet him at every corner since his struggle with Shigemasa. It felt almost as if he had come back to a country where he had been born and raised, after a fifteen-year-long journey to Gwynedd.

This, however, was new. He could not recognise the dishes from the memories he shared with the general. A basket of tiny fish and prawns deep-fried in crispy batter was a taste unknown to him, as were the slices of sweet yellow potato and firm-fleshed orange pumpkin. The rice was too white, the fish too raw and the soy sauce too refined and watery. Everything tasted exquisite though, no matter what it was called or from what it was made. The boy wondered if having the Spirit inside him affected his taste buds as well, or was this food really as perfect as it now seemed?

He was trying not to think too much of what had happened to him back at the pine forest. It was too bizarre to contemplate, trying to make sense of it was like trying to understand a dream. Why was the land of his mind empty, dry and red? Why had the blue sapphire ring appeared in this outlandish scenery, why had it lit up and crumbled the tower of grey stone? He looked at his finger. The stone was calm, quiet, dark. Nothing peculiar about it, he remembered Doctor Campion's words. The ring's appearance in the red darkness must have been merely some figment of his strained imagination.

"Is the food not to your liking, dear guest?" the girl serving the food, the guesthouse keeper's young daughter, enquired with a concerned voice, seeing the straw basket still full of fried fish. "I can bring something else…"

Her extreme politeness towards him contrasted starkly with what he remembered of the *tafarn* wenches in Gwynedd. At first he thought she was kind to him because of his noble status, but he observed she behaved that way to all other guests.

There was nothing here that resembled the sleazy, noisy, dirty western taverns with which he was familiar. The common room was spacious and clean, the guests – mostly – quiet and well-behaved, the food delivered promptly and without fault.

He was awed and humbled by all this civility, until he noticed the sharp swords most men in the inn carried. He remembered the dead samurai he had seen in the street of Kiyō and the warnings of the interpreter. Suddenly the smiles and bows of the guests and the staff no longer seemed as genuine as before.

"We know little of such delicacies in Mikawa," he answered with a practiced smile and a nod.

"Delicacies, *tono*?" The girl laughed coquettishly, partially covering her mouth with her hand, but exposing teeth daubed with black ink – in the fashion he had seen on some women in the city and which repulsed him at first but was now becoming oddly appealing. The long sleeve of her kimono fell loose, revealing a shapely forearm. "It's only some *tenpura*. Surely you eat better food in the north, so close to the capital?"

"Ah, yes, well." Bran coughed. "Maybe in the *daimyo*'s castle, but I come from a small village in the mountains," he bluffed.

"What brings you all the way to Chinzei?"

Bran had no ready answer. He was too busy staring at the girl's impeccably white neckline – surprisingly attractive for a village girl – to think of his new identity. He turned to Nagomi in slight panic – Satō, in his servant's disguise, was not allowed to speak in the presence of "superiors".

The apprentice gave him an odd look before speaking.

"Karasu-*sama* is on a pilgrimage to thank the *kami* for saving his village from the famine."

"Ah, then you've been to Suwa to pray to the Morisaki, god of harvest!" the girl said, beaming approvingly.

"Aye, that is correct." Bran nodded, sighing quietly with relief and smiling gratefully at the apprentice.

Impeccably white neckline, he thought, astonished at himself. *What am I thinking about? What do I care for how a woman's neckline looks?*

He praised Nagomi when the servant girl left them alone.

"That was swift thinking. Thank you."

"I've seen enough pilgrims coming to the shrine from all over Yamato. The ones from the countryside always pray to give thanks for something – salvation from a famine, drought or plague. It's only the rich ones who ask for more."

He leaned over the bowl, preparing to wash himself before sleep. An unfamiliar face stared at him from the reflection in the water. He blinked his narrow eyes, furrowed his flat nose and pulled a couple more funny faces, to make sure it were really his own features.

"*Did you not like the girl?*" a voice in his head enquired.

"I… Eh?" Bran was taken aback by the Spirit's sudden forwardness. "I suppose… she was *comely*… What's it to you, anyway?"

"*Then why did you not take what she was offering?*"

"I ate as much as I could…"

"*I don't mean the food!*" the voice in his head mocked him. "*Did you not see how she revealed the nape of her neck, how she loosened her sleeves? Why, I do believe she would have given it to you for free if only you had asked!*"

"I… I do not understand…"

"*Oh! Don't tell me…*" The general paused. "*You've never had a woman, have you?*"

Bran realised what Shigemasa was talking about. Serving food and drink was not the only source of income for the guesthouse keeper's daughter –and she was, apparently blatantly, offering him her services.

"*Did your father not introduce you into the ways of the floating world?*" the Spirit prodded.

Bran felt his face turn bright crimson and hot. The situation was embarrassing in itself, but *talking* about it made it even worse.

"I… I hope I did not offend anyone…" was all he could say.

"*Eh,*" he could almost sense Shigemasa shrug, "*you're still a* wakashū - *she probably just thought you were inexperienced with women.*"

"I… I am," he admitted shyly, not wanting the conversation to continue.

"*Just my luck, to find myself an unbroken youth,*" Shigemasa said, sighing with exasperation. "*Your school must have been like one of those Satsuma samurai places, right?*"

"I suppose…?"

He decided to just go along with everything.

"*I guessed as much,*" Shigemasa said, grunting, and with that the conversation seemed to have ended, leaving Bran in total confusion.

In the morning, the little boat took Bran and the others to the harbour town of Shimabara, where they caught a ferry across the bay to a place called Kumamoto. It was a much larger vessel, a broad merchant boat with a tall mast and great piece of cloth for a sail, slow, heavy and stable.

"Good of thou to join us," Bran said, seeing Nagomi climb out from below the deck.

"It is not as bad as the other one," the young apprentice replied, although her face was still pale and she visibly struggled with dizziness. "Is all sea travel so tough?"

"This? 'Tis nothing!" he said and laughed. The ship barely rocked on the low waves. "Out in the open sea there are waves that would cover this whole vessel, and the ships ride them up and down like… like…" He couldn't think of an analogy that the girl would understand. "Like leaves in a mountain stream."

"How can people survive this?" she said, turning even paler at the thought.

"It takes some getting used to," Bran admitted, "but there is little else more exhilarating than sailing the open sea. It's almost as good as flying. Of course, on dragon-back it would take us less than an hour to cross this bay."

"Can you still sense your *dorako*?" Satō asked.

He closed his eyes and focused on the Farlink. The ring on his hand warmed up slightly.

"Yes. Somewhere over yonder." He pointed to the south-east. "What is there?"

"You have the map, Bran-*sama*," the boy reminded him.

"Ah, of course."

The dragon rider was the only one who knew how to read Western maps, so it was him whom Lady Kazuko had presented with a rolled up piece of linen cloth she had found in the shrine's library. It was a copy of a Vasconian navigation chart, three hundred years old and badly inaccurate, but it did help Bran to get his bearings in this strange land.

"Where are we…? Ah, I see Kiyō." He was no longer surprised with his ability to read the ink squiggles that formed the Yamato writing. "If this be Qin," he said, pointing to a grey blot on the western edge of the map, "then my ship was somewhere here when it… perished. Flying straight eastwards, the dragon would land ashore somewhere – *here*."

He laid his finger on a crescent-shaped bay on the southernmost tip of Chinzei Island.

"*Hioki*." Satō deciphered the runes and thought for a moment. "That's Satsuma," he said, frowning.

"Is it far?"

"Farther than I thought we would need to go - across the mountains."

"A week?"

"Maybe more. But it's south and we will go through at least two big cities where we can find help and information, if my old man's name still means anything in these parts."

"Does that interfere with the search for thy father?"

"Until we find some clues, we can only hope the Crimson Robe will show himself again. So far all we know is that he's looking for you."

"Kazuko-*hime* said your honoured grandfather had met him before," noted Nagomi.

"It is merely a conjecture. He would be very old now if it were indeed the same person my grandfather saw when he came here on board a Dracalish vessel."

"A Dracalish ship?" Satō glanced at him sharply. "You mean *Phaeton*?"

"Yes, he was a midshipman on board the *Phaeton*."

"My father saw it when he was very young," Satō said. "It inspired him to study *Rangaku*."

"All is bound together by Fate," Nagomi added piously, "just like Kazuko-*hime* said."

"How did your grandfather get the black box? Who's the woman in the medallion?" Satō continued prodding.

Bran explained what little he knew and guessed about the contents of the box, and briefly told the story of his grandfather's life. He could sense Satō did not trust him fully since the incident with Tokojiro and decided hiding the truth would only make this distrust grow.

"What about the dragon figurine?" Nagomi asked when he had finished. "You didn't mention that."

"Oh, it has naught to do with my grandfather. I got it from my father a few months ago."

"Can I see it one more time?"

"It is Yamato work, isn't it?" the dragon rider asked, giving her the figurine.

"Yes, you can buy these things in Kiyō. The Bataavians from Dejima like them."

The man my father got it from must have once been here, Bran realised.

"Then it's not really significant?"

"I don't know, maybe." Satō shrugged. "It seems everything about you is somehow significant."

"I wish it were not so," he said, looking grimly at the steel-grey horizon.

The ferry entered the mouth of a large river and followed it upstream before reaching a harbour and a tall bridge. A massive castle loomed over the city, similar to the one Bran had been seeing in his dreams, but even greater. Its robust stone walls rose upwards in a maze of broad spiralling terraces, culminating in a colossal keep, six storeys tall, its white plastered walls covered with black wooden boards. It was an impressive construction that seemed able to withstand even a barrage of modern cannons, but it was completely exposed from above. Bran could not help thinking how easy it would be to capture it with just a few dragons.

If he needed any more confirmation that there were no dragons in Yamato, this nigh impregnable castle's lack of aerial defences was it. All he had seen of the creatures so far were carvings and paintings. What had happened to them all?

"Did Kazuko-*hime* advise anything about this place?" he asked, turning his eyes away from the ramparts.

"She mentioned a *Butsu* temple to the north of the castle," replied Nagomi, removing a tightly rolled piece of paper from a bamboo container at her belt. "The monks there are aware of most of what goes on in the Southern provinces, and have a great library of strange stories and legends."

"I knew a man in Kumamoto," recalled Satō, "a friend of my father's. If he's still here, I could try and contact him."

"We shall go to the temple first," said Bran.

What was supposed to be a proposition came out as an order, rather forcefully. Satō raised his eyebrows, but said nothing.

"Do you think we're far enough from Kiyō for me to stop disguising myself?" the boy asked.

"It would be safer if you would keep it until we at least move out of the city," Nagomi said, biting her lower lip in thought. "There must be many merchants and samurai from Kiyō coming here on business."

Satō sighed, picked up his heavy bag and headed north. Bran gave one last look to the castle walls – he couldn't shake the feeling of being watched from the tapering towers – and followed after the Yamato boy.

CHAPTER VII

By the time they reached the temple compound, the sky had already turned a gloomy grey. Thick evening fog rolled down from the hills. Nestled between a shadowy mountainside to the west and half-abandoned fields to the east, the temple's dark curly roofs loomed over the poor desolate neighbourhood like a flock of crows.

"Be this really the place?" Bran asked.

"*Honmyōji.*" Satō pointed at a sign carved in a wooden plank above the gate. "Unless there's another one in Kumamoto…"

"We shall need lodgings. It is getting late. Let us enquire this man."

Bran approached a white-robed monk working a small radish patch just beyond the gate.

"Good monk, pray tell us whether thy establishment can provide us with accommodation?" he asked.

The man straightened himself, lifted the brim of his bamboo hat and looked at Bran, bemused.

"He means, can you find us a place to sleep," Nagomi said swiftly.

"Certainly, honourable guests." The monk bowed. "The *shukubō* is in the fifth building to the left, just before the Munatsuki stairs," he said, pointing in the direction of a long stone staircase that disappeared into the menacing darkness of the hillside. Flickers of stone lanterns marked its further path among the pines and cedars. "I don't think there are many other guests today."

"Thank you," Bran said, bowing graciously.

They walked down the stone alley, lined on both sides by clusters of granite gravestones. The monk was right: the *shukubō* – temple lodgings – were almost empty apart from a couple of tired pilgrims dozing on the floor of the dormitory hall, and two monks taking care of the place.

"More visitors!" rejoiced one of them as they entered the dormitory. "A noble samurai among them! We are truly blessed today. *Ingen!*" he shouted down the corridor, "Make sure your broth is at its best, we have fine guests!"

"Oh, that is quite unnecessary, we only need a place to stay," Bran protested after he realised the "noble samurai" was himself, but the monk shook his head, laughing.

"Ingen loves cooking, and I can only eat so much." He patted himself on the belly, which was flat and taut. "He'll be delighted to have a chance to show off his skill. We don't get many visitors here, and most of the pilgrims – well, they are certainly pious, but not what I'd call appreciative of proper cuisine."

From the dining room Bran could see the cook opening boxes and pots with a variety of mysterious ingredients, mixing, slicing, chopping and throwing them into one of the two huge clay pots bubbling away on the stone stove. The guests and the talkative monk, who introduced himself as Itsunen, watched his movements in silent awe. There was no doubt Ingen was a crafty cook. The delicate scent of the vegetable and seaweed broth filled the room and made Bran realise how hungry their journey had made him.

He had discovered early on that the Yamato ate plenty of kelp and laver, something he had not tasted since leaving Gwynedd, and it made him like their cooking even more. He now watched with eager expectation as the monk searched the kitchen for more ingredients to mix into the broth.

Ingen turned to the other monk with an accusing look.

"We're out of tofu," were the first words he uttered.

Itsunen shrugged with an innocent smile.

"The pilgrims ate it all."

"There should always be fresh tofu!" The cook's face turned fierce. "We are monks of Kumamoto, how am I supposed to make *dengaku* now?"

The two monks stared at each other for a moment like some avatars of light and darkness. At last, Ingen slumped.

"You will have to make more at dawn."

Itsunen looked dejected, but agreed.

"The soup is ready," the cook announced without joy, "but I'm not happy with the result. Maybe I should throw it away and start again…"

"*No!*" the three guests cried in unison.

Bran received a steaming bowl of the broth, with plenty of cut vegetables, mushrooms and kelp. It seemed to him the best soup he had ever tasted.

"What, no *noodles?* That's stingy!" Itsunen moaned.

"We're also out of noodles," Ingen replied coldly. "Are you a monk or a gluttonous merchant? You don't need that much food before sleep."

"It's perfect," Nagomi said, and Bran grunted agreement between one mouthful and another.

He was holding the bowl close to his mouth as he saw the others do. It was a much easier way to drink the thick soup.

"It is acceptable," the cook admitted, slurping the broth himself. "Not as terrible as I expected. Alas, I cannot offer you our specialty because *somebody* forgot to restock the cupboard."

He glared at the other monk.

"What brings you to Honmyōji at such a late hour, if you don't mind me asking?" enquired Itsunen after they had emptied their bowls – and asked for second helpings.

"We come from Suwa to speak to Father Ipponin," Nagomi mentioned a name given her by the High Priestess, "to ask him for advice and information."

Both monks turned serious.

"What is it?"

"The Reverend Ipponin passed away a few months ago. We have a new Abbot now," replied Ingen.

"However, I'm sure he will be just as happy to provide you with advice as the old one," the other monk said with a smile.

"We shall see him tomorrow," Bran said, nodding.

"Well, I'm finished," said Satō, standing up. "I can't eat no more. I'll better go where my place is."

He leaned over to Bran's ear and whispered. "I hope the stables here are a bit cleaner than in that poor excuse for a guesthouse we were at yesterday."

"As soon as we're out of the city, thou shall join us in the guest rooms," Bran assured him.

"You bet I will!" he said. "I won't stand another night at the stables. I think I'm starting to get some bugs crawling over me."

White custard-like rectangles of freshly pressed tofu curd simmered on the grid of a grill. Bran eyed them with suspicion. All he knew about the dish was the name, but that knowledge gave him no indication of the taste. Foods like soup, rice or fried fish were straightforward enough, but at times the local cuisine stumped him with dishes like the one Ingen was preparing for breakfast; grilled tofu skewers covered with a brown paste of fermented beans. How could it possibly taste?

Everyone else seemed to enjoy them greatly, praising the cook, so Bran gingerly put a small piece into his mouth. At first it seemed to taste of absolutely nothing, but the soft, sponge-like morsel was warm and full of the energy he needed that early in the morning. He tried another bite, and was now almost sure he could detect a faint aroma of wood from the grill and a savoury sweetness that had to be coming from the beans. He bit again, this time trying the red-brown sauce. The paste was sharp and salty, complimenting the blandness of the tofu cube.

Like most of the food he had been eating since waking up in Yamato, the breakfast in this inconspicuous temple was subtle and refined, only hinting at tastes and aromas. Bran appreciated the skills that went into making all those fine dishes, but he was yearning for a haunch of mutton or a slice of cheese – strong, simple, punchy tastes. Even an apple would have been nice, something he could really stick his teeth into.

"What lies beyond yonder staircase up the hill?" he asked Itsunen, reaching for another skewer, this time of aubergine.

"That's the Jōchibyō, the grave of Kiyomasa-*dono*," the monk explained, "founder of the Kumamoto castle. If you wish, noble guest, we can take you later to pay your respects at his shrine."

"His shrine...?" Bran hesitated, but noticed Nagomi's frown and barely noticeable shaking of her head. "Oh, aye, certainly, I'd be most delighted."

Another monk entered the dining hall, one they had not seen before, and greeted them with a deep bow. Ingen and Itsunen looked at him apprehensively, but said nothing.

"The Abbot wishes to see you as soon as you are ready," the monk said.

"The Abbot – " Bran looked at the man in the white robe in surprise. "We were just going to look for him."

"I know," the monk said, smiling mysteriously, "I will take you to him. All three of you," he added, nodding in the direction of the stables.

"What did they mean *his shrine*?" Bran asked Nagomi on their way to fetch Satō.

"You do not know? I'm sorry, I keep forgetting you're not yet familiar with our customs."

"Not all, it would seem. I guess using chopsticks is easier knowledge to absorb than spiritual matters."

"I see. I'll try to... I never had to explain this to anyone. We pray to the Spirits of our ancestors, great men from the past. This Kiyomasa-*dono* the monk mentioned must have become a worthy ancestor to be enshrined in such a place."

"So his Spirit is still somewhere up there? Like all those souls in the Cave of Scrying?"

"That's different. Those souls, like Shigemasa-*sama*, were never properly purified, so they are stuck to this plane until the day they can move on, but an enshrined Spirit becomes one of the *kami* and watches the world from the Heavenly Plane, answering our prayers - if we are deemed worthy – "

"I knew it. I leave you alone for one night and you've already started talking about Gods," Satō interrupted the lecture, coming out of the stables to meet them. "Where are you off to?"

"Apparently the Abbot wants to see us. *All* of us," Bran added.

The Abbot, a small plump man, surprisingly young for his position, welcomed them in a golden-roofed building off the main path. His guestroom opened on to a huge library filled with old scrolls and newer bamboo-bound books.

"I believe you've been expecting us," noted Nagomi after they sat down at a low table.

"Don't be so surprised, little apprentice," the Abbot replied, laughing and pouring *cha* into black cups. "You priests of the Old Gods are not the only ones who can peer beyond the veil."

Nagomi gasped.

"You're a Scryer?"

"I dabble in divination," the Abbot said, nodding humbly. "This temple has a reputation to keep and we can't afford as many spies and informants as we used to, so we have to resort to other means of keeping up to date."

"Thou knowest what we are here for then?" asked Bran, catching Nagomi's worried glance.

"Only vaguely; divination is not a precise method, as you well know." The Abbot smirked at the apprentice. "You are looking for something, *tono*..."

"Karasu." Bran nodded.

"You have lost something of great value, Karasu-*dono*. I can help you locate it, but I will need time… and resources. The temple has many needs. The roof of the main hall needs a new coat of gilding, for example."

"I understand." Bran glanced at Nagomi. The apprentice was biting her lips in anxiety and staring back at him with alarm. "Let us consider thy proposition, Reverend One."

"It is you who are short of time." The Abbot shrugged. "You know where to find me."

"Thou seemed mightily uneasy, Nagomi-*sama*," Bran remarked when they went outside, "what is the reason for thy apprehension?"

"The *Butsu* monks are banned from using divination," the apprentice explained.

"I thought they're just priests like you."

Nagomi shook her head vigorously.

"They brought their God from Qin, a long time ago. Their rituals and beliefs are different. They have neither healers nor Scryers – at least they shouldn't. There's something very disturbing going on here."

"Didn't the High Priestess say this place is where we should come for help?"

"You heard what the monks said. The old Abbot is dead. This one doesn't seem like somebody Kazuko-*hime* would trust."

"He already knows too much," Satō joined in, 'so the less we tell him, the better."

"There is something menacing about this place," Bran agreed. "I would be loath to share too many secrets with this man. We should leave as soon as possible." Bran turned to the wizardess. "How long is it before that friend of thine arrives here?"

"I have not heard back from him yet, so not before dinner, if today at all."

"Is he to be trusted?"

"I'm not sure of anything now, but he was one of my father's closest associates in Kumamoto – and he despises the *Taikun*. He certainly seems more trustworthy than some fat monk."

"I came as soon as I could. I'm so sorry for your loss, Takashima-*sama*…"

Just as Satō had remembered, the most striking feature in the man's long narrow face were his large flaring nostrils. They gave him the appearance of being constantly agitated. The lips did not help – they were always slightly apart, and quivered as he spoke. The eyes under thin eyebrows were, however, serene.

Satō wore her black and vermillion attire of a Rangakusha for her meeting with the scholar. Master Yokoi was one of those old-fashioned scholars who only knew her as a boy.

"Thank you, Yokoi-*dono*," she said, bowing before the guest, "but my father is still alive."

"What? But we've heard the news – an experiment gone wrong…"

"It's a lie. My father was abducted. I saw it happen."

"I knew I shouldn't have trusted the official channels. Tell me, tell me all!"

The samurai listened to the girl's tale, breathing noisily. Absentmindedly, he straightened creases on his vest, embroidered with the triple dragonscale crest of the Hōjō clan. When she finished, he banged his fist on the floor mat.

"This is exactly the kind of thing that shows how weak the government has become. They allow one of the greatest scholars of our era to simply disappear and do nothing about it! I assure you, I will do what I can to help you find out what's happened to your father – and believe me, I can do plenty."

"You have my eternal gratitude, Yokoi-*dono*."

"What are you doing here in Kumamoto?" he asked, picking up a tofu skewer from a square plate. "In this temple, of all places?"

"We had to flee Kiyō. The magistrate outlawed my entire family. This temple was recommended to us by the High Priestess of Suwa."

"Outlawed? *Preposterous!*" He spat out bits of tofu. "You must come with me to the *daimyo*'s castle, you'll be safe there."

"I… I'm sorry, Yokoi-*dono*, but we have to keep moving south."

Satō glanced at Bran nervously.

"You're not telling me everything, child," guessed the scholar, also looking at the boy with interest.

"No, Yokoi-*dono*," the wizardess admitted.

"You're just as secretive as Shūhan," the samurai said, laughing and slapping his thigh. "We never knew what new spell or device he would come up with! Be that as it may," he turned serious, "I will not prod further. I know you have your father's brains, so I trust your judgement."

"Thank you for understanding."

"My humble means are at your disposal, if you need anything for the journey. I still think you should stay at the castle, though. This place – " he looked around, "it sends shivers down my spine, especially when the mist comes down like tonight. People say these hills are haunted."

"That's why a priestess is with us," said a smiling Satō.

"Thought of everything, eh?" The samurai laughed again. "Are you leaving soon, then?"

"At dawn, if we can't reason with the Abbot."

"I see. Do try to keep in touch, child. I will find out what happened to dear old Shūhan, of that you can be certain."

"I will try."

"Give my regards to the cook; this is some fine *dengaku*. I have to go now. Darkness is coming and I don't fancy going down these hills by night."

"Of course. You understand that all that we've talked about must remain a secret… Even the fact that I'm staying here."

"My boy, I have been conspiring since before you were born!" He put his hand on Satō's shoulder and looked her seriously in the eyes. "As far as I'm concerned - we've never met."

"Maybe we should have gone with him after all," said Bran as they watched old man's palanquin clamber down the hill path.

"We wouldn't be any safer there," replied Satō, "imagine how hard it would be to keep any secrets in a castle."

"The mist descends from the hills," noted Nagomi, wrapping herself up tightly. "Let's go back inside."

Satō entered the guest stables, almost bumping into the groom.

"What ye doin' 'ere?" the boy asked in a rude manner.

"I am..." Satō started politely, but quickly corrected herself, "What d'ye think? I'm off ta sleep."

"Spendin' night in the temple? Are ye daft?"

"Why, what's wrong wi'dat?"

The groom gave her a look one gave to village idiots.

"The mist is a-comin'! I ain't stayin' 'ere wi' the mist comin' down! You'd be'r come wi' me if ye have any brains left!"

"No, I–I'll stay'ere..."

"As ye wish," he said with a shrug, and passed her by, heading for the temple gate in a great hurry.

There was only one horse in the stables, used to send quick messages to the city below. Satō gave it a wide berth. Horse riding, along with archery, was one of the few samurai arts she had never managed to learn. Her father did not keep horses; there was no point in a crowded city. Large animals frightened her. She suddenly felt ashamed of her fear; Bran's dragon must have been far larger and more threatening than this horse, and yet the Westerner was not afraid to ride it – to *fly* it.

An owl hooted in the distance. Satō shivered. *It's cold here in the evenings*, she told herself, trying to explain the goosebumps that covered her skin. She stepped outside and looked towards the gloomy hillside, from which the mist descended upon the compound. Suddenly a dot of light flickered in the darkness then another. Soon there were dozens of them, a line of dancing flames zigzagging like a fiery serpent down the hill, and they kept coming closer.

Ghosts, thought the wizardess, *will-o'-the-wisps?* She felt around and her fingers found a large heavy stick. It would have to do, as her sword was still with Bran. Perhaps she should warn the others – the lights were ever nearer. Would she make it to the guesthouse? What kind of danger would she have to face? She gripped the stick harder...

A lonely, grey-robed monk emerged from the mist, glanced at her with slight surprise and proceeded to light another of the stone lanterns lining the temple's main thoroughfare. Satō breathed out and shook her head.

Fool! Scared of the lanterns! she scolded herself. *I've been pretending to be a servant for so long I'm turning into one!*

She waved the wooden stick. It was roughly the size and weight of a *bokken*. It had been a while since she had practised with one. She assumed a stance and performed a few basic exercises. The stick swished through the air with a satisfying whistle. It felt good. She had not lost any of her skill.

The temple precinct was shrouded in gloomy darkness, pierced only by the flickering lanterns. Deep into the night, the wizardess didn't feel sleepy at all. She was also no longer wary of the mist. Nothing out of ordinary had happened since the coming of dusk. Satō continued her practise with the stick, adding a little magic to the sword exercises. The horse looked at her curiously with big brown eyes and yawned.

She noticed a movement near one of the buildings – the Abbot's house. She sneaked closer. Everyone should have already been asleep at this time of night...

A thin bald man wearing loose black robes knocked on the wall quietly with a staff topped with jingling bells. A panel in the wall slid open, and the Abbot appeared in the opening, lighting his way with a large paper lantern. The bald man grunted something. The Abbot nodded, looked around and, not noticing Satō hidden in the shadows, headed towards the path leading up the hill with the bald man.

The wizardess hesitated. She was intrigued to see what the Abbot was up to, but she was more curious about what she managed to glimpse inside the building, in the light of the lantern, before the little monk slid the secret door shut.

Books – hundreds of books.

The night was thick, dense and humid, the fog seeping through the cracks in the thin wooden walls. Nagomi stood by the window of her room, looking out into the pitch black darkness of the garden, covered in the mist descended from the hills.

She was alone in a room much bigger than she required; she didn't like being alone. Back home, she could always feel her parents and Ine beyond the thin paper walls. At the Shrine she had shared her dormitory with a dozen other apprentices. Here, she could sense no other souls in any of the rooms adjacent to hers. It was an overwhelming sensation.

She raised the clay beaker to her lips and blew. The orange spirit appeared in an instant, flickering merrily. She hummed a made-up melody and it jumped and danced. Heaviness rose from her heart. The mist seemed to float away from the light, revealing a little of the garden. Only now could Nagomi notice the sleeping hydrangeas and a slender sakaki tree near her window. She sensed the tree's young spirit. It was grateful for the orange light which released it briefly from the hold of the dark fog.

There were other spirits in the garden, floating past from the graveyards around the temple and from the forest, not paying her much heed. She felt them all, and she no longer felt so lonely.

There was a rustle in the hydrangea bush and a black pony-tail bobbed up and down underneath her window.

"Nagomi? Is that you?"

Bran dozed in half-sleep. He tossed from side to side, too tired to wake, too restless to dream. He tried to clear his mind of racing thoughts. He could sense Shigemasa, deep inside his soul, louder than usual, babbling like a mountain brook in the distance.

"*Please, just be quiet!*" he shouted at his thoughts. In frustration, he punched the thick beam in the wall. The pain seemed to quieten the general, who continued his brooding in insulted silence.

Moments later, Bran felt the ring on his finger heat up and a new vision overwhelmed him. It had been a while since he had made contact with Emrys. It was as if his mind could only cope with either Shigemasa's or the dragon's presence at any one time. Once the general retreated from his immediate consciousness, the Farlink connection re-emerged.

This time the dragon was calm, sleepy, sedated. There wasn't much detail to the vision, mostly a smell – a faint, sickly sweet smell, oddly familiar. The dragon could not stretch its wings, confined in some tight space.

A man stood before the dragon, a lanky thin man, observing Emrys with great curiosity through horn-rimmed glasses. A crest of a crossed circle decorated his shoulders.

"We can't keep this up much longer," the man said to somebody out of sight. "If we don't find a better method of keeping it sedate, I'm afraid we'll have to – "

The vision was suddenly broken by the sound of rapid knocking at the door.

"Bran-*sama*!"

It was Nagomi, sounding urgent.

"Please, wake up."

He slid the door open and peered carefully into the darkness of the corridor.

"What is it?"

"Sacchan asked us to come outside. Are you alright?" She looked at him with concern. "You seem shaken."

"It's nothing. A bad dream."

Satō was waiting for them under the long eaves of the stables. The boy explained briefly what he had seen and what he wanted them to do.

"You would have us sneak like thieves?" Nagomi asked.

"I know it's not honourable, but I must see what's inside that room," the boy said. "That fat Abbot seemed very knowledgeable, so his archives must be a treasure trove of information."

They crept along the wall of the Abbot's residence. Thick fog concealed their movements and dampened the sound of their feet.

"It's here." Satō slid open a wooden panel slowly and quietly. "The servants sleep on the other side of the house, so we should be safe, let's just try not to make too much noise."

"What if the Abbot comes back?" Bran asked.

"We'll run," Satō said with a shrug, "he'll never catch us on those short fat legs."

They tiptoed into the hall. Bran sneezed into his sleeve. Satō lit a small iron lantern and raised it up to illuminate the room. The bookshelves were covered with a thick layer of dust and cobwebs. The new Abbot did not seem concerned much with the state of the temple's archives.

They found a pair of copper candlesticks in the corner and lit those as well. Now Bran could fully appreciate the number of volumes gathered by consecutive Abbots.

"What are we looking for here, precisely?" he asked, opening one of the volumes and reading by the light of a flamespark.

"Anything that could guide us to the crimson robed man," Satō decided. "It's a long shot, I know, but it's worth a try. This library is huge," he said, admiring the long stretches of cabinets, stacked with silk-stitched volumes and bamboo-bound scrolls, "there must be something here."

"Yes, but how will we find it?"

"Some of the cabinets are marked," Nagomi said, dusting off markings on the shelves, "'*Financial records*' – I think we can omit these."

"There must be a main chronicle somewhere..."

Satō browsed through scrolls.

"*Tale of Heike...*?" Bran picked up a hefty, silk-bound tome. "*The bells of the Gion Temple...*" he started reading aloud.

"No, not this one, leave it."

They searched for a long time, opening book after book, browsing through a few, opening pages and putting them back again if they turned out to be accountancy registers or well-known tales of days past. A few volumes were set aside for further reading.

"*Ach-a-fi!*" Bran exclaimed in Prydain.

"What is it?"

Satō ran up to him.

"Oh, it's... n-nothing," he stuttered.

It was a collection of erotic stories and drawings, the illustrations so explicit that he felt his face immediately turn scarlet with embarrassment. He put the book away on the shelf – but then, when he was sure nobody saw him do it, he took it again and hid it under his sash.

Several hours of fruitless searching later he was all but ready to give up, when Nagomi called him and Satō over.

"Look, I think I've found something."

She was holding a large folding scroll, long and densely written with ancient script.

"It's some kind of lexicon of monsters and magical creatures," the apprentice said, "look at this page."

"*In a cave at the back of the Unganzenji Temple in northern Higo dwelled the Abomination known as the Immortal Swordsman,*" read Bran. "*so called because no living man could remember how long he had lived there, never growing old or sick. The people of…* Kawachi *village describe the Immortal Swordsman as looking almost like any other man, except his eyes were like nuggets of gold, his skin pale, and his teeth blackened like a woman's and sharp like those of a wolf.*"

"That's him!" Satō exclaimed in the high-pitched voice he would sometimes get when excited. "That's exactly what he looked like!"

His sudden cry awoke somebody within the residence. They could hear the shuffling of feet on the wooden floor, and guards shouting.

"We must go," said Satō, "we have stayed here far too long."

"It's all right, we got what we came for," Bran replied, folding the scroll and putting it back on the shelf.

They crept through the fog back towards the lodging house. Suddenly the apprentice halted and stared into the dark mist.

"What is it?"

"There is something… approaching."

"The Crimson Robe?"

The apprentice shook her head.

"I don't think so… It feels like something ancient, stirred from a deep sleep."

"*For once, I agree with the apprentice,*" a voice spoke in Bran's head, "*there is something in those mists that even I wouldn't like to meet.*"

They hurried back to the lodgings. One of the monks, Itsunen, his face grey in the faint light of the stone lanterns, stood in front of the building.

"Noble guests," he said, bowing, "I believe you should leave the temple tonight."

"Why? What's going on?" asked Nagomi.

Bran looked around nervously – the fog was creeping down from the hillside, growing ever denser.

"The hills are restless," Ingen said, emerging from the shadows, "the mist grows thick."

"It's not safe here anymore," added Itsunen, "please hurry."

CHAPTER VIII

The Itō residence at the top of the Sōfukuji Hill was empty. The windows boarded, the doors closed. Sakuma Zōzan watched silently as an old servant, his silver head wrapped in a bandage, locked the outer gate shut and rolled up the *noren* cloth with the Itō crest. There was a sad determination in the way he went about his business.

"*A!*" the servant exclaimed, turning around. "Sakuma-*dono!*"

The scholar nodded politely.

"Where is everybody? What happened here?"

"Ine-*sama* sold the house and is moving to her folk in Nagoya."

"Sold the house... Wasn't there a younger daughter too, the red-haired one?"

"Oh, Nagomi-*sama* is an apprentice now. She lives at Suwa."

"What a pity." Zōzan stroke his pointed beard in thought. *More bad news.* "The Itō were good doctors. There are not many like them left in Kiyō."

The old servant nodded and corrected the bandage that had slipped from his forehead.

"By your leave – I have to deliver these to the harbour," he said, referring to the rolled-up *noren* and a bundle of a few other household items under his arm. Zōzan let him pass and stood for a while yet, watching the abandoned building, trying to think of his next move.

"You seek a doctor?"

A man emerged from under the eaves of the Itō house, his face hidden in a shadow of a dark-purple hooded robe. Sakuma Zōzan stretched his black and white kimono and coughed nervously. He had always felt distraught near strangers.

"Why do you ask?"

"I may be able to help."

"You don't look like a physician."

Zōzan noticed the two sword hilts showing from under the purple robe.

"It is not a physician that your son needs, Sakuma-*dono.*"

The scholar breathed in sharply.

"Who *are* you?"

The stranger cast down the hood of his robe, revealing a calm young face adorned with fine whiskers and a thin beard. His dark, slightly popping eyes seemed to pierce through Zōzan's soul.

"Your last hope, scholar."

Keinosuke lay on a thick silk futon in a small room on the top floor of the Sakuma Mansion. He would seem to be sleeping peacefully, if it wasn't for a scowl twisting his face.

The stranger leaned over the boy.

"Tell me what happened."

"A deer hunter found him on the slopes of Inasa."

"And he's been like this since?"

"Not a sound."

The samurai touched Keinosuke's forehead and winced. He looked around the room.

"I need to see your library."

Zōzan was taken aback.

"Nobody has access to my library, samurai... I don't even know your name."

"My name is not easily given," the stranger said, "and if you want your son to ever wake again, you'll be doing exactly what I tell you."

The scholar grunted uneasily. It'd been six days since the servants brought Keinosuke home. The boy was dying before his eyes. No physician or priest in Kiyō could help, but what they all agreed on was that he wouldn't last long.

"Follow me," he said, standing up and straightening the creases on his kimono.

The door to his library was locked with a complicated Bataavian lock of brass and steel. Zōzan put the heavy key in and turned. The gears whirred, the bolts moved, the mistfire mechanism hissed and the door slid open.

The stranger entered the room, closed his eyes and stretched his neck out, like a sniffing hound.

"What's in there?"

He pointed to a large locked chest under the wall opposite the entrance.

"That's..." Zōzan hesitated, "that's where I keep my most precious scrolls."

"Open it."

"What – no! That's going too far. What does my chest have to do with Keinosuke's state?"

The samurai gave the scholar an impatient look.

"When they found him, was there a lake or a pond nearby?"

"He was found by the White Stag Pool," Zōzan replied, nodding.

"Your son has dabbled in something very dangerous, scholar. I believe he found it inside this chest."

"Preposterous. He wouldn't even be able to open it."

"When was the last time you checked that lock?"

Zōzan approached the chest and touched the padlock.

"It's broken," he stated, astonished. "How...? Why?"

"Show me what's inside." The samurai stood beside him. "Careful."

The scholar lifted the heavy lid with trepidation, but the inside of the chest looked exactly the same as he had remembered it – old scrolls and musty books gathered in a great pile. He saw nothing out of the ordinary, but the strange samurai reached into the pile and pulled out one of the scrolls, a folded length of paper, darkened with age, with red lettering all over it. It smelled of blood and death.

"What's that?" asked Zōzan.

The samurai put a finger to his lips.

"Listen."

Zōzan scoffed, but then heard something. A faint whisper at first, it grew into a voice, annoyed, angry, mean, deep inside the scholar's head.

"*Is that you, Keinosuke? You've awakened already? I should've punished you harder. They've managed to take the foreigner away thanks to your fiasco.*"

"Who…" the scholar started, but the samurai shook his head.

"*Well, do you have something to report?*" the sinister voice continued. "*I don't have time for this. If you want to be useful, find out what's happened to your sensei. She should be in the shrine…*"

The voice paused and Zōzan felt a penetrating presence in his mind.

"*Wait – is there someone else with you? I sense two minds… Sakuma-dono, I'm honoured to meet you at last, and the other one – oh, it's you,*" the voice seethed.

The samurai crushed the scroll in his hands and the paper burst into flames briefly.

"What was that?"

Master Sakuma stared at the pile of ash on the study floor. He was terrified, but a part of him was also fascinated by the immense power he had sensed in the voice. What magic was this? Why didn't *he* discover the old scroll first?

"Bad news," replied the samurai curtly, "what did he mean by *your sensei?*"

"It's… Keinosuke's magic teacher, the Takashima girl. She disappeared after the accident. The police are searching for her."

The samurai looked up sharply.

"The *accident?*"

He's not from around here. Where did he come from?

"One of Takashima-*sama's* experiments went awry. The house was destroyed, everyone inside perished. A terrible tragedy."

"How long ago was that?"

"Five days."

"So a day after they found your son?"

"Yes… You don't think –"

"I think I need to visit the Takashima residence," the samurai said distractedly. Zōzan could see his mind was already elsewhere.

"But what about Keinosuke?"

The machine-servant pressed a piece of moist cotton wool to Keinosuke's lips until all the water had dripped into the boy's mouth. It then whirred another arm, wiped his face with a damp cloth then returned to a standby position, announcing it with a bell.

Master Sakuma reached for the key at the back and wound the automaton up again. There were more of these machines – *karakuri* – than human servants at his household. He trusted in their reliability and tirelessness. A well-oiled *karakuri* could care for his son all day and night, without respite.

Another automaton arrived on its tiny legs with a cup of tea on a lacquer tray. Zōzan sipped it, observing the strange samurai kneeling over his son, holding Keinosuke's head on his lap, focused in silence.

There was a static snapping sound, like an *elekiter* spark. The familiar smell of ozone spread throughout the room. The samurai opened his eyes and nodded with satisfaction.

Keinosuke stirred and woke up.

"*No, stop!*" he cried out. "I can help…" He looked around astonished. "Where am I…?"

"You're home, son." Zōzan couldn't hold back his emotions. "You're safe."

"He's not safe here – and neither are you," the samurai announced, standing up. "I suggest you move as far away from the city as you can. This isn't your true home, is it?" He assessed the room. "An aristocrat like you…"

"I have an estate in Chūbu, where the boy's mother lives. I only brought him here to study at the Takashima school – but now, with them gone…"

The samurai nodded.

"Chūbu sounds good. And keep him away from mirrors and stagnant water for the time being."

"Will you not tell me what happened to my son? What power was in that scroll?"

"If I told you, would you promise not to seek it for yourself?"

There was something in the samurai's eyes that made Zōzan cower. Unable to lie, the scholar bowed his head in shamed silence.

*The interrogation chamber of the magistrate prison was damp and badly lit.

They made it deliberately so, realised Tokojiro, *so the faces of the criminals seemed even more menacing in the murk.*

The guard guided Lady Kazuko in, her hands bound with a single length of knotless rope, more out of fear of some witchcraft than to prevent her escaping. Despite the gloom, her face seemed illuminated with some internal radiance, still proud and gentle despite her precarious situation.

Tokojiro's cheek and eye twitched nervously. The scar on his face, covered with ugly scabs, blisters and painful inflammation, refused to heal since he had crawled away from the Mogi Temple through the dirt and soil of the pine forest, blind and mad with rage and shame. He kept scratching it, which only increased the irritation.

He was sitting along the wall with several witnesses who were to take part in the cross-examination of the priestess. Two of the samurai who had found him in the forest were also present to confess, the third one, Hibiki, still recovering from his injuries, ironically – at the Suwa Shrine.

I never wanted any harm to come to her, he thought, but another part of his mind mocked him: *You should've thought about it before you betrayed her trust, then.*

He never imagined the authorities getting desperate enough to harass the shrine, much less – arrest Lady Kazuko This was unthinkable. How important was this foreigner exactly?

The priestess sat down on the cold floor in front of the panel made of a chief of local police, the *bugyō* himself and a representative of the *Taikun*'s secret service, the *metsuke*, who had arrived from Edo just the night before. The respect with which each of them was treating the priestess depended on their rank – the poor local *doshin*, Koyata, noticeably out of place among the noblemen with his plain grey coat and flushed jovial face, was all bows and apologetic smiles; the *bugyō* seemed decidedly uneasy, unsure whether to treat her as a prisoner or a friendly guest, while the Edo notable looked at her with the simple disdain he reserved for all traitors. It was obvious he had witnessed many such interrogations in his career.

"I can smell a traitor," he scoffed at the beginning of the proceedings, pointing at his nose, "and it sure stinks here."

The *doshin* frowned discreetly, but said nothing. The *bugyō* smiled politely, trying to keep his face a professionally neutral mask, but his discomfort with the *metsuke's* presence was easily discernible. He started the interrogation as politely as he could, but the *metsuke* interrupted him quickly with a snarl.

"No need to belittle yourself before this traitor, dear magistrate-*sama*. We know all about you in Edo." He turned to the priestess. "We've been watching you for a long time, waiting for something like this to come up."

"What do you mean?" the *bugyō* questioned, raising his eyebrows. "This trial deals only with the matter of harbouring a fugitive foreigner."

"Oh, there's far more going on here than that," the *metsuke* said with a snigger.

The priestess remained quiet, smiling serenely all the time. Her smile unnerved Tokojiro greatly. *Doesn't she know that her life is in danger?*

"By your leave."

The *Taikun*'s spy bowed before *bugyō*, with a slightly mocking attitude, pointing to one of the men sitting under the wall. The chief magistrate nodded grudgingly. The man, whom Tokojiro recognised as one of the lesser acolytes of Suwa, stood up in a half-bow, approached the middle of the room holding a large heavy bundle and unravelled it before the astonished eyes of the *bugyō*.

"We found this hidden inside the inner sanctum of the Morisaki *kami*," said the *metsuke* triumphantly.

"You dared to enter the sanctum...?"

Doshin Koyata gasped, but the magistrate silenced him with an annoyed grunt.

"What is this? I don't see that well."

The man brought the item closer. It was some kind of wooden statue, roughly hewn. Tokojiro could not see the details from where he was sitting.

"I would be surprised if you recognised it, dear magistrate, as it would mean you're not beyond suspicion yourself." The *metsuke* grinned. "It's one of the false Gods of the Heretics, the Lion-Headed One."

Tokojiro gasped, as did everyone in the room except the *metsuke*, his servant and the High Priestess herself.

"Kazuko-*hime*... Did you know of this?"

"Of course she did," the *metsuke* barked, "you don't think she-"

"Let her speak," the chief magistrate ordered, cutting him off curtly.

The High Priestess smiled and nodded.

"But... Why? This is much worse than harbouring a Westerner."

"It's obvious, that entire shrine is-" the *metsuke* started again.

"I said, *let her speak!*" the *bugyō* shouted and the other man fell silent at last.

"Mizuno-*dono*..." The priestess spoke, her gentle voice resonating in the room for the first time. "I remember when you first came to this city two years ago. You may not know everything about the complicated situation of Kiyō. There are tangled webs of connections, relationships, interests, debts of gratitude and vendettas going back as far as – "

"I have been thoroughly briefed on my arrival," the chief magistrate said, raising his hand, "and two years is plenty of time to learn what more there was to learn. I implore you, please tell me the meaning of this statue."

"It is no secret. The Suwa Shrine thrives on its kindness. Most of the city is in our debt, one way or another. The safekeeping of this statue was one such favour, going back to the times of the Shimabara Rebellion. A small act of goodwill, compared with what we did for others at the time. It was a decision made by one of my predecessors hundreds of years ago, so who am I to question it?"

The *bugyō* pondered this answer, scratching the back of his neck.

"And you swear you are not, in fact, a secret follower of the Forbidden Faith?"

"*Magistrate!*" The *metsuke* rose up indignantly. "You can't believe the word of this traitor!"

"You will behave in my presence, *o-metsuke-dono!*" The chief magistrate stood up to full height and glowered at the other man. "You may be the *Taikun*'s representative for the case, but I am his *hatamoto* retainer, and still your superior!"

The *metsuke* sat down, scowling in stifled anger. He bowed an abrupt apology.

"My powers, of which you are, I'm certain, aware, come from the *kami*," replied the High Priestess serenely, ignoring the outburst. "The false Gods of the Heretics are impotent in this land."

"Western witchcraft," mumbled the *Taikun*'s spy.

"I see," replied the *bugyō*, "I shall deal with this later. This is a new matter that I must consider carefully. Now, back to more recent events, I trust your answers will be as prompt, Kazuko-*hime*, and we will be able to go home before nightfall."

The priestess nodded gently.

"You have failed to report the *Gaikokujin* to the authorities. Was this another one of your favours?"

"Rather, an old woman's fancy," Lady Kazuko replied.

"Kazuko-*hime*, the seriousness of your charges…"

"I understand. No, this had nothing to do with the shrine."

"Why then?"

"Even if I could tell you, you would not understand."

Does she want to die? Tokojiro struggled to understand. The High Priestess seemed thoroughly resigned to whatever fate held for her. *Is this all part of some greater plan?*

The *bugyō* frowned, obviously as confused as the interpreter.

"What about the outlaw, the Takashima girl? You have harboured her as well."

"The shrine is a holy place. You are well aware we have a right to do that."

"But she's a danger to us all!"

"Oh, and what danger can a wounded, orphaned, seventeen-year old girl possibly pose?"

"A girl who carries a sword," muttered the *metsuke*, "You have tolerated that family for far too long."

"*Doshin-sama.*" The chief magistrate ignored him and turned to Koyata, who looked up in surprise. "Can you tell us the results of your investigation at the Takashima residence?"

So that's why they brought him here, thought Tokojiro. He was observing the interrogation with increasing discomfort. The two men obviously already knew all they wanted about the priestess's crimes, why did they continue with this humiliating performance?

The *doshin* coughed and ran his fingers through thick black sideburns surrounding his round face.

"I… I have concluded that Takashima-*sama* has performed a series of forbidden experiments that resulted in the demise of himself and his entire household."

"And…?" prodded the *bugyō*.

"And that his heir, Takashima Satō, knew about these experiments and was, in all probability, willing to continue them."

"There you go, Kazuko-*hime*. You must admit, all this does not look good for you. An outlawed wizard, a runaway *Gaikokujin*, a *mitorashita* relic in your shrine… Your close familiarity with one of Black Raven's students…"

The magistrate nodded towards Tokojiro, and the interpreter froze. Were they trying to incriminate *him* as well?

"All this points to the highest treason," the *bugyō* continued, "but I hope we can cooperate and explain everything in a satisfactory manner."

Tokojiro felt sorry for the magistrate, who was torn between acting according to the law and trying to save the High Priestess's life or, failing that, her honour.

Lady Kazuko smiled, but did not respond.

"We know you have sent the boy and the girl away from the city on some kind of errand. What was it?"

The priestess turned her head towards Tokojiro. Her eyes seemed to delve into the deepest recesses of his soul.

"You have the interpreter. He knows everything I told the boy. Why don't you ask him?"

"We want to hear it from you."

They trust me less than they trust her.

Lady Kazuko shook her head.

"I have only given them guidance. I don't know which way they took."

"But what is their aim? What are they – and you – trying to achieve?"

There was no response. The *bugyō* sighed. Tokojiro felt somebody's eyes upon himself – it was the *doshin* Koyata, observing his reactions carefully. *He suspects*, the interpreter realised and sweat trickled down his neck.

They had interrogated him, of course – as soon as the three samurai had brought him to Kiyō. He told them the boy and the wizardess were heading straight for Satsuma, to seek help at the Shimazu court. The magistrate believed him, having no other source of information. Besides, it seemed like an obvious path to take for the fugitives: Satsuma was the only place more rebellious and friendly to the foreigners than Kiyō.

He did not know why he had lied; he had no reason to. He cared neither for the *Gaikokujin*'s fate nor the Takashimas girl's. The risk, if he had been caught lying, was fatal.

Because you knew what you did was wrong.

"You must see the truth now, chief magistrate," the *metsuke* spoke. 'she is mocking us with her silence. There is treason afoot in the shrine, we've known about it for years, treason of the highest order, or did you think we haven't heard of your precious *Prophecy*?" he enquired, looking at the priestess, who for the first time stopped smiling.

"*Prophecy*? What are you on about now?" The *bugyō* frowned. "Why wasn't I informed of all these things?"

"It was a plan to overthrow the *Taikun*, disguised in divinations. Naturally, its existence was a state secret."

"Is that true?" The chief magistrate turned his glaring eyes towards the priestess. "Does such a Prophecy exist?"

"You have no idea how our divinations work, *metsuke-sama*," replied Lady Kazuko, not looking at the *bugyō*, "these are not the matters of this world. I respond only to the Gods."

"You're not denying it, then?"

"There are many prophecies. It's what we do at the shrine. We heal injuries and foretell the future."

"And protect criminals and fugitives, it seems," added the *metsuke*.

"Kazuko-*hime*..." the chief magistrate began, rubbing his brow, "you're putting me in a most difficult position."

"I am sorry," was her entire response.

"Not as much as I am. I will have to start treating you like a traitor, not merely like a suspect. May the Gods forgive me..." He stood up and nodded at the guards. "I am tired. We will continue this tomorrow. Take her to the Cage."

"The Cage, *tono*?" One of the guards let out a gasp, but quickly composed himself, wary of questioning the orders of his superior. "Understood."

Tokojiro entered the small square room with walls of plain wood and a dirt floor. In the middle of it stood the Cage, a large box of criss-crossing steel bars. It was not big enough for the person within to stand upright. The priestess was sitting cross-legged on the iron floor, her eyes closed. She opened them when she heard the interpreter enter.

Tokojiro nodded at the guard, who bowed back and left them alone. The interpreter was granted a personal visit to the priestess by the *bugyō* himself, albeit grudgingly.

"I will try to talk some sense into her," Tokojiro had pleaded.

"Very well," the chief magistrate had said, waving his hand, "but don't forget you're not completely beyond suspicions yourself. Any tricks and your head will roll."

Tokojiro knew the *bugyō* was well aware of how he had tried to cheat him out of the *Gaikokujin's* capture, but he was now desperate enough to accept any sort of help. The priestess stubbornly refused to provide any information that could save her life and honour, and the search for the fugitives had stumbled at a dead end. It seemed the next head to roll would be that of the *bugyō* himself.

"What is it about this boy, Kazuko-*hime*?" Tokojiro asked, kneeling on the packed dirt before the Cage. "Why are you willing to risk so much to protect him?"

The priestess looked at him with her wise eyes.

"You haven't told them much yourself."

"That's true," the interpreter admitted, lowering his voice to a whisper.

Neither the *Taikun's* nor the magistrate's men were as yet aware of the Ritual changing the foreigner's face or the disguises the three fugitives had donned. When they had found him crawling around the forest, they had little patience for his incoherent babbling. Later, when it came to confessing before the magistrate court, he had omitted these details deliberately. Another lie added to a tower of lies.

"I... I wasn't sure what I should do."

"And yet you did right." Lady Kazuko smiled. "In your heart you knew what was proper. You've never wanted anybody to get hurt, have you?"

"I only wanted the court to notice me..."

Tokojiro shook his head and touched his scar. His hand reached instinctively to his side, where a sword should be. He still could not understand how the boy could outwit him like that.

"I know," the priestess said, nodding.

The conversation took an unexpectedly distressing direction. He had come with hope of extracting information from the priestess, but instead began to confess himself. It was as if he himself was a criminal in the Cage, and she his interrogator.

"Sooner or later they will question me again, and I... I don't understand why I should not tell them all that I know."

"Oh, but you won't. You are not the kind of man who would betray my trust."

But I already have! He wanted to scream, but the priestess gazed at him with her ancient eyes and the words got stifled in his throat.

She had planned it all. I'm just a pawn in her game.

"They will torture me," he said quietly.

"Leave the city. They will not bother looking for you in all this chaos. There will be plenty to keep them occupied."

"You *are* a traitor," he said, a sudden understanding dawning on him.

The priestess smiled.

"I have never betrayed my loyalties."

Loyalties to whom? he thought, and stood up.

"I must leave. It's too dangerous for me to continue this conversation. I will have to report my failure to the *bugyō*."

She bowed politely and he bowed back.

"You have a brilliant mind, Tokojiro-*sama*," she added as he was about to leave the room, 'so use it for good. A career at the court is not worth losing one's integrity over... especially in these turbulent days."

He breathed in sharply and slid the door closed behind him.

In the calm sleepy quiet of the night water dripped slowly from the tiled eaves of the magistrate gate into a lazy puddle below. Somewhere in the distance, a cat cried its unfulfilled urges. The wind rang a tranquil melody in the rain-chain gutters.

I should be doing this more often, thought Koyata. *I had forgotten how wonderful the nights in this city are.* He approached the gate and knocked on it with a handle of his *jutte* truncheon. A face with a lantern appeared over the wall.

"A – ! *Doshin-sama!*" the guard recognised him and disappeared.

Wood scraped against iron as the heavy bolt was removed from inside and the thick door lifted open.

"What are you doing here at this time of night?"

"I couldn't sleep," Koyata lied, "so I thought I'd check up on the security of our prisoner."

"Kazuko-*hime* is well guarded, Koyata-*sama.*"

The guard looked wounded by the *doshin's* apparent lack of trust.

"No doubt, no doubt, but you can never be too sure, *neh?*"

The guard agreed hesitantly.

"How many soldiers do you have here?"

"Eight at the wall, four inside, and there're Captain Tsukinari's men, of course."

"Good, good," Koyata said, nodding absentmindedly.

He didn't feel good about the numbers at all. If what the purple-hooded samurai had told him was true, it was nowhere near enough...

*The *doshin* was just about to take his evening bath. He disrobed and started to shave himself, leaving the bathroom door slightly ajar as always. He slid the shaving blade along the sideburns; it was a Western fashion he'd picked up from the Bataavians and something he did not trust the town barbers with.

Through the opening, Koyata spotted soft feet clad in black socks treading softly on the tatami mat. *Assassin*, he realised immediately without even looking up. Quietly, he turned the blade around the handle so it changed into a dagger. Dealing with gamblers and smugglers had taught him wariness. As the quiet-footed assailant approached within a few feet of the bathroom, Koyata slid open the door and lunged forwards.

His arm grabbed in a firm clasp, the *doshin's* feet left the floor, his body flipped in the air and he landed with a damp thud on the tatami.

The stranger let out a hearty laugh.

"Formidable reflexes, *doshin-sama!*"

Koyata scrambled up, still cautious, and saw a tall muscular samurai standing in the middle of his room, wearing a purple-hooded cloak over a gaudy blue and yellow kimono.

"Who are you? What are you doing here?" he asked as soapy water dripped down his naked legs in large slow drops.

The samurai turned serious and took something out of the sleeve of his kimono. Koyata tensed, expecting a missile, but it was just a piece of paper, torn off and singed at the edges.

"I believe you have the rest."

The stranger let the piece of paper fly gently down to the floor between the *doshin's* legs. Koyata picked it up and recognised immediately the soft-curved writing of Takashima Shūhan. It was one of the translation pages for the Dragon Book.

"Don't worry, I'm not here to steal it," the samurai said calmly. "I just want to discuss something with you – something regarding the security of the city. Please," he reached out a hand holding the *doshin's* own indigo *yukata*.

"Can you take me to the fire tower?" Koyata asked the guard. "I want to check one more thing."

"Of course, *doshin-sama*, but be careful, it's dark up there…"

The wooden tower rose high above not only the roofs of the magistrate, but above any roofs in the neighbourhood. A brass bell hung from the roof beams, to be used in case of emergency. From this vantage point Koyata could see all the way towards the harbour, the great white ever-burning torch on the top of the wizard spire of the Bataavians and the square island of the Qin, pocked with the tiny red dots of their lanterns. Most of the city slept under the thick familiar cover of the darkness. The deep blue shadow of the holy Tamazono Mountain shrouded the stars to the north, the flat nothingness of the sea spread to the west. He breathed deeply, the salty breeze from the sea tickling his nostrils. Everything seemed as calm and peaceful as it had always been.

Koyata reached into his sleeve and took out a small copper tube enclosed with dark green glass on both sides. He didn't know what the device was called or how it worked – all he knew was that if he looked through it, he could see everything as bright as day, if slightly tinted green.

It was one of several artefacts he had found buried in the dried-up well in the garden of the Takashima Mansion, along with the Dragon Book. By law, he should've reported them all to his superiors, but he knew they would either destroy it all or sell it back to Dejima, and he couldn't admit to the possession of the devices to anyone else. His situation was already precarious enough after the way he had dealt with the Takashima investigation.

He put one end of the copper tube to his eye and looked down into the narrow streets beyond the stone wall of the magistrate.

A swordsman appeared in the alleyway, crouching, sneaking, and then another. Koyata spied further – they were now coming from all sides, gathering slowly underneath the walls, eight, ten, twelve…

He recognised most of them; petty cut-throats, unemployed household samurai, masterless *rōnin*. The usual bunch he had to deal with on a daily basis in his capacity as a *doshin*, but he'd never seen them all gathered together for a purpose. He looked for their leader and found a man clumsily sneaking in front of the first party. For a moment he turned his face straight towards Koyata, easily recognisable due to a great torn scar running halfway through it.

Tokojiro the interpreter… so the *doshin's* suspicions were right: all this time the interpreter had been hiding his real role in the recent events from his interrogators. But where did he find the means – and courage – to organise such an assault?

Koyata turned around and reached for the bell, but stopped halfway. There was some other movement in the shadows on the opposite side of the magistrate. He raised the copper tube to his eye again. It was another troop of swordsmen approaching from the forest on the slopes of Tamazono. These he did not recognise. They were all wearing the same uniform kimonos, grey and drab in the darkness. They moved more stealthily than the first group, and in order. The *doshin* assessed that these new enemies were much more dangerous.

Forgetting about the bell, he half-climbed, half-jumped off the tower and ran towards the guardhouse.

Both assaults started almost at once. Tokojiro's rag-tag band of cut-throats surged over the wall noisily, running at the guards with naked swords glistening in the light of the torches. As per Koyata's suggestion, the guards feigned a feeble defence before dispersing in a fake retreat. The attack from the forest was a much more immediate threat. Captain Tsukinari and his samurai hid in the shadows along the northern wall, waiting patiently for the situation to evolve.

The grey-clad swordsmen leapt down from the battlements straight onto Tokojiro's band. Both groups stared at each other in confused silence. Obviously neither of them had expected the other. A second passed then another, until at last the leader of the grey samurai, a bulbous-eyed, grim-faced young man – they were all young and grim-faced – growled an order.

"Get him," he said, pointing at Tokojiro, "kill the rest."

Koyata observed the battle from behind a stack of building materials piled up in the corner of the courtyard. Tokojiro's swordsmen were more numerous, but they were hardly a match for the grey-clad samurai. Pushed against the wall of the prison, their ranks melted quickly. One by one they were cut down until some of them, having decided death wasn't worth their mercenary pay, began to dash off into the darkness. Soon only a few remained, with Tokojiro standing valiantly in the prison entrance, scowling and waving a dagger – his sword scabbard dangled empty at his side.

At this moment Captain Tsukinari launched his men into an attack at the rear of the grey samurai group. The guards returned simultaneously, this time armed with *naginata* halberds and muskets.

"Round them all up!" Tsukinari ordered over the thunderclaps of the firearms. "Leave some alive."

The commander of the greys turned furiously towards the new threat. He reached for something hanging off his sash and pulled strongly. A round black object, the size of a ripe persimmon, bounced and rolled on the courtyard sand.

"*Look out!*" Koyata shouted from his hideout, but it was too late.

The grenade exploded with a tremendous flash and bang, shrouding everything and everyone in a thick choking cloud of white smoke.

The few remaining of Tokojiro's sellswords emerged from the cloud, coughing and gasping for air. They were quickly subdued by the guards. When the smoke had at last cleared, there was no trace of the grey-clad samurai, only a few puddles of blood remained where some of them had been wounded by gunshot. Gone also was Tokojiro, the interpreter.

Koyata rushed to the prison entrance and breathed a deep sigh of relief. The door was untouched. The prisoner inside was safe – for the time being.

CHAPTER IX

Itsunen stood in the *shukubō's* entrance, observing the street. An odd, hair-raising coldness and the unmistakable reverberating hum of the Otherworld was creeping ever closer. It had been years since he had sensed a presence like this. It felt almost nostalgic.

Together with Ingen they had already woken and escorted all the pilgrims out of the temple – except the three newcomers who had been inexplicably missing from their rooms. When they had finally appeared it was already too late lead them to the main gate, so Itsunen had to explain the way out the back to the raven-haired apprentice while the others packed.

"Through the kitchen to the steel door – it will lead you into the camphor tree grove. There's an old gate there, unused for centuries. Where are you heading?"

"Do you know of a village called Kawachi?"

He froze at the name. *That's no place for a girl like you to look for,* he thought, but then forced a smile. "That old place? There's a path through the fields that will take you around a mountain to the west," he said, "the place you seek is on the other side, on a slope overlooking the sea."

"Try to avoid the main roads," added Ingen, "and the hills."

The girl did not question why. She must have been sensing the oncoming presence herself, Itsunen guessed.

"What about you?" she asked instead.

"Don't worry about us, little apprentice." Itsunen smiled, touched by her concern. "We are the Hosts of the *Shukubō*. Taking care of the guests is our duty."

He watched her join the samurai boy and the servant, and as the three departed through the back doorway he turned to the other monk with a meaningful glance.

"Have you felt it too, Brother?"

Ingen nodded.

"They carry heavy burdens," Itsunen added.

"But the young one carries the heaviest," said Ingen.

Ingen removed a small shrine of Kojin, the three-headed kitchen god, from its stone pedestal and opened a trap door underneath. He climbed inside and started coughing and sneezing furiously.

"I'm sorry, it hasn't been cleaned in a long time," Itsunen said apologetically.

The other monk came out of the dugout carrying two bundles of white fabric and black leather armour. He then disappeared again and brought up a pair of long poles, the ends of which were wrapped in hemp cloth.

"Hurry," he said sternly, "it's close."

"I know."

Itsunen proceeded to put on the old armour made of black leather scales laced together to form a wrap-around coat. He then tied a white cloth cowl around his head and face, and threw a dark cape over his shoulders.

"I hope you were at least sharpening those," Ingen grunted, unwrapping the hemp cloth from the end of his pole, revealing a long glistening blade of a *naginata* halberd.

"Of course, Brother," replied Itsunen, preparing his weapon.

He slashed through the air three times to test the elasticity of the bamboo shaft. The blade buzzed and lit up in a red glow, as if welcoming an old friend.

"Let's see if you still remember how to use this," said Ingen, picking up his *naginata* and heading for the door.

"Your words wound me, Brother Magonojo," Itsunen said, grinning. "Have I not always beaten you in duels?"

"Only because I let you, Brother Motomenosuke," the other monk replied, with a gruesome smile.

The Abbot stood in the middle of the road, misty wisps floating down from the hillside weaving around his short stocky frame. A young man was standing beside him, tall, bald, a staff topped with jingling bells in his hand. His robe was similar to the white cowl that Ingen and Itsunen wore, but jet black, with red pompoms dangling from the sash across his chest and a large conch tied to the waist. A mark of treason was burned into the man's forehead, but he wore it proudly, making no effort to conceal it.

"A renegade," growled Ingen, and spat.

"Not one of us – he's of the mountain hermits," Itsunen said, and turned to the Abbot. "Father, is this really the way to treat our honourable guests?" he asked resolutely. "What about the reputation of our temple?"

"Guests? You mean *thieves*, who sneak into my house at night. Do you know how much it costs to keep the scrolls in pristine condition? I only wanted a little upkeep fee and an offering for a new roof over the archive room." The Abbot spread his hands helplessly. "Was that too much to ask?"

"Who are *you*?" Itsunen asked, referring directly to the silent renegade.

"This gentleman has made a substantial donation to the temple," the Abbot said, "and in exchange he only wished to meet our new guests. Surely you have no problem with that? Please, let us through, there is no need for violence."

"You have dabbled in the dark arts for too long, Abbot." Ingen lowered the humming, glowing blade of his *naginata*. "What's that lurking in the mist behind you?"

"I have done nothing, I assure you. It is all our benefactor's doing."

The man in the black cowl stomped his staff. The bells jingled and out of the darkness emerged a Spirit, white as death, of a great man clad in ghostly armour, wearing a tall conical hat and brandishing a long hunting spear. His eyes burned red like coals, his hair and beard were a blazing flame.

"Behold, the Spear of Shizugatake!" cried the Abbot with glee.

Itsunen stepped back, astonished, recognising the *yōkai* summoned by the renegade.

"Kiyomasa-*dono*!" he whispered in awe.

"You dare to wake the master of Jōchibyō?" Ingen growled. "Have you lost all sense of what is right?"

"Enough of your insolent prattle, I am your Abbot, your superior! Remove yourselves from my path, or suffer the consequences of disobedience."

"May *Butsu-sama* have mercy on your soul, Abbot."

Itsunen raised his halberd above his head, poised to strike.

"You will regret that," the Abbot warned, stepping back. "Move over or you will die!"

"*It is better to live one day with honour than to live to a hundred and die in disgrace,*" Itsunen recited grimly.

The renegade put the conch to his lips and blew. The Spirit of Lord Kiyomasa roared and launched itself upon the two monks in fury.

Even having their way lit by Bran's flamespark and Nagomi's Spirit light, Satō found it hard to navigate in the thick dark mist. The gnarled entwined branches of the ancient camphor trees formed a barely penetrable web of solid black wood.

"There's the wall," she whispered, pointing at a brick surface glimpsed among the trees.

The night around them was completely silent, the mist muffling all sound.

"Then the gate should be nearby as well," replied Bran, "let us venture this way first."

They soon found the remains of the entrance, little more than a pile of wooden beams, blackened with age and rotten to the core. Remnants of gilding on a carved crossbeam were a reminder of the gate's better days. The two planks that had once formed the wings of the door lay buried in the moss, eaten through by time and worms.

Bran reached for one of the planks to heave it out of the way, but Satō stopped him.

"We don't have time for this," she said, "give me my sword." The wizardess pointed the end of her blade at the pile of wood. "*Bevries!*" she cried, and drew a frost rune in the air.

A chain of ice formed around the beams, sharp icicles penetrated inside with a loud crackle. Satō stared into the ice, focusing on the enchantment as the frost spread through the planks, shattering them into splinters in its wintry embrace.

"*Genoeg!*"

She finished the spell, breathing heavily and the ice sublimated, returning its moisture into the mist.

"Most admirable, Satō-*sama*," said Bran. She did not reply to the compliment; the boy may have been impressed, but she remembered how effortlessly the Crimson Robe had shrugged her ice magic off.

"Snuff out that light, we're trying to be stealthy," she said.

A sound of a horn pierced the silence, followed by a blood-curdling roar. The noise of clashing blades came from the direction of the temple grounds. The mist around them thickened. Satō's shoulder burst in pain; she hissed and almost dropped the sword to the ground...

"Art thou all right?"

Bran offered his arm to support her, but she shook her head.

"I'm fine."

Something shifted in the mist behind Nagomi.

"*Look out!*" Bran cried, leaping towards the apprentice and pinning her to the wet ground.

A reddish-grey phantom dashed out and back into the milky haze.

"What was that?" the Westerner asked, staring wide-eyed into the mist.

Instead of replying, Satō raised her sword defensively, the blade covered with hoar frost. The wraith appeared again, and a clawed arm of smoke struck and bounced off the wizardess's sword with an Otherworldly clang. The phantom vanished once more.

"Take Nagomi and run," Satō ordered.

"What... *nay!*" Bran drew his own sword, the runes along the blades lighting up with green radiance. "I shall not leave thee."

"I have trained all my life to fight things like this one." She was adamant. She had not yet recognised the wraith, but could sense its energy. How did the Abbot manage to summon a *yōkai* so powerful? "You stand no chance."

The spectre reappeared from another side, speeding towards them, rolling its eyes and extending its claws. Bran lunged forwards and slashed his sword through the air and through the Spirit's ghostly body. It shrieked and lashed out against the Westerner. He managed to draw back, and the wraith's long red claw merely tore his kimono and lightly touched the skin.

"C-cold!" the boy gasped.

"Western magic is no good," Satō said, blocking another strike of the deadly claws with her icy blade. As she did so, the wound in her shoulder radiated pain again. "Please protect Nagomi. I'll take care of this thing."

Bran nodded and moved aside. The wraith and the wizardess focused on each other.

It was her first real fight, apart from the brief failed encounter with the Crimson Robe. She kept telling herself she had to remain calm and focused, but her hands trembled, her breath escaped her. She was foolish to waste so much energy on those wooden planks when they could have simply been moved away.

Recalling her training, she rolled sideways from under the monster's claws and touched the ground, marking it with a small glowing rune of frost.

The phantom followed her, but it was too slow – before it reached her she was already on its other side casting another rune.

She managed to stamp the third magic seal and then the fourth. This was going well. Her father would have been proud of her. Blood in her veins ran hot with the rush of battle and she almost forgot about the pain in her arm – but when she reached for the last spot, she cried out in agony and fell to her knees, piercing darkness momentarily appearing before her eyes. One of the Spirit's red claws reached her back.

The wizardess braced herself, expecting another blow, but it did not come. Instead she heard the ghost shriek, not in triumph or pain, but in helpless anger.

She turned to see Bran standing between her and the enemy. For the moment, with the light of the moon filtering through the clouds illuminating his stark silhouette, he seemed tall, proud and strong, like a real samurai.

A shimmering magic shield separated him and Satō from the monster outside.

"Western magic be no good?"

The boy winked, his green eyes reflecting the pale rays of the moon.

"Where's Nagomi?"

"Safe beyond the wall," Bran replied, "whatever you plan to do, make haste."

Satō froze the fifth rune promptly. The Pentacle of Seimei was finished.

"*Get back*," she cried and, as Bran leapt aside, she cut through the phantom with great force.

The mystic energies of the five points beamed into the blade, and the Spirit vanished with a noiseless flash, banished into the Void.

This time she accepted Bran's shoulder with gratitude.

Nagomi's heart pounded. She ran through the pine forest, down the slope of the hill upon which the temple stood. Behind her, the mist covered the ground with a heavy blanket. Before her there was only night, cold and dark, lit up only by the comforting flicker of Bran's flamespark.

The shadows of the trees loomed above her. They seemed sinister, spiteful. The branches tore at her skin and dress as if on purpose. The silence of the forest pressed upon her like a heavy blanket. There was evil in these woods and she did not know how to cope with it. The Spirits she had learned to commune with were never malevolent. Neutral at worst, like nature itself, they often required coercing to be helpful, but they never posed any direct threat. She trusted them more than she trusted most humans. The *yōkai* – demons – were the stuff of legends, nightmares.

Only now the reality of their endeavour struck her. This wasn't an excursion around Chinzei. *We could die here.* Was this the kind of threat Lady Kazuko had meant when she sent Nagomi along on the quest? But she could do nothing – she was just a burden, as she had always feared; Satō and the Foreigner had managed the monster well enough on their own.

We should have gone back to the shrine. This is far too dangerous.

The forest ended abruptly and she ran out onto a field of barley. The city below slept, only points of light in the distance marked the watchtowers of the Kumamoto Castle. The thin ribbon of a river reflected the silver light of the moon.

"I think we made it," said Satō, panting.

She dropped her bag onto the ground and sat on it to rest.

"You're bleeding," Nagomi said, reaching towards her with a handkerchief.

"It's nothing," said Satō and wiped her mouth. She had been biting her lips all through the fight.

"Your back," said the apprentice, "you are wounded. Take off that shirt."

"What was that monster?" the boy asked.

The wizardess started to remove her outer garment carefully, hissing. The claw scratch on her shoulder blade was swelling.

"An *enenra*," she replied, 'smoke wraith. I used to train fighting them in my father's school – but those were just illusions, this one was real."

"A *yōkai*…" Nagomi whispered.

"A minor one that must have come down from the mountains. So I was right to fear the mist… What's wrong, Bran-*sama*?"

The boy was staring at the wizardess in astonishment. His eyes focused on the bandages wrapping her chest. When he noticed the girls looking at him, he turned away quickly. His face was red in the light of the Spirit flame.

"Thou… thou art a *female*," Bran mumbled, swallowing loudly.

Satō blinked twice then burst out laughing.

"Oh, of course, you didn't know. You've never seen me in girl's clothes! Was my disguise that good then?"

"It… fooled me," the boy said, still looking away. 'so thou art not… Nagomi-*sama* and thou…?"

Nagomi was the first to understand what he meant.

"*Eeh*? No! We're childhood friends."

The boy grunted something beyond hearing. For some reason he would not turn his face in their direction until Nagomi had finished bandaging the wound, quickly healing under her warm touch, and Satō put on her servant's tunic again.

"I will need to sew it back together when we get to a village," the wizardess said. "You fought well." She nodded at Bran with honest praise. "You have my gratitude."

"It was nothing," the boy replied quietly, looking into the darkness.

"There was something else," said Nagomi.

She could still sense the malignant presence, distant now and weak. The other two looked at her in surprise.

"Even more terrible. It filled the whole place with dread. Did you not feel it?"

Satō shook her head, but Bran spoke slowly.

"'Tis true. I felt… something. The chill, and the humming noise, as if of the Otherworld."

"Whatever it was, we got away," said the wizardess.

"But those two poor monks," Bran said, looking with worry towards the temple, "and the pilgrims…"

"I will pray for their safety," Nagomi said and discreetly stifled a yawn.

"We can't do anything to help them," said Satō, "we're tired and haven't slept all night. We need to rest."

"Is it safe to break camp here?" the dragon rider asked. "We're in the middle of nowhere."

"We won't find a better shelter in this darkness. At least there is cover of trees here."

The dragon rider did not argue. Silently, he nestled himself in a pile of leaves, leaning against the trunk of a massive cedar. Nagomi wrapped herself in the thick travelling cloak and anything else she could find in her bags to stave off the cold. She huddled up to Satō and, exhausted by the long eventful night, fell asleep quickly.

A perfectly round jade glimmered in the darkness, spreading the life-giving light. There was a shadow in the background, a long, serpentine coiled silhouette.

Something – somebody – was lying among the coils.

The green jewel blinked.

A hand gently stirred Nagomi out of her sleep.

She yawned, stretched and looked around. She was the last to wake. The sky was painted pink, the forest rang out with the morning choir of birds and the green barley shoots covered the boundless fields below. By day the landscape was almost idyllic compared to how sinister it seemed in the evening.

There was little as good for one's mood as spending a night in the wild and waking at dawn. The horrors of last night seemed distant and almost forgotten. For a brief moment the apprentice recalled the dread she had felt in the mist, but she shook her head and forced herself to focus on the present. *We can manage. Kazuko-hime trusted in us. But I need to be strong, not just another weight they have to carry.*

"I'm hungry," she complained, rubbing her eyes, "now I wish I had eaten more of that aubergine."

"Nobody could eat more aubergine than you did yesterday," Satō said, laughing.

"What did the monks tell thee about this Unganzenji place?" asked Bran, rummaging inside his satchel.

"It's on the other side of that," the apprentice replied and pointed towards a mountain that rose up from a valley to the west. It wasn't very tall and sloped gently, but it sprawled extensively in either direction.

"I'd say that is easily a day's walk," noted Bran, studying the road ahead through his telescope.

"We're not going to make it on an empty stomach," remarked Satō..

"Why the disguise?" asked Bran, as they descended towards the villages, moving far off the main roads as advised. He was still not sure how to react to what he had learned the night before. The women in the Dracalish military, like Reeve Gwenlian, wore the same uniforms as men and sometimes it was easy to make the mistake – and yet somehow he could not come to terms with the discovery.

"Isn't it obvious? A woman cannot study the art of war," explained Satō, "a girl can't study anything important at all really, unless she's a nun or a priestess. I couldn't wear a sword, couldn't inherit the school... Soon I would have to marry somebody and spend the rest of my days between a lathe and a stove. In Yamato, only men can be truly happy."

"Oh," Bran said simply.

"Is it not that way in your country?"

"It used to be, but not anymore. We have womenfolk in the army and in the Academy. A woman rules all Dracaland from the Dragon Throne – a strong woman."

"Impossible – a female ruler?"

"I assure you 'tis the truth." Her doubt stung him unexpectedly.

"There was a woman *Mikado* in the days of our grandparents," said Nagomi, "and before, in the time of legend."

"Yes, but they never *ruled*. Is your Queen also powerless, Bran-*sama*? Is there a *Taikun* in your country?"

"I'm not sure – who is this *Taikun* exactly? I've heard Tokojiro use this word many times."

"*Eeh!*" She scratched her neck. She seemed surprised that somebody might not know it, even a Westerner like Bran. "He is the true ruler of Yamato. He commands all the armies, controls the ministers, lords over all the *daimyo*."

Bran thought for a moment.

"There are ministers and secretaries in Dracaland, but no man in the kingdom hath more puissance than the Queen."

Satō pondered his words in thoughtful silence.

A small farming hamlet appeared from around the bend. Bran stopped. It seemed as if some disaster had gone through the village. Except one, all of the houses were tiny, single-room huts, even smaller than those in the servants district at Kiyō, and all were half-ruined with neglect and disrepair. High peaked roofs of loose thatch were full of holes and mouldy, as were the walls of bamboo slates tied with reed. The air was filled with the acrid stench of old moisture. Everything looked temporary, more like a gathering of straw-covered sheds than a village. The local shrine was just a box with no offerings, vermillion paint peeling off in patches and the torii gate leaning over to one side. The only road was a narrow path of dirt and mud, overgrown with weeds. A couple of starved cats sleeping in the tall grass and the crying of a child in the distance were the only signs of life.

"So poor...!" Bran was astonished. "What happened here? Where is everybody?"

"Out in the fields," replied Nagomi, leaning over a moss-grown well to draw some water with a cracked pot standing beside it. She tried the water and spat it onto the grass. "It's stale!"

"You mean some poor folk *live here*?"

"Can't be helped," Satō said with a shrug, "it's the mountain soil, not good enough to sustain an entire village. Poor or not, the headman's bound to have some food."

She headed for the largest of the houses, the only building in the village to have a door. Inside they found a plump man with a bushy moustache, counting copper coins on a flat wooden board. The headman stood up suddenly, startled by their appearance, scattering the coins all over the floor.

"*T-tono!*" he stuttered. "To what do I owe... Is it about the new tax?"

"We did not come here from thy master," Bran said, stepping forward. "We became lost on the way to Kawachi. Do you have some – "

"Give us food, peasant," Satō interrupted.

"Of course, of course." The headman bent in a deep bow, his eyes shooting from her to Bran. "I only have some barley gruel, though..."

"Are you trying to lie to my master?" Satō asked, frowning. "You're a village headman, I'm sure you can do better than that. Give us rice and saké."

"Right away, *tono*."

"Didst thou have to be so rude to him?" Bran asked, as they finally sat down to the bowls of plain brown rice and pickled onions. The headman disappeared into the only other room in the house, leaving his guests undisturbed.

"Rude?" The girl looked at him blankly. "That's just how you speak to these people. You can't use the language of noblemen. I doubt they would even understand."

He seemed to understand me *perfectly*, Bran thought.

He heard the sound of a horse stopping on the muddy road outside and somebody leaping down onto the mud. A samurai wearing a dark blue kimono, embroidered with an eight-circle crest Bran saw on the tiles of the Kumamoto Castle, barged into the house calling for the headman. He saw Bran and reeled in surprise. He bowed quickly, acknowledging their presence, but remained aloof.

The headman ran out of the backroom bowing profusely.

"Have you seen anyone suspicious passing through the village?" the samurai asked, interrupting the man's flow of polite platitudes.

The headman glanced towards Bran then shook his head.

"No, *tono*."

"There's a fugitive foreigner on the run from Kiyō, we heard rumours he might be somewhere in this area. You do know the punishment for harbouring foreigners, don't you?"

"Of course, *tono*, I wouldn't even dream – "

"Enough. I don't have time to search this whole village. I trust you, Keichi. Keep an eye out for strangers."

"I will, *tono*."

The samurai then turned to Bran.

"And you are...?"

Bran glanced at Satō and Nagomi; they were silent, their eyes turned downwards. A woman and a servant could not reply to a noble born if they weren't asked directly, he remembered. He felt anger stir within him, struggling to break out. He could barely contain himself.

That's no way to talk to a nobleman. Even a pretend one.

He rose slowly. Already a good head taller than the average Yamato, he was now also standing on the slightly raised part of the floor, so he easily towered over the samurai.

" 'tis polite to introduce oneself first before asking another," he said with indignation.

The samurai took a step backwards. For a moment they were staring at each other. At last, the samurai bowed.

"Apologies, *tono*. I am Matsuo, servant of the Hosokawa clan."

"I am Karasu, of the Aoki clan," replied Bran.

"Honoured to meet you, Aoki-sama," Matsuo said. "Forgive me, but... what are you doing here, in this..." he looked around with disgust, "peasant's hovel?"

"We became lost in the mist. This serf was telling us the way to Kumamoto."

"Ah, yes, there was a terrible mist this morning." The samurai nodded. "Please be careful. There is a dangerous fugitive on the loose."

"Well then, thou best be in pursuit," Bran said, losing his patience.

Matsuo bowed once again and backed out of the headman's house. Bran sat back again, sighing deeply. He looked at his hand in surprise – it was clenched around the hilt of his sword. He thought he heard a chuckle deep inside his head.

"For a moment I thought it was Shigemasa-*sama* again," Nagomi looked at him with concern.

"No, I have him under control," he replied, calming down. His heart was still beating fast, his nostrils wide open. *Why did I get so angry?*

"We should be going." Satō stood up. "You heard that samurai. They know we're here."

Bran let go of the sword with some effort. His hand trembled, covered with sweat.

CHAPTER X

His gag had been removed, his hands untied. Shūhan's throat and mouth were so parched he could only whisper; lack of food and sleep had reduced his life energy to the level where he could not perform even the weakest of spells, and, just in case, his fingers had been shattered at the knuckles. The Crimson Robe no longer feared his magic. He was powerless and drained – or so his captors believed.

The wizard crawled up to a thin straw mat he had been given to sleep on, rolled it away and pressed his broken fingers against the packed dirt. He bit his lips, bravely stopping himself from screaming. The pain was almost unbearable, but he had to endure.

The wounds on his hands opened and started bleeding again. His fingers traced a wavy trembling line of scarlet on the floor, joining with other similarly shaky lines into an increasingly complicated pattern.

This was his last resort – the forbidden, hated, cursed practice. He would fight his tormentor with his own weapon. Shūhan recognised the stench of blood magic right away, the demon in the crimson robe must have been its avid practitioner. Every *Rangakusha* knew of its dangers and disadvantages – but also of its daunting power.

The pattern he was so meticulously and painfully drawing was a beacon spell, a distress signal. Anyone sensitive to magic within range would pick up on this call for help. His tormentor would undoubtedly have noticed it too, but Shūhan had no other choice but to risk it. He only hoped it would reach out far enough.

He tried to guess where he was being kept. The only window in his cell opened to the east. In the day he could hear the shrill cries of black kites and at night, the faint roaring of the waves. Sometimes the wind blew the faint smell of sulphur through the window. He gathered from that he was near some source of the volcanic fumes, by the sea – but there were many places like this on the Chinzei Island, assuming the Crimson Robe had not transported him even further.

The door to the tiny prison opened and the guard cast something large and heavy to the ground before shutting the door. Shūhan's weary eyes could not tell what it was at first. He crawled closer and, in the faint moonlight seeping through the narrow window, recognised it as a human being; a young man with the top of his head shaven - a samurai. The newcomer was almost naked, his skin covered in bloody wounds, scars and bruises. A huge, ugly gash split his face, running through his nose and one eye.

The wizard lowered his ear to the stranger's nose. The man was barely breathing. Shūhan gently touched his shoulder with bloodied knuckles. The slightest of shudders went through the man's body, but he didn't wake.

Shūhan hesitated for a moment, but he could wait no longer. The man was bleeding from his many cuts, the blood sinking into the dirt floor; a terrible waste.

"Poor boy," the old wizard whispered, "I'm sure you won't mind… Your blood is precious to me."

He dipped his shattered knuckles into the young man's blood and, as quickly as he could before the liquid dried up on his hands, crept back to his spot.

"I'm eternally grateful," he whispered, half to the boy, half to himself. "Thanks to you I will finish this much faster."

He repeated the procedure several times until the newcomer's wounds were finally covered with dry scabs and became unusable for Shūhan's ritual.

"No matter, no matter," the wizard murmured, "we'll get back to that later."

At noon – or at least Shūhan judged it to be noon from the way the sun appeared in the narrow window – the newcomer awoke suddenly, gasping with pain.

"Poor boy, poor poor boy," Shūhan whispered, crawling towards him, "what have they done to you? Why? Our captor has no need for torture…"

"I… resisted." The newcomer spoke with great difficulty, turning his face towards the wizard. "I meditated… and overcame the *sokukamibutsu's* power."

"What a great feat!"

"I can think… in two languages… that confused the mind-reader."

"You're an interpreter?"

"I am Namikoshi Tokojiro… Black Raven's student. I know you…" The boy pointed at the wizard with a weak hand. "You're that samurai girl's father, aren't you…Takashima…"

"You've met Satō?" Shūhan was enlivened, finding new strength at the mention of his daughter. "Have you seen her? Is she all right?"

"I…" The young man hesitated. Speaking was causing him visible difficulty. "I accompanied her on her journey."

"A journey – what journey?"

"She left the shrine to search for you."

"Poor Satō… She must be so alone…"

"Not… alone… the Westerner - and the red-hair-"

"Nagomi and the boy…? Why is he there? Why is he not kept safe at the shrine?"

"His *dorako*… is somewhere on Chinzei…"

"But how can he travel? He would be captured in an instant…"

"The – ritual…"

Tokojiro dropped his hand and closed his eyes, exhausted.

"*Ritual?* What ritual?"

Shūhan tried to nudge him awake, but the interpreter remained unconscious.

"Yes, yes," the wizard said, patting the boy gently on his scarred back, "sleep, rest. You will tell me – later. Oh look, one of your wounds opened up – back to work, eh...?"

They were brought food – two bowls of thin gruel containing more water and mud than millet, but it was sustenance – and the portions were much bigger than the last time. They were also given water clean enough to drink.

"Eat boy, eat," Shūhan urged, pressing the edge of the bowl against Tokojiro's lips.

The interpreter managed a single gulp before spilling the rest of the gruel on his chin, coughing.

"What *ritual?*" the wizard asked when Tokojiro pushed the bowl away.

"I'm sorry...?"

"The ritual, you said yesterday, the boy and Satō and Nagomi..."

"Oh, yes... it... changed the Westerner's face. He now looks like one of us. They are all disguised."

"Are they safe? Yes, they must be, or he wouldn't torture you," the wizard answered himself before Tokojiro managed to speak. "Is she going south? Is my girl going south like I told her?"

"Y-yes, she is going south."

"Wonderful! Marvellous! Thank you for the good news."

"It's – nothing... What are you doing?"

Tokojiro gasped with pain and shock as Shūhan inserted his hand into a wound in his side.

"Oh, I'm sorry, I just need a little more of your blood."

"*My blood!* What are you...?"

Tokojiro tried to raise himself and crawl away from the wizard, but the effort caused him to pass out again.

"Don't worry, don't worry, I'm not taking much, just a few drops, that's enough..." Shūhan mumbled before noticing his conversation partner was no longer conscious.

The door to the cell opened and the Crimson Robe walked in, smiling broadly.

"I've given you two enough time," he said and clapped his hands once.

The terrifying living mummy entered the room again, creeping slowly.

"It's no use, you still won't break me," said Tokojiro defiantly.

He had regained a little of his strength by now – enough to crawl away from Shūhan to the other side of the cell. The wizard welcomed this development with disappointment. His pattern under the sleeping mat was almost finished.

The Crimson Robe cackled abruptly.

"I did not come for you, my young friend. I've wasted enough time trying to get through that labyrinthian mind of yours."

Shūhan lifted his eyes, as if only now noticing the demon and his undead abomination.

"You've learned everything I know…" he whispered hoarsely as the *sokukamibutsu* approached him.

"Ah, but that was before you so masterfully interrogated the young interpreter." His tormentor smirked. "I knew it would prove useful to spare you."

At last Shūhan understood, and his eyes widened with terror.

"*No, no! Get away, don't…*"

He then fell silent, his mouth drooped. The living mummy began its patient work on his memories.

By late afternoon at last the three travellers had reached the village of Kawachi. This one did not look as shabby and desolate as the one they had seen in the morning. Bran approached an elderly man sitting on a stone bench outside a small, clean house and asked him about the temple.

With some reluctance, the man raised his hand and pointed towards a low spur of the hill to the west.

"We never get any visitors here," he added, eyeing Bran suspiciously.

The boy smiled, trying to seem confident.

"I have a family buried at the cemetery."

The man nodded. He still seemed doubtful but did not dare to contradict a samurai.

I can get used to being treated like a noble man.

The temple turned out to be very small, at least compared to the vast affluent compound of the Honmyōji. There were only two main buildings and a couple of smaller ones, hidden in the unkempt overgrowth of a long-neglected orchard. Of the rest only the burnt out ruins remained. It seemed almost abandoned.

Nobody came out to meet them, so they started exploring the precinct by themselves, trying to find a way to the cave mentioned in the chronicle. There was a path at the back leading up the hill through the forest, lined with stone statues of sitting monks. Following it they came out onto a wide, sunny hillside glade. Bran looked around. Facing west he could see all the way to the sea, while to the east the spur rose in a rocky outcrop staring at them with a single black eye of a cave. The glade was covered with countless more stone statues, hundreds of them, all positioned in concentric rows around the cave, facing towards it. Most of them were overthrown, some broken in two, all incredibly ancient, covered with lichen.

He noticed Nagomi looking pale-faced staring at the bizarre composition.

"What is it? Do you feel something again?" Satō asked, scratching her shoulder.

"Only a faint remnant… These statues were supposed to keep something inside the cave – but it's no longer there."

"That's good to hear," the wizardess said.

Is it? Where is it now, then?

The condition of the statues worsened the closer they got to the cave. The ones just before the entrance were shattered into pieces, shards of stone, barely visible in the tall grass. Bran hesitated at the cave's entrance. He laid his hand on the hilt of his sword. The cavern was wide and shallow, and with the sun at his back he could easily see that it was empty, yet he could feel some lingering presence within, as if somebody was still inside, hiding in the shadows.

Satō was the first to cross the threshold, with bated breath as if she was submerging herself underwater.

"Somebody did live here," she said, pointing at a few utensils and accessories, including a pipe and tobacco pouch, scattered under the bottom wall, "and not that long ago."

"A samurai," noted Nagomi.

In one corner of the cave was something like a miniature study room; a low wooden table, writing pad, a whetstone, an iron-bound chest and a black lacquered rack for two swords – empty. Satō kneeled to examine it.

"It's very good quality, but has no markings," she said. "Everything is well kept here. This cave was recently inhabited."

"But by whom?"

"It wasn't the Crimson Robe," the wizardess said. "This rack is for katana and wakizashi, and so is the whetstone. There's nothing here for a sword as big as the one he carried."

"Perhaps this chest could reveal something."

Bran touched the lock on the coffer and tried to manipulate it using his pen-knife. He had a little practice unlocking his grandfather's chests back in Gwynedd, but this lock was of a better quality. Satō asked him to step away, getting ready to use her magic to open the chest.

"No, I can do that," he said proudly and summoned what little power of his dragon he could. He wasn't sure if it would work at all with Emrys so far away. The blue stone on his finger lit up briefly and he suddenly smelled methane and sulphur, the Farlink momentarily enhanced. He channelled the power of the dragonflame through his fingers. It was a feeble flame, but focused just enough to burn through the wood around the lock. After a bit of a struggle the lid popped open with a satisfying creak.

There were papers in the chest in neat bundles, dozens of pages written in thick but elegant calligraphy, and drawings in black ink, delicate yet precise, which even Bran could tell were made by someone with great skill and an eye for nature. At the bottom there was a set of at least fifty drawings of the same peony flower, each slightly better than the last, until the final exquisite image, which somehow seemed even more true and genuine than a real live flower would be – an essence of natural beauty captured on a piece of paper.

While Bran admired the ink paintings, Satō browsed through the rest of the papers.

"These are notes to a treaty on swordsmanship," she announced, "but there is no name or date on any of these pages, nothing that could tell us anything about the author."

"Then we're back to where we started," said Bran, placing the drawings back into the chest.

A voice startled him.

"Perhaps I can help you."

A lonely monk in a white robe stood at the entrance to the cave, studying them with great curiosity.

"Yes, I know the legend of the Immortal Swordsman…"

His name was Sozaemon, and he was, as it turned out, the last monk left to take care of the temple. Those who did not die of old age moved away to larger, richer temples.

"Some say he had lived in the cave for countless millennia. Others claim he had only arrived here when Katō-*dono* started building the castle at Kumamoto."

"Who was he? Why was he immortal?" asked Satō.

"I don't know. I have never seen him – the cave had been empty for long decades when I became ordained at the temple."

"But it's not empty now."

"What you saw is how it always has been. Time seems to pass in a different manner inside the cave; everything always looks like new, untouched. Sometimes we used to store food there – it would never spoil."

"Why was the cave surrounded with those statues?"

"To imprison the Swordsman inside. According to what's written in the temple archives, demons of this kind can't suffer anything holy. Sanctified ground, priests and monks whose faith is strong – all this repels them."

"*Them?*" Nagomi asked. "You mean there are more of his kind?"

"There were… other legends. My predecessor studied them, trying to find a way to cure or defeat the cursed creature. The demons were called variously – *kyūketsuki*, Fanged Ones, or simply *Abominations* – but they seemed to appear in stories throughout the Yamato."

"Did this Abbot leave any writings? Can we see them?"

"Yes, by all means. They're in the library, but… Why are you so interested in an old legend?" The monk eyed them with amusement. "You're too young to be scholars."

"We…" Satō hesitated. "I think I met one of them."

Sozaemon's eyes widened. He opened his mouth and then closed it. He scratched his beard in thought.

"Even so, why would you want to find one again? By all accounts, these are very dangerous creatures."

"What happened to the one in the cavern? Where be he now?" asked Bran, evading the question.

"One day, more than a hundred years ago, the Swordsman came out, destroyed all the statues and broke out of the temple. As to where he is…" The monk shrugged. "The land of Yamato is vast, and it's been so long…"

"And thou knowest of nothing that would help us find him, or one of his kind?"

"I'm afraid that is all I know, young *tono*."

Bran nodded. He glanced outside; it was getting dark. "We must go down to the village for the night. We would come back tomorrow to see thy Abbot's writing, if that's all right with thou."

"Oh, there's no need to trouble yourselves; I can give them to you."

"Verily?"

"There's no point in me guarding these scribblings if you can find better use for them. Nobody ever comes here, and when I die they will fall prey to robbers. Just wait here, I'll bring them to you, I have them just here…" He disappeared into the room at the back for a moment and returned with a bundle of notes. "Here you are," he said, "life's work of the fourteenth High Priest."

Satō read the title page in disbelief.

"The Tale of the Blood Sucking Ghost?"

"I believe that's one of the names the legend is known by in the north," replied the monk. "You can stay here, if you wish," he added. "There are lots of empty rooms, and there is no inn in the village."

"Thou hast our thanks," said Bran, grateful for not having to share an inn room with the girls that night.

"This is all very interesting, but I doubt it will give us any new clues." Satō was holding the fourteenth High Priest's notes in her hand, browsing through them idly. "We don't really know where to go from here, and we can't stay in this village longer than one night – they will find us sooner or later."

"I… I think I may have a clue," said Bran hesitantly. "Dost thou know the crest of a cross within a circle?"

"Of course," said Satō. "It's the Shimazu clan, *daimyo*s of Satsuma."

"Where did you see it?" asked Nagomi.

"Last night, just before you came for me, I had a vision through my dragon's eyes. I saw a man wearing this crest, and sensed great puissance within him."

Satō whistled.

"A Shimazu retainer… That's a bit out of our league, although – "

"Yes?"

"My father did tell me to go seek help in the far south. I believe he had even met Lord Nariakira once. Perhaps we could find friends at the Kagoshima court, like we did in Kumamoto."

"It's worth a try," said Nagomi, "at least this gives us a direction to follow."

"How long will it take us to get there?" asked Bran.

"More than a week," replied Satō. She was the only one of the party who knew her way around the Saikaidō, the network of highways criss-crossing the Chinzei Island. "As long as we don't dawdle along the way."

"Let us not *dawdle* then," said Bran with a smile. "I can wake us up at dawn tomorrow."

"Not at *dawn!*" Satō protested. "I will need time to go through these notes."

She'd spent most of the night studying *The Tale of the Blood Sucking Ghost*. She was lying on the straw mat on her stomach, flipping through the pages with one hand, holding a slowly disappearing sticky rice cake in the other.

Nagomi went to sleep early and was peacefully lying on her futon by the wall. The red-haired apprentice was quick to tire, and Satō couldn't blame her – a shrine life was a peaceful one, simple and undemanding compared with what they had endured over the last few days. Nagomi was coping with the strain remarkably well, all things considered. She never complained.

The stories and legends gathered from villages and temples, mostly around Chinzei, differed little in their content from those told about any other kind of magical monster. The Fangeds, as the High Priest referred to them in his work, were immortal, blood-drinking demons invading remote lonely hamlets, killing everyone within and spreading terror throughout the countryside until a Shinto priest or a *Butsu* monk came to exorcise them. An often repeated detail was that the *kyūketsuki* were created from the Spirits and bodies of the dead, animated by a powerful curse, but that, too, was not in itself a unique feature.

One of the pages Satō marked with black ink and put aside read:

The Fangeds were known for wearing clothes of a peculiar manner, long priestly robes of a single colour with no markings. An acolyte in the Hachimangu Shrine on the eastern shore of the lake Biwa reported the colour as crimson red; villagers near Funai said they were dark purple or indigo blue; mostly, though, they were said to be wearing the white of death.

In all these tales the Fangeds behaved like all other demons; ruthless, feral, bloodthirsty, mad with rage and lust. A few black ink drawings, made by the book's author, showed googly-eyed, long-fanged creatures hovering in the air, with sharp claws reaching out and black, snake-like hair flowing in the wind. They looked almost comical. They used no weapons, their victims rather slashed to bits with teeth and talons. There was no mention of any greater agenda that would motivate their actions. Satō could find no explanation as to why one of these creatures would suddenly appear in the middle of Kiyō, searching for Bran and attacking her father.

Perhaps they were looking in the wrong direction. Perhaps the man she saw was not a demon after all, or at least not of the kind that had lived in the cave at Unganzenji. It seemed the Westerner and his dragon were still the best chance she had to stumble upon her father's kidnapper.

She put away the papers and rested her chin on her hands in thought. The Westerner and his dragon. She had been so absorbed in the task of finding the crimson robed man that she had almost forgotten why her house had been attacked in the first place. It was surprising how quickly she had become used to the boy's presence. It did help that, for most of the time, Bran sounded and looked so... ordinary.

It didn't matter to her anymore if the boy was a spy. He stood in her defence when he could have just run away from the *enenra*. In her eyes this had proved Bran's honesty. From now on, they were all in this together.

She yawned and realised the better part of the night had passed. It was time to go to sleep. She stood up and unrolled a futon under the window. The night was muggy, clammy, foreboding of a storm. She slid open the paper blinds to let some fresh air into the room.

A shadow of a bat fluttered from under the eaves, startling her for a moment. A lonely night heron crowed in the distance. The nights in the countryside were so different to those which she was used to back in Kiyō - so full of life. She could smell pine resin and the faint scent of dew on wet soil hanging in the air. She could hear night birds calling to each other in the forest, a choir of frogs in the rice fields and a haunting shriek of a fox. There was something primeval in the darkness, but she wasn't frightened of it. Instead, she felt a part of the scenery outside the window, a sense of belonging to some greater whole. She was part of the Yamato – not only the people, but the land itself. This was what the priests must have felt all the time, she realised, what Nagomi experienced. Perhaps this was why the apprentice had kept her calm on their journey. The land itself was giving her strength.

The wizardess unravelled her travel bundle to hide *The Tale...* inside. Something fell out of the baggage and rolled to the floor with a metallic clang. It was the thaumaturgic device Master Tanaka wanted to give her father. She hadn't even remembered she still carried the artefact. The memory of that fateful day appeared before her eyes all over again. The Crimson Robe, the purple lightning, Shūhan's screams... Satō shook her head. No, she had to be strong and focused. That's what Father had taught her. She was certain he was being strong too, not giving up to whatever tortures the enemy subjected him.

She picked up the leather glove and studied it carefully. She twisted a few gears and adjusted a couple of clockworks at random. The glass dial lit up with blue phosphorescence, but nothing else happened. Master Tanaka had written many pages describing the ways to adjust the cranks and gears, but they were now all buried in the well at the Takashima Mansion.

The bronze needle, however, was pretty straightforward. It was sharp, deadly. Satō pricked herself accidentally trying to pull it out. A single drop of her blood was enough to make the gears start whirling, releasing the power hidden within the mechanism. The wizardess almost dropped the device. The dial went up momentarily before dropping back down to zero and the clockwork went quiet again.

She remembered her father's words.

"Blood magic. It's cruel, it's addictive, it's unreliable and dangerous. It changes you. It drains your soul. It drives you mad."

"Then why do people learn it?" she asked.

"Because it is powerful. No magic is more powerful except perhaps the one the priests use – whatever its true nature. That's why it still fascinates scholars, even though it is largely forbidden in the West."

Master Tanaka had no qualms about creating a device utilising the blood magic. Why did Shūhan order an artefact so blatantly defying the unwritten rules of *Rangaku*? What need did he have for something like this?

Curious, she tried the glove on her right hand. It suited her perfectly. Only somebody who had precise measurements of her palm could have made such a snug fit. Satō realised the truth. A new, expensive Matsubara katana, manufactured to her father's precise directions; a device created by a master mechanician according to Shūhan's guidelines and measurements. These were supposed to be her weapons.

Her father was preparing her for a war.

CHAPTER XI

It had taken them another day of climbing up and down the forested hills before they reached a small farming village on the shores of the Shirakawa River that they thought was far enough from Kumamoto to spend a night in. The next morning they took a ferry across and from there a winding road of flat small cobbles led them east, along the left bank of the great river, to a busy crossroads where, among inns, teahouses and little shops selling all sorts of travel accessories, it joined the main highway heading south.

Along the way Bran observed Satō discreetly. He thought he could now sense tiny differences in the way the girl moved or talked, but he was fooling himself. There was simply no way to tell. Satō spoke the brash manly style of the Yamato tongue, walked straight and fast, both the samurai and the servant boy clothes fitting her perfectly.

"Did you know, General?" he asked Shigemasa.

"*Are you disappointed?*" The voice in his head chuckled. "*I did think the boy seemed effeminate — but then, so do you, to me. I thought you enjoyed his company.*"

"Me?"

"*You did say your school was like a Satsuma one.*"

"I didn't know what you meant."

"*All boys, no women... Friendships changing into passions... You must have been an "under", right?*"

"What..." A sudden understanding dawned on Bran. "*No!* I'd never...!" he shouted out loud with indignation.

"You'd never what?" the wizardess enquired, looking at him curiously.

"Nothing," he replied and looked away, "just a bad memory."

There was a road block across the highway, by the watch tower. Across the sandy road, between a rundown teahouse to the right and a sandal-maker's shop to the left, stood half a dozen soldiers, armed with leaf-blade spears and long-barrelled ornate muskets, and one city official, looking nervously at a paper scroll in his hand. He glanced at the travellers passing him by, but did not stop any of them.

The official was a low-ranking samurai, visibly out of his depth as he tried to perform the difficult duty. Bran, taking a cue from what he had learned so far of the complicated system of Yamato ranks and classes, approached the checkpoint at a proud broad pace, pretending not to notice the soldiers. Nagomi and Satō followed a few steps behind, their heads low. The official looked at him, stepped forwards and bowed deeply. His face was supposed to be a mask of formal detachment, but it twitched nervously. Bran stood back, feigning irritation and appal at the man's behaviour.

"What is this?" he asked, as if he had just noticed the checkpoint.

"I beg your apologies, *tono*, but I have orders to question all strangers going in or out of the city."

"Thou didst not stop any of them."

Bran pointed to a group of travellers in front of him.

"I know who they are, respectable *tono*. Your face I do not recognise."

"By whose authority is this interrogation?"

"Lord of the castle and domain, Hosokawa-*dono*."

Bran pretended to ponder his situation for a moment.

"Very well then, ask away," he said, waving his hand in annoyance.

The official coughed nervously.

"I will need your name and your *terauke*."

"Aoki, Karasu," said Bran, presenting a document showing his allegiance to a *Butsu* temple – a hastily falsified version of the paper belonging to the real samurai Aoki.

"You're affiliated to Sōfukuji?" The official raised his eyebrows. "You do not sound like you're from Kiyō."

"I was raised in Mikawa," explained Bran, this time really growing impatient.

"What is the purpose of your journey?"

"A pilgrimage."

"Ah, you must be on your way to Aoi and Kirishima! Yes, the Kuma Shrines are certainly worth the visit."

"Do not tire me with thy boorish talk, fellow. Dost thou have any more queries?"

"I'm deeply sorry." The official bowed even deeper, unsure of what to make of the stranger and his odd, but noble, manner. "Can you tell me who your two companions are?"

Bran raised his eyebrows.

"What possible interest couldst thou have in a woman and a servant? They are journeying with me. That ought to be knowledge enough."

"Nonetheless, my orders are – "

"*The pox and gout on thee and thine orders! My father was Commander of the Guards at Yoshida Castle!* I shall not be questioned by a common townsfolk scribbler. Now let me through or thy head shall roll!"

Bran put his hand on the hilt of his sword and flared his nostrils, making a fierce frightening face. Despite his age, he was a good head taller than the man before him and the wide sleeves of his kimono made his arms seem much bulkier than they actually were. The soldiers murmured and pulled back, clutching their spears as if they were shields, not weapons. The official's forehead became covered with sweat. Bran grunted and stepped forwards. This was too much for the poor man to handle. He dropped to the ground in prostration, whimpering.

Bran stepped over his quivering body and the girls followed, their heads lowered politely, not looking at the soldiers or the official on the ground. They walked for a while in proud silence. The road turned and entered a grove of old bamboos. Bran made sure they were well out of sight of the checkpoint and then stopped, leaned against a bamboo and breathed deeply.

"That was brilliant!" said a beaming Satō, dropping her bag by the same tree to take a brief respite. "Or was that the old samurai guy talking again?" she questioned, eyeing Bran suspiciously.

"No, I told you I have him under control!" he snapped. Satō reeled back. "I'm sorry," he added hastily. He was strangely exhausted. "It was an act. But I did take my cue from how Shigemasa behaved. Truly, I thought no man would be fooled by it. I'm not... 'Tis not my manner," he finished, catching his breath.

"You'll find that most men of power here are either insanely arrogant or cowards," Satō remarked, "and it's almost always better to be the former, or at least pretend to be. Unless you meet somebody who's really uptight, then you have to duel to see who's the more suicidal."

"I shall remember that."

Bran smiled, but inside he was still shaken. *Duel. Death.* Did these people settle everything with blood?

He had lied to Satō. He wasn't certain if the performance at the road block was just an act. *Commander of the Guards of Yoshida Castle...* he remembered. *How did I come up with that?* The general was changing him, slowly, and he wasn't sure if he liked the direction of the change.

Past the bamboo grove, the highway led them straight south across the vast mud plain separating the mountains from the sea. It then climbed onto a causeway, crossing over many smaller and bigger streams, canals and rivulets flowing down from the mountains.

Bran's overwhelming impression of the Yamato countryside was silence, punctuated only by the cries of peddlers, bird songs, the occasional rowdy chants of the women working in the fields or a distant temple bell. The quietude of the villages unnerved him until he realised the reason for it – there was no livestock in this land. No goats or sheep bleated in the green fields, no cows lowed in the pasture, no chickens clucked, no geese honked. There were a few scraggy dogs lazily lying around the households, but even these were keeping themselves quiet, not minding the passers-by in the least. The only other pets were cats, as idle and indifferent to their surroundings as the dogs.

There were no pastures anywhere, as if the locals believed it to be a waste of space. Every free acre of arable land had been turned into fields. Along the way he had spotted barley, buckwheat and broad-leaved lotus plant but little rice – the tide plain soil must have been too poor to sustain it, he guessed. Where there was not even enough dirt for those crops, the peasants grew rush which, as Satō explained, they then used for covering rice straw mats, or reed for weaving baskets and hats. Higher up the hills, in the distance, he could see flowering orchards of persimmon and tangerine trees. No dry spot was left unused by the industrious farmers.

What the countryside lacked in sounds, it more than made up for in aromas and sights. It was crop planting season, so the fields were sprayed with life-giving manure, the heavy stench of which permeated the air. The villages smelled of vegetables pickling in clay jugs, fish drying on poles and home-made liquor fermenting in barrels. The straw mat makers' workshops reeked of wet rushes. Sometimes a fresh breeze brought the brackish scent of the marsh that separated farmland from the ocean.

The villages along the main road were prosperous communities, with well-maintained shrines and large airy houses and people who liked to laugh and sing. The terrible memory of the deprived hamlets in the hills was slowly fading from Bran's mind.

As the sun rose towards noon and the day grew hotter, the peasants they were passing began to wear fewer and fewer clothes. By midday, both men and women were stripped only to their loincloths, and Bran was finding it increasingly difficult to look any way other than the road ahead.

I have to get used to it, he thought. *Everyone else is. I'm standing out too much.*

By afternoon they decided to make a brief stop on a green glade through which a calm blue brook flowed underneath the weeping willows. There were a few half-naked women there from a nearby village, washing their linen, and Satō and Nagomi decided they wished to take a bath farther upstream. The day was a warm one and Bran agreed without thinking, conscious of the acrid shameful smell of his own sweat. The Yamato people seemed to perspire a lot less than he did, as if they had most of their sweat glands removed at birth.

As soon as they had reached the bathing place, beside a tiny shrine overgrown with moss and ivy, Bran realized his mistake. Satō threw off her servant clothes with an utter lack of modesty. He turned his eyes away quickly, but not quickly enough. Half-consciously he hesitated long enough to catch, for the first time, a glimpse of the girl's entire white-fleshed body. She was built like a boy – which made it all that easier for her to disguise herself as one – narrow-hipped and flat-chested by Western standards, but she was definitely a woman, already well on her way out of adolescence. He felt his face flushing red. Not having any sisters, he had grown up unaccustomed to female nudity. *Don't stare,* he reminded himself, *it's rude to stare.*

The younger girl joined her friend and they both plunged into the water, oblivious of his embarrassment.

"Come on in, Bran-*sama*," said Nagomi invitingly, "the water is lovely."

He didn't know what to say to that. He took off one sandal and a white sock, and put his toes into the stream then pretended to shiver.

"Too cold for me," he said, smiling weakly, "I'll bathe at the inn."

To take his mind – and eyes – off the bathing girls, he proceeded to repack his belongings he carried in the satchel. By the time they had finished splashing about he had cleaned the lenses on his spyglass and goggles, sharpened the pencil and brushed dust off the dragon figurine.

Satō climbed out of the stream and stood just a few feet away, drying herself with a white fleece towel. She let her hair down, took out a short-sleeved, light-blue *kosode* robe from her bundle and started putting it on.

"A womanly dress?" Bran enquired, when he dared to look at the girl again for longer than a glance. The clothes seemed to fit her worse than the samurai outfit.

"No more servant rags," she replied, chucking the tattered tunic to the bottom of the bundle. "Somebody could still recognise my *Rangaku* uniform and crest, besides, I want it neat and clean for when I may need it."

"Sacchan, you carry more clothes than a courtesan," Nagomi said laughing.

"Wilt thou wish for thy sword back?" Bran asked.

"Not looking like this." She shook her head. "I told you, girls can't be warriors; besides, you look good with two blades. Like a proper samurai."

"Thou thinkest so?"

He looked at himself. It still felt awkward to wear these strange clothes, to feel the breeze blow around his ankles in the split skirt and plod along the dirt road in simple straw sandals. His Prydain sword in its metal scabbard was a bit too heavy to hang loosely in the sash, and the constant fixing of it in place soon became Bran's reflex.

"I do, and it's *do you think so*," she corrected him.

She kept doing so whenever she remembered, but Bran was slow to learn the modern way. The general's influence was too strong.

"Why two swords, though?" he asked. "This is a strange custom."

"The katana is for battle in the open field," she said, "the wakizashi is for close quarters, disembowelment and beheading your enemy."

"Disembowelment...?"

He stared at her, his mouth wide open. Satō spoke those cruel words without any hesitation and finished dressing up.

Misreading his surprise, she proceeded to explain.

"Suicide. You stab the blade into your stomach and cut like this," she said, gesturing, "then your second cuts your head off."

"I... I see," he answered, still dumbstruck.

"Not many people do it this way anymore," Satō added, shrugging, "most prefer to take the dagger. These days wearing two swords is mostly just a mark of nobility."

"We should be going," said Nagomi, picking up her bundle. Satō's gruesome tale seemed not to make any impression on her. "We still have a long way to go."

"I only have one room left, honoured guests," the innkeeper said, looking at them as if expecting to lose his head at any moment.

"It's all right, we'll manage," said Nagomi before Satō burst into another unbecoming rant.

It was the third inn they had tried that day, and the first to have any rooms free. There was a millet festival in town, and one of the bridges leading south was damaged in a flash flood, resulting in unexpected crowds filling the city's guesthouses.

"It's our biggest." The innkeeper tried to soften the bad news. "We keep it for our most esteemed guests, *and we serve sea trout today*!" he cried after the travellers as they headed for their room.

The accommodation was indeed quite spacious, fit for a large family. The girls settled themselves along the southern wall, leaving the rest of the floor for Bran.

"We knew it would be difficult to travel during the festival season. Besides, it would have been suspicious for us to take separate rooms anyway," said Nagomi.

"I forgot a woman should not be seen travelling on her own." Satō said with a sigh, unravelling her futon.

This was the first night they were to spend together, all in the same room – until now Satō always had to sleep with the servants – and Bran suddenly became aware of his situation when the wizardess started taking off her clothes before going to sleep. She cast off her *kosode* robe just as unashamedly as she had by the stream. Bran turned his eyes away, but again, not fast enough.

Part of him – the one that accepted all the new information given by the old general – knew this was just how things were in Yamato. *It's only natural,* he tried to convince himself, but he was still a Western boy. The wizards of Gwynedd may have thought themselves modern and rational, but their morality had been inherited from that of Rome and the Sun Priests, even if their religion was no longer universally followed. The edicts of the ancient Imperators, separating the sexes in bath houses and gymnasiums still held more sway over his mind than he would have wished. A conflicting mixture of shame and fascination made him want to flee the room – and at the same time, stay close to the wizardess. He struggled to remain calm and unfazed.

"*The girl is shapely, I admit,*" a voice spoke in his head, "*but inexperienced in womanly arts – you will have no use of her, I assure you. Older women are –* "

"If I want matrimonial advice from a ghost, I will make sure to ask," Bran murmured wryly.

The general harrumphed indignantly.

"Are you cold, Bran-*sama*?" he heard Satō enquire, as if from a distance.

He pretended to busy himself with preparing his own bedding.

"No, why?"

"You're going to sleep in your travelling clothes?"

"I…" he hesitated, "I got used to it on the journey." He made up an explanation on the spot. "On a warship you never know when there will be a call to battle."

His eyes now wandered aimlessly around the room, but, despite himself, his gaze was pulled towards the corner where the girl was lying. He sighed, partly with relief, partly with disappointment – she was already wearing a thin, blue linen jacket and shorts, the sleeping clothes of Yamato boys.

"Suit yourself." She shrugged and covered herself with a blanket. The night was chilly. "I think we're pretty safe for tonight, though."

Why am I lying? he thought. *Why can't I just admit this is not how things are in my country? They know I'm foreign, they will understand.*

He said nothing, just turned his face towards the wall and closed his eyes.

That night he dreamt again of the many women from Shigemasa's past. Their arms were welcoming, their bodies eager – and they all had Satō's face.

"Bevries!"

With a loud crackle, the surface of a muddy pool below the bridge was covered with thick bluish ice spreading for about a dozen yards each way.

"Bravo!"

Bran clapped with enthusiasm. Satō turned to him with surprise.

"That is how Westerners express approval," the boy explained. "That's quite a lot of power, but how about precision?"

She accepted the challenge, stretched out her hand, palm up, and focused on it until sweat started trickling down her brow. She weaved a complicated pattern with her other hand. A column of packed snow started to form on the outstretched palm. Bran leaned down to see closer and the skin on his face started wrinkling up as the spell sucked moisture out of the nearby air. He pulled back to a safer distance and watched with admiration as the column of snow turned into a tiny sculpture of a cherry blossom.

"That… is quite amazing." Bran was astonished. "Rarely have I seen such accuracy in Llambed."

"Surely, the scholars in the West…" Satō protested, feeling her cheeks burn. *There I go, showing off again.*

"Wizardry is a crude and rough school," Bran said, "used for blowing up mineshafts or enslaving elementals. The elementalists are not expected to be meticulous and exact in their work."

"It's beautiful!" exclaimed Nagomi. "I never knew you could do such things."

"It's not really what I was trained for," said the wizardess, "I'm supposed to use magic for fighting."

"Thou would easily pass the third year exams at the Academy," Bran said.

"Why not the fourth?" asked Satō, raising her head up. Bran had already explained to her the basics of the tutoring system at Llambed.

"Thou would fail Prydain," the boy said, smiling, and the wizardess grinned back.

"I keep telling you, it's *you*, not *thou*," she corrected him.

She was trying to sound light-hearted, but the show of magic had dampened her mood. It reminded her again of how she had failed to save her father, despite all her training and skill.

She now realised he had always expected some danger to befall his family, but he couldn't foresee the danger having been brought by his own daughter. By saving the Westerner she had doomed her house. It was because of Bran, because she had found him and saved him, that Shūhan had been abducted.

She found it easy to blame herself for the Crimson Robe's attack, but she couldn't condemn the boy. After all, he wasn't responsible for anything that had happened to him since he had been brought to Yamato by the beam of light… but that wasn't all.

She told herself it was only curiosity. There was something intriguing about the boy, a certain mystery in his behaviour towards her. She had no idea how the matters of heart and flesh were resolved in the West. She only knew men from Dejima often took Kiyō girls for lovers – "Dejima wives", they were called – so there had to be some mutual understanding between the two peoples, something universal, overriding all the cultural differences. Satō was aware of the book Bran had stolen from the library, so at least in some respects he was the same as every other boy she knew, but why was he so awkward about it, secretive, as if it was shameful to read it?

He seemed equally awkward about nudity. Even before discovering she was a girl, he had never undressed in their presence and always took a bath separately even if it meant waiting a long time before everyone else had finished. She wasn't sure how to react. Should she start covering herself in his presence? Plenty of boys saw her nude in the bathhouses and neither she, nor they, ever cared about it one way or the other.

She wondered briefly if his awkwardness would have made him an easier target for seduction… Not by her, of course, by some other woman, never by her. She wouldn't even know how to go about it – although she would be eighteen next year, until now she hadn't even thought about boys in that way.

What am I thinking? I must not get distracted from my mission. In a few weeks he'll be gone, never to return.

The first distant shadows of the mountains appeared menacingly on the southern horizon sooner than Satō had expected. It was raining over the jagged ridge, a heavy, dark, torn veil of clouds descending on the forested mountain tops. The rainwater turned to vapour and rose back to the sky in fast moving billows, giving the mountainside a semblance of being on fire, only to fall back to the ground again in another shower a few miles farther north. The south-easterly wind pushed the clouds towards the coast.

"The rain will be here tomorrow," she said, "and it looks like it's going to stay."

"Surely it's not the rainy season yet?" asked Nagomi.

"That's still a few weeks off, but you never know so close to the mountains. The weather here can be dangerous."

As she had predicted, the clouds descended from the mountains by the next morning, covering the sky with an impenetrable layer of grey. She asked Bran to obtain straw cloaks and bamboo hats for all of them in the nearest village and they trudged slowly on under the first drops of cold rain. Midges and mosquitoes soon rose from the marshes and attacked them with tremendous determination.

"I wish we could ride your *dorako* now," she said, waving the insects away and looking at the low-hanging clouds.

Bran nodded, but did not respond, deep in his own thoughts.

"I still can't believe there are scholars of Western magic here in Yamato," he said after a while, using the more modern manner of speaking, as Satō had taught him. "I have never met or even heard of anyone like you since leaving Brigstow. The Qin ignore it - they have their own ways and they don't care for what we do, since they believe themselves superior to any other race. The beast-heads of Bharata are themselves creatures of magic, so they don't need to study it."

"Oh, if only you could have met my old man," sighed Satō sadly. "I remember him conversing with the Overwizards of Dejima like an equal."

"I'm sure Bran-*sama* and your father will have a chance to meet and talk with each other once all this is over," Nagomi said, and Satō was grateful for this attempt at lightening the mood.

"It will be an honour and a pleasure," said the dragon rider, "but if you have Bataavians teaching you and trading with you, why is there so little Western advancement in your country?"

He waved his hand over the fields.

"You must know, Kiyō is a... special place," replied Satō, "because of all the foreigners with whom we meet and trade, we're much more open-minded. Sometimes the attitude of the Yamato people is as distrustful or ignorant as that which you describe in Qin. Believe me, if you started casting spells in the middle of some village in the north, you"d still get pelted with stones – by those who would not run away, that is."

"I see."

"The government hates and fears change," she added with bile. "They only allow a few licensed premises to study the *Rangaku*, the Western sciences."

"It's not just the *Taikun* though, is it?" said Nagomi. "We all don't like things to change too much. The old ways were always better, that's what you'd hear if you asked anyone in these villages."

"I suppose it's the same in villages all over the world," Bran said with a smile, "but the villages don't set up the national policy."

"That may be true, but in Yamato change always brings disaster of some sort; a war or a revolt. We haven't had one for over two centuries. It's enough to get used to how things are run," said Satō. "My old man often mentioned the 'balance of power' between the great lords, which would collapse if any of them tried to change the existing state of affairs," she added.

"Sometimes a change is a good thing," said Bran, looking pensive. "Those poor people in that rotten village, I'm sure they would welcome any change."

"And how would you propose to help them?" Satō asked dryly.

He started telling them of the machines used by the farmers in his homeland, of how magic, engineering and science produced new crops that gave a greater harvest with less work. Satō politely nodded and feigned interest. She did not care about peasants and farming, she much preferred it when he talked about dragons and war.

He's a country boy, she realised, listening to the lecture. *He may come from a more advanced civilisation, but he's been raised in a countryside, among farmers.* Somehow she had imagined everyone in the West lived in great cities – but of course, the Westerners had to grow food somewhere too. *I wonder if he's even a noble born? I never asked him about his ancestors...*

They walked for a while in silence, interrupted only by the sound of their hands slapping at their necks and faces. The rain changed to a light stinging drizzle. The road became muddy and unstable, barely good enough to walk, and their straw sandals badly needed replacing.

They were halfway through their daily distance, travelling now across a land reclaimed from the sea, mile after mile of perfectly flat polders, divided by a myriad of causeways and dams into neat rectangles of swampy rice paddies, lotus fields and rush ponds.

"So the Bataavians are not helping you with these?" Bran asked.

Satō shook her head, dreading another lecture on agriculture.

"We've been doing this for hundreds of years on our own. By ancient law, anyone who reclaims terrain from the sea gets to keep the land."

"Unbelievable. My house in Gwynedd stands near a dyke like that one." Bran's arm arced the horizon. "There are many sluices and dams at Cantre'r Gwaelod, guarding the most fertile land in all Prydain, but it would all have sunk under the sea a long time ago if we had no magic. Bataavians are particularly good at this sort of thing, that's why I thought – "

"There's no need for magic when you have hard working people," she said with pride, which surprised her. She felt the need to defend the Yamato from this Westerner, maybe because of the way she had ranted about their ignorance and backwardness before.

"One day we will learn all the magic we need," she added firmly, "then we'll be able to change not only the Yamato, but the world."

"Or the world will change you," remarked Bran.

Suddenly he hissed, cursed loudly in his own language and started limping. He crouched and examined his feet. The straps of his left sandal were broken and a wide scratch ran along the side of the foot; he must have stepped on a sharp stone.

"That's my last pair," he stated, "now I have to walk barefoot until we can find another shoemaker who can make sandals to fit my feet."

"That won't be easy," said Satō, giggling.

Bran glanced quickly behind then stood up and looked towards the northern horizon with a frown.

"What is it?" she asked.

She looked back too, but the flood plain lay open and empty all around them as far as the eye could see.

"Nothing..." Bran shook his head. "It was just for a moment... I could swear I saw somebody following us, but there's nobody there."

"It would be difficult to hide anywhere in this bare flatland," said Satō, dismissing his concern.

"I must be seeing things in the rain."

The boy shrugged and moved on, limping slightly.

CHAPTER XII

Hosokawa Narimori, the tenth ruling lord of Kumamoto, was sitting by the reading desk in a study room on the third floor of his formidable black castle. The sliding walls of this small chamber were covered with golden foil and magnificent paintings of green cypresses growing on blue mountaintops, river valleys, waterfalls and cedar tree groves. This was Hosokawa's favourite place in the castle, reminding him there was a more peaceful, more beautiful world outside the walls of the busy city below the keep. He had had the straw mats removed from the floor and put a high chair and a reading desk by the window.

The furniture was of Vasconian make, almost three hundred years old. The desk was of solid dark oak, a rectangular top supported by sculpted columns. The chair was of the same set, with a leather seat studded with brass rivets and a back of ebony, carved with scenes of maritime life, fishermen at sea and great trade galleons. The Eagle of Rome spread its wings proudly over the crest.

Lord Hosokawa preferred to sit by this desk and work in a Western manner, rather than at the usual low table with just a flat cushion for a chair. The ancient exotic furniture reminded him of the glory days of his clan, and he found the rigid upright position helped him to focus better – and focus and peace of mind were what he needed the most. After all, he had an entire province to rule, a province vast, populous and rich.

His ancestors had enjoyed the longest period of peace in known history. Ancient armour of the clan's founder stood, its lacquered scales gleaming white, under the wall of the room, reminding him of the violent past, but it was just a copy ordered by Narimori's father in times of prosperity. Polished daily by the servants, it was never to be used in combat.

Narimori had hoped this peace would last at least throughout his time. Unfortunately, recent events made it seem increasingly unlikely.

He was now reading a seven-centuries-old excerpt from the chronicles of Karatsu Shrine, for the third time. It was written in an archaic language, with archaic alphabet, and Hosokawa struggled with deciphering every line. He wasn't even sure if his work would be worth the effort. So far, he couldn't find anything in the old chronicles to help him solve his conundrum.

Lord Shimazu Nariakira, *daimyo* of Satsuma and Lord Hosokawa's closest ally, had asked him personally for this favour.

"I need your books, Narimori." Nariakira referred to the lord of Kumamoto by his first name, indicating how close they were. "I need your grandfather's libraries, your learned monks. I have many books on engineering, economy, agriculture, magic, all very modern and very useful, but your clan has always been more interested in the past, ancient histories, myths and legends. Perhaps we can find some answers there."

How did one deal with a dragon? Sure, the legends gave vivid descriptions of the creature, its dreadful presence and powers of destruction, and told at length of how heroes and warlords fought and defeated them in valiant combat or how priests and monks placated them and persuaded to leave the populace in peace. However, he had found no clue, no hint as to what one should do with a captive sedated beast, like the one Lord Nariakira had shown him a few days earlier.

Killing it was not an option; it was too precious, too important. If tamed, it would have made a formidable weapon against any enemies of the Southern lords. Hosokawa dared not yet think of using the dragon against the *Taikun* himself. For two hundred and fifty years the *daimyo*s of the Southern provinces had been harbouring their grudges and plotted the demise of the Tokugawa regime. The plans never went any further than annual meetings of the resentful *daimyo*, on the anniversaries of the fateful Battle of Sekigahara, where their ancestors had been so soundly defeated. They all drank lots of saké and raised many patriotic toasts – and rode back to their residences harmlessly… But the discovery and capture of the dragon on the beach of Satsuma had the potential to change everything.

If only they knew how to use it.

He stood up from the desk and walked to a larger window on the other side of the room. From there he could see beyond the castle walls and moat, all the way to the Shirakawa River in its serpentine coils, the river harbour filled with boats and ships, and a merchant district that had grown on the other side of the river, opposite the old city. His subjects were getting ready to sleep as the sun set beyond the western sea, painting the horizon bright red.

The sky today is the colour of steel and blood, he thought. *There's a poem in that.*

"*In the first year of the Angen era we got news of the great white Ryū of Kurama Temple in Heian defeated by a young warrior of sixteen years. There was much jubilation, and the* Mikado *declared a day of gratitude throughout the country.*"

A clear, stern voice read out the words from a book that lay on the *daimyo*'s desk. Startled, Hosokawa turned around, pulling out his tantō dagger from a hidden sheath. A pale-faced man with slightly bulging eyes, Vasconian-style whiskers and a pointed beard stood by the desk, looking at the *daimyo*, smirking.

"*You*! You're back!"

The man bowed.

"That's a splendid desk, *kakka*. Not many like it left in the country, I believe."

"I don't know of anyone else who would have one of this quality, and with a matching chair," agreed the *daimyo*. "Have you returned to discuss furniture? I haven't seen you since my father's days."

"You're reading of dragons? That's unusual."

"I have my reasons." The *daimyo*'s voice contained a command and a warning. *Do not ask anymore.*

"I understand." The intruder bowed. "You seem unhappy, *kakka*."

"Of course I'm unhappy!" Hosokawa hid the blade back into the secret sheath and raised his hands in exasperation. "My best advisor has just disappeared on some random errand. The magistrate of Kiyō pesters me with demands. My soothsayers see only darkness wherever they look. There's been some kind of massacre at one of the city temples – and now *you* appear in my castle, uninvited, bearing no good news, I bet."

The man's face, twisted in a mocking grin all this time, turned serious. "Which of your advisors is missing?"

"Yokoi. I wouldn't have anyone else just wander off like that, but I trust his judgment and wisdom too much to question his decisions. Now your face is as sour as mine," the *daimyo* said, laughing wryly.

"I was hoping to discuss something with Yokoi-*dono* tonight."

"Well, I'm sorry to disappoint." Hosokawa scowled. "You will have to settle for me, his less knowledgeable superior."

The samurai scratched his cheek in thought and frowned.

"Are you familiar with the Society of the Eight-Headed Serpent, *kakka*?"

The *daimyo* nodded.

"I understand that they have all been vanquished a long time ago."

"You understand wrongly. They have never been stronger than now, and if we don't stop them, they may soon grow even more powerful."

Lord Hosokawa stared at the intruder for a moment then inhaled loudly.

"Come with me to the Quiet Room. It's the only place in the castle where I'm sure nobody will spy on us."

For a moment everything fell silent. Not a bird chirped, not an insect buzzed. Even the air stood still as the wind paused in anxious heavy expectation.

The earth moved.

That it was more than just another harmless tremor, Sozaemon first realised when the bottle of sacrificial saké tumbled and rolled off the altar. One by one, the tiny statues of the Bodhisattvas toppled over. The bamboo frame of the wall creaked and heaved. The slates started breaking, the paper tore. The ground groaned and creaked, cracked into hairline fissures that grew dangerously wide with every second.

As abruptly as it had started, it all stopped.

For half a minute more there was silence. Then a lonely frog croaked in the pond and the forest around the shrine erupted in sounds, as if nature was trying to pretend nothing had happened.

Sozaemon crawled out from the futon cupboard and assessed the damage. It was relatively minor. He picked up the statues and fixed the altar trappings. The paper panels would need more work, and money. He dreaded looking at the roof – there were spare tiles under the veranda, but he hated the idea of climbing all the way up.

He sighed. Was it really worth it? There didn't seem to be anybody who would appreciate his efforts. Even the villagers rarely visited, and then only to pay their respects to the local *kami* enshrined in a vermillion chapel behind the Worship Hall. He couldn't remember the last time anybody had made a substantial offering for the upkeep of the temple.

He was the last of the line, the sixth of the Sozaemons. There used to be three Guardians of the Unganzenji – Brother Sozaemon, Brother Magonojo and Brother Motomenosuke – but the other two clans eventually had neither the will nor the means to appoint new heirs to the insignificant, impoverished temple. Now he was alone in the big house. Maybe it was time to shut the door and move on. He could become an itinerant beggar-monk or go back to Honmyōji. He had heard the old Abbot had died recently, so maybe there was still a vacancy for the position?

Sozaemon opened the offering box to see if he could afford to buy new paper for the walls. There was the usual handful of small coins and, shining like the sun among the clouds, a single piece of gold. It must have been left by the three travellers who came looking for the Abomination. They were a strange group – the boy spoke rarely and with an accent he had never heard before, the servant boy behaved like a samurai. They reminded Sozaemon of an old play he had once seen, in which the warrior Yoshitsune and his faithful servant, Benkei, traded places to fool the pursuing guards. He chuckled. Whatever the nature of their mission, they had paid real gold. The coin he rolled in his fingers would be more than sufficient to pay for all the repairs.

The discovery put him in a better mood. Maybe *Butsu-sama* had not abandoned him yet.

Sozaemon climbed up the forest path towards the cave, to see what damage the earthquake had done to the stone statues. He didn't dream of fixing them, he was simply curious. A few large trees lay across the path, felled by the tremors. Having to bypass them made his journey more arduous and longer than usual. By the time he came out onto the glade, he was panting and sweating, out of breath and cursing the moment he had the idea to make the trip.

Four or five more statues had toppled and sunk into the liquefied ground, but the rest had held up remarkably well. He noted with regret that a large crack had appeared across the head of one of his favourite sculptures – the disciple with a peony flower. It would not survive the next quake. He patted the statue on the head, like an old friend, and headed towards the cave.

Nothing ever changed in the cave. The monk came here so often that he now knew the position of every item, every accessory. He could see the disturbances done by the three travellers – some papers rustled, the chest burnt through around the lock - but other than that, everything was as usual. The writing pad on the table, the sword stand by the wall, the smell of tobacco smoke…

He sniffed again. This had never happened before. It was the unmistakable scent of a freshly lit pipe. He looked quickly at the place by the bedding where the pipe and tobacco pouch had always lain. They were gone.

He felt a presence behind him; a dreadful, cold presence. If he had any hairs left unshaven, they would have stood on end. The cold sweat of terror replaced the sweat of fatigue.

"Who…"

"Don't turn around," a voice spoke, icy and sharp like the blade of a sword.

Sozaemon did not repeat the question.

"You came back," he stated the obvious.

"Where is Kiyohide?"

"The fourteenth Abbot? He's been dead for years."

The shadow behind him hissed impatiently.

"I forgot how short-lived you people are."

"Can I… can I sit down?"

Sozaemon was feeling increasingly weary in the presence of the dark being. He *felt* the creature nod, and sat cross-legged on the cave floor.

The Abomination spoke.

"There was somebody here."

"Travellers," he said with a shrug.

"More than that. Where are they now?"

"Why do you care? They didn't take anything from the cave."

"It would be shrewd of you not to question my motives and just answer me."

The voice cut him like a knife and the monk swayed as if he had been physically hit. His heart pounded madly. He felt like a mouse facing a snake. He wondered what it would be like to turn around and look the Abomination in the eyes. Were they really golden, like the legends said?

"They were asking for the best way south, beyond Kumamoto."

"That's better. When did they leave?"

"Two days ago. I… I gave them Kiyohide-*sama*'s writings," he added, sensing it was somehow important.

"I see – interesting."

"Please don't hurt them. They are just some kids," the monk pleaded.

"I will do as I see fit," the voice said calmly, trickling like a wintry waterfall.

There was a pause in the conversation and Sozaemon heard a puffing sound. A cloud of robust sharp tobacco smoke enveloped him.

"Do you still train in the Five-fold Way?" the creature asked, its voice now milder and warmer.

"I… Not as much as I used to," the monk admitted.

The question had surprised him, but only a little.

"That's no good. You should always train. It keeps your mind sharp and your body fit."

"I know, I just – "

He didn't finish. The air around him was not so cold anymore, and he could take a deeper breath. He turned around. The creature was gone, only the scent of tobacco remained, and two sets of wooden prayer beads on the cave floor.

Sozaemon wiped the sweat from his brow and stooped to pick the beads. They were marked with the crests of Magonojo and Motomenosuke clans. He sensed something terrible had happened to their owners.

He sighed. Now he really was all alone. The first drops of rain moistened the bald heads of the statues outside.

A powerful blast shook the brick wall. A soldier dropped his musket and fell down from the battlement with a shriek, but the thirty-foot tall rampart held.

The spider-machine swayed on its thin iron legs, rotated the wooden turret against another target and the long, ornate bronze cannon fired again. This time the cannonball smashed through the wall of a whitewashed steeple on the northern corner of the bastion. The curled pointed roof tumbled to the ground in smoke, and the rebels in and around the machine let out a triumphant cry.

Dylan observed the battle from the safe distance of the Concession, holding the spyglass in his left hand, his right arm in a makeshift sling. The Heavenly Army surrounded the circular walls of the Old City completely, cutting it off from the river to the east and the foreigners' district to the north. It was a matter of days before Huating was taken, but the rebels left the Concession alone. Where else would they get ammunition and fuel for their hellish machines if not from the Western Barbarians?

The Foreign Concession in Huating was a far cry from the splendour and luxury of the Thirteen Factories. Here, the district inhabited by the Westerners was just a random jumble of low wooden buildings, on a malaria-ridden island in the middle of the marsh. Only the headquarters of the trading company in the centre was constructed of local brick and limestone.

But the place had access to a good river harbour, and was much closer to the great cities of the northern Qin than Fan Yu. Dylan was certain it would grow to become a great port one day. *If there is anything left of it*, he thought, as another cannonball whistled over the ramparts and exploded near a tall, yellow-plastered pagoda.

There was a triple knock on the door. Dylan put away a map of the river delta and looked up.

"What is it, Banneret?"

The Tylwyth Teg entered, stamping his heels and nodding.

"It's Reeve Gwenlian, Sir."

"Leave us."

She entered the office limping slightly and sat down on a rickety chair.

"Any luck?"

She shook her head. Her black hair was cut short now that they were in a war zone, but still beautiful.

"The villagers know nothing, or so they say. We tried the Southern camp, but it was too well defended."

Dylan looked at her sternly.

"No casualties, I hope?"

"Nothing but flesh wounds."

He ran his fingers through his scraggly beard. He hadn't shaved since the *Ladon's* disaster, too busy and distressed to think of such minor details.

"I told you not to risk the soldiers for my sake. The boy is in a safe place."

"I'm sorry, Dylan —*Ardian*," she corrected herself hastily, "but, how can you be so sure?"

"You studied in Brigstow, didn't you? So you won't know how the Seal of Llambed works... Trust me, Bran's whereabouts are the least of our worries."

"If you say so."

"How is your leg?"

"I will live," she replied, grinning.

"That's as much as any of us can hope for," he said, nodding.

"What about you? You look as though you haven't slept for days," she said, her black eyes filled with worry.

"I don't sleep that well lately," he agreed. "I still dream about the disaster."

In his long career as a soldier and spy, Dylan had seen his share of death and suffering, but he knew the screams of his men and crew of the *Ladon* being boiled alive in the raging flaming waters of the Qin Sea would haunt him until the end of his days.

There was nothing he could have done to help them. He was the leader of his soldiers and had to make a decision, however difficult it would prove to be. They were over a hundred miles from the nearest land, and the dragons were already tired with battle – some were injured. If they were to have any chance of survival, the squadron had to fly away from the mayhem, unburdened, leaving the poor souls to their doom.

He had never learned what had caused the terrible explosion, but he could guess it was no accident. Only a skilled, well-prepared saboteur could have sunk the greatest ship ever built with one blow. How did he get past the guards? Were there traitors among the crew? He would never know for certain.

At least Bran was safe. Of that he was sure. He had witnessed the white pillar of light pierce the night sky over *Ladon* and knew instantly what it meant – the Seal of Llambed. He had circled over the chaos once to make sure – the boy was nowhere to be seen and his jade green dragon was flying away into the darkness, in the opposite direction to the land, too far to try to catch it. *Good riddance*, Dylan had thought, angry with the dragon for not trying to save its rider. In the end it was just a selfish coward like all its kind.

Nonetheless, he knew Bran's fate was only his own fault. If only he had been more forceful in Fan Yu! He should never have agreed to the boy's demand, and then, just before the explosion – did he have to lose his nerve and enchant Bran with Binding Words? What it must have been like for the boy to see the ship fall apart around him and not be able to move... Still, he was proud of how his son managed to stay calm enough to invoke the power of the White Eagle. He could only hope the Seal's magic did not carry him all the way to Gwynedd. Dylan would never be able to face his wife again.

"I'm sure I could help you forget," the Reeve said with a coy smile.

"Thank you for the offer, Gwen, but I'm afraid I will be too busy tonight."

"Don't overexert yourself, Ardian. We will need all your strength and wits if the battle comes our way."

"Let's hope it won't come to that."

The squadron – whatever was left of it – had landed in Huating at the break of day the morning after the disaster. There was no time to mourn their fallen comrades. By afternoon they realised they were in the middle of a war zone. The right wing of the rebel army besieging the Southern capital moved against the harbour town, defended only by a handful of imperial soldiers and the tall walls of red brick and dark sandstone.

The rebels seemed as numerous as the grains of sand, but even more fearsome than their numbers were their fighting machines. Like the whirligigs of Fan Yu, these monstrous automata were built of bamboo, leather and rope, powered by cranks and gears turned by the arms of men. They were as big as houses, armoured with studded cast iron plates, armed with cannons and pipes spewing Roman Fire. The garrison at Huating had nothing that could even touch the machines.

"If only we still had the *Ladon*," said Edern, standing beside him at the wooden palisade surrounding the Concession – a boundary mark more than a fortification. "One broadside would wipe this entire battlefield clean."

He was also wounded – his left side was tightly wrapped with blood-soaked bandages, but his Faer organism was strong and quickly regenerating. The Ardian and his Banneret suffered their injuries on their first – and, so far, last – patrol over the front line. In an uncharacteristic mistake, Dylan had underestimated the rebels and their ability to quickly gather a strike force against a couple of Western dragons. There were only five of them on patrol and at least fifteen rebel *longs*, white as alabaster, topaz yellow, and green like fresh grass, spewing poisonous mist and lightning. They fought bravely and cast all fifteen from the skies, but failed to come out of the skirmish unscathed. Four of them returned with injuries, the fifth, ensign Dunstone, was thrown off his mount and captured.

Dylan wondered if his son had suffered the same fate – imprisoned by the rebels. There was no way of knowing. No message could get in or out of besieged city except a carrier wisp they had managed to send out on the first day, before the rebels disrupted Huating's ley line.

"The Crown must have already sent reinforcements," he had told Edern, "they should be here in a matter of weeks."

"Will we hold out that long?"

"They wouldn't dare touch us."

"They already have. That's why we're here."

"That was subterfuge. We have no proof of the identity of the perpetrators. It could have been any of the Dracaland's foes. An open attack against a colonial power would bring down the wrath of the entire Western world upon their heads. They must be aware of this."

"I hope you're right, Ardian. *Ho*! There's something flying from the city!"

Dodging the musket shots, zigzagging around rockets and deflecting the rebels' arrows, a fragile whirligig was approaching swiftly across no-man's-land and the marsh separating the Old City from the Concession. It was a large vehicle, powered by at least three men, armoured with silver plate and decorated with the imperial colours.

"What a *twp*," Dylan shook his head. "Flaunting the flag in this situation – are they trying to get themselves killed? Prepare the landing glade."

The vehicle was almost over the palisade when a stray flare hit one of its bamboo propellers. The whirligig turned over and fell to the ground with its landing legs sticking up like a dead beetle.

"*Jawch*! Edern, get the medics!" shouted Dylan, jumping off the palisade.

CHAPTER XIII

A broad-shouldered, balding man with a long oval face stood in front of the cage, peering inside. His eyes were close set and clever. A large cross-and-circle crest adorned his elegant, rich off-white kimono and vest.

"Marvellous," he said quietly, "amazing, and, dare I say, quite terrifying."

"The *dorako* are known to induce irrational fear in anyone unprepared, *kakka*," the lanky man in horn-rimmed glasses said, stepping forwards, "even when they are dormant like that."

"There's nothing irrational about it, my good wizard," the aristocrat said, laughing. "It's as big as a whale and has teeth bigger than a shark. I'm certain this little cage of yours will avail nothing if the beast wakes up."

"We are doing our best to prevent this from happening, *kakka*," the wizard said with a bow.

"Are you prepared for the transfer to Kirishima?"

"Almost, *kakka*. The oxcart will be ready tomorrow."

"Good. We can't wait any longer. I need my daughter to be on her way in a matter of days."

"You will not be accompanying us?"

"I need to sail to Nansei. There's a report of some black-winged monsters I need to investigate."

"More *dorako*?"

"If only we were so lucky!" the aristocrat said. "No, I don't think – "
He stopped abruptly, leaned nearer to the cage and stared closely at the dragon. "Look at its eyes, Heishichi. The beast is not asleep at all – it's watching us."

The wizard frowned then clapped his hands twice. Two more men appeared, reaching their hands out towards the dragon. Together, all three chanted a brief incantation, then the man in glasses puffed a handful of white dust into the air. The dragon's head dropped to the floor of the cage with a thud.

Bran awoke from a half-dream, half-trance. It was the middle of the night and the rain outside the inn's windows lashed in a monotone. The blue light on Bran's finger faded fast, just like the memory of the vision, and soon both the room and his mind were again enveloped in total darkness.

The floor was trembling strangely as if it was alive. At first he thought it was just another part of the dream, but then realised the tremors were real, though now barely felt. The whole thing lasted for less than a minute and he soon fell asleep again, quickly forgetting about the odd experience.

The boat was long, narrow and wobbly, but the oarsman knew his job and the shoddy-looking vessel soon started moving up the Kumagawa at the pace of a brisk walker.

The great Kumagawa, Bear River, tumbled down the mountains into the Yatsushiro Sea, forming the southern boundary of the flatland. On Bran's map the only way farther south was by the sea – a route which they could not choose, fearing the harbour guards might spot them – or up the river, across the wild hills that quickly became ominous rocky summits, hemming the Kuma Valley in between walls of granite and basalt.

An oar-powered boat... Bran had never seen one of this size; the only oar boats he knew were leisure coracles and canoes used for recreation on the rivers and *camlas* of Gwynedd. He remembered the great canal barges, transporting elementals from the Southern mines to the industrial centres of the north. Most of them had mistfire engines, although some were still pulled by kelpies. The Yamato had neither technology nor magical beasts to ease their lot, and the oarsman – just like the palanquin porters, Bran remembered – had only his strong muscles to push the boat against the swift current.

He pondered Satō's words about "changing the world". *She may have been boasting, but there is some truth in it,* he thought. The polders through which they had travelled were an astounding feat for a people who used neither magic nor machines. How many hundreds of years had it taken to reclaim the marshland and turn it into fertile fields? How many thousands of people had struggled against the elements throughout the centuries? The potential of these people was staggering. It seemed once they decided to do something, they would spare no time, effort and resources to achieve it in the best way possible.

The way they performed magic, once they got into it, was amazing too. The Yamato have managed to turn even Western wizardry into art. He wasn't just flattering Satō with praise - with the power and control she exhibited, the girl would have been a star of any school of mystic arts. She said her father was even more talented! Yes, these people had the capacity to change the world, if they were stirred enough to do it. But to what end? He remembered Satō explaining nonchalantly about suicides and executions and a shudder went through his spine. And she was supposed to represent the enlightened ones...

The river meandered across the valleys, canyons and gorges, through deep, dense humid forests of tall proud cedars and spry cypresses. Their trunks shot straight upwards like pillars supporting the skies. He had never seen trees like these, and he would often cry out in admiration at a particularly awe-striking specimen.

"It's just trees, what's so great about them?" asked Satō.

"In my country we cut most of our forests down," he replied sadly. "The Dracaland fleet needed a lot of timber. Only in the mountains the old wood remained, but nothing like this..." he paused, gazing at the striped bark with awe.

"Many great Spirits live in these forests," said Nagomi piously.

The other two looked at her in surprise, as she'd been keeping quiet all day.

"I can sense them. The great trees speak to each other in the rustling of the leaves, the howling of the wind."

"The trees?"

Bran eyed the forest suspiciously. There was a time when he would have dismissed this talk of Gods and Spirits as superstitious nonsense, but now he was curious.

"Of course, look!"

She pointed at an enormous gnarled cedar, its trunk bound with hemp rope and paper tassels, a gate of vermillion logs before it. Bran had seen these decorations many times already and often wondered what they meant.

"This one is old beyond measure, and many come from afar to revere and admire it. Its spirit is ancient and wise. Do your people not worship the mountain and the forest?"

"Our Gods are different, more… distant," Bran replied. He was vaguely aware that there were nature worshippers living somewhere beyond Midgard, but for the most part those faiths had been eradicated by the Sun Priests. "We do not commune with the Spirits as closely as you."

"What does the forest say?" asked Satō.

"They speak of the beginning of the rainy season, of how much water they'll get this year and how great the ocean winds will be in the summer. Some trees will die in the typhoons, and some will be born from their seeds – but the forest will prevail."

"How disappointing - I thought there would be some news."

"The great trees do not concern themselves with mortal matters," Nagomi admonished her friend then her face turned pale and serious.

"What is it?"

"There are also evil Spirits here. They speak of hunger and pain and death," she said shuddering, and turned her back to the forested riverbank.

"Do you think there are some white foxes still left here, or racoon dogs?"

"I don't know," the apprentice replied uneasily, "could be… Perhaps the Yōkai War did not wipe out *all* the magic creatures in the deep forests."

"Goblins maybe?"

"I don't know," Nagomi repeated firmly.

"What was the Yōkai War?" Bran asked.

"It was a war against the creatures of magic," explained Nagomi. "It lasted twenty long years, and the result is the Yamato you see today – only humans and dumb animals remain."

"What? But, why…?"

Bran remembered the Faerie people of his own land. Some of them could have been a menace, but he couldn't think of anyone wishing harm to *all* of them.

"The first Tokugawa *Taikun*s waged it to bring peace to the land, protect humans from demons," replied Nagomi.

"Or so they said," added Satō. "I don't know what harm the foxes or racoon dogs bring to ordinary humans, apart from the occasional prank. I think they just couldn't stand anyone who didn't respect their authority. The Yōkai have always ruled themselves, independent from humans."

"Is this what happened to Yamato's dragons?" Bran asked, dreading the answer.

Satō shook her head.

"The *ryū* were hunted to extinction in the times of legends. The chronicles say they were last seen flying in the Genpei War, and that was six hundred years ago."

"Nothing since? Not even from Qin?"

"If there were any others, they are not mentioned anywhere. The dragon lore is forbidden. My father was the only scholar of the subject that I know of. Still is," she corrected herself quickly.

"What about those Fangeds? Aren't they magical creatures?"

"I don't know," replied Satō, pursing her lips.

"And you really have no other creatures left?"

"Nothing that would have a body that could be killed, but there are still ghosts, Spirits, lesser *kami*..."

Bran listened to this, baffled. To exterminate all races was an idea as preposterous as it was terrifying. One might as well consider destroying all animals. Again, the casual cruelty of the Yamato shocked him, but what intrigued him more was how had it been possible for the *Taikun* to achieve his victory without advanced magic or technology?

"What magic creatures do you have in your land?" Nagomi asked.

"Oh, there are plenty. Apart from dragons there are wyverns, lindworms, kelpies, selkies... all manner of beasts. Then there are the Fair Folk, Tylwyth Teg, and the small ones, Corianiaid, but they are only a little different from us."

"What are they like?"

"The Corianiaid are short and stocky, long-eared and narrow-eyed. The Tylwyth Teg are very tall and slim, their hair is golden or silver – but not what you usually call that, it looks like actual gleaming metal. Their eyes are like those of a cat and they can see at night. One of the Tylwyth was a soldier on *Ladon*. I wonder if he survived the disaster..."

His voice trailed off as he gazed at the cypress grove in quiet contemplation. What happened to the soldiers of the Second Regiment? Were their dragons able to fly all the way to the mainland? They must have been tired after the battle with the rebels. And what of his father? Was he now fighting in the siege of Jiankang or trying to find his son? No, Dylan always put his soldier's duty before family. Bran could only count on himself – and his new found friends.

On a sudden impulse, he reached out, put his hand on Nagomi's shoulder and smiled at her. The girl was startled at first. People in Yamato did not touch each other, he had noticed, except the closest of families. He didn't care. What he did seemed natural enough to him. She smiled back, uncertain. They looked at each other in silence.

The boat halted for the night at Haki, a small timber port built at a confluence of Kumagawa and another unnamed mountain stream. The Kuma River flowed a bit wider here, dark mountains reflecting ominously in its calm shimmering waters.

The riverside inn at Haki was a simple one, used to welcoming lumberjacks and mountain hermits, not samurai, and the landlord would not stand up from his prostration until Bran and Satō told him that it was all right for him not to have the finest horse meat – the specialty of the region – on the menu.

"So tell me, the book from my Academy in Gwynedd," Bran started, as all three settled to a meal of rice, local pickles and dried taro tuber, "how did it find its way here to Yamato?"

Satō sprinkled her rice bowl with some shredded taro before answering.

"If truth be told, I don't know. My father always had smugglers bringing strange things to the house, but they were almost always Bataavian, from Dejima, sometimes from Qin. The man who brought us the Dragon Book... He spoke with a strange accent. I don't believe I have ever heard it before, or since, come to think of it."

"You don't remember what he looked like?"

Satō shook her head.

"I could only hear the conversation between him and my father from my hideout – I was never allowed near the smugglers. I don't think the man realised how valuable the book was, as he was satisfied with just a regular fee. He did seem to be in a hurry, but then thieves and smugglers always do."

"What happened to the book?" asked Bran.

"Oh, it's buried in the well, along with everything else. I figured you can teach me everything I need to know about the *dorako* anyway," the wizardess replied, smiling.

Bran nodded.

"I'm not sure if I will make a good teacher, but I can certainly try to answer any questions you may have."

"I have plenty, don't worry about that! Finish your rice and we can start the first lesson. That taro gets chewy when it's cold."

He reached for the chopsticks, but a sudden trembling of the floor caused him to drop them.

"*It's happening again!*" he exclaimed. 'so it was not a dream!"

"What, you mean the tremors?"

"You can feel it too?"

"Of course, it's just a small earthquake."

"Earthquake...?"

Bran felt cold. He imagined the terrible death and devastation he had associated with the word. The Ruin of Olisippo, the Fall of Ragusa, the Devastation of Trinacria... Eithne had studied earthquakes a lot, he remembered. It had always been the geomancers' main ambition to predict and prevent these disasters. How could Satō be so calm about it?

"Nothing to worry about; the worst that can happen around here is a landslide," the wizardess said with a shrug. "Now look, your taro is completely cold. You should order another one."

On the third morning of the cruise the boat emerged from the deep narrow canyon hemmed in between tall walls of granite onto a wide flat valley where several other mountain streams joined Kuma River as it spilled lazily over the flood plain.

"Who rules from this castle?" Satō asked the tiller, pointing to a large sprawling keep on a flat-topped mound across the river, surrounded by a small trading post town. Unlike all the other castles they had seen since leaving Kumamoto, this one was not a ruin and still seemed to be in use.

Instead of answering, the man laughed broadly and burst into song.

Koko no Hitoyoshi

Yu no deru tokoro!

Sagara otome no

Yuki no hada!

This here is Hitoyoshi

The place to go for a hot bath!

The beauties of Sagara

Have skin white as snow!

"Sagara clan," the man added merrily, "and they have done so for the last seven hundred years."

"So we're not in Satsuma yet?"

"It depends on whom you ask. The Shimazu like to think this land is under their control, but in truth the border lies across these mountains to the south."

The boat moored at a busy harbour across the river from the castle, where countless barges waited for the load of timber from the forested slopes surrounding the valley. Workshops and manufactories lined the shore. Satō sniffed; the air smelled sweetly of fermenting rice. Her mood improved at once.

"There's a hot spring!" Nagomi rejoiced at the sight of a small building with yellowish steam billowing from beyond the bamboo fence.

"You go and have a bath, I'll find us an inn," Bran said, and sneezed. It had been raining since morning and his clothes were all soaked.

"You should go to the hot spring too," said Satō, curious of his reaction, "or you'll catch a cold."

"I'll come in later. I'll go arrange our lodgings first."

Half an hour later they found Bran just outside the hot spring entrance. He tried to seem as if he had just arrived from the inn, but Satō knew he waited deliberately until they emerged from beyond the bamboo fence, in fresh *yukata* gowns, their skin clean and flushed with heat.

"You must try it," said Nagomi, pulling him to the counter.

"Where's the inn?" asked Satō. The hot spring was excellent; a good cold drink would make a perfect ending to the evening. Who'd have thought there was such a nice town so deep in the mountains?

"Across the road from the big shrine," Bran explained, pointing east to where a mighty thatched roof rose high above the houses and bamboo tops.

The Aoi Aso Shrine in Hitoyoshi was the most ancient building Nagomi had ever seen.

Its thick thatch, blackened with age, resembled a giant haystack stuck on top of a wooden frame. The wood was painted black instead of the usual vermillion. She didn't know much about art or architecture, but even she could tell the style in which the shrine had been constructed and decorated was much older than anything she was familiar with.

At every stop since leaving Suwa the apprentice had made sure to visit a local shrine. Some were tiny and poor, chapels served by itinerary priests, where a local *kami* accepted even the merest of offerings. Others were grander, town or castle shrines, dedicated to protectors of clans, great chieftains or the Heavenly *Kami* – Gods of Yamato.

Nagomi prayed at all of them. She prayed for her parents' and Lady Kazuko's health, she prayed that Satō could save her father and Bran would find his *dorako* and a way home. She never asked for anything for herself; she trusted in the protection of the *kami*.

Everywhere around her, in the stones, in the trees, even in the old brooms and sandals she felt their the presence. She was never alone, but now she was *lonely*. She missed her parents, Ine and, most of all, the High Priestess. Unlike Satō, she was used to having people around her. There were always crowds at Suwa, pilgrims, priests, *miko*, servants... Even if some regarded her as a freak and outcast, at least they were *there*.

For many days now they had to hide, flee and avoid people. She endured, with the support of *kami,* but this was not enough. She needed more; she needed something the Spirits could never give her.

She sighed and finished her prayers. As she stood up, she saw a young priest looking at her with a bright smile.

"Rarely do we see such devotion as yours, young priestess-*sama*."

"I'm just an apprentice," she said.

"Which shrine, if I may ask?"

"Su..." She hesitated. Should she be saying that? She was never sure how to behave. This was another thing Satō was better at, having grown up in a household full of plots and conspiracies. "Suwa," she said at last.

"*Eeh*! Suwa!" The young man clapped his hands joyously. "You must see something. Come, *come*!"

She followed him to a building at the back, standing between two great black pines. It looked even more ancient than the rest of the shrine, covered with an thicker layer of thatch. Inside it was dark, damp and filled with strange smelling fumes.

"These are vapours that come all the way from the Aso Mountain," said the priest, seeing recognition in the apprentice's eyes. "They say they are even more potent than your Waters of Scrying."

"Have you tried them?"

"I don't have the Gift," the young priest replied, shaking his head sadly, "do you?"

"A little..."

"*Really*?"

He looked at her with honest admiration. She felt her face redden.

"Would you like to try our mists? I've never seen anyone scry before..."

"It's not that easy..." she started, but his eyes gleamed with such anticipation she could not resist. "I suppose it can't do any harm..."

"Excellent! Please, stand here, priestess..."

"I'm only an apprentice," she reminded him, "and my name is Nagomi."

"This mirror is what the Scryers of old used... Nagomi-*sama*."

"And what are these?"

She pointed to a set of three strange masks carved into a pillar, high by the ceiling, painted white. They were disembodied heads of a child, an adult and an old man.

"I do not know," the priest admitted sheepishly. "They have always been here. This shrine is old, full of things nobody remembers anymore."

She positioned herself in front of the bronze mirror and breathed in. The fumes were stronger than at Suwa, more odorous.

"Do you – do you need anything?" the young priest asked.

"No, just... peace and silence."

What am I doing? Scrying is dangerous. Kazuko-hime isn't here. This boy will have no idea what to do if anything goes wrong. Why did I agree to this?

She could feel the onset of the vision surge through her body, like slowly building lightning. Her hair stood on end, her skin was covered with goosebumps. Everything around disappeared, only the mirror remained – and the three carved heads.

One of them, the head of a child, suddenly opened its eyes and looked straight at Nagomi.

Something appeared in the mirror. The vision, but unlike any she had ever experienced. It was not symbolic or dream-like, it was crisp, vivid and showing something real, familiar.

She saw herself and Bran on the beach in Kiyō, the boy reaching out his hand to touch her hair; then at the infirmary, him looking at her with unabashed curiosity.

"I like your real hair better."

She was reminded of Bran's quiet words at the inn on the day of their departure from Suwa, the dragon figurine from his satchel, the strange markings on the base, neither Yamato nor Bataavian runes. She felt his hand on her shoulder at the boat.

Nagomi did not understand. Why was she shown all this? This was no vision, just memories. She had seen all this before. What kind of scrying fumes were these?

The mirror dimmed and she was ready to step away when the second mask, the one of an adult, turned towards her with a mischievous grin. She was entranced, unable to move. The polished bronze surface revealed another image.

This one was not from her past. It showed the courtyard of the Kiyō magistrate, a rectangle of sand surrounded by a low stone wall. The cherry trees on the looming slopes of Tamazono were dressed in green, waving in the gentle wind. The courtyard was filled with onlookers, many priests and priestesses among them, standing silent, waiting.

A group of men marched out of the magistrate building with an older woman in tow. It took Nagomi a while to recognise Lady Kazuko with her hair uncombed and wearing a ragged gown. She seemed tired and her face was even more wrinkled than usual. The men were all armed and looked hostile. As the entire group reached the middle of the courtyard, the men stopped. One of them unrolled a silk scroll sealed with the mallow crest, and started reading.

"By the order of the great and illustrious *Taikun*, His Excellency Tokugawa Ieyoshi, we sentence one Hosoki Kazuko, former High Priestess of the Suwa Shrine, to death by sword for conspiracy with enemies of the court, harbouring fugitives and treason against the Divine *Mikado*."

The people gathered in the courtyard were ashen-faced, but none dared so much as to gasp. The High Priestess looked up into the sky as if searching for something.

The vision ended, but the apprentice was still entranced. She could feel tears falling slowly down her cheeks, but she couldn't wipe them. The third mask opened its eyes. They glowed red.

The mirror showed her a wide empty road running through the middle of a forest. Tall walls of mountains rose on both sides. A narrow path branched out to the left, into the woods, barely visible, overgrown by ivy and fern. The vision led Nagomi down this path, deep into the dark heart of the forest, until it reached a circular open glade.

A ring of stones surrounded the glade, and in its centre was a mysterious, mound-like construction, walls of flat boulders covered with a thick cap of dirt, moss and grass, with a single narrow entrance leading inside.

There was a man sitting inside with his back to her. She could not see much detail in the darkness of the barrow, only that it was a samurai in elaborate, old-fashioned clothes. The man slowly turned his head. His face was an oval of blackness.

The vision ended. All three masks closed their eyes and rotated back to their positions under the eaves. The shrine around her emerged from the darkness and the young priest ran up to support her as she swayed backwards.

"You seem very distressed… Was it a bad vision?"

"I – I cannot tell you," she said, wiping the tears from her eyes.

"Of course, I understand." The boy's voice betrayed his disappointment. "Shall I take you to the inn? You can barely walk."

"No, thank you, I can manage," she said. She pushed him away and ran out of the shrine.

CHAPTER XIV

Ozun raised himself up on one elbow and gazed admiringly at Azumi's young athletic body. His fingers traced the outline of a *kirin's* horned head tattooed in red, green and blue ink on her arm. The rigid muscles rippled under the smooth taut skin, the magical beast's scales flickering in the light of an oil lamp.

The girl opened her eyes and bashfully covered herself with a straw blanket.

"Don't look at me like that," she said, smiling innocently.

Ozun laughed and bit her gently on the shoulder.

"I can't help it."

"It's almost dawn."

"I know."

He reached his arm around her, but she writhed herself from under it.

"*Stop it!* We need to prepare ourselves."

Ozun sighed and sat up with his arms around his knees. Those fleeting moments where they only had each other were much too brief for his liking.

The bright crimson light of the sunrise peered through a small square window.

"It almost looks like the house is on fire," he remarked.

Azumi shuddered, pursing her full lips.

"Don't say that."

"Oh, I'm sorry. Sometimes I forget."

He reached out to her, but she rolled away, swift like lightning, then jumped up, flipping backwards and landing on her feet behind him without making a single sound. Her hand was on his throat, ready to punch in his windpipe.

"Show-off." Ozun laughed, awed by her supple nakedness.

"Don't be fooled by a woman's tears, hermit," she said, giggling. "I've forgotten all about Koga. I have a new life now, by your side and the Master's."

"I'm also not a mountain hermit anymore," he replied.

"That means you're no longer celibate." She leaned down and kissed the mark of a renegade tattooed onto his bald scalp. "And this makes me the happiest girl in Yamato." She straightened herself abruptly and glanced towards the door. "He's coming."

"Are you sure? I can't hear anything."

"What if he's going to punish you for the failure at Honmyōji?"

He gnashed his teeth. *Those damned pious monks. And I could not even take their spirits.*

"I'm not one of his monsters or sellswords. He can't just – "

The paper panel slid open suddenly and their master appeared in the doorway, his crimson robe seeming almost purple in the shadow. He looked at the two naked lovers indifferently.

"I have a task for you, *kunoichi*," he said to Azumi. His voice carried no emotion.

"Just me, Master?"

"Yes. Hopefully you will fare better than your hermit."

Ozun tensed feeling the cold stare of the golden eyes.

"Be careful," he whispered to the girl as she grabbed her clothes and followed the Master. A faint nod was her only response.

A small, white-furred wolf trotted up and down the side of the causeway, snout close to the wet ground, sniffing. It paused and nudged a piece of dirt with its nose.

"What have you got there?"

Azumi crouched and investigated. She picked up a single long black hair. She tasted it and spat.

"*Dyed.*"

She opened a gourd and poured some saké over the hair. The black dye dissolved, revealing bright red, glistening like pure copper.

"It's beautiful," she whispered with a hint of jealousy. Her own hair was thin, drab, cut neatly at neck-length. "Well done, Inuki."

She scratched the wolf behind the ears. The beast rolled its eyes in bliss. Azumi stood up and blew softly into a bamboo whistle strapped to her sash. The wolf vanished into the mist. A small strip of paper with the character "wolf" written on it floated to the ground.

The *kunoichi* picked up the paper carefully, rolled it up and inserted into one of the many containers at her sash. She then drew the bamboo hat over her face, grasped the iron-ringed staff that completed her mendicant monk disguise and moved on down the road.

She set up her tent on an island of grass in the middle of the marsh, far away from the main road and the prying eyes of passers-by. She much preferred it this way. An assassin needed to be wary of other assassins, and being enclosed within four walls and a roof always made her uneasy. Only when she was with Ozun could she sleep inside a building without waking up in the middle of the night, sweating, remembering the terrible night when the *Taikun*'s father had decided to destroy the Koga assassins – *shinobi* and *kunoichi* - once and for all.

A small bat fluttered in the shadows. Azumi reached out her hand and the creature swooped onto her palm. It chirped quietly, and the *kunoichi* listened, nodding.

"A boat, I understand. Thank you."

She smoothed the tiny hairs on the bat's head and gave it a single cherry. The animal sunk its teeth into the plump flesh of the fruit gratefully.

The bat, like the wolf, Inuki, was a gift from her beloved hermit. She herself had no powers other than her *kunoichi* training, but she had discovered an affinity to communicate with Ozun's Spirits. It was this successful partnership that compelled their Master to endure Ozun's insolence. "Once a rebel, always a rebel", was the hermit's motto.

This time, however, Azumi feared he may have gone too far. He had let the prize get away, and had returned from Honmyōji with nothing. The Master tolerated disobedience in his most trusted servants, but only as long as it was proving effective. A failure put too much strain on his patience. It was now up to her to make up for her lover's shortcoming.

The earth beneath her feet shuddered gently, the tent swayed. The tiny bat was startled and, with the cherry still in its mouth, flew away into the night.

She sighed.

Bran passed hesitantly under the green cloth hanging across the doorway leading into the open air bath.

He knew what hot springs were, but was reluctant to use them. The girls had often reminisced about their favourite bathing places along the journey. He was not yet ready for bathing together with the girls – certainly not with Satō.

He put his clothes in a straw basket and began to wash himself. He examined his feet; three days of rest on a boat helped to heal the blisters a little. Criss-crossing purple lines, however, still marked where the straps of the straw sandals, much too small for his size, cut deep into skin. *Tomorrow we walk again,* he thought with a sigh. *How much farther, I wonder?*

There was only one little old lady in the spring, submerged up to her neck in the steaming water, her eyes closed. With great care Bran stepped into the bath, a large rectangular pit surrounded by cold flat stones – and suppressed a yelp. It was as if he had descended into a cauldron of hellfire. The splash awoke the old woman and she was startled for a moment, but then just smiled and moved aside to make place for the boy. He nodded in silence.

After a while he got used to the heat and started enjoying the soak. His arm and leg muscles relaxed, his sinuses cleared. He could feel the cold perish from his body. He started falling asleep.

"Where are you from, boy?" a squeaky voice asked.

The sudden question stirred him from slumber. It was the old lady, looking at him with interest. She was munching on a thin curly cucumber she had produced from somewhere.

"Mikawa."

"*Oh!* All the way from Mikawa to our little spring! How curious!"

"I'm on a pilgrimage," he explained.

"Ah, of course. The shrines of Satsuma seem quite popular these days."

"How so?"

"There were two girls here earlier who are also on their way to the Southern Shrines, and a troop of samurai passed through the city yesterday, going in the same direction."

"*Samurai?*"

"Yes, about thirty of them, all well-armed and very haughty looking. Their commander stopped to take a soak in this spring and I chatted with him for a while, a very dashing gentleman."

"Do you live in this spring?"

Bran chuckled and the old lady giggled.

"At my age there are few diversions to be had, young man. If you're on a pilgrimage, you should visit our shrine, Aoi," she added a moment later. "*Aoi Shrine gate, best in all of Kuma!*" she sang, and giggled again at the screechy sound of her own voice. "It's very ancient and revered. Not as much as Kirishima, of course. You are going by way of Kirishima, I assume?"

"I suppose," Bran replied vaguely, though the name stirred something in his mind, as if he had already heard it before.

"It's the greatest shrine in all of Satsuma! You must visit it! That's where those samurai were going, by the way."

A troop of samurai going to Kirishima... Bran tried to ponder the news, but the relaxing heat of the pool and the faint smell of rotting eggs disturbed his thoughts. The more he looked at the old lady, the more he noticed there was something odd about her. Casually, trying his best not to show he was doing anything unusual, he cast True Sight and stared at the woman.

In her place he saw a green, reptilian, tortoise-like creature, covered with scales, with a long snout filled with sharp teeth, and webbed feet and hands. It looked at him with the same curious eyes, still snacking on a cucumber, unaware of his penetrating gaze.

"W-what are you?"

The creature realised its true form had been revealed and dived into the water, either out of embarrassment or fear. Bran jumped out of the spring, trying to peer at the creature through the mists and vapours.

"Pleasse, don't kill me!" the creature gurgled from under the water, hissing like a snake. "I am bound by the priestss of Aoi to never harm anyone!"

"I have no intention of hurting you, but – what manner of being are you?"

"Don't you know a *kappa* when you ssee one?" The creature's head, covered with seaweed-like dark hair, emerged onto the surface. "A great *onmyōji* like yoursself surely would recognise a water sprite."

"How did you survive the..." He struggled to remember. "Yōkai War?"

"The good priestss of Aoi provided a refuge to a few of the magical creaturess. The war passed uss by."

"*Us?* How many more of you are there?"

"I'm the lasst of my kind. There could still be ssome goblinss and white foxess hiding in the highesst reaches of the foresst. Pleasse don't let anyone know you've seen me! You must promisse!" The creature swam up to Bran's feet and stared at him eagerly. "Promisse!" it repeated.

"I promise, but you must tell me one thing. Did those samurai say why they were going to Kirishima?"

"They mentioned something about escorting a princessss."

"And they did not say anything about... other magic creatures?"

"No, but – "

"Yes?"

"Ssomething arrived in the mountainss a few days ago, ssomething new and powerful. The foresst iss frightened, there's never been anything like thiss before. Iss that what you sseek?"

Whilst dressing, Bran discovered something round and heavy in the folds of his travelling kimono. It was a golden coin. He smiled to himself, thinking how fairy creatures the world over seemed to have the same idea of rewarding kind strangers.

Just before the inn he saw Nagomi, running from the shrine down the steep bridge spanning a lotus pond. She was pale, trembling.

"Are you all right?"

He reached out to lay his hand on her shoulder, as he had done on the boat. Nagomi shook her head.

"I'm fine, just tired," she said, but then she wrapped her arms around him and broke down in tears, her whole body shaking with sobs.

He awkwardly patted her on the back then just hugged her tightly. He didn't ask, and she wasn't saying anything. She stopped after a short while, swallowed and wiped the tears from her face.

"Thank you," she said very quietly.

"It's... fine." He rubbed her shoulder, trying to think of a way to comfort her. "Everything will be fine."

"Yes."

They entered the inn. Satō was holding a stone flask in an unsteady hand, pouring clear liquid into the cups of some newly found companions, her clothes dangerously dishevelled. A couple of village entertainers were performing a shockingly bawdy song about a housewife and dried eel, with the locals – and Satō – joining in at the rudest parts of the chorus. There was only one other traveller among the revellers. A samurai in a garish purple and yellow kimono was sitting in the corner, quaffing liquor straight from a flask and smoking a long bamboo pipe, grinning broadly.

"Ah, you've come at last!" the wizardess shouted at Bran and Nagomi over the din. "Come on, join in the fun! Try the famous Kuma Shōchu!"

Nagomi drank a little cold *cha* and excused herself with a headache. Bran glanced at her worriedly, but said nothing. Satō grunted something unintelligible and burst into a song about unfaithful samurai wives and the virile men of Kuma.

The apprentice rolled out the futon, changed into her sleeping clothes and lay down on her back. She sniffed. There was a very faint smell of sulphur lingering above the floor. Did the fumes from Aoi Aso seep through even here?

Sleep found her quickly, thick, heavy, like a cotton-padded blanket, merciful. She dreamt she was at Suwa again. Her room was empty, just as she had left it. Dust had settled on the straw mat floor. *Somebody should clean this up,* she thought.

The door slid open and Lady Kazuko entered the room. Nagomi gasped with delight and ran up to her, embracing the woman.

"I thought you were dead! I had this vision..."

The High Priestess caressed the girl's copper hair silently. At last Nagomi stepped away.

"Kazuko-*hime*? Why do you not say anything?"

Only now did Nagomi notice a thin red scar running around Lady Kazuko's neck. She understood.

"You *are* dead..."

"Do not distress yourself, child. I will soon be joining my ancestors," the priestess said quietly and softly. She seemed completely at peace with herself. "I have been ready to meet death for a very long time, since before you were born."

"But... What about the shrine? What about me...?"

"The shrine will endure and so will you. I came only to tell you this – you must continue with your mission."

"I... I don't think that we – that I have the strength..."

"You *have* to," the priestess pressed, "it is even more vital now, since I cannot be there to help you."

"I'm just an apprentice."

"Not anymore. I ordained you before my death."

"But I'm too young! I have not performed the rites!"

"The dying words of a High Priestess mean more than any rites. You are now a priestess of Suwa. Everyone in Yamato will recognise your new position."

"Oh, Kazuko-*hime*." Nagomi wept, the reality of what happened finally reaching her. "Is the *Gaikokujin* really worth all this suffering? First Satō's father, now you – how much more will we need to sacrifice to help him?"

"Somebody else asked me the same question recently..." the priestess said, smiling. "It's not about the boy. It's about the future of all of us, the fate of Yamato – I can see it clearly now..."

"*Fate?* I can't..."

"You can't do it alone, I know. That's why you have each other. Do not distress yourself with my doom. Death is just a transformation. In a way, I'm happy my life ended like this – at least I managed to do something good in the end."

"Everything you did was good."

"If only that was true." The priestess smiled sadly then looked up. "My time has come. I will become one with the *kami*. Remember me in your prayers, child."

"Always."

"You have always been my favourite apprentice," Lady Kazuko said, patting the girl's head one last time, "and the most beautiful."

"You were the only one who ever thought that."

Nagomi smiled through her tears.

"Maybe I was," the priestess said, nodding, "but it will not always be so."

"What do you mean?"

The priestess did not respond. She closed her eyes. A bright, white blinding light filled the room and caused Nagomi to shield her eyes with her hands.

A faint voice reached her from the light, over the distant hum of the Otherworld.

"Oh, of course, I can see it clearly now!" The High Priestess spoke one last time with a dire sense of urgency. "Listen, Nagomi, things are not what they seem. The man you will meet – you must…!"

The vision perished. Bran and Satō stumbled into the room, waking Nagomi abruptly.

"Sorry," muttered the boy.

The wizardess barely managed a mumble.

The way into the Westerner's consciousness lay wide open. The jade dragon snored loudly at the crumbled gates.

Shigemasa did not plan to run this time. He had grown too curious of the Westerner's fate. He decided to wait and see what came out of all this while he waited for his own destiny to unravel.

He still had urges that needed fulfilling, though, needs that had lingered dormant for two hundred years. The Spirits had no life other than the timeless existence in the Cave of Scrying, but once he had possessed the boy's body, the unquenched passions awoke with increased strength.

The general stepped through the crumbling gate and took a deep breath. The air was crisp and moist – and real.

He came down to the common room. The landlord looked up from the counter. Shigemasa presented the golden coin given to the boy by the kappa.

"The maidens of Hitoyoshi," he asked, "are they truly as white as the songs say?"

The landlord rotated the coin in his fingers and licked his lips, greedily.

"For this I can find you Oyuki-*hime* herself, *tono*."

"Good. Bring the woman to my room, and give me thy best shōchū – believe me, I shall know the difference."

The landlord bowed deeply and disappeared into the back.

"You gave a very moving performance tonight, boy."

Shigemasa turned around. The samurai traveller was still sitting there, his bamboo pipe in one hand and a shallow cup in the other, looking greatly bemused. "I haven't heard the *Warrior of Kuroda* being sung in these parts for... oh, many long years."

The general strode the length of the common room in several, quick long steps.

"*Thou*," he said, "I know thee."

The samurai turned serious. He looked deep into Shigemasa's black eyes. At last, he bowed, slowly.

"It is a strange and fateful meeting, Taishō-*dono*," said the samurai.

"What art thou doing here, Swordsman?"

"I heard rumours. I wondered if they were true."

"What rumours?"

"That an ancient prophecy came to pass and the last Shard has returned to Yamato. That the Eight-headed Serpent is awake. That the dragon child is coming."

"Hmph," Shigemasa grunted, "and thou thinkest this boy is the dragon child?"

"I do not know. Perhaps."

Shigemasa grunted again.

"You are displeased, Taishō-*dono*."

"I had hoped the boy would be just a vessel that I might use for my own purposes, to settle whatever holds me to this Earthly plane."

"It still might be true, Taishō-*dono*. Perhaps your path is entwined with the boy's."

Shigemasa contemplated the samurai's answer in silence.

The tavern door opened and the landlord walked in, leading a fragile-looking woman wearing the flowery robes of a courtesan.

"Are you certain of this?" the samurai enquired. "The boy has had a rough night already."

"He is young and strong, and I have waited two hundred years. Do not worry, I shall return the boy to bed long before dawn."

"I'm certain he'll appreciate it."

The samurai sipped from his cup and puffed on a pipe.

The woman proved more than satisfactory. Her eyes were large, brown and unafraid, her skin surprisingly smooth for a woman in her late thirties, perfectly white and glistening with tiny droplets of sweat on her long neck and back. She was politely quiet and patient throughout the ordeal as Shigemasa mounted her awkwardly, unused to the barbarian's long legs and arms. It did not take long before he reached the shuddering explosion he had longed to feel for so many endless years. The woman beneath him squeaked and panted in unison. He knew she pretended, but was impressed that she knew how to do it so convincingly. When he finished, she complimented him on his potency and prowess.

"Do not go yet," he said, as she started picking up her clothes in silence.

She bowed and sat down, covering her nudity modestly with a bunched up red *yukata*.

"Thou hast been trained in a city?" guessed Shigemasa.

"I have, *tono*. My family sold me to a place in Kumamoto."

"What happened?"

"I bore a child... with one of my customers."

"*Ah*! Most unfortunate."

"If I may be so bold, *tono*," the woman said, lifting her eyes, "it is rare to find a boy of your age with such... refined taste."

Shigemasa laughed.

"Thou may travel the length and breadth of Yamato and thou wouldst not find another youth like me," he boasted.

A hint of alarm appeared in the woman's brown eyes as she sensed something odd in the general's voice, and she started rising to her feet. Her fear excited him.

"Do not fear me, woman. I am merely a boy! Come." He reached out his hand. "I can feel this young body regaining its vigour already. Oh, 'tis good to be alive!"

The snow-skinned woman dropped the *yukata* to the ground and stepped forwards, her face becoming the impenetrable mask of politeness and resignation Shigemasa knew so well.

CHAPTER XV

The precious passenger salvaged from the wreckage of the silver whirligig turned out to be the Governor of Huating – incidentally, the nephew of the viceroy who had perished on *Ladon*. He was recovering from concussion, lying on a mattress at the makeshift infirmary prepared in one of the tea warehouses – the Western medics, guarding their precious neutrality, had been treating the injured on both sides of the front line as long as they were paid to do it.

"What on Owain's beard were you trying to do?" Dylan bellowed.

The doctor bandaging the governor's head winced, but said nothing, knowing Ardian ab Ifor was not a man whose anger one could hope to placate.

"Huating… will fall," the governor whispered. "I need your help."

"What makes you think we can help you? We're as trapped here as you are. I have only a dozen dragons and a few hundred armed men behind the palisade. Good enough for a breakout, maybe, but not to relieve a besieged city."

"There are more… coming."

"More Dracalish soldiers?" Dylan moved closer. He wrinkled his nose at the heavy, sweet smell of the Cursed Weed. *An addict, even at such a high position. Our tradesmen have fared exceptionally well in this area.* "How do you know?"

"Last night – a messenger came through the enemy lines from Jiankang. Your Queen… is sending another ship."

"A ship, you say?" Dylan scratched his scar. *At last some good news!* "A troopship? A frigate? Is it ironclad?"

"I do not know. It will come too late to save the city, but with luck you can use it to recapture it…"

"I can use it to get out of this mosquito-infested island!"

"You must help the city," the governor whispered weakly. "If it falls, the Concession is next. I know that's what the rebels are planning. They now feel strong enough not to care about your trade."

"Strong? I admit there are many of them, but they're still just a bunch of rag-tag – "

"No – listen… The messenger did not come just to tell me about your ship. He came bringing news about… Jiankang…"

The man heaved and started retching bile into an enamelled bowl.

"Please, this poor man is obviously – " started the doctor, but Dylan pushed him aside.

"What is it? What about Jiankang?"

"Jiankang…" the governor said, raising his eyes with the effort, "has fallen."

The triangular red flags of the Heavenly Kingdom – as the rebels demanded it to be called – hung from the ramparts and turrets of Huating Old City. The defenders were brutalised, tortured. All officials had their pigtails cut off, and their precious robes torn off in a public humiliation. The common townsfolk were driven away in a long column across the causeways, over the marsh, into the unknown.

Dylan observed all this from the back of Afreolus, using the lull in the fighting to spy on both sides of the conflict. The rebels were too busy with looting the city to pay attention to the silver dragon above their heads. Only when he got too close to the labyrinthine Yunan Gardens, where the rebel commander had established his headquarters, was Dylan shot at by one of the spider machines. The cannonball whizzed past the dragon harmlessly, but Dylan decided he had seen enough.

Heading back to the Concession he passed a lonely *kirin* rider approaching the wooden palisade with the flag of the Heavenly Kingdom at the saddle of his mount, a snow-white horned horse with hooves of flame. The emissary of the rebels was bringing the conditions of surrender.

Dylan entered the brick headquarters and climbed the stairs to the dining room. The Intendant of the Concession and his councillors had already gathered, discussing the message presented by the envoy.

"They are letting us go free!" the Intendant exclaimed, waving a piece of paper. "*We're saved!*"

"On what terms?" asked Dylan, frowning.

"We leave all weapons, munitions and supplies, taking only enough to get us all back to Fan Yu…"

"And…?"

Dylan sensed the intendant had not told him everything.

"And your dragons," another councillor explained.

Dylan banged his fist on the table.

"*Ludicrous!*"

"Ardian, we appreciate your input, but you're not an authorised member of this council," the intendant reminded coldly.

"I've just seen what they did to the people of Huating. If you think they'll just let us go, you're deluded. It will be Gandhara Retreat all over again."

"I understand your concern, but I can't risk the lives of civilians. We're merchants, Ardian, not soldiers. If we have a chance to get away with our health, we must take it."

"They say their leader believes in Mithras. They can't be all that bad," added another councillor.

"Their leader believes he *is* Mithras," Dylan said, eyeing the councillors with narrow eyes, his scar twitching unnervingly. *They can't be serious.*

The Intendant coughed.

"Does anyone else have anything to add?"

The Intendant never managed to give his reply to the rebels. Within half an hour, all councillors were arrested by the soldiers of the Second Dragoons. Dylan effectively took over control of the Concession.

At first he pretended to consider the proposition of the surrender. In reality, he was playing for time, still hoping the ship promised by the messenger from the Southern capital would materialise sooner rather than later.

Two days had passed on fruitless negotiations and the rebels were at last done with waiting. The Heavenly Army began to unravel its lines, surrounding the marsh island from the west and south. To the east was the Huangpu River, and to the north a flooded canal. The walking machines moved forwards, the footmen readied themselves at the rear. The *long* riders patrolled the sky over the Concession, making the dragons of the Second Dragoons agitated and irritated, but largely helpless.

The relief was nowhere to be seen. A few merchants sneaked out of the island in the hope of fleeing, but it was too late to count on the rebels' mercy. The Heavenly Army captured every one of them and cut their throats in front of the wooden palisade, in mockery of the Sun Priests' rituals. After this display, the remaining civilians swelled the ranks of Dylan's tiny army. They preferred to die fighting than to be slaughtered as slaves.

"We are breaking out," Dylan decided at last, "east along the river and then north. All the way to Ta Du if need be."

"It won't be easy," said a grinning Edern.

"It never is."

Dylan turned to his men to give them final orders, when suddenly a barrage of powerful explosions shattered the air, followed by a roar of thunderbolts and a whistle of rockets flying above their heads.

He looked over the palisade to the east. A mighty ironclad battleship, black like the night, chuffed at full speed up the river, cannons blazing, funnels steaming. It was followed by a large stable-ship and a couple of escort vessels. The Queen had sent them not just one ship, but a whole flotilla!

A dozen dragons launched from the deck of the stable-ship. The Qin riders tried to fight them briefly and futilely, overwhelmed by the combined might of flying beasts and the rapid guns of the escort. The marsh to the west of the island filled with smoke and flame, scattered wrecks of the walking machines and bodies of the slain soldiers. The rebels were not yet ready to retreat from the battlefield, but they were certainly much less eager to attack.

A silver dragon landed in front of Dylan and his marines. It carried two men. One of them – a flaxen-haired Seaxe boy - remained mounted, while the rider, a young, brown-eyed soldier of Prydain stock with the shiny new Leader insignia upon his epaulets jumped off with heavy grace and saluted. Dylan noticed the Seal of Llambed on the soldier's chest. *He looks about Bran's age. I wonder if they knew each other.*

"Flight-Leader Hywel ap Cadell, Twelfth Light," the soldier said with a strong Llyn accent, "hope we're not too late."

"Ardian Dylan ab Ifor of the Royal Marines, and interim Commander of the Huating Concession," Dylan said, returning his salute. "You're just in time. First time in combat?" he added, recognising the tell-tale signs in the boy's face, the flushed excitement and hint of fear.

"Green as spring grass, Ardian, but eager," replied Hywel with a grin. "I'm sorry we're not the Guards, but we were the best the Empire could procure at short notice."

"You will have to do." Dylan smiled back. "Whose ship is that?" he asked, nodding towards the black ironclad.

"This fine frigate, Sir, is *Wintoncaestre*, the flagship of Rear Admiral Reynolds of East Bharata and Qin Station."

"Rear Admiral, eh?" Dylan raised an eyebrow. "Come, Flight-Leader, I believe we have a lot to discuss."

The Flight-Leader turned towards the Seaxe.

"Get her to the stables, Wulf. Make sure she's got a nice stall this time!"

"Yes, Sir," replied the blond rider quietly, with only the slightest hint of venom in his voice.

The large sturdy cage of iron bars was much more robust than the previous one. Three men stood around it, feeding a barrier woven closely of many Binding spells. They were wearing vermillion robes with the crest of a circle and cross on their shoulders. He sensed their terror and the immense effort with which they struggled to keep him from breaking out.

Suddenly, with a wild roar, he stood up, stretching his back and wings, shattering the bars of the cage like matchsticks. The wizards tried to fight back, but to no avail. He lunged towards one of them and, in a blink of an eye, snapped his mighty jaws on the man's midriff. Hot warm blood gushed into his starved throat.

Bran woke up strangely sore. His thighs and stomach muscles ached, his shoulders were covered in scratches. He wasn't rested at all, as if he hadn't slept all night. His head was pounding. He remembered scraps of dreams, vivid images. The women from Shigemasa's memories were there again and once more they all had Satō's face. For some reason it annoyed him greatly.

There was something else… a vision of the dragon. Bran could not recall the details of the dream, but could not shake off the feeling that something terrible had happened. He tried to focus and reach out with the Farlink, but received nothing except faint signs of life. The beast must have still been asleep. Perhaps it hadn't eaten for too long – hungry dragons in the wild would sometimes fell into a kind of hibernation, preserving energy until an opportunity to feed presented itself. He dared not to think of another reason for the dragon's silence.

Slowly, he dragged himself from the flat mattress and put on the bottoms of his travelling clothes. With great effort he staggered down to a vegetable garden at the back of the inn, looking for the well.

The mountains around the valley were steaming. The rain had stopped and the dew rose, filling the garden with a milky mist. In the midst of it, by the well, stood Nagomi, looking at her reflection in the dark water, her hair covered with a fresh layer of the black gunk. She nodded and smiled at him weakly. Bran was delighted to see her relaxed and in higher spirits than the day before.

"How do you feel?" she asked.

Before answering, Bran took a bucket of the cold well water and poured it over himself.

He was slowly remembering the events of the previous evening. Satō had been so exhilarated with the opportunity of having a proper night of revelry, she had decided to buy everyone in the inn a round of best local shōchū – then another. With every round, more people had come into the inn, until eventually the whole neighbourhood joined in the merrymaking. One of Satō's golden coins was more than enough to cover the bill.

It had been almost a year since Bran had spent a night at a tavern. He was never big on parties, but this time was different. Was it because the local liquor was stronger, the people more cheerful and friendly – or because Satō's clothes seemed to magically loosen a little bit more with every cup she had gulped?

During the day, as he had already learned, all the conduct of the Yamato people was guided by strict rules. Their manner of speaking, manner of walking, even gestures and facial expressions were always controlled and subdued. However, after a few cups of saké, all this was changing. That night everyone, rich and poor, had joined in singing, dancing and joke telling.

Bran had observed Satō showing off her wealth with concern. She was making them conspicuous. Everyone at the inn had warned them of travelling farther south through a wild mountainous region. As if the rumour of bandits was not enough, there was the water sprite's mention of malevolent creatures hiding in the forests – and Nagomi's strange behaviour a few hours earlier. All of this was very unnerving.

By the end of the night the wizardess had been hanging off Bran's arm, unable to stand, her face deep red. He had dragged her to the room she shared with Nagomi and laid her gently on the futon. For a brief moment she had wrapped her arms around his neck and looked into his eyes daringly, singing in a drunken drawl.

Ima wa ima wa ima wa
Okoran bai ka?
Shita kota gozansan!

Now, now, now,
Why are you angry?
Nothing's happening down there!

Before he could guess what the song meant, she had closed her eyes and was sound asleep.

"I feel fine, thank you," he answered Nagomi's question at last. "Did you sleep well? I'm sorry for waking you up..."

"That's all right." She shook her head. "I slept long enough."

Shadows under her eyes belied her words. Her skin had a greyish, tired hue. Bran felt a pang of guilt. *I should never have allowed the party to last that long into the night*, he thought. *We're far from safe. What if we have to fight today? I'm weak and tired. But she was having such a good time... I haven't seen her so happy before.*

The girl in question appeared in the courtyard. She was wearing her *Rangakusha* clothes, tightly bound this time. She didn't look in good shape, the unfortunate effects of last night's revelries reflected in her tired face and baggy eyes.

A couple of locals staggered towards the well. Bowing clumsily before Bran, they glanced towards Satō and exchanged a few giggly indecent comments. The wizardess clutched the collar of her robe tightly and stared coldly at the men.

Bran dried himself off, threw the towel around his bare shoulders and bowed before the wizardess.

"*Bore da!*" he welcomed her in Prydain.

"How could you have drunk that much and still wake up before me?" asked Satō, wincing. "Is that your soldier training?"

"To be honest, I find your drink rather weak," he boasted, although the back of his head still hurt.

"How long did the party continue after I left?" she asked.

"Not that long." He tried to remember. "In the end only that samurai in the purple kimono remained drinking. He was even tougher than me – flask after flask, as if it was water. He didn't talk much. At last even the innkeeper wanted us to go to sleep," he laughed, but not very loudly.

"I'm not really that used to alcohol, myself. Father always frowned when he saw me drink saké. He said it muddled one's talent."

"He may well have been right. I'm certainly in no mood for spell casting today," he said, laughing again even more quietly. "I had no idea the Yamato were so fond of drinking and singing," he added. "It was almost like one of the nights in a *tafarn* back home, with a harper by the fireside and cold *cwrw* in the tankard..."

His voice trailed off wistfully.

"I had no idea you knew any Yamato songs."

"That was... Shigemasa," he admitted. "The *Kuroda Warrior* was the last song he performed before his death – I felt it decent to let him replay it again."

"Are there many songs in your land, Bran-*sama*?"

"Please," he said, raising his hand, "it's about time you started to call me simply *Bran*. It is a custom in my country that those who drink together, as we did, do not need to refer to each other by anything more than a name."

"Very well," Satō agreed, "are there many songs – *Bran?*"

"Oh, yes," he replied, "children in Gwynedd learn to sing before they learn to speak!"

"You'll have to sing for us one day then"

Oh great, look what your boasting got you into...

"We should be moving," Nagomi said. "The innkeeper said the next lodging place is more than half a day away, in this weather."

"Weather changes quickly in these mountains," remarked Satō, "and I have no intention of staying in this place any longer." She cast a nervous glance at the two locals, who were now swaying their way back to the inn. "I think I would like my sword back today," she added, looking at the wild dark forest rising menacingly over the southern edge of the valley.

Satō was furious with herself. Furious and ashamed.

What she could remember of the last night now was absolutely appalling.

I should never have drunk that much.

It had felt strangely enticing to reveal herself before the foreigner's captivated eyes. It was a new thing for her. The men, she had learned from poems and books, were supposed to be excited by poetic subtleties, the red lining of the *kosode*, the blackened teeth, the purple peony in her hair. But something as common as flesh?

How did the night end? What did she tell him? What did she do? She remembered them struggling up the stairs to the room, her arms around Bran's neck. He smelled so nice... What happened next? Oh no, did she sing *that* song? She hoped he did not understand its real meaning... Had she brought shame to her family?

No, nothing happened. Nagomi was there and Satō would know from her accusing eyes. Bran just left her alone, sleeping on the cheap uncomfortable *futon*. He was that chivalrous, or naïve, or maybe he preferred the company of other boys, like so many young samurai sons she knew...

Stupid, *stupid* girl! All this for what? A few spellbound glances and one drunken embrace. *Get a hold of yourself, Takashima Satō*, she kept reproaching herself as the party climbed the forest road, ever deeper into the dark mountains. *If you need a man, there are plenty of proper Yamato boys. No need to waste your time with this odd, uncouth barbarian.*

She cast one last look at the valley they were leaving behind as the road climbed back into the forest. The sun was still shining at Hitoyoshi, its friendly households and terraced fields, dancing merrily on the tin roofs of the workshops and silver waters of the Kuma River below; but there were heavy clouds gathering around the tops of the mountains and up the hill where she stood the rain started anew – a drizzle at first, but Satō knew it would not end at that. She pulled the hood of her rain cloak tighter and followed Bran and Nagomi up the forest road.

This was the one part of their journey that truly troubled her. Past the last of the lumber mills started a wild country she knew nothing about. The only road winded up and down, left and right, in zigzags and spiral turns through the deep, dark, mystic ancient wood. The trees up here grew even denser and taller than they had along the river, barely touched by a woodcutter's axe, only enough to keep the dirt road passable. There was no sign of any lodgings in the distance and they had not passed a single traveller since leaving the village. By the end of the day the mist started rising from the ground and quickly got so thick she could barely see further than twenty feet or so. The sky turned dark. The evening was fast approaching and the rain became an unpleasant drenching shower. The road narrowed to a slippery path. Her *hakama* was covered in mud.

"It's no use," Bran said. "We'll have to find some shelter for the night."

"Just a bit more. Maybe there will be some lumberjack hut or hermitage," said Satō.

"Or a forest shrine," added Nagomi hopefully.

This was the first the apprentice had spoken since leaving the town. *She's very gloomy today. We're all tired but there's something else...*

She almost bumped into Bran who stopped suddenly. A large tree was lying fallen across the road. The boy moved forwards to look for a way around it, but Satō grabbed him by the sleeve.

"Look out," she said, "they did warn us about the bandits..."

"And quite right they were," a mocking voice spoke behind them.

A tall muscular hulk of a man emerged from the mist. He wore a white tunic, torn at the bulging forearms, and brown trousers. A red band tied his black unruly hair. He held an iron mace, longer than a sword, studded with nails, slung loosely over his shoulder. A little blue electric light wandered along the length of the weapon.

"Well, well, *what is this?*" he boomed loudly, twirling a bushy beard in his fingers. "Three kids on a mountain path? Are you lost? Where are your parents?"

Again a blue flame flickered along the length of the iron mace. The bandit smiled cruelly and scratched his chest with dirty fingers. His tunic spread apart, revealing a tattoo of a five-pointed, interlaced star.

"He's an *onmyōji!*"

Satō pointed at the pentacle on the man's chest.

"*Onmyōji?* What's that?" Bran asked.

"Our own native magic – "

"Have you finished?" the bandit interrupted them. "I don't think you're quite as scared of me as you should be!"

He came a few steps closer, swaying arrogantly, the mace still on his shoulder. Satō pulled out her sword with a metallic whistle. Bran put his right hand on the hilt of his Prydain sword and locked the index and middle fingers of the left hand together.

The bandit stopped and observed them carefully, squinting. He snapped his fingers and out of the forest came three other men, dressed and armed like the samurai, but without any markings on their ragged clothes; *rōnin* – warriors without masters, lethal swords for hire.

The boat hobbled up to the pier, frightening a lazy heron, and the passengers began pouring out. First to disembark were four swordsmen in grey uniforms, grim-faced and silent. The *kunoichi* was the last to step out of the boat, still in her beggar monk's clothes. The ferryman helped her down and bowed with his hands clasped – a devout superstitious man. Azumi bowed back, reaching out with her bowl. No real itinerant monk would pass an occasion like that. A couple of copper coins jingled into the black bowl.

"May *Butsu-sama* bless you with a long life. Tell me, good man, what decent inns are there in this town?"

The ferryman looked at her quizzically, but gave her directions to several establishments.

"We have rich temples, monk-*sama*," he added proudly. "I'm sure they will be happy to accommodate you."

"Saké loosens purses," she said.

"*Ah,* I see!" His face brightened up in a wide honest smile. "How silly of me."

She feared she would be too late again. The boat had trudged so slowly up the mountain river she wondered if it wouldn't be faster on foot, but the ferry moved relentlessly through the tall canyons from dawn to dusk and she needed to be rested for the confrontation, if there was to be one.

It wasn't hard to find the right guesthouse. The memory of the party and the three young travellers was still fresh in the minds of the locals.

"Do you know when they departed?" she asked the landlord.

They couldn't have been more than half a day away – the sun was still high.

"Departed?" The man laughed. "I do believe they haven't even woken up yet!"

Azumi couldn't believe her luck. Could they really have been so reckless?

She hid behind the corner of the inn, opened one of the numerous ivory compartments hanging at her sash and, unrolling a piece of paper, summoned a lizard messenger.

"Tell them to come to the inn by the riverside," she ordered, and the spectral reptile skittered away to where the samurai in grey uniforms were awaiting her orders.

Four skilled swordsmen and herself may have been deemed an overkill, but the *kunoichi* could not afford a failure, and these three kids had defeated an *enenra* already. Two of them knew magic. She wasn't taking any chances.

She watched in astonishment as the three youths passed her by, no more than a few feet away. The youngest – a shrine apprentice, Azumi recalled – even dropped a few pieces of copper into the alms bowl. Azumi bowed and muttered her thanks. They were silent and seemed tired, despite sleeping so late into the day, but they were moving fast even so, and the four swordsmen for whom she waited failed to appear. The children were already on the narrow bridge over Kuma. In a few minutes they would leave Hitoyoshi altogether.

The *kunoichi* could not wait any longer. She merged into the shadows and began to follow the travellers as discreetly as only a trained Koga assassin could.

What had happened to her men? *A betrayal? Impossible, unless...* Was the Master toying with her, testing her? Was she supposed to finish the task by herself to prove her worth? She could do it, she was certain, now that she had seen the targets up close. They were easy targets, unaware of their surroundings, unprepared for a fight. All she had to do was wait until they were out of the town, out of sight of witnesses. This could be one of her easiest assignments yet...

Her keen senses picked up a sudden presence. *She* was being watched. *Who dared...?* She looked around, but could not see anybody. *A Spirit?* No, it had to be a man. She froze, blending even further into the shadows among the cedar trees. The children moved out of her sight, but she didn't mind – the road led straight south through a dense forest, they could not escape her now. The new threat required more immediate attention.

A samurai in a purple robe thrown over a flowery kimono stepped onto the road, looking straight at her. He was brandishing two naked swords, their plain black hilts contrasting with the gaudy colours of his unfashionable outfit. How had she missed him in these clothes?

"Come out, monk," he said, pointing at her with one of the swords.

The blade was caked with fresh blood. She obeyed. There was no point in hiding anymore.

"I know you," she said, remembering at last. "You were in Yatsushiro, by the harbour, but you haven't been on the boat."

"I walked," the samurai stated simply.

It was impossible. He must've travelled day and night without respite to have reached the town before her, and he showed no trace of fatigue.

"What do you want with me?"

"Go back to your Master, monk. These three are *my* prey."

The air around them grew noticeably colder. Azumi shivered. This was not an ordinary opponent. She knew now whose blood was on that blade.

Slowly, within the folds of her robe, she bent the palm of her left hand, reaching for a
hidden blade strapped to her wrist. The samurai's eyes darted towards that hand. He winced.

"Please don't. I don't enjoy killing monks. Even pretend ones."

Smoothly and noiselessly, she let the hidden knife fly towards her enemy's chest. Even as the blade still flew, she pressed a hidden spring on her pilgrim's staff. It split in two, revealing a three-foot long iron chain concealed inside one of the halves, with a weight at the end. Another secret blade popped out at the end of the other half. Hot blood rushing through her veins, she charged at the stranger silently.

She managed to stand against him for several long seconds, and she knew then that this was her greatest moment, the fight she would be most proud of until the end of her days – if she survived the ordeal. His swords were like snakes, living creatures with minds of their own, ribbons of steel, flashes of metallic lightning. The two blades whistled around her a sweet song of triumph and skill, but the samurai's face remained impassioned all through the duel, as if he was trimming a garden.

She felt droplets dripping down her face and she couldn't tell whether it was sweat, blood or tears of exasperation. With a clang, her weapons were torn from her hands, disappearing into the ferns. She tumbled back, just as one of the two inhuman blades whizzed past where her neck had been a fraction of a second earlier. She reached for the smoke grenade and threw it at the samurai, but he cut through it with such force that the air buffeting off the blades dispersed the poison. He was unstoppable.

A white wolf jumped on the samurai's back, snarling, reaching towards the man's neck with its teeth. Azumi didn't have time to think from where the beast had come – it was not her companion… This was the one moment of distraction she could use. Weaponless, she did not consider another attack, but she could still run, and run she did, into the forest, into the mist as far away from the terrifying swordsman as she could.

CHAPTER XVI

"Now," the mage spoke in a calm voice, "you have something that I would very much like to have. Give it to me and I will spare you. I have no desire to hurt children."

"I don't know what you're talking about," Bran replied. Something told him the bandit was not after Satō's gold coins.

"The blue stone, the sapphire shard. This – " He pointed at Bran's left hand. "It is much too precious a thing for a youth like you to carry around these forests."

"This?" Bran looked at his finger with surprise. "My grandfather's ring? Why would you want it?"

The bandit chortled.

"If you don't know what it does, you won't miss it, will you?"

"Tell the Crimson Robe to come and get it himself!"

The bandit blinked in confusion.

"I have no idea who this Crimson Robe is."

Then who – ?

"Come now, this is taking too long," the bandit interrupted his thoughts, "I really only want the jewel, but if you trouble me any longer, I am willing to take your gold too, as compensation."

"Three swordsmen and a mage against three kids?" mocked Bran. He was already observing the scene of battle with True Sight and noticed the three *rōnin* had no magical weapons. This filled him with confidence. "Not taking any chances, eh?"

"You have swords," the bandit replied, shrugging his muscular shoulders. "I like my face unscarred." He rubbed his bearded chin. "Let's finish this, the rain is most annoying. I have given you enough warning."

He stepped forwards and swung his mace, aiming for Bran's head. The strike seemed fatal but Bran stood steady, unwavering, watching the iron weapon buzz off his *tarian* without effect, the shield's surface shimmering softly in the rain.

Satō raised her sword threateningly and the mage pulled back. The three *rōnin* looked at their boss but he shook his head.

"What now?" Satō whispered.

"He can't get through. Not without a Soul Lance or an Unravelling spell," Bran replied confidently.

"A *kekkai*, huh? I see you know a few tricks. So do I…"

The bandit scratched his scraggy beard. From a fold of his shirt he pulled out a strip of paper with Qin characters written on it in black ink. He threw it at the shield. It burst with blue flame. Bran swayed and felt the barrier's collapse around him almost like a physical blow.

"W-what?" he gasped.

"*Get them!*"

The mage waved his hand and the swordsmen rushed to capture the three travellers.

Satō cried out a spell word and slashed the air twice with her sword. Arches of ice struck the closest two opponents in their chests, throwing them backwards. The third swordsman hesitated.

"I knew it!" the *onmyōji* cried. "You're *all* wizards!"

Bran snapped out of his astonishment. His blood rushed in expectation of combat, accelerating his reflexes, but his poise faltered. Without his dragon he was like a cavalryman turned footman. He was trained to rely on shields, Soul Lance and the link with Emrys, but the Farlink was overstretched and could maybe provide him with one or two bursts of dragon flame, and his shield turned out to be useless.

He pointed at the still standing warrior and spoke Binding Words. He put little power into the spell, but it was enough to halt the man's movements completely. He then spread out his palm and tried the same with *onmyōji*, but the mage only smirked and shrugged the spell off.

The dragon rider cursed and drew his sword. A row of runes lit up along the blade. He was not a keen swordsman and the weapon in his hand felt unfamiliar, unwieldy.

"*Are you sure you know what you're doing?*" a voice called in Bran's head.

"Leave me be." The boy struggled to push the general's spirit away. "I have everything under control."

"*He doesn't look that tough. I could cut him down if you'd only let me.*"

"You've chosen a bad time to try your tricks. I need to focus, so be quiet!" the boy cried in his mind with great energy.

The general fell silent, watchful.

The *onmyōji* swung his mace sideways at Bran. The boy leapt up and forwards, quickly calculating the curve of his enhanced jump above the mage's head. He landed hard and turned around, cutting backwards, but the jump had carried him too far and his blade swished through the air futilely. He lost his balance and struggled not to fall face-forwards into the dirt. The Enchanted Acrobatics had failed him once again.

The mage spun around. Bran opened his left hand and summoned dragon flame, spewing a spiralling tongue of fire from between his spread fingers. At last the *onmyōji* stopped smirking as the air filled with the stench of burning skin and hair.

The mage grunted, annoyed. He clearly had not expected to get hurt. He smashed his mace into the ground with full force and the earth around him shook violently.

Bran staggered, dropping to one knee. He attacked with dragon flame again, but this time the mage bit his teeth and endured the pain as the blaze enveloped him. He threw his mace high up into the air then clapped his hands together and murmured a quick mantra before catching the weapon as it fell.

A five-pointed star appeared glowing on the ground around Bran. The dragon rider tried to jump away, but he bounced off an invisible wall – he was trapped within the borders of the pentacle.

The mage towered over Bran with a stern face. His shirt burned to tatters, the five-pointed star tattoo on his chest was fully visible, dancing on rippling muscles. The skin on his torso was covered in fast reddening blisters, but the mage seemed to pay no attention to what must have been a terrible agony.

With lightning speed he swung his iron mace high above his head to bring it down upon the boy, but Bran was just as quick. He dropped his sword and summoned the Soul Lance between his stretched out arms. Blue lightning crackled as the mace clanged against the lance's shaft of solidified life energy. Bran moaned, his shoulders nearly breaking, but the lance held where the sword's blade would have no doubt shattered.

The mage laughed and pushed further against the lance, confident in his pure physical strength. Bran resisted valiantly, but his weapon flickered under the strain and suddenly vanished. The *onmyōji* lost his balance momentarily. The iron mace missed Bran's head by an inch and fell with great force upon the boy's left shoulder, smashing through the collar bone with a loud, nauseating crack.

"*Gwrthyrru!*"

Ignoring the excruciating pain, Bran hit the mage's chest with a Strike of Repel. The enemy launched a few feet into the air with a surprised expression on his face and fell on his back, splashing the mud around.

The road, the forest and the grey sky revolved around Bran, shock quickly overcoming his consciousness. He saw Satō running to his help and then there was nothing but the red darkness.

The fight was too easy. The bandits may have been skilled swordsmen, but they were no match for her magic. She had already frozen two of her opponents to the ground; the third one was struggling to set himself free from Bran's spell.

Satō would have preferred to fight the *onmyōji*. She was curious how her Takashima School training would aid her in a fight against what many wizards perceived as a natural foil to the *Rangakusha* – a native mage, skilled in channelling the destructive aspects of the *kami* power – but the bandit chief focused his efforts on Bran, leaving her to deal with his meagre minions.

She raised her sword to strike the nearest of the swordsmen, when his eyes lit up with red glow and his face twisted and transformed into a blazing demonic mask. He shrugged Bran's enchantment off. The other two men underwent the same metamorphosis and the ice shackles holding them shattered with a loud crackle.

"*Shikigami!*" Satō scowled.

The demonic familiars in human guise! Now the fight became serious. She leapt back as her enemies jumped at her from three sides. She put her left hand to her lips and whispered a quick incantation. Three ice lances shot from her fingers. The demons let out otherworldly howls, but kept on approaching, ignoring their wounds.

This was no good, she realized. She put more energy into her next shot and launched one powerful javelin-shaped missile against the nearest of the assailants. It tore right through him, leaving a gaping hole in his torso. Still the *shikigami* moved forwards as if nothing happened. She parried one blow of his sword, then another, but there seemed to be no stopping the demonic swordsmen. Suddenly she heard Nagomi cry out.

"Sacchan, look out – Bran…!"

Glancing beyond the three demons, the wizardess saw Bran slip and fall down under the pummelling of the *onmyōji's* mace. She noticed the five-pointed star glowing in the sand and cursed loudly.

Fighting the familiars was taking too long and her reserves were draining fast. And now she had to do something to help Bran out of the mage's trap. Desperate, she reached into the sleeve of her vermillion kimono and took out the glove given to her by Master Tanaka. She slid it hastily on her right hand and pressed on the spring. A thick needle popped out, piercing her palm. Blood spurted in a thick stream. The glass dial twitched and lit up brightly as Satō's life energy poured into the enchantment.

"*Bevries!*" the wizardess cried at the top of her lungs.

The nearest bandit immediately turned into an ice statue, frozen solid from head to toe. Satō was as surprised with the result as the other two.

"*Bevries, weder!*" She cast another spell, and another demonic swordsman was stopped in his tracks, his limbs encased in ice. "Blood magic…" she whispered, fascinated by the amount of power she was able to generate.

But that was almost the limit of what the device was capable off. The grip of her sword was slippery with blood and the energy gauge was running low. Worst of all, the wound in her shoulder once more began to throb with pain.

She hissed through gritted teeth, trying to ignore the ache.

Satō dodged a blow from the last swordsman's blade. She pierced the *shikigami* with her sword, but the demon pushed on. Slashing sideways, she sliced the enemy across the stomach. The swordsman glanced at his innards pouring out of the gash, confused. He made a clumsy step forwards and his legs wobbled. Satō pushed him aside and ran towards Bran and the *onmyōji*.

The bulky mage picked himself up off the ground and raised his dreadful mace over Bran one more time. She released all her remaining power, hoping to hamper his movements with strong ice chains. She managed to turn his attention on herself for a moment.

The *onmyōji* swirled his weapon over Satō wildly. She ducked and cut the enemy across the stomach, but her sword bounced off an invisible shield. The mage had his own *kekkai!* Was there no limit to his powers? She lunged forwards, dodging another blow. While the bandit struggled against her icy shackles, the wizardess reached Bran.

She tried to lift him but the boy's body slipped from her grasp. She heard and felt the last of her enchantments shatter, the *onmyōji* breaking free behind her. She turned around and raised her sword feebly, in an attempt to block the final blow from the terrible iron mace as it came crashing down towards her. Parts of the sword covered with frost, but she was too weak to embed the entire blade in ice. Her shoulder was almost paralysed with the agony spreading from the bronze dagger wound.

She stared straight in the mage's eyes, ready to face death…

The moment the three *rōnin* turned into demons, Nagomi hid behind a tree, shivering with terror. She had never experienced such fear in her life, not even when they had to flee from the Honmyōji. She prayed to all her ancestors, but they offered no guidance. She prayed to Lady Kazuko, but the priestess did not appear before her, did not come from the Otherworld at her time of need.

She was on her own and helpless. Again there was nothing she could do but watch her friends struggle, lose and die. Bran was already down, Satō fighting on her own. Still the Gods did not come.

"I must do something," she whispered in despair, "*anything!*"

She felt something warm in her sleeve and reached into it. The Spirit light beaker lit up with the merry orange flame, as if trying to comfort Nagomi in her distress.

"I'm sorry," she whispered and threw the beaker at the *onmyōji* with all her might and little hope.

The hulking bandit's back made for an easy target. The tiny, fragile clay pot smashed against his burly frame and the Spirit light, set free, immediately engulfed the mage's body in flames.

The *onmyōji* howled loudly. He dropped the mace and clasped his hands to his face. Faint pale wisps of bright orange flame whirled around him, penetrating magic defences, scalding his blistered burned skin. The mage reeled to the side of the road.

Satō saw Nagomi standing in the middle of the road with her eyes and mouth wide open, breathing fast, her trembling hands clutching her paper-tasselled wand. Shards of her Spirit fire beaker were scattered on the road. The wisps of shining orange fog spread all over the mage like fiery insects and leapt onto the stumbling *shikigami* behind him, who began to howl and crawl in the dirt just like its master.

But the icy tombs holding the other two were shattering from inside. There was no time to wonder about the miracle. The wizardess pulled Bran up by his right arm, herself still numb with pain.

"Nagomi!"

The apprentice shook off her astonishment and ran up to help raise the boy from the other side. Bran grunted weakly, his consciousness slowly returning.

"There's a hidden path behind that big tree," Nagomi whispered.

The wizardess nodded and the three stumbled into the humid darkness of the misty forest. The undergrowth seemed to part before the girls and, as they carried wounded Bran farther down the narrow muddy path, the woods closed behind their backs defensibly, keeping them safely out of sight.

For all Nagomi knew, they could have been carrying the boy straight into the bandits' lair, but there was no time to think of a better plan. The path was definitely the one she had seen in the revelation the day before. Every fern, every cypress tree, every moss-covered boulder was the same. She could only hope she had interpreted the vision correctly.

She could hear the enemies in the distance, trying to find their way through the dense forest, then there was only the silence of the deep wood and the sound of rain battering on the leaves. Eventually the path ended before a round open glade, surrounded with a circle of roughly hewn, moss-covered stones. Exactly as she had seen in the bronze mirror, in the middle of the glade was an ancient earthen mound with a stone-lined narrow entrance. Remnants of an old straw rope lay in front of it, and a dilapidated wooden door frame showed the inside was still in use long after the mound had been raised.

Nagomi hesitated, remembering the rest of the vision, but there wasn't anyone inside and Satō was urging her to move quickly. They were both at the edge of their strength. The girls entered the mound and put Bran on the floor of flat hard limestone. The chamber was surprisingly dry and warm. Satō sneaked outside to cover up their tracks, while Nagomi sat down by the unconscious boy.

There was very little daylight seeping through the entrance. Nagomi wished she still had her Spirit light with her. Its loss was disheartening. She had been carrying the merry orange flame with her ever since she had become inducted as an apprentice. It had kept her company in any darkness, reminding her of the happy times she had at the shrine. Now her loneliness was even more palpable.

She focused on examining Bran's wounds. The boy's shoulder was dark purple, quickly turning black, swollen to twice its normal size. When she touched it, she could feel the bits of crushed bone move sickeningly underneath the skin. She felt queasy, but at least *now* she knew exactly what to do. She started her healing chant, quietly at first, bowing repeatedly, shaking her wooden wand and sprinkling his arm with dew and rainwater gathered from the floor. There was very little effect – the bleeding did not subside, the swelling remained in place, the shattered bones refused to mend.

"Ooh, it's not working! Why doesn't it work?" she complained. "You're not old enough to be so resistant!"

Bran opened his eyes and looked at her. His pupils were as black as night.

"*His Ancestors are not with him.*"

The guttural roar of the Otherworld coming from deep within the boy's throat accompanied the words spoken by General Shigemasa.

Nagomi backed away, shielding herself with the wooden wand.

"*The boy has great innate resistance,*" the old samurai said, "*even to thy healing power.*"

"What… what do I need to do?" Nagomi whispered.

"*I shall endeavour to open the conduit. Thou wilt have little time, so do thy best.*"

Bran-Shigemasa closed his eyes. A bright blue light surrounded his body and on that cue Nagomi started her chanting once more. The wound started to heal, contract, the bleeding stopped, the swelling receded. The bones and muscles moved around within the flesh and joined together, mending. Soon all that was left was only a dark bruise, a faint memory of the battle. Nagomi leaned back against the wall, panting, exhausted to the very edge of her strength. She had never felt so weak and tired in her life.

"Thank you, Shigemasa-*dono,*" she managed a faint whisper.

"*The boy is no good to me dead. If he perishes out here in the wilderness, I become a wandering Spirit.*"

"You will… not be trying to control him now?"

"*Not today. There would be no honour in that.*"

"I… I don't believe you. He warned us about… your tricks."

The general chuckled.

"*He was right, but the Barbarian deserves this little respite. He fought bravely today – almost like a true samurai. I can appreciate that.*"

Satō barred the narrow entrance with the remnants of the door and sat down next to her friend. The chamber was shrouded in darkness, light barely seeping through the cracks between the stones. The wizardess, too, was tired and dishevelled, her forearm covered with dried blood, her shoulder hanging loose, limp. She loosened her kimono and undid the breast wrap to catch a deeper breath.

"How is he?"

"He should be fine. Do you need that cut looked after?" Nagomi raised a feeble hand but Satō caught it gently and put back on her lap.

"No, it's just a scratch. Don't worry."

"And the… arm?"

"The Suwa priests already did everything that could be done. What about you? You seem exhausted."

"I'm… I'll be all right. I just need to rest."

Bran stirred, opened his eyes and slowly sat up.

"I'm alive," he said.

"For now," said Satō grimly. "They're still out there somewhere."

"Odd…" He rubbed a bruised arm. "I thought it would be crushed to bits."

"It was," the wizardess told him, "you're lucky Nagomi's such a talented healer."

"A healer…?"

"Any priestess would do the same," Nagomi protested shyly.

"I don't understand."

"Nagomi *healed your wound*," repeated Satō slowly as if talking to a child, assuming his mind was still muddled by the shock of the fight.

"But how could she...?"

"*Oh*, you – don't you have healers in the West?"

"No! I've never heard of such thing. Do you mean medicine?" he asked.

"No, that's not it. Your medicine is great when it comes to dealing with diseases and internal ailments," replied Satō, "but for battle wounds or injuries, we have the Spirit healers."

"But... is this true? This is a fantastic power! How did you manage to keep it a secret?"

"*A secret?*" Satō seemed genuinely surprised. "Nobody's keeping it a secret. I thought everyone knew about Spirit healing."

"I assure you if the world outside knew... The Bataavians are certainly not letting this information out." Bran stopped and looked around the dark chamber. "How did we get here? I don't remember..."

"You passed out with pain and we carried you into the forest."

"We've defeated them?"

"No." Satō shook her head. "But we did manage to run away, thanks to Nagomi's sacrifice."

"How do you mean?"

Despite the darkness inside the tomb, Nagomi could feel Bran's incredulous eyes fixed upon her. She avoided their gaze and looked at the floor, wringing the end of her *obi* sash in her hands.

"It wasn't... I didn't..."

"She used her Spirit light to distract the mage," said Satō, patting her gently on the back, "am I right?"

Nagomi nodded.

"Thank you," whispered Bran, "and thank you for the... healing. I still can't – such power...!"

"It's – nothing, really." She felt her throat closing in.

The boy looked around.

"Are we safe here? What is this place?"

"It's a tomb of the Ancients," Nagomi said in a quiet voice, "and a forest shrine, after that." She could faintly sense the *kami* of the place still lingering around, but the altar and all the trappings were long gone.

Maybe if I could purify this place and make an offering, its kami *would yet return...*

"The Ancients?"

Bran flicked a faint flamespark. The hollowed-out chamber was lined with flat limestone flagstones, its surface smooth and cool to touch.

"People who used to live here before the Yamato came," explained Satō.

"*Used to* live? What happened to them?"

"Never mind the history lesson – it was thousands of years ago," Satō said impatiently, "what did those bandits want from us? From *you?* Why were they after your ring?"

"I wish I knew. I thought it was just a curious memento my grandfather retained after his…" He hesitated. "His journey to Yamato. But those bandits thought that shard of sapphire was a more interesting prize than your roll of gold coins."

Nagomi bit her lips. A shard of sapphire… The High Priestess did ask her not to tell anyone about the Prophecy for fear of reprisals – but surely they could not find themselves in a more desperate situation. The priestess was dead, and they were all pursued by some terrible monsters – and all, she guessed, because of the Prophecy; that strange disturbing vision she had saw so many months ago.

They had the right to know.

Before any of them managed to say anything, a twig cracked and a bush rustled outside. Bran immediately vanquished the flamespark.

"They've found us," Satō whispered in the darkness.

Bran joined the wizardess by the narrow entrance, observing the *onmyōji* and his weird companions. There were now six of them, approaching the tomb quietly through the fog in a fan-shaped formation.

Bran reached for the sword readying himself for another battle, but the scabbard was empty. The Prydain blade lay abandoned somewhere in the dirt of the road.

Satō drew her katana with trembling arms.

"I… I don't think we'll make it," she whispered. "I thought I'd covered us well enough. I failed again."

"You did all you could – we're only human," said Bran, trying to console her. "Maybe we can still sneak out…"

She shrugged his hand off.

"I'm a samurai!" she said firmly, "and if I can't fight like one, at least I can die like one. I've been running away long enough. *Takashima!*"

"No, wait…!"

Before anyone could stop her, with a fierce battle cry on her lips she kicked out the door, raised her sword and leapt outside, ready to charge to her death.

Suddenly a blade flashed in the fog behind the bandits' backs, then another. One of the enemies collapsed face down without a sound. Before the others could react, the second also fell victim to the unseen swordsman. The blades flashed once more like twin lightning strikes, and the third tumbled down, flailing bloody stumps of arms. The swords skipped from one enemy to another like two steel vipers hiding in the mist. Within seconds, only the mage remained alive. The *onmyōji* turned to face the enemy and raised his mace with a defiant roar, but it was already too late. The two mysterious swords flashed one last time in a neat, flawless strike and the mage's head rolled slowly off his body, leaving a trace of bloody spurts in the grass.

Silence fell like a death shroud upon the forest.

CHAPTER XVII

The night was hot and uncomfortably muggy. Yezaimon Kayama stirred uneasily in his sleep, throwing off the thin quilt. He had been suffering from nightmares ever since the *Taikun*, in his great wisdom, had resolved to make him the Governor of Defences of the Uraga Channel. The heat and humidity of early summer nights only made the anguish worse.

The position, although ostensibly prestigious, was a burden in the best of days. His wife was right to warn him not to accept it, but it was impossible – nobody refused a gift from the *Taikun* and lived. The domain consisted of miles of empty shoreline, dotted with ancient forts built in times immemorial to thwart some invasion of a forgotten foe. There were no pirates on these seas, no invading fleet sighted in centuries.

Boredom and useless chores filled Kayama's days as he travelled up and down the coast, hopelessly trying to build up some pretence of defence. The local samurai feigned effort only for as long as they could feel his eyes on their backs. Money was short, the treasury almost empty. The breaches in the walls of the coastal forts were covered with grey cloth instead of stone. The cannons remembered the days of the first Tokugawa *Taikun*, some of them had barrels made of wood, painted black to imitate iron. It was all make-believe, a theatre stage with outdated props.

Nobody ever threatened these shores. The Divine Winds protected the islands with a tight impenetrable maze of storms and twisting currents, passable only in one secret place south of Chinzei Island. Once every ten years or so, a barbarian ship tried to break through, but always failed. Sometimes the waves would cast away a few hapless survivors. The regularity with which the barbarians attempted the landings baffled Kayama's mind. Did they not know that as long as the *Taikun*s ruled from their Edo castle, the Gods themselves protected the Sacred Soil of Yamato?

Recently, if the rumours were true, another foreign ship had been sighted off the Nansei Islands, heading north. Like so many times before, the governor had to make sure at least some of his cannons were able to shoot more than blanks, and that a few of his archers and arquebusiers were stationed at their proper posts, in the unlikely event that the barbarians would somehow succeed.

The obviously exaggerated rumours of the size and strength of the barbarian flotilla did little to ease his anxiety. For the last few nights he'd been dreaming of great monsters emerging from the waters of Uraga Bay and devouring towns and villages along the shore. These were ominous menacing dreams and he sincerely wished that the foreigners would already come and go, and leave his poor soul in peace.

The desperate ringing of gongs coming from the beach awoke the governor from an uneasy slumber. Kayama pulled himself off the rice hull-stuffed mattress, grumpily.

"Enough already," he mumbled, "you call yourselves samurai? I thought I'd trained you better than this."

Without haste, he put on his everyday clothes, a plain grey *haori* jacket and sand-yellow, pleated *hakama* skirt, thrust two swords into the sash around his waist and opened the door of the coastal outpost in which he was spending the night.

The ringing continued. He inhaled deeply and instead of the usual scent of sea and wind, he smelled soot and smoke.

Intrigued but not yet worried, Kayama gazed over a high cliff overlooking the port of Kurihama, the gateway to the Uraga Bay. In the pink glow of dawn, a scene of chaos and destruction was unfolding before his eyes. The town was ablaze. The gongs of the military were by now joined by the loud booming drone of the temple bell and the clanging little bells of fire guards. Raging flame was devouring houses along several of the streets, feeding on the wooden frames and thatched roofs. People were running towards the hills in panic, leaving all their possessions to the fire.

Before he could take all this in, a bewildering sound came from the sky, as if a giant lion roared in the clouds. Kayama looked up and reeled in terror. For a moment he thought he was still dreaming or had gone mad. Above the town, far beyond the range of any cannon, bow or matchlock, circled four giant black beasts, like enormous eagles, slowly beating their great wings and weaving long serpentine tails. One of them was greater than the other three, flying higher, as if commanding all this destruction. Every so often, one of the lesser monsters spewed a ball of flame from its mouth which fell into the sea with a deafening blast and a hiss of steam.

There was nothing Kayama could do but admire the destruction from afar. He was, after all, an educated samurai, and could find poetry even in death and ruin. The monsters, he understood quickly, were no doubt Gods or their messengers, coming from the sea to inflict punishment on the unsuspecting sinners. The famines and earthquakes were just a prelude: this was what the prophecies and divinations of the priests had been all about. Kayama sat down on the ground, resigned, as the unbelievable beasts continued to circle above the harbour.

Oh, poor Yamato, the shadow of black wings portends thy doom!

In his head he began to compose the first stanza of an epic poem *On Destruction of Uraga Harbour* when, to his surprise, the black monsters stopped their circling and swooped towards him. As they soared above Kayama with tremendous speed, heating the very wind before them, he noticed tiny silhouettes of men riding atop the beasts, two on each except a lonely figure on the largest one, their faces hidden in the shadows of grey hooded cloaks.

They weren't Gods, he realised with relief, which quickly turned into renewed terror. They were human beings – invaders. They were heading straight for Edo, and he could do nothing to stop them...

BOOK THREE

THE ISLANDS IN THE MIST

P·F·V·S

The spring is a dawn. The vast sky turns pale, the peaks of the mountains brighten gently. In the purple glow, the thin clouds linger towards the horizon.

The Pillow Book

PROLOGUE

The white silk of his robe was stained with the blood of his brethren.

Wet sand squeaked under his bare feet. At the break of dawn the sea was silent, cold and dark like the swords which slaughtered the priests at the Mekari. His brothers had thrown themselves against the blades to protect him and that which he carried away.

The Jewel was not for human hands to hold. The orb of white crystal burned his skin and flesh like a glowing ember. He bit his lips and endured.

The black line of gnarled, twisted pines moved closer with his every breath. He dared not look back; he knew the grey-clad assassins were near. He hoped to lose them in the dark forest growing on the windswept seaward slopes of the nearby dune ridge. If he could only make it to those trees...

Out of the corner of his eye he glimpsed the falling blade and instinctively raised his hand to shield himself. The sword clanged harmlessly. The white sleeve of his robe fell, revealing an arm covered with black scales, glinting in the first rays of the rising sun.

He grasped the blade and snapped it in two. The swordsman stared incredulously at his broken weapon, then at the long, sharp claws reaching for his eyes.

He left the howling assassin to bleed out onto the sand and kept on running. The trees were now less than fifty paces away, their safe shadows beckoning him invitingly. The others were now so close behind he could hear the shuffling of their feet. He stumbled, losing precious seconds. Thirty paces. Twenty. His aching calves cried for him to stop, but he ignored the pain. His heart pounded as if trying to break free from the ribcage. Just a little more effort. Just a few more steps.

He glimpsed them standing among the trees, swords drawn, and realised all was lost. He slowed down and stopped. The men behind him stopped too, waiting, patient. He turned around. There were three of them, all in the same grey, unmarked uniforms, solemn faces without a trace of emotion. Two more approached unhurriedly from the forest.

They could see the Jewel clearly, shining like a beacon through his right hand and the white silk sleeve, but, for the moment, were more concerned with the left hand, armed with its deadly claws. Wary of the fate of their comrade, the swordsmen bid their time until, at last, the first one leapt towards him with the weapon raised. There was no war cry, not even a hastening of breath.

The sun rising over the dunes painted the sea as crimson as the blood of the five men lying in the sand and the robe of the long-haired, gaunt faced man standing before him.

"I'm impressed," the man said, grinning to show his sharp, black teeth. His eyes glinted like nuggets of pure gold. In his right hand he was holding a giant sword, almost four feet in length. "So, this is how the last of the Sea Dragons fights."

The priest said nothing, saving his strength. Two of his claws were broken, his left eye gouged, his stomach and chest cut with many deep wounds but, somehow, he was still standing. He no longer felt any pain, only weariness.

The man in the crimson robe drew his sword and threw away the plain wooden sheath.

"This is where you should say something poignant," he remarked and raised the weapon horizontally above his head. The priest wondered if it was too late to pray to the great Watatsumi for help.

With a sudden roar he lunged forwards. The man in the crimson robe stepped back and brought the sword down. The blade struck the priest's right shoulder, slicing the arm cleanly off his body, but the claws pierced deep into the enemy's chest. No blood pulsed in the swordsman's veins; no heart beat inside the ribcage.

The demon laughed and pushed the priest away. He reached down and wrestled the Jewel, clutched in the hand, though the arm was cut clean off. A frown marred its pale face as the gem's white light burned through the parchment-thin skin.

"That's not right," he murmured to himself. The priest tried to crawl away, slipping and stumbling, but the demon grabbed him by the folds of the white silk robe, turned effortlessly and, with a swift stab, pierced his chest.

With dying eyes, the priest watched as his own blood stained red the Jewel of the Ebbs, turning the stone from a white diamond into the purest of rubies.

CHAPTER I

Slender fingers picked the polished piece of white clamshell up from the wooden bowl and dropped it onto the intersection between the straight black lines with a soft tap.

Atsuko straightened and looked up from the board. Her eyes met those of Komatsu and she smiled encouragingly. He lowered his gaze immediately and pretended to focus on the setup of the black and white stones on the rectangle of golden *kaya* wood.

The boy is very silent today, she thought. *No, not the boy. Komatsu is a man already.* They were both the same age after all. With his top-knot perfectly straight and his black kimono lined on his shoulders without a crease, he seemed very presentable. Any woman he chose for a bride could deem herself fortuitous.

The stone of black slate clicked on the board. Komatsu nodded, acknowledging his move.

"I am to travel to Edo," she said, picking up a white stone and studying its surface carefully. Komatsu looked at her, startled, but composed himself in an instant.

"I know," he replied.

"Ah?"

"Tadayuki-*sama* told me."

"I see."

Tap. The white stone joined four others in a group which seemed hopelessly trapped in a ladder pattern.

"I may never return."

Komatsu swallowed loudly before answering.

"If such be the will of Nariakira-*dono*..."

His fingers reached for another stone.

"I'm leaving in two days."

The black stone dropped back into the bowl with a clatter.

"Two days...? But I thought..."

"Father's request. The auguries for a later date proved inauspicious. Everything is ready for my departure."

"*Hime*..."

He closed his mouth, straightened his back and nodded again.

"I wish you all the best."

"Thank you."

The black stone tapped louder than the others.

"You broke the ladder, Komatsu-*kun*," she noticed, "you haven't got any better since we last played. Have my lessons been so bad?"

"I'm sorry, *hime*. I am a poor student. And your skills at *igo* are unmatched."

"Nonsense," she said sharply, "I can see your mind is elsewhere today."

"I'm sorry," he repeated.

A black kite screeched in the sky. They were sitting in an open room in the summer house overlooking Nariakira Shimazu's famed garden. She could see the summit of the great Sakurajima above the treetops, a thin plume of white ash rising from the tip straight into the sky – or was it the smoke from her father's elemental processing plants?

She looked to the corner of the room where a Bataavian wind machine of brass and polished wood stood, placed there to please the guests with a cooling breeze. Lord Nariakira was very proud of the invention and had one installed in every building in the garden, but she didn't like the clackety sound the device made. She unfolded her paper fan and started to cool herself the traditional way.

"The air is still today," she remarked, "it feels like summer already."

"Yes, *hime*."

"Oh, stop being so formal, Komatsu-*kun*. You act as if we hadn't known each other since childhood."

He looked her straight in the eyes. His face tensed.

"You weren't a princess then, Atsuko."

"No, I suppose not." She sighed. "We all must carry our burdens without complaint."

"Is being the daughter of a *daimyo* really such a burden?"

Atsuko twisted her mouth in a wry smile. She smiled a lot, knowing that her wide, slightly pouty mouth was not one of her best features; smiling helped a little.

"Father has great expectations of my mission to Edo."

Komatsu nodded.

"Nariakira-*dono* is greatly preoccupied with the matters of state."

She touched the stones in the bowl, enjoying their smooth coolness.

"Do you know why I have learned to play *igo* so well?"

"I have often wondered. It is an unusual pastime for a woman."

"It is perhaps because I am a woman."

"Ah?"

"In *shōgi* every piece has a rank and a role. Even the golden general can only move in one way. But in *igo* all stones are equal and their fates are never determined. Depending on the player's actions, an *igo* piece may die a pointless death, or change the fate of the entire battle."

"Like the ladder breaker," he said and smirked. "Are you a ladder breaker, *hime*… Atsuko?"

"I am but a humble woman," she replied softly, "and my fate is what the player wishes it to be."

She heard the tinkling of bells and the whirring of wheels squeaking across the floor of the verandah. Her chaperon automaton was returning to escort her back to the female quarters.

"Promise me," she said, standing up, "that we will finish this game one day."

"Y... yes, *hime*."

Komatsu also stood up and bowed deeply. She felt tears welling up in her throat.

"Thank you. Goodbye, Komatsu-*kun*."

"Goodbye, Atsuko."

The palanquin standing on the slate pavement was the most ornate she had ever seen. *Fit for a princess indeed*, she thought bitterly. Covered entirely in black lacquer and gold leaf ornaments, with the great cross-in-circle emblem of the Shimazu clan on the sides and red silk-covered roof, it was so large and heavy that six of Satsuma's strongest porters only managed to carry it with great difficulty. A brass spout in the shape of a dragon protruded from its roof – the exhaust pipe of a small wind machine. Lord Nariakira spared no expenses to make her portable home as comfortable as he could. After all, she was to spend the next few months inside.

A soft breeze picked up from the sea, scattering the browned petals of the last of the azaleas. The long procession of servants, porters, scribes and retainers waited for her in a rigid line. An unusually large oxcart with an iron studded box stood before the garden gates, surrounded by armed guards. She recognised a few of her father's wizards standing beside it in silence.

A girl approached her with a parasol and gestured towards the palanquin.

"My lady," she said with a slightly trembling voice.

"Are you so eager to get rid of me?" Atsuko asked. The girl gasped and dropped to her hands and knees, apologizing for the rudeness. Atsuko recognised her – the youngest daughter of one of the lowest retainers of the Shimazu clan, destined for eternal servitude to her superiors unless a higher ranking samurai decided to adopt her.

"I'm sorry," Atsuko said, "please, stand up. You're Shosuke-*sama*'s sister, aren't you?"

"Yes, *hime*."

"Is he well?"

"Yes, *hime*."

"Did his facial hair succumb to the barber's knife at last?"

The girl giggled, covering her mouth politely.

"No, *hime*. It still grows in unruly patches."

"I wish he could be here to see me off. And Saigō-*sama*. And Komatsu-*kun*." Her voice trailed off wistfully.

"*Hime?*"

"Oh, nothing. Very well, no point keeping everyone waiting. Are you part of the procession?"

"Only to Akae, *hime*."

"I will be glad of your company."

The girl bowed and then, seeing something behind Atsuko's back, she bowed again.

Atsuko turned around to face her father. Lord Nariakira grimaced in a pretend smile, but she could see sadness in his eyes and was grateful to share this glimpse into his heart.

"Father-*sama*," she nodded.

"Are you ready, child? This will be the longest journey you will ever undertake."

"I am prepared well, Father-*sama*."

"Good."

"Father-*sama*, are you sure this oxcart will fit on a ship?"

"Do not concern yourself with it, Atsuko. It will only go as far as Kirishima."

"But what is it?"

The *daimyo*'s smile was now real and broad.

"A gift from the Gods, some might say. Something *almost* as important for my plans as you."

She remembered something. "Does it have something to do with that fishing village you had destroyed two weeks ago?"

Lord Nariakira's eyes narrowed. "Where did you hear about that?"

She smiled and lowered her gaze in pretend coyness. "The paper walls of the palace are thin and the narrow corridors carry the voices far... I know how you despise killing peasants, Father-*sama*. Something extraordinary must have happened."

The *daimyo* scowled. "You're right. The peasants are the lifeblood of the province, and I wouldn't waste any of them if I didn't have to. Forget about what you've heard, Daughter, and forget about the oxcart. I'll make sure the walls of my palace are reinforced and the voices in the corridors *stifled*."

She shuddered under his angry stare. Lord Nariakira was a man who did not hesitate to strike, even at his own family, if it meant protecting his secrets. She turned towards the palanquin when she felt a gentle shudder under her feet. She swayed and Lord Nariakira caught her arm to assist her.

"Sakurajima is restless today," she said.

"She's saying her goodbyes. From now on, another mountain's shadow will be watching over you – the great Fujisan."

She put her foot into the black and golden box and turned her head one last time towards the garden and the mansion. She wiped her eyes with the sleeve of her kimono.

"You will forget all your woes in Edo," her father reassured her. He was smiling again.

How quickly he changes his mood.

"There're too many distractions to worry about the past."

"Yes, Father-*sama*."

"I will join you in a few months, once I deal with all my matters in Satsuma."

"I shall await you eagerly, Father-*sama*."

She stepped inside the palanquin at last and sat herself down as comfortably as she could among the black silk pillows, scented with plum blossom. She lowered the golden grate, enclosing herself in the darkness. The wind machine attached to the ceiling began to whirr and clack rhythmically.

A cross-shaped shadow passed over his face, waking him from slumber; another albatross far above the clouds. The majestic birds were the only diversions in the featureless azure sky. Even clouds were scarce. The sea and sky were remarkably calm, almost boringly so.

Samuel reached for the barrel and poured the last few drops of fresh water into a tin cup. The raft hobbled dangerously as he let slide the now empty barrel into the sea.

There could be no other way to describe what had happened to him other than a miracle. The old nameless God of his ancestors must have looked upon him with a sympathetic eye on that terrible night.

He still could not remember how he had found himself, soaked and battered, on the piece of wooden decking floating on the dark waves. The *Ladon* burned and sank on the horizon. Screams of the dying carried over the sea for miles and he could do nothing to help them, struggling himself to survive.

When he woke again it was high noon. He was still not far from where the ship had gone down – this was another miracle. A vessel the size of *Ladon* never sinks without a trace – there was an ocean of buoyant debris strewn all around him. Using a wide board as a paddle, Samuel sailed among these riches, trying to gather as much as he could onto his little makeshift raft – barrels of freshwater, crates of rusk, sacks of dried meat. With careful use his finds could have lasted him for weeks.

And then his luck – or Providence's favour – had run out. A storm raged, not strong enough to drown him, but devious enough to destroy all the meticulously prepared provisions. By the time the wind passed and waters calmed, he was left with one crate of hardtacks and a single barrel.

To make matters worse, looking at the stars, Samuel realised he had drifted to the north-east of his original position, into the open sea, far away from any known land.

In his grandmother's fairy tales, which he read from a big old tattered book written in strange letters, the unnamed God was often trying his people. One particular story had always terrified Samuel. As the result of a wager with one of his servants, the God tormented some poor human in increasingly horrendous ways, just to prove his point. Samuel had never learned the end of the story – his mother saw him crying and forbade him to ever read from the book again.

Is this unnamed God now testing me?

The raft bobbed up and down ceaselessly as the current carried him ever farther away into the vast ocean. He had lost count of the days. Food and water had run out a long time ago, and with them – hope. His skin, burned by the sun, was peeling off and covered in painful blisters, his mouth and throat parched, his eyelids stuck together with dust. He lay still, motionless, waiting for death.

A shape appeared in the water, long, vertical and black, like the fin of some strange fish. The sea water bubbled and foamed. A black form emerged slowly out of the waves, larger than the greatest whale. Samuel gathered the last of his strength to raise himself on one elbow and observe the mysterious phenomenon. *So this is how my life will end ...eaten by a monster in the middle of an empty ocean...*

Metal fittings glinted in the sun as the strange object halted just a few yards from the raft. It was no fish – it was a machine! A round hatch screeched and began to unscrew at the top. Samuel waited patiently. As his raft drifted alongside of the vessel, he saw an easily- recognisable crest painted on the black steel hull; a two-headed bear, rampant, holding an axe. The Varyaga Khaganate. What were the Northern people doing in these waters, and what kind of a ship was this?

The hatch unscrewed at last and a bearded sailor emerged, wearing a blue and white uniform and a white flat cap. He shouted something in the stiff, harsh tongue of the Varyaga and reached down to pull out a kisbie ring tied to a rope. The ring-shaped buoy landed with a splash a few feet from Samuel, but he was already too weary to keep hold of it. Seeing this, the sailor jumped into the water and, holding on to the kisbie ring with one hand and to Samuel's raft with the other, let himself be pulled in by another crew member. More curious sailors came out onto the narrow deck to watch the *Ladon's* doctor being brought up a rope ladder.

The inside of the cigar-shaped ship was dark and stuffy, smelling of oil, tar and sweat, filled with the buzzing hum of pumps and engines. Samuel coughed and heaved, but had nothing left to throw up. They carried him down a narrow corridor and laid him on a canvas bunk.

He allowed himself to drift off.

The walking machine waded across the muddy-brown river to the other side. A lonely shell fell into the water a dozen feet away with a whistle and a splash but no explosion – a dud.

The ground was pock-marked with craters and scorched with dragon flame. Remnants of tents, carts, kitchens and destroyed war machines were strewn all over the plain between the walls of the Huating Concession and the river bend. A few rear-guard marauders wandered about the field of battle, assessing what seemed like the complete rout and destruction of their army. The soldiers of Huating garrison wasted a few bullets chasing them off.

"That's the last of them," said Edern, lowering his binoculars.

"They'll be back," said Dylan. "They are merely regrouping. The delta is too important."

A strange clanking and hissing sound came from behind their backs.

"Here comes the Admiral," said Edern, turning. A white-haired, surprisingly lively man, short and stout, approached them from the pier where his cutter had moored. As he walked, steam puffed from a small brass box at his belt. A fetching young aide-de-camp followed, a few feet behind, carrying a large satchel and an old sword.

"*Rear* Admiral," said Dylan quietly and climbed down from the palisade to welcome the newcomer and to introduce himself.

"Ab Ifor?" the Admiral squinted, remembering something. "*Bore da!* I used to have a midshipman called Ifor. Good sailing stock, you Gwynedd folk."

He turned a spigot on the box at his side. The gears in his shoulder and elbow whirred and his hand reached out in a greeting. Dylan clasped it carefully, feeling the cold metal through the calfskin glove. *An automaton.* The Admiral's right arm and right leg were artificial, thaumaturgic devices made of steel rods, brass clockwork and leather straps. The contraptions were noisy and their moves were clumsy, but they seemed to be serving the Admiral well enough.

How could anyone outside the Royal Family afford something like this?

"We have sea in our blood, Sir. Or so my wife says."

"A sailor with a wife!" The Admiral laughed. "Ho! Now there's a dangerous combination. And what about you, Banneret? Is a Faer lass waiting for you back in your forest?"

Edern's eyes darted aside. "No, Sir."

The Admiral stopped laughing and turned back to Dylan.

"Take us to your war room. You have a war room prepared, Ardian?"

"I have requisitioned the council's building. This way, Admiral. Edern, will you take the Admiral's aide to the quartermaster. We need to figure out how to accommodate everyone. I predict we will have a lot more guests coming…"

The Tylwyth Teg looked at the handsome young man standing shyly behind the Rear Admiral and grinned.

Rear Admiral Broughton Reynolds leaned over the map, straightening out a rolling corner with his left hand. The metal arm hung limply along his right side, switched off – the noise and fumes would be too bothersome in the small enclosed space. The map was smudged with soot and blotched with ink and oil.

And I thought Fan Yu was bad, thought Dylan. The "war room" he had managed to procure on short notice was just a small chamber in the basement of the council hall, with a single table, an evertorch on the ceiling and a battered cabinet against the wall.

"And where are the Councillors, Ardian?" the Admiral asked, looking up from the map.

"They wanted to give the concession away to the rebels, so I had them locked up for treason."

Reynolds laughed with the hearty laugh that was beginning to grow on Dylan.

"Dracaland needs more men like you, ab Ifor. Do you know, there are folk back in Lundenburgh who think we should support *the rebels* instead of the rightful rulers?"

Dylan grimaced. "Their ideology can appeal to certain... elements in the Capital."

"Ah, yes. But, it's bad for business, right, lad? Changing regimes like that. Much better the old evil."

"I believe so."

"Politics! Pah," the Admiral snorted. "All I know is that I have my orders to keep this place safe from any barbarians, no matter what side they're on. War! Let's get back to that. What can you tell me about our situation, Ardian?"

Dylan briefly described what his scouts had been reporting. Once the Rear Admiral's flotilla steamed up the Wusung River and removed the immediate threat of the rebel siege, the riders of the Second Dragoons were able to fly once more and the information started trickling again to Dylan's headquarters. The Heavenly Army had indeed captured the old Qin capital of Jiankang and managed to reduce all government-held cities along the great Chang River delta. Huating was the last fortress standing between them and the sea.

"The rivers are the key to all war in this land," Dylan explained. "We must control both riverbanks if we are to even think of successful defence."

"Rivers? I'm not a pike, Ardian, I'm a shark."

"The rivers and canals of Qin are like the straits of the lesser seas, Sir. The Chang is fully navigable for a thousand miles, even for a flotilla like yours. I'm certain we'll be able to use the firepower that you have brought us, wherever the war takes us."

The Admiral scratched his side-burns in thought.

"Well. A man learns all his life – I may yet have to learn how to fight on a river. But what did you have in mind?"

Dylan put his finger on the map and winced, feeling the grease.

"A thirty-mile perimeter, all the way to the Tien-shan Lake here. We will need two thousand people."

"We have two hundred."

"I know. But we can train and arm the people of Huating. They have already requested it. I have the first hundred waiting outside the walls."

The Admiral's eyes widened and he started coughing violently.

"You wish to give *them* our weapons? Have you gone mad, man?"

"Anyone can be trained to use a rifle, Admiral. They are eager to learn."

"I bet they are."

"They are just townsfolk who want to defend their land. The Qin army has abandoned them."

Reynolds squinted one eye.

"What's your history with this place, Ardian? I'm sensing this isn't your first time here."

"I have fought in our previous war with Qin."

"Ah, the *Coronet* affair…"

"There was a bit more to that. It lasted three years."

"I was stationed in Bharata back then. Recovering from this," he said, patting his iron thigh. "Never paid much attention to the issues of the Orient until I got this assignment."

Dylan said nothing. The Admiral seemed a clever enough person. *Let him figure it out.*

"They will need to swear allegiance to the Crown if we're to command them."

"That… may cause problems in the long run."

The Admiral sighed.

"Then we will need to wait for the Emperor's permission."

"Do we have that much time, Sir?"

"How do you think the Qin government will react to us arming their citizens willy-nilly? I may not know these particular people, but politics works the same everywhere. There must be *some* semblance of order."

There were fast steps on the stairs outside and a rapid knock on the door.

"Come in, Banneret."

"Sir, there are dragons coming from the north."

"An attack?" the Admiral asked before Dylan opened his mouth.

"I don't think so. There are only three of them, and the beasts are all yellow."

"What does that mean?" Reynolds turned to Dylan.

"Yellow is the Imperial colour. I believe our wait may be much shorter than we had expected."

The beasts coiled on the landing glade, surrounded by curious soldiers, many of whom had not seen a Qin dragon up close, on the ground. They were smaller and slimmer than the mounts of the Marines, their yellow scales smooth, more like those of a fish than a snake. Their horns branched like deer antlers, and their ends were rounded, not sharp. And of course there was only a vestige of wings in the middle of the long, serpentine body. But there was no doubt of the kinship between the *long* and their Western cousins. The same wise eyes shone above the many-teethed maws, the same sharp claws glistened at the ends of the muscular legs, and the same commanding dread surrounded the creatures. Perhaps even more so; the Qin dragons, especially the Imperial Yellows, spread among their admirers not a primitive, wild fear, but an inspiring awe.

Dylan could see this awe in his men. None dared approach the beasts closer than a few yards. The troops formed a tight circle around the landing glade, murmuring and pointing with respect.

The man who climbed down from the largest of the beasts looked around and smirked with arrogance. "Narrow" was the only word Dylan could come up with to describe this strange person: tall, slim and angular in face and movements. He took off the overcoat, revealing the many-buttoned jacket of yellow silk underneath – sign of the Emperor's favour – and handed it to one of his men. While a servant hastily combed his pointy beard, he put a round blue cloth cap on his bald head, straightened the creases on his clothes and marched proudly towards Dylan and the Admiral.

He barked a few sentences. His words sounded as angular and sharp as he looked.

"The Bohan is taking over the command of this city and all troops within," spoke the interpreter. He was an opposite of his master in every way: crescent-shaped eyebrows and crescent-shaped moustache in a round face. Instead of the rich court robes, he wore a simple dark blue coat with snow-white cuffs. The Dracalish words flew smooth and round from his mouth, with only a hint of an accent.

"Bohan?" whispered the Admiral, "is that the man's name or his title?"

"Both, I would guess."

"The *Bohan* is not on Qin territory," the Admiral said loudly. "Or do I need to remind you of the treaties between our Empires? His troops are over there – ," he added, pointing towards the walls of Huating, " – what's left of them."

"I hear you have been arming the Emperor's subjects. This is a violation of the treaties and reason enough to revoke your concession."

How did he learn about it so fast? How do they always *know about everything?*

"No Imperial subject has yet been given a weapon from our stock," answered Dylan. "We had merely received their request and have been pondering an answer when you arrived."

The two men consulted briefly.

"Whose request was that?"

Not a chance.

"Some of the townsfolk – I do not know their names."

The man called Bohan eyed Dylan suspiciously and barked some more words, pointing at the Ardian and the Admiral.

"Which one of you is the Commander of this place?"

"That will be Ardian ab Ifor," replied Reynolds, "I am merely the commander of the flotilla you see stationed on the river."

The Qinese followed the Admiral's hand and opened his eyes wide, as if only now noticing the imposing line of warships, their guns aimed at Huating and beyond. At last, he nodded.

"You will refrain from answering the petition and from any contact with the civilian populace outside these walls," the Bohan ordered. "This rebellion is an inner matter of Qin. We are grateful for your assistance, but no more will be required at this moment."

With that, he turned back towards the yellow dragons.

"*The Qin army's skills of camouflage are next to none,*" Dylan said quietly in Qin. The Bohan turned again.

"*What did you say?*"

"Admiral, did our scouts spot any Imperial troops coming in Huating's direction?" Dylan asked, pretending to ignore the question.

"Only what seemed like groups of marauders, wandering to and fro north of the river."

"And yet the Bohan here assures us that our assistance will no longer be required. What can he possibly mean?"

"Perhaps his armies are moving underground!" replied the Admiral and they both laughed.

The Bohan's face turned purple.

"The invincible Imperial Army is needed elsewhere," the interpreter said, his calm delivery belying his master's rage. "We do not need to concern ourselves with every stockade in the middle of a cholera-ridden marsh."

"Oh, that's a relief. When the Heavenly Army returns, we can just stand back and watch the city fall for the second time."

The Bohan gnashed his teeth. He spat out his last sentence and marched back to the dragons.

"You will have your answer tomorrow," the interpreter said before joining his master.

CHAPTER II

A gust of wind shook the ferns and the thin branches of the cypress trees surrounding the glade. The mist parted revealing a samurai, tall and heavily-built, wearing a gaudy, colourful kimono of yellow and blue, and a purple hooded cape. A number of small canvas pouches and wooden *inro* containers hung off his *obi* sash. He shook the blood off his twin swords and started to wipe the blades with a piece of paper.

Bran recognised the round, slightly bulging eyes and the whisker above the narrow lips, that were twisted in a strange, disconcerting smile.

"You're the man from the inn!"

"So I am," the samurai replied. He bowed in a greeting as if only now noticing the three travellers. "And you're the boy who can drink like a seasoned warrior," he grinned.

"What are you doing here?"

"Saving your lives," the stranger said. Satisfied with the state of his swords he sheathed them into the plain black scabbards. He said nothing else.

"Did...did Yokoi-*dono* sent you?" asked Satō, lowering her weapon. Bran looked at her sharply. Her hands were trembling, she could barely stand. Nagomi propped her up by the shoulder. Her skin was pale, her lips trembled, her eyes lacked focus. They all badly needed rest, but Nagomi seemed to be in the worst shape.

The samurai looked at her and blinked once before answering.

"Yes, I have been sent by Yokoi-*dono*. I should have introduced myself yesterday; perhaps we could have avoided this... debacle." He nodded at the dead bodies.

Satō let her sword slip to the ground and leaned her back against the earthen wall of the mound.

"You have our gratitude..."

"You may call me Dōraku." The samurai bowed again. "I left food and water by the side of the road. By your leave..."

Samurai disappeared into the forest.

"What luck," the wizardess sighed, collapsing to the ground, "Yokoi-*sama* made good of his promise."

"I'm not so certain," said Bran. He walked up to the dead bandits. The *onmyōji's* headless corpse was covered in blood that was quickly drying; the others seemed as if they had been dead for a long time; their faces had now returned to human form. He still could not detect any magic. *Does my True Sight simply not work on Yamato spells?*

"What do you mean?" asked Satō.

"How do we know he's telling the truth?"

"He did save our lives."

"This could have just been a ruse."

"Why bother? He could have killed us in a blink of an eye."

"There are fates worse than death," said Nagomi quietly.

"Not you too!" Satō raised her hands in exasperation.

"I just think we should be cautious, that's all."

The samurai returned noisily with a large bundle of luggage. He took out a large *bento* box.

"It's not much but you can have it all," he said. "I have already eaten today."

He then presented a dusty sword. "I found this on the road," he said. "I see your sheath is empty." He pointed to Bran's waist.

"This is my weapon. You have my thanks."

"Interesting blade. I have not seen a design like this… for a long time."

Bran bowed stiffly, sheathing the sword without a comment.

Satō looked to the sky. "I suppose we're staying here for the night."

Bran turned to Dōraku.

"Will you not come and sit with us… Dōraku-*sama*?"

The samurai hesitated. He glanced at Nagomi for a moment so brief only Bran managed to notice. "There doesn't seem to be enough room inside. I don't mind the rain and the air is nice and fresh."

"Except for the smell of the dead."

"They do not smell yet," the samurai replied, smirking. "If you need me, I'll be over there," he said, pointing to the remnants of an old wooden shed, half-buried in the ferns and ivy.

By the light of Bran's flamespark, Satō unpacked the *bento* box, reached for the rice ball and started munching it as eagerly as her manners allowed. Nagomi gingerly picked up a piece of broiled eel.

"Aren't you going to eat, Bran?" asked Satō, swallowing the rice loudly.

"I'm fine."

"It's not poisoned."

"I'll have some later."

He did not wish to argue but he couldn't shake the feeling that there was something odd about the whiskered samurai.

"You said wearing two swords was just for show," he said.

She thought for a moment before answering.

"I have never seen anyone *fight* with two blades. I will need to ask Dōraku-*sama* about his technique."

We will need to ask him about many things, Bran thought but decided to keep his doubts to himself. Feeling his strength slowly coming back as he rested, he charged the flamespark a little more. The light, until now the equivalent of a faint, small candle, illuminated the cave like a bright chandelier, revealing the limestone walls around them. He looked up and opened his mouth in silent astonishment.

Nagomi followed Bran's finger with her eyes and, in the flickering light of his magic flame, gazed at the white limestone wall over their heads. It was covered with carvings, etched painstakingly into the soft rock from the top to the bottom of the chamber.

They were primitive drawings, made only of thin straight lines, but they were strangely compelling and seemed to be brimming with ancient primeval power. She could feel their energy. Bran was pointing to a group engraved in the middle of the wall some four feet from the ground. It showed several human beings, stick figures with dots for heads; some of them had horns, others wings. All were gathered around an outline of a circle and inside it, a few specks of bright blue enamel were still stuck to the limestone. The figures were kneeling before the circle. Above the scene were engraved serpent-like creatures, coiling zigzag-like in the air, with bony wings spread wide. The largest of them all, in the most prominent position, had eight long necks ending with eight large heads.

Even she knew at once what they were. *Dorako. Dragons.*

"What is it...?" Bran managed to finally find his words.

"The Ancients," said Nagomi, "they must have carved it while building this tomb."

Bran leaned over to examine the roughly hewn carvings.

"What do you think that round thing is? The Sun? The Moon?"

"I have no idea," Satō said, shrugging. She joined Bran by the wall but pretended not to care much about the discovery. "Nobody really knows anything about the Ancients."

"It's blue," he said, tracing the outline of the circle with the fingers of his left hand, "look, there are still bits of colour left. A blue... stone."

He looked at his hand as if remembering something. Nagomi remembered too. *What through tide stone can you see?*

"I... I have something to tell you," she spoke softly. They turned to her in surprise and all the carefully prepared sentences evaporated.

"Well?" Satō urged her.

With a breaking voice she recollected what she had seen in the Waters of Scrying all those months ago: the red, blue and green stones, the man in the red robe, the sea monster and the ray of jade green light.

"There was more," she added. "Kazuko-*hime* showed me an old scroll with black dragons drawn on it: the rest of the Prophecy. It spoke of the coming of monsters, the Storm God and an eight-headed serpent..."

They stared at her for a long time in silence.

"So you think my grandfather's ring – the blue stone – is somehow involved in all this?" Bran said. "And the eight-headed serpent is this one, here?" he asked, nodding at the largest of the carvings.

"That's an ancient legend," said Satō, "Orochi, the eight-headed dragon, was the father of all the *ryū*. It is said it was slain thousands of years ago. But why haven't you told us all of this before?" she asked Nagomi.

"Kazuko-*hime* believed the Prophecy foretold the… fall of the *Taikun*. She asked me to keep it a secret."

"*Fall of the…!*" Satō gasped.

"Then why are you telling us this now?" asked Bran.

"Because…" Nagomi took a deep breath, "it doesn't matter anymore. The damage is done. The High Priestess is dead."

Satō's face turned grey. Bran narrowed his eyes and then slowly nodded.

"How do you know?" the wizardess asked.

"I saw her in a vision in Hitoyoshi and then in a dream, last night…"

"So you're not certain – "

"I am!" she protested. "The vision was very clear."

"I don't know much about these things," Bran interjected. "You speak of visions, prophecies – is it anything like geomancy?"

"I don't know what – " Nagomi started, but Satō interrupted her.

"It's just as vague and enigmatic. There are many interpretations – "

"Not this time," said Nagomi. "I know what I saw!" she started coughing. Exhausted, she leaned back against the wall and could not speak for a while.

"I don't doubt that," the wizardess said, "But what if you saw something in the future, not the present?"

"I know…what…I saw," Nagomi repeated. She reached for the water flask and both Bran and Satō rushed to help her; the boy was faster, pressing the bottle's mouth to her lips.

"How did she die?" asked Bran when she finished drinking.

"Executed by the Magistrate."

Only when she spoke those words did she understand and accept their meaning. Her heart was surprisingly calm.

"It's my fault," the boy said.

"Everything she did was of her own accord," she said. "I'm sure she wouldn't have helped you if she didn't believe it was important…"

"Important? Why? I'm just a castaway. You should have left me on that beach."

"Haven't you been listening?" she protested, "the Prophecy…"

"Even if my ring *is* somehow involved, it's not like *I* have anything to do with it. I just carry it around."

"What about the other two stones?" asked Satō, "what of the blood stone and the jade?"

Bran's eyes glinted in the light of the flamespark and Nagomi thought of her own interpretation of the Prophecy, the one she hadn't even shared with the High Priestess.

"I don't know… those remain a mystery."

"All my ring ever does is light up whenever I contact my dragon," the boy said.

"You've never mentioned it before," Satō eyed Bran's hand.

"It never occurred to me that it was important. I thought it was just some magireactive mineral, like Carmot."

"And yet the *onmyōji* attacked us because of your ring. I wonder how he knew?"

"I bet that man outside knows about it too," Bran said, nodding towards the tomb's entrance. "I noticed him glancing at my hand a few times."

"That doesn't mean anything. People in Yamato don't wear rings, so it's natural he was curious."

"You seem very eager to trust him."

"Dōraku-*sama* saved us all. I just think he deserves a little more confidence."

"We don't know *anything* about this swordsman. We don't know anything about those bandits. All that happened today could have been an elaborate trap. How did you even manage to find this tomb?"

Satō's hand, holding a pickled plum, stopped halfway between the box and her open mouth. She turned to Nagomi.

"That's a good question – how *did* we get here? I was following your lead."

"I… I had another vision yesterday," Nagomi admitted and told them about the third of Aoi Aso Shrine's revelations. The first one, concerning her and Bran, she chose to keep to herself. She finished by recounting the last message she had received from Lady Kazuko's spirit.

"Do you think she meant Dōraku-*sama*?" Satō said, biting her lip in doubt.

"Who else?" Bran shook his head in exasperation. "But what was she trying to tell us? 'You must…' what? Trust him? Follow him? Fear him? *Kill him?*"

"I don't know. I'm sorry," Nagomi replied.

"You don't have to apologise," said Satō, "we're all stumbling aimlessly in the dark."

In the silence that filled the tomb they heard the pitter-patter of the rain upon the wooden door frame and the rustling of the cypress trees in the wind. Nagomi raised a hand to cover her mouth.

"We should go to sleep," said Satō, packing the *bento* box and stowing it away in the corner of the chamber, underneath the ancient carvings. "We've learned much today, but we need to think it through in the morning. My father always says there are two things one shouldn't do in excess before night: eating and thinking."

The girls soon fell asleep, despite having to lie on the packed dirt floor without so much as cloaks to cover themselves. Everything they had, except what they carried on them, was lost somewhere on the road.

Bran sat with his back against the limestone wall, his hands wrapped around the hilt of his sword. He was wide awake. The rain poured outside, and the water found its way through the earthen mound and a crack in the stone, dripping rhythmically into a small puddle on the floor. A thunder clapped in the distance.

"*Well, well, so the old witch is dead at last,*" the spirit in his head spoke suddenly.

"What do you care? You didn't know her."

"*On the contrary, boy,*" Shigemasa replied, "*you're forgetting I was one of the Scrying spirits of Suwa. I've known her since she first came down to perform her divinations.*"

"What was she like?"

"*Very noble, I suppose,*" the General admitted with some reluctance, "*and with great insight. She was the only one who could read straight through me whenever I tried to play with the visions too much.*"

"You liked her!" Bran realised with surprise. He got used to thinking of Shigemasa only as a malevolent presence in his head. Now for the first time he had to consider him a real human being.

"*She knew she would die because of what she had been doing – I foretold it myself – but had no fear of death. I respected that.*"

The general fell silent for a while, and when he spoke again, he picked a new subject.

"*Your beast... it is asleep all the time.*"

"How do you know that?"

"*I can see it snoring in front of the gates of your Innermost Keep. I could walk past it now without a problem.*"

Innermost Keep...? The red-eye tower!

"Don't you dare try anything!"

The general laughed bitterly. "*If I wanted to, you couldn't stop me. I can see the walls of your castle crumble all around me. I know how the battle must have exhausted you.*"

"Then why – ?"

"*I am now intrigued with you, Barbarian. This talk of prophecies tonight... I know how they work. I've been there. If what the red-hair says is true... I have waited so long, I can wait a little more ...*"

"That's... a relief, I suppose. Of sorts."

"*Make no mistake, it's not because I'm growing soft on you or anything.*"

"I'll remember that."

He wanted to ask about their new companion, but the spirit had already slid away into the dark silence, leaving Bran alone with his thoughts.

He flicked a weak light and directed it towards the carvings on the wall. Their strange inner power continued to intrigue him. He took out his pencil and notepad and copied the drawings as well as he could.

No Westerner has seen these things before me, he realised. *I'm an explorer, like Cook or Brendan. I should have been noting everything all along.*

Some of the human silhouettes had wings drawn in the same way as the dragons above them. What did it mean? Were they shamans disguised as dragons, or was there some greater mystery behind it?

He touched his ring and it lit up lightly. Satō was right, nobody in Yamato wore this kind of jewellery. Obviously it had been drawing everyone's attention. How could he have missed it? His entire disguise could have been ruined by the tiny trinket. He slipped the ring off his finger and put it inside the black lacquer box. It was safer that way.

The blue stone and the dragons – he had dismissed the connection as coincidence earlier, but now he wasn't so sure any more. All the questions that had made him embark on the sea adventure in the first place were now coming back. What secret had his grandfather bestowed upon him? Who was the Yamato beauty, the beloved Omon? He dared not think yet of Nagomi's divinations. Satō had said so herself, the prophecies were often vague...

He turned away from the wall and looked at the girls, sleeping on the naked floor in their travelling clothes, their silhouettes faintly illuminated by the flamespark. The apprentice lay still, on her back, her dark red hair, with traces of henna washed off by rain, spread on the floor. She seemed barely alive, like some enchanted princess in a fairy-tale. Satō kept moving about, changing position, unable to keep still even in her sleep. She had uneasy dreams.

He needed to stay awake, to protect them from whatever lurked outside. With his father so often absent, he had felt it his duty to protect their small family from whatever dangers he had imagined. And right now, he realised, Satō and Nagomi were the closest he had to a family in this strange land. *I can't let any of them get hurt*, he thought. *I owe it to them.* The brave wizardess who had lost her father because of him, and the copper-haired girl who had performed what amounted in his eyes to a miracle – and yet remained so humble about it all; these were debts that were difficult to repay.

The girl was a *healer* – and apparently, one of the many in Yamato. His mother, being a Cunning Folk, knew how to brew restorative poultices and soothing concoctions and he had heard of some experiments in using strong, precise thaumaturgy for medical uses, but the conflicting Potentials of the patient and physician made it an expensive and difficult matter. The ability to heal a broken arm within mere minutes remained the stuff of dreams and legends.

His thoughts raced back to his father and the Marines. What would the army of the Dracaland do with the power of healing the wounded on a battlefield? The first modern nation to get its hands on this magic could easily bid for mastery of the whole world. It was a good thing the Yamato were so isolated after all. The Bataavians in Dejima must have known about this, but they chose not to share the news with anyone. The small republic could never defend itself or the Yamato from the likes of Dracaland, Breizh or Midgard, if any of these powers discovered there was something worth fighting for here.

He could not even begin to grasp the rules of the native magic. What good was his knowledge of Potentials, Willpower, Energy Equivalence or Conduits if the spirits of the dead themselves were able to come from beyond the veil to assist the caster? The spirits of the Yamato dead – the *kami*, as Nagomi called them – seemed to simply bypass all the barriers, disregard the laws of nature; and that mage – shattering his *tarian*, fed with Bran's own life energy, with a piece of paper… Summoning demons to aid him… None of this made any sense. How could he try to protect the girls if his magic proved so powerless? Perhaps they did need a bodyguard after all…

The night passed slowly – or so he guessed, unable to see the sky and the stars. The damp air inside the tomb induced a fit of coughing. Satō stirred, almost woken up.

He started quietly chanting the lullaby his mother used to sing, a long time ago on the long winter nights, when they waited for Dylan's return:

> *Huna'n dawel, heno, huna,*
>
> *Huna'n fwyn, y tlws ei lun;*
>
> *Pam yr wyt yn awr yn gwenu,*
>
> *Gwenu'n dirion yn dy hun?*

He remembered Rhian's face by the bed, the carved oaken frame and the cold white-washed walls of his bedroom, illuminated by a dancing fire fae trapped in a jar on the shelf.

> *Paid ag ofni, dim ond deilen*
>
> *Gura, gura ar y ddôr-*

There was a shrieking yelp and a brawling noise outside. Bran leapt to his feet at once, extinguishing the light. He looked through the slit in the door, but could not see anything in the darkness. He heard growling, which subsided to gurgling and then silence.

Carefully, he removed the door boards and peeked outside, but could see nothing in the darkness. He lit the flamespark again and walked out into the rain, sword in hand. He walked past the bodies of the bandits and further into the forest, crossing the circle of stones, towards a ruined shack, where the strange samurai was supposed to be sleeping.

How could he possibly sleep in this rain? The shed had barely any roof and only faint remains of walls. In the flickering light Bran glimpsed a large shadow to his right. With a heart beating feverishly, he turned towards it. There was a man-sized shape of a creature, sinister in the darkness, slouching, silent. Bran approached the mysterious figure, the grip of his sword now slippery with sweat and rain. Every step he took filled his heart with ever more dread. The night was filled with the smell of death and blood.

What am I doing? I should be running away. No, I should wake the girls and then we should run away.

"Halt, demon!" he cried out. The spectre turned around. For a blink of an eye, in a flash of lightning, the shadow twisted its face into an evil, hellish, inhuman mask, but in the next moment, Bran realised it was Dōraku.

The samurai sighed with relief and put a hand on his chest, jokingly.

"You've frightened me, boy! And not many managed that and lived to tell the tale."

"What... what are you doing?"

"What does it look like? I've been taking a night's piss!" the samurai replied, adjusting his *hakama*, "what are *you* doing in this cursed weather? Go back inside, you'll catch a cold."

"I... heard something... You haven't noticed anything strange?"

"Apart from seven corpses lying in front of an old shrine?" Dōraku grinned. "No, it's as peaceful as it gets tonight. You must have been dreaming."

Purple-green rays of a forest dawn penetrated the tomb, casting playful reflections on the limestone wall. The wind had chased the clouds and the mists away, the morning was bright and almost cheerful.

There was a knock on the door. Carefully, with sword in hand, Bran looked outside to see Dōraku holding a couple of sodden-through bundles of cloth in his arms. The samurai observed the boy for a while before speaking.

"I found your luggage on the road," he announced, presenting the bundles.

Bran did not respond, so the samurai laid them on the shrine's porch.

"And I believe I've discovered the source of your nightly fears. Please, come with me."

Reluctantly, Bran followed. Dōraku parted the ferns on the eastern side of the dale revealing the body of a wolf, with its throat gruesomely torn off.

"The wolves must have fought over the meat. Will you help me dispose of the corpses?"

"We do not have time to dig graves," Bran replied.

"I've dug a pit already. It would be unwise to leave the traces of battle out in the open."

The bodies were stiff, cold and heavy. Having grown up in the countryside, Bran had seen a few dead bodies in his life, but never handled any, certainly none as gruesome as the corpse of the *onmyōji*. Flies and woodland creepers had already started nibbling on the bloodied stump of the neck and the chest, blistered and charred by Bran's dragon flame. The samurai kicked the head unceremoniously into the grave before picking up the body by the shoulders. Bran lifted the *onmyōji*'s legs and together they hauled the rigid carcass across the glade.

"*Eeh*, would you look at that!"

Dōraku pointed to the *onmyōji*'s chest. The pentacle tattoo was half-washed off with rain.

"What does it mean?" asked Bran. Looking at the headless body he could barely contain nausea.

"It means he wasn't an outlaw, only pretending to be one. He must have been licensed to work at the court."

"The *Taikun*...?"

"That's what I'm trying to find out," the samurai said, ruffling through what remained of the dead mage's clothes. Bran turned his eyes away.

"Ah, there it is. This will have the crest of his lord..."

Dōraku picked up what looked like a golden coin, covered in dried blood. He spat and cleaned it off. He then stared at the golden disc for a long time, scratching his beard.

"Well, what is it?"

"Most interesting. That's the crest of the Hosokawa," the samurai said, casting the coin over to Bran. It was decorated with the eight circles pattern he had seen everywhere in Kumamoto.

"Wait – isn't Yokoi-*dono* serving under the lord Hosokawa of Kumamoto Castle?"

"Last time I checked," the samurai replied, nodding. His bushy eyebrows moved closer together and his brow furrowed.

"Then I don't understand..."

Why are you showing me this? This proves you've been in league with those bandits.

"The *daimyo* has no need to consult all his moves with his retainers, and a retainer doesn't share all his secrets with his samurai. There are some very complex games being played, boy."

And I'm the prize, Bran realised.

CHAPTER III

He heard Satō call out to them. She was looking through the bundles brought by Dōraku.

"I found these all over the road," the samurai said, "I brought what I could."

The wizardess unpacked one of the lacquer boxes with delight. "That's the food I bought in Hitoyoshi! It's still dry. Nagomi, wake up!" she cried inside the tomb. "Karasu-*sama*, come, maybe you'll want to eat *this* one."

Bran glanced nervously at the samurai.

"Karasu-*sama*?" Dōraku said, bemused.

"Karasu of the Aoki clan," Bran murmured, bowing slightly.

"I see."

"Oh, I'm sorry," said the wizardess standing up, "we haven't been introduced properly." She bowed politely and, before Bran managed to stop her, said:

"Takashima Satō, heir of Takashima Shūhan."

He winced. She was being so careless in the presence of the samurai! Of course, if this Dōraku was really in Yokoi-*dono*'s service, he'd know about Satō already, but if he wasn't...

Nagomi clambered out of the mound, rubbing her eyes. Sleep did her well. Her skin had healthy colour, only her hair remained mousey and drab.

"Nagomi-*sama*, is it?" said Dōraku, "that will be Itō Keisuke-*sama*'s young daughter, isn't it?"

"Yes," the girl opened her eyes wide, "how did you know?"

"I have been quite recently to Kiyō. The city is full of rumours...and certain names are often repeated."

"You have news from Kiyō?" Satō looked at the samurai curiously, "have you heard anything of my father?"

"I've heard some say he's not as... *dead* as the Magistrate thinks."

"And what of the High Priestess of Suwa? Is she really..." she stopped, glancing at Nagomi.

"When I left the city she was still in the Magistrate's prison. I'm sorry Nagomi-*sama*, as her apprentice, you must be – "

"She's dead," the red-haired girl said with confidence, reaching for the food. "And I'm a priestess, not an apprentice."

Bran and Satō stared at her in surprise.

"Kazuko-hime had me ordained as a priestess of Suwa before passing away," Nagomi said. "Are these our things?"

She started to unravel her bundle.

"Congratulations, priestess," Dōraku said, bowing. "The High Priestess must have held you in high esteem. Now, I'll scout the way ahead. We should be moving out soon."

"But you don't even know where we're going yet," protested Bran.

The samurai smirked.

"The road goes in only one direction. I'm sure I'll figure it out eventually."

They trudged through the dense woodland, Dōraku in front, cutting the trail along the animal paths and lumberjack tracks through the tall ferns and young, slender camphor trees. Bran followed close behind him, with the girls at the back. He preferred to keep an eye on their guide.

The samurai insisted they didn't follow the main road, wary of more unpleasant surprises waiting further on. He led them down the mountainside, avoiding the densest parts of the woods, bypassing the gullies and the windthrows. It was certainly a safer way than the road, but it meant they were moving at a much slower pace. By evening they were still in the deepest part of the forest. As the twilight grew around them, the trees seemed to grow closer, the green canopy above them tightened into an impenetrable roof. They walked now in a dark, humid tunnel, tripping over the roots and dodging the low-hanging branches. Bran mumbled curses under his nose directed towards their guide, but Satō and Nagomi said nothing.

At last they reached the side of a small babbling brook; a cascade of liquid ice shimmering in the starlight. The brook turned north here and its gentle bend formed a cosy, sandy cove, shaded by a large weeping *katsura* tree.

"We sleep here," decided Dōraku, dropping his luggage on the grass underneath a camphor tree.

"What, just like that?" Bran protested. "Shouldn't we at least start a fire?"

"Too risky," the samurai said, "it might draw more bandits or… other things."

"*Other things?*" Bran felt cold, remembering the warnings of the creature from the hot spring.

"It's an old forest."

"We'll be fine," said Satō, "it's not the first time we have had to sleep under the stars. Let's just be glad the weather turned out fine."

Bran looked up. The stars twinkled brightly in the sky; as far as he could tell, this meant no rain for at least one more day. The forest air was surprisingly warm.

Satō stepped up to him with a smile. "I too would have preferred a bed at an inn," she said, "but there is soft grass and thick moss here that should be enough of a mattress, considering the circumstances."

The mention of the inn and her closeness reminded him of the night in Hitoyoshi. *How much does she remember?* he wondered. She behaved as if nothing important had happened between them. *Maybe she's right. Maybe I'm just imagining something where there was nothing.*

A strange buzzing noise woke Satō up, as if a huge bumblebee droned among the trees. When she listened closer she also heard electric crackling and the sound of splintering wood .

She waited until her eyes adjusted to the dim starlight and sneaked carefully towards the sound. Soon she could see a white light flickering among the cedars and a blue streak of lightning jumping from tree to tree.

There was a round glade where a large tree had fallen not long ago and other plants had not yet grown over it. In the middle of the glade stood Bran, panting, holding in his hand a six-foot long shaft of solid blue light. A flamespark hovered above his head. All the tree trunks around the glade bore scorched scars.

He heard her come through the undergrowth and pointed one end of the shaft towards her.

"It's me, Satō."

The dragon rider breathed out and the blue light in his hands flickered and disappeared.

"What was that?"

"Soul Lance. A dragon rider's weapon. Did you not see me use it in battle yesterday?"

"I was busy enough with my own fight. How does it work?"

"It is part of my life energy. Instead of using it to power spells, like the wizards do, I use it to create this long, unbreakable piece of light… umm… crystal."

"Can anyone do that? Or only dragon riders?"

"Anyone with magic talent, I think. But it's really only good for dragon combat. It's the only weapon that is certain to withstand dragon flame and penetrate a fully grown dragon's armour. It's virtually unbreakable."

"But…?" she asked, sensing Bran was not telling her everything.

"It's only as strong as the rider that's wielding it. And it failed me yesterday."

"This is why you're here, training," she guessed.

He summoned the lance again with a buzz.

"A trained soldier's lance is nine feet long. My father's is at least twelve feet, the blade as broad as a glaive. This…" he said, giving the lance a shake. Air shimmered around the blade. "…this is pathetic. If we are to face a real enemy – one that is likely to be much more powerful than that *onmyōji* – I *need* to make it work."

"If we are to face an enemy, you need to be rested," she said, smiling.

"You're right." He opened his palm and the lance vanished with a flicker. He moved back towards the camp, but just as he was passing her, he stopped, turned and looked her straight in the eyes.

"What is it?"

"That song you sang in Hitoyoshi... what does it mean?"

"What song?" She looked away, feeling suddenly hot. "I sang many songs. So did everyone."

"*Now, now, now...*" he hummed.

"It's just a song," she lied, feeling her cheeks burn up. "It doesn't mean anything."

"I...was thinking about that night."

She looked back at him. Even though his Yamato face was familiar, she could not penetrate the stare of his alien, jade eyes.

What does he...

She held her breath, feeling his fingers on her cheek. She wanted to run, but made no move. All fell silent; she could only hear the thudding of her own heart. She closed her eyes and shivered.

"What was that?"

His touch vanished and she heard a buzz of summoned lance.

What?

She opened her eyes and saw him crouching defensively, pointing the lance towards the treetops.

"There's something up there. Look!"

A black shadow jumped from tree to tree noiselessly and disappeared into the darkness.

"Let's go back to the others," Satō said quickly. "Dōraku-*sama* might know what it was."

"Yes." He scowled at her mentioning the samurai's name. "*He* might."

They found Dōraku waiting for them under the *katsura* tree, trying to light his long bamboo pipe.

"The *tabako* got wet," he said. He gave up and hid the pipe away into the sleeve. "Do you still have trouble sleeping, Karasu-*sama?*"

"There is some... *thing* in the forest," Bran said quietly, careful not to wake Nagomi.

"I told you. It's an old forest. There are always *things*."

"Still, we thought it'd be best to keep watch," added Satō. "For the rest of the night."

The samurai nodded. "All right, I'll take the first shift."

"No," said Bran, "*I* will keep watch first. Then Satō. Then you."

Dōraku chuckled. "Very well. Have a good night." And with that, he got back to his bedding.

"What?" Bran asked. He could not see Satō's face clearly in the gloom, but he could sense her anger.

"That was extremely rude!" she fumed. "The way you spoke to Dōraku-*sama*, that mistrust in your voice..."

He raised his arms in exasperation. "He knows I don't trust him. Why should I pretend otherwise? Our lives are at stake. I grow tired of all these Yamato niceties!"

The last sentence came out as a shout. She stepped back.

"You... you may speak our language, but you still have a lot to learn about *us*!" she said and turned around in a huff, leaving him alone in the night.

Bran watched the silver-lined wisp of a cloud move slowly across the night sky. He put his fingers to his mouth, remembering the touch of Satō's skin.

I wonder if her lips taste different than Eithne's...

She hadn't run or shirked away from his touch. He no longer doubted – there had definitely been *something* between them. Except now he'd ruined it all.

He bit his lips and clenched his fist on the hilt of the sword.

I may not get another chance.

There was a change in the wind. The silver-lined cloud obscured the moon; the forest fell silent, shrouded in pitch blackness.

An army of bandits could sneak up on me in this darkness. He remembered his duty and summoned the power of True Sight to sweep the area around him.

Contrary to what many laymen thought, it wasn't a real "see-in-the-darkness" spell. What he saw were subtle differences in the layout of mystic energies and ley lines caused by physical objects around him – and, of course, any spells or magic objects. Since he wasn't a trained wizard, the True Sight always put a great strain on his eyes whenever he used it for more than a blink. After a few seconds of studying the forest his head started aching and he was forced to return to normal vision – but not before he spotted a brightly shining shape in the branches of a tree before him.

Things in the forest.

Slowly and quietly, he slid his sword from the sheath and lay it on his lap. Whatever the creature was, it did not make any attempt to attack them – it just sat on a branch, watching.

What is that?

"*Nothing worth losing sleep over,*" a voice spoke in his head. Bran jumped up.

"*Taishō!*"

The general chuckled. "*I see you're learning to refer properly to your superiors.*"

"Do you know what it is?"

"*I can't see with your magic eyes, boy. But I sense no malice in the creature. If I were you, I'd be more worried about your new companion than whatever lurks in these forests...*"

"Dōraku? Why?"

There was a long silence and Bran thought Shigemasa had once again wandered off, but the voice spoke again.

"*Be cautious. Listen, observe. Strangers you meet on the road are rarely what they at first seem.*"

Bran sensed the general retreating. "No, wait! You must tell me more!"

"*I must?*" the voice resounded with sudden anger. "*Child, you presume too much!*"

This time, the old spirit's voice vanished from his head for good.

Bran sighed. *Tonight I manage to annoy everyone I speak to.* He looked up at the tree before him. The watching creature was gone. The forest was so quiet that he could hear Satō and Nagomi breathe in their sleep. The wizardess muttered, suffering again from another nightmare. But there was a sound missing. The third breath.

Listen, observe. Bran rose softly and snuck up towards the massive dark frame of the sleeping samurai. His chest seemed to make no move under the silk kimono.

Is he dead?

Bran reached out to touch Dōraku's hand. Moonlight seeped through a gap in the cloud and fell on the samurai's face. He snored loudly and turned to the other side. An owl hooted. The wood came back to life with a myriad of night voices.

Bran shook his head and returned to his post.

Tiny fish danced around Nagomi's toes as the priestess stepped into the freezing stream to refresh herself before breakfast.

"This place is beautiful," she said, sighing. The sunlight danced on the babbling water. The spirits in this part of the forest were calm, joyful. The stream was too cold and shallow to bathe in, so she just washed her face and hands.

"It is pretty in the daylight," agreed Bran, taking a bite off a large, flat rice cracker, "but how long will it take us to get down from these mountains at this pace? Are we sleeping rough tonight again? We're running out of food."

The samurai puffed on his pipe.

"Don't worry, I know a safe place we can stay today," he said, "and tomorrow we should descend into the valleys."

"How long are you planning to accompany us?" Bran asked.

Satō gave him an angry look, but the dragon rider either failed to notice it or decided to ignore it.

What's up with these two again?

"As long as it's necessary to keep you safe," the samurai replied, "or do you wish me to leave you alone?"

"No!" Satō said hastily. "Please. We're glad to have a swordsman of your skill on our side, Dōraku-*sama*."

The samurai bowed politely.

"I have never seen anyone fight like you," the wizardess said. "Who was your teacher?"

"I had no teacher. I invented this style myself."

Satō gasped.

"*Impossible!*"

"You fared well yourself against those bandits, Takashima-*sama*. That mage was a difficult opponent for one so young."

The girl looked down in embarrassment.

"We would perish without your help."

"You're being too modest."

He's playing with her, Nagomi realized. *Why can I see it but she can't?*

Bran stood up abruptly, knocking over the water flask.

"Shouldn't we be moving on already?" he spoke through clenched teeth.

He noticed it too.

Dōraku smirked and reached for his bag.

"As you wish, Karasu-*sama*."

Dōraku led them for a few more hours down a slightly descending path, along the hollows and ravines, across cold streams and over the crags, until they reached a cliff-side, a sheer drop of rock barring their path. He pushed the ferns aside and gestured them to have a look.

Nagomi stood beside Bran, taking in a magnificent view spreading below. A vast, low-lying plain stretched all the way to the horizon, flooded by the mists, steams and vapours coming down from a jagged line of mighty cone-shaped peaks bordering the valley to the south. The fire mountains rose from the haze below like an archipelago of small islands rising over the ocean of mist, a few of them bellowing out thin wisps of grey, ashy smoke.

There was a town in the middle of the plain, crouched on both sides of a silver ribbon of a river among the fields of tall, pinkish grass, sweet potato farms, tea groves and citrus orchards.

Bran opened his satchel and put the spyglass to his eye, studying the landscape.

"This is Kyomachi on the Sendai River. Beyond that, *Ebi no Kogen*, the Highland of Shrimp Grass," explained Dōraku. "See how the grass turns pink in the sun? Like boiled shrimp."

"And those peaks on the horizon?" asked Bran.

"That's Kirishima, the Island in the Mist."

"*Kirishima...!*" Bran exclaimed, almost dropping the telescope. The samurai looked at him curiously.

"I… I've heard it has a magnificent shrine."

Where did he hear that? thought Nagomi.

"How do we get down there?" asked Satō, peering over the cliff.

"There's a gully further east we can use to descend," the samurai replied, "but that's not for today. We need to reach our lodgings before the night."

Bran raised an eyebrow.

"There is lodging, here, in this wilderness?"

"You'd be surprised. I know I was the first time I found it."

This was by far the greatest tree Nagomi had seen in these mountains: an enormous cedar shooting straight towards the clouds like a pillar supporting the heavens. The twisted maze of roots thicker than a man's thigh sprawled like veins and tendons of some ancient creature at its base. There was a well dug out among the roots, lined with round stones and covered with a bamboo mat, and a tiny box shrine nailed to the trunk. She bowed a quick greeting to the tree's ancient spirit, then looked around, searching for a dwelling. She found none.

"Who lives here?"

Samurai pointed upwards with a grin.

Half-way up the trunk was a rectangular platform of wooden planks with walls of bamboo and reed.

"Wait here," said Dōraku and approached the tree. Finding hidden leverages in the trunk, the samurai climbed up to the tree-house with the speed and deftness of a hungry bear.

A minute later a trap door opened and a rope ladder unrolled to the ground. Dōraku's head appeared in the opening.

"Come up. He's not here."

"He? Who's *he?*" asked Bran, grabbing the ladder and testing the strength of the ropes.

Nagomi scaled the ladder after him. The tree-house was neat and surprisingly spacious. A small clay stove stood in the middle with a cast iron pot on top, a bed of thickly packed straw by one of the walls, a small chest of heavy wood, darkened with age, and little else.

"Is this a *yamabushi*'s hut?" she asked.

"Of sorts," agreed Dōraku.

"Can we really stay here? Won't the host mind?"

"We'll have to wait and see. Sit down, I'll make some tea."

The pot bubbled merrily away on the stove. Nagomi tried to take as little place on the floor as possible, in case the mysterious owner of the tree-house returned. The samurai opened the wooden chest unceremoniously.

"There should be... ah, there they are."

He produced five tea cups and put each before one of the travellers, setting the fifth one aside. The cups were of superb quality, each a slightly different style, but they had all seen better days. Nagomi's vessel was burnt orange in colour, chipped and cracked in several places, with markings of some ancient master still discernible near the bottom.

"*Eeh!* These are worthy of a *daimyo*'s treasure" Satō said in admiration. Her bowl, black and metallic, was perfectly irregular, blotched with white glaze like snow clouds in the winter sky.

Bran paid little attention to his cup – red with silver streaks - absentmindedly contemplating the wall ahead.

Dōraku poured the hot brew into all five cups and raised one to his lips. Before taking a sip he turned towards the same wall that Bran stared at.

"Aren't you going to join us, Kabuto-*sama?*"

"Why are you bringing strangers to my house uninvited, Swordsman?" a disembodied voice croaked.

"Come now, Kabuto-*sama,* you know very well that would be impossible. You invited me here a long time ago."

For a moment nothing happened and then something started revealing itself in the corner, as if from under an invisible mantle. A humanoid creature, tall and slender, clad in the red robes of the mountain hermit. A single wing of black feathers twitched nervously over the creature's shoulder. In the middle of its red face, between two golden, eagle-like eyes, protruded a long sharp beak.

Nagomi cried out and jumped away in terror, reaching for her wand.

"A *tengu!*"

Satō drew her sword a few inches. Only Bran remained calm.

"You're one of the *kappa's* friends, aren't you?" the boy said matter-of-factly. "I saw you last night."

The bird-like creature's eagle eyes narrowed. "It takes a keen eye to spot a *tengu* in the darkness wearing its mantle."

"What are you talking about?" Satō leaned over to Bran "What *kappa?*"

"I met one in Hitoyoshi. In all the commotion since then I almost forgot about her."

"The old lady from the hot spring!"

Kappa? Tengu? All those fairy tale creatures were supposed to be extinct, hunted down by the *Taikun's* armies generations ago…

"If you're referring to Kuma-*hime*," the *tengu* croaked, "then yes, I have the honour to be her acquaintance."

Dōraku laughed heartily.

"You are full of surprises, Karasu-*sama!*"

"Karasu-*sama?*" the creature turned its head to one side, studying Bran with curiosity.

"That is my name. Aoki Karasu," the boy replied.

"What a coincidence. So is mine. Karasu Kabuto – Kabuto of the Crows."

The *tengu* bowed clumsily, spreading its wing in greeting.

"Your tea is getting cold, old friend," Dōraku noted, pointing to the cup.

"What cause do you have to disturb my isolation – again?" the *tengu* asked, lifting the tea bowl. It opened the beak, stretched out a long thin tongue like a woodpecker, and started slurping the drink loudly.

"We are simply passing through the mountains, trying to avoid the main road – again," the samurai answered, smirking.

"When last you had to hide you were alone, Swordsman, but now you have a priestess and two wizards for company. Have your enemies grown so strong since?"

"How did you know…" Satō asked.

The *tengu* let out a screeching sound which terrified Nagomi until she realized the creature was laughing.

"I am Kabuto of the Crows. It was I who conversed with Kobayakawa-*dono* on the summit of Mount Hiko. You think a fledgling like you can keep a secret from me?"

Satō hid her face inside the teacup.

"You are here because of the Great Magic, aren't you?"

"The Great –?" Bran started, but Dōraku interrupted him.

"We do not wish to burden you with our tale. Can you spare us a roof for the night?"

"As long as you promise to leave in the morning," the goblin replied, "there are blankets in the chest – as well you know."

"Excuse me," Satō spoke, her voice trembling, "but do you have any food to spare? We can pay…"

The *tengu* scoffed.

"Look around – what good is your gold for me? There's plenty of rice and bamboo shoots in the larder, but you'll have to go down among the roots to find it. You may wash yourselves while you're at it. What are *you* looking at, priestess?" the goblin said gruffly, turning towards Nagomi. She almost dropped her cup.

"I'm sorry!" she said and bowed deeply, her head touching the floor, "I was just wondering… about your other wing."

The *tengu's* face turned sour – or so Nagomi guessed.

"Matsudaira Nobutsuna himself slashed it off with his great sword *Daihanya*. He wanted to make me a gift for the *Taikun* – the last *tengu* of Chinzei. With only one wing I could no longer fly or use my magic… still I escaped."

A rattling sound made everyone turn their attention to Bran. The boy's cup lay overturned, his hand clenched around the hilt of his sword.

"Nobutsuna…" the dragon rider struggled to speak. His eyes darkened.

The Spirit! Nagomi realised. *What does he want now?*

"Matsudaira Nobutsuna led the *Taikun's* armies to victory at Shimabara," explained Dōraku, observing the boy carefully. "He subdued this island all the way to Satsuma. Why does his name anger you so?"

Bran breathed in deeply and loosened his grip on the blade.

"It is his deed that angered me, that's all."

"You intrigue me, Aoki-*sama*," the *tengu* tilted its head from one side to another, "first you keep a *kappa's* secret, now you take pity on a goblin?"

"Didn't I tell you last time we met, Kabuto-*sama*," Dōraku said, grinning. "The Yamato is changing."

"So you did, Swordsman. Perhaps there is yet hope for the likes of us in this world."

CHAPTER IV

Torii Heishichi, the Arch Wizard of Satsuma, had no way of knowing whether the spell had worked. He had been designing the pattern ever since he had received Lord Nariakira's mysterious order, four days ago. Two more days it had taken himself and six of his best students to weave it into place, infusing the bars of the great iron cage with complex magic. He could only hope it was enough to hold the beast down.

It lay asleep peacefully in its cage, but it could have been a hunger and weariness-induced lethargy, rather than effects of his spellcraft. Heishichi knew enough of the *Rangaku* scientific method not to put too much trust in a simple correlation of facts. The Court zoologist had found records that seemed to confirm his fears – there were dragon-like creatures living in the rivers of Bharata which could survive for weeks without food in this dormant state... They could only wait and observe.

An old scholar who had once helped Lord Nariakira's father with his financial and agricultural reforms was now tasked with calculating how much a beast of this size would need to eat, and how often it should feed. It was all guesswork, based on old legends, ancient chronicles studied by Lord Hosokawa in Kumamoto, and secretly smuggled bits of Western knowledge. Was the *dorako's* metabolism more akin to that of an ox, or a wolf? Or maybe a giant snake? In the end, the scholar cautiously estimated that it should be fed a wild boar or a deer at least once every three days just to keep it alive.

This posed another difficulty. Should they wake the dragon to feed it? If they hadn't, would it perish of hunger in its sleep? He could only guess the extent of Lord Nariakira's wrath if the beast died through neglect of its keepers. Getting away with a disembowelment order would be lucky. The dragon's well-being was his own responsibility – whether the beast perished of hunger or ran away, his blame would be the same.

Heishichi hated the dragon and the new situation he had found himself in because of it. He held the post of a *Daisen,* the Arch Wizard, but now he had been turned from an academic to a farmer. As one of the few who had unlimited access to the beast, he had to take care of its needs. His hands reeked of raw meat. And he was running out of time.

They were scheduled to leave soon for Kirishima, where he hoped to utilise the power of the magic nexus to make the binding spell stronger and reduce the number of wizards needed to sustain it to a more manageable number. But to make it to Kirishima, the dragon had to feed.

"On a count of four, disrupt the channelling," Heishichi commanded and winced, seeing hesitation on the faces five of the wizards. Only Sugimoto, the young Earth Wizard, remained composed.

Four was an unlucky number, foreboding death. He had chosen it deliberately; there was nothing he disliked more than foolish superstition. His students were quick to learn of this particular quirk of his character, but old customs took long to get rid of.

A heap of untouched carcasses lay before the beast, its nauseating stench permeating the air. Days had passed uneventfully. The dragon did not wake of its own accord, so Heishichi decided to risk it and remove carefully the enchantments binding the beast inside the iron cage.

"…*four!*" he shouted.

The wizards broke their concentration and dispersed their energies, unravelling the enchantment – just by a fraction, to see what would happen. The beast did not move.

"Should we unravel the second coil?" asked Sugimoto.

"Yes, prepare to… no, wait."

The dragon stirred at last. Its nostrils flared. Picking up the scent of the meat, its eyes started opening slowly, narrow slits at first.

"Careful now."

Fast like a whip, the beast's head snapped forward. Teeth clenched on a wild boar's carcass and pulled back before anyone could react. Heishichi had never seen anything so big move so fast. He heard others whisper astonished prayers.

The dragon swallowed the boar in a few gulps, then reached for another carcass. It was then that it noticed the presence of the humans. Heishichi's eyes met the beast's gaze and his skin was covered with a cold sweat and his throat tightened. The *Daisen* felt for the first time the legendary fear gripping the soul to the core.

"Enough," he whispered what was supposed to be a sharp command.

The six wizards raised their arms and tightened the spell's pattern. The dragon shook its head from side to side, struggling with dizziness. Heishichi reached into his sleeve and pulled out a pouch of white powder. He blew it into the air around the dragon's maw. The beast succumbed, lowering its head to the ground and fell back into a heavy sleep.

The *Daisen* breathed a sigh of relief. The white powder, a strong concentrate of purest Cursed Weed smuggled from Qin at great expense, was his own invention. As with everything else regarding the *dorako*, this was also a never tried before experiment.

"Prepare it for transport," Heishichi commanded, fixing his horn-rimmed glasses.

The buzz of a lazy fly added to the monotonous drone of the priest's prayer. The small cemetery glade was surrounded by tall pine trees, cutting it off from the refreshing sea winds. In the stale air of a warm midday Heishichi struggled with lethargy.

He knew he had to at least show that he cared. This was, after all, the funeral of one of his students. The wizard's body lay on the funeral pyre covered with a white shroud so that the gathered would not have to see its terrible state.

The family would not be told of what had really happened, but they had accepted their fate a long time ago. A wizard's life in Lord Nariakira's service was never a long one. Ever pushed to the limits of their knowledge and power, the *Rangakusha* of Satsuma perished in their prime whenever an experiment went wrong or the forces unleashed proved too strong.

In his position as the Satsuma's *Daisen*, Heishichi had presided over many such funerals – too many to remember. This, however, was the first time he had to say farewell to the victim of a dragon.

He had been trying to figure out what went wrong all night; why did the *dorako* wake and snap like that? Was there an error in the holding spell, or did he mix up the proportions of the sleeping powder? In the end he had to concede he had not enough information. This worried him much more than the loss of a student. Men could be replaced. They only had one dragon.

Perhaps, perhaps… he lost the train of thought. He had a feeling the solution to the problem was within his grasp. If only he could focus. If only the priest stopped mumbling!

He became aware of the sudden silence. Everyone was staring at him. *Did I say that out loud?*

"I'm sorry," he said with a bow.

"It's all right," the celebrant replied, "it must be difficult for you. You were his teacher, I am told."

"I was."

"I am finished with my prayers. The ceremony can proceed."

"You are aware of our custom, priest?"

"I have been made aware, yes," the celebrant replied, the polite smile disappearing momentarily from his lips.

"Step aside, then."

Heishichi and two other fire wizards approached the body of their slain comrade and put their hands on what remained of his chest. The *Daisen* summoned a white flame which started to devour the flesh from inside. Within seconds the corpse incinerated, leaving nothing but a pile of ash underneath the white shroud.

At Heishichi's signal, Sugimoto stepped up to the pyre and whispered a spell word: "*Aardse Nor.*" Earth parted beneath the pyre, burying it along with the shroud and the ashes.

"There will be no tombstone necessary," Heishichi announced.

"But the Spirit of the deceased must be…"

"None of my students has ever come back to haunt me. I doubt this one will."

"I cannot agree to this."

"You are free to argue your point with Nariakira-*dono*."

The priest made no answer, aware of the *Daisen's* elevated position at the Satsuma court.

"Good. You may clean this up. I must return to my duties, I have wasted enough time on these pointless rituals."

He turned on his heel and headed back towards the shrine. By the time he had passed the last of the stone grave marks, he had forgotten all about the deceased student of *Rangaku*.

Councillor Hotta Naosuke climbed the narrow road leading up the Shiba Hill, past the long row of thousands of little bodhisattvas wearing red bibs that marked the border of the Zojō Temple, along the stone walls of the Okubo Clan residence, through a small pine grove and further on, still upwards.

Near the top he stopped for a moment, catching his breath, took off the tall black cloth cap that indicated his status as a government official, and wiped his face with it. The sun was merciless. The road here wound westwards along the slope, and the glade where he chose to rest commanded a magnificent view in three directions. Naosuke looked north, back whence he came. From the hill he could see almost all of Edo, all the way to the *Taikun's* Castle, rising in its many tiers like a mountain of white, dazzling in the sun. The city of wood, stone and noise sprawled around it in all directions endlessly, except to the East where the reclaimed land encroached on the uneasy ocean.

Southwards lay the marshlands and the rice fields of the Kantō Plain, the water in the muddy ponds glittering like mica dust. But the eye was quickly drawn away from these vistas to the only view truly worth seeing in all of Yamato: rising in a perfect cone, with its top forever hidden in the clouds, snow-covered slopes dazzling with golden light, at once majestic, beautiful and terrifying; the unparalleled Fujisan.

If we were to clear the hilltop and build a viewing tower, thousands would flock to this place, he reflected. *I should propose it on the next Council meeting.* He took one last look at the city and then gazed up, into the azure sky. A large black bird with a long tail and broad wings soared high above the sparse clouds.

On the northern slope of the hill there was a long deep dell, hidden in the shadows of tall silvery firs and black pine trees. Long before reaching the hollow, Naosuke smelled the heady odour of brimstone filling the forest and heard the strange hissing and gurgling sounds coming from beyond a rocky outcrop. But there were no volcanic fissures or hot springs in this part of Edo.

The Councillor climbed the sharp boulders, hid among the roots of an old pine tree and looked down. The hissing repeated, even louder now, followed by a screech and a cracking noise, as of tree branches being broken. On a narrow sward of grass nine tall men were sitting by the campfire, wearing hooded cloaks of dark grey cloth. Further down the valley, beyond a circle of white tents, coiled three monstrous creatures, resting. Each as big as a rice ship, their reptilian bodies, massive heads and long, spiked tails were covered with jet-black, glistening scales. The terrible jaws, dripping foul slobber, seemed capable of swallowing a human whole. Leathery, bat-like wings, folded along the sides, heaved up and down as the beasts breathed in and out.

The hissing was the sound of a plume of steam and smoke, wafting from the monstrous nostrils with every breath. The cracking sound was the bones of a deer – one of several piled in a nook of the dale – that one of the creatures devoured in a few snaps of giant teeth.

Naosuke observed the monsters with curiosity. He had read the reports and studied the legends, but he was little prepared for the sight of the black-winged monsters. He had not been in Edo when the dragons had arrived. The Council had been called immediately to deal with the threat, but still it had taken him a few days to reach the city from his summer house in the mountains. By the time he had arrived, a semblance of calm returned to the capital, although the city buzzed with rumours and tall tales. The invaders did not yet wish or dare to attack the *Taikun*'s castle, instead they had set up their camp on the slopes of the Shiba Hill, out of sight, and waited.

Not even the *Taikun*'s scouts dared get close to the barbarian encampment. Nobody knew what it was that they wanted or what they were waiting for in the shadowy vale. They had sent no envoys, they had made no threats, although their presence was enough to cast a dark shroud over the entire neighbourhood. Only the monks at Zojō remained steadfast, everyone else had moved out of the vicinity of Shiba. Looking at the resting dragons, Naosuke could not blame them. A primeval terror reaching deep into the soul gripped anyone
who got near to the three beasts.

Three? There should be one more… he gazed upwards once again and realised that what he took for a bird at first was in fact the fourth of the dragons – the largest one. The monster was circling above Edo slowly like a vulture, far beyond the range of muskets and arrows.

The Councillor decided he had seen enough and started climbing down from his lookout point. A small stone escaped from under his feet, triggering an abrupt avalanche. It would have been too quiet for any human to hear. But one of the grey cloaks stood up in an instant and turned towards Naosuke, searching the precipice for the intruder. The Councillor could not see the eyes under the hood's shadow, but he sensed their piercing power. One of the black monsters paused between gulping one deer carcass and the next and also looked up.

There was no point running away. He stood up straight and, with as much dignity as he could muster under the terrifying gaze of the beast's eyes, spoke loudly:

"I am Hotta Naosuke, son of Hotta Naonake, representative of the Council of Elders of Yamato. I came to hear you out."

The Councillor passed through the imposing Shōin-mon gate, nodding out of respect to the giant chrysanthemum crest made of pure gold, attached to the dark wooden beams.

The guard bowed deeply.

"Your weapon please, Hotta-*dono*."

He pulled out his ceremonial *wakizashi* and lay it on the guard's outstretched arms. None could enter the inner court with a sword, not even he, one of the five most important men in the country excepting the *Taikun*.

He tightened his sash and walked on, passing the paper lanterns marked with the sign of the mallow crest. The guard waited until he thought Naosuke was well out of sight, before speaking to the other.

"I don't know why, but I always get the chills when he walks by."

"I know what you mean. Makes my hair stand on end. There is something odd about this Councillor."

Naosuke chuckled as he walked through the pillared corridor of the Outer Palace of Edo Castle. His hearing was much better than the guards suspected, but he made nothing of their insolence. He had not got to where he was by having petty quarrels with commoners.

He passed the golden-walled reception chambers, where the *daimyo* waited for an audience, then the white room, where the *Taikun* met the imperial messenger on the rare occasion one was sent from the *Mikado*'s Palace. All this he was leaving behind. Long ago he would have been one of the lords in the inner room, hanging on to *Taikun*'s every word, bickering among themselves for the master's attention, quarrelling for every extra *koku* of rice given or taken on the Master's whim. Now he had access to the Naka-ōku, the Middle Palace, where the *Taikun* met with his closest advisers. Beyond it lay only the private rooms of the ruler's family and concubines.

He entered the Great Room. The paintings on its gilded panel walls showed the bay of Edo, surrounded by tall, snow-capped mountains, with merchant ships and fishing boats scattered on the waters. This reminded the council of what mattered most in the politics and survival of the island nation: the Sea.

Naosuke was the first to arrive. He prided himself in diligence and punctuality. Others could be "fashionably late", but not him. He sat down on a silk cushion, admiring the view to a small stone garden of the inner courtyard. The gleaming white gravel was spread before the verandah like a beautiful shingle beach in front of the sea painted on the walls. His dark brown eyes glittered and his waxen, pale skin wrinkled in a grin.

A servant slid open the door to the Great Room. Masahiro Abe peered carefully inside. Somebody was already there, sitting by the garden.

"Councillor Hotta. First as always."

The Councillor turned around to face him and bowed. "Chief Councillor. I wonder how long before others arrive?"

"I've seen old Tadamasa-*dono* on his way here. Ah, here he is."

An old man with a face wrinkled like a pickled *ume* plum appeared in the corridor. A staunch ally of Abe, he greeted the Chief Councillor with a light nod and sat on a cushion beside him before bowing to Hotta.

Next came young Kuze Hirochika. He was only a few months older than Abe. As such, he had had a chance to observe the Chief Councillor's rise to power first-hand. This made him admire Masahiro's abilities, but despise his conciliatory character. Master Kuze was a man of quick action and a few words, the hot-headed leader of the War Party. Lastly, the two Matsudairas entered the room. They were a confident pair, almost to the point of insolence, certain of their position in the Council as a decision could rarely be made without the consent of them both.

They had all come from various parts of the Empire, mostly the central provinces, except the Matsudairas, who had come the longest, from Izumi in the south.

"Please slide the screens behind you, Noriyasu-*dono*," Abe addressed the elder of the two cousins. The Councillor pulled the paper screens together, enclosing them all in an octagonal space.

"I shall be brief, for the matter is pressing. Councillor Hotta here claims he has news about the invaders that require our urgent attention."

The Councillors looked at Naosuke with vague interest.

"I hope you have found a way to drive them out of our sacred land," said young Hirochika.

Councillor Hotta smiled and bowed lightly.

"I'm afraid not."

"What is it then?"

"I have spoken to the barbarian commander."

They all gasped loudly, except Abe who had already heard the story. Now they paid more attention to what Naosuke had to say.

"They have an interpreter with them," the Councillor answered a silent question, "a man from Chūbu they found cast away on the Great Ocean some years ago."

"Traitor," murmured Hirochika.

"Who are they? What do they want?" asked the Matsudairas almost in unison. "Why did they attack the Uraga Harbour?"

Abe raised his hand and they fell silent.

"They come from a land across the Great Ocean, but they are of the Western race, as far as I could tell. Their language is strange to me. They hide their faces under the grey hoods so you never know which of the twelve you're looking at."

"There's only twelve of them?" Hirochika asked, "that's not even enough to bother the army. The city guards should be enough to deal with the Barbarians!"

Are there no limits to his stupidity? wondered Abe.

"As for Uraga, they did not attack it – although they might as well have," Naosuke continued, ignoring the interjection, "I have been to Uraga myself, to see the destruction up close. Only the forests on the cliffs were scorched by the dragon flame, as a show of strength. The fires in the city were caused by panicking crowds. Overturned braziers and kitchen fires, as is usually the case."

"You have not yet told us what the barbarians *want*," said the younger of the Matsudairas.

"At first their commander demanded to speak to... and I beg you to withhold your anger... His Imperial Excellency."

"*Preposterous!*"

"I told him that even if a thousand dragons descended on the Imperial Capital, the people would rather perish in fire than allow them to sully the *Mikado* with so much as their presence."

I'm sure you have.

"Well said!" Hirochika clapped his thigh.

"At length, I have convinced them to present their demands... *requests* in a missive to the Council. I have made five copies of the letter," Naosuke said, handing out the folded papers to the Councillors.

Abe waited until all of them finished reading. He observed their reactions carefully. Kuze Hirochika's hands trembled, his face turned purple with anger and by the end he tore the paper into pieces. Old Makino put the letter close to his nose, squinting to read Naosuke's squiggly characters. He harrumphed and put the missive away with a face grim and sour. The two Matsudairas exchanged whispered remarks and grunts full of meaning.

"It is this Council's task to decide what response – if any – we give to the enemy commander," Abe said at last.

"The barbarians are not deserving of our response. The missive is obviously aimed to insult us and provoke our anger," snorted Makino. He and Abe represented the conservative party, favouring the status quo. To him, there was no force under the Heavens strong enough to impose a change on the *Taikunate* and the *Mikado*.

"If that was their aim then they've certainly succeeded!" Hirochika banged his fist on the floor. "Send out the army to wipe the scum out and let's hear no more of it."

Naosuke scratched his long, crooked nose in a gesture he was famous for; this indicated an utter disdain to his interlocutor's proposition. He gazed at Kuze with his shallow set eyes.

"Unlike you, my dear Councillor, I have seen the Black Wings with my own eyes, up close. The commander of the Westerners demonstrated to me how little harm our arrows and muskets can do to these monsters. Obviously we're dealing with something far more dangerous than ever before."

"We must treat them as we treat all barbarians," Kuzo was adamant. "Make them suffer for what they have done. Landing on Imperial land without permission is an act of war."

"Makino-*dono*, you're the minister for capital defences," Abe said, turning to the old man, "How long, do you reckon before we can gather enough force to thwart the Black Wings?"

The minister wiped sweat off his forehead with a silk handkerchief and gathered his blue robe nervously. "The treasure is rather empty until the end of the year. We've only just started building the new forts to Bataavian design. We are yet to receive new canons, and we would have to call upon the *onmyōji* and warriors from the outer provinces..."

Well played. The two had been practising this exchange all morning.

"There you have it," Abe turned back to Kuze, "the Westerners are here to stay, at least for a while. And if you read the missive carefully, they warn of an even greater force awaiting their signal off-shore. We must negotiate."

"That would be regarded as a sign of weakness," Naosuke said, unexpectedly supporting the hawk party, "not only by the barbarians, but internally. The *tozama* clans would use it as proof of our failure to govern."

"There is virtue to be found in prudence," said the younger of the Matsudairas, "The *Taikun's* rule would not spread over a unified Yamato if his divine ancestor had resorted to attacking overwhelming odds headfirst without preparation."

"What do you propose, Tadakata-*dono*?" inquired Abe.

"Open negotiations, agree to some of their initial demands, but no more. Give them access to the Kiyō corridor – they will be easier to contain there. You know my opinion on dealing with foreigners. It's high time to open our country up to their trade and science."

"Preposterous," replied Kuze, "the *Taikun* will never agree to this."

"And where *is* the *Taikun* at this hour of national emergency?" asked Councillor Hotta, raising his eyebrow.

"His Excellency is still indisposed," said Abe, annoyed at Naosuke for bringing this up. *You know very well where the* Taikun *is. In the Inner Palace, with his many concubines.* "Kuze-*sama*, may I remind you of the fate of the Qin Empire when it stood against the powers of the West without due preparation?"

"The downfall of Qin started with letting the barbarian ships too near their coast," snorted Hirochika, "they were weak in the face of the enemy."

"So are we!" Tadakata rose himself up from his cushion. "How do you propose to defend Edo from the Black Wings? With bow and arrow? Or with the primitive tricks of our court magicians?"

"With a strong will and iron heart, if you have them!" Hirochika stood up as well, his hand inadvertently reaching for where his sword would have been, had he not left it at the gate.

"Enough!" Abe clapped the floor. "Let us not forget who our real enemy is! Sit down, Councillors. Your shouting will disturb his Excellency's rest."

"The esteemed Tadakata-*dono* is right, but, in a way, so are you, Kuze-*sama*," he continued when both lords sat back down, "we cannot afford to antagonize the Westerners just yet, but we also need, as the *Taikun's* government, to present a strong and unified front against the internal opposition. We know there are forces in the south that would too easily jump on the opportunity to exploit any weakness shown by this council."

And there are forces in Edo who would love nothing more than a hastily gathered army they could take control of, he thought, looking at Councillor Kuze. He couldn't say that out loud, but he hoped the majority of the Council understood that as well as he did.

"What we need is time. And only negotiations can give us enough time," said Naosuke. "Anything else would be invitation to a war we can't afford. But what if we run the negotiations covertly? The *daimyo*s need not know about anything. That way all sides would be appeased."

"Can we even do such a thing?" Tadakata straightened himself up in surprise. "How do you conceal four dragons from the public? Everyone knows they're here."

"The commander of the Westerners is willing to co-operate," said Naosuke and Abe couldn't help wondering what the Councillor had promised the barbarians in exchange for their co-operation. "He's agreed to fly the Black Wings away from Edo, in a pretend retreat. We just need to provide them with a place to hide, and enough meat so the dragons don't need to hunt in broad daylight. If we play our cards right, we might convince everyone that the Westerners have gone for good."

"It's a bold idea," said the older of the Matsudairas, "if the secret is revealed, the damage to our prestige might be irrevocable."

"If the secret *is* revealed, it will mean one of us failed to keep it."

Naosuke looked intently at Councillor Kuze.

"Are you suggesting I could betray the Council?"

Chief Councillor raised his hand to silence young Kuze from bursting out again in anger.

"We have ways of dealing with disagreements in the council. Now, please, everyone, calm down. The motion proposed by the esteemed Councillor Hotta is a valid one. I suggest we vote on it now. Should we open the clandestine negotiations with the invaders?"

He and Hotta Naosuke raised their hands. Kuze and Makino voted against the motion. This was a surprising development. The oldest of Councillors only very rarely disagreed with Abe. *What's he playing at? Surely it's not a sudden influx of patriotic feelings...*

The two Matsudairas looked at each other and smiled knowingly. Only one of them raised his hand; the other remained silent.

"Interesting," observed Abe, trying his best not to let annoyance show in his voice. *Tricks and ploys. Can't they see we're trying to decide the future of the entire nation?* "Seems like we have a stalemate. I adjourn the meeting until next week. Let us discuss the matter among our own advisers and then maybe we can provide the *Taikun* with a decision."

CHAPTER V

A soft singing woke up Bran. He looked down the entrance hatch. Nagomi was crouching by the square well, washing her hair, sparkling copper and gold in the morning sun, humming. Her travel clothes were folded neatly on a flat stone. She smiled brightly seeing him climb down the rope ladder.

"The tree spirit has taught me a new song," she said, "from the days when it was young."

"You… you really can *talk* to them…?"

"Not always… But this one is as old as Yamato and taught itself to speak to anyone who can listen. I'm sure if we'd spent some more time here you'd start hearing it too."

"And what does the tree… tell you?"

"Stories from days gone by. There used to be an entire village of the *tengu* here, a long time ago. And before that, a holy place of the Ancients…"

"It remembers the Ancients? Perhaps we could ask it – "

She shook her head. "It was just a sapling back then. The Ancients worshipped its parent tree, long since felled by the winds."

The forest reverberated with the sound of an axe. It was the samurai, chopping firewood in exchange for their host's generosity.

"I've noticed you share my concern about our new companion," Bran remarked.

"Dōraku-*sama*? I'm… not sure. He seems well-meaning, but there is something very strange about him. *Oh!*" She clasped her hand on her mouth. "Maybe he also has a Spirit within him, like you do!"

"Maybe that's what it is. I think Shigemasa… the *Taishō* knows something about him, but he's not telling."

Bran drew a bucket of icy cold water from the well and splashed it on his face. A pheasant cawed in the distance. The boy looked around and saw a large black silhouette perched on a thick branch of a nearby tree.

"Kabuto-*sama* is watching us again."

"I wonder if he had any family of his own, living in this village. Maybe we remind him of his children."

"Have there been many of his kind before the Yōkai War?"

"The forests in the old stories are full of them. They must have been at least as numerous as the *kappa*. Was the old lady really a water sprite?"

Bran nodded. "She even gave me a golden coin as a reward for not telling on her, but I must have lost it in all the running."

Nagomi washed off the last remnants of greyish lather off her hair and reached for the towel.

"I too have lost something in the running," she said, "I have only one portion of Kazuko-*hime's* black paint left."

"We're so far from Kiyō now – maybe you don't need it anymore?"

"Perhaps… I wonder how the people in the valley will react when they will see me. Maybe they will think *I'm* a goblin." She giggled.

"Everyone I've seen so far in Yamato and Qin has hair as black as raven's feathers," Bran said.

"I've never met anyone like me," she said.

"So how come yours is that colour – if you don't mind me asking?"

"Not at all – it's no big secret. It's because I'm a *Dejima daughter.*"

"What does it mean?"

"It means my father was a Bataavian – a physician from Dejima. His hair was the colour of fire as well."

"Your father…? But I thought…"

"Itō Keisuke-*sama* was one of my father's disciples. He felt it his duty to take care of his master's family after the Bataavian was banished from Yamato."

"Banished?"

"He was accused of spying when a map of Yamato was found in his luggage. He was only using it for his research! That was some three years after Ine was born – she told me she still remembers saying farewell to him from the pier and Mother hiding her tears behind a paper fan…"

"So, what about you?"

"He managed to return to Dejima in secret ten years later, for one last meeting with my mother."

"And how did your stepfather react to that?"

"How should he react? He accepted me as his daughter also. It was the only honourable thing to do."

"He didn't mind that his wife had slept with another man?"

"There was never any passion between my parents, so there was no resentment," Nagomi answered, very matter-of-factly.

In Gwynedd a family like theirs would be the talk of the town…

"So you've never even seen your real father."

"Only in a picture. I don't even know his full name, other than "*Firippu*", which was what my mother called him. The few letters she got from him were signed with just the initials, *P.F.V.S.*"

"P.F.V.S…" Bran repeated.

He was certain he had seen these four initials somewhere. Before he could remember, Satō called on them from the tree-house above.

"Rice is ready!"

The *tengu* followed them down the forest path, skipping from branch to branch, watching them with its large sad eyes in silence. At last they reached the cliff-side again and the path started to wind down the gully mentioned by Dōraku the day before. A large ship-shaped rock split the path in two. Before any of them managed to pass it by, Bran heard a loud crow. He looked back; it was Kabuto, with its head thrown back and the beak opened wide. Dōraku bade them stop.

"This is the limit of my domain, Swordsman."

"Till our next meeting, Kabuto-*sama*," Dōraku bowed.

"No," the *tengu* said, shaking its head.

"Oh?"

"I may have lost most of my magic but I still have a little of the Gift. One way or another, we shall never meet again."

"It saddens me greatly."

"We've lived long enough, Swordsman. I bid you fare well."

With that, the mysterious creature leapt away into the deep wood, leaving them to contemplate its ominous warning.

What did he mean, "we"? wondered Bran. *We, the tengu or we – me and the samurai?*

By noon the path led them back onto the main road. It was no longer an empty forest track but a lively thoroughfare, connecting the many farms and villages of the Sendai Valley with the shores of the meandering river.

"I hope we will reach Kyomachi tonight," the samurai said. "It's the last town before this road splits in different directions."

They marched into the crossroads town shortly before dinner time. It differed little from Hitoyoshi. There was another timber harbour here, another hot spring and a few inns serving those coming down from the mountains in the direction of Satsuma. Taking the matters of the lodging in her own hands this time, Satō managed to find the most expensive inn in the town, a large, three-storey white-plastered building on the outskirts, almost in the forest, with its own garden, dining hall and an outside bath sourced directly from the hot springs beaming underneath the town.

"This is the first decent guesthouse since Kumamoto," she said, her ears closed to Bran and Nagomi's pleas for caution. "I'm a samurai and I can afford a good room in some mountain backwater."

Without even stopping to unpack she went straight for the hot spring, while Dōraku sat down in the common room to try the various liquors available at the inn. It was up to Bran and Nagomi to go to the market to resupply for the onward journey.

A small vermillion *torii* gate marked the entrance to the shrine. So near the marketplace and the harbour, the shrine had to be dedicated to the *kami* of good trade and luck in fishing, Nagomi guessed. It didn't matter.

"Wait here a moment, please," she asked Bran.

She picked up a wooden ladle from the fountain at the entrance and splashed water on her hands and face. Passing by a bronze statue of a sitting cow – polished to brightness by countless pious hands – the priestess approached the modest, tile-roofed Prayer Hall.

The shrine was neither particularly ancient nor rich; the decorations were modest, unassuming. The humble townspeople prayed here for everyday blessings and protections. There was nothing unusual about the place.

This was a welcome change for Nagomi, a well needed respite from the overwhelming events of the past few days. She took a few deep, calm breaths, revelling in the tranquillity of her surroundings before approaching the altar. She started with the usual thanks to the *kami* and Ancestors for their protection and good will towards her and her friends and family, for being alive and healthy. But then her voice broke.

"Please," she started, feeling her eyes well up, "I have never asked for anything before. But now I... I just don't know what to do anymore. It's all just too much... I need guidance."

She pressed her hands together and closed her eyes.

"Kazuko-*hime*, please tell me what did you mean to say about Dōraku-*sama*. Sacchan trusts him but he scares me so... I can sense something's not right, but I can't tell what it is."

She clapped her hands twice and shook the bell rope.

"I feel so alone... You're gone forever, my family is far away... I have only Sacchan now, and... and..."

Bran's green eyes appeared in her mind. She remembered the warmth of his touch. Satō rarely touched her like that. *I suppose I'm still a child,* she thought, *and Satō's all grown up now. It's no longer proper.*

She shook her head and focused on her prayer. "It doesn't matter. I just need strength to carry on. But... if I only knew we were on the right track. That we're doing the right thing... Just a sign..."

She clapped one more time and opened her eyes. Nothing happened. Nothing would, of course. It was silly of her to hope otherwise. She sighed and turned away from the altar. Bran was waiting for her outside the shrine gates.

The sun was nearing the rooftops and the marketplace was closing down. Bran and Nagomi had to squeeze their way through surprising crowds of shoppers going the opposite way. They walked along the river bank, past the fishing boats lined on the pebble beach. As in every harbour, the vendors sold mostly fish from the river – fresh to locals, salted to travellers – but other produce drew Bran's attention, great stone jars of yellow *mikan* fruits, pickled from last winter, and sacks full of sweet potatoes prepared in every manner imaginable; fried, baked, boiled, and just plain raw.

Bran and Nagomi, their mouths sticky with sweet *mikan* juice, packed bags full of fruit, baked potatoes, pickles and freshly harvested bamboo shoots, first of the year, boiled to perfect softness.

"We either bought too much or too little," said Bran. "Either way, Satō will be mad at us."

"It's her own fault. She should have come with us, instead of moping about in the bath. Why is everyone looking at us?" she stopped.

"I think it's your hair – your hood is off..."

The girl quickly pulled the straw hood back over her amber hair, but it was too late. Some raised their fists in a gesture against evil, others clapped their hands in prayer but mostly they just seemed intrigued. A small crowd started gathering around Bran and Nagomi.

"Come," Bran grabbed the girl by the hand and pulled her out of the circle of people, out of the marketplace, leaving the curious crowd behind.

He was hoping the commotion would end once they got back to the inn, but it was a futile hope. The rumour overtook them; the townsfolk had already begun to gather at the inn, frightened and confused. The landlady watched the growing crowd for a while, and then approached the travellers with a concerned face.

"I'm sorry, but your rooms are... not fit for your esteemed persons."

"What do you mean?" Satō asked, rising from the floor.

"They, um, they are infested by lice."

She's not even trying.

"We'll take another room."

"All other rooms are full, *tono*. I'm very sorry. Perhaps another inn."

"We will pay more," Satō insisted, "isn't this the best place in town?"

"Your money will only turn to leaves in the morning!" the landlady blurted, unable to keep her fright beneath the mask of politeness anymore. She glanced at Nagomi, who tried, futilely, to keep her copper locks under the hood of her cloak.

Satō's face tensed. She reached for her sword, but Bran was faster. His blade was already drawn and pointed straight at the landlady's widened eyes.

"I have a good mind to slay thee for this insolence," he said, seething. The landlady stepped back, but still she refused to kneel. Bran looked around. The crowd fell quiet and anxious. Satō froze with her sword drawn half-way, staring at him in surprise.

He found Dōraku, observing the scene with some amusement. He was smoking his long pipe and sipping from a large bowl-like cup in silence. The locals gave his table a wide berth. He poured himself another cup and sipped it.

Their eyes met. The samurai frowned and stood up, in a few long steps came up to the anxious landlady and leaned towards her. He whispered something in her ear. The woman's face turned white. She quickly bowed before him and started placating the agitated crowd and removing them from the inn.

"It's all right now," Dōraku said after they were gone.

"What did you tell her?"

The samurai smiled vaguely. "I simply gave her a warning. You can put that away."

Bran looked at his own sword as if seeing it for the first time. He sheathed it with a clank. Dōraku smiled again and got back to his table.

"I'm sorry," he mumbled. *I really was ready to kill that woman,* he realised with a shudder.

"Sorry for what?" asked Satō. "She was asking to have her head cut off. I've never been so insulted in my life. I'm not sure if I want to stay here anymore."

Nagomi stood up. Her face was pale and her lips pursed together fiercely.

"I'm tired. I'll be in our room," she said.

"Wait!" Bran moved to follow her, but Satō gripped his arm. The priestess disappeared up the stairs without turning back.

"Will she be all right on her own?" he asked.

"She *wants* to be on her own now. She's learned to handle her... condition this way."

"Condition...?"

"She may not seem so to you, but to the people of Yamato she's a freak, an aberration. And it's worse here, in the countryside, among the commoners."

"Now I wish I hadn't convinced her..."

Satō shook her head.

"Don't worry. She's survived fifteen years of this, she'll manage."

Bran sat down and played with his chopstick in pensive silence for a while, then stuck them in the pile of rice in his bowl.

"Don't do that," said Satō sternly. "It brings bad luck."

"Sorry," he mumbled and put the chopsticks on the wooden rest.

So many things to remember.

"Look, I... I never apologised for that...outburst in the forest."

She looked at him, puzzled, then remembered. "It's Dōraku-*sama* you should apologise to, not me."

I couldn't care less about him.

"I ...will, but I wanted to talk with you, first."

She sighed. "It's all right. We were all stressed. Still are."

Tentatively, he reached out his hand to cover hers. She twitched, but didn't move it.

"I... " He struggled for words.

This would be so much easier if I knew at all what I wanted to say.

A bottle of saké appeared on the table with a soft clank. Satō immediately withdrew her hand.

The landlady bowed with an apologetic smile. "It's a flask of our finest," she said. "I hope you will forget this little... incident, client-*sama*."

"I'll go check on Nagomi," said Satō, standing up.

The inside of his satchel was filled with blue light.

Bran had opened the bag to take out the notepad and pencil. He wanted to make some notes to clear his mind, as he had been doing since the night in the tomb of the Ancients, but seeing the light seeping through the hinges of the black lacquer box made him forget all about the journal.

He took the ring out of the box and the brightness almost blinded him at first. He guessed quickly the reason for the jewel's dazzling radiance. Since they had descended into the valley, Bran had been feeling his connection with Emrys greatly increased. The dragon was really close now, the Farlink amplified. Even though the beast was still fast asleep, he could now sense the direction and distance precisely to where it was being kept. The blue stone must have been reacting to this proximity.

Now I definitely can't be wearing it in public, he thought with regret.

To fit the box and notepad neatly back into the satchel he first had to take out the dragon figurine. He had almost forgotten about it. He had seen so many other dragon sculptures and carvings all over the Yamato that the little statuette seemed no longer to hold any importance. He kept it out of sentiment – it reminded him of Samuel and the crew of MFS Ladon, of the birthday on board the great ship. But if there ever came the need to discard any items from his luggage, the red dragon would have been among the first to go…

He was about to put it back and close the bag for the day, when the carved letters on the figurine's base caught his attention. He scratched his nose in thought.

There was a knock on the door. Nagomi quickly wiped her eyes.

"It's me," said the boy, "I… I brought some fruit."

She nodded at Satō to slide the door open. Bran sat down by Nagomi's *futon* with a reassuring smile.

"Here," he said, handing her the peeled fruit.

"Thank you."

She wasn't hungry, but was grateful for the gesture. The boy opened his satchel.

"That's not really what I came here for. I just remembered something."

He took out the red lacquer figurine of the dragon, the cheap and tacky Kiyō souvenir.

"You said your father – your real father – signed his letters to your mother with four letters."

"Yes."

"I thought it may have been a coincidence, but… I doubt there would be two men with such strange initials."

He showed her the figurine's base, scratched with four symbols.

"I… I can't read that."

Satō leaned over.

"Are these letters of some kind? I noticed these marks when you first showed us the statuette."

"These are Latin letters, the alphabet they use in Rome."

"What do they say?"

Nagomi's heart was beating furiously, as if after a long run, though she didn't know why.

"P – F – V – S."

"No!" she cried and turned away. The tears returned and started flowing down her cheeks uncontrollably. "That's a very bad joke."

"It's true. I promise."

"But how?" asked Satō, "how is this possible?"

"My father said he got it from a Bataavian physician. It must have been your – "

"It's too much of a coincidence," Nagomi said firmly, holding back the sobs. She could not help her tears and did not know how to stop them. "This... this must have been some other Bataavian. Maybe it's a common name."

"That's not what Kazuko-*hime* would have said," Bran replied.

She sniffed and turned back to him. She reached out her hand.

"Can I..."

"Of course," Bran replied, "it belongs to you."

It was smooth and warm, like Bran's hand when he had taken her away from the marketplace.

"Kazuko-*hime*..."

Is this your sign? Is this your response to my prayers?

Yellow sulphurous mist descended on the Sendai valley in the morning. The air was warm and thick with dew, making it difficult to breathe, not to mention walk. Dark clouds returned, coming from all directions like a besieging army.

She had on her straw hood, but decided not to dye her hair after all. Bran's miraculous discovery had cheered her up greatly and restored her fortitude.

They halted at the crossroad, on the outskirts of the town. Several bridleways were spreading from here, all leading roughly south.

"Which road do you wish to take?" asked Dōraku.

"Which one leads to *Kirishima*?" Bran replied with a question.

Why Kirishima? She looked at Satō, but the wizardess only shook her head and shrugged. *We might as well,* her eyes seemed to say.

"The town or the shrine?"

"Is there a difference?"

"The shrine is farther up. Closer to the fire mountains."

"The shrine, then."

The samurai nodded. "This way."

He stepped upon the path leading straight towards the tallest of the sharp mountaintops on the southern horizon.

"I hope you bought enough supplies."

"Why?"

"Because it will take us three days to reach the shrine and we're not stopping anywhere along the way."

"*Three days?* I can't wait that long," Bran whispered. The three of them marched a short distance behind their guide. The road was rarely used and badly in need of repairs.

"Why are you in such a hurry? What's in Kirishima?" asked Satō.

"My dragon," the boy replied and winced, "we need to hurry."

She drew her breath, a little too loud. Master Dōraku turned to them.

"Is something wrong?"

"No, it's fine. Is this the fastest route to the shrine?"

The samurai chuckled.

"You should already know you can't afford to follow the fast routes. Whoever your enemies are, they will be expecting you."

"He's leading us into a trap," Bran murmured.

"You said the same when he guided us to the *tengu's* house, and then when we climbed down the mountains," she replied, "and he's right about the enemies – the Crimson Robe *would* expect us to take the main road."

"I thought we *wanted* the Crimson Robe to find us. How else are you going to find out what happened to your father?"

"I thought you might want to get your *dorako* first. We could use it in a fight."

He did not respond, picking up the pace instead.

We never discussed it before, she realised as the boy marched a few paces before her. *What if he doesn't want to help us? What if he only cares about his beast?*

Not everyone was as selfless as Master Dōraku, after all. The samurai guided them tirelessly through the towns and wilderness, just because Yōkoi-*dono* had asked him to. She was growing weary of Bran's suspicions. Even Nagomi seemed apprehensive towards their guide. Why couldn't they just let him be? He was as cheerful and open as the few men she had met. So what if he had secrets – who among them didn't have any?

He was following the Way of the Sword and, she was raised to believe, wielding the swords with utmost skill required a clear mind and a pure heart. She only had to remember that knave, Tokojirō – a coward and a traitor who managed to get himself disarmed by a confused Westerner.

And he *was* guiding them well. The volcanic peaks emerging from the mist seemed much closer by afternoon. The road started climbing upwards again. The villages and fields grew sparse, replaced by low growing, thin islands of forest in the sea of short, bright green grass growing over the ancient lava flows. The weather turned for the worse. It was the beginning of the rainy season in this southernmost corner of Yamato. The clouds, gathering since morning, finally released their waters in a torrential downpour, beating upon the travellers with a force of a mountain waterfall. Shivering under their straw raincoats, they climbed still upwards across the rocky, torn highland. The stinking brimstone vapours had been dispersed by the rain.

"At least now I know we won't suffocate – we'll drown," Bran remarked wryly.

In these conditions they managed to traverse a far shorter distance than she had expected before having to stop, exhausted. Master Dōraku led them to a small copse of thin, gnarled pine trees. He pulled out a large measure of tent cloth from the bag and wrapped it around the branches, forming a very rudimentary shelter from the elements.

"I'd prefer to face our enemies than this weather," said Bran, preparing his bedding on the wet soil.

Will his whining never stop?

Satō rolled her eyes.

And to think I almost let him kiss me. Again.

What was she thinking? And after she had *promised* herself...

"You'll be fine. We'll soon start a fire," said the samurai.

The bleak weather managed to turn even him grim and sullen. He picked up some wood from around the thicket, but it was all wet. Satō tried to help him light the campfire, but the firesticks got damp and could not produce even the tiniest of sparks.

"Or maybe not," Master Dōraku commented their efforts with a joyless smile.

"Oh by the Dragon's Breath..."

Bran reached out towards the pile of firewood and flicked his fingers. A wide tongue of flame spewed from his hand and the wood burst with a bright blaze.

The samurai looked genuinely surprised for the first time since they had met him. He scratched his thin beard in wonder.

"I couldn't stand another night in the cold," the boy said with a shrug, "besides, it wasn't that easy before. We're now much closer to the..."

He glanced at the samurai nervously.

"...source of power."

"Yes, there is a strong vortex of mystic energies nearby," Master Dōraku agreed. "All magic in its vicinity will probably be similarly strengthened."

"And how do *you* know that?" Bran asked suspiciously, "are you a wizard as well? Is he telling the truth?" he turned to the wizardess.

Satō wasn't sure what to answer, but then she remembered her glove – she took it from her bag and studied the dial. It was fluctuating, trembling, as if great streams of magical energies flowed through it.

"He's right!"

Eager to test the discovery, she scrambled out of her bedding and cast a small freezing spell at a branch of a nearby tree. To her surprise, the whole tree became covered with solid ice from root to top. She jumped back, startled by her own power.

"*Eeh*! A fire wizard and an ice wizard!" the samurai exclaimed, "what fascinating company I find myself in! Are *you* a mage as well, priestess-*sama*?" he asked Nagomi. The priestess raised her eyes as if frightened that somebody would mention her.

"None of your business," barked Bran before Nagomi could answer.

"Bran!"

Satō clasped her mouth, shocked. The samurai glanced at the boy in amusement.

"What about that vortex of energies you've mentioned?" Bran asked quickly, avoiding her accusing stare.

"The Takachiho Mountain."

"Takachiho Mountain..." Nagomi repeated, whispering the words like a prayer.

"*Ame no Uzume asked again — where shall you go and where shall the August Grandchild go? He answered and said — the child of the Heavenly Deity will proceed to the peak of Kushifuru at Takachiho, and I will go to the upper waters of Isuzu at Sanada in Ise*," Master Dōraku recited.

"What is it?"

"An excerpt from an ancient chronicle," explained Nagomi. "The peak of Takachiho, where the August Grandchild Ninigi no Mikoto descended from Heavens, bearing the three Imperial Regalia. The Dwelling of the Gods. I never dreamed I would..."

"It's just over that summit," the samurai said nodding south, where in the last rays of the setting sun they could see a tall volcanic cone hiding in the clouds, one of several in the chain of Islands in the Mist. "We should reach it by tomorrow. If you get well rested tonight, that is."

He stood up and stepped out of the shelter, immediately disappearing from sight into the rainy darkness.

"Where are you going?" Bran asked nervously, but there was no answer. "I don't like to have him around, but when he's gone it makes me even more anxious," he mumbled.

"If he hasn't killed us yet, I don't think he will," replied Satō.

"He could be bringing his men now to capture us and carry us away to some dark prison."

"You worry too much."

"And you're too trusting."

"I have lived in this place for seventeen years. You only arrived a month ago," she said, feeling her anger rising. *How many times will we have to go through this?* "I will choose my allies as I please, thank you very much."

"But I never – "

"Good night, Bran-*sama*." She turned his back to him huffily, covering her head with a blanket.

CHAPTER VI

Chief Councillor finished reading the documents from the pile he had marked with a sign of a "Horse" and moved on to a pile marked with the sign of a "Ram". As the head of the government, the matters of the Empire lay solely on his thin, bony shoulders. Without some kind of sorting system he would soon be buried under the weight of documents, missives, reports and letters. At first he had them divided into three categories of urgency, but by now he had twelve separate stacks of papers, each stamped with a character from the Qin zodiac.

Even with this system, a lesser man would break down under the weight of single-handedly ruling the islands. Abe did not like to rely on secretaries and courtiers, like his predecessors. Their minds did not work fast enough for him. He had kept the ones he inherited with the job on court salaries, but never called on their services, leaving them largely to their own devices. That way, everybody was happy.

He had retained only one man at his side, the personal aide to the previous Chief Councillor himself, Hotta Naosuke. Master Hotta had appeared in the *Taikun*'s court in service of one of Ogasawara lords and had risen to the top almost as fast as Abe. Naosuke's unremarkable physiognomy, accented only by the cunning glint of his eyes, hid one of the brightest minds Abe had ever worked with. It almost seemed as if the Councillor needed no sleep, food or drink. He worked constantly and without fail.

It was Naosuke who laboured on dividing the documents into zodiac-marked stacks as they arrived to the Chief Councillor's office. The "Ram" pile was for all matters of coastal defence, and it had grown so large lately, that it had to be divided into two, one of the stacks dedicated solely to the defence of Edo and surroundings. He fingered through the letters from the many *daimyo*s who had been ordered to provide Edo with men, supplies and arms.

"A thousand samurai from Aizu with armour and horse, a dozen war boats and five battle mages," he read to Naosuke, who scribbled down some notes. "Yes, the Aizu are reliable as always. The Matsuyama, the Takamatsu, the Kuwana... not as much as they could send. Note: admonish them for avarice." He continued going through the stack until he reached the bottom.

"Is there no answer from the southern provinces?"

"No, *tono*. Only Nabeshima-*dono* has responded. The Saga province is sending a token force of samurai now and preparing a larger detachment for later."

"What about Tosa? Chōshu? Higo?"

"They seem to have ignored your... the *Taikun*'s orders." Naosuke's face remained perfectly still, but his eyes glinted, betraying how satisfied he was with the news. Abe recognized a familiar ambition in the Councillor. He had no doubt that, sooner or later, Naosuke would replace him in the position. It did not matter in the long run; the court was like a boiling pot of *oden* – some would rise to the surface, others fall to the bottom. Such was the way of politics. If anyone were to take over the reins of government, Chief Councillor preferred it to be the wily, moderate Hotta rather than the hot-headed Kuze or one of the self-confident Matsudairas.

"The Southerners have mingled with the Westerners too much. They are no better than the Barbarians. I don't suppose Nariakira's response was any different?"

"He did not even bother with one."

Abe rubbed his eyes with a tired gesture.

"I know you two used to be close. Why don't you write him a personal letter? For old time's sake."

Naosuke shrugged lightly. "I may try, but we have not spoken to each other in years. Not since he stopped coming to Edo."

"Ah, yes. That's another thing. We will need to remind him about his duties. The Alternate Attendance system must be obeyed."

"He will not come," said Naosuke firmly. "You would have to drag him by force."

Abe smiled knowingly.

"That may not be necessary. Did you know he's sending his daughter to the Castle?"

Naosuke raised his eyes. "I didn't even know he had a daughter."

"Adopted, I believe. I'm not sure what he's planning exactly. Help with administrative duties, officially, but this is obviously just a ruse."

"Obviously."

For a moment they were both silent, pondering the mysterious plans of the Satsuma *daimyo*.

"What about Kiyō?" Abe said, picking up another piece of paper. "What do the *Rangaku* wizards say? Will they help?"

"Their answer is in the "Dog" pile, but I can tell they won't be terribly committed to the cause. Not after how the *Taikun* treated them."

"I will change these laws. I need the cooperation of the wizards. If a war with the West were to break out... I know what might convince them. That scholar under house arrest, what's his name – Takashima? I want him released."

"That might be difficult. He and his family have been outlawed."

"By whose orders?"

"Bugyō of Kiyō."

Fool.

"I will override it. Send the dispatch with the first post."

Naosuke nodded, but still looked doubtful. The wizards were notorious for their anti-government sentiments.

"What will you do if that isn't enough?"

"Then whoever takes my place will have to find a way to deal with those rebellious half-barbarians, one way or another. Whatever the cost, we need national unity in these difficult times. We cannot share the fate of Qin just because of some petty squabbles."

The other man nodded again in silence. At least on this, they were both in agreement.

Chief Councillor put away the bunch of papers and wiped the sweat off his brow.

"Tell you what, Hotta-*sama*. Why don't we leave this for now and go to get some saké?"

Naosuke looked up in surprise.

"Are you thirsty, Chief Councillor? Should I call for the servant?"

"No, no. I meant going to an inn. Have some leisure time."

Abe realised how unusual his request must have sounded. Normally he was the last person to be seen drinking and merry-making when he should be working. But these were not normal circumstances.

A smile slowly appeared on Naosuke's face. "Very well, Abe-*dono*. I know just the place."

The girl finished her dance, picked up the fan from the floor, bowed and left, followed by the *shamisen* player. The two men remained alone with their flasks of saké in an octagonal, Qin-style pavilion in the middle of a small garden at the back of an opulent guesthouse. A nightingale sang inside a large hydrangea bush; blue-tinted buds swayed in the wind.

Chief Councillor picked up a strip of grilled chicken meat on a stick and chewed it for a while, deep in thought.

"If we fail this test, history will know us as the last Councillors," he said.

"And who would write this history?" asked Naosuke.

"The Barbarians, no doubt."

"That's very pessimistic. Bordering on treason."

"We both know there are none more faithful servants to the *Taikun* than the two of us. But we must acknowledge the facts. The Qin fell to the Barbarians in two months. Do you remember when the news first broke out about the war?"

Councillor Hotta nodded. "Of course. I will never forget it."

It had been ten years earlier almost to the day. Like many young idealists of the age, Hotta Naosuke had at the time been studying law and history at the famous Mito school, under Aizawa-*sensei*. He was just becoming aware of Yamato's dreadful situation under the facade of the *Taikun*'s "peaceful reforms".

He had been late that day. He noticed from a distance that the students had gathered on the main courtyard in a great crowd, instead of attending lectures or working on the Great History as they should have been doing at that time of day.

"Is this true? Is it really true? So fast... total rout!" He heard the voices as he approached the crowd. He grabbed one of his friends by the shoulder – it was Shimazu Nariakira, then son of the *daimyo* of Satsuma. They disagreed on matters of politics, but enjoyed each other's company whenever copious amounts of saké – or better yet, shōchū, of which Nariakira had always plenty – were involved.

"What's going on?"

"News from Qin. The Barbarians have destroyed their fleet and broken through the Barrier. They've captured Huating and Fan Yu."

"What? But the war's only just started..."

"And now it's finished. The Barbarians are at the gates of Jiankang. The Empire is pleading for peace."

"Is this news confirmed?"

"As much as any news from abroad can be."

The crowd hushed momentarily, as Aizawa-*sensei* walked into the courtyard. He was already an ancient man, wrinkle-faced, dry-skinned, his lips always pursed and twisted as if he had eaten something sour. He was a renowned scholar and tutor to the *daimyo*s of Mito, but his greatest claim to fame had been an incident twenty years earlier, when he was delegated to translate for the Western barbarian sailors who got captured while shipwrecked on the coast of the province. This meeting shook him to the core and he had devoted the rest of his life to developing a way for the Yamato to deal with future foreign threats.

The old headmaster approached the message board and squinted to read the black squiggly letters. He then harrumphed, shook his head and turned to the gathered students.

"There will be no lectures today. You are free to ponder this momentous event however you see fit. If anyone wants to discuss anything with me, I'll be in the garden, meditating."

"Say, Nariakira, do you still have that barrel of black yeast stuff you got for the harvest holiday?" Naosuke prodded his friend and, with a couple of other drinking and debating companions, Tenkō and Nobumitsu, moved in the direction of Shimazu's lodgings, ostentatiously to discuss the latest news, but in reality to have a taste of the famous liquor.

"Old Sourface must be overjoyed," Naosuke said. "Isn't this what he's always predicted? That the Barbarians will come and gobble us all one by one, like a pack of wolves eating up a herd of deer?"

"I don't think being right makes him happy today," replied Nariakira.

"The *Taikun*ate must react to this," Tenkō said, banging his fist on the table. He had one cup too many and his face was flushed. "If they ignore even this news, then, then…"

"Then what?" goaded Nariakira.

"Well then they're no longer fit to rule! And by the will of Heavens, they should be removed!"

"Don't you start with your Confucian fairy-tales," Naosuke said, waving his hand, "will of Heavens indeed! That's a traitor's talk."

"A traitor to what? The nation? The *Mikado*? The Tokugawas gained their power by force, not by legacy or divine intervention. They can be removed by force."

"And what would you have instead? Civil war all over again? There is no *daimyo* strong enough to take the *Taikun*'s place."

"You know very well whom I would have instead. We all think alike here, except you, don't we, lads?"

Tenkō looked around himself, trying to find support for his rebellious words. Nobumitsu said nothing. He was an expert in deciphering ancient texts, but modern politics was not his strongest point. But Nariakira nodded and grunted in agreement.

"There is a family that ruled Yamato for hundreds if not thousands of years," said future lord of Satsuma, "their line is unbroken, and they still are nominally monarchs of this country. Their legitimacy to rule is much greater than that of any *daimyo*."

"I can't believe you're being serious," Naosuke scoffed, "Bring the *Mikado* back to power? That puppet? You might as well put *Butsu-sama* on the throne, or Amaterasu herself! What good would that do?"

"It would be a symbol behind which everyone could rally. You know this might work. There will be no war if we all unite behind the Chrysanthemum Throne."

"That's just a dream. Tokugawas have half the *daimyo*s supporting them, if not more. There would be a war. More bloody than the last one. And while we fight amongst each other, the Barbarians will swallow us up, just like they did in Bharata."

"Well then, what is your solution, o wise Hotta-*dono*?" Tenko mocked him, pouring himself yet another cup, not noticing the warning look he was given by Nariakira.

"I don't know yet. But I don't believe the problem lies with the institution. It's the people who are the problem. As long as they rule, Tokugawas guarantee peace. Peace and time is what we need right now, not hot-headed intellectuals pursuing dreams of divine legacy. But there is stagnation creeping in, and with it, indolence and corruption."

"That's why we need a revolution!" Tenkō banged the table again.

"A revolution is chaos, and chaos would be used by our enemies. We need better reforms, smarter reformers."

"How many reforms have there been in the past century? And after each one, things get worse."

"That's why we need smarter people in the government. People like us. Isn't that what we study here for? To learn how to rule the country better?"

"We'll never get anywhere near the government," said Nariakira softly, his inner calm cooling the heads of the quarrelling friends, as always. "You're the only one of us who is from a *fudai* family, and you're what, thirteenth in line to succeed? The rest of us are *tozama*, outsiders. All our skill and knowledge will amount to nothing as long as the current system is in place."

"There must be another way than revolution," Naosuke put down his cup, deep in thought. "And I would give anything to find it."

"And have you found it? The way, I mean," asked the Chief Councillor having listened to the entire tale.

"I like to think so," Naosuke replied, but said nothing more, keeping the secret to himself.

"So that's what the conversations were like at Mito," said Abe, looking into his saké cup. "I've often wondered."

"We were young and hot-headed, all of us. Some have changed little – like Nariakira-*dono*."

"Do you think he still considers replacing the *Taikun* with the Divine *Mikado*?"

"His mind is too fast to dwell on one idea for too long. No doubt he has come up with a dozen different plans since then."

"I used to dread waking up one day to see Satsuma's banners at the gates of Edo. Now I would welcome them."

"They would certainly be of great help against the Black Wings," agreed Naosuke. "Unless, that is, Nariakira-*dono* deemed it more useful for his cause to *join* the invaders..."

"He'd never... do you think...?"

"He's always been a patriot at heart, but his sense of what's best for the nation can sometimes be... misguided."

Councillor Hotta's crooked smile and raised eyebrows expressed his distrust much more strongly than his words. He reached for the saké flask, put it to his ear and shook it.

"Alas! No more."

"*Under the budding hydrangeas,*
I reach for the white clay bottle:
Like my head, it is empty," chanted Abe and both men erupted in drunken laughter.

A hundred Qinese men stood in a loose column in the middle of the plain, holding on to their self-repeating rifles, their heads sweating under the green turbans in the sweltering sun. The navy blue of their uniforms stood out against the brick-brown of the muddy earth.

On the other side of the plain waited a thousand or so soldiers, wearing mostly grey studded kaftans and red trousers. The men brandished an assortment of weapons of all sorts, broad swords, spears, halberds, pitch forks and a few matchlocks. The arrangement was supposed to imitate a rebel rabble, but Dylan had strong suspicions that this was how the Imperial Army really looked.

"How ever did you convince old Pointy Beard to give us this demonstration?" asked Admiral Reynolds, observing the field.

"It was his proposition. I tried to convince him for three days and then suddenly he came back in the morning with this." Dylan waved his hand.

He had been training the hundred men for a week, with the help of other dragoons. The blue uniforms they wore were spares from the Admiral's stores, as were the rifles and ammunition. He knew the safety of the Concession depended on the success of this demonstration of the Western art of war – already the scouts were reporting that the rebels had been regrouping a large number of troops to the south of the Cheng River in preparation for a renewed assault.

As if we hadn't shown them enough how superior our tactics are, he thought bitterly. But he knew this wasn't the case. The Qin officials had to be convinced that the Western tactics could be applied to the mentality of the Eastern soldiers. And of that even Dylan himself wasn't certain.

"I must admit, you've done a great job, Ardian. They look almost human."

Dylan winced and scratched his scar nervously. He was trying to stamp out this sort of attitude in his own men, but he could do nothing about the Admiral's old fashioned prejudice.

"I had plenty of valuable help from that Lee fellow."

"The interpreter?"

"He turned out to be more than an interpreter. He's a sort of lieutenant to the Bohan, or a protégé. I have a feeling it was his whispers that led to us having this exercise."

He stood up in the stirrups and raised his hand. A hush spread throughout the battlefield. Both sides watched him, a small human figure on top of a great silver dragon. The respective assigned commanders – Edern led the blue-clad hundred – raised their own banners in anticipation. The Banneret's men screwed on their bayonets.

At the signal, the thousand men charged ahead with a variety of battle cries. A perfectly executed rifle salvo thundered and a flood of bullets whistled over the heads of the running rabble.

The first line of the attackers was to drop to the ground after the first salvo. This was, after all, supposed to be just an exercise. But nothing of the sort happened.

What are they doing?

"Cheating bastards!" the Admiral cried, waving his fist.

Edern cried a new order, but Dylan couldn't hear what it was. The blue-clad men aimed the rifles again, slightly lower this time. Another thunder of shots echoed throughout the mud plain and this time, a row of running soldiers stumbled and fell. Nine hundred men ran past their comrades rolling on the ground, wailing and groaning in pain.

The Admiral laughed a wheezing laugh, but Dylan frowned. He didn't want to start *another* war when the first one wasn't yet finished... but he trusted Edern knew what he was doing.

The Banneret's men shot twice more – two more lines tumbled under the feet of those running behind them – and then split into three groups, in a classic flanking formation.

Dylan's heart rose as he watched the perfectly performed manoeuvre. And they only had a week of training! The Qinese were proving to be just as good soldiers as his own men. He glanced at the Admiral. The old soldier was engrossed in the spectacle, his eyes wide open. His hand clapped against his thigh when the flanking troops pierced the now seven-hundred-strong battalion from both sides. The bayonets flashed against the swords and halberds. Most of the attackers wore heavy studded armour and their weapons were hefty while Edern's men bore themselves lightly and moved swiftly, and their bayoneted rifles held a nasty surprise that no spear or halberd could counter: once in a while a shot was heard, followed by a cry of anguish.

The Qin battalion fell into confusion and disarray when the middle group of the blue-clad soldiers charged head on, led by Edern whose hair and Lance shone like silver stars in the melee.

"Observe now, Admiral," said Dylan, "this is a modification to our usual tactics that Lee had advised us would suit best the Qin style."

Edern led a wedge of soldiers straight for the heart of the "enemy" formation. Disregarding their "losses", they charged onwards. For a moment, the silver haired head disappeared in the sea of blades and banners, but then a loud cry of triumph was heard and the remaining Qin dropped their weapons and surrendered. The battle was over.

"Aim for the head and the body will fail," Dylan said. "It's old fashioned, but seems to work here still."

The Bohan and his entourage marched quickly across the battlefield, stopping only for a moment to assess the injuries of his men. None of them were life-threatening. Edern's riflemen had been aiming for the feet and shins of the attackers, and their aim was accurate.

"How many of the rifles and uniforms can you procure?" the Bohan asked as soon as he climbed to the top of the small mound upon which Dylan and Reynolds stood.

His face was an impenetrable mask. No discussion of the result, no explanation for his men's behaviour during the exercise. The Bohan acknowledged his utter defeat without so much as a twitch. Dylan couldn't help but smile in admiration.

"I can send for a transport of three thousand from the Fragrant Harbour. It would be here in two weeks."

"Slow."

"It would be faster if we could sail past Ederra. And the messages take longer since the ley line's disruption."

The Bohan snorted and then grinned. His mood changed surprisingly fast.

"Come, Ardian. The Qin have secrets of their own – it's time I showed you one of them."

"What's going on? Where is he taking you?" the Admiral demanded. The entire conversation had been in Qin and he caught no word of it.

"I have no idea, Admiral, but I bet it will be an interesting trip."

CHAPTER VII

The three travellers lay around the fireplace in silence, the beating of the rain on the tent cloth the only sound of the night. The wizardess wrapped her cloak and blanket around her like a mummy. Nagomi lay on her back, hands on her stomach, in her usual pose. Bran turned away from the fire, facing the rain and darkness beyond the makeshift tent, contemplating what Satō had said.

She had the right to say it. It was her land, her people. Whoever he was, Dōraku, a *real* samurai who had lived in Yamato for his entire life, was closer to the wizardess than a Westerner. The boy felt a sudden, surprising pang of jealousy. He shook his head. He could not lose focus now. He had a mission to perform; a dragon to rescue. Emrys was now almost within his reach, no more than a couple of days walk away. He could feel the beast almost as strongly as if it was right beside him.

He reached a hand into the night and conjured a dancing sparkle of dragon flame. It came effortlessly, like a child's illusion. Dōraku was right – it was very easy to perform magic in this place. He could sense the currents of energies surging through him from all directions. With a wave of hand, he formed it into the shape of a rampant dragon, its wings spread widely. Then, just to see if he could, he sculpted the flame to show his own figure, dressed in the Yamato clothes, sword at his side. It seemed odd when viewed like this, it did not feel like him at all. The samurai uniform and haircut did not suit him. Another flick of the fingers and the dancing figure of fire changed to resemble the wizardess, with her tomboy posture and the *katana* in her hand. In his fiery vision, Satō wore the samurai gear much more comfortably and with more confidence. Just like Dōraku... Bran weaved his hand again and the flame split into two figures, one of him, one of Satō. The figures got closer. With another flicker, they were naked...

A twig cracked in the darkness. Dōraku returned from whatever his nightly errand was. Bran closed his hand, extinguishing the flickering flame sculptures, and pretended to sleep. The rain poured around the camp without respite.

The sweet smell of sizzling meat tickled her nostrils. She opened one eye and saw Dōraku, sitting by the campfire, holding a makeshift roost of long, sharpened sticks.

"Fish!"

She sat up immediately. Oil dripped from two fat trouts into the fire, sending out aromatic sparks.

"Where did you get it?"

"There are streams full of fish in these mountains, if you know where to look."

"So you're a fisherman now, too," said Bran, picking himself up on the other side of the campfire. "You are a man of many talents."

The samurai only smiled and turned the fish to the other side. He reached for his baggage and rummaged for a while. He took out a small bamboo box from which he poured some dark sauce on the fish, but something else caught Satō's attention; she glimpsed a corner of something round and white.

"Is that a… a theatre mask?"

Dōraku looked at her curiously and took out the mask. It was old, yellowed, fractured in places, trimmed with patches of white fur and painted in fierce red and black patterns.

"You like theatre?" he asked.

"I love it!"

The samurai gazed at the mask for a long time, then up to the sky with a faint smile, as if remembering something. He then turned to Bran.

"Will you hold the fish for me, Karasu-*sama*?"

Bran sighed grumpily, reaching for the roost. *What is it now?*

The samurai stood up, stretched himself and waited until Satō woke up the priestess. When he had the full audience at last, he put on the mask, bent his back and stretched his arms.

He began a strange wail, one in which Bran, at first, could barely discern the words. It was unlike any song he had ever heard, with no rhythm and scarcely any melody, yet strangely harmonious and haunting. It wasn't until he began to understand the lyrics that he realised Dōraku was telling a story.

Sore koso sashimo Atsumori ga saigo

Made michishi fuetake no…

Indeed until the last moment

Did Atsumori keep the bamboo flute…

The samurai began to pace around the campfire on tiptoe, shaking his head and waving his arms, miming to the words. It was a tale of some duel in the middle of the battle, between a youth called Atsumori and an older warrior, Kumagai of Musashi province. The story was reaching its climax, and the song and Dōraku's movements were picking up the pace.

Uma no ue nite hikkunde

Namiuchigiwa ni

Ochikasanatte…

And on their horses they wrestled,

Then, falling into the waves,

Dropped one against another

At last…

"The fish!" cried Dōraku, tearing off the mask and leaping towards the campfire. He grabbed the roost from Bran's hands at the last moment – the sticks had almost burnt through; any second later, the trouts would have fallen into the fire.

"What happened?" asked Satō. "Who won the duel?"

"Kumagai," said the samurai, "but he did not rejoice in victory. Atsumori was the same age as Kumagai's son. The old warrior became a monk, dedicating his life to the atonement for his sins."

"But it was death on the battlefield. There is no wrong in that."

Dōraku looked at her with sad and strangely solemn eyes. "I pray that you never have to ponder this dilemma yourself, young warrior. But look, the fish is ready. Eat well, we have a long way to go."

As he sank his teeth in the tender white flesh of the trout, Bran heard a soft humming. He glanced at Dōraku. The samurai was looking into the fire, singing the rest of the song so quietly that Bran was certain only he could hear the words.

Kataki nite wa, nakarikeri

Ato tomuraite, tabitamae

Ato tomuraite, tabitamae.

If thou art not my enemy

Pray for me often,

Pray for me often.

By midday, the terrain got even tougher, as the travellers had to climb ever higher upwards, towards the summit of the mountain, along the needle-sharp, rocky ridges and jagged, weathered bluffs.

The black and grey mountaintops, naked, save for a few tufts of the shrimp grass or lichen-covered boulders, seemed to Bran indeed a good home for Gods and Demons to roam. This was how the world must have looked like when it was still young, in the age of Unbridled Fire. The red earth here was warm to touch. Plumes of steam spewed from fissures and rifts in the rock. Small, round craters were filled with clear blue-green water, boiling hot. There certainly was beauty in all this rough, rugged landscape, but overall Bran was thankful that they only needed to spend two more days climbing these volcanic slopes.

Based on the phases of the moon he was noting in his diary, less than a month had passed since they had left the Suwa Shrine. It seemed like a year. This journey had been by far the longest he had ever had to undertake. Any distance longer than a few miles back in Gwynedd, he would have just mounted Emrys and flown. The thin straw sandals the Yamato used for long-distance travel were barely any better than walking barefoot. His legs burned, his arms ached, his whole body cried "Enough! Get rest!"

He dared not complain. The journey was hard, but if the girls were managing to walk all this distance without so much as a whimper, so could he.

They never complain, he thought. *Not even Nagomi.* The priestess seemed excited to leave the city at first, but he could see clearly the recent events had taken their toll on her. She was more focused, more serious than when he had first met her.

She was the only one in Yamato who did not hide her feelings. She cried openly, and she laughed without restraint. All the other people he had met so far had worn masks of politeness, cheerfulness and indifference as impenetrable as Dōraku's theatre mask.

Satō is really good at this game, he thought. She played her role perfectly throughout the day. Seeing her, one could almost believe she was just on some country holiday with her friends. It was only at night that Bran could sometimes hear her sob, quietly. He never mentioned it. *I don't need to give her another reason to be angry.*

Before evening they had climbed almost to the top of Mount Takachiho, into the clouds covering the jagged summit, a gruelling trek through the empty and dusty lava fields. Weather up here changed abruptly. The day before they'd had to suffer a torrential shower, now Bran would have been grateful for a drop of water or a gust of wind to disperse the stale, humid, hot air. Below, spread the valleys of Kirishima; seas of tall, bushy grass. But he could not see far beyond the hellish steams and sulphurous mists emerging from the cracked slopes of the mountain.

There was, at last, a patch of greenery, a clump of low azaleas blooming bright pink, huddled on the southern incline, which provided them with some welcome shade and shelter. They ate a brief meal there and, at Dōraku's advice, drank the last of their boiled water.

"Below that ridge the mountains end and, from there," the samurai said, pointing with his bamboo pipe, "tomorrow we start our descent straight to

Kirishima. It's a cedar forest all the way down, pleasantly cool and dark at this time of year."

Satō moaned, discarding the ruined straw sandals and picking new ones from the bag. She was down to her last pair. "I can understand not going by the main roads… but this is not even a road!"

"It would be too easy to follow us through the woods. I needed us to stay out in the open, to see any incoming danger. From here, we can see far down but remain unseen from below."

Even Bran had to admit this sounded reasonable. How many enemies were now after them? The Magistrate, the Crimson Robe, the lord of the Kumamoto Castle… and whoever kept Emrys imprisoned. It seemed as if all of Yamato had turned against them.

This was the most desolate, miserable place he had ever had the misfortune to see. He had once flown to the top of a volcano on Brendan's Island, but it was surrounded with greenery, vineyards and orange orchards. There was nothing so abundant growing here, nothing to make a fire with. Only the lonely clump of wild azaleas, exposed to the elements.

He reached over and fluttered his fingers over the pink bloom. He knew a real samurai would at this moment think about the flowers in some poetic terms. Here was life, clinging desperately to a hellish wasteland, flourishing, ever hopeful in its fragile beauty. He tried to think like a cultured Yamato warrior, come up with a way to capture the beauty in words, but couldn't. His Western mind tried instead to assign a taxonomic rank to the plant, analyse the way the soil composition was reflected in the colour and size of blossom. At the Academy he had been taught botany, not poetry.

I will never be like them.

He picked a large, five-fold flower and, without thinking, crushed it between his fingers. A mocking chuckle resonated in his head.

Bran stirred, moaned and threw his head from side to side in his sleep before finally opening his eyes. They were black as the night around the camp.

General Shigemasa sat up and stretched the muscles of the boy's body. He looked around. The campfire was sizzling away into ashes, giving just enough light to illuminate the girls lying close together underneath their blankets and the dark silhouette of Dōraku who sat outside the tent cloth, cross-legged, in the pouring rain.

The General rose and crept quietly up to the samurai.

"I may be deep in meditation, but I can still hear you coming, *Taishō-dono.*"

Shigemasa chuckled. "And thou canst even tell 'tis me?"

"The boy does not know how to sneak like that. Why do you disturb my exercise?"

"I see… things. This close to Mount Takachiho my senses are as sharp as in the Caves."

"Oh? And what do you see in the darkness and mist?"

"I see a head of the eight-headed serpent reaching out towards us. I see monsters coming from beyond the sea. I see one of the three perish, but I know not which one. And I'd rather it not be the boy."

"Two of these I am aware of," nodded Dōraku, "but what is this about the monsters from beyond the sea?"

"I do not see it clearly yet. I am worried, Swordsman. I require this body. I need it safe."

"I will do what I can to protect the boy."

Shigemasa scoffed.

"It is *thee* that I am worried about."

Dōraku uncrossed his legs and turned around. His eyes glistened in the campfire light.

"I am not like the…others."

"So thou sayest, but how can I believe thee?"

"Have I ever betrayed your trust, *Taishō-dono*? When we fought at Shimabara… have I ever done anything improper?"

"That was more than ten score years ago. A lot has changed since then, even the way people speak."

"I have not. Not like that."

Shigemasa looked into the night for a long while in silence.

"I will have to tell the boy about thee," he spoke at last. "Let him decide what to do."

Dōraku stood up.

"I would advise against it, *Taishō-dono*. He would likely do something unwise."

He stepped forward. Shigemasa shuffled backwards.

"Thou threatens *me*? By what power?" he said and laughed, but the laughter died in his throat when Dōraku stepped even closer and his eyes glinted gold.

"I was hoping I could trust you to keep a secret," the samurai said, "but if there be no trust between us…"

Like a striking serpent, Dōraku's hand flashed forward towards Bran-Shigemasa's face. And then there was darkness.

He was back on the plain of the red dust. The light from the tower on the horizon was dimmed, hazed by the distance. Shigemasa sighed and started walking back towards it when he heard heavy footsteps thumping in the dust behind him.

He turned around and saw a giant. More than twice the size of a man, he wore a cloak of darkness and wielded twin blades of silver light, each as big as a glaive. Eyes like two pieces of gold shone brightly from under the hood.

"Thy tricks do not scare me, S-swordsman," Shigemasa started defiantly, but ended on a stutter. He drew his own sword – here he had his old armour and weapons – but it seemed a mere toothpick in comparison.

"These are no tricks, *Taishō*. Here, everyone shows their true form."

"If thou wishest to strive with me, then do it honourably, like the nobleman thou art."

"As you wish." The air shimmered and in place of the giant appeared the Dōraku as he was outside, with his ridiculous yellow and purple kimono and old-fashioned whiskers.

"Now – " he started, but Shigemasa did not let him finish. He charged with a short yell, so suddenly, he almost succeeded in surprising the samurai.

The blades clanged – once – twice. Shigemasa's sword raised a plume of red dust. A tip of one of Dōraku's swords hovered an inch from the general's neck, the other – at his heart.

"I don't even know what killing you here would do to you," the samurai whispered hoarsely, "but I am itching to find out." His eyes glowed like lanterns, his breath smelled of death.

Shigemasa blinked then threw back his head and laughed, genuinely this time.

"Dost thou expect me to beg for mercy? I am a samurai!"

Dōraku lowered his weapons and his figure seemed to shrink and darken even further.

"No, you're right. It is not proper."

He closed his eyes and whispered something unintelligible, then sheathed his swords and turned on his heels. Shigemasa tried to follow, but he couldn't budge. His feet sank into the red dirt like quicksand and the more he struggled the deeper he fell.

"What hast thou done to me?"

"I will release you when it's safe," said Dōraku without turning, "I cannot have you interfere with my plans."

The general snickered. "Plans? I could have told thee about thy plans. It is not *I* that shall be the cause of thy failure."

Dōraku stopped.

"Thy ears are pricked now, eh? But it's too late. I shall tell thee nothing."

The samurai's shoulders dropped. "Good," he said, "your prophecies were growing tiresome."

With that, he walked away into the darkness. A nameless wind blew across the featureless plain, picking up the dirt and shrouding the horizon in a blood red haze.

They huddled together in the darkness, in a large cave on the shore of the Kuma River, not daring to light a fire, not daring to make a sound.

Bats were their only companions, flying in their hundreds to roost as the evening fell. Further in, the cave expanded to a magnificent palace of limestone formations, but they stayed near the entrance, watchful, observant.

"He will find us," Azumi said, shivering. Rain and fog drenched her clothes and hair as they fled through the forest, but she had nothing to change into. "He will find us and destroy us."

Ozun kissed her on the forehead. A thunder struck in the distance and she shuddered. The rain started anew.

"You're a brave *kunoichi*. Surely you're not afraid of a storm now?"

"Don't mock me. You know what He's capable of."

"We will be all right," said Ozun, caressing her wet, cold back. "Tomorrow we will reach the sea, and from there we can sail to wherever we want."

"But where to? He'll find us anywhere in Yamato."

"Then we will leave Yamato. We will go to Nansei. His power doesn't reach there."

"I have a villa in Nansei," a darkly sweet voice said behind them, "although it's a bit too warm this time of the year."

They jumped up and turned around. In a flash of the thunderclap they saw a tall figure in a long robe of crimson, with eyes glowing gold. Stench of death and blood filled the cave.

Ozun stepped in front of Azumi, rising his jingling staff in defence.

"How brave," the Crimson Robe said, smiling. "And romantic."

"You can kill me, but leave her. She did nothing wrong."

"Kill? Who said anything about killing?" the Crimson Robe feigned surprise.

"But I thought…" Ozun lowered his weapon.

The Crimson Robe waved his hand and a powerful force cast the hermit against the cavern wall, knocking him out. Azumi cried and tried to run but she couldn't move; one word whispered by the Master was enough to hold her in a bind.

"Kill you, after what you've done for me?"

"I don't understand," she whispered. "What good have I done?"

"You've forced my old friend to come out of hiding! That must count for *something*. Thanks to you he had to show off his fencing skills and my other spies – you didn't think you were alone? – could have confirmed it was really him?"

"You… know this …swordsman?"

"Know him!" He laughed again. "Yes, I *knew* him."

Ozun stirred and moaned, trying to rise up, but the Crimson Robe snapped his fingers and the hermit's head was smashed against the wall again.

"Please stop it!" she cried. "You said you would not kill him!"

"I've decided to change my tactics," her master continued unperturbed. "Sending you out one by one will not do, not when that… man is around. I am summoning everyone from the old team – and once we're done here, I will need you both back."

"Done with what?" she asked and the way his golden eyes looked at her made her immediately regret the question.

"The tracks from the road lead here," Azumi said in a hoarse voice. Her ashen skin was almost the same colour as her tight-fitting uniform of the Koga province assassins. Her cheek twitched nervously whenever she had to address her master. His punishments left no trace on her body but drove deep scars into her spirit.

The Crimson Robe was standing atop a fallen tree, careful not to stain his robe with mud. His men were searching the forest floor around the earthen mound as he watched from beyond the stone circle. Azumi observed his unease with satisfaction. The power of the Ancients was still strong enough to keep the likes of him at a distance. The remnants of their presence permeated this primeval forest.

"Somebody made a very good effort at concealing them," she added.

"This is what I have spared you for," he said, smiling. She gulped and continued.

"There was a battle here as well, but much more … lethal."

"We found them!" cried one of the members of the searching party, shovelling away a pack of fresh dirt. The men all wore the grey uniforms. They were very reliable – and very disposable.

The Crimson Robe knelt by the bodies, already starting to swell and turn blue in the hot and humid spring air. A cloud of hungry flies buzzed irritatingly above until he snarled and made an impatient gesture; the insects dropped dead. He traced the pattern of the wounds with his hand and examined the way the head had been cut off the mage's body. His golden eyes glimmered with recognition. He chuckled.

"Only one man uses that technique with such precision."

He turned to the *kunoichi*.

"Have you found anything else of interest?"

"There was a dead wolf buried along with the bodies. It looks… familiar."

"Show it to me."

The men brought out the carcass of the slain animal. The Crimson Robe examined the wounds and let out a surprised laugh.

"How quaint. With all these dead bodies around… chivalrous as ever."

"I also found this on the floor of the mound," Azumi said, showing him several long hairs of deep red colour.

"The young priestess who was a friend of Shūhan's daughter... what was her name again?"

"Nagomi, I believe."

"So she's no longer dying her hair. That should make things easier."

He stood up and looked at the headless body of an *onmyōji*, thinking something over. He then looked at the people gathered around him.

"One of them is a wizard, right? I believe that gives them an unfair advantage…"

He leaned over and examined the corpse once more.

"Take this body with you. Burn the rest." He spat. "No, wait. One more idea. Ozun!"

The hermit appeared before him and Azumi winced. His left arm hung limply along his body and he slouched slightly, but in his eyes still glimmered the rebellious streak she loved him for.

Ozun's eyes narrowed when he saw the wolf's mangled body.

"I need your powers to hunt down the owner of this beautiful red hair," the Crimson Robe said and let the thin copper-coloured thread float down with the wind onto the *yamabushi*'s outstretched palm.

"The spirits of the forest yearn for revenge," Ozun said, looking at the dead animal.

"Do they, now?" The Master looked at the hermit with interest. "Fine. Let them have it, then. But! The dragon rider must be unharmed."

Ozun nodded.

"I need fresh blood. This is useless."

The Master whistled at one of the grey-clads. The man came up and knelt down. Azumi turned her eyes away, knowing what was about to happen. The great *nodachi* blade fell and the *rōnin's* head rolled on the grass. Blood splattered the dead wolf's body.

Ozun crouched by the animal and patted it gently on the side, sighing. His fingers caressed the grey fur, now turned red. He stood up, put the conch to his lips and blew a solemn melody. At first nothing happened, but then white-and-blue will-o'-the-wisps appeared in the crowns of cedar trees. Spiralling, they descended to the ground all around the glade, in their dozens. The forest reverberated with the sound of the shell, and the wind and leaves joined in with their own morbid song. The entire wood mourned the death of the noble animal.

Wherever the wisps touched the ground, they turned into ghostly wolf shapes. Soon there was a great pack of them before the shrine, howling for vengeance. The largest one approached Ozun, who let the beast sniff the glimmering copper strand of hair. The hermit leant down and whispered something to the leader of the pack, then stamped the jingling staff twice. The wolf snarled and launched into a chase. The other spirits followed in deadly silence.

"And you are certain they will find their prey?" the Crimson Robe asked.

Ozun nodded, pale and frail after casting the spell. "Nothing escapes my *yōkai*."

The Crimson Robe turned to the rest of his men who awaited further orders.

"Destroy this eyesore," he said, pointing at the earthen mound, his eyes glinting with grisly satisfaction, "I don't want a trace of the Ancients to remain."

CHAPTER VIII

Captain Kiyomasa came up to the campfire and poked it with a stick.

"This fire will go out in an hour," he said, "bring more wood."

Two guardsmen rushed to carry out the order. He clasped his eyes with his palm in exasperation.

"No, no, no, no! Never leave your post together, how many times have I told you?"

"Apologies, Captain Kiyomasa," the two soldiers bowed.

Kiyomasa sighed.

"You stay here – you get the firewood," he ordered. When the younger of the watchmen disappeared into the dark cedar forest, the Captain sat down on a log and gestured to the older of the soldiers to join him.

"I know what you think. I'm too rigid. A martinet. No, don't protest. Every night I make sure the watch is set up properly, the fires are lit, the weapons are at the ready. But you must understand, I don't do it for my own benefit."

He waited for a prompt, but the soldier was too overwhelmed by the presence of his superior to speak out.

"It's because of those highborn, the samurai," he continued, "they are not used to being in an army. You've seen them, a band of arrogant snobs. Each thinks himself equal to another – and they all think they're better than me. They would never follow my orders. I can't command them, but I can give them an example. Perhaps observing how disciplined you common footmen are will inspire them to act as warriors should."

The soldier nodded, then opened his mouth and licked his lips.

"You may speak."

"Forgive me, Captain… I don't understand. What are we even doing here?"

"You know the reason. We are to escort Nariakira-*dono*'s daughter across these wild mountains."

"But… thirty of Kumamoto's finest samurai and a troop of footmen? Who would dare to even think of attacking such a force?"

"I don't know. These matters are as over my head as yours. All I know is that I've got my orders and you have yours, and we must do our best not to neglect our duties."

Kiyomasa was lying. He had received his own secret orders directly from the *daimyo* on the day of their departure. He was one of the two people in the entire entourage who knew about the real treasure hidden at the Kirishima Shrine.

Twice already had a messenger arrived on horseback from the castle, carrying a coded message from lord Hosokawa, and rode back with the answer. The missives exchanged did not bring him peace of mind. The *daimyo* was just as unsure of what to do as the Captain. Were they to charge the shrine and capture the dragon by force from Satsuma guards? But that would mean an open conflict between the two *daimyo*, who had until now been staunch allies and, ostentatiously, friends. Wait and observe, hoping for a solution to arrive? They did not have that much time; the princess was expected at Edo in a month and that meant she had to depart Kirishima at most within a week from now.

"He's taking his time," he said, nodding towards the trees.

"There's something wrong with this forest, don't you think, Captain? It gives me goose bumps whenever I stray too far from the camp."

Kiyomasa nodded. The wood sprawling the steep slopes of Mount Takachiho was unlike any he had ever seen. The cedar trees grew into twisted and bent shapes instead of straight majestic pillars. Outcrops of sharp volcanic rock scattered among the wild ferns were bathed in the yellow vapours descending from the summits. No animals lived here apart from snakes and crows.

He stared into the evening mist and spat in disgust. He had never wished so badly to be back in Kumamoto.

Bran woke at dawn and looked around. The girls were still asleep, but Dōraku was sitting a few feet away, observing an azalea bush, a paper scroll on his lap and a painting brush in hand.

He yawned and walked behind the samurai to look at the paper over his shoulder. He expected to see a simple sketch, one that a pretentious warrior would draw to while away a sleepless night. The flower on paper, though marked with a few quick strokes of black ink, seemed more real, more alive than the one hanging from a twig. Again, Bran felt a twang of envy, recalling his own clumsy attempts at drawing.

Is there no limit to this man's talents?

Dōraku finished his sketch, stretched out the scroll, looked at it and nodded with satisfaction. He left the paper to dry, pinning it to the warm ground with four pebbles.

"Ah, you're awake," he said, noticing Bran behind him. His face was even more pale than usual, and his movements seemed slower, less energetic.

So even he can get tired.

"What do you think?" the samurai asked, nodding at the scroll.

"It's… astonishing." Bran couldn't lie.

"Yes, I'm rather glad of it myself," the samurai smiled and for the first time Bran saw him genuinely pleased about something. "You know, I once spent five years trying to capture the beauty of a peony flower."

A peony flower…?

The samurai put the writing utensils into one of the containers hanging from his sash.

"What do you keep in all those pouches?" Bran asked.

"Ink pillow, thread and needle, *tabako*, *yuzu* sauce, *shichimi* spice…" the samurai recited out. "Everything a man needs on the road."

"And the big one?"

"That's salt."

"*Salt?*"

"I guess I'm a little superstitious," Dōraku said, chuckling quietly. "They say some kinds of demons are afraid of salt."

"That's a lot to carry around just because of some superstition."

The samurai smirked.

"Some demons are bigger than others."

Bran started rolling up the bedding. The clouds had cleared a little, and from their position near the summit of Takachiho he could see far down towards the cedar forests covering the slope, and beyond, into the valleys.

"Is that the town of Kirishima?" he asked, looking at the chequered board of fields and orchards below the forest. There was a blue ribbon of a river flowing down from the mountains to the north and, where it turned west to circumnavigate another mountain, spread a small town of grey- and blue-roofed houses.

Dōraku nodded.

Several large structures of red brick stood on a hill on the outskirts of the town, across the river. They looked out of place in this otherwise idyllic landscape; the sprawling buildings reminded Bran of sleeping monsters, spewing white smoke from their nostrils high into the sky. It had taken him a while to realise what he was looking at. The last time he had seen buildings like those was in Brigstow.

"Are these… " Bran struggled to speak. His knowledge of Yamato failed him: there seemed to be no word for a *factory* in this language. "What *are* these?" he asked at last, pointing to the red brick buildings.

"The great workshops of Satsuma, boy; the first of many. That's a brewery, if I'm not mistaken, and that's a steel plant. The third one wasn't there the last time I was here."

"Where's the Shrine?"

"Higher up the slope, on the edge of the forest. You can't see it from here."

"I'm not sure we'll make it there this afternoon."

"There's a good road halfway down that lumberjacks use. It's not going to be like the last two days."

For an instant he tensed, his eyes narrowed.

"What is it?"

"Wake the others. There is something… odd in the air."

The girls woke and, after quickly eating a small, dry breakfast of pickles and rice cakes, they moved out hurriedly, urged on by Dōraku.

Bran kept thinking about the peony drawings. The memory lingered at the back of his mind, irritatingly. It was the same with Nagomi and her father. Another stirred recollection. If only he could stop, clear his head…

They walked for about a mile at a hurried pace. Dōraku's serious mood spread, and Bran was now also sensing some kind of hard to pinpoint dread. He looked to the girls – they were also silent, grim. None of them was saying anything.

He heard a faint howl in the distance, then another. Dōraku slowed down; he looked back toward the volcanic road as if searching something along the northern horizon, his whole body rigid and alert, like a hound that had caught the scent of its prey.

"What's going on?" asked Satō, but the samurai gestured to them to keep quiet and continue their march towards the trees. He sniffed the air. His neck stiffened, his gaze focused at a point along the ridge. His hands wrapped around the hilts of the two swords stuck in the sash.

"Keep walking at a normal pace," he said sternly, "but when I say run, run into the forest. Try to get to the road, there should be people there."

"What is it?" Bran repeated Satō's question. "More bandits?"

"I don't know yet – it's… something else. Look, there it is."

A grey dot appeared over the ridge, then another, and more. Soon there were dozens of them, running down the mountain in a tight pack.

Bran reached into the satchel for his spyglass.

"Are these… wolves?" The pack easily numbered twenty, thirty, maybe more animals. And still more were coming.

Dōraku drew his swords in a smooth, perfect, noiseless move. The blades glittered in the sun. The swords thirsted for blood.

"Go, now," he said.

"We can fight them," opposed Satō, "it's just some wolves. We are stronger here, near the vortex."

"These are not normal wolves. And they are after me, not you."

"How do you know? *What's going on?*"

"Does it matter? He's right, we need to get to that forest, it's too dangerous here in the open," Bran said, thrusting his spyglass into the satchel. He pulled Nagomi with him towards the trees.

"Satō! Come, I'm sure he'll manage."

"But…"

"Run, now!" the samurai barked at the wizardess. His cold, fierce eyes demanded obedience. For a moment, Satō hesitated. But the pack now grew to a horde, a sea of grey poured over the ridge down the slope, an immeasurable, unnatural multitude of blood-thirsty animals. There couldn't possibly have been so many of them in the entire forest. At last the wizardess started running alongside Bran and Nagomi.

They were a few hundred yards nearer the trees when the first two of the pack reached Dōraku. His swords moved faster than a human eye could register and, with a yowl, both animals were slain. Instead of falling to the ground, however, they perished into thin air with a quiet flash. Three more wolves jumped on the samurai. He cut them down in one smooth strike. Still more came, and still more appeared over the ridge, an unending army of vengeful ghosts. Dōraku's arms turned into a whirlwind of steel as he fought against the onslaught, but his body remained calm and still.

"They're coming towards us," Bran said. A few of the ghostly attackers ran past the samurai. He tried to pick up the pace, but Nagomi could not run any faster.

"I'm… sorry…" she started, panting, but Bran silenced her.

"Save your energy. We're almost there."

Far in the distance, on the barren mountainside, Dōraku's outline was barely visible under the attack of countless wolves, now swarming from every direction, swamping him under the sea of grey fur.

They ran into the shadows of the tall cedar trees, but the wolves kept on running. One of them caught the hem of Satō's *hakama* in its teeth. The girl stumbled, drew her sword and cut through the animal's body. It disappeared in the same white flash as those slain by Dōraku. The other two wolves turned away and started running alongside the runaways, safely out of range of Satō's sword.

"The blade works against them!"

"If we stop now there will be too many for us to fight," said Bran, "if we get to the road, maybe we can find help."

As he glanced at the wolves running beside them – two more appeared on their left, seeking to encircle their prey – he thought he noticed something else in the forest, deeper among the trees. A glimpse of… crimson? His blood froze. *Are the wolves just a ruse?*

He ran out onto a wide dirt road. The wolves jumped behind them, but hesitated to attack, growling uncertainly. Bran turned around to see what made the animals stop. On the road before him stood a company of about thirty samurai, accompanied by foot soldiers, servants and porters.

"What's the hold-up?" a voice asked in a commanding tone. An important-looking samurai came forth to the front. He was short, stocky and round-faced.

"Why are we not moving? I want to be in the Shrine by evening! Oh…"

He stopped, seeing the three travellers and the wolves behind them. He frowned.

Bran noticed the symbol embroidered on the samurai's kimono. The same symbol had been stitched onto the soldiers' cloaks and banners on the horses. The eight circles; the crest of lord Hosokawa of Kumamoto.

He clenched the hilt of his sword tightly and made a step forward.

Two young samurai and a girl wearing the travelling clothes of a priestess stood on the road; a straw hood fell from her head, revealing her hair – red like a fox's fur…

The wolf growled, then another came out onto the road, head low, teeth bared. More howled, hidden among the trees. Kiyomasa counted at least a dozen of the beasts. What got into them? He had never heard of the wolves behaving in such manner, not even in the harshest of winters.

One of the boys, wearing a dark blue kimono, stepped forward, holding a long sword. There was fear and determination in his eyes.

"I am Captain Kiyomasa Katō, son of Kiyotada, of Kumamoto castle guards," the Captain introduced himself formally, "who are you?"

The boy eased a little and looked back to his companions.

"Please help us," said the other of the youths in a high-pitched voice. "We are pilgrims on our way to Kirishima". His vest was black and his kimono vermillion, like the pillars of a *torii* gate. Kiyomasa had never seen one of this colour.

The wolves, apprehensive at first, now started moving towards the group, growling quietly. The eyes of their brethren blazed among the trees. The horses in the train started neighing in fright, as they felt the pack close in from both sides.

His men whispered among themselves.

"Goblins! Demons! This damned forest..."

"Come," he said, gesturing at the three youths to join the convoy. "I don't think those wolves will attack thirty samurai, but even if they do, we're sure to make short work of them," he boasted, trying to encourage himself as well as the strangers.

"Thank you, Captain," the boy in the blue kimono said, bowing – though not deeply enough, Kiyomasa noted. He bore himself with the arrogance of a high-born samurai.

Kiyomasa gave the signal to march onwards, but nothing happened.

"What now?"

"It's the wolves, Captain," reported the sergeant, "they're not moving." The animals stood a few paces from the front of the group, growling fiercely. The soldiers lowered their halberds and the wolves' eyes lit up with an unnatural glow. The air in the forest turned cold, the mist smelled of blood.

The Captain, his hair standing on end, murmured a short prayer to the Goddess of War. *Benzaiten-sama, give me strength in combat and valour in death.* He drew his sword and marched towards the closest of the wolves. He stomped the ground in an attempt to frighten the animal, but the wolf only growled back, showing its sharp teeth.

"Kuso!"

Kiyomasa slashed his sword, aiming for the head. The wolf disappeared in a flash. The Captain fell on his bottom in surprise, and everyone else gasped in terror.

"Inugami! The *yōkai* are back!"

The wolves sprang from all sides in silence. Lord Hosokawa's samurai started slashing around at random, some hid behind the horses and the wagons.

The servants dropped their loads and ran away. But Kiyomasa's soldiers stood their ground, forming a triangle of spears around him and the three travellers.

"They may be ghosts, but they can be cut by steel," Kiyomasa cried to his men. He noticed the two boys joining him in the fray. The girl stood in the middle of the convoy, praying. A pale aura of sanctity surrounded her, repelling the *yōkai*. The beasts attacked in waves, without fear or remorse. One of Kumamoto's retainers fell down with a ghostly animal at his throat, then another. There seemed to be no end to the demonic pack; the samurai got pushed away from the footmen; the defenders were stretched dangerously thin, their line breaking. Another soldier fell down with a gurgling cry.

Like a herd of deer, thought Kiyomasa. *They will pick us off one by one. But the deer don't fight back!*

"Form an arrowhead!" he cried an order. The soldiers obeyed instantly, setting themselves up in a tight wedge of glistening spears.

"Charge!"

His fear disappeared completely, replaced by the rush of exhilaration. This was no exercise! This was a real battle, the likes of which he had only dreamt of. His entire soldier's training led up to this moment.

He led the charge against the wolves, chasing the demons back into the forest from which they were emerging. His men cried and died, their throats, thighs and stomachs torn by the ghostly fangs, but they pushed on. Out of the corner of his eye he saw the two boys fighting alongside the soldiers. They fought well.

And then, as suddenly as they had appeared, all the wolves vanished. The forest was silent.

The losses were grave. Five of Kumamoto's retainers were dead, either slain by their own companions' indiscriminate hacking, or torn apart by the wolves. Six more were too wounded to walk on their own and had to be carried on stretchers. Of the footmen, a third were either dead or incapacitated. Blood turned the sand of the road into mud.

"I lost many good men here!" the Captain burst out, feeling his face turn hot. "I demand to know what just happened! It's no coincidence –"

"Captain Kiyomasa!"

He scowled hearing the shrill voice.

"Gensai-*dono*," he said calmly, bowing before the young, fierce-faced samurai. Kawakami Gensai was one of lord Hosokawa's most trusted men. He emerged from the battle unscathed, but Kiyomasa knew it was not because he had strayed from a fight.

"There are wounded men awaiting your attention, Captain. I will take care of our noble guests."

The military convoy turned into a funeral procession as the bodies of the slain samurai were put on the wagons. The servants and soldiers were buried on the spot in the hard volcanic soil. At Master Kawakami's request Nagomi had agreed to oversee the funeral rites.

The samurai poured saké from his own flask into two small white cups and offered it to Bran and Satō.

"I've heard stories about the *yōkai* of Satsuma forests, but I never imagined I'd see them with my own eyes," he said. The corners of his mouth twitched slightly under the thin moustache and Bran realised this was Master Kawakami's way of smiling.

Thick, dark eyebrows accentuated a plain, strong face. His hair was tied in a tight ball-like bun, stretching the skin on his forehead in what must have caused constant irritation. A thin, badly stitched scar ran from the corner of his right eye towards the ear.

"We were just as surprised," said Satō.

"Oh, I'm sure, I'm sure. But what were you doing off the main road? These mountains are not hospitable to lonely strangers, even without demons roaming about."

"We... got lost in the mist," Bran said. This excuse had worked once before. The samurai narrowed his eyes and his lips twitched again.

"I hear you're both good with the sword," he changed the subject. "We must spar later. You're on your way to the Kirishima Shrine, aren't you?"

"Yes."

"This little affair set us back a few hours, but we should reach it before night. Ah, I believe the young priestess returns. That hair of hers is quite remarkable. We best be on our way, lest Captain Kiyomasa gets all irritable again."

The samurai's lip twitched one last time.

"He suspects something," Bran said to Satō quietly.

"Obviously. You should've let me speak to him."

"And what would you have told him?"

"I'd certainly come up with a better explanation than being *lost in the mist.*"

Nagomi joined them, wiping water off her hands.

"Do you think Dōraku-*sama...?*"

"Who knows," said Bran, "but we must assume the worst."

"That's twice he's saved our lives," said Satō, "we need to honour his memory."

Bran let his mind wander, observing the soldiers marching around him with curiosity. The only other time he had seen Yamato footmen was at the picket in Kumamoto, but Captain Kiyomasa's men seemed much more like a real army than those shivering guardsmen. They bore a range of weapons, spears, swords, long-barrelled rifles of antiquated design, but he was most interested in their *naginata* glaives. They consisted of long curved, widening blades attached to wobbly bamboo poles. They looked remarkably similar to his father's golden

Soul Lance. He asked one of the soldiers to let him hold it for a while; it was well balanced and hefty. It felt good in his hands.

Once out of the cedar forest, the road descended steeply towards the market town spread below the Kirishima Shrine, amongst a thick carpet of pink-blooming azaleas and, further down, vast tea plantations. The sky was hazy grey.

It was the time of the harvest. The white headscarves and pointy straw hats of peasants bobbed up and down between the bushes as they filled baskets with freshly picked leaves. Bran had never seen a tea plantation up close. He wondered how the thick, moist green leaves were transformed into the hard, black brick with which he was more familiar. The Yamato *cha* was served either as a bright green, foamy, soup-like liquid or a yellowish-green drink, bitter and refreshing. Neither of those resembled the 'tea' he knew from home.

"Milk and sugar," he said, tracing his fingers over the young tea leaves.

"What?"

"We drink *cha* with milk and sugar," he repeated.

"Ugh!" Satō said. "Why would anyone do that?"

Bran shrugged. "It's just a custom... we like sweet things. I've heard that in Shambhala, in the mountains west of Qin, they eat the leaves with butter and salt. Everyone has their own way."

"Did you hear about the Way of Tea?" Satō asked. "I studied it, but only got as far as folding the cloth. It's very difficult."

"The Way of Tea?"

"The *Cha* Ceremony, a proper way to drink powdered *cha*." She then started to describe a complex and highly ritualised procedure. He tried his best to feign interest, but quickly got lost in the many small rules.

"You'll have to teach me later, when this is all over," he said when she finished and thought, *Liar. There will be no "later".*

A group of nearby labourers in red sashes and dark blue tunics erupted into song. The first harvest must have been a joyous occasion to the entire community.

Without the Cursed Weed money, you would have no tea for breakfast, Bran remembered his father's words from Fan Yu. He imagined the Yamato peasants lying on the side of the road, their minds addled with laudanum, as clipper ships filled with cheap tea sailed from Kiyō harbour to Lundenburgh.

Satō shook him by the shoulder – the road turned abruptly and he was almost about to walk straight through the tea bushes.

"What is it?" she asked with concern. "Suddenly you've grown all dour."

"You told me once your father desired a change for Yamato... but what if the change brought only more suffering?"

"You mean like in Qin?"

"You know what happened in Qin?"

"Of course! Everyone was shocked to hear of the humiliation brought upon the Emperor..."

"It's not the Emperor you need to worry about, but the people."

"How do you mean?"

He told her briefly of his experiences in Fan Yu. She stared at him with her eyes growing wide, but when he finished, she shook her head.

"This would never have happened here. The days of Qin's glory are long past, but Yamato is still strong and virile. It just needs some reforms…"

"I may know little of the situation here, but I've seen enough of the world outside. If the Westerners – if *we* come in force, do you think we will be impressed by your reforms? By your swordsmanship, by your calligraphy, by your *cha* ceremonies?"

"If your people do come in force, we will fight them and remove them from our lands – or die trying," she said with defiance, her hand inadvertently reaching for the sword.

"Then you will die trying," he replied unhappily.

CHAPTER IX

Ardian ab Ifor was sitting at his desk in the cabin on the first deck, buried in some papers. Samuel tried to discuss with him Bran's upcoming birthday, but the Ardian paid him no attention, mumbling something in response.

"I'm sorry?" said Samuel.

The Ardian raised his head and repeated the murmuring. It had a strange, droning quality, like the monotone hum of a mistfire engine. It filled the entire cabin, drowning out all other sounds.

The Doctor woke up. He was on a canvas bunk bed. The droning sound continued in the darkness. He reached out and his hand touched a cold metal surface, vibrating in tune with the hum.

A curtain opened, letting in some light from a table lamp. A bearded man in a green cloak looked at him intensely.

"*Gut*. You waked," he said with the harsh Varyagan accent.

"I… yes, I am awake," Samuel replied weakly. "Are you a doctor?"

He was still dizzy and nauseated. The bearded man nodded and handed him a bowl to retch into; Samuel gestured it wasn't necessary.

"I'm a doctor too. Samuel Ben Hagin," he said.

"I am Magnus Ingvarsson," the other man said, shaking Samuel's hand. "You rest now. I bring Admiral."

Admiral?

"Please, just tell me – where am I? What is this place?"

Ingvarsson smiled but said nothing. He turned around and disappeared down a long, narrow corridor.

The Admiral was a short man, like all sailors on this mysterious vessel but, unlike the others, was clean shaven except for abundant sideburns, flaxen yellow like the rest of his hair. A large, straight nose dominated a determined face.

The cabin they were in had rounded walls, made of thick metal sheets joined with thick iron rivets, and was very sparsely equipped except for a console filled with gauges, switches and dials beside the Admiral's table. There was a small, thick-framed round window in one of the walls, but Samuel could see nothing but darkness behind it. The constant, irritating humming filled this place as well. The air was stuffy, smelling of dozens of men cramped in tight quarters.

"Fridrik Otterson," he said simply instead of a greeting.

"Admiral, I hear."

"Well, *ja*, but let's not dwell on *formalitaet* too much. What were you doing in the middle of the ocean? We saw no other castaways and heard of no Western shipwrecks in these seas."

"I drifted off far from where my ship sank. We were at anchor before Huating."

"That is far indeed! You were very lucky we found you at all. We're *tva* hundred and fifty miles north-by-northeast from Huating."

Samuel recalled the navigation charts with some difficulty – his head was still spinning.

"You're headed for Chosun?"

The Admiral laughed.

"*Nej, herr Doktor.*"

"But… there is no other land between here and Tyr Gorllewin. Unless you're trying to reach…"

"The fabled islands of Yamato? *Ja,* that is exactly where we're going."

Samuel leaned back in his chair and tried to gather his thoughts.

"The storms… the maze of waves… the navigation problems," he said, trying to remember all the many reasons he knew for nobody but the Bataavians being able to reach Yamato.

"All of this, we have discovered, working only on the surface of the sea," said the admiral, smiling.

"This ship…" Samuel understood at last. "We're sailing under water!"

A buzzer sounded on the steel wall. The admiral pressed a button on his console. The heavy round door swung open and into the cabin came another man, silver-haired, wearing a dinner jacket and round metal glasses. In his hand he held a pocket watch on a chain that he kept checking nervously.

"*Doktor* Nobelius," the admiral introduced him. "The finest naval inventor in the *Khaganatet.*"

"Honoured," said Samuel.

"Likewise," said Nobelius swiftly. "*Amiral,* in ten minutes we need to make another *tryckkontroll*… A pressure check," he added for Samuel's benefit.

"*Ach, ja, Doktor.* We'll be right with you."

The inventor left hastily.

"I'm guessing the existence of this ship is supposed to be a secret," said Samuel.

"Oh, it is – for now. But you won't be telling anyone in the West about it for a while. We've set our course and will not surface until we are in *Dejeema.*"

Dejeema. The name invoked an even greater sense of mystery.

"The *Khaganatet* has been trying to chart these seas for years," the Admiral continued, "ever since we've reached the coast of the *Stora Havet* – the Great Ocean – and built the harbour at Alexisborg. We have learned many *sekret* – the Bataavians are not as good at keeping them as they think. But, we wanted to make sure we knew what we were doing. There is only one such *boot* in the world and we didn't want to lose her."

"Just like *Ladon,*" said Samuel quietly, remembering the vastness of his own ship.

Each nation is trying to outdo everyone else in making the machines of war… where will this race end?

"Pardon? Anyway, we found out we were late to the party. Another power is heading for Yamato as we speak. Hence our hurry – and the poor *Doktor*'s *angslan*… uneasiness. This *boot* was never properly tested."

"Another power? Not the Dracaland – I would know…"

"You wouldn't," said the Admiral with a laugh, "but *nej*, it's not the Dracaland. Nor Breizh, nor Midgard, nor any of the old ones. There's a new child in the nursery, as they say, and it's eyeing Yamato as its new *leksak*… new toy. And if we don't hurry there will be nothing left of it to share."

A sailor appeared in the cabin's round door and cleared his throat.

"*Ach, ja, naturligtvis.* Nobelius is waiting. Excuse me, *Doktor* – you may return to the infirmary. And it's probably best if you hold on to something for the next ten minutes."

Three loud whistles echoed throughout the vessel. He heard many heavy boots running to and fro around the deck amid barked orders. The tongue of the Varyagas, like those of their Western kin in Midgard and Niflheimr, was most suited to pronouncing orders, he had always thought.

Their vast empire stretched across two continents, from the cold Venedian Sea in the West all the way to the borders of Qin in the East. Most of this enormous landmass was poor and inhospitable – dark northern forests or arid open steppe, with little value other than some furs and fish; but the Varyagas possessed an insatiable hunger for land and discovery, a legacy of their Norse ancestry. It did not surprise Samuel that once the Varyaga explorers had reached the Great Ocean, the Khaganate decided to push still further eastwards, beyond the known charts.

He felt the change in the air pressure in his ears and then the bulkheads started creaking and groaning worryingly. Within five minutes everything was over; another three whistles announced the end of the pressure test.

He lost count of the many exercises and training routines the crew of the *Diana*, the underwater ship, had performed over the past two weeks. He would have lost the count of days if it hadn't been for the calendars hanging on the wall of almost every cabin. The vessel surfaced only by night, to replenish the air stored in Doctor Nobelius's ingenious tanks, and nobody but the maintenance crew was allowed outside.

Samuel had been allowed to see the outside world through the round window in the Admiral's cabin, but he saw only the gloomy, dusty murkiness, barely illuminated by a faint evertorch. On one occasion the Admiral showed him the surface through *Diana's* periscope. He realised immediately they were in the middle of the famous sea maze. The storm waves rolled back and forth in random directions, heedless of the prevailing winds; the clouds and mists covered the sky and the horizon with an impenetrable curtain of grey. All the navigation devices behaved as if broken. Only after submerging the ship to below a hundred feet the compass started showing north again.

"How do the Bataavians get through this?" he asked the Admiral later.

"There is one route always open clear for them. Every year they send only one ship. A sailing ship, mind – the Yamato do not allow *maskines*... engines. And when it returns with cargo it also brings the details of what the route will be the next year – for it always changes. It is a much more elaborate system than the crude *barriaer* of the Qin."

"Is Yamato really worth all this effort?"

"I have spoken to a *Midgaerd* spy who sailed on their ship once – he told me of the riches the land keeps; there is *koppar*, *kamfor*, silks, cotton, *porselin*... but most of all, there are people who were, he said, among the most ingenious he had ever met. The years he had spent on *Dejeema* had been the best of his life – and he had travelled far and wide. And they are fiendishly clever. It is a waste to keep a nation like that under lock and key."

"But they obviously wish to keep their doors closed from us."

"The rulers, maybe. But Philip – the *spion* – told me there were many people in Yamato who demanded a change. All they need is a little... *assistans* from outside. The Bataavians are too weak and too set in their ways for this."

"So this is not just about taking the Bataavians' place," Samuel guessed. "You want to start a revolution. That's a bold ambition for a commander of a single ship."

"A ship that can sail under water, mind. But my mission is just a beginning. If I succeed, we will build more ships like *Diana*, merchant ships and war ships and eventually the rulers of Yamato will realise the *futilitet* of their boundaries."

"And what about that other... *Power* you've mentioned?"

"One thing at a time, *Doktor*. For now my greatest worry is reaching *Dejeema* in one piece. The closer we seem to be to Yamato, the deeper we have to go to avoid the effects of this sea *labyrint*. Hence all the tests and exercises."

"How deep can this ship go, if need be?"

"We don't know," Otterson smiled. "We have never sailed as deep as we are at the moment."

Samuel wriggled uneasily in his chair. The creaking of the bulkheads overhead suddenly seemed a lot more ominous.

The Bohan had set up his headquarters in the same stone-and-water gardens that the Heavenly Army had used during their brief hold on Huating. Dylan landed his dragon on a square in the middle of the walled city, surrounded on all sides with tall buildings of white walls and black tile roofs. The town was loud and crowded with refugees, soldiers and merchants. The guards led him through a sculpted gate past a tall wall and immediately the din quietened, replaced by the babbling of water and the chirping of sparrows.

The paths in the garden were as angular as the wrinkles on Bohan's face, a convoluted labyrinth of bridges and gates designed, not out of convenience, but following some greater, Heavenly scheme. At select places stood intricately eroded stones or statues, pavilions overlooking flower ponds or grand old trees, with boughs sprawling like wooden snakes, supported by bamboo poles. Dylan knew there was nothing random about the placement of these features; the Qin left nothing to chance.

Following the guards, he was trying instinctively to map the garden paths in his head, but soon gave up. He had seen the Gardens from dragonback; it was just a tiny space in the middle of the bustling city. But they had been walking now for far longer than it would take to traverse this space from one side to another in a straight line, and they seemed no closer to their destination.

I am literally a-mazed, he thought, with a chuckle which made one of the guards look back at him and frown.

Another gate and another wall appeared before him on top of which coiled a dragon sculpted out of blue clay tiles. Past this wall the garden was even quieter, only an early cicada buzzed in the top of a great pine tree.

This tree must have been planted when this place was just a village, Dylan thought, admiring the gnarled, twisted, blackened trunk.

The guards stopped.

"Please," the Bohan gestured him to follow further, into an expansive bungalow, the walls of which were open and airy, carved with intricate latticework of wood and lacquer. This was the largest and most opulent building Dylan had seen so far in the Gardens.

The Bohan led him along a corridor of wooden planks, polished to such perfection that they seemed to be covered with glass. Water trickled in a covered gutter alongside, cooling the entire house down. His navy boots squeaked on the slippery surface and he was finding it hard to keep up with the pointy-bearded man without stumbling. At last they reached their destination – a small square room. Red lanterns stood on black iron stands in the corner; a golden screen showing a coiling dragon adorned the opposite wall. The Bohan closed the door behind them carefully.

A table of polished wood stood in the middle of the room on four tall legs of eroded stone. On the table lay several thick brushes, an ink stone, several pieces of paper, a lacquer tray filled with what looked like sand and a copper brazier in which blue fire burned. Dylan immediately sensed magic.

"Sit, please," the Bohan pointed to two chairs on both sides of the table. "We shall write a formal request to the *tai-pan* at Fan Yu."

He reached for the brush and paper and Dylan dictated what should be written. When they finished, the Bohan blew on the ink, rolled the paper carefully and dropped it into the flaming brazier.

He turned to Dylan with a smile.

"It will take a moment to decipher the message and deliver a reply. Let's have some tea."

The Ardian knew better not to question what had just happened. At his host's signal the golden screen slid apart, revealing a hidden entrance. Two men entered the room. One was a servant carrying a pot of fragrant, straw-coloured tea and two white china cups. The other wore the robes and the hat of a priest. He held a sharpened bamboo rod in his hands.

The Bohan poured the tea from on high, splashing it all over the tray – a sign of luxury. By the time Dylan had finished his second cup, the priest staggered, touching his forehead with his fingers.

"Ah, good," said the Bohan, "it was faster than I expected."

The priest rolled his eyes up and started to shiver in spiritual ecstasy. The servant who had brought the tea now guided his hand holding the bamboo rod over the sand tray.

The rod trembled and started moving, as if on its own, writing Qin letters in the sand. The Bohan copied them onto paper. The message was brief, but the priest seemed exhausted by the ordeal and the servant had to escort him out of the room.

"The ship will be dispatched in two days, with the right of passage through Ederra Strait," the Bohan read out the characters.

"That means they will be here in a week," said Dylan, still reeling from what he had just seen. At last, here was the explanation of the astonishing speed with which information seemed to travel throughout the Qin Empire. He pointed to the sand tray.

"What – what was that?"

"Magic," the Bohan replied with a self-satisfied grin.

The vast watery expanse of the Qian River spread like a narrow sea between the tall pagoda underneath which Dylan had set up camp and the opposite shore, almost two miles away.

"You were right, Ardian," the Admiral said, studying the brown, stormy waters through the long, heavy telescope attached to his iron hand. "Hard to believe that's not the Sea. I could wage an entire battle between these shores."

"Perhaps you will have it, if we fail to establish a bridgehead."

"Are you certain this is necessary? I could defend this crossing with a few gunboats for years."

"It's not just the crossing. There's a trade port on the other side that the rebels might use as an alternative to Huating. We have orders to assist the Imperial Army in its capture, if we can."

The Admiral ran his fingers through the balding hair and sighed.

"Ah, politics. How I loathe it. Interfering with a good war."

"Sir?"

"I also got new orders yesterday. Once this here battle is over, I'm taking my ships up north, to Ta Du. Don't worry – there are a few gunboats coming to take my place, and the Qin fleet is supposedly on its way. You shouldn't be lacking in ships."

Dylan frowned. "I haven't heard of any new developments over there."

"I don't know what's going on either – but we can both guess it's going to be something big."

They both nodded in silence. The storm clouds and crow flocks had not yet been fully dispersed here in the south and already they had started gathering elsewhere.

There is always war in Qin, he remembered his son's words. Bran – for the first time in weeks he recalled the boy's face, his voice. He looked eastwards, where the great river entered a broad, funnel-shaped bay of the Qin Sea. A line of Reynolds's warships obscured the horizon, reminding him instantly of the upcoming battle.

"Let's make the best of what time we have, then," Dylan said with a dry smile.

He gazed down on the camp. Three thousand men in blue uniforms busied themselves among the white tents – an army with no name. It seemed an impossible task to train so many soldiers in such a short time, and yet he had succeeded – with great help from his lieutenants and officers of the Twelfth Light Dragoons. The dragons of both regiments rested in the hastily built stables a bit further to the west. There had been little need for them so far – the rebel scouting parties had fled as soon as they saw their glinting scales in the sky. Both the men and the beasts itched for a fight.

"You know, Ardian," the Admiral spoke just as they were about to return to the camp, "I've been thinking lately about what happened to your son."

Over the few weeks, the two men had exchanged many tales. Reynolds knew now with details the story of *Ladon*'s final journey, and they had both agreed that the Ifor serving under the Admiral in the days of the Kyrnosian Emperor must have been Dylan's father.

"Sir?"

"I had a certain idea of my own… but it will have to wait until after the battle. Look, here she comes," the Admiral said, pointing downstream, "our signal."

A ripple formed on the horizon, which grew fast to a white foaming wave, stretching from shore to shore. A giant tidal bore, many times greater than the famous wave at Môr Hafren in Gwynedd, rushed towards them with the speed – and sound – of a steaming omnibus, taking everything with it. Only the most tightly anchored vessels could withstand its terrible force.

Dylan knew that the Heavenly Army on the other shore also waited for the wave to pass towards the floodplains upstream. There would be a full day to attempt the crossing before another bore came rumbling down from the sea.

"Now there's a sight," the Admiral said, his eyes gleaming with youthful joy, "I'm glad I came all this way to see it. Ardian – " he continued, turning to Dylan as the crest of the wave roared deeply beneath them, "I believe it is time. To battle!"

"To battle!"

There was a soft knock on the workshop door, barely a scratch, so quiet that Master Tanaka had not heard it at first, too busy with adjusting the pressure points of his new mistfire engine.

The knocking repeated, louder this time.

"I'm busy," the mechanician murmured.

"Hisashige-*sama*!" A commanding voice spoke.

Master Tanaka dropped the octagometer and hurried to open the door. He lay prostrate on the floor.

"*Kakka!* I am most sorry, I was not informed of your visit – "

"I am glad to hear that. This is not an official visit, and I'm not here in my capacity of the *daimyo*. Please, stand up, Tanaka-*sensei.*"

The lord of the Saga province, Nabeshima Naomasa, entered the room. Even wearing the plain indigo clothes of a low-ranking samurai, the well-groomed, weary-eyed man exerted an unmistakable presence. Here was a man born and bred to rule. His ancestors were friends to the *Taikun*s, his domain's forces guarded the entry to the Kiyō harbour – arguably one of the most important positions in the Empire.

"Is this the engine you were telling me about?" the *daimyo* asked, stepping up to the desktop.

"Oh no, *kakka*. This is just a toy, a testing piece. The other one I had already brought down to the harbour."

"Do you think the boat is going to be faster than the Satsuma one?"

"Difficult to tell. They had the Bataavian plans, I had to figure out everything from scratch... I will be trying it out next week."

"I may need you to do it sooner."

"*Kakka?*"

The *daimyo* reached into his sleeve and took out a curious item: a small ball of cork with a dozen long black feathers glued to it.

"A Bataavian shuttlecock," said Hisashige. "I have received one too. But I do not yet know what it means."

"It's a message from the Overwizard of Dejima. It means one of *our own* is in danger, and we are called on to help in any way we can. And there is more. There have been many messages coming from Kiyō – strange and dire news."

"I was too busy with my experiments..."

"I know. That's why I decided to visit you and explain the situation personally."

The *daimyo* sat down on the straw matting and gestured the mechanician to do the same. Master Tanaka listened to the tale with increasing disquiet.

"So that's why I never heard from Shūhan-*sama* again... and here I thought he was just busy, like me. And Sakuma-*dono* returned to his Chūbu home... none of this bodes well."

"No," the *daimyo* agreed, "and this is why I have come to you for help. I need your divination machine."

Hisashige's face turned dark. "Why not ask the priests of Yutoku?"

"I have asked them for a general prophecy, but nothing detailed. I do not trust them as much as I trust you, *sensei*. Is something the matter?"

"My divinations are... not as accurate as they once have been. The future is strangely clouded. But I will endeavour my best."

The Inari Shrine of Yutoku, where Master Tanaka had his home and workshop set up, rose in many-pillared, vermillion terraces on a wooded slope overlooking a rapid, broad river. A tunnel of bright red *torii* gates lined the path descending towards the pier. The dawning sun cast a crimson shadow on the water.

He stood on the pier with two other men and a boy, his adopted son Daikichi. A long and narrow boat, of the kind used for cormorant fishing, was moored to a thick bollard, bobbing in the fast current. A great ironbound chest rested in the middle.

"I should be sending a detachment of my samurai," said Lord Naomasa. "They would be ready to go in one day."

"And they would reach Shimabara in four," replied Hisashige. "The eighth hexagram speaks plainly: *Whoever comes too late, meets with misfortune.* But if I'm not back in a week, please send your samurai, *kakka.*"

"At least allow me to accompany you, *sensei.* Or failing that, go in your place. It is a dangerous quest and you are not young."

The mechanician bowed his grey head. "The boat takes two, and only I know how to control the engine. Do not fear, *kakka*; for the eighth hexagram also says *there is a movement towards the union of the greats, and good fortune.* And the fifteenth hexagram adds *he who is humble employs the strength of his allies. Modesty brings good fortune.*"

Lord Naomasa laughed quietly. "How can a lowly *daimyo* discuss with the mighty oracle! Very well. Etō-*sama* will have to suffice for the entire force of the Saga province."

The third man bowed swiftly at the mention of his name. He was short and tense, his eyes darting left to right as if in constant expectation of a foe, his hand held on to the hilt of his sword.

Master Tanaka bowed back and then turned to the boy standing aside.

"Daikichi, take good care of my machines while I'm gone."

"Yes, Father."

"Remember to oil the gears and clean the pipes, as I have instructed you."

"Of course, Father."

The old mechanician opened his mouth once more, but then found nothing more to say and closed it again.

"Well, I'd better be off," he said, turning back to the *daimyo.*

"And you are certain of the direction of your journey?" asked Naomasa.

"The blood signal is still fresh in my head. I'm surprised you can't sense it."

"One more proof, if proof were needed, of my lack of any magical talent," said Naomasa with a sigh.

The intense pulsing of the blood magic beacon had reached Hisashige in his workshop the night before, when he still busy calibrating the divination circuit on his clock. He had recognised the spell signature right away; it was similar to the blood pattern he had been given by Shūhan to weave into the glove. Now he understood what the beacon meant. Takashima Shūhan was alive and desperate enough to call for help using the most forbidden type of Western magic.

"I will bring him back, *kakka,*" Master Tanaka said firmly.

He climbed into the narrow, wobbly boat carefully and held on to the mooring ropes waiting for Etō to join him. Daikichi untied the ropes and pushed the boat into the current. Etō stood up, grasping an oar and guided them downstream. The pier, the *daimyo* and the little boy soon disappeared into the dawn haze.

The river carried them swiftly past the small town and a bridge into the narrow inlet of the Ariake Sea. Hisashige waited until they were out in the open waters, out of sight of the shore. Morning sun was already high upon them when he reached for the iron-bound chest in the middle of the boat and opened it with a creak.

Inside was the small mistfire engine, a tangled mass of copper pipes, coils, valves, shafts and gears. He grasped a brass lever and pushed it forward, then turned two valves on the side of a large glass cylinder. He spoke the words of command. The elementals awoke slowly, released from their copper prisons into the cylinder. Steam rose inside an iron funnel when the seawater mixed with the emanations of the fire sprites. The entire boat trembled as the crankshaft turned.

"Careful, Etō-*sama,*" the mechanician said, pointing to the glistening iron rod rotating furiously under their feet without any protection. "I'm sorry, I did not have time to build a cover."

The samurai mumbled something and focused on the oar in his hand, now serving as the tiller. Hisashige pulled another switch inside the chest; a large gear clicked into place and suddenly the boat leapt forwards. Etō almost fell into the water, but held on to the edge of the boat valiantly. The water rippled behind them in a broad v-shaped wake.

"It worked, at first try!" Hisashige rejoiced. "And she *is* fast. Let's take it as a good omen for the rest of our journey!"

Etō only grunted as he struggled to keep the boat on course against the rolling waves.

CHAPTER X

A small square building of unpainted cypress wood stood not far from the shrine's main gate, overlooking the wide platform of the dance stage.

"It will be a noisy and smelly place in the evening," said Satō, wrinkling her nose.

The landlord bowed, his narrow eyes squinting apologetically.

"I beg your forgiveness, noble guests, but all other rooms have been reserved for Atsu-*hime* and her entourage. Perhaps you may find something more suitable in the town below?"

"Perhaps we should," she said, eyeing the building with contempt. *This is almost like going back to the stables.*

Bran pulled her aside.

"Remember what that monk at Unganzenji said? The demons can't stand anything holy. It may be just a legend, but I wouldn't take my chances. We're safer here, on the Shrine grounds."

"Very well, we'll take what you have left," Satō told the landlord.

"Settling yourselves in?"

Master Kawakami approached them from the direction of a larger, far richer building nearer the main hall, where he and other Hosokawa retainers had their accommodation.

"Almost, Gensai-*sama*," Satō said with a bow.

"Let me know if you need anything. I still want to clash swords with you later."

"It's a wonder he hasn't recognized us yet," Satō whispered as the samurai passed under the main gate and descended towards the town, "with Nagomi's hair and my *Rangakusha* outfit…"

"These men were ahead of us in Hitoyoshi, and were moving slow," said Bran, "they must have marched out of Kumamoto a long time ago. Let's just hope they take that princess they came for and leave before they realise who we are."

"I don't think they're here just for the princess. That's not an escort, that's a war party."

"You don't think…"

They looked at each other in mutual understanding.

"Can you… sense the *dorako*?"

Bran closed his eyes and breathed in.

"Over there," he said, pointing towards a tall fence separating the shrine's public space from the inner sanctum. "They keep it in a cage. It's still asleep, but not for long… I can feel Emrys struggling to waken."

"*Emu- emris?*" she repeated.

He blinked at her.

"Emrys – my dragon. I never told you its name?"

"I didn't even know dragons had names."

"Of course they do. How do you think I call him? *Come here, dragon?*"

He chuckled.

"Naming a dragon is important," he added, "much more than a horse or a dog. It's a creature of magic, so there must be some magic in the name as well."

"And what does *Emris* mean?"

The dragon rider opened his mouth to speak, but then shook his head.

"That is a long tale to tell. Let's wait for supper, when Nagomi joins us."

"Ah! Supper! That's right."

She hadn't eaten a proper meal since leaving the shores of the Sendai River. The shrine fare was not much to expect, but at least it would have been warm – and made by somebody else.

The priestess was luckier than the two of them. She was allowed to live with the other priests and, in this way, she had gained access beyond the shrine's fence.

"They're making some repairs to the inner compound," she told them at supper. "Preparations for the festival – or so they said."

"A festival?" Satō asked.

"In three days there will be a *kagura* dance on that stage over there."

"There will be crowds."

"Hundreds, the priests tell me."

"This will be a good time to strike."

"*Strike?*"

Bran stared at her over the bowl of buckwheat noodles, frowning. He took a bite of a pickled herring and chewed it in silence for a moment.

"We haven't really thought this through, have we," he said, chuckling.

"No, we haven't."

Satō started to laugh as well. She had no idea what was so funny, but she couldn't stop until her sides started hurting. Nagomi looked at them both and then joined the laughter.

"We... we do have to come up with a plan now," the wizardess said at last, wiping tears from her eyes.

"First we need to find out exactly where and how Emrys is being held captive."

"*Emris?*" It was Nagomi's time to ask.

"You were supposed to tell us the story of the *dorako*'s name," said Satō.

Bran slurped the remaining noodles and gulped the broth from the bowl before speaking again.

"This is how my mother told me the tale, when I was a child," he began.

Satō leaned closer. Bran had never told her any legends from his country before.

"A long time ago – in the Age of Heroes – our land, the Island of Prydain, was invaded from across the Sea. The enemy flew on dragons white as snow, and was unstoppable for there were no dragons on the island at the time. We lost battle after battle and, in the end, the Kingdom of Prydain was reduced to a small country in the westernmost corner of the island, defended by a king from the Faer race, called Arthur."

Bran sipped some *cha*, his eyes wandering about as he tried to remember the story.

"King Arthur was trying to build a great fortress to make a last stand against the invaders, but the walls of the fortress kept crumbling. At last, there came a boy with the powers of prophecy." He nodded towards Nagomi and she smiled. "The boy guided the warriors to a cave. There was a pool inside the cave, of water dazzling bright like liquid silver. The boy ordered King Arthur's warriors to search the bottom of the pool. When they did so, they found a giant round stone."

"What was it?" Satō asked eagerly.

"A dragon egg, of course. Its magic was so powerful that it prevented the construction of the fortress. Once King Arthur ordered the egg taken out of the cave, it hatched into an enormous red dragon, larger than any ever seen by mortal eyes. With a dragon like this by their side, the Prydain warriors finally had a chance to fight against the invaders."

"Have the invaders been defeated?"

"That's another tale, I'm afraid," Bran smiled.

"So, I take it that the red dragon's name was Emrys," Satō guessed.

Bran shook his head.

"It had no name other than Y Ddraig Goch, which simply means 'The Red Dragon' in our language. But the boy was called Emrys Wledig. He later grew into a great warrior and a poet."

"Your warriors are poets too? Like the samurai?"

"Not anymore," Bran replied sadly.

She pondered the tale in silence. A shy servant girl came out of the kitchen to take away the empty bowls. Satō glanced at her and reached out her hand.

"You, girl, wait! Show me your face."

The servant lifted her head, frightened. Her eyes were blank, covered with the mist of blindness, but there was no mistaking her face.

"Don't you have a sister in Suwa?"

"Y-yes, *tono*," she stuttered.

"I knew it! What's your name?"

"Yōko."

Satō smiled.

"Your sister is in good health and well taken care of," she said.

"Thank you, *tono!*" the girl fell on her knees. "That is great news."

"Are you happy enough here? Do you need anything?"

"I am, *tono*. No, *tono*. T' priests provide me wit' all I need."

"You have your sister's smile. I will let her know I've met you."

Yōko lay prostrate on the floor in gratitude, but Satō bade her get up, slightly embarrassed.

"What is it?" Satō asked Bran and Nagomi when girl left the room. Both looked at her bemused.

"Nothing," Bran said, shrugging and pretending to focus on his food.

"You've never seemed more like a samurai than now," said Nagomi, "it's as if you've suddenly grown up."

We both have, the wizardess thought. Sudden heaviness pressed on her heart. Her friend's face somehow seemed no longer as innocently childish as it used to be. She didn't smile so much, and blue crescents under her eyes showed plainly how much trouble they had been having lately.

Do I look the same? She wondered. *I feel worse. All the running, all the fighting – it's drained me so much…*

Bran yawned and stretched his arms

"I know we should be thinking up strategies, but all *I* can think of is a well-stuffed *futon*."

She could not agree more.

When he had first arrived in Yamato, Bran had trouble telling its people apart. All the men and women on the streets of Kiyō seemed too similar, with their uniformly black hair, brown eyes and flat, pale-cream faces.

Looking at the crowds filling the main courtyard of the shrine, a square of polished stone floor surrounded by a colonnade of vermillion pillars, he understood his early mistake. Every person in the multitude of pilgrims looked different. A commoner with a nose like a squashed *taro*; a noble lady, her face covered with white paint, one eye slightly larger than the other; a samurai with thick eyebrows joined above the nose and an innocent expression, oddly unsuitable for one who wore two sharp swords at his side.

There must have been hundreds of people here, coming and going, stopping for a moment before the talisman shops, then proceeding to the Offertory Hall where they had only enough time to clap, bow and throw a small coin before another of the pilgrims pushed their way in. How many thousands of copper coins jingled daily against the sides of the offertory boxes? And this was an ordinary day – how this place would look like on the day of the festival!

He was confident they had made a good decision to stay within the Shrine grounds. With crowds like these even the Crimson Robe would think twice before attacking. *Was it his shadow I saw in the forest?* The wolves must have been the demon's doing – and Bran suspected a lurking presence beyond the Shrine walls. *Will he come just for me, or for the dragon, too?*

He stood among the pillars, observing the crowds, sketching the details of the shrine precinct in his notepad, noting what he had learned throughout the day. The inner compound spread to the north and east, up the slope of the Takachiho Mountain in what looked like three terraces. The majestic undulating gables of the Inner Sanctuary rose above the ochre-coloured roof of the Offertory Hall. The shrine, he had learned, had been dedicated to some ancient *Mikado* and his family, all now deemed Gods by the priests and their following.

A path branching east of the courtyard led past the dance stage to the cemetery, laid out among the pine trees. Earlier in the day the funeral procession of the slain Hosokawa's retainers had passed through the shrine. Bran managed to stay out of sight of Master Kawakami, who no doubt would have insisted on him and the girls joining the ritual. They had no time for this.

Bran noted the dimensions of the fence surrounding the inner precinct and wondered if it was so high and strong on all sides, when a sudden commotion caught his eye. A group of burly bodyguards were making their way through the crowds, pushing people to the sides with their hands and bamboo poles.

"Make way for Shimazu Atsu-*hime*!"

Shimazu! The crest of a cross in the circle flashed in Bran's mind. The Shimazu were the ones holding Emrys captive. Overwhelmed with curiosity, Bran squeezed through the crowds, hoping to catch a glimpse of the mysterious "princess".

First came the servants and retinue, carrying banners with the circle-cross, then six strong men hauled a massive palanquin, decorated with black and gold, with a brass spout sticking out of the roof. But the palanquin was empty, its grid open. A woman walked slowly in silence beside it, accompanied by a servant girl. Her long kimono of black silk embroidered in brightly red and purple flowers, bound with a wide, pink *obi* sash, reached the ground, hiding her feet so that the woman seemed to slide over the grey stones. She was wearing a straw hat with a wide rim folded to the sides, concealing her face from the crowd. Bran could not make out any of her features, or tell whether she was old or young, beautiful or ugly, even though she passed him so close he could smell the faint scent of sandalwood perfume from her hair and clothes.

A light punch with an end of the bamboo pole reminded Bran he had got too close. He pulled back and made his way back to the house by the dance stage.

The cedar trees cast short, flickering shadows in the light of a flamespark hovering faintly over Bran's shoulder. Confused moths and night flies flapped distractingly about his head. A bat fluttered from tree to tree. He adjusted the black scarf covering his entire head except his eyes and mouth – a technique Satō had taught him before he had set out on the nightly escapade – and moved on.

He walked carefully along the outer fence of the shrine. Seven feet tall wooden planks surrounded the compound on all sides. There was a small gate in the north-western corner of the perimeter, but no other openings. Bran knew the rough layout of the inner precinct from Nagomi's description. There was a storage area immediately beyond the corner gate, living quarters for the priests beyond that and, to the west, a garden and a small villa where the Shimazu princess had her dwelling. The storage area was his best bet when looking for a place where Emrys could have been kept, but the two armed guards posted outside the gate were discouragement enough from trying to get through that way.

Whoever had prepared the shrine's defences had made a thorough job of it. The fence boards were all well-maintained, freshly lacquered, any loose or rotten planks recently replaced with new ones. The trees in the immediate vicinity of the fence had their branches cut so that no spy or assassin could use them to climb over the wall.

But Bran had certain advantages over any regular spy. He found his way to the darkest, most remote part of the compound, halfway down the mountainside. He used the sword's scabbard to calculate the distance and angle. There could be no mistake. He calmed his breath, closed his eyes, focused on the centre of gravity of his body, just above the sternum. He weaved his hands in a spiral move, tracing a ballistic curve, a line of sparkling light in the darkness.

When he was happy with the projected trajectory, Bran made one step back and bounced himself off the ground with a light tap. He let his body be carried over the fence in a somersault along the spiral line of kinetic energy, hoping at least this time his enhanced acrobatics skill would not fail.

It was a smooth jump all the way to the top. He caught a glimpse of the inside of the precinct, a small pond surrounded by flowering reeds, when his foot tripped over one of the planks in the fence. He waved his arms futilely and the damp grass hit him in the face.

He heard a soft outburst of laughter.

A pair of brown eyes stared straight into his. A woman in a rich, cream-coloured kimono was sitting no more than ten feet away from him. A paper lantern in her hand illuminated the whole scene with a faint, pale light. In the other hand she was holding a white folding fan.

Her skin was smooth, unpainted; the lantern's light gave it an almost angelic glow. Her face was flawless, symmetrical, exquisitely proportioned, with cheekbones and chin prominent but not offensive and a small, pointed nose over full, slightly pouted lips. Eyes of a roe deer, almond-shape, deep, reddish brown, glistening like a polished carnelian, stared at him with piercing intelligence from under the thin, gently curved, raised eyebrows and elaborate hair-do. She was a girl, really, no more than a few years older than him, but there was maturity and wisdom in those eyes belying her age.

She showed no fear and made no sound or movement. Bran sniffed, and smelled the familiar scent of sandalwood. The garden was silent, a single frog croaked in the lily pond. His face stung where he fell.

"You are the clumsiest *shinobi* I've ever seen," she said. "Are you here to kill me?"

Who is she?

"N... no."

"Did my father send you, then?"

"My business is with the shrine, not you," he replied.

"I see," she said and pouted her lips. "Come closer."

He hesitated. The girl stood up and approached him instead, lifting the lantern to his face. She was surprisingly tall for a Yamato woman, only a few inches shorter than Bran. The sweet smell of sandalwood overwhelmed his nostrils.

"What strange eyes," she said upon closer examination. "Green like jade."

"So I've been told."

She touched the black scarf.

"Are you hurt?"

"I'm fine."

"You're not an assassin."

"No."

"I know who you are," she said.

"Oh?"

"You're one of those three pilgrims Gensai-*sama* met in the forest. He told me all about you. I've seen the red-haired priestess in the afternoon, helping with the altar."

He didn't know what to say to that.

"You must tell me why you are here," she decided suddenly, "or I will cry for help."

Bran glanced behind – he could try and jump back, but he wasn't sure he was able to focus clearly enough in this situation. And even if he did, she would then no doubt alert the temple guards. The advantage of surprise would be lost, and he would probably never get another chance to steal his way into the inner premises. Worse still, the security of the shrine would have been compromised and the dragon would no doubt be moved to another secret location.

"You can trust me," she said, still looking boldly into his eyes. "All I want is a good story. I'm so bored here. Everyone is so old, polite and tedious. Please?"

She looked at him pleadingly with the carnelian eyes. He felt his heart melting.

"Are we safe here? Will nobody eavesdrop on us?"

"This is my private part of the garden," she assured him, "and everyone's asleep by now."

She motioned him to sit beside her on a long stone bench on the bank of a lily pond.

"It's about the treasure, isn't it?" she asked before he could say anything.

"The treasure?" Bran's heart started beating even faster than it already was.

"Nobody ever tells me anything, but I am smarter than they think. There are two dozen samurai armed to the teeth guarding this shrine. My father had a great iron oxcart accompany my entourage. He told me it contained a gift from the Gods. You're here to steal it, aren't you?"

She grinned.

Her father...?

"Not steal. It belongs to me," he said.

"How exciting! But what is it, tell me?"

He opened his mouth but a female voice cried in the distance.

"Princess Atsu! Please come back, it's late."

"Oh, how I hate that woman," the girl said, standing up. "A living chaperone is such a nuisance compared to an automaton!"

An automaton?

"Atsu... you are the Shimazu princess!"

"Of course! Who did you think? I have to go. You must visit me again tomorrow!"

"I will," he blurted, "I mean... I'll try."

"I shall wait," she smiled at him with a smile warm like summer sun and ran off into the garden.

He shook his head, trying to maintain focus. He measured his distance again and leapt over the fence. He almost made it this time.

There was a rope hanging across the fence, tied to a black pine growing on the other side. He tugged it to check if it held fast and climbed across, as quietly as he could. She was already waiting for him by the lily pond.

"I thought a rope might be of use to you," she explained, "I found some in the gardener's shed."

"That was very thoughtful... but what if somebody noticed?"

"I told you, nobody ever comes here. Now sit down and tell me your story. My chaperone thinks I'm meditating – we have all night."

He gulped.

"You must first tell me yours, princess," he said.

He had spent all day thinking about the girl, wondering what she was doing in the shrine.

"Oh, but my story is nowhere near as interesting as yours!"

"Such is my condition, *hime*."

"Very well, but don't blame me if you're disappointed. And don't call me *hime*, all my friends call me simply Atsuko."

"But we've only just met..." he started, but seeing her pout again, he added, "Atsuko."

She smiled, looking not at him but at the floating lilies, their buds closed for the night.

"My current life started when the *daimyo* of Satsuma, Shimazu Nariakira-*dono* adopted me as his only daughter. My real parents came from a poor, distant branch of the clan, so they were glad to be rid of me. Later my father had to commit suicide for some minor offense and my mother died soon after."

No shadow marred her beautiful face as she was saying these words, only the light of the lantern flickered in her big brown eyes.

"I have lived alone in the Kagoshima Castle for years, trying to learn as much as I could about the world from the books in my new father's library."

"Satsuma is so far south – it's almost outside Yamato," she explained, "so we're more connected to the seas than to the land beyond the mountains. My father was always very keen to expand his knowledge of the Western magic and technology and there were always some foreign envoys or scholars in the castle, sneaked in secretly from Dejima or the Nansei islands in the south. Sometimes I've managed to talk to them."

"You speak Bataavian?"

"Just a little. Not as well as my father."

"Have you ever been to Kiyō yourself?"

She shook her head with sadness.

"This is the first time I travel out of Kagoshima. It is not acceptable for a woman of my standing to journey without good reason."

"And where are you going?"

"Edo."

From the map he had seen in Lady Kazuko's room Bran knew the *Taikun*'s capital city was weeks away from Satsuma.

"That's a long journey! Aren't you excited?"

"Maybe," she said with a shrug, "but I fear I will not see much. They carry me around in a shuttered palanquin everywhere. They will put me in a windowless cabin on the boat, and then lock me somewhere in the *Taikun*'s palace, where I am to do secretarial work for my father and his officials."

"So what are you doing in this place?"

"Oh, I was just waiting for those samurai from Kumamoto to escort me across the mountains. Now that they're here, in a few days, I will have to leave."

Bran felt a sudden pang of sadness. He turned his eyes away from Atsuko's face, pretending to admire the reflection of the moon in the pond.

"Now, your turn," she insisted, "what is the treasure you seek?"

"A *dorako*," he said without a moment's hesitation.

"*Ah!*"

The excitement and admiration in her almond brown eyes was worth betraying his greatest secret.

"I am a dragon rider. I come from a land far away, and I lost my dragon in battle off the shores of Qin…"

She pouted, irritated.

"Now you're making fun of me. I can tell you're just a Yamato boy underneath that mask."

"I'm telling the truth! Wait here."

He knelt at the edge of the pond, cooling his face with the water to lessen the pain of the transformation.

"Are you all right?" she asked.

He turned to her, removing the black scarf. She gasped and hid her face behind the paper fan.

"I am Bran ap Dylan o Cantre'r Gwaelod," he said proudly.

"Fantastic!" She clapped her hands. "How did you do that?"

At first he spoke cautiously, in short, broken sentences, but she was so eager to hear more and looked at him with such expecting admiration that, before he noticed, he was telling her of all his adventures in Yamato, from waking up at the infirmary, through the visit to the Cave of Scrying, to the clash with the *onmyōji*. By the time he had finished, it was well past midnight.

Her next question threw him off balance.

"That samurai girl and the priestess... are they pretty?"

"I... I think Nagomi is regarded as a pretty girl..."

She giggled.

"But not the other one?"

"It's difficult for me to judge people of your race. I – "

He looked into her almond eyes, staring at him expectantly.

"I never thought I would find an Eastern woman as beautiful as you," he blurted.

What am I saying?

Atsuko was as unlike all the other girls he had fancied as a rose was different from a field daisy: mature, bright, polite... and her smile, sincere and wise... there was no fault in her smooth, shapely face and carnelian eyes.

She startled at his confession and turned her eyes away. For a while they enjoyed the sounds of the night and each other's company in silence.

"I will help you," she said, "I know the man who will tell me everything. His name is Torii Heishichi-*sama*, and he's my father's *Daisen* – Arch Wizard. I wondered why he was chosen to accompany me on this journey! And I can demand access to every room and every building in this shrine. I will find your *dorako*."

"You really shouldn't... it's dangerous."

"I know!" she said, beaming. "That's what makes it exciting. Oh, it's like I'm in a *kabuki* play. A secret prince who comes at dusk and disappears at dawn, a dragon, mystery, magic and action!"

Bran felt his cheeks redden at the words "secret prince".

"Tell me something in your native tongue!" she asked.

He thought for a moment and then started singing, softly at first, ending on a louder, though shaky note as the song's melody brought with it the memory of the rolling hills of Gwynedd and the slate walls of his home in Caer Wyddno.

Ar lan y môr mae rhosys cochion

Ar lan y môr mae lilis gwynion

Ar lan y môr mae 'nghariad inne

Yn cysgu'r nos a chodi'r bore.

"What does it mean?" she whispered a question after a long pause.

"Beside the sea red roses grow,

Beside the sea white lilies show,

Beside the sea my love resides,

By day she walks, by night she hides."

He choked on the last verse of the translation.

"So you're also a poet."

"No!" He laughed. "That is an old song, a fireplace song."

"Your tongue is strange. At once harsh and sweet. And so unlike Bataavian."

"It is much older than Bataavian. When the oaks at Mona were yet acorns, my people already spoke Prydain. Some say its roots are in the speech of the Faeries."

"The Faeries?"

He told her of how the golden-haired Tylwyth Teg danced under the stars in the old elm woods along the Taf Fechan, in the Great Forest of Brycheiniog. He hadn't spoken these names in such a long time they sounded strange to his ears, still they rolled smoothly off his tongue.

"There is nothing in my father's books about all this!" She clasped her hands together in awe. "I have learned so many new things tonight."

He tried to smile but it came out as a yawn. His eyelids felt heavy and sticky.

"Oh, how thoughtless of me. I've been keeping you awake all night."

"It's all right," he said, stifling another yawn.

"No, no, your days must be busy while I spend mine lazing about and strolling in the gardens."

"I... I haven't really slept since yesterday," he admitted.

"Then go and rest. But you *must* return tomorrow."

"I will," he said, this time with certainty.

CHAPTER XI

The dream was a story.

Out in the middle of a vast plain, covered with tall grass that waved like the sea in the wind, stood a great castle, once magnificent and white, now fallen in disrepair and ruin after long years of neglect.

Three men desired to enter the castle; one had a long beard, the other wore a grey hood, and the third had eyes as green as jade. But try as they might, they could not breach the mighty wall of grey stone that encircled it.

The fourth man, a red-haired merchant, had the key to the single gate in the wall. He would come to the castle once a year with a cartload of goods from the valleys and mountains beyond the grassy plain. The lord of the castle shunned him, but coveted the exotic wares from the cart.

After many long years, each of the three men devised a different way of breaking through the castle walls. The bearded one dug a tunnel underneath it. The grey hooded one rode a flying beast over it. And the jade-eyed one ambushed the merchant and stole from him the key to the single gate.

All three met at the courtyard and the lord of the castle came out to greet them and he was old, frail and trembling. They drew their swords.

Lady Kazuko was right. The priests at Kirishima had recognised her status and guided her to the more luxurious accommodation higher up the slope of Mount Takachiho.

She had not seen such opulence in Suwa, rich though the Kiyō shrine was. There was gold leaf and jade everywhere, precious silks and exotic woods. Her mattress was soft as snow, the clothes chest was encrusted with red lacquer and ivory. A servant maiden, who brought tea in an expensive Qin pot, wore richer robes than Nagomi herself.

Wandering around the compound she noticed the priests had put her in a room far away and separated from everyone else. She quickly guessed the reason. They may have been too polite to make any mention of her hair, but their nervous glances gave them away.

Their nervousness increased after the funeral of the fallen samurai, when the rumours of the wolf attack spread around the shrine. She caught a whispered "goblin" or "*yōkai*" whenever she passed by a group of younger acolytes or maidens. The elders still smiled and bowed at her welcomingly, though their smile disappeared as soon as she pretended to turn away.

There was plenty she could help with around the precinct. Of late a small earthquake had caused a landslide near the Offertory Hall and once

Nagomi had rested she was more than happy to put her hands to some physical work to take care of the injured workers.

After a day of such work one of the chief priests took her aside.

"We appreciate your assistance, priestess," he said, "but it does not speak well of our hospitality that we let a guest do such hard work."

"Really, I don't mind."

The priest lowered his head.

"I must insist…"

"Oh."

"The workers are simple people, they would not understand all the… circumstances. Any other time, perhaps, but not with all the rumours of the *yōkai* coming down from the mountains…"

"I see."

"I'm sure there is enough to keep one as industrious as yourself busy. Is there anything I can help you with?"

"Can you tell me what's over there?"

She pointed to a fenced-off area to the north-west of the main compound.

"Oh, that's… that's just a storage area. Nothing of interest."

"That's a lot of guards for just storage. And a big fence."

"*Eeh*! Very perceptive." He laughed and lowered his voice. "It is actually our main treasury, priestess. We don't need the thieves to know where we keep our most precious offerings, do we?" he said and winked.

"Of course not," she said, winking back, feeling slightly sickened.

She was picking up the withered flowers at the altar of *Mikado* Jimmu to replace them with fresh ones, when she noticed Bran, browsing the souvenir stalls. She came up to greet him.

"You're working?" he asked. "Aren't you supposed to be a guest of the shrine?"

"I can't stay restless for long. At Suwa I was always busy with something."

"Did you find out anything interesting yet?"

"There's a closed-off area in the north-western corner – I could see the roof of a large building over it. The priests say they store most precious treasures in there."

"I'll try to check it out tonight."

"Be careful, there are many guards."

"Oh, now, that definitely sounds interesting," he said with an absent smile. He was twirling an *obidame* buckle in his fingers, a simple souvenir piece carved out of a deer's horn in the shape of an orchid.

"What *are* these things, actually?" he asked.

"Noble ladies wear them around their waist sashes, tied on a cord – like that one," she lowered her voice and pointed to an elderly, heavily built woman passing by, wearing too much make-up. Her kimono was as noisy and gaudy as herself, and her *obidame* was golden, encrusted with jewels.

"How is your arm?" she asked, as she had been asking every day. With Bran's increased resistance and lack of attunement to the spirits, she worried his wounds might never fully heal.

"It's barely a bruise now."

"You seemed so surprised, back then. Don't you have priests in the West?"

"We do, but they are not healers..."

"Miracle workers then? How do you call them... thauma...?"

"No, they're not thaumaturgists, either, unless they decide to learn some magic on their own."

"Then what is their power? I have never spoken to the Bataavians about their religion."

"I... Nothing like this, certainly." Bran hesitated. "I have rarely paid much attention to the Sun Priests," he said at last. "Matters of religion are left to the Church and, in exchange, the Church tries not to interfere in the matters of wizards. These days, I don't think they have any *real* power."

Nagomi looked at Bran curiously, not sure if she understood him properly.

"No power? Then what good are they?"

Bran shrugged, "What priests are usually good for? They preach, they teach, they offer advice to the confused and help to the poor. The Church used to fight the wizards in the old days, blaming them for all sorts of calamities... Now, priests and mages mostly ignore each other."

The priestess nodded.

"I see. I've heard about something like that. Sometimes a priest would be abandoned by the *kami*, lose the power of healing, and start some new cult claiming he's found new, better Gods."

Bran chuckled. "Sounds about right to me."

He studied her for a moment.

"You look healthy," he said. "This place serves you well."

"It's a busy shrine," she said, shrugging, "and that reminds me of Suwa... but I wouldn't like to stay in this place too long. The priests here are... different."

"We won't be long here, anyway. In a few days it will be all over, one way or another."

There was gloom in his words and she didn't like it. It reminded her of her own dark visions that kept haunting her in the night.

"You can see the future, right?" he asked, as if reading her mind.

"Sort of... sometimes..."

"Can't you tell how this story ends? Can't you see if we are succesful?"

"Well..." she stumbled on words, "scrying's not as simple as that."

"But surely you have seen *something* about our future?"

"I have seen nothing that would show that we are going to fail," she lied with a smile.

Satō wandered aimlessly about the shrine's courtyard in the sizzling noonday sun. She came up to the talisman stall, picked up a few cloth pouches embroidered with lucky spells and then put them back without looking. She bought a few joss sticks, but forgot to light them. She drank some cold tea and ate some sweet bean *mochi* at the pilgrims' teahouse.

She was feeling increasingly useless. She had neither Bran's sixth sense nor Nagomi's authority to investigate the shrine and its surroundings. In the end, she climbed up the hill towards the *Butsu* chapel beyond the cemetery, to pay for a prayer in Master Dōraku's memory.

She could not understand why the other two did not seem to mourn their guide in the slightest. He had sacrificed himself to save their lives! But Nagomi and Bran never mentioned his name again.

What is wrong with them?

As she stood before the chapel's statue of the bodhisattva Jizō, her head bowed in prayer, she noticed somebody standing beside her.

"Who do you pray for, young man?" Kawakami Gensai asked. He was wearing a fine kimono of soft grey silk and only the short sword at his side.

"A friend."

"Do you mind if I join you? I also have fallen friends to mourn."

"Not at all," she said, stepping aside. "I'm sorry for the deaths of your comrades."

"Such is the samurai's lot."

They prayed for a while in silence, then bowed before the statue and to each other.

"Is that a Matsubara?" Master Kawakami asked, glancing at the handle of her sword.

"Yes."

"*Eeh!*" I have never fought anyone wielding a Matsubara before."

It was the first time she had seen his face take on a genuine expression of joy. She gave it not a moment's thought.

"I have little else to do today," she said eagerly, "so whenever you have the time…"

"Most excellent. I will send a messenger in a short while – you're staying in the annex, aren't you?"

"Unfortunately, yes," she said, embarrassed.

She stepped under the vermillion gate with some apprehension, hoping Bran would not notice. He was very vocal about them not leaving the precincts of the Kirishima Shrine, fearing the Crimson Robe's attack. But she could not refuse Master Kawakami's invitation and they obviously could not fight on the sacred ground.

The samurai's servant led her off the main road, onto a glade of freshly mowed grass. Master Kawakami was there already, dressed in his grey and blue fighting clothes. A flask of saké and two cups rested on a lacquer tray on a tree stump.

"Welcome," the samurai said, bowing.

"What is this place?"

"A duelling glade – for those who felt insulted on the grounds of the shrine. It is still maintained, though not used as much as it used to be."

He gestured to them to sit down by the tree stump. Satō poured saké into his cup and then hers. She gulped the liquor.

"It's sweet," she said, surprised. It tasted quite unlike her father's sakés.

"Northern style, from Aizu," Master Kawakami replied. "You like it?"

She nodded. "It's exquisite."

"A refined taste for one so young. Now then, let's see if your swordsmanship is just as good," he said, standing up and drawing his sword. It was wider and longer than most *katanas* she had seen, a thick, heavy blade that seemed almost crude to an untrained eye; but she recognised it at once.

"*Dōtanuki?*" she raised her eyebrows.

"I know, I know. My teacher mastered one and I got used to the heft. It's not as bad as you might think – of course, if you have the original, not a copy."

He had the right part of his kimono pulled down for more freedom of movement. Veiny muscles rippled on his arm and torso, developed by years of carrying a blade a good pound heavier than usual. A grim, fierce tiger stared at Satō from an elaborate tattoo spread across the samurai's chest.

She assumed a stance and noticed a glint of interest in Master Kawakami's eyes. The stance of the Takashima school was significantly different from the more well-known styles; the blade closer to the chest, the hands on the hilt closer together. His stance also surprised her. She was expecting one of the slow, precise styles, suited to the heavy blade, but Master Kawakami stood softly and lightly on his feet, more like a martial artist than a swordsman.

He's going to be fa –

She barely managed to reflect the coming blade. Her shoulder shook with the power of the blow. Her opponent gave her no time for respite; another cut came from above, then another from below, a quick one-two. She felt her wrist twisting dangerously, almost spraining. She jumped back, the samurai's blade swishing where her head had just been.

That would have gouged my eyes!

She blocked another blow and stepped back again. She had to be careful: the grass under her feet was moist and slippery. *If I could use my magic… but that would be against the –*

Master Kawakami pushed on with the attack, thrusting and slicing without pause, not letting Sato strike even once. Blood flowed away from his face, giving it a morbid pale hue, like a *kabuki* mask. His expression was solid, focused, only his eyes moved swiftly, following and anticipating her every move.

Is he mad?

Her back touched a tree trunk. There was nowhere else to retreat. The *dōtanuki* blade flashed again before her eyes. She cast her head back and hit herself on the tree behind. In a daze, she slashed wildly, without looking. The two weapons clashed, and she let out a cry of pain as her left wrist finally gave way. Her sword whirled in the air before falling into the grass. The tip of her opponent's weapon hovered an inch from her eyes. The samurai's face as fierce and focused as that of the tiger on his chest.

"I yield!"

He smiled, took a step back and bowed, before sheathing his sword. He hardly even broke a sweat, but Satō felt so tired she feared she'd throw up.

"Well done," the samurai said, handing her the dropped weapon, "but why were you holding back?"

"I did not!" she protested, panting. She needed to sit down.

"You hesitated. You have skill, but lack confidence." He studied her for a moment. "You have fought recently, and lost."

"I have," she said.

"Why does it trouble you so? You are still young. There will be many fights you will lose."

"I chose a coward's way."

"You ran from a fight – so what? Don't believe all that *bushido* nonsense. These are just some rules in an old book. The real war has no rules."

She stared at him in confusion.

"I did not get to where I am now by dying whenever somebody bested me in combat," he said. "If you survive now, you get a chance to win later. Take time to train, study your opponent, grow stronger, and come back to fight again. Shinmen-*sama* often had to run away from a fight before he became the master."

"Shinmen-*sama*...?"

"Have you not heard of Shinmen Takezō, the greatest swordsman in Higo?" He seemed taken aback by her ignorance, and she was herself surprised that there was a famous samurai she had not yet heard of. "I have to send you one of his books later. My master learned everything he knew about fighting from his works, and so did I."

"I will be most grateful," she bowed deeply.

"And if I may offer more practical advice, you will be slightly faster on the upper block if you hold the sword like this," he said, taking her hand in his and guiding her in slow motion. "Oh, I'm sorry," he added, seeing her wince, "you need that wrist looked after by a priest."

"It's... nothing, really," she said, stepping quickly away. Her ears were burning. The samurai looked at her curiously.

Did he see through my disguise?

She sheathed the sword and tightened her kimono. "I was not aware Kumamoto Castle had not one but two such great swordsmen."

"Two? My teacher is long dead, and though I loathe boasting, I'm not sure who might be the other man you speak of."

"What about Dōraku-*sama?*"

Master Kawakami frowned.

"I am not familiar with this name."

"He came from Kumamoto .He said he was a retainer of Yōkoi-*dono*."

"A retainer? What did he look like?"

She described the fallen samurai in great detail, including the two swords he had wielded with so much prowess. Master Kawakami was silent for a long time after she had finished speaking.

"I have never heard of such a man, either in Kumamoto or anywhere else on Chinzei – and believe me, I would. I know the school of sword you describe – it was one of the styles invented by Shinmen Takezō – so he must have been trained locally. How did you meet him?"

"He… on the road from Hitoyoshi."

"And where is this elusive swordsman now?"

"He fell defending us from the same wolves that killed your comrades. It was him that I prayed for at the chapel."

"Ah. Well. Nothing to worry about then." The samurai's lips twitched in a smile. "An odd story, no doubt, but finished now."

He tilted the flask, but it was empty. He let out a short "Hah!" and gestured at the servant to take it away.

"I need to go down to the market," he told Satō, "I cannot trust my servants to pick the right flask by themselves."

She raised her eyes. "Oh – can I go with you?" she asked without hesitation. It was her best chance to go down to the town safely. Surely, not even the Crimson Robe would dare attack a samurai of Kawakami Gensai's stature.

"I'll be honoured," he said with a smile.

The small town below, huddled between the mountain and the river, was filled with visitors from all over the province, here to see the famous *kagura* dance of the Kirishima Shrine. All the guesthouses were full, all the tea and saké shops were brimming with patrons, loud and rowdy, their faces flushed from too much of Kirishima's famous black yeast spirit, shōchū. The main street was lined with stalls on both sides, and the crowd moved slowly from one vendor to another like a giant, easily distracted caterpillar.

Master Kawakami disappeared inside a large liquor warehouse, leaving the two girls to themselves. Satō had taken Nagomi along. The priestess had been at first reluctant to leave the shrine but once they reached the lively market she forgot all her fears.

"Look here!" she led Satō to a stall marked with a dial of a Batavian clock.

Here were sold items which were rarely seen out in the open anywhere other than Satsuma. These were Batavian goods – from toys and sugar candies to simple magic items, like perpetual whirligigs, bouncing balls or tiny glass baubles with electric sparks trapped within for eternity.

"How much for this?" asked Satō, pointing at a glass lens hidden among mostly worthless colourful trinkets.

"Ah, excellent eye, *tono*," the vendor bowed, "I had it delivered only last week. That's ten silver *monme*."

"*Eeh*! That's less than half of what it's worth in Kiyō," Satō shook her head in astonishment. "And so easily available!"

She moved to another stall. This one was full of books and scrolls, mostly samurai adventures.

"I loved these when I was little," she said, flipping through the pages. "Look, this one's about the warrior monks of Mii-dera."

"One of my favourites as well, young swordsman," Master Kawakami spoke behind them, giving the girls a fright.

"*Ah*! Gensai-sama! Have you found what you've been looking for?"

"Somewhat," he grimaced, "all they care about here is shōchū. I have pressed the landlord long enough and it turns out he had a whole batch of the Fukushima's finest."

A few drops of rain fell on the books and the vendor began to hastily cover them up.

"We should go back," Nagomi said.

"Oh, can't we stay a while yet?" said Satō, "I wanted to go and see the workshops across the river. I've heard so much about them..."

"Karasu-*sama* will be worried," the priestess gave her a telling look. "Maybe some other time."

Master Kawakami looked to the dark clouds. "It will pass soon. But as you wish."

The crowds split into two currents. One flow headed for the inns clustered on the southern edge of the town, the other – for the shrine, where some of the pilgrims were yet hoping to find some accommodation. Satō, Nagomi and Master Kawakami joined the former, moving slowly forwards as the rain changed from a spitting drizzle to a drenching torrent. His servant strove to keep them all under one bamboo umbrella, pummelled by the sudden onset of wind.

Just before the bridge to the shrine the samurai stopped abruptly, causing the entire crowd behind them to also stop and wait in the downpour.

"What is it?" Satō asked.

"For a moment there I thought I felt – a presence..." his hand released the hilt of his long sword. "Nothing. Never mind me. Let's press on!"

Satō looked at the colourful multitude around them but saw nothing. She felt Nagomi grasp her by the hand and pull her closer.

"We must not get separated in this crowd," the priestess whispered. "And let's stick close to Gensai-*sama*, just in case."

"In case of what? What did you see?"

"Nothing, but... somehow I don't feel safe here."

Only when they were safely back beyond the shrine's great red *torii* and behind the closed door of her room, did the priestess sigh with relief.

"What happened there?" asked Satō.

"Didn't you feel it?"

The wizardess shook her head.

"I think something is out there, waiting for us."

"The Crimson Robe?"

Nagomi shrugged. "It could be anything. That evil presence from Honmyōji, whatever it was… or something we stirred in the forest… We must tell Bran."

"He will be angry at us for leaving the shrine. But I guess we have no choice. Where is he, anyway?"

"He must have gone on his nightly scouting mission already."

There was a knock on the door. Satō reached for her sword.

"I bring a gift from Kawakami Gensai-*dono*," a servant's voice announced.

She was wearing a different kimono this night, of plain black, glistening silk with crescent moon and stars embroidered in silver. The dark robe enhanced the lightness and smoothness of her skin and neck and made her seem even more mature and regal. She smelled of rosewood.

"Come with me, my secret prince," she said with a slight giggle and led him by the hand, beyond the lily pond and her lodgings, into the outer precinct. By the faint light of the paper lantern they passed along an ancient clay wall, covered with thick moss and mould. The grass was wet with fresh rain.

"This is where the priests live – and your red-haired friend," Atsuko explained.

Manoeuvring between some sheds, pavilions and huts of unknown purpose, they reached a massive storehouse in the middle of the storage area, a rectangular building supported on tall pillars of cedar. The thick stone walls had no windows.

"I think it's here. It's the only place in the shrine I'm not allowed in," she whispered, "and I've seen Heishichi-*sama* coming in and out of it every few hours."

They were huddled in azaleas behind a low wall. There were two guards stationed outside the storehouse, whom he recognised as Hosokawa's retainers. Bran could feel his heart beat faster than ever. Atsuko was so close he could now smell not only the rosewood on her clothes, but also the faint, chalky aroma of her make-up. He felt the warmth of her skin, heard her quiet breath.

"Well, what do you think?" she asked.

I think you're wonderful. I think I want to stay here forever.

Reluctantly, he turned his attention to the storehouse. He cast True Sight and the sheer amount of energy surrounding the structure almost blinded him. Magic currents surged through and around the building, powerful fields and multiple knotted spell threads interconnected with each other. In the middle of it all the silhouette of Emrys shone with a familiar bright green light. Bran's head began to hurt.

"Yes, this is the place. Why are Kumamoto soldiers guarding it instead of your Father's men?"

He didn't like them being here. The eight-circle crest of the Hosokawas on their clothes brought back memories of the fight in the forest.

"They are my escort. Kumamoto is famous for its warriors, and has more of them to spare. Lord Nariakira agreed to this to strengthen the alliance between the two domains."

"And you're not afraid of betrayal? What if something happened to… to you?"

She shook her head.

"They wouldn't dare. It would bring shame upon the entire clan. But if they did… My Father would proudly accept my sacrifice."

"You're a *bait?*"

"I am just one stone of many on the *igo* board," she said. He did not know what game she was referring to, but he understood the metaphor well.

"Let us return to the garden. Will you know how to get here on your own?"

"I think so." He looked around to get his bearings. "There's the Jimmu shrine, and beyond it – the main offertory and worship hall, right?"

She nodded and turned to leave.

"Wait, I want to try something."

He closed his eyes and focused on the Farlink connection. There was a resistance at first, and not only because of the magic barriers around the cage. Emrys was fighting him back. Bran pressed on, forcefully at first, then, when this only made the dragon resist more, gently, soothingly, caressing the beast with his mind. At last the dragon yielded, recognising its master. It stirred in its cage uneasily, snorted and grunted. Even the guards outside heard the noise and stepped away from the warehouse with a start.

A slim man wearing *Rangakusha* clothes appeared on the garden path, pacing quickly towards the building. Bran recognised the lanky face and horn-rimmed glasses from the visions he had shared with Emrys. The wizard entered the warehouse and shortly Bran could feel the dragon fall asleep again, the mind link between the beast and its rider weakened. Whatever the wizard did, it had worked – for now. Bran was satisfied with the results of his little experiment, though more than a little perturbed by the initial resistance.

"Who was that?"

"That was the *Daisen,* Heishichi-*sama*. You need to watch out for him. Now come, before we're found out," she said and pulled him back towards the lily pond.

They sat down on the stone bench in silence. Stars frolicked on the surface of the pond, rippled by the wind. Bran noticed she did not let go of his hand.

"I… I brought something for you," he said and presented her with the *obidame* buckle.

It had taken him all day to come up with a gift fit for a princess before remembering his grandfather's black box.

"Oh – it's beautiful!"

The intertwined golden dragons glistened in the light of the lantern as if alive.

"I'm afraid it's missing a stone…" he said.

She shook her head.

"It doesn't matter. I haven't seen such craftsmanship outside my father's treasure chest. Thank you."

"It belonged to the woman my grandfather met in Kiyō."

"But it's such an important thing! Are you sure you want me to have it?"

"Yes. Please."

Moon danced for a moment in her eyes, but then her gaze dimmed back again and she turned her face to the lily pond; still she did not let go of his hand.

"I wish I could wear it to the shrine dance," she said.

It took him a while to realise what she was telling him.

"I see."

"I asked them if I could yet stay a day more, but they won't let me. Gensai-*sama* insists I must leave tomorrow."

"Can they take you away just like that? Aren't you a noble woman?"

"Oh, my prince!" she said, laughing bitterly, "I may be a noble woman, but I'm still a woman, and my words mean nothing in this world of men."

"The wizardess, Satō… she once told me that in Yamato, only men can be truly happy."

"I should very much like to meet that girl in samurai clothes one day. But tell me, oh stranger from far away land." There was no mockery in how she addressed him, only wistfulness. "Surely the women of your people are also slaves to the men? They are also bound to a life of misery and imprisonment in their golden cages?"

"I… don't think it happens that often anymore," he said, "not among mages, at least."

"Then they must become lonely spinsters, mocked by their families, free to be taken by any man strong and willing enough?"

"No!" Bran cried out with genuine surprise. "They just – live their own lives, I suppose, have lovers, husbands… I'm sure my mother always loved my father, and that's why they're married. Maybe the royals or high nobles arrange families to keep blood purity… but those are rare occurrences these days."

He fell silent. All this talk of mother and father made him remember his little home, with walls of slate, by the beach, on a green hill, far beyond the three oceans. He suppressed tears swelling in his throat.

"Oh, my secret prince! What wondrous tales you tell me, how heavenly is your land!" Atsuko cried and suddenly started sobbing discreetly. Awkwardly, unsure, he pulled her to his chest and embraced tightly, letting her tears wet his kimono.

She raised her head. Tears destroyed her make-up, tracing lines of dark mascara on her cheeks, but her beauty was undiminished.

"Thank you, prince. I will always remember you and your tales. They will give me hope in the dark, dull life that awaits me, even if they sound like fairy stories."

She brought her face close to his until their lips met for one fleeting moment, a heartbeat. She pressed something in his hand and then stood up and disappeared into the darkness of the garden; only the paper lantern yet flickered for a moment, like a trapped firefly.

He opened his hand. It was a small carved wooden container, of the sort the samurai attached to their sashes when they needed to store small items, with a bead of carnelian stone as a fastener. With trembling hands he opened it and unrolled a piece of paper hidden inside. It smelled of rosewood.

Edo is a great and faraway place
But the world is even greater
If East and West met once
They may yet meet again.

My secret prince,

Tomorrow I leave for Edo; maybe I will see you in the crowd, but not recognize you. It is as it should be; our meeting was just a bright spark, a candle in the darkness that envelops my life. If it lasted any longer, it would burn a hole in my heart too big to heal. As chance had it, it only burned out a memory.

I hope all goes well with your plans. I will pray for you and your friends. If you ever find yourself in Kagoshima and are in need of help, remember this: my father's name is Shimazu Nariakira, and our family code word is "Shōhei" — "Tranquillity".

And now, the spark dies down, the black curtain falls. The lily pond grows over with weed.

Atsuko

Bran gazed at the surface of the pool, rippled by the soft night breeze. A sad, lonely owl hooted in the distance.

Since dawn there had been preparations all around the wooden stage. Guests at the nearby lodging house had been woken by hammering, sawing and polishing of decorations, cries of carpenters and builders, mixed with the stomping and shouting of dancers rehearsing before the big day.

In the morning, on the hour of the Snake, a double cordon of samurai formed a corridor from the northern compound to the gate at the end of the main courtyard, separating the crowds of pilgrims from the stone path.

With heavy feet and heavy heart Bran moved through the crowds to a raised platform near the talisman shops from where he could observe Atsuko's entourage leaving the shrine. She was carried slowly in the black and golden palanquin. Hosokawa's retainers surrounded the vehicle, with Captain Kiyomasa leading the convoy at the head of his soldiers.

The princess did not wear her straw hat this time, and had the blinds of her vehicle open so that everyone around could witness her mysterious beauty. The commoners prostrated themselves in the presence of a great lady and only Bran and a few nobles remained upright, bending over in a polite bow as she passed them.

She was looking around, as if trying to find somebody. Bran's heart sunk when he realized she had no way of recognizing him. She had not seen his Yamato face under the mask. To her, he was now just another samurai in a crowd of onlookers. He tried to catch her eye, hoping to somehow convey all his feelings in a single look, but her gaze just slid over him without noticing, and she passed by, leaving only the scent of rosewood behind.

Behind the palanquin, marched Master Kawakami. He did notice Bran and bowed slightly, his lips twitching up and down in his imitation of a smile.

"She's so pretty," said Satō with a sigh. Bran spotted her only now, standing beside him on the platform. She had a pained look in her eyes.

"Oh, to have her looks and her position... If any woman could find happiness in life it would have to be her."

"Sometimes beauty and wealth are not enough," he replied, his eyes still fixed on the procession now leaving the shrine through the main gate.

"Aren't you philosophic today," she said but then turned serious. "Is something wrong? You look as if you're sick."

There I go, showing my feelings to everyone, like the Barbarian that I am.

He tried to force his face into a cheerful mask, as he had seen the wizardess do so often.

"I'm fine, just... a little tired, that's all."

Satō stepped off the platform and winced.

"You don't seem so good yourself. Does your wrist still hurt?"

"No, it's healed. It's just a headache. I've had it since morning," she said and laughed. "Look at us. You'd think we've already been through a battle, not just preparing for one."

He nodded with a smile. The shrine gong rang out the hour.

"The dances start soon," said Satō and took him by the arm. "We should find Nagomi before the crowd grows."

CHAPTER XII

The instructor put another painted board onto the stand. All riders craned their necks trying to see the drawing. The shape of the creature drawn in ink and water colours on the board was roughly humanoid, but its face was bright red and its body was covered in thick blue hair.

"This one is a Sheng-Sheng," the instructor said. "Don't be fooled by their appearance – these are more than just some mountain apes. They are cunning, fast and stronger than five of you together. Avoid getting in the melee range – let your dragon deal with them. Luckily, they are most likely to fight in tight groups, separate from the humans."

"Will lightning to the head stop them?" one of the soldiers asked, waving a thunder pistol. He was of the fresh draft, same age as Wulfhere, and kept asking the same question about every magical creature the instructor described.

"Once again, Eadweard, the answer is yes. If you manage to hit it from dragonback. Their heads don't make the best targets, as you can see."

"Is it smaller than an apple, sir?"

The instructor sighed "No, it is not smaller than an apple. And if you try to bore us again with your tale of shooting apples off your cousin's head, I'll have to assign you to first aid duty."

Laughter rippled through the regiment and Eadweard sat down, his cheeks red.

Wulfhere ignored the exchange, focusing on his notes. "Big, red, strong. Dragon flame and pistols, no melee," he noted. This time, he was going to be extra careful with his choice of enemy. He had lost Eolhsand, his old mount, on patrol north of Fan Yu. Recklessly, he had charged a camp of the rebel scouts without waiting for backup. The rebel war machines proved more than a match to the dragon. He managed to fly away from the battle, but the beast was too heavily wounded and had to be put down.

His father's name had prevented him from being stripped of rank but, not being an officer, he had not been given a spare mount. Instead, he had been assigned as co-rider to the Flight Leader.

Hywel ap Cadell. It had taken him weeks to swallow the insult. He, a Warwick, serving under a peasant from some backwater beyond the Dyke! He still shuddered with anger thinking about it. How long would he have to suffer this humiliation?

There was a rumour of a transport of spares coming from the south. A battle was at hand, and there were always casualties in battle – dragons more likely to fall than the riders. A regiment of light dragoons could afford one mountless rider, especially one as unpopular as Wulfhere was among his comrades, but further losses had to be replaced if the troop was to remain operative.

All he had to do was survive.

It started with a single white flare, shooting up into the grey clouds. Then the line of ships standing at anchor at the river mouth erupted in bright flashes. A second later a prolonged thunder rolled through the river, the smoke trails of rockets covered the sky and suddenly, the opposite shore turned into one great explosion, spanning half a mile. The ground shook first, before the sound of the barrage reached the soldiers gathered in the barges on the northern side.

"That's our prompt," murmured Hywel as the bombardment moved further south. The commander raised his Soul Lance and, one by one, the dragons of the Twelfth Light sprang into the skies. Their task was to cover the western flank of the landing party – the Second Marines doing the same thing on the opposite side. The first wave of the barges launched from the moorings.

"Where's the enemy?" Wulfhere asked, straining to see anything among the smoke and dust raised by the shelling. The barges were almost halfway across the river and there was still no response from the rebels. He felt nervous. The dragons flew slowly, to let the barges keep up. *We're sitting ducks here*, he thought.

"Maybe they ran away," replied Hywel hopefully.

"Look, they dug trenches along the river bank."

Several rows of dugouts ran parallel to the shoreline, now mangled and partially buried by the barrage. Nothing seemed to move inside.

"We're flying too low," said Wulfhere. "Why are we flying so low?"

"Don't be a coward, Wulf," said Hywel, but his voice trembled.

An easterly wind picked up, dispersing the smoke clouds, and they saw a line of the rebel war machines, standing on the top of a tall cliff like patient spiders, their cannons aimed at the middle of the river.

"There they are," said Hywel.

"For the Dragon Throne!" the commander yelled. The dragons roared in response, and fifty winged beasts swooped down as one.

They were sitting in the canteen tent, by the long table, finishing their meal. Fighting still raged on the other side of the river, but half of the regiment was allowed to fly back to the camp for a brief respite. The battle was obviously going in their favour.

"Our naval guns are making mincemeat out of the enemy," said Berthun, a black-haired, thick-browed rider from Rheged. His voice was not boastful and his face was grim, a face of a man who had seen too much for one day. "This battle will be over before nightfall."

"Mincemeat... now there's something I'd like to eat instead of all this rice and fish!" replied another boy and many laughed, though not all.

"You're not drinking your rum?" Hywel asked. Wulfhere sat quietly over his bowl, a tin mug filled with muddled brown liquid untouched.

You call this swill "rum", he thought bitterly. *In my father's house we would drink the finest of Burdigala wines.*

He wasn't sure where the sudden memory came from. He shook his head.

"I have a feeling we may yet need our clear heads."

"You worry too much. Berthun is right, with the ironclads on our side nothing can stand in our way."

"I've heard a rumour the fleet is ordered to set sail on the morrow."

The Gwynedd boy looked at him sharply. Wulfhere may not have been a reliable soldier most of the time, but his good connections made him a valuable source of gossip.

"It will be all over by tomorrow," Hywel said at last.

He grabbed the Seaxe's mug and drank the rum in one gulp, snorting.

"Did you know Bran was supposed to be here with his father?" he asked.

Wulfhere shook his head. "I thought he stayed at the Academy."

"No, apparently he's gone missing in the *Ladon* disaster."

"Dead, you mean."

"Nobody here seems to think so. The Seal of Llambed saved him, but nobody knows where he is. Imagine if he was here, though – three boys from the same year on one battlefield!"

Hywel laughed, his cheeks already rosy from the drink. Wulfhere sat silent. The memory of Bran, and of his humiliation at the Red Dragon *tafarn* spoiled his mood completely. He pushed back the bowl and stood up.

"I'll go check on the dragon."

Hywel nodded. "We'll be flying again in ten minutes anyway."

Wulfhere stepped outside the flapping tent door and gazed across the muddy river. The waters flowed calmly now, unaware of the carnage on the southern shore, undisturbed by the smoke and flares.

There was a sudden quiet thunder strike in the distance, and a great flash in the sky. A ball of flame hurtled, rolling and tumbling from beyond the southern horizon, like a meteor. Long before it reached its destination, Wulfhere guessed what the strange missile was aiming for. The flaming rock hit one of the warships dead on, smashing through all the decks, straight for the ammunition storage. A blink of an eye later a tremendous explosion tore the hapless ship asunder.

For a moment everything was deadly quiet. Then the debris started falling down on the camp – half a mile from the blast – and the dragon riders poured from the tent to see what was happening.

"By the Red Dragon's Breath…" Hywel whispered, sobering up in an instant. "That was the Admiral's frigate!"

A swarm of Qin dragons headed towards them like a cloud of colourful ribbons in the wind.

"Look at that," whispered Hywel, "there must be dozens of them."

The regiment divided into two groups; one squadron, led by the commander, flew upwards and to the West, to strike at the enemy dragons with the sun at their backs. The other split further, into individual flights, to deal with the danger on the ground. Hywel was a Flight Leader – a rare promotion for one so young – and so he and Wulfhere found themselves leading a group of four riders, speeding low over the heads of both the enemy and friendly soldiers in the direction from which the flaming boulders were coming. The mysterious cannon – if cannon it was – took a long time to reload. It had shot only twice more since the Twelfth had scrambled. Neither of the shots was as precise and deadly as the first one, but the ships were forced to stop their bombardment and engage in evasive manoeuvres. It was imperative to locate it and destroy it fast, before the enemy regained their initiative.

"It came from beyond that low line of hills," said Wulfhere, one of the few who had seen the first shot fired. Hywel's flight turned along an irrigation canal running south-west across the rice fields towards a crest of sand dunes.

Something was running towards them down from the hills. At first it seemed like a cavalry of ponies, or a battalion of warhounds.

"Watch out!" Hywel cried to the other riders, "It's what's-their-faces, the leaping lions!"

"Bishiu," Wulfhere corrected him grimly.

In his notepad the name Bishiu was circled in red. Though the vestigial wings on the backs of the horned, lion-shaped creatures did not give them the power of flight, they could still pounce a hundred feet or more into the air to bring down any beast unfortunate enough to fly so low. Their strength and fierceness were legendary, and although one-on-one they were no match for even the smallest of dragons, they always travelled and fought in great packs.

"Up twenty!" Hywel commanded and the four dragons climbed to two hundred feet. The Bishiu were now following the flying beasts at speed, howling and barking, and leaping without much effect.

"Let them howl!" Hywel said, laughing, but at the same moment one of the lions leapt farther than any before it and its claws grasped a hind leg of one of the dragons. The mount snorted and dropped a few yards, flapping its wings desperately, trying to shake the beast off.

Two more of the Bishiu reached the dragon, pulling it further downwards. Hywel turned the flight back to save the hapless rider. Lightning and flame poured like rain on the heads of the leaping lions and the beasts scattered, squealing like pigs on fire. Soon, however, they began regrouping again at the foot of the hills, growling menacingly.

"Up ten," shouted Hywel with a tired voice, "and keep those shields on! Next time you're caught, you have to fend for yourselves. We've had enough delay as it is. That infernal cannon is about to make another try at our ships, I bet. Onwards, men of the Twelfth!"

It was difficult to assess the size of the enormous mortar until they got close enough to see the crew and soldiers bustling around it, and even then it was hard to comprehend. Each of the six wheels upon which the heavy wooden platform rested was at least twelve feet in diameter. The barrel of the gun, painted bright red and decorated with coiling hieroglyphs, rose menacingly into the sky like a giant chimney, leaning at a slight angle towards the battlefield.

"If *these* are the rebels," asked Wulfhere, "how come they have access to such weapons and not the Qin army?"

Hywel shrugged. "You want to switch sides?"

The Seaxe did not answer.

The cannon was manned and guarded by what seemed at first like very large men in bluish-green uniforms.

"*Sheng-sheng,*" whispered Wulfhere when they got closer.

A hail of musket balls and flaming arrows bounced uselessly off the *tarians*. A few rockets exploded between the dragons without harm.

Hywel reached out his right hand and summoned a bluish Soul Lance. He gestured to the rider at his left side – grey-eyed Eadgyth – ordering her to take out the rocket launchers and war machines on a ridge to the south. Hywel and one other dragon, led by a silent, tattooed man from Alba called Nechtan, swooped down towards the gun. There were only three of them left in the flight; the fourth rider flew back to the rest of the army to announce the discovery of the gun's position.

"Shouldn't we wait for the others?" Wulfhere asked.

"No time. At the least we can distract them from making another shot."

The *sheng-sheng* dispersed, cowering before their dragons and the gun halted its slow rotation. But the dragon flame could not penetrate the casing. The gun carriage was magic-proofed. Only the iron bindings of the wheels started melting in the fire, settling the entire machinery deep into the ground.

"Cover me, I'm going down," announced Hywel, standing in his stirrups.

"*What?*"

"You heard me. I'm going to dismantle that thing from the ground."

"That's insane! Didn't you hear the instructor? Those furry apes will rip you apart!"

Hywel's eyes glinted with battle rush and pride. "That's why I need you to cover me. You should be happy – if I die, you get to keep the dragon."

"But – "

"That's an *order*, ensign. Bring us close to that cupola at the back, that's where the steering mechanism must be."

Reluctantly, Wulfhere took over the reins and guided the dragon down. He could see Hywel's lips move wordlessly as the Gwyneddian calculated the trajectory of the enhanced jump. Nechtan circled above them, checking the crowd of the *sheng-shengs* with precisely aimed balls of dragon flame.

Hywel leapt down, somersaulting in the air before landing upon the platform. His Lance flashed, cutting an opening in the iron dome and he disappeared inside.

Wulfhere cursed, bringing the dragon to heel. There were more enemy soldiers swarming from all sides, and there was no sign of their own reinforcements coming, except Eadgyth returning from her mission. Several war machines smouldered on the ridge.

He's as good as dead, the fool.

Wulfhere and Nechtan were doing their best to keep the enemy from returning to the gun carriage, but both they and their mounts were growing tired with the prolonging battle. His mount struggled to keep airborne. Now that he was in charge of the dragon, he could feel the chaotic whirlwind of magic currents around the machine, disrupting the flow of the Ninth Wind. It was like flying through a tornado.

There was a small explosion inside the vehicle and one of the great wheels broke off, falling down with a thud, burying a few of the *sheng-sheng* combatants underneath.

Nechtan whooped, but the cry of joy died in his throat. Wulfhere felt it too. There was a dark *presence* on the battlefield beneath them. It did not take him long to find its source. A Qin man in simple red robes and long uncut hair was walking unhurriedly towards the gun, accompanied by several soldiers carrying long bronze tubes. The ranks of rebel soldiers parted before him like grass. The *sheng-shengs* dropped to their hairy knees.

The Alba rider, recognising an officer of some sort, let out a battle cry and dived down. The strange man looked up with eyes shining gold and Wulfhere was certain he smiled wickedly, though it was too far to see his features. The man raised a hand. His soldiers aimed their bronze tubes and launched flaming spears carrying what seemed to be fishing nets made of silver, glittering thread.

Wulfhere pulled up out of the range of the missiles, but Nechtan was too late. His dragon's wings got entangled in the nets and the beast tumbled down to the ground. The *sheng-shengs* swarmed to it, swamping both the dragon and its rider with their bodies.

"We need to retreat! Where's the Flight Leader?" shouted Eadgyth.

"Inside," Wulfhere pointed grimly at the gun carriage, from which the sounds of a fierce battle were still coming. The two riders tried to get close to the bombard but the nets launched again, keeping them at bay. The enemy footmen were now climbing onto the platform on all sides and the strange Qin man was reaching for a rope ladder.

"*Swyfen!*" the Seaxe cursed, "I'm coming after him. Cover me!"

He dived in and, swerving back and forth to avoid the nets, he landed the dragon on the carriage, in the middle of a troop of the *sheng-shengs*, who dispersed in an instant.

"Stay here," Wulfhere commanded the beast. The dragon had enough sense of its own to understand the order, despite their weak Farlink connection. "Guard the entrance."

The Seaxe looked up one last time towards Eadgyth circling above and then leapt through the opening in the iron dome.

He found Hywel on a narrow staircase reaching deep into the bowels of the war machine. The Gwyneddian was limping towards the exit, his side covered in blood and his cavalry sword broken, but a broad grin lightened his face.

"That gun won't move again. But what are you doing here? I told you to stay up."

"We have to get out of here. The others have still not arrived and there are enemy reinforcements outside. Can you fly?"

"I can try."

With Hywel hanging on his shoulder, Wulfhere climbed out onto the platform only to see a swarm of strong arms covered in blue fur reaching towards him. He pulled back inside, hacking at the *sheng-shengs* furiously. Hywel joined him, but with a broken sword and not enough power to sustain the Soul Lance any more, he could do little against the onslaught.

Several of the creatures grasped the jagged iron edges of the opening and, with tremendous strength, tore it apart. Others poured in through the breach, forcing the two riders further down the wooden stairs. Rocks and arrows flew, bouncing off Wulfhere's *tarian* with a shimmer. One of the beasts moved forward, wielding a heavy spear with a blunt bronze head. The blade penetrated the shield with a crackle, hitting Wulfhere's side and pinning him to the wall. He hit his head and his legs gave in. The *sheng-shengs* trampled and tumbled over him and a red darkness shrouded everything around.

The cold wind woke him up, but he dared not stir or open his eyes. The harsh, ineligible howls and barks around him told him he was still among the *sheng-sheng*. He wasn't bound – they must have thought he was dead. The wound in his side ached.

Very carefully, he opened one eye by a slit, just to get his bearings. He was laid on the gun platform, not far from the iron cupola. Hywel lay beside him, to the left, not showing any signs of life. Further along the Seaxe could make out the outlines of two more bodies: Eadgyth and Nechtan, he guessed. The *sheng-sheng* stood around them in a circle, agitated.

What are they doing to us? Some kind of sacrifice?

Another kind of cold passed through his body and he sensed the strange Qin man coming up to the riders. Wulfhere's skin got covered with goose bumps. The *sheng-sheng* fell silent and stepped aside. The man reached for the first of the bodies – Nechtan, judging by the hair colour, though the body was mangled almost beyond recognition – and raised it to his face. A sleeve of the robe slid down, revealing a tattoo of a black lotus flower on the forearm.

The Qin man's eyes turned from gold to black and he plunged his teeth into Nechtan's neck. The Alba soldier woke suddenly, gasped and twitched briefly, before falling limply to the floor.

Their tormentor moved to Eadgyth. Wulfhere closed his eyes and tried to calm his breath and heart to stay undetected. What was this *creature*? No briefing mentioned anything like it.

The man – the *demon* – now leaned over the body of Hywel. He turned his back to Wulfhere for a brief moment. This was all the boy needed. A Soul Lance appeared in his right hand and he leapt up, striking the enemy under the ribs. The Lance went straight through the lungs and heart. The Qinese let out a terrible shriek which made all the *sheng-shengs* fall down on their faces in fright.

Gathering all his strength, Wulfhere pulled the Lance downwards and to the side. There was no blood, no guts spilled from the gash, just rotting flesh. The creature reached back with a hand blackened with blood, but the dragon rider pushed on the Lance and the demon tripped over Hywel's body, falling.

It's still alive. How is it still alive?

The creature flailed its arms, trying to stand up. Wulfhere grabbed Hywel and, dragging him along the platform, hewed his way through the crowd of terrified *sheng-shengs*.

A ball of flame dropped from the skies, then another, then a lightning bolt. He looked up. Coming from over the sand dunes, the dragons of the Second Marines were coming to the rescue on the northerly wind, led by a man wielding a shining golden Soul Lance.

He sighed with relief and turned around. The platform was empty. There was no trace of the *sheng-sheng* soldiers, the two dead dragon riders – or the mysterious demon.

CHAPTER XIII

Dry wind blew volcanic dust across the arid highland. Particles of dark grey fell onto the torn and tattered remains of Dōraku's kimono and covered gaping, open wounds with a thin layer of ash. The samurai lay sprawled on the ground. His arms, thrown apart, still held on to both swords, but most of his upper body was ripped and slashed to pieces by ghostly fangs and claws, which pierced through the clothes and the mail shirt underneath like paper.

The wolf spirits disappeared, having fulfilled their purpose, leaving Dōraku's corpse exposed to the elements but also allowing it to slowly regenerate. The spell started working its way through the wounds as soon as the battle was over. Shredded veins and tendons linked up, nerve connections began slowly rebuilding themselves, muscles and skin grew back over the gashes and lacerations.

Dōraku needed neither blood nor oxygen to function. His heart, even fully regenerated, lay still in his chest without a single beat. His lungs did not move, no air pumped in or out of the trachea even as it grew fully back from the damage done by the wolf spirit's jaw. Even though they did not perform any vital functions anymore, the spell's power unhurriedly restored his inner organs to their former state.

His consciousness slowly returning, Dōraku moved fingers first of his right, then left hand, making sure he could feel the hilts of his swords. The muscles and tendons in his limbs were not yet fully regenerated and all he could do was lie and wait for full control of his motor functions to come back eventually. He felt the warm rays of the midday sun on his newly regrown skin and concluded it was a pleasant feeling, like lying half-asleep in a warm bed, long into the late morning hours.

He knew not how many hours or days had passed since the battle with the wolf ghosts. Since he could open his eyes, a night and half a day had gone by and that was his only frame of reference. At noon he could bend his wrists and wiggle his toes, move muscles of his face. In the afternoon, he could move his hand to where his waist had been and touch the soft leather of the salt pouch. The lungs and throat were not yet reinstated enough for him to speak comfortably, but it was only a matter of hours at worst.

A shadow fell across his face. A tall man towered over him, blocking the sun.

"It's your own fault, you know, old friend. Why drink a wolf's blood when there were so many humans to choose from?"

"Ganryū," Dōraku whispered hoarsely, straining his newly reborn voice box, "I have never been your friend."

The crimson clad Fanged stood leaning on the scabbard of his great two-handed *nodachi* sword, his long hair flowing in the dry hot wind, his silhouette black against the midday sun. He chuckled.

"Now, now. Don't you remember all the good times we had?"

"Have you come to reminisce, or to brag?"

"I have no time for either. I only wanted to make sure you won't be standing in my way tonight."

"Tonight? What day is it?"

"The seventh."

"Four days and you still haven't made your move?"

Ganryū shrugged, "There's been a troop of Hosokawa's retainers in the shrine. I don't wish to antagonize Kumamoto right now through impatience."

"Hosokawa will never join your cause."

"We'll see about that once I get my hands on the dragon."

"The dragon is in the shrine?" Dōraku tried to laugh but his throat failed him. "Then you can't get anywhere near it."

"Unlike you, I don't work alone. My people don't share our hindrances. All I have to do is to wait for them to come back with the *dorako*. Isn't it precious, Takezō? Or whatever name you are using for yourself these days."

The man in the crimson robe leaned closer towards Dōraku's tense face.

"I can't join my team, but neither can you help your companions. I wonder who will prevail in this contest; three city kids or a troop of trained warriors and assassins?"

"You underestimate them."

"Perhaps. I wouldn't mind a challenge for a change. Your performance against my wolves was sorely disappointing."

He examined Dōraku's body. "You regenerate faster than I expected."

"It's the Takachiho Mountain."

Ganryū pulled out the great sword from its sheath in a slow, deliberate move.

"I've always wondered how long it would take you to regrow your head."

He raised the *nodachi* to strike down, but at the same instant Dōraku swung his right arm at the Fanged's feet. Ganryū leapt at the last moment, somersaulting back a few steps. The *katana* cut through the air with a whistle. Dōraku brought his left hand up, throwing the pouch of salt at his opponent.

Ganryū cried out and spluttered, cursing and rubbing the white crystals out of his eyes.

"I don't have time for this," he snorted, "by the time you'll be able to stand up, I'll be long gone."

With that, the Crimson Robe turned away and walked down the slope towards Kirishima.

The Admiral seemed frail, weak and somehow older. The green cloth of the infirmary tent cast an unhealthy hue on his wrinkled face.

"That was a good battle," he said quietly and burst into a dry cough.

"We were reckless," said Dylan. He, Edern and the Admiral's *aide-de-camp* were sitting by the old man's bed. "That's the second ship I lost to the Rebels on my watch."

"Every ship's destiny is to sink," the Admiral said. "Victory is all that matters."

"And we've won splendidly," said Edern, "though our losses were great."

"The enemy's losses were much greater," said Dylan with a bitter smile. "The Ever Victorious Army is what our troops are called now. By the Emperor's edict!"

"And by my edict, they will now have a Commodore to lead them."

Reynolds gestured feebly at his *aide-de-camp*. The young man reached into his pocket and gave Dylan a sealed envelope.

"If I could make you an Admiral, I would," the old man said. "A better soldier I have not seen since my father's death. And the Pointy-Beard will respect you more if you have a proper rank. I could see how uneasy he was, having to deal with a mere Ardian."

"Thank you, Sir, that's a great honour."

"I only wish I could see all the victories you will win, Commodore."

"Perhaps after you return from your assignment at Ta Du – "

The Admiral laughed and then started coughing again. Blood spattered the bed sheet. He looked at the mangled, twisted remains of what was once his right arm. His iron leg was torn off at the knee.

"I am nothing but a broken machine… I should have died with my ship, but I won't fall far behind her. It doesn't matter. I had a long life. All my old crew mates are gone – from the Culloden, the Terpsichore, the Phaeton…"

His eyes opened wide.

"The Phaeton! That's what I wanted to tell you about!"

"Sir?"

The Admiral looked around him. "This is too confidential even for our lieutenants."

Edern and the other young man nodded and left.

"Tell me, Commodore, did your father ever tell you about the time we invaded Yamato?"

Yamato? Is he delirious?

"No, Sir."

"Good." The Admiral chuckled lightly. "So he had kept his oath. We were all sworn to secrecy as soon as we returned from that accursed place – and paid well to keep it."

"Paid?"

"How else do you think I could have afforded all this?" He pointed to the remains of his automated limbs and chuckled again. "Even after I was abandoned by my own men in shark-infested waters… But it doesn't matter. I've kept my part of the bargain. But it didn't mean I forgot – oh no, I never forgot it, and I bet neither did Ifor, for his own particular reasons."

With an increasingly weakening voice, in short sentences interspersed with bouts of coughing, the Admiral told the astonishing story of the Phaeton's raid on the city of *Keeyo* and the harbour of *Dejeema* and of the mysterious woman they had brought back to Dracaland.

"*Dejeema!*" Dylan whispered, remembering suddenly. "Bran asked me about that place the night before the disaster."

The Admiral nodded. "That would confirm my suspicions. I figured if your boy was somewhere in Qin, we'd have heard about it already. Even if the magic transported him all the way to Fan Yu or Temasek, we would have had some news by now. But there is nothing. And there is only one place secretive enough for this to happen."

He wheezed loudly, but managed to stop himself from coughing. What he had to say was too important.

"What if your son had found some information about his grandfather's journey? Maybe even some souvenir from it? Something Ifor had brought with him to Gwynedd? Could this have influenced the way the Seal worked?"

"The ring…"

"What's that?"

"My father gave Bran a ring and told him to always keep it with him. We never learned where it came from. A shard of a blue stone."

The Admiral closed his eyes, straining to remember.

"The memories are faint after so many years… That woman. She wore a brooch of gold with a blue stone around her waist. She and Ifor were very close. I don't remember what happened to her – I think she was taken away when we moored at Brigstow."

"But if all this is true…" Dylan said, thinking quickly, "and if Bran really is in Yamato right now, then that means – he's lost to me! Nobody knows the way to Yamato."

"Ah! But – no!" the Admiral cried, raising himself off the pillow, "there is a greater secret than the Phaeton's journey!"

He fell back and breathed hard for a while.

"My *aide* will give you access to all my papers," he continued at last, "what's left of them after the *Wintoncaestre* blew up. There you will find coded notes – the boy knows the code."

"The Bataavians changed the course of their ships after the *Phaeton* incident. I have tried to figure out where the new passage was, but then… my crew got restless again… and I was reassigned to the Cape Colony, not long after we got it from Bataavians.. It was there that I met a certain doctor, a spy in Bataavian employ. He told me everything."

The Admiral paused, gathering strength.

"There is only one ship in the year, and only its pilot knows the route. It sets sail from New Bataave in the late spring, past Temasek and Tagalogs. You will find all this in the notes."

"Late spring – that's… right now."

"Exactly."

The Admiral closed his eyes and focused on breathing. Dylan could see life trickling away from the frail body.

"You will do with this knowledge as you see fit," the Admiral whispered with increasing difficulty. "I trust you will... make the right decision."

He said nothing else. Dylan waited a moment and then touched the Admiral's wrist; there was no pulse. He stood up quietly and went outside.

He woke up feeling something was not right. The tent seemed somehow different in the pink light of dawn, the bedding was in the wrong position, and the table was folded.

A warm, soft hand touched his shoulder and then he remembered.

"Good morning, Commodore," said Gwenllian. He sighed.

"The night was too short."

"And now you're off again."

"There's a war on, you know," he said, smiling.

"Not right now. The battle is over."

"The Bohan's armies are still besieging Shanglin. They will need our help."

"Let them fight it out themselves. I'm still not sure we should be helping the Emperor rather than the Heavenly Army."

He chuckled. "Not you too! I find it hard enough to quell rebellious moods among the ensigns."

"And who can blame them? I despise the Ta Du court. Have you seen what they are doing with their women?"

"You mean the feet? It's been like that for centuries."

"The Rebels have disallowed that custom. And they are giving away the land to the poor peasants for free."

"But they refuse to trade with the West. They decline our envoys and kill our smugglers."

"And that is reason enough? That they don't want to peddle the Cursed Weed?"

"You sound like Bran." He shook his head and sat up, reaching for the uniform.

"Don't go yet," she pleaded. "I'm sorry."

She ran her fingers down his back, scratching the scars left on his body by all the dragons he had once ridden. A pleasant shiver ran down his spine. He thought about something for a moment, looking through the white canvas walls at the rising sun.

"Come with me," he said. "There is still some time before the siege recommences. I want to show you something."

They flew on the back of Afreolus over the vast, flat plain south of the river, a battlefield stretching from where the Ever Victorious Army had first made its landfall to the walls of Shanglin overlooking a long and narrow lake. The Bohan's army encircled the city on all sides.

"Is this what you wanted to show me?" asked Gwenllian. "How the Emperor's Army destroys the last Rebel stronghold between here and Jiangkang?"

"No."

The silver dragon dived towards the southern end of the lake. Dylan landed it on a spur of land between two outflows, beside a ruined villa of some Qin dignitary. He led her down an overgrown path to a green mound. Bits of white protruded from among the grass.

"Are these... bones?" she said with a shudder.

"Porcelain. But come over here."

She joined him at the top of the mound and, looking down, gasped. The ground beneath was strewn with shards of pottery as far as the eye could see, white, ivory and celadon green.

"These are the great celadon kilns of Yue – or what's left of them after the centuries of wars that rolled through these plains."

"Why are you showing me this?"

He did not answer. Something caught his eye, glinting in the sun. He came down and rustled through the pot shards. He found a piece of celadon pottery, a large round bead, an inch in diameter, polished so smoothly it seemed like a true gemstone – a piece of beryl or jade. Some hair-thin Qin characters were carved carefully into the clay, but they were eroded beyond recognition. There was some magic still left in the stone; Dylan could feel its slight buzz in his hand.

On an impulse, he pulled out the leather cord from the hood of his cape. He threaded the bead onto it and climbed back to the top of the mound, where he tied the cord around Gwenllian's white neck.

"It's... it's beautiful," she whispered, admiring the jewel's green shimmer. Her black eyes turned sad.

"Something troubles you."

He said nothing again, just gazed eastwards, beyond the besieged city, towards the sea.

A sudden roar of guns broke his meditation.

"I have to go," he said, "that's the Bohan's army, breaching the walls of Shanglin."

CHAPTER XIV

The messenger from Kumamoto galloped for a full night and day across the mountains, without respite, changing horses several times before reaching the procession. He was now resting in the Captain's palanquin while Kiyomasa walked beside it, carefully perusing his orders, written in the *daimyo*'s personal code.

"Silk is cheaper than jade. Make friends with the wizards for the time being. The winds blow strong from Higo, but the tide is higher in Sasshu."

The Captain frowned. The courier was almost too late – Lady Atsuko's entourage had already departed from the shrine, but they were still close enough to turn back. The first words of the missive meant that the protection of the *dorako* was more important to Lord Hosokawa than the safety of his ally's daughter. Kiyomasa was to take as many of his men as he deemed reasonable and go back to Kirishima. It was a risky gamble and a costly one.

The last sentence was an unnecessary reminder of his precarious situation. Lord Hosokawa had sent reinforcements from Kumamoto – Higo in the *daimyo*'s code – but so had Atsu-*hime*'s father – Sasshu indicated Satsuma – and these would arrive first. If Lord Nariakira decided to move the *dorako* again somewhere else, the Captain would be unable to stop him.

"You're back," Heishichi said, not even looking up from the scroll he was studying. "Did something happen to the princess?"

There was no sign of worry in his voice, not even a feigned interest.

"Atsu-*hime* is safely on her way, with the rest of my men. I have returned to aid you with the protection of the Treasure."

"I don't remember Shimazu-*dono* agreeing to this arrangement."

"I take my orders from Kumamoto, not Kagoshima."

The wizard finally raised his eyes. He removed his horn-rimmed spectacles and his sad eyes seemed suddenly smaller, narrower. His hands trembled slightly.

"My men are more than capable of taking care of the safety of the shrine."

"You have not seen what our enemies are capable of."

"You mean the ghost wolves? Pah!" Heishichi scoffed. "Those *onmyōdo* tricks are no match for the power of my wizards."

Kiyomasa struggled not to scowl. Everyone had warned him that *Daisen* Torii Heishichi was as arrogant as he was bright. *"Too clever for his own good"* was an often repeated description of the wizard. Too radical, even for the Kiyō community, this merchant's son could only find a refuge and recognition for his skills at the Satsuma court.

"How many men do you have?"

"Six – and me. The best in Satsuma. I picked them myself."

"And I have twice that – also hand-picked. I'm sure the shrine can accommodate for all of us without a quarrel."

"Do as you wish," the wizard waved his hand, "just try not to disturb me too much. I have a lot of work to do."

"I would like to see what security you already have in place," the Captain remained standing. Heishichi crumbled the scroll in his hand and sighed deeply.

"Captain… Kiyomasa, was it? Do you know what we have in there?" he asked, pointing vaguely with his Western-style pencil in the direction of the storehouse. "Something that could change the fate of Yamato. And all the combined powers of Satsuma's best wizards can do is to keep it bound safely in the cage. I have already lost two men to this beast's uncontrollable wrath; one of them died. I'm at the end of my wits here, trying to make it do our bidding. And you want to check my *security detail?*"

Kiyomasa waited patiently for the rant to end.

"All your research and sacrifice will come to naught if somebody steals it from us."

"*Let them have it!* I want to see how *they* deal with the monster! But no, you're right." He calmed down as abruptly as he had exploded. "Very well. It is time for the changing of the guards anyway. Come, Captain."

Three mages in ill-fitting black and vermillion *Rangakusha* robes stood in the corners of an equilateral triangle, their hands outstretched towards the centre of the warehouse's floor, where an eight foot tall cage had been set up. Within the cage, bound with heavy steel chains, lay a celadon-scaled dragon, half-asleep, half-stunned by the efforts of the mages. A large thaumaturgic device – a tangled mass of pipes and gears – tick-tocked rhythmically in the corner, serving some unknown purpose.

This was the first time Kiyomasa had laid his eyes on the terrible beast and cold sweat trickled down his back. It took all his soldier's training not to run away screaming. He gained a new respect for Heishichi, who calmly paced around the dragon making notes. At the end of his round, the wizard leaned over to the machine in the corner and adjusted some dial.

Two more wizards entered the chamber, ready to replace their colleagues. All five men looked at their superior. The *Daisen* nodded and raised a hand with four fingers extended. At the count of four, the two of the standing mages quickly switched positions with the newcomers. The dragon snorted, but remained motionless.

Heishichi nodded with satisfaction. The replaced wizards stretched their hands and backs and quickly left the warehouse.

"Six times a day," the wizard replied to an unspoken question.

"And you're here every time this happens?"

"Of course. Somebody has to control the situation."

"Aren't you tired? All this and your research?"

"Exhausted. If it wasn't for the extract from the *maō* plant, I think I would be dead by now."

Kiyomasa looked into Heishichi's eyes. His pupils were large and the whites of his eyes blood-shot. A barely discernible twitch pinched his lower left eyelid.

"*Maō* plant?"

"A certain physician from Kiyō prepares this wondrous concoction. I have had no need for sleep in a week."

"Do your men also take this... extract?"

"Of course! Though not as much. I do let them sleep for a few hours a day, that's why the shifts rotate."

"And you said you only have these six men?"

Heishichi gave him a long look.

"I know what you're driving at, Captain, and I can assure you, the risk is —"

"Never mind. Hopefully this situation will not last too long. I just needed to know what our resources are."

"So I'm free to go back to my studies now?"

"I will let you know about my own arrangements later."

The wizard rolled his eyes and it was obvious he cared little for Captain Kiyomasa's "arrangements".

Satō mingled into the throng of pilgrims surrounding the stage. The performance was to start at noon and last well into night. People of all classes and professions had gathered to witness the dance, a colourful throng of craftsmen, merchants, local samurai and travellers from neighbouring towns and villages. The men were accompanied by their wives, mothers and daughters in pastel-dyed spring *yukatas*, or by mistresses in gaudy kimonos and overdone make-up. As the multitude of people grew in the courtyard, the usual hangers-on appeared: street hawkers, snack vendors and an occasional pick-pocket.

"So what's all this about, then?" Bran asked. He had been looking gloomy all day and Satō was growing increasingly exasperated with his moping. The headache she'd been suffering all day didn't help her irritation.

"They're going to perform a *kagura*," explained Nagomi, "a holy dance. It will tell the story of the shrine and its *kami*."

"And what is the story?"

"You'll see for yourself. Most will unveil long before dark."

They had planned to make their strike after nightfall, but not before the crowds dispersed, hoping that the performance provided just enough distraction.

"It's about Watatsumi, the King of the Dragons, and his daughter Otohime," she added.

"How apt," said Bran.

"Shh, it starts now!" Satō tugged him on the sleeve. "Let's come closer."

In a flash of smoke and fireworks, the announcer appeared: a priest in a fiery-red robe and a white dragon mask. He spoke loudly, in an archaic, theatrical manner, waving his hands and stomping his feet exaggeratedly. He greeted the audience and told a few bawdy jokes to put them in a good mood. When he decided they had had enough, he stepped back and a puff of white smoke appeared from behind the curtain.

"See now the first tale of the Dragon Dance - a tale of how the Great Creators, the Goddess Izanami and her husband the God Izanagi, created the world."

Two actors in long, flowing white robes, in male and female disguise, came onto the stage. To the haunting sounds of bamboo flute, drum and wooden beaters, they performed a slow, majestic piece known as the Birth of Gods. The crowd was obviously familiar with the traditional dance, for it cheered and reacted in all the right places, sometimes even slightly before the appropriate moment for applause arrived.

"In their wisdom the Gods spawn the three Dragon Kings to rule the Upper Sea, the Middle Sea and the Bottom Sea", said the announcer, "but as the last of the dragons passes through the divine mother Izanami, it burns her so badly she dies!"

The "Goddess" lay still on the wooden floor, the other actor weeping over her body. Suddenly his face burst with bright red light of the setting sun.

"From the tears of divine father Izanagi," the announcer cried from behind the curtain, "comes forth the Sun Goddess Amaterasu!"

At this prompt, the crowd murmured a brief chanting prayer. Satō noticed Nagomi bend piously in a deep bow. Even if she was only represented by a prop on the theatre stage, the Goddess's presence was almost tangible.

The next scene was the dance of Ninigi, grandson of Amaterasu, descending upon Mount Takachiho with the Imperial Jewels, to rule the world from its top. This was met with great applause from the locals in the crowd, as Takachiho, rising majestically beyond the shrine, formed a natural backdrop to the performance. The actor's dance was long and exhausting, martial in its nature. Ninigi danced with a wooden lance, a bow and a sword, conveying the many battles he and his father had to win in order to conquer and rule the land of Yamato.

Near the end of this part of the performance the actor in female guise reappeared on stage. The two performed a symbolic marriage dance. The announcer spoke once more:

"Many were the victories of Ninigi, and at last the land was subdued. He wedded an Earth Goddess and she bore him a child – a brave and strong son, prince Hikohohodemi, the Hunter prince."

Satō joined the enthusiastic applause, but when she turned to Bran she caught him yawning.

"You did not like it?"

"I'm sorry, I'm sure it is all very impressive and symbolic for you, but most of it just goes over my head. I don't even understand half of what is going on."

"Maybe that general in your head could narrate you an explanation." She was joking, but Bran frowned.

"Shigemasa is keeping silent lately. I think he's too overwhelmed by all the magical energies of this place."

It was a hot, humid day. Dark clouds hovered above the shrine, but not a drop of rain yet fell. A nearby vendor was selling cold *amazake*. Bran bought a whole flask of the drink and gulped half of it in one go before passing it over to Satō. It was sweet and refreshing. Just then, the announcer reappeared on stage.

"And now for the tale of love, love found in the strangest of places. See how prince Hikohohodemi descends into the depths of the sea and discovers his beloved Otohime!"

The prince's descent was another long and complex dance in which the journey to the bottom of the sea was created through minor illusions, conjured images of exotic fish, shellfish, corals and other "wonders of the deep". At long last, the prince arrived at the Dragon King's castle. The actor climbed an imaginary fence, and saw the princess sitting alone in the coral garden. Together they performed a complicated courtship dance. Their moves were exceptionally smooth and attractive, at times almost acrobatic.

The music got more dramatic as the princess's father, the Dragon King, appeared on stage. Smoke and sparks blew from its nostrils. The King was played by two actors in a dragon costume, its body and head fiery red, rolling its artificial eyes, lolling the cloth tongue and gnashing wooden teeth to the great amusement of the audience, especially the children. The prince and the princess managed to calm the Dragon King with another bout of dancing, and the prince was allowed to marry Otohime and remain in the undersea castle.

This time Bran joined the applause at the end.

"You've enjoyed this one?" Satō asked.

"Oh, yes! Very much. Have you noticed the magic?"

"You mean the illusions in the Sea Dance?"

"There's a wizard backstage, I can see his aura. Must be one of Hei – " he stopped.

"One of what?"

"One of the troop," he finished, though she was certain this was not what he meant.

The crowd around them started to thin out.

"Is it over?" asked Bran with a rather disappointing voice.

"No, it's just a break, the actors need to rest and eat," Satō replied, laughing. "Come on, we should eat something too."

The dining room was full of people and they had to wait an unusually long time for their meal of rice, cold soymilk skin and stewed vegetables.

"Have you noticed anyone suspicious?" Bran asked the girls.

"In this crowd? Impossible," Satō shook her head, "there could be a whole army hiding among the visitors. Listen, what if the Crimson Robe decides to strike today? He too must know this is the best moment."

The night before, Bran had at last shared his suspicions with them. Satō and Nagomi agreed that there was a dark presence prowling outside the shrine walls and together they concluded it could have been none other than the Crimson Robe – even though only the wizardess had seen the enemy up close, and long weeks had passed since then.

Perhaps we want it to be him, Bran thought. *Better the demon you know…*

He turned to the priestess. "What do you think, Nagomi?"

"Me?" the girl looked at him, startled.

"You're the only one who's not here to fight. You are with us because you want to be here, not because you have to. It ought to be your decision."

"I…" Nagomi took a deep breath. "We will fight, of course."

"Are you sure?"

"What other choice do we have? Your dragon, Sacchan's honoured father… it's not like we can run away."

"But what about you? This could be a battle to the death. It would be safer-"

"You're my friends!" she interrupted him. "Do you think I will just stand by and let you get hurt?"

Friends? We've only known each other for a month… He looked to Satō. Their eyes met and she smiled reassuringly.

Friends it is, then.

"It's decided then. Let us prepare ourselves and meet back in my room. Listen – " He paused for a moment. "I'm not sure how this will end, but we may find ourselves having to flee again. If you have anything you feel will come in useful on the run, take it with you."

"No, no, no, NO!"

Hurrying feet thumped on the corridor and Satō's alarmed face appeared in the door of Bran's room.

"What happe – "

She stopped, noticing the mess on the floor. Bran was kneeling among the items thrown mercilessly around, holding his leather satchel.

"They stole the ring," he said.

"*Eeh!* Who did?"

Bran shrugged. He was calming down now and started to put the items back into the bag.

"Did they take anything else?"

"No. These weren't common thieves."

A servant girl walked past the door with a tray.

"Yōko!" Satō called her over. "Have you noticed anything suspicious?"

"What happened, *tono?*"

The girl touched her way into the room and bowed.

"There were thieves here," explained Bran.

"Oh no! I must tell t'landlord!"

"First tell us if you've heard anything."

Yōko wrinkled her nose in thought.

"There were some… samurai. I could tell by t'way they walked. It seemed strange that they did not greet me – now I think they thought they could just sneak past me."

Satō dismissed the girl and turned back to Bran.

"Hosokawa's men," he said.

"*Eeh?* What would they want from your ring?"

Bran asked the wizardess to sit down and explained what he and Dōraku had discovered about the *onmyōji* and the involvement of Lord Hosokawa in the ambush.

"We are harassed constantly since Kumamoto. That *daimyo* is onto something. All those samurai we met on the way here, they're not just here to protect the princess – you said so yourself."

"You don't think he's in league with the Crimson Robe…?"

"No." Bran shook his head. "We would be in much worse trouble if that were the case. I think he's got his own agenda."

"You should've told me sooner. I wouldn't have spent so much time with Gensai-*sama*."

He looked at her sharply.

"What have you told him?"

"Not much," she shrugged, "he doesn't even know my name. But I – I told him about Dōraku-*sama,* thinking they knew each other."

"And did they?"

"He's never heard that name."

"*Strangers you meet on the road,*" said Bran pensively. "We should have been more careful. It must have been that Captain, Kiyomasa."

"Captain Kiyomasa hasn't left with the others. I've seen him outside, just now, discussing something with the priests."

Nagomi entered the room. The priestess wore a thick hooded cloak and carried a small bundle.

"I have some soap, a towel, a flask of water, bandages… couldn't think of anything – what's happened?"

Bran gathered his belongings back into the satchel and stood up. "Somebody stole my ring. But we'll deal with that later. Let's solve one problem at a time."

Just as they made their way back to the stage, the announcer jumped on it again. He was wearing a blue robe now, and his dragon mask was red.

"You have seen how love was found in the depths of the sea. But alas! Nothing lasts forever. Three years have passed and prince Hikohohodemi is feeling homesick. His land is on the surface after all, not in the depths of the blue ocean!"

The prince and the princess reappeared. Their costumes were now richer, indicating how their status and wealth had grown over time. But the prince's dance was melancholic, his moves and gestures wistful and nostalgic, his whole body pointing upwards where his kingdom lay.

The dancers moved in the same disjointed, purposeful manner as Dōraku had on the night of his performance. The haunting music, based on strange, jarring harmonies, resembled the samurai's song. The memory of their rugged camp in the desolate, wild mountains seemed like a dream to Bran, as he stood in the measureless crowd of onlookers.

Has it really been just a few days?

At last, the princess allowed the prince to return to the surface. The Dragon King then came on stage, bearing gifts for the prince's departure: a fish-hook and two magical jewels, orange-sized orbs, glowing white and blue. As the announcer explained, these were the *kanju* and *manju*, stones that controlled the ebb and flow of the tides. With these, the prince returned to his homeland and, as a mercifully brief dancing routine showed, won a war against his former fishing companion, recapturing the land.

The announcer returned on the stage.

"A few months have passed and princess Otohime sends a message – she is with child. She agrees to give birth to her son on land, not under the sea, but she bids the prince promise he would not spy on her at childbirth."

The princess came from under the sea with her fish-like entourage. She hid inside a wooden hut to give birth. But the prince, sneakily, crept up to the birthing shed, among bursts of laughter from the audience.

In the most impressive flash of special effects and fireworks so far – it was already getting dark – the princess disappeared and in her stead emerged a writhing, fiery, blue-headed dragon. It spotted the prince and, ashamed, flew away, leaving the new-born child on the sand.

"The princess closed her heart before the prince, and closed the sea before all men," explained the announcer. "Their love was but brief, like a candle in the darkness, but the memory of it remained forever."

Bran stood transfixed. It was no coincidence. *Their love was but brief, like a candle in the darkness...* Atsuko must have hoped he would watch the Dance and understand.

Satō pulled him back into the crowd.

"The sun is almost down. We have to go."

"I... yes, of course. But what about the dance? Will it really continue into the night? The story seems over."

"That's just the first part," Satō waved her hand. "Now they will show the tale of Jimmu, the first *Mikado*, who was born of Otohime's child. There're a lot of stories left to tell."

"I heard they're going to do 'Amaterasu in the Cave' at dawn, at the special request of the High Priest," added Nagomi.

"Oh, that would have been nice! Too bad we can't stay. Come on, Bran! I'm starting to think you don't really care about our quest anymore."

The sun set beyond the cedar trees. Bran led them into the forest, along the compound's western fence. They reached a place he assumed to be near enough to the big storehouse, but out of sight of the guards by the forest gate. He made ready to burn through the boards in the wooden fence. There was no need for ropes or acrobatics this time.

"Bran?" Nagomi asked quietly just as he was about to cast his spell.

"Yes?"

"What are you planning to do once you get your dragon back?"

He turned around and saw Nagomi look at him intently, waiting for an answer. Her face, in the flickering light of a flamespark, was serious and sad.

"We'll run away and hide somewhere in the forest. Emrys should manage all three of us for a brief flight."

"That's not what I mean. What will you do *after* that?"

What was she expecting him to say? He was a stranger in a foreign land, a fugitive with a price on his head. His home was Gwynedd, far beyond the western horizon, not the alien land of Yamato...

"I... I'm not sure," he lied. "I should probably fly to Dejima, and get some help there... find out what happened to my father, maybe, if he's still alive..."

"I see," replied Nagomi and said no more. Her lips were pursed tightly, and her eyes darted away from Bran, into darkness.

Satō sighed and stood between him and the priestess. "Let's leave that until we have made it through, shall we?"

Nagomi nodded.

Bran touched the fence with his open palm.

"*Llwch!*" he whispered, and with a flash, the boards turned to sawdust, leaving an opening big enough for them to squeeze through.

Suddenly he staggered back and almost fell. Satō supported him.

"What is it? Surely that little spell – "

"No, that's not it. It's Emrys, for a moment I thought it…" Bran frowned and shook his head. "Now it's gone. Let's hurry. I've got a bad feeling."

Captain Kiyomasa's battle instinct told him this was the perfect night for a surprise assault. Everyone in the shrine was busy preparing, watching or taking part in the *kagura* performance. There were crowds in the courtyards and among buildings of the outer enclosure; there was chaos, loud noise and bright lights. There had already been a disturbance the night before, when the dragon suddenly awoke in the middle of the night. It turned out to be a false alarm, but it was enough for the Captain to order all of his men to stand guard throughout the night of the *kagura*.

Satsuma's wizards were also agitated, though none of them could quite tell why. Their magically enhanced intuitions warned them about some vague threat. Between them and Kiyomasa's men, whoever decided to attack the shrine would have to be desperate, mad, or have access to resources available only at the rank of a *daimyo*.

There had been no open conflict between the *daimyo*s since the last of the rebellions, over two hundred years ago. Any lord who dared to wage war on a neighbour faced the full wrath of the *Taikun*'s armies – and utter disgrace. Besides, which *daimyo* would be able to strike undetected, here, in the middle of Satsuma territory? Saga was too far away, Sagara too weak...

Logic, then, advised against there being any threat of a major strike against the shrine, either on this night or any other. But this was not the time or place to depend on logic and reason. There was a real, living and breathing dragon kept asleep in the inner compound. There were wolf spirits attacking armed men in the middle of the road. Some evil lurked in the dark woods around Kirishima. No, logic could not be trusted anymore. Something was bound to happen on this night, the Captain could feel it with every hair on his body.

Once again he made sure that the sentries were awake and watchful, that the weapon and armour racks were in place and that Heishichi's wizards were doing their job, whatever it was.

As night fell, evening fog began to rise from the wet grass. It thickened quickly in the stale, damp air.

"This is just what I needed," he scoffed, "mist so thick you can barely see the end of your sword. Where did it come from? I don't remember it being so bad last night."

He shrugged and wrapped his kimono sash tighter.

"Can't be helped, I suppose. It's been a muggy evening."

He ordered the lookouts to announce their position loudly once in a while and went towards the outer compound, hoping to catch at least a glimpse of the performance before the change of guards.

They hurried between two long houses with wide colonnades of cedar under broad eaves, towards the storehouse. Bran could still hear the noises coming from the dance stage, the fireworks and sound effects going off and the cries and applause of the enthusiastic crowd.

In contrast, the inner shrine was eerily quiet and empty. There were no birds singing, no frogs croaking, no insects buzzing, none of the background noises he remembered from the previous nights. It was as if all the living things had disappeared from the shrine. The compound was filled with an evening fog so thick and pale it seemed unnatural.

Nagomi whispered, confirming his fears.

"I know this mist."

"How?" asked Satō.

"It's the same mist as in Honmyōji."

As they ventured deeper into the shrine, the fog thickened even more around them. Bran could only see for less than thirty feet ahead.

"It's going to be hard to find our way around if it gets any worse," said Bran.

They found a low wall and azalea bushes to hide behind and tried to crawl as close to the storehouse as they could without arousing suspicion. Was it the same wall he had hidden behind with Atsuko; the same bushes where he had smelled her skin?

He soon spotted the great, dark blue shadow of the stilted building, carved out of the gloom by a few stone lanterns spread throughout the compound. The fog seemed to be at its densest here, as if emanating from the storehouse itself.

"Something's wrong," Bran whispered. "There should be guards."

As a waft of wind spread the curtain of fog apart for a brief moment, they saw the bodies of five samurai lying face-down on the grass before the storehouse. The building's gate had been shattered open. Bran closed his eyes, trying to contact Emrys. The link was still there, but it was much more subdued, as if the dragon had been hidden behind some new kind of barrier, even stronger than Heishichi's spell. In that instant, the noise from the outer courtyard quietened as there was a pause in the performance.

"I hear battle!" Satō stood up from behind the wall, trying to pierce through the fog. The clanging of weapons and the sound of battle cries came from the direction of the forest gate.

"It's over there!"

"I know," replied Bran, "that's where my dragon is."

"Then the Crimson Robe must be there too," said Satō with blazing eyes.

CHAPTER XV

He woke up with a headache more intense than any pain he had ever suffered. Every heartbeat released lightning strikes from the corners of his eyes. He could barely stand up. Moaning, he crawled to the basin in the bathroom and splashed his face with icy cold water. It helped a little, enough for him to gather his senses.

With his head bandaged with wet cloth, Koyata staggered to the street and then wandered the merchant district in search of a herbalist open at such an early hour. He found one, as expected, nearer the harbour, where the taverns started. Many a late night reveller queued up at the counter of old Nagayoshi.

The pharmacist took only one glance at Koyata's pained expression and bandaged head and reached for a well-worn cupboard. He took out a large square tablet of pressed brown powder.

"Break off a chunk and dissolve it in a cup of water – or saké, if you feel brave enough."

"I'm not drunk," the *doshin* said, weakly.

"It doesn't matter. This will deal with any pain."

"What is it?"

The pharmacist smiled. "For you, *doshin-sama*, this is sugar and rice flour." Koyata shrugged – he didn't care if it was Cursed Weed as long as it eased his ache. He took the tablet and reached for the money, but the pharmacist stopped his hand.

"On the house, *doshin-sama*."

I have to remember to check his warehouse one day, Koyata thought and winced. Even thinking was painful.

He returned home and lay on the floor, waiting for the brown powder to start working. He was in no shape to work today. Lately he was doing much more than was expected of him anyway. He had led several raids on the dens of the *rōnin* connected to the night attack on the Magistrate. He had been trying to discover where the grey-clad samurai had come from and gone to. He had investigated the rumours of the man in the purple cloak who had been asking many strange questions and then vanished without a trace.

He deserved rest. Perhaps it was the exhaustion that brought on the headache. Koyata was not young anymore. He reached for the basin he had brought near his bedding and changed the wet cloth on his forehead. The lightning strikes continued to pound mercilessly.

At length the medicine seemed to have started working. The ache lessened, but disturbingly, the flashes of light under his closed eyelids intensified.

There seemed to be a pattern to them, a complicated design of red lines. Koyata opened his eyes and then closed them again. The pattern continued to flash, and now there was no doubt – he was beginning to see other vivid images, blinking bright against the black screen of his eyelids.

A dirt floor – a man crawling in his own blood – a stone watchtower concealed among pillars of black rock – a dark valley on a slope of jagged boulders – a fuming mountain overlooking the sea...

The images flashed in repeated succession and all the while the red pattern pulsed in the background. After what seemed like an hour, the pain started returning – the powder's effectiveness was subsiding. As his head began to throb again, the images under his eyelids melted away, replaced by the familiar lightning strikes.

He stood up abruptly; blood rushed from his head and he almost fainted, but he swayed to the cupboard and broke off another chunk of the brown tablet. This time he simply swallowed it. He had to know what the strange vision was. He had no power of prophecy like the priests – of that he was certain. It was almost as if somebody was sending him a signal...

He waited for the images to return. They were weaker this time, but since he was prepared, he could spot more details. The red pattern was drawn in blood on the dirt floor. The fuming mountain was scarred on the sea-ward slope. The man was tortured and beaten but alive and, beside him, lay another man with a face torn by a jagged scar. Koyata had seen this scar somewhere before.

The interpreter. And the other man – was he the wizard, Takashima?

He knew the mountain. His grandfather was a fireman in Shimabara and had died on that broken slope, rescuing villagers from the lava flow. It was far away, but he could reach it in a day, perhaps, if he made haste.

Koyata grabbed the brown tablet, thrust his *jute* truncheon into his sash beside the short *kodachi* sword and ran out.

"No, I don't care about your cousin's inn. We're not stopping at Kuchinotsu."

The old steersman snapped his toothless mouth shut and shook his head. The sky was turning dark and the waves grew higher on the evening breeze.

"*Kuso!* Here's a golden coin – do you recognise it? Have you seen so much money in your life?" Koyata shook the piece before the steersman's face. "This is what you will get if we reach Shimabara before night. And this," he said, tapping the truncheon's handle, "is what you will get if we won't."

The steersman's arms drooped. He turned the boat to the wind and raised the sail as high as he could. The boat picked up some speed but it wasn't enough.

When the evening star twinkled above the horizon, Koyata gave up at last.

"Just put us to shore wherever you can. I will walk the rest of the way."

When he reached a tavern on the outskirts of Shimabara it was past the Hour of the Rat and, at first, the landlord refused to let him in. Even calling on his authority helped little – this wasn't Kiyō, after all, and the people here had little respect for the city guards. At last, a mixture of pleading, threats and calling on the virtues of his grandfather, caused the door to slide open.

"All right, all right, you will wake up the guests! What have you been eating?" the landlord cried, waving his hand before his nose, "you reek!"

"Medicine – for my head. Please, I just need a roof to sleep under, I will be gone at dawn."

"So you've said – and trust me, I'll make sure of it."

Why is he so hostile? What is wrong with this place?

He bit off another chunk of the brown tablet and swallowed. The bitter taste no longer disturbed him; in fact, it was now sweetly pleasant. Soon the powder started working its magic and he was able to fall asleep.

It was dawn again when the boat wobbled up to one of the many piers of the Shimabara harbour. All through the night Master Tanaka had guided it around the crescent-shaped peninsula, following the blood beacon's weakening call, making notes, trying to determine with more precision where the signal was coming from.

"We will rest a while and then start on our way up the Unzen Mountain," he decided, upon consulting his notes and maps. His companion nodded silently.

What an odd fellow, thought Hisashige. Etō was, reputedly, one of the most trusted and skilled of *daimyo* Naomasa's retainers, but his constant grim vigilance was most unnerving.

He knew the road to the top well. Mount Unzen was just across the narrow sea from Saga and he had often taken the trail. All along the winding path there were countless hot springs flowing from the volcanic rock, bringing relief to aching backs and limbs. If only they were not in such a hurry he would gladly soak his old weary body once again.

As they sat down to a quick breakfast, Hisashige noticed a familiar narrow face at another table. The flared nostrils were unmistakable, as were the triple dragon-scale markings of the Hōjō clan on his vest. The other samurai noticed them also and rose to greet them.

"Yokoi-*dono*!" Master Tanaka bowed, "what a timely meeting. What are you doing in Shimabara?"

"I'm on my way from Kiyō where I had some errands to run. You've met young Motoda, my pupil?" A barely adolescent man standing behind Yokoi bowed deeply, silently.

"Kiyō?" the old mechanician eyed him suspiciously. He knew Yokoi Tokiari was a mutual acquaintance, but he wasn't certain how much the man could be trusted.

The samurai leaned down and lowered his voice.

"Truth be told, I am investigating a disappearance of a certain *Rangakusha*."

"On whose authority?"

Why would Kumamoto be interested in the Takashimas?

"My own," replied Yokoi, straightening back. "Or rather, his heir."

"You've seen Satō-*sama?* Is the boy all right?"

The samurai nodded with a smile. "I see you know which family I'm talking about. He was fine when I last met him – although it was in the strangest of circumstances and I can't vouch for his safety now. I was hoping I could help in the search for his father, but alas, I could find no clues."

"Then what are you doing *here?*"

"What do you mean? I'm waiting for the ferry back to Kumamoto. My mission has failed."

"But – " Hisashige hesitated. He still wasn't sure how much the other man could be trusted. Then he remembered the divination. *The strength of allies…* " – but Takashima-*sama* is here!" he finished in a whisper, "on Mount Unzen."

Yokoi stared at him in amazement for a while then clapped his knee in joy.

"Good fortune brought us together! Tell me, tell me all, how come you know of this? But I will let you finish your breakfast first. We shall be waiting outside, pondering the twisted paths of Fate!"

Master Yokoi travelled in an elaborate, four-man palanquin and so, to keep up with him on the journey, Master Tanaka reluctantly had to rent one as well. His was a light, two-man piece, a little more than a cushioned chair with curtains. It allowed him to soak in the scenery of the mountain path and inhale the sulphur-infused air which he knew were good for his old lungs.

Etō refused a transport and instead walked at a hurried pace beside the two palanquins, ever watchful, as did young Motoda on the other side. The blood trail was now faint but it led them unmistakably straight up the mountain slope, a dome of black lava a few *ri* east of the main peak. The entire eastern mountain-side was sliced off as if with a great knife, a terrible mark left upon the earth by the devastating earthquake.

Master Yokoi loudly expressed his dissatisfaction with their chosen route, but had no choice but to follow. As the palanquins climbed up the path the wind whistled through the rocky outcrops and it seemed to Hisashige that the spirits of the thousands that perished in the Shimabara catastrophe still filled the land with their wails and despair. Even sixty years on, no plants grew upon the black, scarred stone. Past the huts of the quarry workers and poor farmers who struggled with their buckwheat and radishes on the hardy soil there were no settlements and the path seemed to end amid the rubble and outcrops of lava.

"Time to leave the palanquins," said Hisashige, climbing out of his vehicle. The wind dispersed the clouds and the sulphuric fumes and the pale sun was high up. He looked down, towards the harbour and the sea stretching to the azure horizon. Through some phenomenon of echoes the sound of the crashing waves reached his ears even here, mixed with the cries of the kites and the shouts of the fishermen.

"Are you certain of this, Tanaka-*sensei*?" Yokoi asked. He came up to the chunks of lava rock, perforated like a petrified sponge, piled across the path and searched for a way forward.

Hisashige focused on the beacon. He could barely sense it now, its power almost spent. He opened a small round box at his sash and looked at the geomantic compass inside. The needle wobbled and stabilised, pointing towards the peak of Mount Unzen.

"We're not far," he said.

Etō came up to them and said quietly: "I found a passage on the left side of the rubble. It's narrow, but we can make it."

They ordered young Motoda to stay with the increasingly uneasy porters and either wait until nightfall or follow if they could find another way. Then, one by one, they sneaked through an opening among two large boulders. Once past this obstacle, the path wound onwards, into an even more inhospitable land. There were no birds here bar a few carrion crows observing them curiously from the tops of the lava outcrops. The rock formations took on more fantastic shapes; sharp, jagged pillars and arches of black stone. Still they could see no trace of any place where the missing *Rangaku* scholar could be held captive.

The mountain top was within their sight and Master Tanaka was beginning to lose hope. What if Shūhan had only been carried through this dire place when he had sent his signal? He could be somewhere entirely different by now...

Just then, Etō discreetly tapped him on the shoulder.

"We are being followed," the samurai whispered.

"Are you sure?"

Etō looked offended for a brief moment, then nodded. "Let us hide around that next corner and wait," he said.

They referred the matter to Yokoi and all three hid behind a massive pillar of volcanic rubble. Etō drew his sword noiselessly and raised it above his head.

"Careful. It might not be an enemy," cautioned Hisashige, wary of his divinations.

A man walked slowly and carefully from around the pillar, holding one hand to his head with pained expression. Etō waited until they were certain the stranger was alone and then leapt out from the shadow, blade aimed at the man's chest.

"*Halt!* Who are you and why are you trailing us?"

"I could ask the same of you."

His hand reached for the handle of his truncheon but the fierce-looking samurai twitched the blade threateningly. Koyata tensed. He ran out of the brown powder some time ago and his head was beginning to thump again, though noticeably weaker than before.

"You could, but there's three of us and one of you," the samurai said coldly. "Besides, it's you who had been following us since Shimabara."

"I'm not following anyone. You are merely going in the same direction as me – it seems."

He could not decide whether they were friends or foes. They may have been allied with whoever was keeping Takashima captive, but one of the samurai wore the triple-scales of Hōjō and the other two bore the bamboo-shoots of Saga, the protectors of Kiyō. These were good credentials.

"I am following the red pattern," he said. "Perhaps you could explain to me what it is."

The oldest of the three stepped forward with an astonished expression. His head and beard were grey, almost silver, and his eyes were wise and well-meaning.

"You're a wizard?"

"I am *doshin* Koyata of the Kiyō town guards," he bowed low, "and although I know many *Rangaku* scholars, I am not one myself."

The grey-haired man whispered something to the other two. The one who bore the Hōjō markings nodded in agreement, but the other one remained unconvinced. At last he, too, lowered his sword.

"The pattern you seek is a beacon of help," explained Master Tanaka after they finished their introductions. "Sent by a friend of ours. Though why or how it reached you all the way in Kiyō, I cannot tell."

Koyata decided not to share with them the details of his investigation into the mystery of the Takashima mansion. He trusted them, but not much.

"Have you found the gorge of jagged stones yet?" he asked. They looked at him blankly.

"The black watchtower then?"

"We don't know what you mean," said Master Tanaka. "I was guiding us using divinations and geomancy."

"In fact, we were at a loss as to our direction," added Yokoi, "the path doesn't seem to go any farther."

Koyata looked around. The landscape was familiar; he had seen it before, flashing in his mind. He ran up to the next bend in the road and looked down.

"Over there," he said, pointing to a cluster of boulders with a lonely crippled pine struggling to take root in the cracks of the lava. "Follow me."

Past the boulders was a narrow gully which soon grew to the valley of jagged stones he had seen in his visions. He bade them crouch down and they made their way carefully between the rocks.

The lowest part of the gorge was green, overgrown with lichen and moss and a few gnarly trees. Water trickled from some spring in the mountainside, yellow and smelly. Beyond the spring rose a high tower of black stone, a square base with tapering walls supporting the slender second floor, reachable only by a ladder. The third level, rising above the edge of the gully, was built of cedar beams, once golden but now darkened with soot and smoke, underneath a triangular roof of black tiles.

Two spearmen in familiar grey uniforms guarded the entrance. A few more patrolled the valley, while a group of men and women worked behind the watchtower tending what looked like a very poor vegetable patch. There was one more building at the very end of the gorge – a living quarters for the guards and servants, guessed Koyata.

"The servants are here, but the master is away," said Master Tanaka, consulting his geomantic compass. "Can you smell the stench of blood?"

"I can smell nothing but brimstone," said Yokoi, shaking his head.

"It's faint, but it's there," agreed Koyata. "What does it mean?"

"I don't know. Evil things. But the needle is steady and I detect no more magic in this place than is present in an average *Rangaku* abode."

"Perhaps Takashima-*sama* is no longer here," said Yokoi.

"There's only one way to find out," said Koyata, drawing his short *kodachi* sword. He noticed the silent samurai, Etō, do the same with his weapon.

"There must be at least eight swordsmen in this valley," said Yokoi, "are you sure it's wise to just charge them like that? I mean, I can aid you with my blade but Tanaka-*sensei* here is, if you'll excuse me, past his prime…"

Hisashige's eyes glinted. "I would not insist on coming here if I thought I'd be a burden, Yokoi-*dono*."

"I did not mean…"

"Observe."

The mechanician took the lacquer sheath hanging by his belt and instead of drawing a sword he unscrewed the hilt and pulled out a short iron rod with copper wire coiled around it.

"*Teppō!*" gasped Yokoi.

"A Bataavian thunder gun," said Koyata studying the weapon. "I've read about them but never seen one. Are you a good shooter?"

"Good enough. But I reckon I can only charge this toy enough for one shot before the fight is over."

"Then make it count. I suggest the commander of that patrol on the right. He seems to me the toughest of the bunch."

They huddled behind a wall of piled rocks, waiting for the three-man patrol to come within range. Hisashige turned a gear on his gun and the copper coil lit up red. He aimed it carefully and pulled the trigger. The recoil almost threw the weapon from his hand, but the lightning hit the grey-clad swordsman straight in the chest, killing him instantly. Forking bolts grazed the other two men, throwing them into a daze.

Koyata and Etō leapt over the rocks and struck the other two *rōnin* down before they managed to recover from the stun. The *doshin* noticed that Yokoi stood back, only feigning a fight. *Two against six*, he counted quickly, *and they're not bad with swords, I bet. What was I thinking?*

Three more swordsmen ran up to them from the other side of the gorge. Koyata drew his *jutte* truncheon, trapped an enemy's sword in the hook protruding from the handle and pushed forward, tripping the grey-clad man's left leg. The swordsman fell down and never got up, a *kodachi* blade firmly embedded in his chest.

This felt nice. This was just like in the old days, fighting the smugglers and the bandits on the streets of Kiyō harbour. Koyata looked up – Etō fought two men at once, with three more running towards them. *Spears. Kuso. Doshin's* short weapons were no match against the pole arms. He turned to Yokoi, still waving the sword harmlessly at the back.

"Be useful!"

He grabbed the samurai by the sleeve and swung him around. Yokoi fell forwards, bumping into one of the grey uniforms. Etō did not waste the opportunity; one of his opponents was dead within seconds. Koyata finished the other one with a truncheon blow to the head.

"You fight well for a town guard," the samurai spoke, catching a quick breath.

"But now I'm afraid we've met our match," Koyata said, nodding towards the spearmen. Etō prepared himself, but his grim face twitched, betraying nervousness.

A sudden thunder echoed throughout the valley and one of the spearmen fell on his face with a cry. The other two halted and turned, looking for the owner of the gun. Etō yelled and jumped at the closest of them; Koyata followed, although he could only hope to distract his opponent. He dodged too late, tripped on a stone and the spearman thrust and pierced his side, almost pinning him to the rock. Koyata grabbed the shaft and struggled with the *rōnin*, disregarding the pain.

A sword struck the bamboo shaft, splintering it in two. The spearman stumbled, losing his balance, falling straight onto the blade. Koyata rolled aside, letting the *rōnin* drop to the ground before finishing him off with the short sword.

"You're hurt!" Yokoi-*dono* helped him up. The *doshin* knelt on one knee, breathing hard, holding his bleeding side. As far as he could tell, his vital organs were still intact. All the enemies were dead. Etō was also bleeding from a cut, though not a severe one. Master Tanaka climbed out of his hiding place among the rocks, where he had crept during the fight, and helped to bandage the *doshin's* wound with a strap of cloth. Yokoi's nostrils were wider than ever, as were his eyes. His sword was bloodied. Koyata realised it was this blade that shattered the spear.

"Thank you, *tono*. And apologies for earlier. I was unspeakably rude."

"No, no, that's quite understandable. We were all fighting for life. But now we must hurry into the tower. I'm afraid the ladder…"

"It's fine. I'll keep watch."

The men and women tending to the garden had already disappeared into some nooks and crannies of the mountainside. The way to the tower lay open. Etō and Master Tanaka climbed the ladder first, followed by the ever cautious Yokoi-*dono*.

More sounds of battle came from inside the tower, followed by another thunder clap from Master Tanaka's gun. Soon the door opened from inside and Master Tanaka appeared carrying a bloodied, battered body. Yokoi climbed the ladder behind him, with another man in his arms. Last came Etō; his sword was broken and his right arm hung limply along his side. When the silent samurai reached the ground he staggered and fell to his knees.

"What now?" the *doshin* asked wearily. The make-shift bandage around his stomach was soaked through; he was badly in need of a doctor or a priest. "We'll never drag them back to the path. I'm struggling to stay up as it is."

"We won't have to," said Master Tanaka smiling. He pointed to the ridge of the valley where the young Motoda stood waving and shouting.

"It was madness," the *doshin* said, laughing quietly and wincing as the wound in his side twitched. The old priest taking care of the local shrine had barely enough power to stem the internal bleeding. "I would never have dreamed of charging a fortress like that with just four men."

"All my divinations confirmed my endeavour would succeed, but even I did not believe them in the end," said Master Tanaka, shaking his head.

They were sitting in the common room of the headman's house near the foot of the mountain. The porters managed to carry them down only to the first village; there the injured had to rest, waiting for the more skilled healers to arrive from Shimabara.

With Etō out cold in the headman's bedroom alongside the men they had brought from the watchtower, there were now just three of them left to decide the next important matter: what to do with the freed captives.

"I'm not sure I understand," said Master Tanaka when Yokoi-*dono* raised the question.

"Surely each of us had his reasons for coming here. Who of us will take the scholar back home with them?"

"Naomasa-*dono* has already prepared a house in which Takashima-*sama* will rest far from prying eyes," replied Tanaka.

"He could do the same in one of my Kumamoto villas," said the other man, "What about you, *doshin*? What were your orders?"

"I have no orders, *tono* – I told you, I came here of my own accord. The Magistrate officially announced the scholar dead. But if they ever found out he was alive and I helped him escape…"

"Do you have any family in Kiyō?" Master Tanaka asked.

"I don't – but I don't see what that's got to do – "

"My master's domain may be small, but Naomasa-*dono* has many connections in high places. He would gladly arrange a position for you somewhere else. A better position, in a more prestigious city."

Koyata noticed Yokoi-*dono*'s nostrils flare like two mountain caves. *He's started bargaining already. There's three of us and my vote decides. What can* you *offer, Hōjō clansman?*

He knew Master Tanaka's proposition was hard to beat. Hosokawa may have been a powerful *daimyo* here in the south, but he was one of the outer lords, with no access to the *Taikun*'s court. The lords of Saga, on the other hand, were welcomed even to the *Mikado*'s palace.

"The treasury of Kumamoto would be at your disposal," Hosokawa's retainer said uneasily.

A bribe, then. Not bad, but not good enough, either. Why was that injured scholar so important, anyway?

"I will have to think about it," Koyata said at last, standing up from the low table and bowing. "The wounded can't be moved until the priests arrive, so we're not in a hurry."

"Of course," both old men agreed eagerly.

"Oh, and what do you want me to do with the interpreter?" he asked.

"Who?"

"The other prisoner."

Yokoi-*dono* shrugged. "We didn't even know he was there, did we, Tanaka-*sama*? Is he of any interest to you?"

"I have a few questions to ask when he wakes."

Yokoi-*dono* waved his hand. "Do whatever you wish."

CHAPTER XVI

As the evening turned into night, the guards began to grow bored and restless.

In the north-western corner of the inner compound, a dirt path led through a small, simple gate deep into the forest. Once, it must have been built for transporting lumber for construction and repairs straight from the woods, but nowadays it was mostly used by those of the priests who went into the forest to gather herbs and mushrooms.

Apart from the gate leading towards the main courtyard, this was the only way in. Captain Kiyomasa, aware of the strategic value of this point, made sure to put a strong watch around it. Two of Hosokawa's retainers agreed to stand at the gate alongside several of Kiyomasa's own spearmen.

"Damn this fog," said the younger of the two, almost a boy, wearing striped *hakama* and blue kimono, "have you ever seen anything like it? It appeared so quickly, almost as if conjured."

"Hold your tongue," the other samurai reprimanded sharply, "you'll bring us bad luck with your superstitious talk. We should be glad the fog is here, nobody will attack in this kind of weather."

"Do you really think somebody would want to assault this shrine?"

"The Captain seems to think so, and that should be good enough. He's getting his orders directly from Hosokawa-*dono*, so we can't argue."

The younger guard scoffed.

"That upstart. I don't see why – "

"He's a good soldier. And he comes from a great family."

"A distant, impoverished offshoot. Thinks too much of himself, if you ask me."

"Good thing nobody asks you, then."

The younger samurai scowled and paced around the brazier to keep himself warm.

"There's nothing worth taking here," he said.

"I'm not so sure. Have you seen that great storehouse in the middle? There's three of our own posted in front of it and those mages keep coming in and out. I think there's some kind of barbarian weapon inside. You know what they say about those Satsuma folks."

The other retainer nodded. There was no need to add anything more, the Shimazu clan were well known in the South for their illicit contacts with the Westerners and it only made sense that there was some kind of device or magical treasure stored in the shrine that had something to do with the barbarians.

"I wonder how long we are supposed to endure this schedule," he said. "Night is for sleeping, not for standing outside in the fog."

"It shouldn't be more than a day or two; I think we're supposed to get some reinforcements from Kagoshima."

The guard in the striped *hakama* raised his eyebrows.

"Shimazu samurai are coming here? That should be interesting."

"I hope they will bring something to drink. This place is supposed to be famous for booze, but I haven't seen so much as a flask of saké since we've been stationed here!"

"What do you expect, it's a shrine. The only saké they have is the one on the sacrificial altar."

"Too bad Gensai-*sama* has gone with the princess. He always had something to wet one's lips."

The older guard started to laugh along with his companion, but the laughter died in his throat.

"Hark! Did you hear that?"

There was a strange, gurgling noise on the other side of the gate, where two of Kiyomasa's footmen stood guard. The old samurai stood up, grasping the hilt of his sword in anticipation.

"Everything all right over there?" he shouted. There was no response.

"Should we raise the alarm?" asked the other.

"Not until we know what's going on. You, man, go and see what's going on the other side."

Kiyomasa's spearmen, as ordered, opened a small wicket in the gate and peeped outside. A cry of terror froze in his throat.

In an instant, the gate burst open with a terrible force, showering the two samurai with shards and splinters of wood. Retainers drew their swords, ready for a fight. The soldiers stood alongside them, except one, who started running towards the alarm gong. The runaway was the first to die, slain by a dart thrown by an invisible enemy from within the mist.

"Who's there? Show yourself!" the older samurai cried, but there was nothing in front of them, only the milky white wall of the fog. A great spear blade cut through the air with a metallic whistle and one of the soldiers fell down without a sound, slashed almost in two. The blade struck again, but this time it clanged against the retainer's sword.

"Not so good against a real swordsman, eh?" the samurai boasted. "Come out and fight like a man, coward!"

A blood-curdling cackle rang out and the owner of the halberd moved into the light. It was no man, but a dark human-shaped shadow, hovering one foot above ground. It held the spear in its long, thin arms with confidence. Its head had no face, just a blank surface, but even without a mouth, it laughed.

The other retainer froze in panic and dropped his sword to the ground. The demon moved towards him in a flash and slashed his torso in two, then turned against the first one. The old samurai managed to parry another blow of the great spear, but he felt his shoulders stiffen with unearthly cold. *This is no match for a mortal man,* he thought briefly.

"Fall back to the storehouse!" he cried to the remaining soldiers. "Alert the priests!"

Before he could add anything more, the spear's blade pierced his chest. He slashed his sword at the ghostly shadow, but it went through the enemy as if through thin air.

With dying eyes, he saw the shadow move further into the mist and darkness in search of other prey. A human appeared in the gate, barely visible in his black *yamabushi* robes. He was leading two pairs of oxen by the reins. The animals were pulling a large, four-wheeled cart with a flat platform. The hermit looked down at the dying samurai with pity, then whistled. Immediately, six samurai appeared around him, dressed in identical grey uniforms.

The three guards posted at the storehouse huddled around a flaming tripod brazier. The day was warm but as night fell and the evening fog rose from the dewed grass, it got cold.

"I wanted to see today's *kagura*," complained one of the samurai, sporting a large moustache in the fashion popular in the southern islands. It made him look older and more distinguished from the other two.

"Worthless rural circus tricks," scoffed another, shortest of the three, but wearing the most elaborate armour, old style, inherited from some belligerent ancestors. "I'm telling you, there's nothing like the Hakata theatre. These peasants don't know proper entertainment; it's just illusions and smoke for them."

"It would still be better than sitting here in this fog," replied the first one and sneezed, "only *shinobi* enjoy nights like this."

"There's no such thing as the *shinobi* anymore. The *Taikun* made sure of it."

Azumi scowled under her hood and clenched her fists. She was sitting a few yards away from the brazier, and had been observing the outpost for the last couple of hours, waiting for the signal to strike. They did not see her, of course; the *tengu*'s invisibility cloak was flawless.

"I know that! It's just a turn of phrase," the guard sneezed again.

"Here, have some of this," the third guard reached out to the first one with a gourd, "it's local, powerful stuff."

"Aaah, excellent! *Kanpai!*" the moustachioed samurai raised the gourd straight to his lips and took a great swig. "Enough!" laughed the owner of the gourd, "leave some for us."

"That hit the spot. Those Satsuma folk sure know how to brew!"

"Wait, did you hear that?" the armoured guard stood up, listening to something in the distance.

"I can't hear anything but the music and clapping from the stage."
It's enough that I heard it.

"It sounded like a cry coming from the lumber gate."

"Well, it's about time those lazy oafs announced their position. We should too, come to think of it," the moustachioed guard rose and cried out, "All clear at the store – !"

He didn't finish. A throwing dagger stuck into his throat. The other two jumped to their feet, swords drawn. "Attack! We're under attack!" cried the short samurai, slashing wildly into the air in front of him, searching for the shadowy attacker. Azumi observed this with slight bemusement, standing just a few feet away. *This is too easy.*

"Strike the gong!" the armoured guard cried. The other samurai leapt towards the alarm bell but before he could reach it, three sharp, small missiles whistled through the air and embedded themselves in his neck. Gurgling, he fell on his back. The remaining guard's eyes widened in fright as he recognized the star-shaped missiles for what they were.

"It's impossible… you have been vanquished! The *Taikun* had you all killed!"

"Not all of us," said Azumi, casting the hood of the *tengu's* cloak enough to reveal only her cold eyes. They were the last thing the guard saw before the swift sickle blade on a long iron chain bypassed his parry and slashed through his trachea. His spinal cord severed, he died in an instant.

The lid creaked open. Inside the plain lacquer box lay three slim vials of crystal glass, enclosed with porcelain stoppers. The contents of one was brown and murky, the other grass-yellow, like weak *sencha*. The third liquid was clear, transparent.

Brown was for sleep. Yellow was for waking. Clear was for death and glory.

Sugimoto took a gulp from the yellow vial. It was his time to join his brothers in the storehouse. The liquid itself was cool and bitter, but soon the familiar warmth and sweetness spread throughout his body. He felt his veins swell – this was the most unpleasant effect of taking the extract of the *maó* plant. This and the cramps that started wandering from his calf muscles to the shoulders. He shook his head and opened his eyes wide. He felt refreshed and fully wakened.

The earth wizard opened the door of the long, one-story building in which they had been settled and stepped outside, into the fog. Everything seemed bright and crisp. He knew the effects of the extract would soon subside and then he would have to take another sip to be able to stand through the night. And then another. The intervals between sips had been decreasing in an alarming manner.

His task was dull and dangerous, but he took pride in it. Master Heishichi had chosen Sugimoto and five other wizards from among many dozens. He deemed them most trustworthy, most reliable, and most skilled. Trained at the best of schools, by the best of teachers. Entrusted with the protection of Satsuma's greatest secret.

He stumbled over something in the mist. He looked down and saw, at his feet, the body of a dead samurai with a long, needle-thin blade sticking out of the neck.

"Look, there's somebody still alive!" the wizardess cried and, ignoring Bran's plea for caution, darted across the small courtyard in front of the warehouse towards a lonely figure, leaning its back against the pillar. The man raised his sword against them with a shaking hand.

"The pilgrims from the forest?"

"Captain Kiyomasa!"

"What are you doing here?"

Bran passed him by and ran up the short stair, through the burst open gate into the storehouse.

"It's gone," he cried from inside. "There're more bodies here."

He ran back out.

"You're too late," Kiyomasa said and started coughing.

"What happened?" Bran asked, looking at the five dead bodies.

"What does it look like? We were attacked by all sorts of enemies. *Shinobi*, ghosts, *rōnin*, you name it. The wizards came to help us and they're now fighting at the gate," the Captain said, pointing towards the fighting. The mist in the direction of the gate flashed with explosions and thunderclaps like clouds during a storm.

"Have you seen a man dressed in a crimson robe?"

"That I have not," the Captain replied and winced as blood spurted from the wound in his side. Nagomi knelt to examine it, but Bran stopped her.

"We don't have time for this, he'll be fine."

"I'm no use in a fight anyway," the priestess protested, shaking his hand off her shoulder. "Go on, I'll join you soon."

He hesitated for a moment, uncertain what to do. Satō made the decision for him.

"Come on, they're getting away!" she cried and pulled him into the mist.

The wheels of the oxcart squeaked away in the distance, accompanied by the shuffling of four pairs of hooves. The mist muffled the sounds.

"Wait," the *Daisen* commanded, stopping his students from pursuing the attackers. "Let Kiyomasa's men bleed them out first. We must act smart if we are to avenge our brothers."

Only Sugimoto and two others remained from the onslaught. Three mages lay dead inside the storehouse; the corpses made for a gruesome sight. They had no chance to defend themselves. The sudden assault disrupted the spell patterns and the backlash of magical energies destroyed their bodies even before the blades of the assassins reached them. That one of the grey-uniformed *rōnin* had also been caught in the torrent and torn apart was little consolation.

"Spread out," said the *Daisen*. "Ishida, go right, along the wall. Try to find out how they manage to control that damned *dorako* on their own." Somehow the enemy had succeeded in safely transporting the beast onto an oxcart. "Takano, help those soldiers out before they make a mess of themselves."

As the other two disappeared into the mist, the *Daisen* looked at Sugimoto and said:

"Stop that oxcart. At any cost."

The dense fog was no trouble for him; on the contrary – he could see the enemy without being seen himself. Sugimoto was adept at using the True Sight, a secret technique he had learned directly from a Bataavian tutor at Nansei. From a safe distance he was able to assess the situation and choose the best course of action undisturbed.

His attuned element was Earth. A rare, unpopular element, not as spectacular as Fire or Air. He could not bring down lightning or summon walls of flame like his brothers; but he felt comfortable and calm manipulating the slow, steady rhythms of the rock and sand, safe in the knowledge that, when the time came for action, he could be just as effective as the other wizards.

He knelt down on one knee and touched the ground with both hands, sensing the miniature ley lines like mole-tracks in the moist soil. He whispered the spell word and tugged at one of the invisible strings.

A ripple passed under the dirt like a giant earthworm and headed straight towards the oxcart surrounded by enemy soldiers. Several men fell down as the ground quaked beneath their feet. The wheels of the cart buckled and one of them snapped.

The earth so close to the magical nexus was pliable, yielding. With little effort the wizard turned the flow of the ripple against the bullocks pulling the cart. The animals lowed in panic as the earth beneath them started trembling and cracking. The man leading the oxen, a *yamabushi* in black robes, stopped and looked around, searching for the unseen enemy but Sugimoto was safely hidden in the thick, impenetrable mist.

The wizard was so concentrated on the task that he only noticed the shadowy demon behind him at the last moment. He turned around quickly to face the new danger. The spear's blade, aimed at his back, pierced the chest.

But Sugimoto was not one to go down easily. His dying hands grabbed the spear's pole. The grey shadow tried to wrestle it from the wizard, but his grip was strong. With freezing hands, he reached inside his sleeve and took out the third of the crystal vials. Pouring its contents down his throat, he felt a sudden surge of power. He knew the energies released would destroy him just like the mages in the storehouse, but it was too late to worry about it. With the last breath, with the last surge of power, Sugimoto cried the words of the most dreadful of his spells; the Earth Tomb.

"*Aardse Nor!*"

The earth opened beneath his feet and swallowed the wizard, the spear and the bewildered *yōkai*.

A jolt went through Ozun's body, and the *yamabushi* dropped to his knees, supporting himself on the staff. Azumi appeared at his side promptly, helping him up.

"What is it?"

"I lost the *yōkai* – the one from Honmyōji."

"Lost? How?"

"I don't know, but ... it cost me dearly."

"Do you need help?"

"No." Ozun shook his head and wiped the trickle of blood from his nose. "Get back to the others. They need you now more than I do. I sense more danger coming."

She nodded and slipped back to the rear of the convoy.

He pulled on the reins strongly, forcing the oxen to press on. The animals lowed in protest, the broken wheel snapped away and the axle ground in the mud, but the cart moved slowly on. There was yet hope. The cart was their passage to freedom. The load had to be delivered to the Master; only then would he set them free from his service.

The ground around the cart was scorched, cratered and scarred with fire and lightning. The few remaining *rōnin* and Nanseians – masters of unarmed combat recruited from the southern islands – huddled behind a *kekkai* shield, helpless. The enemy wizards, out of range of any counterattack, were launching missile after missile against the weakening barrier.

"What happened to your other men?" Azumi asked the commander of the grey-shirts, a bulbous-eyed youth with big ears and a gloomy face. There should have been at least a dozen of his *rōnin* in the troop but she could see only half that number.

"We were ambushed by a bunch of samurai while you were flirting with your lover-boy," he snapped. "At least we got all of them."

"That shield won't hold for much longer," she said.

"You think I don't know that?" He ducked as another missile exploded a mere foot ahead of them.

"There's another wizard hiding in the fog; much more powerful than those two," explained one of the Nanseians. His bald head was covered with sweat and burn marks. "He keeps us in check whenever we try anything."

"Why don't you make yourself useful, *kunoichi*, and do something about it," said the grim-faced *rōnin*.

"Useless brawlers," she scoffed. She wrapped herself in the cloak of black feathers and disappeared into the shadows and fog.

From behind, the enemy wizard in glasses seemed almost unassuming. Thin, long-limbed, awkward in movements, a weakling by any measure. While Azumi approached him under cover of her magical garment, he performed a series of strange dance-like movements, waving arms in wide curves that left fiery traces in the air; a powerful incantation that even she, otherwise blind to magic, could sense through her quivering skin.

"Behind you!" a voice shouted a warning. The wizard turned around, losing focus; his incantation fizzled out in a noiseless flash.

Who dares?

Nobody should have spotted her. The black feather cloak was a powerful artefact – the old *tengu* fought long and hard defending it. Who could have peered through its magic?

She glanced to the side. Two youths ran, without stopping, towards the oxcart. One in *Rangakusha* clothes, paid her no attention. The other, in an indigo kimono, looked straight at her with a puzzled expression as he ran past. She recognized them in an instant.

Them! Here?

Was the red-haired girl somewhere here as well? She quickly shook off her surprise and started after them, forgetting all about the wizard.

He, however, would not let her go so easily.

"Show yourself, filth," the wizard cried and whirled his hands in half-circle, igniting the very air before him.

Her feather cloak caught fire.

CHAPTER XVII

The priestess tied the bandage and rose from her knees. Her hands felt warm on his cuts; blue light spread from her fingers and where she touched, the wounds closed.

"We need to help them," the girl said, ready to run after her friends.

"No, child," he said shaking his head. "Heishichi-*sama*'s wizards will hold out, and if they don't, we won't help them. But we can get help. Come with me."

He led her away from the battle, towards the outer court. As they got closer, the lights grew brighter and the cheerful din of crowds grew louder. The pilgrims were oblivious to the massacre in the inner compound and the Captain could almost forget about the fighting himself. The *kagura* dance entered its most frantic, loud and magical phase, the tale of *Mikado* Jimmu's battles with the Long-legged Man.

"Gather as many priests as you can," the Captain shouted over the noise, "and meet me back here. But don't take long."

"They... they may not hear me out," said the priestess.

"Tell them I sent you. Tell them it's about the Treasure."

The priestess nodded and her red hair disappeared into the crowd. Kiyōmasa himself ran to the Offertory Hall, where he was hoping to find the head priest and his retinue. If his suspicions were right, they would need all the holy hands they could find.

Near the gate the fog thinned out and Satō could see everything more clearly. It was a regular battle; the *Rangakusha* wizards, led by the lanky man in glasses, and Captain Kiyomasa's soldiers, strove against a few *rōnin* swordsmen in grey uniforms. There was a mage also among the enemies, some *onmyōji* who cast protective spells from behind, but she could not see him very well in the fog.

An oxcart was stuck in the middle of the lumber gate, one of its wheels shattered. The bullocks whined, trying to pull the broken wagon across the muddy road. On the cart's platform lay a large box-shaped container covered with a black cloth. The cargo was guarded only by two *rōnin*.

"Do you see the Crimson Robe anywhere?" asked Bran.

Satō shook her head.

"This is still sacred ground. He must be hiding somewhere outside."

"Can you take care of those two swordsmen?"

"Easily." She could feel the energies of the nexus surging through her. It made her dizzy and exhilarated at the same time. Even the headache disappeared. "Leave them to me."

She put on the leather glove and drew her sword. The gears whirred, the brass arrow reached half-way through the dial. She focused her power into the blade and the feedback, multiplied in the air sizzling with the energies of the nexus, made the sword jolt so hard she almost dropped it.

She had not been trained in using the True Sight, but even she could now faintly see the flow of energies around the blade; sparkling currents of blue and white light. When she drew the first frost rune, its image hovered for a moment in the air.

"*Bevries*," she whispered. The word thundered and echoed throughout the space between her and the *rōnin*. A wave of cold air spread from Satō's sword and froze both of the warriors into solid blocks of ice.

Such a powerful spell should have left her exhausted and spent, but she was barely tired, only a bit short of breath. She felt almost omnipotent. What would happen if she used blood magic here? *Would I even survive so much power?*

The box of the cart burst open in a flash which blinded her for a second. She laughed. Bran must have also discovered the ease with which magic worked in the shrine. Smouldering splinters and bits of molten iron showered the ground around her.

The oxcart was still moving, although even more slowly and laboriously than before. She saw Bran scramble off the ground, shake his head and jump onto the moving platform. The boy struggled with the chains wrapped around some large dirt-green metallic bulk lying on the cart. It had taken Satō a long while to realise what she was looking at through the mist and smoke. When she did, her heart skipped a beat. The dragon, asleep, bound and famished, was a far more magnificent sight than she could have imagined. No pictures or description could have given it justice. Greater than any animal she had ever seen, dwarfing the two oxen with its immense girth; in its sleep it seemed more like a statue carved of a single piece of jade, a pile of green jewels heaped into the form of a beast. Moonlight shimmered off its scales and black sickle-like claws. She knew she should feel the onset of the dragon fear just looking at it, but all she could feel now was awe.

Bran struggled with the chains and at last he managed to burn them through, but the dragon still would not waken, the leathery wings – *wings!* – still folded neatly along its sides. The boy noticed something outside the gate, jumped off the wagon and disappeared beyond the wooden fence.

The two *rōnin* in front of her were still encased in their icy tombs – she wondered if they had already suffocated or froze to death; for a moment she did not care. She could not care about anything now that she had seen the dragon. But there were more enemies to worry about, the other swordsmen and Nanseians were busy with their own fight somewhere in the fog – and she could now see more clearly the mage standing behind the oxcart, casting shields and deflecting the magical onslaught with a heavy iron mace.

She recognised the pattern of his magic first, then the weapon, and then, as the smoke from another explosion parted, she noticed that the mage had no head.

Pressing his hands and face to the scales, he felt the heat inside and smelled the faint brimstone of the dragon's breath. At last, after so many days, so many miles, so many misadventures they had been reunited. But even this close, he could no longer get through. His Farlink signals bounced off a powerful barrier; an envelope of strange, unfamiliar magic surrounded the dragon's mind and what little he could glimpse through the gaps in the barrier did not bode well. All he was getting was hunger, fury and confusion, the first symptoms of feralisation.

The spell maintained by the wizards inside the storehouse he could penetrate easily. But this was a new spell that no human could sustain alone. There had to be either a conclave of mages somewhere nearby or a focus artefact of immense power. Bran looked around quickly. Behind the oxcart the balance of the fierce battle of wizards and swordsmen was slowly tipping against the defenders of the shrine, but Bran had no time to worry about that. In front of the cart, holding the oxen reins, stood a man clad in black garb with a bell staff in his right hand. Their eyes met for a moment as the man struggled with the whining animals, forcing them to drag the vehicle despite a broken wheel. They were some twenty yards from a vermillion *torii* gate which stood further down the forest path, indicating a symbolic boundary of the holy ground. The driver was desperate to reach it, ignoring the fact that the cage and the box around the dragon was no more, ignoring even Bran who was standing at the platform with the sword drawn.

Looking further along the road, Bran saw somebody in the shadows of the trees, a silhouette ominously black with streaks of red light in the True Sight. In the stranger's hand an orb of dazzling white light shone like a tiny sun, a nexus of energies flowing around Emrys. Whatever spell held the dragon, this must have been its source.

With a yell, Bran leapt from the cart and started towards the *torii* gate; only now did the man in black let go of the reins and stood before Bran, the jingling staff raised like a lance in defence.

"Out of my way!"

Bran slashed wildly. His sword bounced off the staff with a loud clang and as he flung himself forward, the enemy swung around and suddenly appeared behind, grabbing him by the neck with the shaft of the staff and pulling him close.

"You're out of your league, child," he whispered "Get out of here while you still can."

Bran struggled but couldn't set himself free. He hit the enemy under the ribs with the pummel of his sword, but it was futile. *If it was my old sword, it would punch the breath out of him*, a thought flashed through his mind.

He grasped the arm of his captor and cried *"Rhew!"* The sleeve of the black robe lit up in flames. Its owner released Bran for a moment, but then caught the boy by the shoulder and spun him around. The last thing Bran saw was the butt of the staff heading for his face.

The oxcart was still lodged between the gate posts when they arrived. The battle seemed to have moved beyond it; the Captain Kiyōmasa could not see well through the smoke and mist, but he heard the clashing of the swords clearly. He did not know who was fighting whom. All his men, he had found dead. Of the wizards, the only one still standing was *Daisen* Heishichi, whom he discovered wounded and staggering by the side of the road. One of the priests healed his most threatening wounds and the *Daisen,* after gulping some of his life-giving extract, soon rejoined the fray.

The *dorako*! The priests halted seeing what lay on the oxcart. Only Nagomi kept on running.

"Come on! Look, a child is braver than you," the Captain shouted, prodding the priests onwards. Shaking off their fear, they grasped their weapons – long, iron-bound sticks – and followed the red-haired girl.

Bran came to seconds later, lying in the dirt of the road, his sword flung away from his hand. His nose was swelling up quickly and he was nauseated with dizziness. There was an odd buzzing in his head, a sort of murmur growing slowly from deep within. The man in the black robe was standing above him, putting out the flames on his sleeve.

"Ozun!" a strong, dark, commanding voice cried out of Bran's sight, "this is the rider! Bring him to me."

Ozun leaned over Bran and reached out to lift the helpless boy from the ground when a red shadow appeared behind him. He turned around; a sword flashed. Instinctively, he raised his left arm in a vain attempt to block the falling blade. The Matsubara sword cut through the forearm with ease, lodging itself deeply into the man's skull. The severed hand dropped to the ground. The hermit threw his arms apart and fell backwards, without a sound.

Satō was standing in the middle of the road, her sword chipped and bloody. She was trembling and breathing hard. The man in black robes lay in the dirt beside Bran, his skull cleaved through. Blood and gore oozed from the crack onto the road. Bran scrambled to his feet hastily and tightened the satchel straps. He felt the acrid taste of vomit gathering in his throat.

He stepped over the dead body towards the girl and touched her on the shoulder. She raised her eyes to him, wide open, blank and black, but then shook her head and was almost back to normal; only her hands kept trembling. Looking down he noticed one of her hands, clad in a leather glove, was covered with fresh blood.

"You're hurt!"

"It's nothing. Bran, back there is the *onmyōji* – the one from the forest! I did all I could but he just won't die. I think the body must be animated by the Crimson Robe, he must be somewhere near – "

She stopped and narrowed her eyes looking past Bran's shoulder. He turned and saw the man behind the *torii* gate, now fully visible, standing in the middle of the road. His eyes gleamed golden in the gaunt, smooth face, his long black hair flowed gently over the shoulders draped in a robe of bloody crimson. The jewel in his head, an orange-sized orb, was also the colour of blood.

"*You...!*" Satō let out a hoarse cry, but before she could leap towards the Crimson Robe, out of the fog and shadows appeared a woman in a tight ashen-grey uniform. Her face and arms were burned, her eyes sweltering with fear and hatred. She saw the cleaved skull in the dirt and a wordless, feral howl escaped her lips. Madly she spun back towards Bran and Satō, flinging a deadly chain-and-sickle weapon towards them.

The wizardess barely managed to dodge the throw, more by instinct and luck than skill. The sickle's bronze blade grazed Bran's cheek, drawing blood. Weapon-less and struggling to keep focus required for spell-casting, he pulled back, knowing he would just get in Satō's way for the moment.

It was an equal match. The woman's skill with her weapon was far superior to Satō's swordsmanship, but the wizardess had her magic to rely on, flinging icy missiles and freezing the ground beneath her opponent's feet to catch her off balance. Bran had never seen anyone fight like that, so seamlessly matching magic and fencing. This must have been how the battle mages of old fought, in the Age of Unbridled Flame.

There was no time to admire the duel. Still more enemies ran towards them, as if answering to the unspoken summons of their master beyond the vermillion gate. Bran wondered briefly whether they had defeated everyone in the shrine already, or whether they chose him and Satō as the greater danger to their plans. The grey-clads and the unarmed warriors had gone past the oxcart and were almost upon them, but a greater danger loomed in the fog, slowly lumbering its way towards Bran. He could see it now without the need for True Sight – the headless, rotting body of the mage slain in the forest by Dōraku's twin blades.

Bran swooped underneath another flight of the sickle-chain, rolled and, jumping to a stand, summoned his Soul Lance. He hesitated. He could not strike a woman in the back, even in fierce combat. He shouted a challenge.

The woman produced a glass ball from her sleeve and shattered it on the ground. A cloud of smoke burst forth and by the time it cleared, she was gone.

Satō blinked and turned immediately towards the newly arrived enemies, clashing swords with the first of the grey-clad *rōnin*. Ice shards shattered around her, a cold wave covered the swordsman's arms with hoar. Bran looked around and, not seeing the woman in grey anywhere, joined the wizardess at her side, protecting them both with a front-facing *tarian*. His lance flickered worryingly. When did he lose so much energy? He had barely cast any spells...

Our last stand, he thought grimly, watching as more enemies arrived. *Where's Nagomi? Did they get her as well?*

He caught a movement behind his back, to the right. He turned quickly, but not quickly enough. The sickle blade, hurled in a smooth, precise motion, flew towards Satō's back.

As in slow motion, Bran saw a white, blurry figure leap in between Satō and the blade, arms apart, red hair billowing. The bronze blade struck, wedging itself between ribs. Nagomi cried out and fell down.

Satō turned around, releasing the full power of her enchanted blade against the woman appearing from the shadows, cutting through the deadly weapon. The links shattered, the ice covered the rest of the chain and, through it, the assassin's entire arm.

The wizardess dropped to her knees beside Nagomi. The priestess gasped a few times and then collapsed limply into the arms of her friend.

Captain Kiyomasa arrived a mere few seconds too late. The little priestess lay dying in her friend's arms. And the boy… something strange was happening to the boy. He grew in stature, taller and broader than any man. Wings sprouted from his back, spreading across the width of the road. He roared like a tiger and spewed hot smoke and steam from his reptilian snout.

Even the ever stoic *Daisen* reeled from the monstrosity. The enemies pulled away. The creature made one giant leap towards a female assassin who was clutching the remnant of a chain and handle in half-frozen arms, and cast her aside like a rag doll. The woman hit a tree and collapsed to the ground. Several of the *rōnin* ran up to creature, trying to stop it, but the swords failed to penetrate the celadon scales, serving only to irritate the monster as it continued on towards the *torii* gate.

One more person stood in the creature's way. *No, not a person*, Kiyomasa realised. *A headless corpse.* By some unholy magic it still moved, casting all manner of spells against the approaching monster, waving a heavy iron mace threateningly.

The creature's clawed arm reached out and ripped the mace out of the corpse's hands, snapping it in two like a stick of bamboo. It then grabbed the animated body and in a swift move ripped it in two.

Kiyomasa did not even try to comprehend what he was seeing. The dragon, sleeping on the oxcart, would be enough to rid anyone of their senses. Now he observed a battle between a moving, headless corpse and a boy transformed into a giant lizard-like beast. He knew only one way to react.

He drew his sword and with a battle cry – "*Hosokawa!*" – he rushed towards the enemy swordsmen.

CHAPTER XVIII

Nagomi!

Something snapped within him. He cried and lunged forward in fury. There was nothing in his heart but hatred; hatred towards the woman who attacked his friends, towards the Crimson Robe, towards the men who had kept him chained in the cage for so long…

Wait, that's not me. That's Emrys.

Does it matter?

Pent-up energy surged within him; the dragon had plenty of it to spare. A grey-clad swordsman ran up to him – small and weak in Bran's eyes. One swipe of a clawed arm and the man fell down, blood spurting from a shattered hand. Another of the *rōnin* came up from behind; his sword broke on the scaled back. Bran turned with a fierce cry, which turned into a dragon's rumbling growl. He grasped the swordsman's head in his hand. The skull gave in with a satisfying crack.

These are not the men I want to fight. Where is the one with the spectacles?

He shook his head. *No, not that one either.* He turned again, towards the *torii* gate, where the creature in the crimson robe stood in the shadows, still calm, still smirking.

The demon stretched out a hand holding a large blood-red orb. His lips moved and the orb lit up with bright crimson light. Bran swayed as if some unseen force had hit him, but managed to swipe one of his claws and hit the enemy on its outstretched hand. The red jewel flew away. The smirk vanished from the demon's face. Another of Bran's swipes reached the face, leaving bloody claw-marks on its cheek.

The demon leapt back and drew his weapon, a giant, two-handed sword. Magic shimmered along the blade.

We don't want to fight it. Bran staggered away, trying to refocus. Emrys was growing stronger and, somewhere deeper, another will was stirring. *Shigemasa! If I have to balance all three inside me, I'll go crazy.*

The enemy. Concentrate on the enemy. But it was too late. In the crowd of clashing warriors, Emrys spotted the lanky man in the horn-rimmed spectacles. Bran tried to pull his attention back to the Crimson Robe, but the dragon's fury was too strong. He felt the beast's mind yank away and suddenly he was alone. The Farlink was broken.

A roar sounded behind Kiyomasa's back, a roar so tremendous it silenced all other noises. Even the sounds of the festival in the distance quietened down.

The Captain turned around and watched in terror as the green dragon rose, shook off the chains and spread its majestic wings. It roared again and in the wrath of its bellow the Captain heard the words of an ancient cry. He stood transfixed, unable to move or even blink.

"Down, fool!"

Daisen grabbed him to the ground and covered with his own body as the dragon lowered its head towards them and spewed a tongue of flame as hot as the Sun itself.

The dragon beat its wings twice, as if testing, before leaping off . It flew towards the shrine, fast like the wind, spewing flame and steam, setting fire to the thatched buildings of the inner compound, destroying everything in its path. In a few seconds, it was gone.

Bran's strength quickly waned. The Dragonform could no longer be sustained with Emrys awakened, away and unheeding his call. He was confused, lost, for the first time in long years not sensing the Farlink connection. He made a step towards the Crimson Robe. The red orb lay in the ferns by the roadside, shining with a pulsating light, making him dizzy and nauseated. Something was amiss, but he couldn't think straight enough to realise what it was.

The Crimson Robe scrambled towards the jewel. Bran tried to stop him but was too slow, too lumbering in his still transformed body. The demon rose, clutching the orb triumphantly. The gem beamed brightly and Bran swayed again under its spell. He felt tired and sleepy. Waves of negative energy flowed from the jewel. What little of the dragon power remained within him subsided; he could feel it seeping away.

The *Daisen* crawled off the Captain with a moan, holding his hands over his face. Kiyomasa scrambled to his feet, ready to fight again, but all around him was deadly quiet. Many of the priests and the grey-clad *rōnin* lay dead, scorched by the dragon's breath; the others were afraid to get up.

In this silence, the Captain watched the boy-turned-beast sway aimlessly to and fro, disoriented. He seemed to be shrinking in size. A long-haired man clad in a dark red robe emerged from the shadows of the *torii* carrying a great *nodachi*, a horse-slaying sword, effortlessly in one hand, and an orb of red crystal in the other. The man stuck his weapon into the ground, reached with the freed hand inside the folds of his garment and drew a bunch of white paper dolls. He scattered them on the ground under his feet.

"Ozun!" the man spoke with a voice that sounded like death itself. "I have not yet released thee from my service. *Fight for me!*"

At this signal a dark, sinister spirit rose from the dead man's body. It grabbed the bell staff and stomped it one-two-three times. In answer to the summons, the spirits of all who had been slain until now also abandoned their bodies and appeared, hovering above ground, holding ghostly, translucent weapons.

"Abomination!" cried the Head Priest. The surviving acolytes and the samurai picked themselves off the ground, ready to continue the fight. "These spirits must be put to rest!"

The battle broke out anew around the oxcart. Magic, holy power, ghostly energies and steel blades clashed in deadly strife. Wherever a man fell, the jingling staff brought him back to life. But whenever a ghost was slain, either by cold blade or by a priest's exorcism, one of the paper dolls at the Crimson Robe's feet burned out.

Somebody was calling Bran's name. A despairing voice slowly made its way through to his brain, muddled with fury, bloodlust and confusion. *Satō...* She was still kneeling on the road, clutching the priestess in her arms. Blood trickled slow and thick from the wound in Nagomi's chest. The priestess was pale, her lips blue, her chest no longer rising in frantic gasps.

"*We need to run, boy,*" a familiar voice in Bran's head broke through the dizziness.

"Shigemasa! Where have *you* been?"

"*No time to explain now! Trust me, I've seen many battles in my life, and this one's already lost. We'll be slaughtered if we stay here.*"

"But there's ...nowhere to go."

They were now cut off from the shrine by the heat of the fighting. Even the female assassin was getting back up, ready to attack again. In the opposite direction stood the Crimson Robe, the orb in his hand shining with cold red flame.

A few men led by Captain Kiyomasa broke through towards Bran. They all stopped between him and the Crimson Robe, but for one youngster who charged at the demon.

The Crimson Robe's great sword flashed forward, cutting right through the man. Black fangs dug deep into the priest's neck. The man died with a gurgling cry and the demon cast him aside.

Bran stared at the dead body which shrivelled and shrunk, like a quickly drying piece of meat. The Captain's voice broke him out of the stupor.

"I don't know who or what you are or what you want, but I won't have a priestess's death on my conscience. If she's still alive, save the girl and yourself," said Kiyomasa. "We'll guard your retreat. *Run!*"

Bran cast a final look at the oxcart and the remnants of the chains. Emrys was lost from him, a dot of green flame in the night sky, flying westwards first, then turning north in a blind rage.

"I'll come for you," he sent a thought through the Farlink, without a hope of an answer. "I'll find you again."

"*You'll find your death in a moment,*" a nagging voice in his head urged him on. Having a little of the Dragonform strength still left in his arms, Bran lifted the unconscious priestess gently from the road, nodded at Satō to follow him and darted into the deep forest.

The right sleeve of her kimono felt wet. Surprised, she looked down – it was soaked with her own blood. At some point in the heat of the battle, either the assassin's sickle or one of the grey-clad swordsmen's blades must have reached her.

Though Nagomi was dying, she was not dead yet, and Bran – if it was still him under the dragon-like disguise – was carrying her off into darkness, into safety. She noticed a sword lying on the road, and a leather satchel with a broken strap. She picked them up, thrust the weapon into her sash alongside the Matsubara sword and, clutching the bleeding arm, she followed the transformed boy, crying with pain.

The Crimson Robe noticed the escape and tried to follow, but she did not let him. She now had no need for the glove's needle; she had plenty of fresh blood to spare. She put her left palm on her right arm, and the right hand on the trunk of a nearby cedar tree, discharging all the power she had left and could yet summon. A web of thick ice spread from tree to tree, halting the demon's pursuit.

The release made her tremble with ecstasy. She gasped. *So much power! If only I could wield it all of the time...*

She heard the sound of a bugle conch in the distance, but there was no time to wonder what it meant. Bran was already out of sight. She forced herself to run.

The dense forest muffled the noise of the battle and suppressed the lights from the blazing shrine. She was running in silence and darkness now, up the hill, along animal paths and lumberjack cuttings. The Westerner in front of her grew smaller. She was too exhausted to wonder at what had happened to Bran. His monstrous form now all but subdued, he looked almost human again. He seemed to barely have enough strength remaining to carry Nagomi's body over the gnarled roots and wet, mossy stones.

"Are they... following us?" he asked, breathing heavily. His voice was croaking, guttural.

"They must be – but I don't see anyone yet."

"I... have to... rest."

They halted by a large rocky outcrop, a wall of sheer black basalt. Bran laid Nagomi down. Part of the assassin's sickle blade, snapped off by the ice, was still sticking out from her breast, as they were afraid to remove it without a way to stem the resulting bleeding. The priestess was pale like a sheet of paper but she was still breathing.

"I can't run with her anymore," Bran explained feebly. "My strength is gone."

"We'll just have to carry – no! They're already here!"

A glimpse of crimson appeared among the trees in the light of the moon. The pursuit was almost upon them.

"Young *tono*! Over here!"

Satō looked at where the voice was coming from. A girl was crouching on top of the outcrop, her hands reaching down towards them, touching about blindly.

"Yōko! How did you…"

"Please hurry!"

The wizardess pulled herself up the ridge and, together with the servant girl, took Nagomi's limp body from Bran, who soon followed to the top.

"It's no use, he'll find us here," said Bran quietly, as the Crimson Robe appeared at the glade, accompanied by the ashen-clad assassin and a bald Nanseian warrior.

"Please come," Yōko whispered and led them, crouching, into a small niche in the rock. The nook seemed barely large enough to fit one person, but turned out to be an entrance to a long cave. When they were all inside, Bran lit a flamespark. They were in a tunnel.

"What is this place?"

"I do not know," Yōko replied, "but there are tunnels like this all over t' mountain. As old as Gods, some say. This one will lead you to safety. Please hurry."

"How did you know we'd be here?" Satō asked. They were now running down the damp corridor lined with limestone flags. Bran was still carrying the priestess, but he was now only his normal height and strength, and could barely keep up the pace.

"I – 'tis a curse," the girl said shyly. "Sometimes I have visions of t'future… sometimes I can see things others can't. Like the samurai inside you, *tono*," she said. "This is how I learn'd about them tunnels in the mountains. I saw terrible danger befalling you all, and I jus' had to try and help."

"And with a gift like that, you are still just a kitchen servant?"

"T'priests say there is no *kami* presence about me and that only a demon could grant such powers. It is a grace that they allow me to stay at t'shrine at all."

It was obvious to Satō that the girl had latent magical powers and, with proper training, could grow into a great wizardess. *The priests must have known it, too. They keep her hidden from Shimazu…*

"This is the end of t'tunnel," Yōko pushed open a wall in front of them. There was nothing but darkness and silence outside. "You are far from t'shrine, and from your enemies. I hope yer' not too far from help," she said.

"What about you?" asked Satō. The girl smiled.

"My place is in t'shrine. The priests will need all help they can get."

The girl rummaged for a while in the clump of tall ferns.

"'ere, take this."

She handed them a small, shallow clay vessel and a bundle of grey cloth.

"What is this?"

"It's a holy light that the priests carry 'round. Your friend will need it."

"These are my things!" Satō said astonished, checking the inside of the cloth bundle. "My books, my notes!"

"Thank you," Bran put the vessel into his satchel. "A day will come when we will repay our gratitude properly.

"Please, just let me sister know I am well, young *tono*."

"I will, Yōko," said Satō.

The hatch closed behind the girl and the tunnel exit blended into a rock wall. They were in the middle of the cedar forest, somewhere high up on the slopes of Mount Takachiho. Bran laid Nagomi's body on the damp ground and lit a faint flamespark. Satō knelt beside the priestess to assess her injuries. Around them, the wood was dark and deadly quiet.

Satō took out a dagger and cut through Nagomi's sash. He turned his eyes away as she parted the priestess's robe to reveal the pale, soft skin underneath.

"Don't be so squeamish," the wizardess said, misunderstanding his embarrassment. "Can you still do magic? I am spent."

He nodded. "It's fading away without my dragon, but I still have a little left..."

"I need you to cauterise the wound."

She guided his hand. "Here." Bran produced a small, hot flame from his fingers at the same moment when Satō pulled out the sickle shard. Nagomi stirred in pain, but the wound bled only for a second. Pink dribble trickled out of the corner of the priestess's mouth.

"We need to find some help," said Bran, "or find a way back to the town."

"The Crimson Robe must have his men all over that place. Besides, I don't even know how to get back. I lost my orientation in that winding tunnel."

She tore a strip off her sleeve and prepared a makeshift bandage.

"There must be *something* around here," she added, looking around. "Why else would a tunnel lead into the middle of the forest?"

"I'll go look for some shelter. It's starting to rain. Will you manage on your own?"

"I may not be a spirit healer, but I've observed Ine and Itō-*sama* at work many times. I'll do what I can."

He returned a few minutes later. The rain was beating on the leaves above, but not much of it was yet getting through the canopy.

"How is she?"

"I don't know. She's still breathing... barely... she may be bleeding inside – there's no way to tell. Have you found something?"

"There's a cave nearby. But the path is slippery. We need to be careful."

They wrapped Nagomi in her robe and carried her slowly along an old, long-overgrown path leading up the hill. The priestess seemed fragile, as if her body was made of fine china. She moaned and whimpered quietly a few times when Satō or Bran tripped on the slippery stones.

Using his sword like a machete, Bran cut through the vines, ferns and bracken to clear the way. The path wound for a few hundred feet over slick outcrops and lichen-covered boughs. At last it reached a large cave, carved by a trickling waterfall in the volcanic rock of Mount Takachiho. Bran's faint flamespark could not light all of it, but he could see the remains of a camp on the floor.

Hunters or poachers, he thought, seeing remnants of traps, bits of rotten rope and broken-off shards of spearheads and harpoons.

"It smells," Satō wrinkled her nose.

Somewhere at the back there had to be a fissure leading to the depths of the volcano, from which seeped the fumes, filling the cave with the faint stench of brimstone – but also making it drier and warmer than it at first seemed.

"It's a shelter. And look, there's water," Bran said, pointing to a waterfall trickling away in the corner. "Lay her here, I'll start a fire."

He gathered all the bits and pieces of wood scattered around the cave floor, brought in some of the drier deadwood from the forest and set the shoddy campfire aflame. It burned fast, bright yellow in the sulphur-infused air.

Satō crouched over her unconscious friend, washing the wound with the pitiful amount of water she managed to bring from the waterfall in the clay beaker the servant girl had given them – the only container they had.. Her movements became automatic, rigid, as she struggled to cope with pain, exhaustion, and the shock of battle.

"You're hurt as well," Bran said, touching Satō's shoulder gently where the enemy blade had cut the deepest. The silk of her kimono was soaked red.

She shook her head.

"It's nothing. I've had worse at swordplay trainings."

"It still needs to be looked after…"

"Not until we find help for Nagomi."

"Will she make it through the night like that?"

"We can but pray."

Gently, but forcefully, he sat her down away from the priestess. She had neither strength nor will to oppose him.

"You can do no more now," he said. "In the morning it will be easier to look for help."

"Yes," she answered feebly. "What about you…?" She raised her hand to his face.

Now that the battle rush in his veins had gone, he was feeling the dumb ache in his broken nose again, and the stinging on the cheek where the assassin's blade cut him.

"I got lucky," he said with a forced smile. "Scars only make a man more handsome."

That's what my mother used to say about my father. Am I too going to be covered in scars when I'm old?

He took the clay beaker from Satō's trembling hands.

If I ever manage to grow old…

"What do we do with this?" he asked.

"I don't know…"

Bran put the vessel into Nagomi's hands. A tiny orange wisp of light appeared inside the shallow bowl, flickering weakly. It seemed the priestess's face became more peaceful and relaxed, but it may have been just a trick of the dancing light.

"Look there, by the waterfall."

As if in answer to the holy flame, a tiny sparkling dot appeared above the stream, then another, and another. A cloud of fireflies danced in the shadows like a school of fairies.

"So beautiful," whispered Bran, but Satō rose, picked up a stone and threw it at the fireflies.

"No! Get away!"

The dancing lights vanished.

"What are you doing?"

"It's the souls of the dead coming for Nagomi! I won't let them!"

She threw another stone and then slumped down to the ground, exhausted and dejected. Bran reached his hand towards her.

"We must rest. I'm sure in the morning everything will work out – somehow."

They lay down on the damp, rocky floor. The flames of the campfire illuminated the cave walls, casting strange, trembling shadows. They did not even have blankets to cover themselves from the cold of the night; they had used both their cloaks to wrap up the priestess.

"What was that… charm you were under?" Satō asked.

"Dragonform, the last resort of a rider… I was channelling Emrys's raw magic power – at least for as long as I had contact with it."

"I'm sorry you lost your *dorako*… again."

Bran did not reply. He was trying to remember his actions under the spell's power.

Did I… did I kill somebody?

"I have seen it," said Satō. "Up close. It was magnificent, even bound and locked like that. And then when it rose and spewed the flames… I could feel its power – it was immense."

"Emrys is yet small and not fully grown. You should've seen my father's dragon…"

She sneaked closer to him in the darkness, shivering from cold. He reached his arm around and embraced her.

"Tell me something about it," she urged.

In the darkness he could hear her laboured breathing.

He spoke at last. "Nine years ago my father took me to the hatchery by the Pont-y-Pair Falls on River Llugwy, to let me choose my first dragon."

"You were seven and you were given a *dorako*?"

"I would not get to own it for three more years, while it grew in the hatchery. And it hadn't even hatched yet when we arrived. There were just three eggs to choose from, the baby dragons ready to break out. While we watched, two green heads emerged from the eggs. Viridians of Gwydyr Forest, proud, stout beasts of ancient lineage. Father liked one of them immediately. *Take this one, son,"* he said, *"look at how bright its eyes are."*

"Was it Emrys?"

"No!" Bran said with a quiet chuckle. "Emrys started hatching last. Its egg was smaller, less shiny. As soon as it came out, the hatchmaster wanted to take it away and drown it."

"Why?"

"It was a swamp wyrm. We knew it immediately by the smell. A poor, cheap breed that must have got mixed up with the others. Nobody would offer one of these to the son of Dylan ab Ifor. It would have been an insult."

"What happened?"

"It fought back. It bit the hatchmaster's hand and leapt towards us – it couldn't fly yet. My father wanted to kill it, but I stopped him. The dragon jumped on my lap. It stank of the swamp – it still does – but I didn't mind. It snuggled up to me, seeking protection. I knew then that I never wanted another dragon. Since then, it never threw me off, never bolted, and although I've had it for six years now, it never showed any signs of going feral – until we got here. And now… it is lost."

He fell silent. Satō had stopped paying attention to his story a while ago, dozing off between the sentences with her head resting against his chest.

I lost everything. Emrys, Nagomi, a chance to go home – I couldn't even keep the ring…

It was his last thought before he fell into an exhausted, dreamless sleep.

CHAPTER XIX

The forest air was unpleasantly hot and humid; the wind machine had spluttered and died as soon as they had left Kirishima. With the wizards gone, nobody in her escort knew how to fix it. Atsuko opened the shutters of her palanquin to let the air in, but it did not help much. She yearned for some rain. This year the beginning of the rainy season was remarkably dry.

There will be drought, she thought, *and poor harvest again.* Her heart went out to peasants, striving against bad weather. Satsuma would survive – her adoptive father was a good administrator and made sure there was always enough surplus rice in the villages. But other provinces might not be so lucky, especially if the drought repeated itself the next year, as it often did.

She hoped there would be no famine, like in the year after her birth. People still told dreadful tales of the time. It hit the Northern provinces worst, but Chinzei had been affected by a flood of refugees. It had taken years for the samurai and merchant families to recover from the crisis.

The princess looked around and noticed something amiss about her escort. She motioned to an officer walking nearby.

"Sergeant, where is Captain Kiyomasa?"

"I'm sorry, *hime*, but he received urgent orders from Hosokawa-*dono*."

Atsu quickly counted the samurai surrounding her palanquin.

"Did he also have to take half of my escort with him?"

The officer avoided her gaze, staring at his sandals uneasily. "Yes, *hime*. Those were the orders."

"And is he going to catch up to us eventually?"

"I'm afraid I don't know. But there is nothing to worry about," the sergeant raised his head, "we are safe."

"That's not what I heard. I heard there are bandits in this part of the mountains."

"Merely rumours, *hime*. Besides, the escort is still strong. No bandits would dare attack a troop of samurai!"

"I hope you're right. And I hope your master has good enough reason for ridding me of half the guard. I will have to report to my father about this, of course."

"Of course," the sergeant stared at his sandals again.

"When do you expect us to leave these stuffy forests behind?"

"Tomorrow we descend onto the plains of Hyūga. The winds there blow from the Eastern Sea, so the weather should be more pleasant. Do you need anything, *hime*?"

"Bring me some more water, Sergeant."

"Right away *hime.*"

The inn and the small village that grew around it were both perched on the edge of a mountain spur reaching east, deep into the valley of Oyodo River. These were the last vestiges of the great cedar forests. One of the windows in Atsuko's room looked out onto the valley and the vast plain of the Hyūga Province. The Sergeant was right – even here, so many *ri* from the coast, the breeze speeding up the river carried with it the memory of the sea, the promise of the rolling waves and the crying of the kites.

She tried not to think of the journey ahead of her. In a week or so they would reach Akae Harbour and from there embark on a month-long sail to Edo. A month at sea! Stopping for the nights, of course, and with longer interludes along the way in Naniwa and Chūbu; still – she could hardly imagine a voyage so long.

She touched the *obidame*. She had resolved to wear it on her sash at times; it was pretty enough, even with the stone missing, and it reminded her of the green-eyed boy she would never see again. She wondered if his quest had succeeded… *He would have laughed at my fears.* He must have spent months out in the open ocean, suffering storms and typhoons – and maybe even sea monsters... And if he managed to endure all this, what right had she to complain of her little escapade? *No,* she decided, *I will not moan. My father expects me to do my duty and nothing else.*

She heard a horse outside, galloping at first then coming to a stop. She looked out the west window at the road before the inn. A messenger from Kumamoto. What did he want? Was it to take away even more of her escort?

The courier did not dismount. A samurai came out to greet him – Atsuko recognised Kawakami Gensai's thick topknot. The two men exchanged a few quick words and then Kawakami handed the messenger some small item, a piece of jewellery. Sunlight glinted briefly off its azure surface. The messenger hid it in a lacquer container at his waist, nodded and galloped away.

She had little time to wonder what she had just witnessed. As soon as the courier disappeared into the forest, another commotion drew her attention. Cries rose from the direction of the village. Commoners appeared, running down the road, panicking. The patrons poured from the inn, pointing at something and shouting.

Atsuko tried to see what everyone was so agitated about, but the west window was barred with bamboo poles and she could see nothing beyond the stretch of the road in front of the inn.

There was a knock on the door.

"*Hime!* We must be on our way," the servant said.

"What is going on?"

"I don't know. The locals are saying something about the mountain being… on fire. Kawakami-*sama* insists on us leaving immediately."

Eruption? Atsuko shuddered. No volcano had erupted on Chinzei within her lifetime, but she had heard enough terrible stories to fear any mention of the "mountain on fire".

"I will get myself ready."

In a few minutes she was guided by the servants to the courtyard where the black-and-gold palanquin awaited her. Before going inside she stopped and looked up towards the peaks of the Kirishima ridge.

Far away, near the top of one of the conical summits, a long, narrow patch of a dark, hazy wood had been set ablaze. This did not look like an eruption, rather, a strangely regular forest fire. Suddenly, as she was looking, another patch of the forest burst into flames in a straight line going sideways across the mountain slope.

"*Hime,*" the servant girl insisted. Her eyes were full of terror, but in Atsuko's heart curiosity replaced fear. What was going on over there?

She shaded her eyes and looked towards the peak one last time. She thought she could see a dark dot soaring over the mountains, like an eagle but much, much larger. But then it disappeared in the haze and she was no longer sure whether it was just a trick of the eyes.

With a sigh, she climbed into the palanquin and closed the shutters, sealing herself from the world outside.

BOOK FOUR

THE RISING TIDE

If I see a bridge of flying magpies
Across the frost-white sky
I know the night is almost over.

Chunagon Yakamochi

PROLOGUE

The grounds of the Imperial Palace of the Divine *Mikado* were as tranquil as the blue, cloudless sky above. Noble men shuffled along gravel paths in silence. Thrushes sang softly in the gingko trees. Water trickled in the canals along the avenues into the ponds where frogs croaked the coming of the evening.

Crown Prince Mutsuhito sat down on the springy grass beside one such pond, looking at the great white wall stretching all around the palace gardens. Beyond lay the bustle of Heian, the Imperial Capital. The streets of the city he had seen only once, when, as a child, he had to run from a fire to the Shimogamo Shrine across the river.

"Trapped in a palace like *Butsu-sama* himself," he said quietly. Nobody heard him beyond the silk curtain. Since he was three years old and could express himself formally, the Crown Prince had insisted that his path, wherever he went, was concealed from the outside world. Nobody protested, of course; nobody questioned. The word of the imperial heir was a command of the God.

"How is my Divine Father doing today?" he asked louder.

"His Imperial Majesty is busy writing another letter," an unnamed servant answered from beyond the curtain. All his servants were nobles themselves, of course, from the finest aristocratic families.

"He is angry, then," the prince guessed. He imagined his father's jowls shaking with fury. *Mikado* Kōmei was often angry, and when he was angry, he wrote letters.

"There is... disturbing news from the Taikun's court."

"Oh?"

"I am not sure, *denka*. We did not have an official report yet, so we must rely on rumours."

"What is it, then?"

"There is a rumour of – unspeakable as it sounds – the barbarians landing in Edo."

"Invasion?"

The prince stood up abruptly. A frightened frog leapt from under his feet.

"A scouting party, perhaps... I believe if it was indeed an invasion, we would have more news about it by now."

But how? The Divine Winds were supposed to be impenetrable... have the Bataavians betrayed us?

"Prepare the curtain," Mutsuhito ordered, "I think I shall visit my Father."

An acrid, unpleasant smell filled the imperial chambers; the stench of alcohol and women. Mutsuhito covered his nose with a handkerchief and entered his father's study.

The *Mikado* ordered the woman away. The Prince recognised her – one of the ladies-in-waiting. The woman picked up her kimono, giggled and disappeared through the back door.

"I thought you were writing letters, Father-*sama*."

The *Mikado* tried to rise with dignity, but swayed back onto the silk cushions. His face was purple.

"I was! I am! Look, here it is. It's almost ready."

Mutsuhito reached for the scroll and browsed through. Despite his state, his father's writing remained calm and dignified. It was a missive reminding the *Taikun* of his duty to protect the Divine Land and the need of expulsion of any barbarians who dared to stand on it.

"What happened in Edo?" the Prince asked.

"The barbarians have set up a camp south of the city and demand to speak to the *Taikun*. Why they have not yet been annihilated or how they even got so far inland, I don't know. They are not telling me everything – but I *will* find out. I have my own ways."

The barbarians, Mutsuhito thought, *what were they like?* They were not all bad – he touched the burned-out circle of skin on his arm where he had been secretly vaccinated against the pox by a red-haired physician. Not even his father knew about it – all Western medicine was forbidden in the palace.

"I like the toys the Westerners make," he said, "the dolls that move of their own accord, the birds that sing when you turn the key..."

"Mere tricks to gain our confidence!" the *Mikado* cried. "I will order these toys burned!"

The prince said nothing, not risking his father's wrath turning against him. There would always be more toys sent from the south.

"I can see you are busy, Father-*sama*," he said, glancing towards the back door. "I will leave you to your... duties."

The *Mikado*'s lips wobbled. He raised his hand feebly, holding the wooden sceptre, the symbol of his power.

"It's all my fault," he said.

"What is?"

"If the land suffers it means the sovereign is to blame. It's the punishment of the Heavens. The fires, the earthquakes, and now this... I have been frail and I have neglected my duty as the Divine Father."

"There has never been a more dutiful *Mikado* than you."

His father hid his face in his hands and started sobbing. Mutsuhito felt it best to leave him alone.

The Prince studied his reflection in the round bronze mirror. He untied the ribbons holding his long black tresses in place and the hair fell down onto his shoulders.

His fingers smelled of fish, despite frequent washing. It was customary to present the Crown Prince with fresh sea fish on any special occasion, these having been of old an item of luxury in the landlocked capital city. Neither jewels nor gold adorned his room. The Imperial Family lived in traditional austerity and was dependant on gifts from the courtiers and a meagre yearly stipend.

There were some more gifts coming his way, and slightly more opulent. His Coming of Age day was swiftly approaching. Soon his long boyish hair would be cut off and his plain robes replaced with the clothes of an adult.

It seemed to him ominous to have such an important ceremony at such a critical time. There was more news of the barbarians coming from Edo and none of it served to calm Mutsuhito's father down. The *Mikado* had ordered prayers for Yamato's prosperity in the seven shrines and seven temples of the capital and then sat down to write another angry missive to the *Taikun*.

Mutsuhito wondered if anyone ever read the letters. *Probably not.* Why would the all-powerful overlord and Commodore of all the Yamato armies care what the Imperial Puppet had to say on matters of state? The *Mikado* represented a symbolic and spiritual power without any real influence. It was said that all the healing power of the shrine priests depended on the *Mikado*'s well-being, but Mutsuhito suspected this was just a story made up by the chroniclers in the ancient times to justify the need for the existence of the Imperial Family. His father had only very limited command over the spirits. His biological mother, he remembered, a daughter of a noble family from Chinzei, had become a skilled healer, but only once she had retired to a temple in the mountains.

A tiny bell tinkled, signifying the water had reached the desired temperature. He stepped towards the bath, untied the silk sash and dropped his red robe. Nobody attended his baths, not even the chamber maids. This was a breach of the custom but, again, nobody dared to question his command. They just assumed it was one of his divine whims.

But there was another, much more important reason for his seclusion. One that only his mother and his physician knew about. At first – they told him – it was just a small spot of infarction on his upper thigh, a bit of hard, dead skin. But as the prince had grown, so had the blemish and by now it covered most of his thigh, descending below the knee in places.

It didn't hurt or itch. In fact, somehow it felt even more natural than his human skin. He sat on the bath's edge and scratched the thigh absent-mindedly; the soft light green scales shimmered in the candle light.

CHAPTER I

There was fresh blood on Dylan's boots.

It came from a puddle he had stepped into, a street earlier. Or maybe from another, a block away. There was no way to know for certain; all the streets of Shanglin were bathed in blood.

He walked over a dead body and stumbled over another lying just beside it. He didn't look down; not anymore. They were all the same, anyway: stripped naked, mangled, slashed with swords and burned with gunshots. Only the size and gender differed. The conquerors of Shanglin did not discriminate. Old men, children, women... all were piled along the walls and blood-filled gutters. The dead, black window holes of the burnt-out houses stared down at the carnage in silent accusation.

Dylan didn't bother to count the slain. How many people had lived in Shanglin before the war? Ten thousand? Twenty thousand? How many more gathered here fleeing from the besieging Imperial Army? Only a few hundred women survived, spared for the soldiers' entertainment. Another hundred may have fled into the marshes. That was all.

There's always war in Qin, he thought. *But not like this...*

He heard cries. He rushed into the narrow cul-de-sac between a burnt out brick warehouse and a ruined inn. Three Imperial soldiers, flushed with drink, were standing over an old woman, beating and abusing her. The woman was still alive, though barely, and her cries for help weakened with every blow.

Red mist swam before Dylan's eyes. He raised both hands. *"Rhew!"* he cried, letting the dragon's fire flow freely from his fingers, at full force. The nearest of the soldiers stood up in flames and screamed in agony before succumbing to the fire and folding down like burning paper. The other two swayed drunkenly at Dylan. He dodged a clumsy blow, grabbed the attacker's arm with one hand and pressed the other to his chest.

"Gwrthyrru!"

The repelled soldier flew back, his shoulder torn right out of the socket. He put a hand to his chest and pink foam spewed from his mouth. He made a few steps and fell on the ground, trashing in dead throes. One man remained, sobered by the deaths of his comrades; he raised the broad Qin sword. Dylan did not waste magic, and simply punched him in the throat with the edge of his palm, smashing his windpipe. The man dropped his weapon and fell to his knees, gasping and choking.

Weakened by the magic outburst and anger, Dylan knelt by the old woman; she was breathing rapidly, her eyes wide open. She noticed him and shuddered. She reached shaking fingers out to him, crooked into the sign against evil.

"Curse you, Westerner! Curse your guns and your dragons!"

She took one last, hoarse gasp, and died.

He climbed the arch of a wide bridge spanning one of the city's many canals, and passed Qin soldiers guarding the passage. They let him through without a word, or even a bow. Dylan was too numb to take offence, although he did make a mental note of the guards' behaviour.

Beyond the canal lay the Tianyi Gardens, where the conquering army had made their headquarters. Traces of destruction and fire and blood had been scoured from the gravel and all the dead had been removed from the paths. Rose and camellia bushes had been cut down to make place for tents. Soldiers sat on moss-covered boulders and stone benches around ponds, playing *ma jiang* for bits of Cursed Weed. Gold and silver coins, looted from the city's treasure houses, were strewn all over the grass.

No discipline at all, thought Dylan bitterly, *this rabble would never have taken the city without our help.*

The words of the dying woman echoed in his head.

She blamed me for her fate, not the Qin soldiers torturing her.

The Bohan set his staff up in the main lecture hall of the great Library Pavilion; a long, two-storey building with eaves like sickle blades pointing to the skies. Dylan found him there, studying a large map; several other maps lay scattered around the floor and tables. The upper half of a discarded automaton lay in the corner, its glass eyes and metal hand raised accusingly into the air.

"Ah, Commodore *Dí Lán!*" the Bohan welcomed him with a grin and open arms. "Come, join us. We are planning our next stratagem. What do you think of moving on Chansu?"

"Another siege?" Dylan asked. He dismissed a servant who offered him a cup of tea.

"I know you Dracalish like moving swiftly, but this is how this war will have to be fought for now, until we push those vermin beyond the walls of our cities."

Vermin.

"Perhaps it would be easier to capture the cities if the defenders were given a chance to survive."

The *Bohan* looked him in the eyes and smiled.

"You don't approve of our methods, Commodore."

"No, I can't say I do. I will write a report to Fan Yu of all that's happened here."

Bohan's smile vanished. He stood straight, letting go of the map; it rolled up with a rustle.

"These... rats dared to stand against the Mandate of Heaven. They got what they deserved. Besides, they had plenty of time to surrender without bloodshed."

"Plenty of time? The siege lasted less than a week – thanks to *our* guns and *our* dragons."

"That was a week too long."

"Her Majesty will not take kindly to having her troops associated with this massacre."

The *Bohan* smirked and stroke his beard.

"Do not presume to deceive me, Commodore. I know your orders as well as you do. You are to provide us with any assistance we require in defence of your country's trade interests – and provide us you shall. Speaking of which, I will need half a dozen of your dragons to-"

"Enough!" Dylan slapped his hands on the table. The outburst surprised him. The *Bohan* raised a sharp eyebrow.

"My men are not butchers! You can capture your cities yourself. Huating is safe, and that's all that matters for our trade interests."

The *Bohan* blinked, and then laughed.

"You want to teach *me* about butchery? You, a Westerner? I know *you*. You've destroyed entire nations and you'd destroy Qin if you thought this was in your... *interests*. Oh, but you're too shrewd for that - you prefer to kill slowly."

"I don't know what you're talking about," said Dylan.

"You don't know? How many of my people died because of your accursed trade? How many died of famine in Bangla because you took their fields to plant more Weed? Don't *you* lecture *me* about butchery, Commodore *Dí Lán;* unless you want me to get better at it. Play war like the nice soldier you are, and we'll all be free to go home in no time. Isn't that what you want?"

Dylan gritted his teeth. He knew he couldn't give the Qin official the satisfaction of another outburst. He inhaled and exhaled slowly.

"Tell your soldiers to stay out of my way," he said, forcing himself to sound calm. "I'm going back to the main camp."

"I will send my requests to your tent, Commodore," the *Bohan* replied.

"You will have a prompt reply."

Dylan nodded sharply, turned on his heels and stomped outside.

Makino Tadamasa returned to his apartment at the guesthouse, put his two swords on the rack and the padded raincoat on the chest, and paid homage to the household spirits at the tiny shrine above the entrance. He then slid away the paper panels forming the western wall of the room and sat down on a narrow veranda overlooking a small garden.

As one of the inner circle of hereditary *fudai* daimyo, Tadamasa could easily afford a private residence of his own, but he preferred to live in one of the lavish, extravagant guesthouses in the middle of Edo, near the walled pleasure district. He had his wife and son neatly cooped up in a mansion just outside the city; near enough for them to fall under the rules of alternate attendance which required the daimyo's family to live under Edo's surveillance as glorified hostages – and yet too far to interfere in Tadamasa's everyday duties and entertainments. These days the visitors would arrive mostly from the nearby pleasure district, but sometimes they were his feudal clients or representatives of other, lesser daimyo, basking in the light of his influential position.

He had just spent half a day negotiating an important contract for the delivery of cannon barrels and compressed air to the *Taikun*'s new harbour fortress at Daiba and all he wanted to do was to soak in a relaxing bath and watch the moon reflecting in the pond in the small garden. He was understandably annoyed when a servant knocked on the door of his apartment and announced a guest.

"I told you I'm not seeing anyone today!"

"I beg your apologies, *kakka*, but it is the esteemed Councillor Hotta-*dono* who wants to see you."

"Keep it brief, Naosuke, I have a bath waiting," barked Tadamasa, sitting at the low table.

"I will, Councillor-*dono*. I come to you with a proposition. As you well know, I need one more vote behind my motion for the next month's meeting. The Matsudairas are beyond my reach for now; young Kuze is – well, I have not found any leverage on him yet. So, only you remain, Tadamasa-*dono*. Now, before I tell you what my offer is, I wonder if there is anything that could sway you to my side?"

"Nothing," the old man said and grunted. "I don't know what makes you think I would do such a thing. I have made up my mind."

"Money? Prestige? Women? Men? How about a little blackmail, no?" Naosuke pressed.

"Listen, Naosuke. I am an old, rich, powerful man. You may think to threaten me or bully me or bribe me or whatever it is you have done to your opponents to get as high as you have, but none of this will help you with me."

Naosuke nodded sadly.

"I was afraid you'd say that."

He clapped his hands and, out of the shadows, came a burly *rōnin* pushing before him a young boy who was bound and gagged. Tears streamed from under the blindfold. Tadamasa recognized his nine-year old grandson.

"Tadakuni! How *dare* you..." He raised an accusing hand at Naosuke. "My family is under the *Taikun's* personal care!"

"That may well be," Naosuke said with a self-confident shrug. "But it makes you wonder, *eh* – if I can get my hands on the *Taikun*'s hostages, what more *am* I capable of?"

Tadamasa's shoulders slumped in defeat. If he was younger, he would find more strength to fight; but he was old. Next year he was planning to retire from the Council altogether...

"What do you want from me?"

"I only need one vote. That is all. And your immediate retirement after that, of course. I already have a more... pliable... replacement prepared to take over your position."

"You have it. Now give me back my grandson."

"After the vote, dear Makino-*dono*. After the vote," said Naosuke, smiling.

Hanpeita crouched at the roof of the guesthouse, observing the entrance. He first saw the burly *rōnin*, carrying a large rolled *futon* on his shoulders. Councillor Hotta followed, deliberately turning in the direction opposite from the *rōnin*.

Hanpeita waved a lantern. From a roof across the street another lantern waved; one of his men – he didn't know which one, it was safer this way – confirmed he was going to follow the *rōnin*, letting Hanpeita and his group follow the Councillor.

They moved softly from roof to roof, using the skills Hanpeita had learned in Tosa, his home province, before coming to Edo.

When is Gensai-sama *going to arrive?* He wondered briefly, leaping noiselessly across a narrow cul-de-sac. No action could start without the master swordsman joining the group. But it was a long way from Kumamoto and the spring storms kept delaying the journey.

Hotta stopped in the middle of a brightly-lit alley running towards the southern gate of the city. Hanpeita and his men lay flat on the roof; the Councillor looked around slowly, his hand reaching for the short *kodachi* sword. His eyes glinted gold in the light of the lanterns.

It is *him,* Hanpeita thought, clutching the hilt of his katana in a sweaty hand. He felt as if the Councillor was looking straight through him, even though he couldn't possibly see any of them hidden in the shadows.

The contact was right. He is no longer human.

Hotta smiled and his grip on the hilt relaxed; he continued on his way. Hanpeita bade his men stop.

"It's too dangerous tonight," he whispered. "He'll spot us. We'll have to try again some other time."

A clay beaker rested on Nagomi's chest, with the spirit light burning bright orange. She couldn't remember where she got it from – it wasn't the Suwa light, that one she had lost on the road from Hitoyoshi…Something inside her body hurt. She heard the whining sound of a bamboo flute that soon grew louder and louder and then the whinging of a *hichiriki* oboe joined in. A waft of a breeze brought with it the scent of cherry blossom.

It's too late for cherry blossom, she thought.

She sat up carefully and the pain inside made her wince. She touched her chest and looked around. In the flickering orange light, she saw Bran and Satō sleeping on the cave floor, entwined in an embrace. She turned her eyes away, towards the shimmering waterfall and a babbling stream flowing from it into the forest.

A cloud of gold and green fireflies, the tiny flickers darting to and fro, hovered over the brook. The heady scent of cherry blossom made Nagomi dizzy. She took a deep breath and felt warmth spread all over her body. The pain subsided.

A cloud of white mist appeared on the other side the stream, and from it emerged a wispy shape of a woman in a long flowing robe the pink colour of cherry blossom. Her face was lime-white, her thick eyebrows were painted with charcoal in the ancient fashion. The fireflies surrounded her, drawn to the soft light emanating from her body. A white fox purred and rubbed against her like a cat. The woman beckoned the priestess with a slender hand.

Nagomi stood up and staggered towards the figure across the stone cave floor and grass moist and cold with dew of the coming morning. The white fox perked up, its ears twitching. The figure reached out her arms across the stream. Her face beamed white light, too strong for Nagomi to bear; she lowered her gaze and raised the beaker up.

The woman's hands touched hers; they felt like warm, soft leaves. The beaker's flame burst bright; Nagomi closed her eyes and shivered, as strong, cold wind blew against her naked skin. The sound of the flute and oboe grew faint, until it was barely audible.

When she opened her eyes again, she was standing on the peak of an imposing steep mountain, shooting high above the layer of dense white fog. The wind whirled and parted the mists and she could see all of the Chinzei Island and further, all the way towards Heian, the Imperial Capital. Somewhere beyond the curving horizon lay Edo and the Northern provinces.

The dawn rose threatening and ominous, blood red over the eastern seas. Black clouds were gathering over the northern horizon where the *Taikun*'s castle lay, in Edo, and more dark billows were coming on the Westerly winds over the sea from the direction of Qin. Nagomi saw that the clouds were giant flocks of carrion crows and ravens, circling the skies in hungry anticipation.

The beaker in her hands burned brighter again, the cold wind blew once more, and she found herself back in the forest. The woman in the cherry blossom robe was smiling sadly. Nagomi felt an overwhelming desire to join her on the other side of the stream, feel the warm, motherly embrace of her willowy arms, to never again feel the pain and sadness... She stepped forward into the water. But the woman shook her head and floated back towards the white mist behind her.

The fireflies buzzed over the stream towards the priestess, and gathered around her. One by one, they landed on Nagomi's body, extinguishing their flame and dying. As they touched her, she sensed their tiny, burning spirits; they seemed familiar, as if she had met them before somewhere.

It's the old Mushi from Shofukuji Temple, she realized. *And the homeless woman from Shinbashi. And the porter from Omura. All my strays...*

She felt the pain inside slowly disappear, the fatigue give way to vigour. The spirit light in her beaker was vibrant and dancing.

The music intensified again, the unseen zither and drums joining the flute in quick, mad rhythm. The woman waved her hand, showing Nagomi the cave behind her. The white mist enveloped her and she disappeared. Gone were the fireflies, but the white fox remained, staring at Nagomi with cunning, glowing eyes. The priestess turned and walked towards the cave. On its threshold she looked back; the fox was still there, twitching its whiskers anxiously.

The music grew to a frenzy and then stopped. Nagomi lay down on the cave floor, wrapped herself back in the tattered clothes and cloaks and put the spirit light on her chest. The white fox barked once and vanished into the forest, its bright white tail visible among the trees for a second more.

She smiled and closed her eyes.

CHAPTER II

Bran's first thought was that he did not wish to wake up. The world outside was cold, and he was warm and snug here, nestled as if in his mother's embrace.

Five minutes more…

Someone sighed. He opened his eyes.

He shuddered as the freezing wind blew against his back. Satō must have felt it too, for she huddled up closer. Her black hair tickled his nose. He caressed her head. She stirred and frowned, but she did not waken.

Through the haze of exhaustion, he was remembering the battle in the Shrine, the dragon, his transformation, the Crimson Robe, and the flight into the tunnels. His side was sore from lying on the rocky floor of the cave. The makeshift campfire burned out. Dawn peered through the trees, faintly illuminating the cave with greyish gold.

He unwrapped himself carefully from Satō's embrace, threw a few more pieces of wood and summoned a little spark; barely enough to light the fire back again.

This was the last of my dragon magic left.

He squatted by Nagomi's side and brushed hair from her forehead; she was running a slight fever, but her breath was calm and stable. He adjusted the cloaks around her – she must have been stirring in her sleep – and then went to the stream to wash in the icy cold water. This helped him clear his mind a little. He scratched his cheek where the *shinobi*'s sickle blade had drawn deep blood. The scar was still fresh and painful.

What now?

Getting help for Nagomi was the priority, as was finding some food. He could only hope they were safe enough from any pursuit in the cave. He patted the sword at his side reassuringly.

At least I still have the blade.

He felt a stir at the back of his mind, a nudging presence. At first he thought it was the Farlink returning and a jolt of joy came through him, but his delight was short-lived.

"What do you want?" he asked, annoyed.

"*I will overlook your impertinence considering the circumstances, boy,*" said Shigemasa graciously. "*I have something very important to tell you.*"

"Do you know a way out of here, *Taishō?*"

"*That I do not…*"

"Then whatever it is will have to wait until we're safe."

By the time Bran returned to the cave, Satō was awake and leaning over the unconscious friend.

"She is still feverish," he said.

"And the wound is swollen again," Satō said and sat down; her face crumpled.

"This is hopeless."

"She will all be alright," he said. He sounded unconvincing even to himself.

"I'll go look for help. There must be some village nearby where those people came from," he added, pointing at the remnants of the hunting gear strewn on the cave floor.

He stepped outside and heard loud voices and the sound of several people trudging noisily through the forest somewhere downhill.

"Somebody's coming," he said and frowned.

"The hunters! They will help us!" Satō stood up, excited.

"*Shh*! We don't know if they're friendly. Let's hide and see what they're up to, first."

He extinguished the campfire and helped Satō move Nagomi into the bushes, from where they observed the men arriving at the cave.

There were three of them, all in crude hunting gear – deerskin trousers and fur hats, bows and long knives in tree bark scabbards. A large yellow hound accompanied them, its nose to the ground. They were loud, not caring for stealth. Two of the hunters carried their game hung over a bamboo pole.

"Look!" Satō whispered with horror, pointing at the pole. Tied to it by the wrists and ankles was a tall man, naked and hairy. The third hunter prodded him with a stick and baited him with the tip of his knife. The man's body was cut and slashed in many places and full of bruises.

"What are they? Slave traders? Cannibals?"

The hunters came into the cave's entrance and threw their prey roughly at the cold rock.

"That's 'nuff. Throw t'trinket back on it," said the third hunter, and one of the other two took a string of jade jewels. Bran could not see what he did with it from his hiding place.

"Make sure it's tied up well," the chief hunter warned.

"Wait! Somebody's been 'ere," said the man holding the necklace. Immediately the hunters fell silent, pulling out their long hunting knives and eyeing the forest around them suspiciously. Bran and Satō dropped to the ground.

The birds chirped and the wind rustled the bamboo leaves.

"Do you have any power left?" whispered Satō.

"No dragon magic. I can do simple illusions, but-"

Before he could finish, the hound stood rigid, sniffing towards them.

"Look at the dog!" the chief hunter cried. "Over there, in the bushes!"

The other two aimed their bows at the hideout.

"Come out of there!" the chief hunter ordered.

Bran waved his fingers. A growl and a roar rang out at the back of the cave.

"What the…"

The hunters turned back in fright. The dog started to bark madly.

"Was that you?" asked Satō. He shook his head and focused on the illusion.

"*Ystlumod*," he spoke.

At that moment, a dark, large flock of bats flew out of the cave over the heads of the bowmen, who released their arrows, aimless, into the air, shouting in surprise.

"Now!" cried Bran, drawing his sword. Satō leapt out with a katana in her hands, releasing a rain of icy sparks on the leader and his dog. Hoar covered the animal's hair and it yelped in pain. The hunter shielded his eyes with his arm.

Bran cast bright sparks into the eyes of the other two and attacked them with the flat of his blade. He did not wish any more men to die; he still remembered the nauseating stench of blood and death from the battle at the Shrine. With a couple of hefty blows, he forced the two men to drop their bows and run off down the hill.

But Satō's opponent refused to give up easily. Her sword clashed against the hunter's long knife. The man was stronger than the wizardess, and well-rested. His dog caught on the girl's hakama and tugged at it with a mad growl, making it harder for her to move. In short quarters, Satō's long blade was a hindrance; the hunter pushed her against the tree, grabbed her wrist and forced her to release the weapon. He let out a leering chuckle, noticing the curves under the girl's torn kimono. He dropped the knife and reached for her.

"Stay away!"

Bran lashed out at the man blindly, only for his face to meet the hunter's fist. Lightning flashed before the boy's eyes; he reeled back, stunned and disoriented. Blood sprouted from his broken nose again. An irritated voice spoke in his head.

"*Good. I'll take it from here.*"

In an instant, Bran's sword arm drew a perfect curve which bypassed the hunter's parry. The blade lodged itself in the hunter's neck. Blood spurted from the wound and the man fell gurgling to his knees.

Bran could do nothing to prevent the hunter's death. Shigemasa's spirit was as strong as ever, unlike the weak and spent boy.

"Let me back in," he protested feebly.

"*I don't think so,*" replied Shigemasa.

"You fiend! Of all the moments…"

"*It is a pity,*" admitted the General, "*but you were too keen to die lately, and that doesn't suit me at all, boy.*"

Satō noticed the change in Bran's posture before he turned around and looked at her with eyes as black as the night. She picked up her sword and pressed its sharp, icy edge to his neck.

"Drop your sword and let him go," she said calmly.

The General licked his – Bran's – lips, eyeing the blade.

"Thou wouldst not hurt him."

"It would hurt *you*, first."

"I will be of much more use to thee than the lad," the General said, smiling. "I know my way around this island. I am a better fighter. I could protect thee... young woman."

In response she pressed the sword closer. A droplet of blood appeared on his skin.

I can't keep it up for long.

"We are of the same stock, thou and I," he continued with a smile. "Samurai both. Thou canst trust me." He began to slowly raise his hand towards the blade, but before he could move it away from his neck, she pressed even harder.

"I trust *Bran*!"

His sword-hand moved faster than she could blink, but somehow she managed to pull back and parry the powerful blow aimed at her neck. Sparks flew from the clashing blades.

Bran stood right in front of the door to the red-light tower, trying to calm himself down.

Don't panic. Focus. You can do it.

It was his body; he managed to get it back once already.

But I had Emrys then. And my ring.

He looked at his ring-finger; it was empty.

So it's gone here as well.

But Shigemasa was in a hurry, and had made a sloppy job of banishing Bran from his mind. The boy pressed at the door and it budged a little with a creak. He sensed the General was trying to push him back, but at the same time was distracted by Satō. At last, the strain of dealing with two diversions at once irritated Shigemasa to the point of bursting. Bran read his quick thought: he was going to *kill the insolent bitch!*

No!

Bran rammed at the door with all his strength at the same time that Shigemasa's sword flashed towards Satō's neck. He leapt inside the tower and, with great effort, he tore the General away and cast him far out onto the red dust plain, into the deepest recesses of his soul.

Exhausted, he fell down onto the forest floor.

Satō splashed water on Bran's face. He opened his eyes and she breathed with relief – they were jade green.

She helped him up. The dead hunter's dog was sniffing its slain master, whimpering. She stomped her feet and the animal ran away into the forest with a yowl.

"What about the other two?" asked Bran.

"I don't think they'll come back," she replied. She was still shaking after the encounter. "Can you get Nagomi into the cave? I'll check on that poor man they were carrying."

She passed the threshold and reeled back in terror.

In the back of the cavern, instead of the naked man, lay a large black bear. Its fore and rear legs were tied with strong rope. Its fur was shaggy and dirty and its sides collapsed with hunger. She fought the primal fear taking her over, making her want to flee. She stepped back and bumped into Bran, who had just brought Nagomi over the cave's threshold.

"What's going – ? Oh…"

The dragon rider laid the priestess down and moved carefully forward.

"Look out!" Satō warned him earnestly, "it can slice your head off with one blow!"

"It doesn't look like it has any strength left.." Bran said. "And what happened to the human?"

She studied the bear more closely. The animal looked at them with strangely intelligent eyes, exposing its teeth in an effort to look threatening. Around its neck was hung a necklace of jade stones.

"You don't think…"

"I don't know, you tell me! Have you ever heard of something like this?"

She scoured her memory for the old tales.

Nagomi would know better, she always loved those stories…

"Well, there are… there were foxes and raccoon dogs which could shapeshift… but I never heard of bears. Can you use True Sight?"

He shook his head.

"I'm too exhausted for that. But that necklace…" Bran walked past her. The bear grunted and waved its head. The boy jumped back, startled, but then slowly came even nearer the animal.

"*Eeh!* What are you doing?" Satō cried, as the boy reached for the jewels.

"I want to see what that necklace is for."

"Maybe it keeps the bear sedated! Maybe it's sapping its strength and if you take it off, the bear will jump and eat you! Why can't you just leave it alone?"

"I… I'm just curious, that's all. I think…Look, it's letting me touch it."

The bear lay its head sideways on the cave floor and did not move, only breathed heavily as Bran examined the jade gems wrapped around the animal's huge neck on a piece of leather cord.

"Yes, of course it would let you touch it, if it meant it could get its strength back and kill us all."

But Bran did not listen. He reached out his hand.

"Give me your dagger," he said.

"You're insane," said Satō, but she gave him the weapon. After all a man was thrown into the cave where the animal now rested…

The boy cut through the cord. The jade gems scattered on the floor of the cage with a tinkle. Nothing happened.

"Well at least it didn't bite your a— look out, it's moving!"

The bear started writhing on the cave floor. Bran quickly jumped back and Satō pulled out her blade by a few inches. But the bear did not attack. The animal's body twisted and tossed around as it groaned in agony.

"Is it...dying?" she asked.

"No. And I know what's happening..." whispered Bran. "It's *transforming...*"

The bear muscles and bones started to relocate and half a minute later a tall, muscular, hairy naked man lay unconscious on the cage floor.

"The day just keeps getting better," said Satō, sighing. "Now we have *two* casualties to take care of."

With some effort, Bran and Satō carried the man towards the campfire.

"I've never heard of bears changing into humans, or the other way around," repeated Satō, "I wonder which way it is. The hunters treated it like an animal."

"I've heard stories... Of werebears and other such creatures living in the frozen forests of the deep north, beyond the Varyaga Khaganate."

"But what's it doing here? It looks almost like a Yamato, only taller."

Bran shook his head.

"I don't know. But we really need to find some help now. For both of them," said Bran. He stood up from the campfire.

"Don't leave me." Satō tugged on his sleeve. "What if that bear-man wakes up and attacks me? What if the hunters return?"

He looked at her surprised. She suddenly seemed frail and vulnerable as never before.

Is this the real Satō ... or just another mask?

As if in answer to the girl's fears, the hairy stranger stirred and moaned. Satō jumped away, reaching for her sword, but Bran remained motionless. The man raised himself on his arms, his movements still resembling an animal. He shook his head and looked up. He saw them and stepped back on all fours. His body was covered in old and new scars. Powerful muscles bulged on his shoulders and thighs, but he was visibly famished, with a stomach caved in under the protruding ribs. Long hair and a short, shaggy beard surrounded a sunken face, with eyes rounder and the nose longer than those of the Yamato. The hairs on his chest were discoloured in the shape of a white crescent that the black bears bore below their necks.

The stranger opened his mouth to speak, but produced only a low growl. He coughed a few times, clearing his throat before trying again.

"You... you're not the hunters."

"The hunters are gone," said Bran. "You're safe now."

"Safe," he repeated hoarsely, sitting down in a bear-like manner, with his legs straight and supporting himself on his knuckles. For a while he bobbed sideways, before speaking again.

"They... took my clothes."

Bran untied his sash and gave it to the man, who wrapped it around his waist like a loincloth. He grunted in thanks.

"Who – or what – are you?" asked Satō, tapping her fingers on the hilt of the sword.

The man bowed, or rather, rocked deeply forward.

"I am Chief of the Kumaso, the Bear People. Torishi."

"*Bear People*? There are more of you?"

"No more," the man shook his head.

"Not much of a Chief, then," Satō remarked.

"But I thought... *werebears* only lived in the far north," said Bran.

The bear-man looked up and squinted.

"Before the Yamato came... my people lived on these islands. Then we were pushed to the edges."

"And now you're the only one left?"

"That I know," the bear-man said, lowering his head, "and what of you?" He glanced at their tattered, bloodied clothes and noticed the unconscious priestess.

"We lost a battle yesterday and had to run," explained Satō in as vague terms as she could. "Our friend was wounded. We need to go down to the valley and find help."

"Help?" Torishi shook his head and stood up. He towered above them, taller even than Dōraku, and more broad-shouldered. He did not seem as weak now. He ran his hand sideways across his beard.

"The Chief of the Bear People will help you."

Satō eyed him suspiciously.

"You look as if you need help yourself. I'm afraid we don't have any food to share."

"Come with me," said Torishi, "I have plenty."

"*Bear* food?"

The man guffawed. "Come!"

He stooped over Nagomi and hesitated. Finally he reached out and gently caressed her red hair. Then he frowned.

"Your friend... is a priestess?"

"Yes," said Bran. "What of it?"

Torishi laughed wistfully.

"To think I would help one of their kind..."

He leaned to pick the girl up.

Satō bit her lips. The man lifted the priestess's limp body without effort.

"My house is not far," he said and without waiting for them, walked off into the forest. Satō looked at Bran. They both shrugged and followed outside.

CHAPTER III

Satō trudged alongside Bran and the bear-man for about a quarter of a *ri* through the thick undergrowth, slipping and cursing, out of breath and out of strength. At last, they reached what looked like an impassable tangle of poison ivy stretching from tree to tree, and stopped. The man nodded at them.

"Move those two branches away. Do not touch the leaves."

The ivy parted with ease, revealing a comfortable entrance to a large, round, open glade. Stepping through it, she saw a large hut with walls of bamboo and straw, and a roof of tightly-woven grass. It stood beside a small stream flowing across the glade. There were remnants of several other huts, all dismantled or burnt down a long time ago.

"But – this is like a normal house!" she cried out.

"This used to be a village," noticed Bran, stepping over a few broken bamboo poles.

"Eight families lived upon this stream," the bear-man said, "the last of the Kumaso."

He entered the house, and she followed hesitantly. It was dark and tight, with just a little light falling through a tiny window, but it was also warm and dry. An unpleasant, sweet smell was coming from the opposite wall, but she couldn't see through the gloom. Torishi laid Nagomi on a long, low bench beside the fireplace in the middle of the hut and covered her with skins.

"There is food in those crates and jugs by the door."

"What about Nagomi?"

"The young priestess? I need to prepare while you eat."

Satō opened one of the crates and reeled back.

"What is this?"

Bran picked up what looked like a dark-red log and sniffed it.

"It's smoked meat." He licked it. "Venison," he said. "Wild boar?"

She gave the boy a stare, but he was busy biting his teeth into the tough meat and didn't seem to notice.

Torishi laughed again.

"Tasty, eh? There is more here, fresher. Deer."

He reached into the gloom and took a long haunch, blackened with age and glistening with fat. He then put on a long tunic of light brown cloth that reached to his knees. He offered Bran his sash back, but the boy raised his hand in protest.

"Er... you can keep it."

"Meat, meat and more meat," Satō opened one crate after another, holding her nose with her fingers, "you wouldn't have anything without legs?"

"Fish in that round box," the bear-man said. He threw some wood on the fireplace and started lighting it up with a flint.

"Thank *Butsu-sama* for that!"

There was about a dozen small, silvery fish inside the bamboo box, cured in some sour-smelling paste. The girl devoured them quickly.

"I suppose rice is out of the question," she said. Torishi shook his head; every time he did so, his thick, long mane of black hair shook wildly from side to side.

"We grew millet, when there were hands enough to work... And we used to buy rice from the valleys. But it's been a long time since I ate either."

The fire started and was now crackling merrily. Smoke rose up through a hole in the grass roof. Torishi reached for some clay pots on the wooden shelf by the only window and put them around the bench where Nagomi lay.

"Now. What happened to her?"

"She's been stabbed through her lungs," Satō said grimly. "She's lost a lot of blood, and I don't know what's going on inside her."

The bear-man sucked air through his teeth and stroked the back of his head. He reached under the bed – a sleeping platform raised about a foot over the floor on wooden logs - and pulled out a small deerskin drum, and a sealed lacquer box.

"What are you doing?" she asked.

"I must commune with the Spirits."

"*Eeh!* You're a *healer* then?"

"I am Chief of the Kumaso," he said, as if that explained everything. "I did not save my people from the Blistering Sickness, but I can deal with injuries."

"Blistering Sickness?" Bran whispered.

"He means smallpox," replied Satō. "Is that what happened to your village?"

Torishi opened the lacquer box carefully.

"The hunters brought the Blistering Sickness into the forest," he explained. "And we, shamans, could not deal with it. But I survived. The Spirits chose me to witness my kindred suffer and die."

His face took on a grim, determined expression as he tied a tightly woven scarf around his head. He picked up a spruce twig, a blade of grass and some dried leaves from the box and tossed them on the fire. A dark, thick smoke spewed from the fireplace.

"The young one will live. The Spirits owe me that much."

He then poured water into a small bowl, mixed in something that looked like dried seaweed, and drank it, wincing. He stuck two small carved bamboo slats into the ground by Nagomi's head.

"Into these sticks I move the pain and the sickness," he said, "when the sticks turn black you must throw them out."

Bran nodded and moved closer to the window. The bear-man started banging out a simple, steady rhythm on the deerskin drum and chucked a few more twigs and leaves onto the fireplace. Thick white smoke filled the inside of the house. The drumming grew faster and louder. Torishi threw back his head and started chanting in a strange, ancient-sounding language.

Ku koh tobochi tan anchi kanne

tani asi ku kon tuntumi ku-tata

Tamb e'tahne ku shirao venara

Ku koh tobochi utarakhe echi mauhe pirikano

Inkoshishchuka yanua, Isomaraykire!

Tan ven ainu kuru-kasihi

Esiohteya mau tambe, ponno ponno

Tan ukuran echi-kochari chiki, pirika!

His body started writhing in a trance, the drum beating grew frenzied. His chanting became garbled, eventually turning into a simple, wordless "*Ya, ya, ya, ya!*" interspersed with whistles and groans. Sweat trickled down his brow.

"Nothing's happening," Bran said when a good half an hour had passed.

The white smoke hovered over Nagomi's body like a dark spirit.

"Look, the sticks!" Satō whispered, pointing. The pieces of carved bamboo turned solid black, obsidian. Bran grabbed them and scowled.

"Hot!"

"Get them out!"

The boy threw the sticks out the window. They fell into the stream with a hiss of steam. The black smoke disappeared; the air in the room was clear again.

Torishi was still in a trance, but his movements were slower now, more relaxed, and the beating was steady again. She could once again make out words in his chanting.

Ashim puhara,

kamui akah kata

E-kom pashuhi

Tu kamui sonko,

Re kamui sonko,

Anokote!

He stopped and dropped his head until his chin touched his chest. He rocked back and forth for a moment yet, eyes closed, murmuring some quiet prayer.

The priestess moaned and stirred. Blood started returning to her cheeks. She opened her eyes and gasped for air.

"Nagomi!" Satō leapt to her feet. The priestess winced, but smiled weakly.

Bran came up to the bench where the priestess lay. He took her hand and held it tightly, not saying a word.

"I'm... sorry..." Nagomi said with effort, "for worrying... you."

"Don't be stupid," said Satō with visible effort. She turned to the bear-man.

"Is she really alright?"

He nodded heavily.

"See for yourself."

Satō uncovered the place where the sickle blade pierced Nagomi's chest. There was barely a trace of a wound, little more than a white scar she traced down with her finger.

"Are you... are we safe?" the priestess asked.

"We're safe," said Bran. "Here, have some water."

The priestess lapped up a few mouthfuls from a clay pot and lay back on the bench, closing her eyes.

"You must rest now. We'll tell you about everything later," he added.

"It looks like we are even, Torishi-*sama*," Satō said, bowing before their host.

"The Spirits repaid their debt," the bear-man said, shaking his head. He leaned towards her. He smelled of raw meat and soil. He touched her arm with a long, dirty finger. She fought the urge to step back.

"You too are wounded."

He took a small container from the box and handed it to her. It reeked of animal fat.

"Put it on the wound. *Kudzu* root. Keeps it clean."

She looked at Bran, slightly panicked. The boy glanced at Nagomi.

"He helped her – maybe he can help you, too."

The blood-soaked and tattered sleeve of her kimono fell apart in her hands when she tried to roll it up. She tentatively scooped some of the white goo and put it onto the red, swollen wound. It stung, but she endured in silence.

The noon turned to afternoon, and the inside of the hut grew even darker and gloomier with all the smoke and soot. Nagomi was still asleep, but her skin had a healthy glow again, and her breathing was regular. Satō had her arm bandaged and was eating the last of Torishi's fish, while Bran devoured another portion of cured venison. He caught her repulsed gaze.

"Stop looking at me like that," he said. "I'm not a Sun Priest. I haven't had meat for a month. Why don't *you* eat meat, anyway?"

"I… I just don't," she replied, realizing she had only a faint idea of the reason. "It's gross."

Torishi handed them each a wooden cup filled with some misty liquid. She smelled it suspiciously.

"Another medicine?"

The bear-man chuckled.

"Yes, medicine… for the head."

She sipped. It had a bitter and fermented taste, like bad saké. She gulped the cup in one go and felt the warmth spreading throughout her body. She reached out for seconds, but Torishi took the cup from her.

"One is enough."

"So…" Bran started. "What happened to your people? Did they all die from this sickness?"

Torishi shook his head again.

"That was just the end. First the Valley People kept on coming… always up, always deeper into the forest," he said in a monotone, resigned voice, staring at the flames. "Cutting down trees… building homes of wood and paper… planting fields… hunting our game… taking our women."

He raised a hand to the light. His arm was covered in ancient scars and burns.

"They had metal and fire, and the Bear People only had wood and stone and claw. After they took our land they started hunting *us*."

"Like the hunters we fought today," said Bran. "But *why* hunt you?"

"Our insides hold powerful magic. Or so the Valley People believe. But only if cut from a bear. That's what the jade necklace was for – to seal me in bear; strong but dumb. Easy to trap."

"And they would've left you to starve?" asked Satō.

"Bad luck to slay one of us. Much better to let one die of hunger."

"Somehow I… I knew I had to remove the necklace," said Bran. "Was that you?"

Torishi nodded.

"It's a call from one Kumaso hunter to another. But there are no more Kumaso hunters in the mountain." He looked into the darkness. "And the Valley People were deaf to our calls."

Nagomi stirred and moaned. Torishi touched her head with a fatherly gesture and the girl calmed down.

"You asked whether Nagomi was a priestess," remembered Satō.

"Your priests were the chief of our enemies. They rallied the Valleys against us. But… it doesn't matter now. The crimes of others are not her fault."

He paused. "My daughter had fox hair, too."

Satō blinked, surprised.

"A Dejima child? In this forest?" Satō could think of no other reason.

"Many fox-haired cubs laughed and played in this village before the Blistering Sickness silenced them forever."

He lowered his head and let out a long, sad grunt, then looked back up at them with a smile.

"No, let's not dwell on the past. You must be tired."

It was still early, but Satō felt weak and weary. She nodded. Torishi stood up and moved Nagomi gingerly onto the raised bed.

He unrolled a couple of old boar skins on the floor.

"I need to check the traps," he said, heading for the door. "Maybe catch a fish."

He left the house. Satō ran her fingers through the bristles and a few bugs skittered onto the floor. She recoiled in disgust.

"Blistering Disease," she murmured.

"What?" asked Bran.

"What if it's still here? Aren't you worried?"

"Don't be silly, nobody dies of smallpox anymore."

"Not here. At least Nagomi's vaccinated, but I…"

"You'll be fine. The disease must be long gone."

It wasn't very reassuring, but there was little else she could do. *He's our host,* she thought with her eyes closed. *And saved Nagomi's life. I have to take what he has to offer.*

She saw Bran shake the skin with a swift motion and tried to do the same, but a needle of pain pierced her arm.

"Are you alright?" the boy asked.

"I'm fine."

She lay down on the boar skin, carefully, trying to touch as little of it as possible, and closed her eyes.

"Looks like we were lucky again," she heard Bran's voice nearby.

"Yes… the *kami* take good care of Nagomi – and us."

"Did you mean it?" he asked.

"Mean what?"

"When you said you trusted me."

There was a long pause as she mulled over the answer.

"We have to trust each other. There's nobody else left."

"Thank you."

He sighed. She heard the fur rustle underneath him.

"I killed a man today."

"It was the old Spirit, not you," she said, not sure where he was going with it.

"I think I slew some more yesterday."

She tried to recall the details of the battle, but it was all a blur; only the death of the man in the black *yamabushi* robes she remembered clearly, the sound of cracking skull, her blooded sword.

"I thought you were a soldier."

He sighed again.

"I was taught how to fight, yes, but not how to take a life. It's… not at all how I imagined."

"I wouldn't know," she said, "I am a samurai. Killing is in my blood."

But when she closed her eyes she could still see the anguish on the slain man's face; after all it was her first kill, too.

Does death hurt that much?

"An old doctor once told me," said Bran, "not to dwell too long on killing. If I do, I might start… enjoying it."

"That's what my Father taught me, too. Not to give in to bloodlust. The doom of the samurai, he called it. But I yearned to kill this demon so much!"

Father…

Shūhan's gentle face appeared before her eyes. What would he have said about the way she conducted herself in the battle?

"It was close. We could have all died there."

"Nagomi almost did."

"Eh… Our host is right. No point dwelling on the past. We're alive, that's all that matters. As soon as Nagomi is healed and rested, we will…"

He hung his voice.

"We will go down from these mountains," she finished for him. "And the first thing I'll do when we get to a town is take a bath and buy some new clothes. Good thing I still have my gold."

This was as far ahead as she could think right now.

Bran turned on his side; from the soft rhythm of Satō's breath he could tell she was already asleep. The priestess lay on the platform on her back with her hands clasped over her stomach, hair spread like red fire on the dark skins. The door to the hut squeaked open and in came Torishi, quietly, with three large fish tied to a pole. The bear-man sat down in the corner and began to work on his catch in utter silence.

They had avoided the subject all day, but now that Bran was alone with his thoughts it had returned at last.

What are we going to do now? What am I going to do?

There was a void in his mind; the dragon was gone. Broken away, it was roaming somewhere over Yamato.

I could still hunt it down, he thought, *follow the news and rumours. A rampaging dragon is an easy thing to track after all.*

But he dreaded what he had to do to Emrys, as he also knew, after the Farlink was gone, it was too late for anything else.

Father was right, he thought bitterly. He imagined Dylan, shaking his finger.

"I told you. You can't trust a dragon."

I still need to get back home after that. The Bataavian ship will be here in a month, if I manage to get back to Kiyō. He sighed. Suddenly everything seemed that much more complicated and depressing. Get to Emrys, and fly away; that was all he had ever thought about - until now.

And what about the girls? It had been an insane idea to take Nagomi on this dangerous journey in the first place. Whatever had Lady Kazuko been thinking? And Satō? Without a dragon, was Bran still a target for the Crimson Robe?

Unlikely. She would be better off chasing him on her own. Or better yet, find somebody more suitable for the job... like that Gensai man from Kirishima.

He didn't sleep much that night; by morning he had made up his mind.

"I'm going after the dragon. Alone. We will get you two down to the Valleys and find a way to transport Nagomi back to Kiyō."

They looked at him puzzled.

"It's my dragon and it's my quest," he proceeded to explain. "You both are no longer a part of it. Satō, you had better look for your father without me. And I don't care about the Prophecies or whatever the High Priestess told you, Nagomi – it's got too dangerous."

"Do you think... I followed you because... Kazuko-*hime* told me to?" asked the priestess quietly. Talking still was an effort for her.

"No, that's not what I –"

"It was not your decision to have us join you, and it will not be your decision to make us leave," said Satō.

"Look, you got it all wrong!" Bran struggled, "I only do this because I don't want you to get hurt! Because I *care* about you."

"And you think that we don't care... about you?" Nagomi said and turned her face to the wall. She would not say anything more.

"Idiot," said Satō, standing up. "Don't make her angry, she's still not well. Come, let's talk outside."

Bran followed her and they sat on the bank of the cold stream.

"I want to track the dragon down. But I can do it all by myself," he said, scratching the scab on his cheek. "You don't need to follow me anymore. You can go searching for your father, and Nagomi can rest in some shrine in Kagoshima. I would only be getting in your way."

Satō sighed and wrapped her arms around her knees.

"I'll tell you a secret, Bran. I don't think my old man is still alive."

He looked at her, surprised.

"I never said anything because I didn't want to worry Nagomi, but... it's been so long. The Crimson Robe must have decided it's not worth keeping him around anymore."

"Then why...?"

"I want revenge. And don't you want one too? It's partly because of that demon that your dragon has gone – how do you say it?"

"Feral."

She pondered it for a while.

"I understand what you're trying to do, and I think it's very honourable," she said at last, "but it's too late."

She put her hand on his arm in a gesture she must have picked up from him.

"We're friends now, Bran. We fought together; we've been through hardships together. We've saved each other's lives. And if there's anything you need help with, you can count on us."

He nodded slowly and smiled, somehow relieved.

"And you can count on me."

"Great." She stood up. "So what's the *real* plan?"

By the next morning, Nagomi stood up from the bed on her own. She swayed at first, but refused the support of Satō's arm.

"I'm fine, really. I need to stretch my legs, they're too weak."

She paced slowly around the hut; there wasn't a lot of space in the low, dark building, so she stepped outside, where Torishi was preparing a morning soup of bracken and roots. The bear-man saw her and smiled, welcoming her to sit beside him.

"You're well, little cub."

"Yes. All thanks to you, I hear, Torishi-*sama*."

She bowed.

"Thanks to the Spirits. You know it as well as I do."

"You're a priest, too?"

A shadow marred his face for a moment.

"I speak to the Spirits, but in a different way."

In the silence that followed, she sensed the presence of many *kami* all around her. They studied her in curious silence; the place felt almost like... like...

"This entire glade is a shrine!" she said, astonished.

Torishi nodded. "We do not build shrines. Our Spirits dwell with us."

"Did you stay here to keep the Spirits company after everyone died?"

"You might say that," he said and threw another split root into the pot. There was little emotion in his voice, but Nagomi suddenly felt an overwhelming sadness and loneliness.

"I heard that you... your people lived here before the Yamato came."

He nodded.

"Are you one of the Ancients, then?"

"Oh, no," he said, shaking his hairy head. "But I know *of* them. They lived alongside us, a long time ago. The Little Folk, we called them. We learned the bear lore from them, and the secrets of the Forest."

"What happened to them?"

"They were already a dying race when we came. That's what the legends say. Sick and poor. They hid in the tunnels they dug deep into the mountains, in the earth barrows... praying to their dragon gods to come and save them. None ever did."

The dragon gods?

"This is ready," he added, picking up the pot. "Time to put it on the fire."

"There's no point wasting your time because of me", said Nagomi, "the sooner we leave, the sooner we will find Bran's dragon and your honoured Father."

Satō cast Bran a meaningful look and said, "It shouldn't take us more than two, three days to reach Kagoshima, and it's a city as big as Kiyō."

"Did your father know anyone in Kagoshima?" asked Bran.

"There are a few wizards who moved there from Kiyō. I'm sure I can ask around. We'll be safe from the *Taikun* there, too."

She noticed the bear-man listening to their conversation with great interest and, as soon as they finished planning, he stood up and started packing his belongings into a large canvas bag: his shaman's box, little drum, ointments and herbs.

"What are you doing?" she asked.

"There is nothing to keep me here."

He reached for the weapons hanging on the wall – a long, curved hunting knife in antler sheath and a bow with two dozen flint head arrows.

"But what about the Spirits?" asked Nagomi.

"They agree. Your coming was a sign. Time to forget about the past."

"You don't even know our purpose."

"I don't need to."

Satō leaned over to Bran and whispered in his ear.

"What do you think?"

"We could use his protection," replied Bran, eyeing Torishi's muscular arms and chest, "if we can trust another stranger. He seems kind though..."

"He is a *werebear*. What if it's dangerous, like your Dragonform?"

Satō felt Nagomi's hand on hers.

"I believe in this man's good intentions," the red-haired girl said. "Please, Sacchan, let him join us."

"All right, then," said Satō with a sigh. "We're moving out in an hour. I just hope the people in the valleys don't shoot you on sight."

The noon sun stood high in the sky. Satō picked up her bundle – thanking quietly the servant girl from Kirishima for salvaging so much of their belongings – and headed towards the fence of poison ivy.

"Wait, please," said Torishi. He entered the bamboo hut and emerged with a burning log from the fireplace.

What is he doing?

The bear-man chanted in his strange language and started walking around the building, singing and setting fire to the dry straw walls. The hut quickly burst into flames, like a giant funeral pyre.

He cast the burning log into the stream and stood for a while in front of the blazing house with his head hung low; a giant black silhouette against the yellow flames. In his light brown tunic, woven of bark cloth and richly decorated with black patterns, and embroidered red and blue headscarf, he looked truly regal, as the great chieftain of a proud race should. Finally, he turned around. His face was grave, but calm.

"Thus perished the last village of the Kumaso," he said. "Let us leave this forsaken place."

CHAPTER IV

"We will now vote for the second time on Hotta-*dono*'s proposal from the previous meeting. And if this time we have a stalemate, then, according to the law, we will refer to His Excellency's decision. Are we all in agreement?"

Chief Councillor Abe waited until all the other councillors grunted their confirmation.

"In that case, please raise your hands if you believe we should initiate our secret negotiations with the Barbarians."

He raised his hand, as did Naosuke; this was expected. The two Matsudairas voted in the same split way as before. Young Kuze looked at them with contempt. It seemed there would be a stalemate again, after all. This suited him; the *Taikun* was bound to disagree with the motion.

But then the old Councillor Tadamasa also raised his hand, slowly, with a visible effort.

"Makino-*dono*," the elder of the Matsudairas asked with a frown, "are you sure you understood the question?"

"I may be old, but I'm not senile," replied Tadamasa angrily.

"May I ask what changed your mind?" asked Kuze, struggling to keep calm. His right hand twitched close and open.

"No, you may not," the old Councillor said and lowered his eyes, seemingly fascinated with the dark lining separating the *tatami* mats on the floor.

There was a long silence. At last, Chief Councillor Abe coughed and spoke.

"Then I declare the vote to have passed. We will send the message to… no… I will go meet the foreigners myself. Hotta-*dono* will accompany me."

Kuze Hirochika rose in indignation.

"Then there is nothing for me to do here. While you talk like weaklings, I shall prepare the defences of the capital. Let's see whose way will prevail, a clerk's - or a warrior's."

He turned to Naosuke and seethed through his teeth.

"It's your fault, Hotta-*dono*. I don't know how, but I know *you* did this. It's another one of your tricks. But you'll regret this, mark my words. Your days as the Councillor are numbered."

"Titles are meaningless. I exist only to serve the *Taikun*," said Naosuke and bowed.

The interior of the Inner Palace was austere, contemplative, compared to the lavishness of the Outer and Middle courts. Those ones were designed to awe and overwhelm the *Taikun*'s guests with gold flakes, priceless paintings, ancient scrolls and vases, and rich gardens. The Inner Palace was where the *Taikun* and his family relaxed. The walls were plain black and white lattice of bamboo and paper, with all the effort put into harmony and balance rather than decoration. Beyond the *Taikun*'s private rooms lay the great *Ōku* hall, the many-corridored harem where his wives and concubines spent days painting, playing instruments and engaging in ceaseless intrigues and power struggles. And surrounding all this was the *Taikun*'s private garden, with moon viewing verandas, tea houses and delicate pavilions overlooking decorative ponds teeming with koi carps and small brown turtles.

It was on one of the garden verandas that the great *Taikun*, Tokugawa Ieyoshi, lay on his side, admiring the plum trees growing around a small, circular pond. They bloomed for the second time this year and were an unusual colour of pure scarlet, their petals floating like drops of blood on the surface of the pool. Ieyoshi was not superstitious, but even he wondered if it wasn't some kind of an omen.

The *Taikun* was an old man; tired of life. His efforts at reforms had failed, his treasury empty, his borders undefended; he was all too aware of the shortcomings and dangers facing his nation. He glanced with worry at his only son, Iesada, who sat beside him, observing the flowers with a blank look. A weak-minded and weak-bodied boy, he was not an heir fit for the challenges of ruling a country in these difficult times. Ieyoshi could have only hoped he would live long enough to guide the Yamato nave across the seas of trouble before an untimely death.

The squeaking of the nightingale floor in the Corridor of Bells announced the arrival of the boy messenger at the veranda. The *Taikun* slowly turned his aching body towards him.

"What news of the Council, boy?"

"The Council has voted to open secret negotiations with the Western Barbarians, *kakka*."

The *Taikun* suddenly jumped to his feet with agility defying his age and health.

"What!?" he roared. A flock of startled sparrows flew from the peony bush. "How did that happen? Abe was supposed to make sure there would be no talks!"

"Word in the palace is, Makino-*dono* was convinced by Councillor Hotta to support the motion. Abe-*dono* was simply outvoted."

"And who proposed the motion in the first place?"

"Councillor Hotta, *kakka*."

The *Taikun* closed his hands in fists and gnashed his teeth.

"He will pay for the insolence. His usefulness has at last expired. I will force the little pale devil to resign. Come, Iesada, you should learn from this."

Reluctantly, the *Taikun*'s heir picked himself up from the veranda floor and followed his father down the Corridor of Bells to the Room of Scrolls, where the old *Taikun* liked to prepare his edicts and despatches before officially dictating them to his secretary.

"Make me some ink, son, my arm is weary. Now, let's see... we shall do it the old fashioned way. *To Hotta Naosuke, the esteemed Councillor, etc., from Tokugawa Ieyoshi, Great Commodore of Yamato, etc.* The secretary will fill up all the required titles. *Please accept this gift as an expression of our gratitude for your services. We trust this ancient cha ceremony set, said to belong to Sen Sōsa himself, the first headmaster of the Omotesenke School, will be to your liking. We know how fond you are of the Ceremony, and we hope in the near future you will find sufficient time to fully appreciate its beauty.*"

"That's it? We're sending him a tea pot?" Iesada blinked, his face showing utter lack of understanding.

"Have none of my teachings reached through that thick skull of yours?" Ieyoshi said and sighed. "Read between the lines, boy! You need time to practice Way of *Cha*, time you can't spare if you are busy running the government. That's the way we deal with things at the court. *Subtle and refined.* Do you understand?"

"Yes, Father..."

"Do you? Sometimes I wonder. Come with me to the Middle Palace, we shall make this letter known. And you," he said to the boy messenger who waited patiently in the door. "Get me Abe. I need to remind him the Council is just an *advisory* body."

Dōraku examined the surroundings of the shrine, discovering the tracks by the burned-out remains of a gate leading into the forest. It was the middle of the night, the forest was pitch black, but his eyes could easily spot the signs of a battle which had taken place around the *torii* gate: the earth torn and the trees shattered by magic, the discarded weapons; the charred remains of an oxcart and a few links of a shattered iron chain. But the bodies had been taken away for funeral, and the rain washed off the footsteps; even he could not tell them apart.

Everyone in town spoke of nothing else but the fire and devastation of a large part of the shrine and the death of many priests and samurai in the conflagration. Those who spoke the loudest were blaming it on some careless kitchen maid or a rogue lightning strike. After greasing a few palms here and making a scary face there, Dōraku soon learned a different story: that of a flying monster, coming down the mountain and destroying everything in its path.

Two days had passed since he had come to his senses on the rocky slope of the Takachiho Mountain. The day before, he had to kill a deer; but an animal's blood was not enough to sustain him after the exhausting regeneration.

Cursed thirst. If only I had more time to rest...

There was an odd set of tracks leading east, up the slope; it seemed as if some bulky giant had run through the forest, followed by more hurried steps in the same direction. He traced all these tracks down to a line of tall, grey rocks. Here the first set seemed to disappear into thin air, while the other group scoured the ground searching for clues, much like Dōraku himself was now doing. They then departed north along the rock face.

"They aren't here anymore." A young voice surprised him. He turned around to see a girl dressed in the simple clothes of a shrine servant.

"And how do you know who I'm looking for?" he asked and frowned. He didn't like being surprised.

How can she see me?

"I helped them escape. They went up there," she said, pointing to the east, over the rocks, "but I can't tell you how they got away. It's a secret."

She covered her lips with her hand and giggled.

"Who are you? How did you find me?"

"I'm just a servant girl, samurai-*dono*. But I can see... things."

"Have you seen the battle?"

"No, samurai-*dono*. I can't stand the sight of *blood*."

He stepped closer and saw the girl was blind.

She senses my thirst.

"Are you going to help them?" she asked.

"I'll try," he replied and turned north.

"What are you doing, samurai-*dono*? That's not where they went!"

"Now that I know they survived, I can see where those people have gone too," he said.

"But they may be in danger."

"And *are they* in danger now, girl?"

"N...no," she admitted. "For the moment they are in safe hands."

Dōraku looked at the servant girl carefully.

"That's a remarkable gift you have, child."

"The priests think it comes from a demon."

"The priests are all dead," he said, "and believe me, I would know if it was a demon. Here," he added, throwing her a large silver coin, "this should pay off whatever debt is keeping you here. Move to some other shrine, where they will recognize your talent."

"Thank you, samurai-*dono*."

The old, bald Nanseian, Shō, threw a thick piece of firewood into the air and chopped at it with the edge of his hand. Two cleanly sliced parts fell to the ground. He grunted, satisfied.

"Show off," mumbled Azumi.

She was crouching against a cedar tree, clutching a large straw basket in her arms.

"Why can't you just use an axe, like everyone else?"

"I need to stay fit. You could do with some exercise too."

She shrugged.

"I don't care."

"You may want to watch your tongue, woman."

She stared at him in cold fury.

"And who's going to tell him? You can't even find three lost kids!"

"You were there too," he barked.

"I'm not a tracker. And *I* was wounded."

"They used magic. I can't deal with magic."

"Neither can I. Makes you wonder why he chose *us* to pursue them."

"The Master is after the *dorako*. His magic is needed there. We'll be fine, they can't have just disappeared. It's only a matter of time."

She kept staring at him. He ran his hand over his bald head. He was always uneasy near her.

Is it because I'm an shinobi… or because I'm a woman?

"What did he promise you, Nanseian?" she asked. "What would you do with the Reward?"

"My father is the king of Nansei," he replied proudly. "A *rightful* king. Yet he has to pay tribute to Satsuma. I would change that."

He punched a nearby tree, to show what he would do with the masters of Satsuma. The blow left a satisfying, fist-size crater in the trunk.

As if in answer, the bushes parted and a tired, grey-clad swordsman appeared on the glade before Shō.

"What is it?" the Nanseian asked.

"We found this in the forest, Shō-*sama*." The *rōnin* handed him a tattered, bloodied piece of white cloth. Shō studied it for a moment.

"The priestess," he said, picking up a red hair. "You haven't found the body, then?"

"No, just this. The rest of the group followed the tracks into the woods; they sent me here to report."

"Very well." Shō nodded. "Get up, Azumi. We have a hunt on our hands."

The assassin rose and started tying the straw basket to a sash on her back.

What was that?

She turned around swiftly, but there was only the forest.

"What is it?" he asked.

"I thought I saw something, over there in the trees."

"Must have been a deer."

"A climbing deer?"

"A monkey, then. Hurry up, woman."

There are no monkeys in these forests, Nanseian.

It was already dark by the time Azumi and Shō reached the camp the grey-clads had set up around the waterfall cave.

"We found them running through the woods," one of the swordsmen said, casting two frightened men onto their knees before Shō. The Nanseian squinted to see their faces better in the light of the torch.

Poachers.

"They have an interesting story to tell."

One of the men told the tale of their meeting with two armed, spell-casting youths.

"Only two?" the Nanseian asked.

"Yes, Shō-*sama*."

Shō nodded at the *ronin*. One of the poachers understood the gesture and raised his hands in despair. His pleas for mercy were cut abruptly by a quick sword cut. His companion jumped up and tried to run away. As he was passing Azumi, she raised her hand in silence. The sickle blade pierced the poacher's neck; the man fell to the ground, clutching the wound and gurgling.

"Have you found anything else in the cave?" Shō asked, turning away from the dying poacher crawling in the grass.

"Only traces of campfire and this," one of the men presented a handful of jade comma-shaped jewels and a piece of string. The Nanseian furrowed his brow in thought.

"Magic", he said and spat. "Who's the best tracker here?" he asked.

"That is me," said the swordsman who spoke first.

"Take a torch and try to figure out what went on here. As soon as the day breaks we follow the trail further. They can't have gone far; they're tired and injured. Somebody finish that man off!" he added, annoyed.

The tracker returned shortly before dawn.

"There were two of them coming in – and one carried – but three left. They either got help or somebody captured them. Big feet, lots of hair," he added, presenting a bundle of long, black hair he had gathered from the branches around the cave.

"Black hair? You recognize any of this?" the Nanseian asked Azumi.

How can you not recognize it?

"It's a bear," she said.

"Right. A big man in bear skin should be easy to find. Wake up you lazy oafs!" he shouted and started kicking those who would not get up quickly enough, "the trail is fresh."

In half an hour the camp was packed and the group made ready to follow the tracker up the mountainside, deeper into the forest. They walked for a quarter of a *ri* when the tracker stood up and sniffed.

"Smoke."

He wrinkled his nose.

"Strange smoke. That's no campfire. Stay here; I'll see what's going on."

Minutes passed, and the tracker failed to reappear. Shō scratched the top of his bald head.

"You," he said to another of the grey-clad swordsmen. They all looked the same to him.

"Check what's up with him. But be careful."

As soon as the swordsman disappeared in the bushes, Shō selected three others.

"Shadow him. Run back if there's any danger. Don't get heroic."

He didn't have to wait long before an abruptly cut shout echoed through the forest.

"Shō-*sama!* It's a tra-"

The Nanseian clapped his hands and motioned others to follow him. There were six warriors still left, and a few hired hunters, armed with bows;

Azumi followed behind. They all hurried in the direction of the shout and ran through an opening in the wall of poison ivy out onto a wide, sunny glade. Remains of a small house built of straw and twigs were still smouldering near a calm stream. A tall man, clad in a purple hooded cloak, stood in the middle of the glade, with his back, towards Shō. He held twin swords in his hands; the blades dripped with blood. Her heart skipped a beat.

"No... no, no, no," said Azumi, stepping back.

"What's wrong?" asked Shō, but he couldn't wait for an answer. The man in the hooded cloak turned around to face them. His eyes were golden, and his face pale like old paper: just like Azumi remembered. The six grey-clad swordsmen surrounded him in a narrow circle.

The Nanseian took a long, cautious look at the two bloodied swords and ordered his men to step further back. The hunters drew their bows and targeted the man, but Shō told them to put down the weapons.

"Arrows can't hurt him."

He stepped closer, though sweat covered his bald head.

"What is your quarrel with us, Fanged?"

Fanged?

"I will have no quarrel if you turn around now and go back to your master, Nanseian," the Swordsman spoke.

"That I cannot do. Step aside and let us continue the hunt."

"I said, leave this place now - while you're still alive."

"I serve one of the Eight Heads. You *will* stand aside."

"Your master told you of the Serpent? How reckless of him." The Swordsman smiled wryly. "I do not care for them, and do not fear them."

What are they talking about?

"Cut him to pieces," Shō ordered, and the six warriors leapt into battle.

As soon as the grey-clads launched their attack, Azumi decided discretion was a far better part of valour and vanished from the glade. From a nearby tree, she observed the fight. It was brief.

The Swordsman's eyes turned from gold to black; his face seemed even paler in contrast. His body became one with his swords, a whirlwind of blades, a flurry of cuts. He undercut the first warrior's grip with such force that the man's katana flew high into the air. The swords moved faster than the eye could see, with inhuman speed and unnatural strength, whistling through the air, breaking through mail and bone with ease.

His opponents were highly trained swordsmen and killers in their own right. But before the flying katana dropped to the ground, the fight was over. The demon stood alone in a pool of red; the six swordsmen around him dead or dying, some sprawled on the grass, some still kneeling, clutching their gushing wounds in agony for a few more seconds. The hunters fled into the forest. The Swordsman shook the blood off his swords, in the same move wiped and sheathed them. His kimono was splattered with crimson, but there was not even a scratch on his body. Shō reeled back; he looked to his sides, searching for Azumi, only to discover that he was alone.

You may think me a coward, she thought, *but at least I will live to warn the Master.*

"Did you not know who I am, Nanseian?" the Swordsman spoke, his voice icy cold. "Did my name not reach the southern islands yet?"

The old man shook his head, speechless.

"I am Niten Dōraku; I am Shinmen Takezō; I am the Immortal Swordsman. I have never been defeated in a fair fight. I gave you the chance to live, but you threw it away. And now, because of you, I hunger even more…"

Shō raised his hands in combat stance; the Swordsman leapt towards him. The sinewy man struck a powerful blow on the demon's chest, but it made no impression on the samurai, who grabbed Shō's outstretched arm and snapped it at the elbow like a twig. Glistening fangs plunged into his neck and the demon started lapping up bright blood spewing from the vein. Shō gurgled and flailed his arms desperately.

The Swordsman threw the bloodless body to the ground and wiped his lips. The colour of his eyes returned to gold. He looked at the Nanseian's corpse.

"Poor fool… were Ganryū's promises really worth so much?"

He closed his eyes, bowed his head and started praying.

Azumi did not wait to see him finish.

CHAPTER V

Bran felt as if he had seen all this before. They were climbing down a narrow, forested gully, following their new guide, just as they had been following Dōraku not that long ago.

How come we keep doing this?

The gully had been carved in the slope of the Takachiho Mountain by the same stream that ran through Torishi's village. By now it had grown into a raging mountain river, foaming and skipping over the boulders on its journey down to the sea. It was nearing the end of the day and the rain started pouring down again.

"There is a village right below that ridge," the bear-man said. "Good people, if easily frightened."

"What do we tell them?" asked Nagomi. "We don't look like normal travellers."

Their clothes were still tattered, singed and bloodied in places. Satō and Torishi had tried hard to repair them over the previous couple of days, but they could only do so much with bone needle and vine thread and cold stream water. The wizardess had her arm wrapped in bandages, Bran's broken nose was still bruised and swollen.

"We don't need to tell them anything," replied Bran. "They're just peasants."

Satō raised an eyebrow but said nothing.

Nobody welcomed them at the entrance to the village; the only road was empty and quickly turning into a quagmire in the rain.

Another desolate hamlet, thought Bran, and his heart sank.

The sharply angled thatched roof of the headman's house loomed over the centre of the village. As they drew closer, heads started appearing in the doors and windows of the huts, curious faces of children and their mothers.

We must be the most visitors this place has seen in years.

That the two of them wore noblemen's clothes – albeit torn and tattered – made it even more of an event. By the time they reached the village centre – a wider and less muddy bit of the road in front of the headman's house – they were followed by a small, silent, curious gathering.

A far larger crowd had gathered on the square, made up of men and women in field clothes. They were not there to welcome the visitors; in fact, Bran saw only their backs. The crowd listened to the headman, who was standing on a tree stump, shouting and waving his arms, trying to calm the agitated villagers down.

"Yes, there will be new taxes," Bran heard him say, "and we will have to work harder through the harvest season to rebuild our shrine."

So they know already.

Angry murmurs rippled through the crowd.

"But who knows – there may be work at the rebuilding! Carpenters, porters, all sorts of construction workers... I'll send a man to Kirishima tomorrow to see if there's any word of what they may need."

"There's never any work in town!" somebody cried. "They have their own craftsmen."

"All they want is more rice, more barley, more buckwheat, never more workers," complained another. "At this rate we'll have no grain left for the sowing season!"

Others hollered in agreement. Bran turned to one of the old women in the group that had followed them through the village.

"What's going on?" he asked.

"Oh, terrible news, *tono*," she replied, bowing. "The Great Shrine has burned down! Many dead, many wounded. Priests and even... some samurai."

"How awful!" he said avoiding her gaze.

The men in the square finally took notice of the strangers, as did the headman. He raised his hands again.

"Be quiet, all of you!" he cried, "let me welcome our noble guests."

This had the effect opposite to what he intended. The villagers became even more aggravated, their anger now turned toward the mysterious visitors.

"Noble guests?" said one, a burly, strong-looking fellow with a few teeth missing and a bruise under his eye. "They don't look noble to me! Look at the girl's hair - only demons have hair like that! And that bearded giant, isn't he one of the mountain goblins?" He spat.

Bran's hand wandered to the sword at his side.

How dare you...

"What noblemen have no horse, no bags, no servants?" added another peasant, a woman in dirty-brown *monpe* and red headscarf.

"First a burned shrine, and now *they* are coming down from the mountains?" shouted someone else. "Funny that!"

"Silence, serf!"

Bran stepped forward, with the sword drawn by a few inches. The crowd pulled back and quietened, but then the woman in the red headscarf cried again.

"Look at his eyes! Bright green! It's a goblin! A goblin!"

She grabbed his kimono and shook him, as if to see if he was real. A handful of gravel flew towards his face. Sudden outrage turned his vision red. In one swift move, Bran drew the sword and slashed her across the chest.

"Aiyeeee!" She fell down with a brief, shrieking yell. Red splattered over the mud.

Everything fell silent for a brief moment; and then the crowd charged. They fell on Bran with fists, clubs and stones. He slipped in the mud, letting go of his sword. Instinctively, he summoned a weak *tarian,* but the sight of magic only roused the peasants into further frenzy.

The barrage stopped as abruptly as it had started. A villager was thrown aside with great force, then another, and the crowd scattered in fright. Torishi's bulking frame loomed over Bran and a muscular, hairy arm reached out to help him up. Satō was standing in the middle of the road, waving her blade threateningly at any peasant who dared to get near. A man was lying at her feet, screaming and clutching a stump of an arm.

The bear-man handed Bran his bloodied and muddy weapon. He stared at it, as if seeing it for the first time, then at the peasant woman at his feet, and the wide gash across her chest still spurting blood in a weakening rhythm, its edges bright red and glistening in the rain. He felt nauseous. He looked around. Only the headman remained on the road, prostrated, not daring to look up.

He felt somebody grabbing him by the arm.

"We'd better go," Nagomi said quietly. "Looks like we won't be staying here for the night, after all."

It was too late to look for another village, so they decided to break camp off the road, an hour's walk down the mountain. The forest here was not as wild as higher up, with young trees planted in place of the old ones by the woodsmen, and all the fern and bracken cleared regularly.

"We'll find a bed and bath tomorrow," said Satō, smiling. She bumped Bran in a friendly way, trying to cheer him up. The boy had been gloomy and silent since leaving the village. He nodded, absentmindedly.

"What's wrong with him?" Torishi asked.

"It's complicated," she replied, herself unsure.

Bran looked up, overhearing their exchange.

"It was me this time," he said in a blank voice. "Not Emrys, not Shigemasa. I slew her because I was angry. Because she touched me."

"You did nothing wrong," said Satō. "They were about to attack you, right? She showed no respect for a samurai. She got what she deserved. You should rest now."

"I'm fine," Bran replied and stood up. "I need to be alone for a while."

He followed a path deeper into the woods and a clearing freshly cut by the lumberjacks. He sat down on a stump of cedar tree and closed his eyes.

He was trying to recede from consciousness the way he had all those days ago in Mogi. At last it worked; when he opened his eyes, he found himself looking down from the top of the red-eye tower, out onto the measureless red dust plain.

"*Taishō!*" he cried at the top of his lungs. The shout echoed throughout the flatland, the only sound in this vast emptiness.

He waited. Eventually, a lonely dot appeared on the horizon, moving slowly. When Shigemasa neared the tower, Bran shouted again.

"That's enough! Don't come closer."

The old General looked up to him with a wry, mocking smile.

"What are you doing to me?" the boy asked.

"I haven't done anything," Shigemasa replied. "That's just the way things are, boy. You didn't think there wouldn't be a price? You're becoming one of *us*."

"No!" Bran cried and the power of his protest raised a gust of wind so strong it slid Shigemasa away by a few feet.

"It's your whispers, your... mind tricks!"

Shigemasa chuckled.

"I told you, didn't I? The old hag from Suwa had no idea what she was unleashing. To bind the spirit of a Barbarian with that of a samurai... Nobody ever tried anything like it."

"I don't care. I want you to *stop*."

"I can't - ! As long as I'm here, you will keep changing. You should be happy, Barbarian."

Bran gnashed his teeth.

"Why are you so upset anyway?" the General asked. "It was just some peasant scum. They should *all* have been put to death."

"No. You wouldn't understand. It's not how things are done in *my* country. We are *not* killing innocent people."

A smile vanished from General's face.

"Oh but I *do* understand. I understand you Barbarians very well. I fought alongside the Red Heads at Shimabara, remember? You like to think yourselves all high and moral. You don't kill like us, facing your enemies. You'd rather stab us in the back..."

"Shut up," said Bran.

"*Insolent brat!* You think I came here just to listen to your childish whinging?"

There was a short pause. Brain sighed.

"Oh, yes," he said, "You had something to tell me. That *very important* thing a few days ago. *Before* you tried to steal my body."

Shigemasa shrugged.

"You were about to be killed. I had no choice. I saved you."

"Your help is much appreciated," said Bran with an angry sneer.

Shigemasa looked at him with amusement, and Bran expected another outburst. But the General started laughing, patting himself on the belly with glee.

"You even *talk* like an old samurai now!"

He's right. I sound just like him.

He shook his head and stood straight.

"All right. I'm listening now."

The General stopped laughing and scratched his beard in a slow, deliberate manner before speaking.

"It's about the man who was your guide. The one who called himself Dōraku. What you must know is that he's –"

"The Immortal Swordsman?" interrupted Bran. Shigemasa opened his eyes and mouth wide, in genuine surprise.

"*You knew?*"

"It was obvious. There were too many clues. All I needed was some time to gather my thoughts and remember all the facts. But why bring it now? He's long dead."

"It's not that easy to kill one like him, boy. 'Immortal' is not just a *name.*"

This did intrigue Bran.

"How do you know him?"

"He was at Shimabara, too, as one of the *Taikun's* assassins. Back when all the Abominations like him were yet under our control... or that of the Rebels."

Our control...

"The Rebels used the Fanged?"

The General nodded gravely. "They were the first to do so. No trick was beneath them."

"So you *did* recognise Dōraku at once. Why didn't you tell me sooner?"

"I had my reasons then. I have my reasons now."

You were scared of him.

"You think he's still alive, then? That he will come after us?"

"That the wolves did not kill him, I'm certain. I've seen him come out of worse in the war. But who knows what his plans are now..."

Bran closed his eyes.

We have enough trouble as it is.

"I...thank you for letting me know," he said with a sincerity which surprised even him. The General opened his mouth to speak, but Bran warped himself back to the real world before Shigemasa could add anything else.

He opened his eyes to see Nagomi appearing from among the trees. Her face beamed with relief.

"There you are! You've been gone for hours."

"I was... meditating."

The priestess sat down beside him on the tree stump.

"Sacchan said you shouldn't be so upset about what happened."

"That's just the thing. I'm *not* upset. No shame, no remorse. And I should be."

It was clear from her expression that she did not understand.

"Weren't you just defending yourself?"

"What I did stands against everything I was ever taught. It's one thing to kill in a battle, but to slay an innocent..."

"Sacchan said —"

"Yes, but what do *you* think?" he interrupted her. "You are a healer, from a family of physicians. Isn't it your duty to save lives?"

"I..." she pulled back at first, but then composed herself.

"Look – we are all tired and strained. With everything that's been happening to us lately… all the fighting and running away, and – you just made a mistake, that's all."

"A *mistake*."

He laughed, bitterly.

"When this is all over, if you're still worried about that woman, we can come back here and pray for her."

"And that will… help?"

"Of course! This will placate her soul and restore the peace in yours. Everything will be fine."

He stifled a bitter laugh, not wanting to hurt her feelings.

Is killing really that simple here?

Despite their doctrinal differences, most wizards shared with the Sun Priests the ideal of the sanctity of life. As the ancient Roman philosophers had taught, it was a spark of the Divine Essence, identical in its nature to the Creator, and intended to return to its holy origin in its own time. Any other fate destined it to roam the vastness of the Otherworld, diminishing the Creation forever.

In a more down-to-earth version, slaying was believed to decrease the magic potential in the vicinity of the killer, as well as his own. The theory, though never fully scientifically proven, was popular among the Dracalish and Prydain scholars. That the magic academies like Llambed ostensibly trained future soldiers did not contradict the belief and wars were acceptable as long as they were fought far from Dracaland's vulnerable shores.

Bran wasn't sure if the weakness he had been feeling after the incident was just the power of suggestion, or a true loss of energy.

Placate her soul and restore the peace in yours.

The Yamato, living in a world crowded by the Gods and Spirits, had developed more practical ways of dealing with death. He wondered if these were just meaningless gestures, or was there something in the priestly rituals which helped restore the balance of nature.

A nighthawk began its long, loud call, and they both sat for a while listening to the haunting shrill.

"There's something else bothering you, isn't there," said Nagomi, observing his face.

He shrugged with resignation.

"It's all just too much. My *dorako* … the battle… and you almost died…"

He looked up at her and smiled.

"Back then in the shrine you said we wouldn't fail – so there is still some hope I guess."

"I lied," she said.

"What?"

"I have dreamed of the battle at the shrine, the night before it happened. I saw your *dorako* burning the place down. I saw myself die."

"Then *why* didn't you tell us?"

She looked down and played with the loose straps of her travel cloak.

"I believe… sometimes you can change what the vision shows. I hoped I could… I had to try."

"You knew and yet you threw yourself on the blade."

She nodded.

He reached out and pulled her to himself, hugging her tightly.

"You're the bravest of us all," he told her. She protested feebly.

"My dragon is gone," he said after a short pause, "I may have to kill it."

He caught a glimpse of Satō's vermillion kimono among the cedar trees.

"Dōraku is still alive," he whispered quickly in Nagomi's ear. "He's the Immortal Swordsman."

He let her go and stood up. It was beginning to rain.

It rained for four days straight.

Where is the damn sea?

Satō cursed the moment they decided to cut short across the valleys in their race towards the sea. Their new guide seemed at ease just wandering around the woods, the concept of being in a hurry meaningless for him, leading them only roughly south as much as his knowledge of the forest allowed. Finally, they got lost among the gullies and hills. What was supposed to be a two-day trek now reached into its fifth, with no end in sight. The food was running scarce; they were left with thin barley gruel and some forest vegetables and roots found by the bear-man, tasteless and smelly, and some bitter herbal concoction Torishi brew in place of *cha*. It gave her energy enough to walk on, and staved off illness, but did nothing to improve her mood. Bran and the Kumaso ate an occasional hare or wood pigeon caught in Torishi's traps, but neither Satō nor Nagomi could force themselves to swallow flesh.

I'm not starving yet.

The forest seemed to spread endlessly in all directions, a grey-green wall of cedars, cypresses and camphor trees overgrown with weeds reaching into the air to swallow the moisture, and lichen hanging in great curtains from the branches. Any other time, she would find this a wondrous sight: there were great camphor trees on the slopes of Suwa, but not that tall and in such great numbers. But the rain and the cold made her look only down, to the sodden ground, where Torishi's big footprints marked the path through the thick cushion moss and dense bracken. She noticed a reddish-brown *habu* adder slithering away slowly among the roots.

We need to get out of here.

She worried about her friends more than herself. The priestess claimed to have fully recovered from her wounds, but she was pale, silent and gloomy, struggling to put on a brave face whenever she noticed somebody was looking at her. Bran was absent, spending most of his evenings and mornings trying to make contact with his *dorako*, apparently to no avail.

On the third evening she had noticed Torishi leaning down to Nagomi and saying something quietly. The priestess smiled, nodded and stood up from the campfire, wiping tired eyes.

"Where are you two going?" Satō asked, putting down the book she'd been reading – the collection of samurai stories she had received as a gift from Master Kawakami in Kirishima. She had just finished the chapter about a nameless swordsman of the Bunroku era, during the Civil Wars, who had slaughtered one hundred students of the Ichijōji fencing school in a single battle. She was disappointed with how far into the realm of fantasy the tale had gone.

A hundred men defeated by one swordsman? What a ridiculous idea.

"She asked me to teach her the bow," replied the bear-man. "All the Kumaso girls knew how to shoot."

"A bow? What do you need that for?" she asked Nagomi.

"I can't rely forever on Luck and the Gods to help me," the priestess said, "and it sounds like fun, too."

Nagomi followed Torishi towards a nearby open glade. Satō reached for the book, but did not open it again. Her eyes fell on Bran, leaning against a camphor tree. He was staring into the fire.

That's not such a bad idea, she thought. *Training helps take one's mind off life's hardships.*

"I can teach you how to use a Yamato sword, if you want," she offered. Bran looked up.

"I'm sorry?"

"I was a teacher in my father's dōjō, after all."

"I know how to fence. I had a soldier's training."

She couldn't help bursting out with laughter.

"You call that waving about fencing? Come with me, I'll show you fencing."

He looked wounded for a moment, but then smiled and stood up.

A hot spring burst forth from among the stones, covered with white, sulphurous residue, and ran down the glade a pale blue, steaming stream. Satō put her foot into the rippling brook and sighed.

"Too bad it's so small. I could really use a hot bath."

Bran inadvertently imagined the girl naked in the water. The jarring sound of a sword being unsheathed brought him back to reality.

"Stand like this," she ordered. "Left foot forward, right foot to the back and at an angle. Both bent slightly. A bit more."

Bran obeyed, although the stance felt unnatural to him, strained.

"Bring the sword to your right shoulder, pointing straight up, a bit towards the rear. Elbow up. That's the Shadow Frost Stance, the basic form of the Takashima School."

"All right."

"My form is the standard Metal," she said, hiding the blade behind her so that he could only see the pommel. Bran didn't really try to remember the names.

"Try to strike me from above."

"The girl is good," Shigemasa's voice spoke in Bran's head. *"Her footwork is flawless."*

Bran raised the blade and brought it down at Satō, half-heartedly. The girl dodged aside without moving the sword.

"No, no. You have to really try to hit me. Don't worry, you won't manage," she said, grinning.

"She's right. There's no way you can touch her."

He repeated his strike harder, and this time her sword flashed and clanged against Bran's blade; its tip hovered by his neck.

"Good," she said.

"That was good?"

"Yes," she laughed. "For a beginner."

They clashed a few more times, each time Satō's blade ended flawlessly near one of Bran's vital points, while his own sword flew in some random direction.

I don't see how this is teaching me anything, he thought, growing annoyed. *Hold on, I can show you a trick or two as well.*

He raised the sword deliberately too high. He noticed her loosen her stance, certain of herself. He stepped forward and, when she was raising her weapon to block him, pretended to slip on the wet moss. Satō's sword swished past his head as he lunged forward, grabbing her by the waist and pulling her to the ground with him. He pressed the edge of his blade against her neck.

They were both covered in mud and breathing heavily.

"Well... done," her lips moved in a whisper. He put the sword aside slowly and leaned down to kiss her, gently at first, but when she didn't resist, more passionately. She ran her fingers through his hair, pulling him closer.

"Bran? Sacchan? Where are you?"

Satō broke off the kiss and pushed him off. She stood up hastily, adjusting her kimono. She leaned over the hot stream and washed her face.

"You did well," she said, not looking back at him. "We... we should try it again some day. Fencing. We should try fencing again."

"What is this silver ribbon? Mist?" Torishi asked, pointing to the southern horizon when Satō and the others joined him on the bald top of the pass. The bear-man was always in front of the group, his long legs carrying him eagerly onwards despite the heavy bag of supplies he carried. His strength was inexhaustible.

"It's the sea," Satō corrected him and sighed with relief. "This is the Kinko Bay. And look, that must be Sakurajima – just like in the pictures. At last!"

The mountain rose in a perfect cone from the middle of the bay. Looking down from the ridge, Satō saw an affluent-looking market town, surrounded by citrus orchards and tobacco fields.

"The Sea!" Torishi said with wonder. His hand encompassed the coastal flatland.

"Then this must be the ancient kingdom of my people."

As if in answer, Sakurajima billowed a puff of thick smoke and ash. The cloud rose tall and wide, shaped like a giant sprawling pine tree, until it dwarfed the mountain itself. The perfect cone of the mountain rising from the middle of the round bay was the most beautiful sight she had ever seen. She expected at any moment to hear ringing of alarm gongs and panicked cries in the town below, but nobody seemed to pay any attention to the eruption. Before long, the winds scattered the cloud over the bay, and all the ash fell down from the sky like grey rain. They watched the spectacle for several long minutes in complete silence.

"The Fire Mountain..." said Torishi in an awestruck whisper. "The first thing the Kumaso kings saw when arriving from the Sun Lands. They settled in a flat valley beside the Great Lake in the shade of the Fire Mountain."

"Try not to exert your birth right too keenly," Satō said finally. "The people down there may be more terrified of you than peasants. Come, let's try to get to the town before nightfall."

By the time they reached the lowlands, Satō understood why none of the locals paid any attention to Sakurajima's eruption. The mountain spewed ash and smoke twice more that day, each time the cloud dispersing harmlessly before reaching the land.

Everything seemed calmer, brighter and nicer on the plain. The sea breeze pushed the rain clouds northwards up the mountains – which explained the wretched weather the travellers had had to suffer for the last couple of days. The sky over the lowlands was the colour of pure, bright azure, the air crisp and fresh, smelled faintly of damp and sea salt. For the first time in a very long while, Satō had to shield her eyes from the bright sun.

As they passed through the fields and orchards, the farmers stopped their work and watched them with curiosity; their eyes were focused mostly on Torishi's great, hairy form, much to the bear man's unease.

But the farmers, or rather their equipment, were an equally curious sight to Satō. Even Bran halted in surprise when they had first encountered the strange machine.

In the middle of a tobacco field stood a black cylinder, taller than a man, with a narrow funnel spewing white steam. Attached to it was a set of gears, pulleys and flywheels increasing in size; the last one, as big as an oxcart wheel, pulled a thick hemp rope. At the other end of the rope was a plough, pulled against the dirt by the power unleashed by the cylinder. There were three such machines in the fields around them, each serviced by a team of samurai and scholars bearing Satsuma crests on their clothes.

"That's a traction engine," said Bran, astonished. "Only the richest farmers in Gwynedd have them."

"Welcome to Satsuma," said Satō with a grin.

CHAPTER VI

At the edge of the town stood a wooden watchtower; it was empty. A single samurai rested in a ditch on the side of the road, chewing on a straw, his face covered with a bamboo hat. He heard them approach and raised the brim lazily. Seeing Torishi, he jumped up immediately, spitting out the straw and straightening his clothes.

"Halt!"

He put on the air of a proud, militant bureaucrat. He bowed before Bran and the girls, before turning to the bear-man.

"You can't carry those here," he said, pointing at the bow and the long knife. "You're far away from your forest, hunter."

Torishi looked helplessly to his companions.

"He's right," said Satō. "We will carry your weapons for the time being."

She took the bow and quiver and Bran took the knife. With their clothes and hair in disarray, they could both easily pass for the mountain hunters, if it wasn't for the clan crests still visible on their kimonos through the dirt and stains.

The samurai let them pass, eyeing them curiously. Before long, Satō heard his feet thumping on the dirt road.

"If I may be so bold," he said, after catching his breath, "you seem to be in some distress. May I offer you lodgings in my house? It's not far, by the harbour."

"My son has gone to the wizardry school in Kagoshima," explained the samurai, showing them an entire empty wing of his residence. "You can use any room."

"You're very kind," said Satō weakly. The warm, cozy inside of the house made her drowsy; she was wearier than she had realised.

"The servant will prepare a bath. If you excuse me, I need to send for somebody to take my place at the tower."

The samurai's plump, rosy-cheeked wife appeared to take over the duties of a host. Seeing the state they were in, she raised her hands to her head in a comic display of grief.

"*Eeh!* What terrible thing happened to you? Did you get lost? Were you attacked?"

"Both," said Satō, quickly coming up with a story of a group of bandits they had to fight off in the deep forest, with the help of Torishi, who had agreed to escort them for the rest of their journey.

"So close to Hayato! I always knew you shouldn't trust those highlanders," the woman said, glancing nervously at Torishi, before leading Satō and Nagomi to the bath room. "It's all those vapours and fog up the mountains, makes them go crazy. Do you have any other clothes?"

The wizardess shook her head. Nagomi's travel clothes almost fell apart as she took them off; Satō's vermillion kimono was in no better shape.

"I'll take you to the market tomorrow," declared the samurai's wife, "for now, please use our *yukatas*."

"We are in a hurry to reach Kagoshima-" started Satō, but the woman interrupted her, waving her hands.

"Nonsense! My husband will get you a fast boat, you'll reach the city in no time. You take your time, girls."

"Well, this is nice," said Satō after the woman had left them alone. The cypress-lined bath was almost as large and luxurious as the one at the Takashima Mansion and, for the first time in many weeks, the wizardess allowed herself to completely relax.

"I can't believe we survived so much," she added, shaking her head, "it feels almost like a bad dream right now."

"I'm just glad we're all still together," Nagomi said, splashing her face with hot water.

"Don't ever do that again," said Satō, turning serious.

"Do what?"

"Sacrifice yourself for me! Bran told me about your vision."

"I had to do *something*..."

"I understand, and I'm grateful. But we can't lose you. *I* can't lose you."

Satō reached out and touched the thin scar running between Nagomi's breasts.

"If I'm wounded, you could just heal me, right? But if *you* are injured, I am helpless. I never want to feel that helpless again."

Nagomi submerged herself till the tip of her chin touched the hot water.

"It's not like the old days, when I could mend your broken bones without breaking a sweat," she said and smiled.

"I'm not *that* old," said Satō in a pretend indignation; she smiled too.

Nagomi regarded Satō's naked body.

"You're a woman now," she said, "everyone can see that. When you are not wearing your male clothes, all men turn their heads. No wonder Bran – "

She stopped and covered her mouth with her hand. Satō blushed; they both fell silent. A magpie screeched outside.

Bran lay in the darkness of the vast, eight-mat room he had been given all to his own and felt terribly lonely. It had been long since he had to spend the night alone in a single room, without so much as hearing any of the girls' breath as they slept. They always chatted in whisper for a while before going to sleep.

He wanted to go home. He wanted to see his mother again, reading a book by the fireplace. He wanted to find out what had happened to his father, to Edern, to Gwennlian, to all those people he had so much more in common with. The girls now called him a "friend" – and he appreciated this rare privilege – but how many times had Satō pointed out he was a stranger here?

The wizardess never mentioned the episode by the brook again; she avoided his gaze, his touch. It was driving him mad. *What is wrong with me? Am I not good enough for her? Too alien?*

Out of nowhere, Atsuko's face appeared in his thoughts. The alabaster skin, the almond eyes, the smell of rosewood... the faint touch of her lips on his, like a butterfly landing. He was not too alien for *her*. She might have been attracted to him because he was a spark of unfamiliarity to her dull life, but what was wrong in that? Who could tell what reasons compelled people to be with each other, to spending time in each other's presence?

The silence inside his mind only exacerbated the loneliness. With the Farlink gone even Shigemasa's brooding murmur could not replace the resounding hollowness left by Emrys.

"I may have found something that will help you with that," said the General.

"I really dislike it when you read my thoughts."

"I can't help it, boy. You think I enjoy your wallowing? I preferred it when you were in a rage."

Arguing with the old Spirit was the last thing on Bran's mind.

"What have you found?"

"It will be best if you follow me."

Bran closed his eyes and transported himself onto the red dust plain. It was getting easier every time. The General was already waiting for him. He seemed haggard, wind-worn. His lacquer armour had lost its sheen and several of the metal scales.

"When you last cast me away I found myself in a strange part of this place, one that I have not seen before," Shigemasa explained, leading the way towards the horizon, "it takes a while to get there, but with little else to do around here, exploring it was a welcome distraction."

The plain, flat and featureless so far, began to rise and fall in a chain of hills and canyons. The earth turned from red to grey and then black. Bran cast a worried glance behind: the red-eye tower was barely visible.

Will I be able to get back on my own?

They climbed to the top of a tall black mound and the General pointed into the narrow canyon below. Something moved at the bottom, glinting green. Bran started down the slope to look closer. Half-way down he finally realised what he was seeing.

"Emrys!" he cried and ran the rest of the way.

"Be careful, boy," the General shouted a warning, his voice surprisingly anxious, almost afraid. "It's completely wild."

He was right. The dragon paid no attention to Bran. It hopped madly from rock to rock, from crag to crag, flapping its wings in vain and roaring helplessly. Something was keeping it from leaving the canyon. As the boy approached, the beast calmed down a little, but there was no recognition in its snake-like eyes. The dragon crouched with its claws forward, baring its teeth and hissing.

Bran sensed fear suffused with anger. It took him a while to realise what it meant: whatever this creature inside his mind was he could reach it with his thoughts. Did it mean anything in the real world? That remained to be seen, but he *had* to try.

He came forward with a hand reached out, sending soothing, calming thoughts. He had no idea how to tame a wild dragon, and didn't even know something like this was even possible.

This is not a real dragon, he reminded himself. *This is all in your head.*

"Easy, easy," he said, "good boy, good Emrys…"

The beast's flared nostrils narrowed, its jaw clenched. His snake eyes glinted. With a great effort Bran took another step, and then another. He was trembling, affected by the dragon's aura of fear. He summoned a *tarian* almost inadvertently. With one more step he was close enough to touch the beast. He moved his hand slowly.

The dragon spat fire; it was just a warning shot, but without the *tarian* it would burn him badly. The boy ignored the flames and pressed on. The dragon twitched its wings. Finally Bran laid his trembling hand on the warm, jade green scales and a jolt came through his body, like an electric spark. The dragon snorted and puffed sparks and smoke, but did not move away. Bran felt its emotions flow clearly without disruptions; he sent back an order. The dragon lowered its head in submission. The Farlink between phantom dragon and its rider had been established.

Bran leapt onto the mount's neck. Even though the dragon wasn't real, it felt great to be able to fly again. He flew back to the top of the black hill and landed – with some effort – near Shigemasa.

"Come, *Taishō!*" he said, laughing. "This will be faster than walking!"

"You seem perky today," said Satō. She was grinning herself, wearing an over-sized blue kimono she had borrowed from their host – her vermillion *Rangaku* outfit sadly damaged beyond repair. She still avoided looking him too long in the eyes, though.

"Things don't look as bleak when you're rested," the boy replied with a smile. He had no heart to worry today.

"Are we going already?" he asked, seeing her and Nagomi step down from the porch and into the sandals. "I thought – "

"We're going to the town. And so are you. Hurry up."

"No, I'll stay here with Torishi. I don't need anything."

Satō covered her month and sniggered. "Have you seen yourself lately? You need new clothes. And a *barber.*"

A barber?

He picked up a small glass mirror lying on the shoe cupboard and studied his still unfamiliar Yamato face. His hair had grown long and unruly, sticking out in tufts and clumps. The scar left by the sickle had healed up by now, but there seemed to be a layer of dirt on his cheeks... He touched his face.

I need a shave.

He hadn't shaved before; the Prydain grew beards late and slow. He wasn't even sure he knew how to do it. Dylan used magically imbued razors, which made the task much easier, and Bran doubted they had such devices here.

"All right," he said, putting the mirror down. Only now did he notice the Bataavian runes 'V.O.C.' on the back.

Western glass.

"But let's try to be back before lunch."

It was well past noon when, rested and refreshed, they followed the samurai and his wife to the Hayato Harbour. They were all wearing their new clothes: Satō wore a plain grey kimono and black hakama; Nagomi's travel clothes were pale yellow, and Bran managed to find a robe of the same dark indigo colour as his previous one. The Aoki crest of a mountain reflecting in the water had been hastily transferred onto the shoulders of the new outfit by the old tailor.

Their new travel bundles had been filled with necessary supplies: a waterskin and a small flask of saké, seaweed-rolled rice buns and dried rice crackers, straw sandals, bandages, a folded razor marked with Bataavian runes and a sharpening stone for the swords. To Bran's delight, the Hayato cobblers had a small supply of sandals large enough for his Western feet. For the first time in a long while he could walk the cobbled streets comfortably.

Hayato was just a small fishing port, but their host managed to find a merchant boat heading for Kagoshima that was big enough to fit all of four of them.

"I hope you will have a swift and pleasant journey," the samurai said.

"I'm sorry for your trouble," said Satō.

"It's no trouble at all!" the samurai's wife replied, waving her hands, "it's the least we could do after what happened to you in the mountains. We wouldn't want you to think badly of Satsuma."

"I forgot to ask," Bran turned to the samurai just before boarding the boat, "were the machines in the fields yours?"

"Oh, no, no. They belong to His Excellency, Shimazu-*dono*. He's just testing them out on my fields. You should check out the wizardry school near His Excellency's castle, if that's the sort of thing you're after."

"And if you happen to meet a young man named Sugimoto, tell him his mother is very proud," added the woman, wiping a tear from her eye.

The couple stood on the pier, waving to the departing boat until they were just two specks on the horizon.

"It must be a long time since they've seen their son," said Nagomi, waving back. "I wonder what my parents are doing right now..."

A sudden gust of wind filled the ship's sail and she had to sit down and hold on to the bench.

"A school of wizards…" said Satō after a while, "I wonder if they were the ones we met in Kirishima."

"I'm surprised they haven't heard anything from the shrine yet," said Bran, scratching his cheek; his skin felt itchy after the barber's blade, especially around the scar. "It's been what, a week?"

"They are a bit out of the way here," replied Satō, "I suspect the news has to reach Kagoshima first."

"What's it like, this Kagoshima? Have you ever been there?"

The wizardess nodded.

"A few times with my father. It's a big city, almost as big as Kiyō. Maybe even larger, now – it keeps on growing."

The boat rocked again on a rogue wave. The enclosed bay was calmer than the open sea; still the girls sat tightly on their bench, not daring to look over the edge of the boat. Bran looked up to Torishi who stood on the prow proudly, like some old sea dog, unflinching as the salty waves splashed against his face. It was the first time Bran saw him happy.

"I've never seen anything so flat before," the bear-man yelled over the wind. "All the way to the horizon in every direction. It's like standing on top of the tallest mountain in the world! And look, the Fire Mountain is ablaze again!"

The boat slowed down, entering the narrow strait. They were approaching Kagoshima Harbour, and the waters of the Kinko Bay grew crowded with fishing boats and cargo ships. The wharf was flanked by a massive, slanting, stone wall, topped with what looked to Bran like modern cannons. On the opposite side of the strait the majestic Sakurajima loomed over the bay like a fist aimed towards the Heavens in defiance.

The ground shook as if in earthquake as three hundred *kin* of flesh slammed against the sand of the arena.

The crowd went wild, shouting the name of their champion: *Kyūkichi! Kyūkichi!* The wrestler stood calm, with his head modestly bowed, grinning discreetly.

The referee waited until Kyūkichi's opponent gathered his huge bulk off the ground, and then pointed the wooden paddle at the winner.

"Undefeated for a record twenty five games. The strongest man in Chinzei – Unryū Kyūkichi!"

The spectators cheered for more than a minute before the referee raised his paddle once again, prompting them to silence.

"This concludes today's tournament – unless there is another contender amongst you?"

Shakushain pushed his way through and stepped into the light.

"I will fight."

The crowd jeered and booed him. Not only was he too lean and slim to be a wrestler, his thick beard and long hair betrayed a foreigner. There was no place for the likes of him at the sacred arena.

The assistants rushed to remove him from the sand, but the reigning champion raised his hand to stop them.

"No, wait. Let him in."

Shakushain took off his cloak and handed it to the little dark-skinned man standing beside him. The crowd fell silent; they had never seen anyone whose muscles were so taut and perfectly toned; the geometric tattoos which covered his entire body were also a sight to behold. He basked in the spectators' amazement for a while before crouching down to the starting line.

"I know you," said Kyūkichi. "You're the Northerner who defeated Taniemon last year."

"He said I cheated. I was banned from the East Division."

"He was lying. I saw the fight. You beat him fair and square. I haven't seen a *Mitokorozeme* like that in a long time."

Shakushain smiled and bowed. The champion performed a brief ritual dance and stomped his legs, then entered the ring, threw salt on the sand to banish evil spirits, and crouched in front of his opponent.

Will he be the one who gives me a good fight? The Northerner thought, hopeful, assessing Kyūkichi's frame and stance.

His quest so far had been a series of disappointments. The *Shamo* – or Yamato, as the Southerners called themselves – liked to brag about being the greatest warriors on Earth. But most of them learned to fight with spears, swords and bows; and he had defeated all the sumo wrestlers with little difficulty and no satisfaction. The bears and sea lions in his frozen northern homeland had put up more of a fight than these walking mountains of fat.

The referee marked the start of the fight. A lesser wrestler would have charged instantly at Shakushain, hoping to throw him off balance with the pure mass of his body. Kyūkichi just stared at the Northerner, studying his posture, the way his muscles rippled underneath the tattoos. Shakushain did the same, looking for weak points; there was no flaw in Kyūkichi's stance.

"Go on! Go on!" the referee urged them.

At last, the *Shamo* wrestler charged. Shakushain's muscles tensed and he let out a cry when the full weight of his opponent slammed into his chest. His feet slid dangerously on the sand, but he managed to hold just before the edge of the arena. The two men grappled with each other, trying to force one another to make an error of judgment. Sweat made their bodies slippery, making it difficult for Shakushain to get a grip.

This is no time for cheap tricks.

The *Shamo*'s skill left no place for special throws or undercuts; however Shakushain tried to pull or push, Kyūkichi responded in kind, his body nimble and pliable.

Only pure strength can settle this one.

At last, Shakushain managed to grab his opponent's thick loincloth in both hands. The crowd gasped as Kyūkichi's feet left the ground. The *Shamo* twisted and turned in Shakushain's grasp, but in vain. Straining his muscles almost to the limit, the Northerner took a step back, then another. His calves trembled under the wrestler's weight. Feeling the rope surrounding the ring touch his heels, he turned around and let go; Kyūkichi flew outside the arena and landed, with a great thud, on the wooden floor.

In the silence that followed, Kyūkichi's laughter and clapping resonated loudly.

"Come with me!" the wrestler said, not bothering to get up from the floor. "Join my stable! I will make you rich."

Shakushain forced a smile, bowed, took his symbolic trophy from the stunned referee's hands and picked up his cloak from the little dark-skinned man. He had no mood for celebrating the victory. He spotted a glimpse of crimson in the audience and that spoiled his humour for the rest of the day.

The Crimson Robe found him outside the hall. He slid his hand across his chest in the Northern greeting.

"*Irankarapte,*" he said.

"*He.*"

"And who might that be?" the Crimson Robe looked at the little man at Shakushain's side.

"A friend from the North."

"That's a curious necklace."

The little man was wearing a jagged shard of blue glass tied on a leather cord. He covered it with his hand.

"What do you want?" barked Shakushain. "I don't need you anymore."

The Fanged smiled. "It is I that needs you. For a hunt."

"I don't hunt people."

"I know. This time I'm after a beast."

A beast?

"I'm listening."

CHAPTER VII

The fine black dust screeched under Bran's feet. The street sweepers may have all gone to sleep, but the Sakurajima Mountain was still awake, blowing up ash almost incessantly through the night, among the silent lightning strikes. The city of Kagoshima was the first he had seen in Yamato where the streets had not been immaculately clean. Not even an army of dedicated cleaners could defeat the inexhaustible power of the volcano.

Bran walked the swiftly darkening streets of the trade district, past the shops and inns closing, and saké stores and pleasure joints opening for the evening. He had an unusual guide into the night life of the bustling city: the General Itakura Shigemasa.

It started with a conversation they had had a few hours earlier. Bran and the others had eaten a rich supper at an inn Satō remembered from her travels with her father. Almost all the dishes served were fish – deep-fried in bronze paste, tiny marinated herrings, big chunks of rockfish, which tasted remarkably like the chicken, slices of succulent raw tuna – all this served with lashings of buckwheat noodles, polished rice and crisp pickles, and doused with *cha* and best local shōchū mixed with hot water. Later they had been asking around for some news and rumours that could lead Bran towards the dragon, but with no results, and Satō had decided they would have to visit the wizardry school the next morning.

"*They* will know," she said, before going to the room she shared with Nagomi.

Bran had retreated into his mind again and found the jade dragon still there, strolling about the red dust plain not far from the tower. Shigemasa was sitting at a safe distance from the beast, observing it curiously.

Bran approached the dragon, and this time it let him touch its scales without objection. The buzz of the Farlink once again filled the boy's head. It was very faint, barely a murmur, but Bran was almost certain this time that he had reached through to the *real* Emrys. There was no trace of sentience in the stream of emotions he received, just the beastly rage, the confusion and the hunger… He let go, and the dragon trotted off by a few paces before lying down to sleep. Bran turned to the General.

"Why have you shown me this, *Taishō*?"

Shigemasa chortled and stroked his beard.

"For too long I had to watch you and your little troupe wander aimlessly the length and breadth of Chinzei. A dragon hunt sounds much more exciting. But tell me boy, did it work?"

Bran looked back at the phantom dragon.

"It… seems to be working. But I never heard about anything like this being attempted before. When a dragon goes wild it cannot be re-tamed and there is no other way but to kill it."

"But isn't that what you were planning to do?" Shigemasa raised his eyebrows. "I thought I was just giving you a way to track the beast down and slay it."

"I don't want to slay Emrys," Bran said, "I want to *save* him."

The General scratched his chin in thought.

"I can't say I know a lot about these things, boy, but I trust your judgement. I'm glad we can start doing something useful for a change."

Bran felt a change in the way the Spirit was treating him.

"*We,*" *he said.*

"I'm grateful for your help," said Bran. "If there's anything I can do…"

The samurai's eyes glinted and his face brightened in a grin.

"Tell me, did the wizard girl give you some more of her gold coins?"

"We split the treasure among the three of us, but what —"

"Put on your kimono, boy," said Shigemasa, standing up, "I'll show you the side of Yamato you haven't yet seen."

Kagoshima was a narrow city, hemmed in between the sea and the hills, and there was only one direction to cross it – north to south along the main street, across the river, past the merchant storehouses and into a district that was built-up more densely. Two- and three-story buildings lined the narrow, criss-crossing alleyways.

"*I've only been in this city once,*" said Shigemasa, "*but it shouldn't be hard to find the right place. Just follow the noise!*"

There was nothing of Kiyo's nightly quiet here. The part of the city Bran ventured into seemed more alive after dusk than by day. The streets, illuminated by red paper lanterns, teemed with people, a forest of colourful paper umbrellas protecting their heads and clothes from the omnipresent dust. It didn't take Bran long to realise that the crowds were made predominantly of adult men, and that all the women either hung off the shoulders of their male companions, or stood in small groups in the doorways, laughing and shouting at the passers-by, revealing their painted necks and white ankles seductively.

"Wait a minute," said Bran, stopping in the middle of the street, "I may not be experienced in these matters, but even I know what this place is."

"*Ignore them, boy. Tonight we seek a more refined pleasure. Turn here, after that palanquin.*"

Bran followed the ornate vehicle carried by four tall porters into another street. This one was wider and not as crowded, paved with small square stones. There were only a few buildings here, sprawling mansions hiding behind tall earthwork walls daubed with red plaster. Armed guards stood before each gate.

Shigemasa made Bran stroll the street up and down, while he assessed which residence they had the best chance to get into.

"The best one will be fully booked," the General said, *"so will the cheapest one. Try the one with the plum blossom on the* noren.*"*

The guard eyed Bran carefully, studying his face, clothes and the crest of the Aoki clan on his shoulders, and then bowed slightly – *too slightly,* for Bran's liking – and stood aside.

The inside of the strange residence was lush, by Yamato standards. The walls and floors were laid of delicate, sweet-smelling timber; the corridors were decorated with vases, paintings and flowers. A group of young women in the vestibule studied Bran unabashedly as he approached the counter. He heard them whisper and giggle among each other.

"Look at his eyes! He must be from Kiyō. One of them half-bloods."

"Impossible! He's far too high born for that."

"He seems so shy – do you think he's unbroken yet?"

The last sentence amused them greatly and they broke into another fit of giggles.

Bran felt his face burn bright red. Following Shigemasa's advice, he asked for a single table in the common room and "one shamisen girl".

"We don't want to spend too much on your first time."

He was then led into a large hall where several other men were already sitting at the low benches, drinking and conversing in hushed tones, accompanied by women in opulent, many-layered kimonos and elaborate make-up. They reminded Bran of the high-born ladies he had seen in his dreams.

A flask of saké and two cups waited for Bran on his table and, before long, a young girl came into the room. She headed towards him, holding a long-necked string instrument. She smiled gently and nodded her head. Her every move and gesture was deliberate, yet perfectly smooth. Underneath the thick make-up, she was almost as beautiful and gracious as Atsuko.

"Does my noble guest have any wishes for the music?" she asked in a soft, sensuous voice.

"A… anything you like."

She plucked the strings with the grace of a prowling cat and started humming a sad, slow song.

Hana wa Kirishima, tabako wa Kokubu

Moete agaru wa Sakurajima

Kawaigararete neta yoru mo gozaru

Naite akashita yoru mo gozaru

Flowers of Kirishima, tobacco of Kokubu

Fires of Sakurajima

Caressed in the evening

I cried until morning

Bran stared at her, transfixed. Her fingers were long and slender; her voice was like that of a nightingale, and her lips...

"Don't fall for her, boy," Shigemasa chuckled, breaking the solemn mood, *"she's just one of many. Offer her some saké."*

The girl batted her eyelashes and sipped like a sparrow from the white cup. She re-tuned her instrument and started on another melancholy song.

The *shamisen's* sound brought him a memory of a bard's harp back in Gwynedd. His mind was transported by the melody to the sprawling green hills and the slow-rolling rivers of his homeland, the calm, golden-leaved forests where the only danger awaiting a traveller was getting lost in the subtle beauty of the hazel groves, the sea-side dunes of Cantre'r Gwaelod, the narrow, cobbled streets of Caer Wyddno... He saw the stone towers of the Academy; the dried-up marshes of the Teifi; and, as the song grew to a chorus, the red-washed walls of his home.

Wasuregataki furusato

Iika ni imasu chichi haha

Tsutuga nashi ya tomogaki

I miss my home town,

How are my mother and father?

Are my friends alright?

He saw Rhian holding a basket of freshly cut herbs and talking to Dylan who was cleaning the scales of the Azure dragon. They were laughing and both looked happy then.

How old is this memory? Bran wondered. He hadn't seen his parents together like that in years. The dragon was not Afreolus, but one of Dylan's previous mounts.

Home. It was strange; he had spent months out on sea without ever missing Gwynedd, but now, this beautiful girl's sad song made him almost weep from home sickness. His eyes welled up. He shook his head.

"Stop," he croaked, then coughed, pretending there was something in his throat. The girl blinked in confusion. "Sing something else."

The girl nodded and retuned her instrument to a more cheerful key. He gulped his saké and poured himself another cup right away and then another.

The evening passed briskly; the girl sang and played some more and once, at Shigemasa's request, performed a slow, graceful dance with two paper fans. By the end of the night – and of the third or fourth bottle of saké – Bran's thoughts and emotions were elevated to the point where he wanted to write a poem or paint a picture that would capture an impression of the scene.

The girl sat back down after another dance; the sleeve of her kimono dropped, revealing a naked shoulder. She did not adjust it; Bran leaned forward, his face burning. The girl was more subtle than the eager, flirty women from Shigemasa's memories, but she made him burn with the same desire; he recalled the vivid dreams he shared with the General, including one he hadn't remembered before – of a pale-faced woman in a red kimono, in what looked strangely similar to his inn room back at the Hitoyoshi …

"*You won't get that sort of thing here,*" the voice in his head said with a lewd chuckle.

"That's not… I've never even…"

"*Oh, but you* have. *I should have told you earlier.*"

This sobered Bran somewhat.

Hitoyoshi wasn't a dream…?

"You…you took the liberty of my own body to…!"

"*I'm not a monk, boy! But I can make it up to you. There was a place not far, I bet it's still in business. If you want I will take you there.*"

Bran hesitated for longer than he thought he would.

"N-no."

"*Why not? It's only natural. The little wizardess does not seem willing to give you what your body needs, so I thought…*"

"I'll be just fine," he replied, his mood soured.

The girl looked at him patiently, waiting for another order. He smiled and raised a silent toast to her. She put her instrument down and relaxed a little.

He could now hear the conversations by the neighbouring tables. Saké seemed to have enhanced his hearing at the expense of other senses. It was clear that the other men came here not just to admire the girls' performances, but to discuss important matters in a tranquil atmosphere. The two samurai to his left deliberated on the prices of rice and sweet potatoes, but the group to the right – three men whose clothes of soft silk were all marked with the cross-circle emblem of Satsuma – dropped a name in their conversation which made Bran prick his ears.

"I heard the daimyo's plan fell out."

"Some terrible disaster. All news is suppressed."

"Might be wise to invite daimyo's honourable brother to our next get-together."

The elder samurai nodded. "I will let Hisamitsu-*sama* know. But, have you heard? The *Daisen* Heishichi has returned from Kirishima. I passed him at the castle gates. He'll be with the daimyo now."

Bran had heard enough. He faked a yawn and dismissed the girl.

"You have been exquisite, but I am tired now."

"Of course, noble guest."

She remained with her head bowed until he left the hall. Once out of the residence and onto the sudden cool quiet of the street outside, he stopped and leaned against the red-plaster wall for a moment. His head was spinning a bit.

"That was…" He searched for the right word, "magnificent."

The General said nothing, but Bran could sense his satisfaction.

"*Are you sure you don't want me to take you to that other place now?*"

"Maybe later," he said with a smile. "I have to go somewhere else first."

He looked around; the street was darker and emptier than when he had entered the establishment. He breathed in the scent, not unlike that of Kiyō on that first fateful night. The noises on the main street were muffled, and in the silence, Bran heard a nightingale singing in the garden of one of the mansions.

I will miss this place, he realized, *just as much as I miss Gwynedd now.*

Once past the trade district, Bran drew the hood of his travel cloak over his head and returned his face to its Gwynedd look. He crossed a narrow canal and approached the deceptively small castle of the daimyo of Satsuma. The guards stopped him before the narrow bridge over the castle's moat.

"Halt! The gates are closed for the night. Whatever your business with the daimyo, come tomorrow."

Bran threw down the hood and looked up, noting the effect his foreign face had on the captain of the guards.

"I only seek tranquillity," he said, using the archaic code word '*shōhei*'. The captain drew breath loudly, then said "keep him here until I come back," to the other guard and left in a hurry.

He returned five minutes later.

"Come with me," he said and led the boy, not to the main gate, but to the southern side of the castle wall. He pulled a hidden lever; steam spewed from a concealed valve. Bran heard brass pulleys turn inside the wall, and a small postern opened with a clunk. They walked down the narrow, winding corridors, up the stair to the second floor of the keep.

"Wait here, you will be announced," the captain said and left the dragon rider in the company of a servant.

Upon entering the daimyo's room, Bran became acutely aware of the magic energies permeating inside. A round paper lantern hovered over the floor on its own, illuminating the room with a faint light. A grid of magic trip-wire ley alarms was scattered around the painted walls and paper-covered windows. Even the inkstone glowed slightly with some minor enchantment. This was the room of a man who was not afraid of magic and did not care much for the *Taikun*'s restrictions in its use.

Shimazu Nariakira was a broad-shouldered man, with a long, oval face, a large, straight nose protruding between close set, clever eyes. Bran tried to find similarities between Atsuko and her father, before recalling she was an adopted child. The aristocrat was sitting at a table made of a single slab of walnut wood, supporting his head on his hand, studying a board game in complete silence. A thin wisp of white smoke rose from the incense bowl on the table, filling the room with the familiar scent of sandalwood.

Bran said his greetings and stood, waiting, for a minute, then another; his patience began to grow thin. The daimyo remained unflinching. Bran cleared his throat.

Lord Nariakira raised his head slowly. There was something odd in the nobleman's eyes and face, but Bran couldn't quite put his finger on it. The atmosphere in the room, and the ALCOHOL in Bran's head unnerved him. The daimyo still did not speak.

"I... I was hoping I could request your assistance, *kakka*," said Bran at last.

A deep chuckle came from beyond a thin wall. It slid open, revealing another room, almost a mirror image of the one Bran was in, except brightly lit. A man who could have been Lord Nariakira's twin looked at Bran with great amusement.

"*Gaikokujin!*" he said. "Insolent as ever. Do you not know you should always wait until your superior speaks, no matter how long it takes?"

The boy glanced from one man to another in confusion. At last, he used True Sight on both of them.

"An automaton!"

"Yes," said the real daimyo. "A new creation of my mechanicians. You have the privilege to be one of the first guests I have tested it on."

"It's... remarkably life-like."

In the West, automatons were mere toys, their practical pursuit abandoned long before Bran's birth. Now he understood what Atsuko had meant when she spoke of her chaperon.

"Come here, boy, let me look at you in better light."

The daimyo studied Bran for a while.

"You are shorter than I expected," he said at last.

"*Kakka?*"

Bran was ready to provide the *daimyo* with a long explanation regarding his presence in the castle and his knowledge of the secret password, but Lord Nariakira's blatant statement threw him off guard.

"Sit down," the daimyo gestured at another walnut table identical to the first one in every detail. Even the pawns on the game board were all in the same position.

"Two days ago I received a letter from my dear daughter Atsu," he continued, "in which she describes a meeting with a young Westerner whose name she fails to mention."

Bran gulped. *How much did she tell him?*

"In describing the man, my daughter paid particular attention to his, as she puts it, 'emerald green eyes.' By the end of the letter, she entreats me to hear his fascinating story and provide him with anything he may require, if we were to ever meet."

He paused. Bran kept silent, waiting for him to continue. The daimyo grunted with satisfaction.

"You are either brave or unwise to come here," he said. "I could easily have your head off. Maybe I should, *eh*? I can only imagine the circumstances in which you two have met. My daughter was to be kept under strict surveillance, so you had to be pretty sneaky - or reckless. Those responsible for allowing your meeting will, of course, be punished."

Bran opened his mouth to protest, but thought better of it.

They can't be helped and I'm in enough trouble as it is.

"However," the daimyo continued, "my daughter is not easily impressed, and I put great trust in her judgement of people. If she puts a good word in for you – and grants you access to our family code word – my interest is piqued. Let me hear you out first – and bear in mind, your life is in my hands. Let us start with introductions – who are you, boy?"

"I am Bran ap Dylan gan Cantre'r Gwaelod - the *dorako* rider," Bran replied.

Lord Nariakira digested the information before clapping his knee in joy.

"*Unnh!* It makes sense now. I take it you know it was I who kept your *dorako* imprisoned – and yet you come to me of your own will? "

"I… I hoped you might help me… find it, *kakka*."

"You seem to have done it with no problems before."

"I lost that ability after what happened at Kirishima."

"And *what* happened at Kirishima? Tell me about it, or better yet, tell me all about your adventures. I need to know what kind of a man comes alone at night requesting the help of a daimyo."

Of all the people Bran had recounted his adventures to since coming to Yamato, Lord Nariakira was by far the best, most informed, and avid listener. His knowledge of the outside world, familiarity with matters of global politics, and Western magic was uncanny. The story took Bran much shorter to tell than he had expected. When questioned about it, the daimyo chuckled.

"Yes, I suppose I do know a bit more about the world than your average country samurai. But, you shouldn't be so surprised. You have seen some of my machines and workshops on your way here."

"Yes, *kakka*."

"So, Kirishima… you did not see the battle to the end, then?"

"We ran away to save the priestess."

"And have you?"

"Yes, *kakka*. She is alive and well. If I may inquire, have there been any survivors?"

"Yes, though not many. My soldiers reached the shrine just in time to drive the attackers off."

"Is… Captain Kiyomasa among those alive?"

"He suffered the worst injuries, but I am told he will survive."

"That makes me glad. He was… is a good soldier."

"That he is," the daimyo said with a nod. "*Yoshi!*" he added, standing up, "I will not have your head just *yet*. Whether or not I will assist you, is another matter. Tell me, young *dorako* rider, what were you planning to do once you got to Kagoshima?"

Bran had realised by now that honesty was the only way to gain this odd man's trust.

"I thought I might sail north following any hints and rumours I could find."

Lord Nariakira turned his back to Bran, looking out the open window. This seemed a reckless gesture – they were alone in the room, and the dragon rider had not been searched for concealed weapons. Bran cast True Sight again and saw the shimmering magical shield protecting daimyo's body – as well as silhouettes of two men sitting behind yet another fake wall. One of them was a wizard, protecting the Lord with his magic. The other's power signature was strangely familiar...

"It's a shame you haven't seen for certain who stole that ring of yours," said Lord Nariakira.

I'm sure you already know whom to suspect, Bran thought, but refrained from commenting.

"There is one more thing left out of your story, boy," the daimyo said, running his finger along a wooden slate in the window frame, "what do you know of this... Dōraku-*sama?*"

"I know that he's the Immortal Swordsman. An *Abomination.*"

"That's a very loaded word."

"That's what the stories call him."

The daimyo turned around and stepped towards Bran.

"I take it he did not manage to gain your trust during the journey."

The boy hesitated.

"Even though he saved your lives twice," Lord Nariakira pressed.

"He... I may have misjudged him in the end. Did you know of him, *kakka?*"

The daimyo smiled.

"I knew *of* him, yes."

"And... would you trust him?"

"I am a daimyo. It is my job to trust no one. But I would like to have him on my side; in battle and in a debate."

"But I thought... Immortal Swordsman... *a blood-sucking demon,*" Bran recalled the words of the Unganzenji abbot. The daimyo raised a finger to his lips in thought.

"Yes, he is all that. But he is also an outcast of his own kind. A renegade. One day the other Fanged will find a way to dispose of him for good, and it will be the biggest loss for Yamato since Taiko-*dono* mentioned to Rikyū-*sama* he no longer enjoyed his *cha.*"

"You embarrass me, Shimazu-*sama.*" A familiar voice spoke from behind the fake wall. It slid open and a looming figure in a purple cloak emerged from the hidden alcove.

"Let us hope we'll never find out whether you were right."

"You!" Bran jumped up, reaching automatically for his sword, before remembering he had to leave it with the servant outside.

"The same," the Swordsman said with a slight bow. "And let me congratulate you on impeccable timing, Karasu-*sama* – or should I call you Bran? I have only arrived in Kagoshima last night. Are the others alright?"

"*Eh*... yes. They are resting at the guesthouse."

"That's splendid news. I'm glad you came out of this alive."

Lord Nariakira waved his hand dismissively.

"It's time for you to leave," the Swordsman added, noticing the gesture. "Shimazu-*dono* and I still have a lot to discuss."

A servant slid open the door to the study and waited to accompany Bran outside.

"*Kakka.*" The boy bowed.

"Dōraku-*sama* will notify you of my decision," said the daimyo, and with a voice used to giving orders that could not be refused, added, "and you shall accept it, whatever it may be."

CHAPTER VIII

At Lord Nariakira's invitation, Dōraku sat down to the shōgi board.

"That was a performance worthy of Ginza, *kakka*," he said, taking out his pipe and stuffing it with tobacco.

"I needed to know if the boy was telling the truth. Or what he thought was the truth."

"And what do you make of it all?"

"Combined with what Heishichi and Atsuko have told me? All very disturbing news. That Crimson Robe is one of *yours* – do you know him?"

"Yes."

"Whom do you think he serves?"

"No one. I have never seen him do anyone's bidding – other than the Eight-headed Serpent, back in the days."

"Not even the Kumamoto?"

"He did mention not wanting to irritate Hosokawa. So there may be an alliance of convenience. But working for a mortal… no, if anything, it would be the other way around."

"I see. Either way, between this and the rumours of my brother Hisamitsu conspiring against me, it looks like Hosokawa Narimori-*dono* is no longer a useful ally. Now, where were we…"

The daimyo moved the Foot Soldier piece, reinforcing his defensive position. Dōraku chuckled.

"How very much like you, to worry more about your alliances than about a dragon let loose," he said, picking up a Lance and moving it two places forward in a casual scouting movement.

"The dragon, according to my spies, is rampaging in the north, far beyond the borders of Satsuma. Before the boy came, I thought it was no longer my concern."

"One *dorako* may be enough to tip the balance to one side in the conflict."

Nariakira moved another Foot Soldier one field forward.

"A valuable asset lost, certainly, but nothing worth losing my sleep over."

"And you are not at all worried about the *Taikun* learning you had a dragon – and then lost it?"

"The *Taikun* has plenty enough to worry about for the moment."

"Oh?" Dōraku reached for a captured Angle Mover, to put it back onto his side of the board.

"There was some disaster at Uraga Bay. Complete lack of communication from Edo since."

The Swordsman's hand hovered over the board.

"That is new."

"Of course, no word of it was supposed to get out to the outer provinces."

"I take it the town criers of Kagoshima will have an interesting tale to tell tomorrow."

The daimyo smiled. Dōraku finally put the Angle Mover down in an offensive position.

"Uraga Bay is the gate to Edo. A gate to all of Yamato."

"Indeed."

"You don't think it's an attack?"

"Anything is possible. But they wouldn't keep a tsunami or a typhoon in such secrecy, would they?"

"I heard the soothsayers are anxious. All they can see is Darkness."

"*Unnh*," Nariakira grunted in agreement. "All the more reason to secure one's position against whatever may happen." He slid his Flying Chariot to the left to fill up an empty slot in the wall of his castle.

"I am surrounded by enemies on all sides."

"You said you will consider the boy's situation, *kakka*, but something tells me you've already made a decision," said Dōraku. He moved a Lance forward, capturing Nariakira's flying chariot. The daimyo frowned.

"I will not let another *asset* out of my hands. The rider stays in Kagoshima until I decide what to do with him." The daimyo moved another piece back towards his Great General, strengthening his castle. This was his usual tactics, building up a strong position on one side of the board, from which he would send out massed attacks against the enemy's flank. Loss of one piece was insignificant in the long run.

"An *asset*," said Dōraku. "You mean like Anjin-*sama*, all those centuries ago."

Nariakira looked up. "That Seaxe in the first Taikun's employ? You remember him?"

"I met him once. Most curious fellow. Old Ieyasu was very fond of him. But in the end, he wasn't of much use to anyone."

The daimyo shrugged.

"We all know the story. When he arrived to Yamato, there wasn't anyone like him, and Ieyasu needed him to play the Vasconians. But we're in another age now. I have my wizards, I have my Bataavians... the boy is not as unique and precious as he likes to think."

"And what about the wizard girl? Wasn't Takashima-*sama* one of your allies in Kiyō?"

"Oh, Shūhan is safe," the daimyo said with a wave of his hand. "I have it on good authority. Keep this a secret, though, I may yet use this knowledge as leverage."

"Hmm." Dōraku puffed on his pipe.

"You disagree."

"You have plenty of wizards and scholars at your disposal. What good is another one?"

"I don't follow."

"A dragon rider without a *dorako* is just a minor magic user."

One of the Swordsman's lances charged the castle head-on.

"Better to have this than nothing at all. If I let him go, he'll only get himself killed or captured by my enemies – that Crimson Robe, whoever he is, or Hosokawa. And if he succeeds, it's even worse: he will fly away to Qin." The daimyo moved another Foot Soldier into sacrifice position to defend the Generals. "No *dorako*, no rider."

"He could be... *coerced* to help us." Dōraku duly gobbled up the sacrificed pawn.

"I hope so! That's why I need him here. As an advisor, not a fighter. I don't have many scholars of dragon lore in my court."

"And you would give up on the *dorako*?"

"There will be more where that one came from. If one got through, others will follow. For now I'm glad to leave the *dorako* where it is. Maybe it will fly to Kumamoto and deal with Hosokawa before I get my hands on him," the daimyo chuckled gleefully. He moved the first of his Lances, building up to a massed assault on Dōraku's right flank. In a few moves he was going to smash through Swordsman's defences and gain total dominance of the field.

"I'm afraid that, as usual, you underestimate the power of an individual's actions, *kakka*."

Dōraku took the captured Flying Chariot from the wooden stand and placed it one field away from the promotion zone. The daimyo's eyes widened as he reasserted the situation on the board.

"Impossible."

"Do you see now? The Flying Chariot on its own is just a pawn, useful only for a sacrifice. But transform it into a Dragon King..."

A skilled player like Nariakira could clearly see there was only one possible outcome. The Dragon King was one of the most powerful figures in *shōgi*, and in the position where Dōraku had put his piece it posed a danger to the entire meticulously prepared castle. It was not enough on its own to threaten the King General, but it would require the daimyo to reconstruct his whole strategy.

"Hmpf," was all Nariakira had to say for a long time as he leaned over the board. "Hmpf," he repeated.

"*Yoshi*, you've made your point, Fanged," the daimyo spoke at last, straightening his back. "But what guarantee can you give me that your plan will work?"

"Only that of my honour, *kakka*."

The daimyo nodded and grunted approvingly.

"*Unnh*. Well said."

He stood up, indicating the audience was over.

Bran found Nagomi sitting at the doorstep of his room, in the darkness, wearing her sheer night *yukata*.

"What are you doing here?"

"I couldn't sleep."

He sat down beside her, drowsy and tired.

"Bad dreams?"

"Too many dreams. I saw you with Dōraku-*sama*. He looks fine."

Bran nodded.

"I just met him. He's coming here tomorrow to bring us news from the daimyo of Satsuma."

"You've had a busy night."

"And you don't seem at all surprised."

"We need to tell Sacchan," she said, ignoring his remark. "She will be mad we've kept it from her."

"I didn't think it mattered. I hoped we wouldn't see him anymore."

"Is he going to join us again?"

"I don't know. He seems to be mingling with more important men now."

He saw the silhouette of her head nod in silence.

"You saw something else," he guessed.

"Your *dorako*."

He lit a faint flamespark and looked at her. The light danced on her hair, making it seem like a roaring flame.

"Emrys? Was it alive?" he asked.

"Yes, just... asleep. I don't know... it was dark and cold. A metal box. Underground, I think..."

"Then it's captured already..."

She shook her head. "I don't think it's happened yet. But it will, soon."

"Have you...always been able to see the future?"

Nagomi nodded.

"When I was little, I had... intuitions. Vague premonitions. If I had visions, I did not understand them without hindsight. One summer, when I was ten, I sensed a great misfortune approaching, but I didn't know what it was and whom to warn."

"And what was it?"

"A typhoon. It would have been disastrous to the city, luckily the priests of Suwa foresaw it too and there was enough time to prepare."

"So you went to Suwa to train your talent?"

"Kazuko-*hime* requested it. And with her help my skills grew... I used to need to get into a trance, inhale the sacred fumes to see the visions, but since..."

She stopped and bit her lips.

Since the High Priestess died, Bran guessed. *She can't bring herself to say it.*

"You mean since you've become a priestess," he helped. She nodded again.

"It's as if a window had been opened into the future. I've been having more of these dreams, even on ordinary nights like tonight."

"You do seem more tired than the rest of us," he said. He hadn't noticed it before, but there were deep blue bags under her eyes. He felt sorry for her.

"If there's anything I can do to help..."

"*Un-n*, it's fine." She shook her head and yawned discreetly, standing up. "I'd better go. Maybe I can still catch some sleep tonight. Don't worry about Sacchan, I'll explain to her somehow."

"Thank you."

Bran stood up as well and for a moment they were standing against each other, face to face. Suddenly, Nagomi stood on her toes, threw her arms around him and pressed her lips firmly against his – then ran off down the corridor, without looking back.

"Is it true? Are you really the Immortal Swordsman?"

"Hush!" The samurai put a hand to his lips with an amused smile. "This is supposed to be a secret."

It's a joke, she thought. *They're all playing a joke on me.*

Satō was still reeling from the revelation Nagomi had shared with her the night before, when Master Dōraku entered the Sugi Inn and approached them with arms open, as if welcoming long lost friends. Even though a lot about the samurai suddenly made sense, she still didn't want to believe it.

We didn't see him die, after all.

Master Dōraku finished greeting everyone else – bowing deeply and rubbing his chest in front of Torishi – and cast a doubtful glance around the inn. "This is not a good place to discuss important matters. Why don't you come with me?"

"So... how *old* are you?" asked Satō, as soon as they sat down to breakfast. The place Master Dōraku had led them to was an opulent teahouse, adjacent to the castle walls. She noticed everyone else in the common room was either an aristocrat or a member of the daimyo's family. The guests were staring at Torishi far longer than was considered polite, but the staff had welcomed the Swordsman like a frequent guest and led the group to a cozy, secluded alcove, where the cast iron tea-kettle hovered, suspended on a rope over the fireplace.

"Let's see... I was born in the twelfth year of Tenshō era, in the Yoshino district of Mimasaka province," recited Master Dōraku. The wizardess paused, doing quick calculations in her head. The Yamato reckoning of years was needlessly complicated, she had always thought.

"That's two hundred and fifty years ago!" Her eyes widened.

If it's really all a joke, it's a very well thought-out one.

"You're thinking of the Bunroku era, Tenshō was the one before. So it's two hundred and seventy."

"*Eeh!* But that would mean… you'd have seen all those wars, all those battles…!"

Master Dōraku nodded, twirling his moustache.

"I was a young boy in the rear echelon at Sekigahara, yes. I climbed the walls of Naniwa Castle. I fought the rebels of Shimabara."

"This is where you have met the *Taishō,*" added Bran. "And you've made a great impression on him."

"I'm honoured to hear that."

"Not a *good* impression," said the boy. "I can sense he loathes you."

The samurai chuckled.

"When you've lived – or sort of lived – as long as the two of us have, some differences of opinion are inevitable."

"Wait." Satō put her hand on the table with a loud smack. "Hold on. How do we know you're telling the truth? How do we know you and this old Spirit did not make it all up?"

Before any of them could react, a *tantō* flashed in his hand and a long, straight gash appeared down his forearm. The stench of blood filled the alcove momentarily, but the wound was dry and dull in colour. As Satō watched, it began to mend rapidly, as if under a priest's spell. Within seconds, it vanished without a trace, leaving just a patch of smooth skin.

She sniffed. The smell was unmistakable.

"Blood magic," she said.

The samurai nodded and wiped his dagger before sheathing it.

"Blood magic, yes. It's what keeps me alive. We were all born out of a Blood Magic."

"We?"

"Whatever you call our kind," he said and smiled. "All the Fanged. Abominations. Blood-sucking ghosts."

"*Demons.* But you look so… human. Not like him."

He looked straight at her. For a blink of an eye so brief she wasn't certain if she really saw it, his face turned paper-white, his eyes golden and his teeth long, sharp and black.

"We can disguise ourselves well. He just chooses not to."

Torishi, silent until now, smoothed his beard and spoke in a solemn voice.

"I've heard of you, Swordsman. Or at least someone *like* you. Stories about an immortal man visiting the Kumaso villages, in the days of my grandmother and her mother."

Dōraku smiled. "I'm surprised your people remembered me. I was just a passing traveller."

"You can certainly make an impression," remarked Satō.

She had not touched her food since the Swordsman's demonstration. All she could think of was the "curse".

Blood magic can make you immortal.

The energy drawn from the tiny needle in her glove was enough to make her spells fantastically powerful. What would it be like to use more blood? For example, all blood drawn from some animal? Or... *a human?*

"The addiction," she blurted. The others looked at her blankly, except Master Dōraku.

"You have truly a scholar's mind," he said. "Inquisitive from the start. Yes, the blood is addictive. But there are ways to deal with it. If you try hard enough – "

"Why are you here, Dōraku-*sama?*" interrupted Nagomi. She positioned herself opposite the samurai, as far away as was possible, in the small alcove, and kept her eyes fixed on him all the time. Bran was sitting close beside her, their knees almost touching. For some unfathomable reason this annoyed Satō.

The samurai turned serious. "I bring word from Shimazu Nariakira-*dono.*"

"The daimyo?" Satō reeled back. "What does *he* want with us?"

Master Dōraku turned a meaningful glance at Bran.

"I... I asked him for help," the boy said.

"*Eeh?* What exactly is going on here?"

Questions rushed through Satō's head. *How did he get to meet a daimyo? Why nobody ever tells me anything? Why is he sitting so close to Nagomi?*

"I figured he would be the best-informed person on the matter."

"And you've made the right choice," said the Swordsman, filling his pipe. "The Lord of Kagoshima Castle has agreed to your request. You are all invited to his summer palace tomorrow morning," the samurai said with a mysterious smile.

"*Another* day's delay?" Bran slumped. "I was hoping we would move out as soon as possible."

"I'm sure you will not be disappointed with what His Excellency will show you tomorrow. Ah, the *cha* is ready," said Dōraku, reaching for the iron kettle.

"Let's eat. I'm eager to hear of your adventures since we parted company."

Bran closed his eyes and descended into the red dust plain. It was easier every time he tried it, and he was beginning to enjoy those moments. At the top of the tower there was complete silence and isolation, disturbed only by the wind blowing from nowhere to nowhere.

Earlier Satō had tried to convince him he should prepare himself for their meeting with Lord Nariakira.

"These are not the clothes you wear to meet the lord of the province," she insisted.

"But I already *met* him."

"Yes, but that wasn't formal. There is a hierarchy to these things even *you* can't ignore."

"The Shimazu are one of the Great Clans," added Nagomi, "above them are only the *Taikun* and the Divine *Mikado*… A common physician's daughter like me would never dream of meeting such an esteemed person."

"Is that why you are putting on make-up?" Bran didn't think much of the priestess's efforts with the white paint and lip carmin. Satō, too, was at her most feminine, practicing a girly giggle and blushing on command.

"I just don't understand why suddenly – "

"It's *what's proper*," said the wizardess, futilely trying to put charcoal paste on her eyelashes. Her hand shook.

"Now go away, you're making me nervous with your staring."

The *Taishō* was nowhere to be seen. Had he wandered somewhere off, or was he not *always* present here in a physical form? Either way, his existence on this featureless plain must have been excruciatingly boring. Bran felt sorry for the old General. At least in the cave back in Suwa there were other Spirits to keep him company.

Bran came down to the green dragon and touched its neck. This time he penetrated farther, trying to learn more about Emrys' whereabouts. For a moment nothing seemed to happen; but when he pressed harder, his head began to spin and he found himself in the middle of a storm of unintelligible signals, a hurricane of raw emotions, impressions and visions. Wild yearning. Anger. Bloodlust. Fear. Freedom. The idea of a forest, a mountain-top, a rice field; the taste of fresh meat; the buffeting of wind.

Exhausted, Bran let go of the jade-green phantom and slid down to the ground. It seemed the dragon was both further away physically, and further into the process of going wild and Bran was unable to pick up any sense of direction.

The General appeared out of nowhere and came up to the boy.

"Trouble, eh?"

"I can't get through. I need to… I need to stop thinking, somehow. There's too much noise in my head."

"I can teach you how to do that."

"Really?"

Shigemasa scoffed.

"All well-educated samurai know how to meditate. Of course, it takes years of training, but I can teach you a trick or two today. Now sit straight, like a Man."

Bran knelt down with the body resting on his heels, with feet turned outwards. He usually could not withstand this position for longer than a few minutes.

"Good. Fold your hands like this and don't move. Now we need something for you to focus on. Look at the red light on top of the tower, and don't let your eyes wander off it."

The boy duly stared at the light. He waited for about a minute for further instruction, but nothing happened.

"What – "

The General hit him in the back with his sword's scabbard.

"Quiet! Think of nothing but your *breath*. In and out. In and out. Look at the light."

Bran soon lost track of time – there was, after all, nothing on the red plain to help him to orient his thoughts. He tried to count seconds, but lost count after a hundred. He continued to force his eyes on the gently pulsating red light…

Another slap on the back woke him up.

"No sleeping!"

"Surely I'm ready now–"

"It's not even ten minutes since you started. Your mind is still full of random thoughts."

It feels like school now, Bran was annoyed, but stared into the light again. He focused on his breath. Finally the light at the top of the tower began to subdue, its pulsations grew slow and soft, as did Bran's heartbeat. The *Taishō* grunted with satisfaction.

"Enough. Try your magic now."

Bran felt light-headed and awake, but mostly, he felt his feet and legs burn with terrible pain. He stood up, made a few steps and staggered; falling, he reached out a hand and touched the warm, green scales again.

Images and sensations flooded him. An enormous, lush green valley, perfectly round. Tall, sheer cliffs on all sides. White-washed villages scattered about its bottom like snowflakes. In the middle, a high fire mountain, gushing steam from several outlets.

A ruby-hued light on the top, a beacon he couldn't resist, summoning him closer…

"Then it's captured already…"

No, don't go there!

Bran tried to call the dragon away; he sent out a powerful Word of command, but the strain of conflicting pulls proved too much. The thin link broke, and the beast cast him away.

He swayed back; the General supported him and helped him stand straight.

"Did it work?"

"I saw – a great round valley, with steep edges and a fire mountain inside."

"*Unnh.* Must be Aso-san. Anyone on Chinzei will know how to get there."

"Aso-san. I'll remember."

The General smiled lightly.

"Be careful in your dealings with the daimyo of Satsuma. I knew the first one, Tadatsuna-*dono*. He drew off hundred thousand Qin soldiers with just eight thousand men. His descendant looks equally cunning."

"I'll be careful," Bran replied.

When he departed, the image of the green valley and the ruby-hued light was still clear in his mind; but there was something else he recalled from the vision: a nagging, odd feeling of *another* Farlink. As if there was another dragon and rider pair somewhere near – somewhere in Yamato.

Is my father coming to my rescue at last?

CHAPTER IX

The naked torsos gleamed with the omnipresent black pumice powder, covering the body with a thin layer the moment the porters cleaned themselves. The men lifted the four boxes marked with the circle-cross crest of Satsuma and carried them swiftly down the streets of Kagoshima, along its main road. One of the vehicles remained empty: Torishi insisted on running along with the porters.

"I don't like being locked," he said. Bran quietly agreed with the bear-man.

Sakurajima loomed on the right; this meant they were moving north. Soon they entered the outskirts of the city, passing at least one "great workshop", belching white and yellow smoke from its red-brick chimney stacks, and started climbing up and down some low hills, before crossing the gate of thick wooden beams.

It was a long journey, and as Bran left the confines of his black box, he felt pins and needles running all over his limbs. He was still jumping up and down trying to relax his tense muscles, when Lord Shimazu Nariakira came down from a flower-topped hill to welcome them. The porters immediately fell to the ground while Bran and his party bowed deeply.

"How do you like my garden?"

Bran looked around and spotted the garden's most striking feature: from where he was standing, the trees and flowers seemed to form a window frame through which the mighty Sakurajima appeared like a part of the continuing garden arrangement, with the blue waters of the Kinkō Bay flowing before it like a decorative pond.

"It is magnificent, my Lord," replied Satō, her eyes hidden behind a paper fan. She was wearing a many-layered, long-sleeved kimono with summer motif she had rented a day earlier especially for the occasion. Tense and nervous, she had already tripped on its hem a couple of times; the blush of embarrassment visible even through the thick make-up which seemed to freeze a trained smile in place.

"You're Takashima Satō, aren't you?" Lord Nariakira said and smiled. Satō looked as if she was about to faint.

"I met your father once, you know. What a mind! Didn't he tell you to come to me if there was any trouble? Naturally, I would do anything to help Shūhan-*sama* and his family."

The wizardess could only nod.

"And you are Itō-*sama*'s daughter! How is he these days?"

"He... he is well, *kakka*. He's in Chubu, fighting smallpox."

"The man's a hero! Just think of the lives he's saving with his art... Men like him should be rich and powerful – not us, old wrinkly bats who've inherited their wealth because of what their great-great-great-grandfather did in one battle or another."

The daimyo chuckled and then turned to the towering Torishi – who hardly broke a sweat along the journey – and pretended to flinch.

"And who is that? A forest giant of the Kumaso! I never thought I'd meet one of your people."

"I am the last one," replied the bear-man. Meeting Lord Nariakira didn't seem to make any impression on him. The daimyo's face turned serious for a moment, "I'm sorry to hear that. My power does not reach far enough into the mountains."

Finally, the daimyo looked at Bran. He stared at the boy's transformed Yamato face for a moment, perplexed, before bursting with laughter – though his eyes remained ever serious.

"Yes! I see, I see. Come, come, my noble guests. I will show you something of interest!"

They followed him down a steep flight of stairs carved in stone, to a narrow inlet, cut off from the rest of the bay with a tall, thick lock gate. Moored to a wooden pier was a ship unlike any Bran had seen in Yamato. It was about sixty feet long, its hull was sleek, narrow, streamlined, covered with copper plate and painted black. Three masts rose from the deck, but there was also a thin funnel above a long, rectangular cabin. A brass lightning box hung from the foremast in place of a storm lantern and brass tubes and vents pierced the stern deck above the boiler room.

"But this is a... mistfire ship!" Satō forgot her decorum momentarily, picked up the hem of her kimono and ran down the pier to see the vessel up close. Lord Nariakira climbed on board and looked down an open hatch in the middle of the deck.

"Captain Kawamura! Are you there?"

A tall, robust, solemn-eyed man emerged from the hatch in a hurry. He was stripped to the waist, wearing only a pair of baggy *monpe* pantaloons. His upper body was smeared with oil and soot, and he held a big wrench in his hand, which he dropped, and pressed his forehead to the ground before the daimyo.

"*Kakka!* I did not expect you today!"

"Get up, Kawamura. How is she?"

"Ready to set sail at your command, *kakka!*"

"So, what do you think of my *Iroha Maru?*" Lord Nariakira said, turning to his guests, beaming with pride. "You won't find a faster ship in all of Yamato."

"This is incredible! I had no idea anyone was building something like this!"

Satō ran up and down the deck, before leaning down the hatch and examining the boiler room, "How big is this engine?"

"There's sixty-four elementals trapped in the Great Cauldron, noble lady," replied Kawamura, visibly abashed at being questioned in matters of engineering by a woman and guest of the daimyo.

"Sixty-four! To think Hisashige-*sama* was so proud of his eight!"

"Old Tanaka is pretty close to building such an engine himself, last I heard," said the daimyo. "And how do you like the ship, young *Gaikokujin-sama*?" he asked Bran, "How does it compare with what you're used to?"

"Very favourably, Nariakira-*dono*. I've seen yachts in the Brigstow harbour not unlike this boat."

The boy did not say out loud what his immediate thought was.

I could take it out to the open ocean and sail back to Qin.

At this moment he felt he was closer to home than ever since he woke up in Kiyō. Even if something happened to his dragon, even if the daimyo would not agree to lend him the ship, he could just steal it. With some effort and a bit of luck, using the knowledge he had gained on *Ladon*, Bran was sure he would be able to navigate his way towards the Qin coast.

All I have to do is to follow the setting sun...

He was nudged out from his musings by Nagomi. Her eyes pointed at Lord Nariakira.

"I'm sorry, *kakka*... I was admiring the lightning box."

"Ah yes. An intricate piece. I got it freshly made in Bataave. Anyway, Captain Kawamura will be in command of the ship on your journey. He will show you around. Kawamura, you will sail wherever these people tell you to."

"Of course, *kakka*."

"There is one more person I'd like you to meet. Heishichi!"

A lanky man came down the stairs onto the pier, wearing a long, hooded vermillion robe.

Heishichi!

"You're the Chief Wizard! You are the one that kept Emrys in its cage!"

The man dropped the hood, revealing his face. The entire left half of it was scorched into terrible, swollen scars and blisters. His left eye twitched constantly.

"Is that... did my dragon did this to you?"

Heishichi nodded.

"But the priests at Kirishima...!" said Nagomi.

"I wear these scars as a reminder of my disgrace."

"He wanted to kill himself," said the daimyo. "I didn't permit it, of course. My best wizard," he patted the *Daisen* on the back.

Heishichi bowed his head.

"I allowed my Lord's possession to be stolen. I have brought shame upon myself and all my family."

"Yes, well, you'll pay it back with your continuing service, of that you can be certain. You may start by joining these four noble travellers on their journey."

Heishichi bowed again in silence; the right half of his face twitched. The daimyo turned to Bran again.

"I will have your things brought from the inn before long."

"When do we leave, *kakka?*" asked Bran, darting away from Heishichi's pained stare.

I don't suppose we get to choose our travel companions.

"At dusk. I will be sailing before you, in my own official ship. This will draw the eyes of the spies."

"Will Dōraku-*sama* be joining us?" asked Satō.

"For now he's coming with me."

"I'm sorry, *kakka*" intruded Nagomi, "but where are we going?"

"That's a good question, young priestess-*sama*." The daimyo looked at Bran. "What do *you* think?"

"I think... I think we should go to a place called Aso-san," the boy replied.

"You managed to contact your *dorako* then?" Satō asked.

Bran nodded.

"Heishichi?" the daimyo turned to the wizard.

"It makes sense, *kakka,*" the *Daisen* replied. "It is a nexus of power even greater than Mount Takachiho. A creature attuned to the magical energies would be drawn to it."

"But it will not be there by the time you reach Aso," added the daimyo. "Even on *Iroha Maru* it shall take several days to sail that far north. You will have to adjust your course along the way."

"I will try my best," Bran said, bowing.

"Of course you will", Lord Nariakira said, smiling; Bran felt uneasy under his stare. The daimyo seemed to be guessing at his deepest thoughts.

"And now I must leave you. I have to prepare for my own journey."

The daimyo bid them farewell and climbed back up the stone stairs. Captain Kawamura shifted his wrench nervously from one hand to another.

"Follow me, please, I will show you the cabin..."

Satō had spent half a day in the engine room, observing preparations for the launch and making note of the various valves, gauges and transformation chambers. The entire engine was of Bataavian make, and built so that even a person without magical talent could maintain it with ease.

The great cauldron had a small glass window in its cast iron wall, through which she could observe the elementals inside. The orange and blue wisps seemed to dance, or fight with each other within the confines of the chamber.

"I never really understood what the elementals are," she said, more to herself than to the Captain, who was busy adjusting a flange on a copper pipe. "They look so... alive."

"In a way, they are," a hoarse voice spoke behind her. She turned around to see the *Daisen* Torii Heishichi. His scarred face was hidden in the shadows.

"They grow, like crystals, but they can't multiply on their own, so they can't be said to be alive like us or animals."

"Some of them seem to have little faces," the wizardess observed. She had never seen elementals as big as these. The ones her father had worked on, obtained at a great cost from Dejima smugglers, or products of his own experiments, were just wisps of luminous air, barely longer than a man's thumb.

"Yes, that's something my students find most disturbing when they start working with the elementals. As they grow, they are beginning to look more and more human. Some Western scholars believe that that's how the magical creatures came about in the first place. And I've even seen an elemental larger than a new-born child."

"What did it look like?"

"Almost like a new-born child," the *Daisen* said, smirking. "It had a face and what could almost pass as limbs… But it was very unstable and soon perished. With a terrible cry."

With that, the lanky man stepped back into the shadows. Satō felt a shiver running through her spine. She wasn't certain if the wizard was telling the truth or was having a dark joke at her expense.

A cry? Does it mean the elementals feel pain?

She looked into the cauldron once more. The wisps whizzed back and forth all around the chamber and whenever one of fire met with one of water, a white flash of mistfire was produced which travelled up towards the funnel outlet.

Does it hurt when they do that?

Captain Kawamura finished working with the flange and clapped his hands.

"Right, time to increase the pressure."

He turned a great red valve, and even more elementals poured from their holding chambers, now a full thirty-two pairs of fire and water sprites. The inside of the cauldron filled with white smoke and its walls heated up.

Satō tried to listen to the tiny cries of the elementals, but all she heard was the rushing of mistfire up the pipes and the rhythmical beat of the firesteel and brass pistons.

In the quickly falling dusk, the *Iroha Maru* puffed inconspicuously away from the secret wharf. As the boat increased its speed, cutting through the waves of Kinkō Bay like a frolicking whale, excessive emanations of the elementals' magical energy transformations rose in a column of grey smoke from a narrow chimney. The paddle wheels rammed the water with a rhythmic roar, like a dozen waterfalls at once.

"We will sail her far into the open ocean," the Captain explained to Satō, "and circumnavigate Chinzei beyond the range of patrol boats."

"How far have you sailed this ship before?" she asked.

"She's been to Amami and back once. That's seventy *ri* each way. She's quite capable," Kawamura patted the steering wheel with a caring smile.

The fishing boats had all come back for the night already, and the waters of the strait between Sakurajima and the city were still and empty, cleared for the passage of the daimyo's ship. Satō could barely see anything before her, except the ominous shadow of the mountain concealing the stars lighting up in the darkening skies.

She was about to ask the Captain how he was planning to steer them in the night, when a bright yellow spark appeared in front of them.

"What's that?"

"That's the lighthouse on the Okagashima battery, Takashima-*sama*. There's five more between us and the Kaimondake cape where we turn westwards. I've sailed this route many times at night. Before dawn we'll be out in the open ocean – and then you'll see what she's really capable of!"

It was *Minazuki*, Month of Water, according to the Yamato calendar, Bran remembered; somewhere between May and June by Western reckoning, he guessed, but had no way to be certain. He had lost count of days a long time ago, when wandering the dark forests and high mountains of Chinzei.

The scorching sun stood high at noon, a slight cooling breeze having blown all the clouds away towards the land. The ocean was still and the weather was as perfect as they could ever wish for. Everything had a warm, fuzzy, dreamy quality to it.

Nagomi decided to stay on deck during the day, lying lethargic on a bench with her face turned to the sun and her eyes half-closed.

"This is like a holiday," she sighed, relaxed, "I never knew sea travel could be so pleasant."

Bran grunted back too lazy to answer. With Captain Kawamura at the wheel, there was nothing for any of them to do but watch the sea. He was leaning on the stern bulwark, munching on a juicy mikan. They had a whole crate of the fruits in the ship's hold, and in the heat of a summer's day this was about all the food they needed to sustain themselves.

Heishichi came out of the engine bay and sat on a bench, studying some square-shaped measuring instrument. Bran turned serious at once. He threw the fruit into the sea, wiped his hands on his clothes and came up to the wizard.

"I'm sorry," he said, "for what my *dorako* did."

Heishichi looked up, blinking with one eye. The burned half of his face remained still.

"At least I'm *alive*," he said, darkly. "Your *dorako* snapped one of my men in half."

A faint half-memory, half-dream returned to Bran; a sense of dread and fear.

"I... I didn't know."

The *Daisen* shrugged.

"We all understood the risk. It doesn't matter now. All my men are dead anyway."

Bran felt sorry for the wizard, and slightly guilty until he remembered this was the man who had held Emrys in its cage all this time, preventing their reunion until it was too late.

Heishichi returned to studying the device and adjusting the dials. He frowned and raised it to the sun.

"How good are you with Octagonometry?" he asked Bran.

"Terrible," the boy replied with a weak smile. He sat down on the bench beside the wizard and played with a piece of thin copper wire he had found lying on the deck.

It looks like Nagomi's hair, Bran thought.

"Riding a dragon is my only talent, really."

"When you got separated... how did you know how to find it again?"

Bran scratched his nose in thought.

"It's a power all dragon riders have... we call it *Farlink*. We can command dragons during flight and in combat. But I can also sense my mount wherever it is."

The wizard listened intently, from time to time turning to his device to adjust another gear.

"And what happens when your *dorako* dies or is lost for good?"

"The rider will be assigned a new mount, but it takes a while to readjust. A few weeks to make it listen to basic commands, months to reach the full union. Some riders are better at it than others."

"And are *you* better than others?"

Bran hesitated.

You are a good rider, he remembered Madam Magnusdottir. *One of our best.*

"So I've been told," he said at last.

Heishichi nodded.

"So you can't just take a *dorako* and make it yield to your will in an instant?"

"No. That would be a great feat."

"Then how did this... Crimson Robe manage to steal your beast at Kirishima?"

So that's what he's been getting at.

"He had some kind of an artefact. A ruby orb, about this size," Bran said, showing a clutched hand, "he could control my dragon and weaken *me*, when I transformed."

Heishichi looked at him sharply.

"A ruby orb? Are you sure?"

Bran nodded.

"I almost touched it. In True Sight it glowed like the Sun. Do you know about it?"

The *Daisen* didn't answer. He leaned over his instrument and carefully bent a thick copper wire. A bluish electric arc sparked across the device.

He stood up abruptly and pointed one edge of the device towards the horizon.

"Captain Kawamura, I have the radius!"

Bran stared in the direction Heishichi to which had pointed. All along the southern edge of the sky ran a thick, black, ominous wall of clouds, illuminated from inside by countless flashes of lightning; a massive storm, the likes of which he had never seen before.

The *Iroha Maru* continued to skirt the edge of the great storm all through the day. By evening a worried Bran joined Satō and Captain Kawamura in the helmsman's cockpit.

"Shouldn't we be turning back towards the land soon?" he asked, studying a navigation chart. It was oriented with the West to the top, so it had taken him a while to learn to read it.

"Soon, *tono*. We'll be taking a wide turn around these islands here, and I hope to get you near Aso-san in two days."

"And where is Aso-san?"

The Captain put his finger roughly in the middle of the map of Chinzei.

"So we're going back to Kumamoto," remarked Satō, pointing to the nearest harbour.

Kawamura shook his head.

"No, Takashima-*sama*. We can't be seen anywhere near the city. That's where His Excellency will be heading to draw attention from us. We will land somewhere in the marshes of Saga, to the north. Unless you tell me otherwise, *tono*."

"Me?" Bran looked up, startled.

"That's what I've been ordered. Listen to the boy with green eyes if he orders a change of course."

"Oh."

When Emrys moves somewhere else.

"Of course."

What if I order him to sail to Qin?

He looked through the left window, where the black wall of clouds still loomed, crested with white billows, neither grown nor lessened since he had first seen it.

"And if we had to go through this storm?"

The Captain blinked and laughed.

"That's no storm, *tono*. Those are the Divine Winds, *Kamikaze*. And we're not going *there* even on *Taikun's* orders."

Divine Winds?

There was something his father had told him... what seemed a very long time ago...

The Sea Maze! We're so close!

"How do the Bataavians get through that?" he asked.

"Believe me, if we knew the secret, His Excellency would have already sent ships to survey the Great Ocean."

Emrys got through on its own. And if it did, so could others.

He had sensed the other beast – or beasts – again last night, soaring through the dark sky. He was certain now the dragons were somewhere in Yamato.

The air cooled a little by the evening. Bran stepped out of the bridge, leaving Captain Kawamura leaning lazily over the steering wheel, chewing a chunk of tobacco.

The middle deck was illuminated by a single evertorch, powered by the lightning box on the mast. The faint beam obscured all but the brightest stars in the dark blue sky, and Bran moved to fore to see more of them. It was a curious thought: despite Bran being half-way across the globe, the stars looked the same as in his home country. There were one or two constellations he had only seen in the southern seas, but all the old summer familiars were there. He recalled Doctor Campion's lessons: Pisces, Aquarius, Capricorn... The Moon was just beginning to wane. Venus rose proudly from the East, and Vega, Bran's favourite, shone brightly to the Northwest. The Polaris hung to the right of the bowsprit, indicating they were headed north-west.

Nagomi stood on the prow with Torishi, eagerly discussing something. Her hair glowed warmly in the evertorch's light. Bran came up to them. The bear-man gave him a quick glance, smiled and left.

The priestess lowered her eyes and stepped aside to let Bran stand beside her by the gunwale.

"Do you know the names of the stars?" he asked.

"Some of them, yes."

"What do you call that big one?" he asked, pointing at Vega.

"That's Orihime, the Weaving Princess. And that's Hikoboshi the Shepherd," she replied, nodding at Altair hovering low above the horizon on the other side of the Milky Way.

"Her... lover," she added and flushed.

"What did you talk about with Torishi-*sama*?"

"His people have... had... a different way of communicating with Spirits than the priests. It's more... intimate. They did things I didn't think possible."

"Such as?"

"Travelling into the Otherworld or speaking with the *kami* directly."

Otherworld?

"Did he tell you what that place looked like?" he asked.

"A great, flat plain of red dust at first. A spirit guide can help you to reach other lands, where the *kami* dwell. For the Kumaso a spirit guide was the bear."

Is Emrys my spirit guide, then?

The waves lapped softly against the hull of the ship. The deck vibrated lightly under Bran's feet. Underneath, in the engine room, Satō and Heishichi were working on some experiment. With the bear-man gone to his cabin, Bran and Nagomi were all alone on the deck.

The priestess was clutching the rail tightly, facing the breeze.

"The years I spent in the shrine were an endless cycle of …seasons, festivals, rituals and chores," she started, "I was sure that was how I would spend the rest of my life. I got used to it. This… simplicity and repetitiveness. I felt at home with it. But when I was… dying," her voice broke a little, "all I could think of was 'too short'. 'My life was too short.' Those last few weeks with you and Sacchan… I was so scared that would be all I would ever know and – " She paused.

She's cute when she's sad, thought Bran. He shuddered, remembering her heartbeat slowing down, her body growing cold in his hands as he carried her up the forest path. Then he remembered her kiss – clumsy, naïve, and so unlike Satō's thirsty caress. It had taken him completely by surprise.

It must have been her first.

He reached his arm around her and pulled her close. She didn't resist, but didn't look up to him, either. She let out a quiet sigh and he felt her body relax; it seemed she was content just standing near him. She looked up to the sky and sung in a soft voice:

Ohoshi-sama kirakira

Sora-kara miteiru…

The stars twinkle in the sky

Looking at us from above…

"I've never heard you sing before."

"It's a song of the Tanabata festival… the story of Orihime and Hikoboshi. They can only meet once a year, on a bridge of magpies thrown over the River of Stars…"

She fell silent again. He didn't know how long they stood like that, looking at the moon and the sky splattered with bright pin pricks. His breath slowed down and his mind was clear; he realised he inadvertently slipped into the meditation Shigemasa was teaching him. Outside the red dust plain – the *Otherworld* - he couldn't quite sense his dragon yet, just a certain weak buzz, like a droning insect. He raised his hand and focused. A tiny flame, no greater than a burning match, appeared in the middle of his palm.

"Oh!" Nagomi clasped her hands. "You can do magic again!"

The flame disappeared.

"Yes, though only this much, and with great effort."

"Does that mean you'll be able to ride your *dorako* again?"

"I hope so," he replied.

A sudden movement in the water caught Bran's eye.

"What in *Annwn* – "

A long, black shape cut swiftly through the dark sea across their path. Captain Kawamura had no chance to avoid it – it was too low and too fast for him to see. At the last moment, the shape swerved aside – but it was too late. *Iroha Maru*'s prow jumped up and the entire ship rocked from side to side, throwing Bran and Nagomi onto the deck.

By the time Bran scrambled to his feet and helped Nagomi up, the ship was listing at a few degrees to starboard. He had spent enough time on sea to know what it meant; the hull was breached and they were taking in water.

Not again...

CHAPTER X

Wulfhere of Warwick woke up, raised a hand to wipe his tired eyes and hissed in pain.

"Careful. That arm is still healing."

I don't remember being wounded in the arm.

He opened his eyes. Hywel was sitting by his bed, half-smiling, his shoulder in a binding, his head swollen and wrapped in thick bandages.

"What happened?"

"They say it's because you struck that... *thing.* It will be sore for a few days."

"What was it?"

Hywel shrugged with one shoulder.

"Only the Qin know."

Wulfhere spotted two Qin faces in the tent's entrance. They disappeared the moment they saw him look at them.

"And who are they?" he asked Hywel.

"Your worshippers," the Prydain boy said with a chuckle.

A Qin man entered the tent; round-faced, sporting a crescent moustache over narrow
lips.

"You've made quite a name for yourself, Lieutenant," the Qinese said in good, slightly lisping Seaxe.

"I'm just an Ensign."

"Not anymore," said Hywel. "You were promoted."

"Why? And what do you mean, 'worshippers'?"

"You've struck down a Black Lotus," the Qin man said.

"Black Lotus... is that what you call it?"

"It, and others like it, yes. They are members of a secret society, attaching themselves to any disturbance in hope of profit."

"But I... I didn't kill it."

"Nobody can kill a Black Lotus – or so they say... but you've harmed it and made it leave the battlefield, Lieutenant. That is a feat worthy of a great warrior," the Qin main said. He wrapped his right fist with his left hand and bowed.

"I was lucky," replied Wulfhere in a subdued voice.

"What is wrong with you, Wulf!" Hywel said, laughing. "I thought you'd be bragging about this to everyone!"

The Seaxe closed his eyes and took a deep breath. The sight of Nechtan, twitching and dying in the creature's grasp, flashed under his eyelids.

"I'm still tired, that's all."

"Sure, sure. I'll let you rest."

Hywel stood up and left the tent. The Qin man remained.

"Who are you?" asked Wulfhere.

"My name is Li," the man replied, bowing again. "I am merely a servant of my Lord Bohan, the Commander of the Imperial Army."

"What do you want from me?"

"To see the hero and wish him good health."

"Thank you."

Uninvited, Li pulled himself up a stool.

"I hear you have royal blood in your veins."

How in Hel *does he know that?*

"My ancestor was a king of Dracaland, yes."

"Forgive me asking, but why then were you a mere ensign until now? And one without a dragon, too? In Qin, you would be a high-ranking officer already."

As I should be!

"My commanders aren't fond of me. They are mostly *waelesc.*"

"*Waelesc?*"

"Prydain. They are of a different, older race. A race we once conquered. They hold many grudges against us, Seaxe."

Li nodded. His face brightened.

"Ah, now I understand. My commander is of the Hunan people, from the South. We seem to have similar... misunderstandings. But, Commodore *Dí Lán* is a Prydain, no?"

"I don't know much about him. His son..."

"His son?"

"Why are you interested in the Commodore anyway, Li?"

"I am a curious man," Li replied with a smile. "And the Commodore is an interesting person. I didn't know he had a son?"

"I studied with him at the Academy. He would be here if it wasn't for the disaster at sea."

"He is dead, then. How unfortunate."

"No, no," Wulfhere said, waving his hands excitedly. "He's got a Llambed Seal. That would have saved his life."

"A Llambed Seal?"

"A spell all graduates of Llambed have. The rumour has it he's been transported out of Qin, nobody knows where. Somewhere safe."

"Out of Qin? And the Commodore is not trying to look for him?"

Wulfhere shrugged. "He's a soldier. He's got his orders."

"Fascinating. Well, it's been an interesting chat," the Qinese said, standing up. "I certainly enjoyed it. Do you mind if I come here again?"

"Not at all."

Li bowed and left the tent.

What a nice fellow, thought Wulfhere.

Gwenlian woke up; in the darkness of the tent, she saw the silhouette of a man sitting on the edge of her bed, with his head in his hands.

She was just a Flight Leader when they had first met, five years earlier. He was commanding her regiment at the time. Dashing, handsome, bright, with a scarred, mature face, he was popular among both the women and men of the Second Royal alike. They all loved and respected him and it was no surprise that she had fallen for him at once.

She preferred not to ask, but sometimes she wondered about his feelings. Who was she for him? Their relationship lasted too long to count as a passing distraction in time of war. She knew he had a wife in Gwynedd, Bran's mother, but he never talked about her and she was grateful for that.

She reached out to him and caressed his back.

"What's wrong, Dylan?"

He raised his head slowly.

"Do you think Edern would make a good commander?"

What brought that on?

"He's proving himself well in the field," she replied.

"Yes, he does, doesn't he? He's got an affinity with the Qin he trains. They like him."

"They like you, too. They like anyone who brings guns and victory. What's wrong?" she repeated, twirling the jade necklace he gave her at Shanglin.

Dylan sighed and lay back by her side.

"I can't do it anymore. I think I'm growing old."

"Is it about Shanglin? This has nothing to do with us."

"You know they couldn't have done it without our help."

"I warned you there would be trouble."

"What was I to do? I had my orders."

"Well, you're thinking of doing something *now*. I can tell."

"I can't betray my country. I've sworn to serve until... until..."

"What? You're not planning something *stupid*, Dylan? Think about your son."

"I am thinking about him. Gwen, I was wrong. I should be out there, looking for him. I should be in Yamato."

"*Yamato?* How do you know – "

"I *know*. I was guessing before, but now I'm certain."

"You've already decided," she said, after studying him for a while. She knew that look; there was nothing she could say or do to change his mind.

"Will you help me?" he asked, taking her by the wrist.

"We'll be court-martialled if they find out. You'll be stripped of rank, and your family will get no pension. We'll be lucky to get out of it alive."

"But you *will* help me."

"I know you, Dylan ab Ifor. You've already planned how to get out of all possible trouble."

He smiled and leaned to kiss her.

Dylan knocked on the flaps of Edern's tent.

"Banneret?"

"Coming!"

The Tylwyth's head appeared in the opening. His face was flushed, his hair unkempt. "Yes, Commodore?"

"I need you at the headquarters."

"What's going on? I didn't hear an alarm."

"We have to plan our next attack. I want to move before the Imperial Army does."

"Oh. Right, I'll be there in ten minutes."

"Who have you got there, Edern?" Dylan asked.

Edern glanced around with shifty eyes and then grinned, mischievously. "Admiral's *aide*," he whispered.

Dylan chuckled.

"You sly fox. You have ten minutes. I'll be waiting."

"What's all this about, then?" asked Edern, running his slender fingers through his silver hair.

Dylan traced the staff map with his finger, leaving a golden trail where he touched the paper. A grid of such lines in different colours marked the imagined movements of the wings and squadrons, all concentrating on a small town, some forty miles north-west of Huating.

He stood up and looked around. There were just a few of them in the room – the Ardian of the Twelfth Light, the Commander of a small squadron of gunboats which had recently arrived to replace Admiral Reynolds's fleet, Gwen and Edern; it was still the same sparse brick warehouse in the Concession he had been using when the Second had first appeared in Huating. Dylan preferred this place to any other of the proposed locations for the staff headquarters: it was the only one where he was certain there were no Qin spies.

"Chansu," Edern deciphered. "That's in an opposite direction to where our main forces are."

Dylan nodded. "But this is where the *Bohan* will strike next. I want that city *ours*."

"Why the hurry? Were there some new orders from Lundenburgh?" asked Seton, the Ardian of the Twelfth. Dylan glanced at him and caught himself inadvertently biting his lips. The man had an indecipherable, blank face, hidden behind a great Seaxe moustache.

"Yes," replied Dylan, looking Seton straight in the eyes.

They had met once before, a year earlier: Seton was the commander of the Foot detachment saved from the Birkenhead disaster. His exemplary conduct on board the ship had earned him quick promotion.

Since arriving in Huating, he had made it clear on several occasions that he would not let the debt of gratitude get in the way of his sense of duty.

"May we see those orders, Commodore?" Seton asked.

"They are for my eyes only."

I won't have another massacre on my hands.

Seton's eyes narrowed, but he said nothing. Edern leaned over the map, rubbing his chin. "Will we make it, though? With just two regiments of dragons and without the *Bohan*'s infantry…"

"The city lies near the coast. The gunboats will be more than enough replacement for the Imperial Army."

The navy man nodded sharply. He didn't seem to be bothered with the sudden change of plans.

There would be no trouble with this one, at least.

"I want us to fly in three days. The Rebels will not expect us so soon; they think the *Bohan* is still in the South."

Seton's finger traced a red line between Chansu and the rebel headquarters at Suchou, and stopped at a complex of several large bodies of water.

"That's only twenty miles to send reinforcements, and we won't be able to stop them beyond those lakes."

"Me and my men will take care of the left flank," said Dylan.

"Oh?" Seton raised an eyebrow.

"I will leave the glory of entering the city to yourself, Ardian." Dylan smiled.

Maybe that will get you off my back.

Wulfhere's task required discretion and skill, but he struggled to even keep his dragon in a straight line. His arm was still sore, his command of reins not up to scratch and proper Farlink was out of the question; this was one of the fresh batch of mounts, barely broken. And it wasn't even a typical military breed, but a Highland Grey – a Shadowcloud, like the one ridden by Dean Magnusdottir.

The other soldier in his detail was a quiet, dark-haired Kernow girl, Keyna. She was riding a tiny Kernow Crimson, a most unusual mount for a Light Dragoon.

It's even smaller than that frog Bran was riding.

The Crimson was fast, but not very strong. Together, the two riders were an odd pair. Wulf had no say in who was assigned as his newly acquired command. Keyna accepted his orders with just a nod of the head and a mumbled *yessir* from under a long fringe. She had expressed no surprise when he told her where they were going.

"We are assigned to the Royal Marines, to Commodore's guards," Wulf had said, "at Ardian Seton's request. It's an honour, you see. Because of what I did."

Keyna nodded, not impressed in the slightest. He sighed; he was getting used to everyone knowing him as the Hero of Qiang River.

Commodore Dylan was leading a charge of Silvers and Azures on a rebel column trying to get across a narrow strip of land between two large lakes. The battle was brief; the rebels had only a few dragons of their own, and there were no heavy weapons or mysterious tricks like at the Shanglin. Below, the footmen of the Ever Victorious Army were moving in to mop-up the survivors and secure the perimeter among the burning remains of the oxcarts and walking machines.

But the Commodore did not seem satisfied with the outcome of the fight. To Wulfhere's surprise, he and several other dragons split from the main skein and flew north, across one of the lakes, towards a line of old rebel fortifications.

What's he doing?

Wulf spurred his mount to fly higher, into the low-hanging clouds, and follow the Commodore. He noticed Keyna dragging behind.

She can't keep up. He rolled his eyes. *That's the problem with those small dragons. No stamina at all.*

"Go back to Ardian Seton," he cried an order. "Tell him what happened."

The girl nodded and turned around. Wulf was now alone inside the grey-white fog. He could still see the Commodore's silver mount clearly, but his own dragon's scales turned a shimmering, semi-translucent grey that made it so perfect for the mission he had been tasked with.

He hadn't told Keyna the other reason for his assignment.

"Keep an eye on the Commodore," the Ardian had told Wulf after the main debriefing. "That's why I'm giving you a Shadowcloud. Let me know if you see anything suspicious."

Well this is certainly suspicious, he thought. The Commodore's detachment – five riders altogether, Wulf counted – dived towards the fortifications. The rebels manning them opened fire from all sorts of weapons – rockets, cannons, muskets and repeating rifles; the sky filled with smoke and explosions. The dragons spewed fire and lightning, but where one gun was silenced, two more barrels answered in a hellish cackle.

A squadron of Qin *long* appeared from over the hills to the West – a dozen beasts at least. Wulf was reminded of his own patrol mistake, when he had lost his own dragon.

There's too few of them. They will be massacred!

A tactical error of this scale was very unlike the Commodore. The Qin descended upon the five Western mounts from three sides. One of the Dracalish dragons broke off and, in a wounded zigzag, headed back across the lake, then another. The third spiralled down, its rider stunned by a near explosion; the mount recovered just above the ground and retreated as well.

When just the two riders remained, the Commodore turned sharply north and, breaking through the cloud of enemy with ease, sped along the lake shore, soon finding himself out of the range of the rebel guns. The *longs* soon abandoned their pursuit, unable to keep up. Only Wulfhere's Grey could match the full speed of a Mountain Silver.

This was a no-man's land between the frontlines of the two armies; camps of marauders strewn among abandoned villages and ruined fields, flooded by swollen rivers and canals unbound from the confines of shattered dams and broken levees.

What are they doing here?

Wulfhere kept up a safe distance, unnoticed by both the pair of riders and anyone on the ground. Trying to navigate in the thickening clouds, he almost missed the Commodore and the other dragon land beyond a ridge of low, steep dunes bordering the lake on the north-east, lined with birch and willow.

Wulf pulled on the reins and directed his mount to the bottom of the ridge; he flew below the tree canopies, thankful for the new dragon's natural stealth.

I would make a mess of this landing on any other mount, he thought.

The dragon touched down in the sand silently like a cat. Wulfhere jumped off and climbed carefully to the top of the dune, where he dropped to the ground and crawled the rest of the way through wild wheat and tall grass.

He found the Commodore and the other rider – Wulf recognized the Reeve of the Second Marines – in a narrow ridge on the dune slope. The Commodore was tracing a complex pattern on the sand with black powder.

"But you used up all three charges of your Seal years ago," said the Reeve.

The Commodore finished the rune and shook the powder off his hands.

"Only you and Edern know that."

"And have you told Edern of your plan?"

"He will guess what happened when he sees this. Now move back. I know it's just an illusion, but it's the most powerful one I've ever made."

The Commodore knelt down and touched the pattern. He spoke a sequence of spell words too quietly for Wulfhere to hear. The sand exploded with blinding white light.

When Wulf's sight returned, he saw a column of radiance rising high above the dunes, piercing and tearing through the clouds.

This must be visible for miles around... he thought, and then he realized what it was – or rather, supposed to be.

The Seal of Llambed! He's faked the Seal!

He looked back down. The Commodore and the Reeve were mounting a dragon – only one, the great Silver of the Commodore.

The other Silver was in its death throes, tearing the dune's slope with its claws.

She used the Kill Word, Wulf realized with a shudder. The Commodore raised a hand and shot a tongue of flame at the dying dragon. It added little to its suffering, but the scorched scales made the death seem even more violent.

"I'm sorry, Gwen," the Commodore said to the Reeve, "it was the only way."

"I understand," she replied, "but are you sure we'll make it to the Bataavian ship on just one dragon?"

"It shouldn't be more than a day's flight from here. They couldn't reach to Yamato yet. And Afroleus is strong."

"Edern will be angry you didn't take him with you."

"He will understand. The Ever Victorious Army needs a commander if they are to reach Chansu before the Imperial Army."

The great Silver beast spread its wings, oblivious to the fate of the other beast. Wulf shuffled to the side, to hide himself underneath the branches of a weeping willow as the Commodore flew above him. He waited a couple of minutes to make sure neither he nor his Shadowcloud were spotted, and then made his way back down the slope.

He had heard a lot – but it didn't mean anything to him. And something told him Ardian Seton would know just as little.

But there was somebody else who *might* know…

The ocean was big, empty and the colour of pure lapis lazuli under the cloudless sky.

"I'm having second thoughts, Dylan," said Gwen. They had been flying in a zigzag line for a whole day. Since leaving the shores of Qin and passing through the Barrier, they saw no ship or even a boat.

She removed her goggles and put the spyglass to her eye.

"How can we possibly find anything in this vastness?"

"I've studied these seas. There are only so many ways a sail ship can pass through. The winds, the currents… the Bataavians *must* be here somewhere."

"What if we missed them?"

"Let's hope not."

Afreolus roared and buckled. Dylan sensed the beast's irritation with the long journey, and growing restlessness.

"Afreolus is nasty today," remarked Gwen.

"Yes, it's been like that for a while."

"It can't be going feral yet? You only got it after the first Panjab."

"It's been ten years now."

"I remember your previous mount. An Azure, not Silver."

"I lost it to the jungle madness. Pity. I liked it."

"You always said you preferred the Azures."

He nodded. "They make fine companions."

He regarded his mount's long silver neck and horned head. Always an unruly beast, Afreolus was growing ever more stubborn as years went by.

Not long now, he thought. *A year at best, if all goes well.*

"Are you alright?" asked Gwen. "After the Kill Word, I mean."

"I'm fine, really. A bit disoriented without my dragon's wind sense. Where are we?" asked Gwen, looking at the featureless sea below. Dylan traced the rough light map in the air.

"About two hundred and fifty miles south-east of Huating. Another hundred miles this way there's a chain of islands which lie beyond the Sea Maze."

"Can we land there?"

"If we fail to find the ship. But there's still a day or so of flying left in Afreolus. Let's make the best of it."

Gwen rummaged in the saddle bags.

"Do you want some bread?"

"No, I'm fine. I'll have *cwrw*, maybe, if there's still some left in the canteen."

She leaned back to open another bag.

"There! Look! Five o'clock!"

Dylan turned his head and followed her finger with his eyes. On the edge of the curving horizon a sharp, white, triangular dot stood out against the canvas of lapis lazuli. The unmistakable trace of a ship's wake.

"Could be them," said Dylan and spurred Afreolus around. The dragon growled, struggling in the reins.

"Come here, you dumb beast!"

The mount resisted again, ignoring the Farlink command and the tugging reins. Dylan cursed and summoned a Soul Lance with a buzz. He touched the dragon's scales with its tip; he knew to a dragon it felt like being prodded with a red hot poker. Afreolus yowled and shook its head but obeyed at last.

The brass letters on the stern spelled the name "Soembing".

"It looks so… ancient!" cried Dylan.

The Bataavian ship was a two-hundred feet long three-master, with a single thin funnel between fore- and mizzen-masts. The engine was silent; the wind was good, and all the sails were up. The single row of six antique cannons may have been impressive in native ports, but were useless against any modern vessel.

Dylan scratched his scar.

"I've seen Bataavian ships. They're just as good as ours. I don't even know if I can land on this shell."

"They don't seem to expect a fight," said Gwen.

They swooped towards the ship. Afreolus sensed an incoming fight and shook its head triumphantly, nearly tearing the reins out of Dylan's hands. The Bataavians noticed them when it was almost too late. Most sailors fled under deck, unable to withstand the dragon fear. A few remained, valiantly, and responded to the attack with small arms fire; rifle bullets and lightning bolts struck the *tarian* surrounding the dragon, bouncing harmlessly off. Dylan circled the ship a couple of times, looking for a good place to land.

I could sink it in moments, he thought. *It should be in a museum!*

A hatch on the bow opened and the multi-barrelled mouth of a rocket-launcher spat missiles after Afreolus. Dylan pulled on the upper reins, turning the dragon on its back in a half-roll. The beast spewed flame, scorching the first wave of the rockets. But one got through; it exploded underneath the dragon's right wing in a hail of sparks and shrapnel. The *tarian* held, but the noise and flash angered and frightened the beast. For a second, Dylan lost the link with his mount altogether.

It's over, he thought in sudden desperation. *I was wrong. Its mind is gone.*

"Dylan, we need to land!"

"I'm trying!"

It's on the brink of going feral! How in Annwn *did I miss that earlier?*

Struggling to retain control over the dragon, Dylan dived for the poop deck, the only surface wide enough for a landing. Just as the dragon's claws were about to touch the deck, another, stray rocket burst above his head. The dragon landed with a huge crash, rolled on its side and, losing its grip on the boards, slid down onto the quarterdeck with a terrible crackle; it broke through the rigging and smashed against the mizzen-mast, snapping it in two with the force of the massive impact. With a deafening creek, the mast slowly fell, covering Dylan, Gwen, the dragon and some of the Bataavian crew with the heavy shroud of white canvas sails.

Dylan felt the dreaded *snap* in his mind, and then the all-too-familiar emptiness. The beast growled and threw both riders off in a spasm of fury, tearing its way out through the sail, helping itself with bursts of dragonflame. Dylan dodged the splinters of timber flying all over the place; a stray tongue of flame reached the main mast, and the course sail caught fire. Some of the Bataavian sailors tried to stop the beast with their thunder guns, but that only made it more angry and frightened.

Dylan finally found his way out from under the fallen mast. He saw Gwen standing against the gunwale, defending herself with the Soul Lance and shield from several panicked Bataavians. She was staggering. A long gash ran down her left leg. The sailors' efforts to subdue her were half-hearted; they were more concerned with the dragon wrecking the ship behind their backs.

He focused and sent a command through the Farlink; then another, stronger. A wave of anger was the only response. The beast was too far gone. It attacked a man now, ripping him in two with its claws and biting the other through with the mighty jaw. Blood and guts spilled on the deck.

It's too late.

Dylan closed his eyes and focused again. His lips moved noiselessly as he pronounced the Kill Word.

Afreolus raised its head and screamed an ear-splitting, devastating yell; it buckled in spasms, tearing the planking apart with its claws. It coughed, spitting several great balls of flame, which ignited everything in its path. It beat its wings and jumped, trying to fly away. Its death throes rolled the ship from side to side, and the beast started sliding off the bloodied deck. In a last effort, it held on to the gunwale with teeth and claw. The ship listed dangerously, and for a moment it seemed the dragon would pull it down to the bottom of the sea with it. At last, the wooden planks snapped away and Afreolus fell, splashing, into the water.

Dylan fell to his knees; the backlash of the dragon's death made him briefly deaf and blind, leaving what he knew would be a great mental scar – another one to add to the many. He wiped a nose-bleed and as the sight slowly returned to him, looked up.

He was staring straight into four barrels of a repeating air gun.

"What are we going to do about them, *Kapitein*?" a sailor, holding Dylan at gunpoint, asked a tall, red-haired, long-faced man in a black-and-orange uniform.

"We can't risk any more delay," the Captain replied. "Throw them overboard."

Dylan smirked. He was standing against the shattered bulwark next to Gwenlian, with his hands on the back of his head. He glanced at the planks and noticed something curious: from under the wooden boarding torn off by Afreolus military-grade steel showed through.

This is an ironclad, after all!

"What are *you* laughing about," the sailor barked, pushing the barrel closer.

"I've survived worse," said Dylan.

"You speak Bataavian?"

"I've spent two years at Bretten, Captain… Fabius, isn't it? I remember you commanding a rather more… contemporary vessel."

The Captain frowned.

"Who *are* you?"

"I am Commodore Dylan ab Ifor of the Royal Marines. I need to get to Yamato."

"Commodore? Dracaland is at peace with Bataave! Why did you attack us?"

"I'm not here on behalf of my country. All the damage was unintended, and I will recompense you as soon as we reach a friendly shore."

"I have men dead."

"I'm sorry."

"Why *are* you here, Commodore?"

"I'm looking for my son."

Captain Fabius gave Dylan a long, curious look, then waved his hand at the sailor with the gun.

"Lock them down. I want to hear this story."

Before Dylan opened his mouth, a cry came from the quarterdeck, where the Soembing's crew was busy putting down fires started by the dying Afreolus.

"*Kapitein! Andere draak!*"

The Captain looked up; the Commodore and the Reeve did the same. High above the Soembing's two remaining masts, beyond the range of any of the ship's cannons, circled a great Qin dragon, gleaming golden in the sun.

"Friends of yours?" Fabius asked.

"No," said Dylan, "but I think I know who it is. I would advise you let *this* one land."

CHAPTER XI

Shakushain breathed in the crisp, sulphuric air and gazed down from the summit of the volcanic cone. The peak of the fire mountain rose tall from the bottom of a vast, bowl-shaped valley, the rim of which loomed in a vertical cliff on the horizon. Several craters spewed yellow smoke and grey ash all over the rough slope. The raw, savage landscape reminded Shakushain of his homeland, far in the freezing North.

"This is a good place, demon!" he cried. The Crimson Robe turned around with a grin.

"Glad you like it."

"Are you sure it will come *here*?"

"Sooner or later. This is where all of Chinzei's magic is centred. And a beast like that will follow the lines of magic, unbeknownst to itself. When will your trap be ready?"

"Soon, demon. Soon."

He picked up a couple of wooden stakes from a pile and proceeded to insert them into holes dug in the living, steaming rock. He had spent two days preparing the stakes – shaving the wood of the young alder tree; carving the magic patterns; summoning the *kamuy* spirits to inhabit each and every one of the pieces of wood. This was going to be the greatest sacred enclosure the world had seen. Only fitting for the greatest prey ever caught.

He reached the seventh slot when a quarrel caught his ear. He saw three of the Crimson Robe's men – the grey-clad *rōnin* – standing over his dark-skinned companion, mocking him and laughing at the orders the small man tried to give them in his strained, guttural accent.

Shakushain threw the stakes to the ground and in few quick strides approached the laughing men. Without warning, he punched the nearer one in the face. The swordsman fell down senseless; blood trickled from his ears and nose.

"You will all do as Koro says," he said, pointing a finger at the remaining two. "He's a better man than all of you put together."

They bowed and departed quickly, mumbling curses. Koro followed after them, waving his small fist. There was still a lot of work to do before the circle was finished.

He bent the last of the willow boughs, slotted it through a loop made of stripped bark and stepped back to admire his work. The figure was as tall as a man, and twice as long, woven densely out of willow, bamboo and birch. The wings were the most difficult, a delicate structure tied together with vines. A covering of butterbur leaves imitated the green scales.

Shakushain hadn't seen the dragon he was trying to replicate in the sculpture, but it didn't matter. The figurines of bears and wolves he made as a young shaman's apprentice always came out resembling disfigured pigs, but they worked nonetheless. This one was the same – only bigger.

With Koro's help, Shakushain carefully transported the fragile structure into the middle of the sacred enclosure, then he tied its delicate limbs and wings with a chain woven of poison ivy. *Like for like,* such was the rule of the Northern magic. To trap the real dragon, he had to first shackle the imitation.

He lit up two bonfires, one on each side of the circle – beacons for the crazed beast. It was near; the demon's spies had brought the news of it ravaging the pastures on the southern rim of the Aso Valley. That meant they should see its flames tonight; he hoped the beast would fall into the trap by midnight.

Koro cried out excitedly and waved his hands. His blue necklace was glowing. Shakushain ran up to him and looked in the direction where the little man pointed. A dot of light flashed against the dark shadow of the southern cliff-side, followed by a blast, and a bright line of flame. A second later a whoosh of hurricane-like wind and a sound of explosion reached where they were standing.

It's coming.

Samuel fell off his bunk and slid across the floor, hitting the opposite wall with his shoulder. The entire ship shook from some heavy impact, rolling to one side and then back again.

All the alarm bells rang out at once, all the evertorches lit up. The bearded sailors ran past Samuel back and forth, shouting orders and repeating them further. The ship was listing and, as far as Samuel could tell by the changes in air pressure, rapidly descending.

The doctor's instincts kicked in.

There may be wounded. I should be in the infirmary.

But the layout of the vessel was yet unfamiliar to him and instead of the infirmary, he found himself in a corridor he hadn't seen before. It was eerily empty and quiet compared to the chaos everywhere else. A door at the end caught his eye. It was unlike any other on the ship. He approached it slowly. Made of a slab of patinaed bronze, it had no visible handle, just a red locking rune blinking slowly where a keyhole should be. Samuel touched the metal surface; it was freezing cold.

I shouldn't be here.

He realised his hands were shaking and his throat felt dry. He turned back and hurried down another corridor, down a flight of metal stairs. This led him straight to the ship's bridge. An officer shot out through the round door and Samuel had never been so happy to see another human being. The crewman looked at Samuel in bewilderment, waved him aside and ran on with some important orders. Inside, the Admiral was sitting at his desk of many knobs and buttons, holding the steering wheel with one hand and pushing levers with another. He, too, was shouting something at the navigator, who was clutching a broken, bleeding nose and trying helplessly to plot a course on the map which seemed to consist mostly of a blank space and a few scattered navigation points.

Samuel's grasp of the basics of the Varyagan language allowed him to understand some of the Admiral's yells and curses.

"*Vad fan!* That was a *mistfirer*! What's a *mistfirer* doing in these waters?"

"I don't know, *Amiral*. We are definitely in the right place."

Somebody pushed Samuel aside and barged into the cabin.

"Nobelius!" the Admiral hollered, "do you have the *skaderappor*?"

"The *komandotorn* is breached and the *roder* is stuck."

"Can we hold her up?"

"Only if we blow all the ballast."

The old engineer and the Admiral began to exchange technical naval jargon at great speed, and Samuel lost track of the conversation. He decided to depart from the bridge and look for the sick bay elsewhere.

"*Doktor!*" the Admiral shouted after him. "Shouldn't you be at the infirmary?"

Satō woke up in pitch-black darkness. Her head throbbed and her left shoulder was sore from where she had hit the floor. She stood up on wobbly legs; the cold seawater, rushing through the narrow, jagged breach in the ship's iron hull, reached her knees and was rising fast. The only light she could see was the small glass window in the cauldron, where the elementals frantically continued to exchange their magical energies.

The ladder should be somewhere to the left... or was it right?

She stumbled and grabbed some handle; a valve opened, letting out steam.

Oh no! I broke something!

She tried to set the handle back to its original position, but slipped and dropped to the floor again with a splash.

The trap door opened above her head and somebody leapt into the water. A strong arm grabbed her and led her towards the ladder.

"It's alright," she said weakly, "I can manage..."

Somebody pulled her up onto the deck, somebody's hands loosened her clothes and held her while she retched out the seawater.

"Get this hose down," somebody shouted.

Captain Kawamura.

She was beginning to recognize the voices and the faces around her. Red hair – Nagomi, standing closest, worried. The Captain, setting up some heavy iron device with a long leather hose attached. The bear-man's storm of hair.

"Where's Bran?" she asked.

"Downstairs," answered Nagomi.

The Westerner appeared up the ladder, soaked through, spurting water.

"I got him out of the water, but won't manage to bring him up here."

"Bring whom?" asked Satō. She had a nagging feeling she was forgetting somebody.

"The *Daisen*! He's unconscious."

"I can help," the priestess stood up, but the Captain stopped her.

"Nobody's coming down until we stabilize the ship," he said. "If that cauldron floods, you'll be boiled alive. Come, Kumaso, I will need all your strength."

Torishi rushed up to the device Captain Kawamura had set up.

"Keep pressing that end of the lever," the Captain ordered. "Try to synchronize with me. Can you do that?"

Torishi nodded.

"One of you needs to make sure the hose isn't crooked and the water flows freely," the Captain said to Bran and Nagomi. The priestess straightened the coils and dropped the end of the hose overboard.

"What about the breach?" asked Bran. "The water is still coming in."

"One thing at a time. We'd need a wizard to fix it and our only one just got himself knocked out."

"I'm a wizard," said Satō. The Captain looked at her and stopped pumping for a moment.

"You're hurt," he said.

"It's just a bruise. What needs to be done?"

"How good a swimmer are you?"

She slumped.

There was never time to learn...

"Not very good."

"I'll help you," said Bran. "The sea is calm enough; I can hold you while you cast spells."

He dropped his clothes quickly, leaving only the linen loincloth, and leapt into the sea. She heard him yell and, fearing something terrible had happened, ran up to the bulwark.

"Cold!" he shouted, spitting. "Come on, I'll catch you!"

She stood against the rail, paralyzed with fear at the thought of leaping into the dark abyss.

He's shaming me again. I can't swim, I can't ride a horse... what kind of samurai am I?

She took a deep breath and jumped over the edge. Freezing water enveloped her.

I'm drowning, she thought. *I'm going to die.*

She started thrashing about in panic, until a strong pair of hands embraced her tightly and pulled her up to the surface.

"Calm down," said Bran. "It's harder when you move about."

With one arm wrapped around her waist, he swam slowly towards the stern, helping himself along the way by holding onto the spokes of the silenced paddle-wheel. The pistons were quiet, and the ship drifted sideways on the waves.

"The breach is under the water-line. Can you hold your breath for long?" he asked.

She nodded. She was certain she could do at least that much. He pulled her down and she inadvertently opened her mouth. Instantly, they emerged back to the surface.

"It's all right, we'll try again. Did you see the breach?"

"No," she said, coughing. "I had my eyes closed."

He chuckled. "I'll try to guide you. Can you cast with your eyes closed?"

"I have to say the word."

"As long as you remember to only exhale. Right, one more time – on the count of three. One, two, *three!*"

They submerged much more gently this time. She felt his hand on hers, holding it straight and steady. He tapped her gently on the waist with his other hand.

"*Bebblubblu!*" she cried. The sound of the spell word was distorted by the water, but it didn't matter, what was important was her mental focus on the incantation. She felt her hand turn cold as the bolt of ice shot from her fingers, freezing the water around it.

They were back on the surface.

"Almost there. One more try," said Bran. "Deep breath. One, two, three."

She repeated the spell, this time trying to keep her eyes open. The salt stung, but she endured, making sure she covered the bubbling breach with a thick layer of frost.

"I've never... done... magic under water," she said, coughing and spluttering and trying to wipe salt from her eyes.

"Don't touch your eyes," said Bran, "it will only make it worse. You need to wash it with fresh water."

They swam back towards the stern, where Nagomi threw down a rope ladder. Now that the immediate danger was gone, Satō relaxed, letting Bran drag her freely against the waves; she felt the warmth of his body pressing against hers through soaked clothes.

No, she scolded herself. *You promised yourself.*

She climbed down to the engine room to secure the breach from inside. The water was now just up to her ankles, too low for the pump to be of any use, so Bran, Torishi and the Captain were pouring it out with buckets.

"That was quite a whale," said Captain Kawamura, assessing the breach.

"A whale?"

"What else? There are no reefs here."

"That spell won't last long," said Satō.

"We'll bring her to port in the morning," the Captain replied, "I know a place where we'll be safe from prying eyes."

Satō came up to Nagomi, who was kneeling by the still unconscious Heishichi, trying her best to wake him up.

"How is he?" the wizardess asked.

"Not badly injured."

The priestess's fingers glowed light blue, and the girl murmured a brief prayer. The *Daisen* coughed, gasped and opened his eyes. He sat up and shook his head. Satō turned her eyes away; the wizard's scorched face still made her nauseous.

"My glasses..."

"Here," said Nagomi, handing him the wire-framed pair. "I'm afraid one of the lenses broke..."

"Thank you."

"You should thank Bran," said Satō, nodding towards the boy. "He got you out of the water."

Heishichi stood up, cast Bran an empty stare and went to examine the damage to the ship.

"Did you do this?" he asked Satō, pointing at the ice.

"Yes."

"We could use a talent like you in our school. Our last ice mage died in Kirishima."

She couldn't help smiling.

"Thank you, but I have my own *dōjō* to run in Kiyō."

He smirked. "That's not what I heard."

The smile perished from her face.

The *Iroha Maru* moored at a low stone pier with a bump. Bran jumped off under Kawamura's direction to assist with tying the ship's hawsers to the bollards.

The place they landed in was a small town, little more than a village, hidden at the northern end of a long, narrow gulf. It was surrounded on all sides by tall, steep hills covered with lush green forest, except for one narrow pass to the west, where some farmers toiled what looked like barley fields.

There was only the one pier in the harbour. The small fishing boats used by the villagers had been towed out onto the wide beach of fine grey volcanic sand. Sparkling in the noon sun, the shallow sea had the colour of bright jade.

"This is wonderful!" said Nagomi. "What is this place?"

"Sakitsu on Amakusa Island," the Captain said. "We're almost at the edge of Yamato."

"Wait," said Satō, stopping half-way down the gangway, "I know that name. Isn't this part of *Taikun*'s personal domain? Are we really safe here?"

"They can answer your question, Takashima-*sama*," the Captain replied, nodding towards the end of the pier. There was already a group of curious children waiting there, and one or two fishermen coming to see the strange boat. An official looking man came up to greet the newcomers. He was wearing a long black robe, tied with hemp rope, and a tall Phrygian cap. He greeted them with a singing accent. Bran hesitated.

"If I didn't know better, I'd say you were..." he struggled to find a Yamato word, but could only come up with a Latin equivalent, "a *pater*."

"I am, indeed, *pater*. My name is Kukai."

"You are a Sun Worshipper!"

The man nodded.

"Driven to these islands by persecution, we remain faithful to the religion of our fathers. What is this strange vessel?" he added, pointing at the ship.

The Captain leaned over the edge.

"This is the private yacht of His Excellency, Shimazu Nariakira of Satsuma," he said. "We need to stay the night to make some repairs, if it's alright with you."

"Any subject of Shimazu-*dono* is welcome on Amakusa. We have long enjoyed his friendship and assistance."

"You kids go see the town," the Captain said, spitting tobacco discreetly into a handkerchief, "me and *Daisen-sama* will get to work."

"Please, let me show you around," said the man in the Phrygian cap.

The settlement had just a few narrow streets, lined with modest, simple houses, huddled on the edge of a cliff. The farther from the pier Bran went, the stronger a certain emotion he failed to recognize grew within from the very depths of his soul. It was directed at the *pater* and his congregation and absorbed him so much he barely noticed what went on around him.

"So many children..." he heard Nagomi say. "The town must be rich."

"On the contrary," said *pater* Kukai, "the soil here is poor – what little of it there is – and the fish avoid these coasts. But the *Taikun* keeps sending new colonist families every year."

"So I was right. This place does belong to the *Taikun*," said Satō.

"In name only... There is a *bugyō* on the island, but he lives across the mountains, on the Kumamoto side. All he's interested in is sending the colonists as far away as possible. Most of them end up here."

"And you turn them all into Sun Worshippers?" asked Bran.

"If they so wish. Whatever scary stories you might have heard in the past, we're a peaceful people. And here is our place of worship," said *pater* Kukai, stopping in front of a dark, windowless, foreboding building, imitating a vaulted cavern.

The girls went in, followed by Bran, who instantly recognized the shape of a *mithraeum*. The inside was also familiar with long benches along the walls and a painted altar opposite the entrance.

"Today is a special day: Mercuralia," *pater* Kukai said, "you're welcome to witness our ceremony."

For the first time since his arrival in Yamato Bran could tell the proper date.

Mercuralia – the Feast of Water. That's mid-May...

"Who is this man fighting an ox? And the woman in the blue robe? Are they your ancestors?" Nagomi asked, approaching the altar with great curiosity.

"These are their main *kami*," replied Bran, before the *pater* could answer. "*Isis,* the Earth Mother and *Mithras,* the Sun Warrior. A mockery of our Gods."

Eh, our *Gods? What am I saying?*

"I see you know something of our faith, young man" the *pater* said, dryly, "but we do *not* mock your beliefs: ours are much older. You're welcome to see our rituals for yourself tonight."

"I... I don't..."

Bran shook his head, trying to clear his mind. He realized his hands were clenched tightly into fists, and his breath was quickened. He felt sick.

"Are you alright?" Nagomi touched him on the shoulder.

"I... I'm sorry. I don't feel that well. I'd better go back to the boat."

He left before they could stop him. He knew now the emotion surging within him, making his hands shake, his teeth chatter. It was hate – pure, seething hate.

He looked down on the red dirt plain from the top of the tower. A great storm blew across the plain, shrouding the horizon in red haze, raising billowing clouds of dust. In the middle of the hurricane stood Shigemasa; fierce and somehow taller than usual.

"What is the meaning of this?" Bran cried against the wind.

The General raised his head but did not answer. The storm changed again, forming the clouds of dust into images. Haunting visions, moving sand sculptures.

Bran saw the Sun-worshipping rebels attack temples, shrines and those of the villagers who refused to join them. He saw a boy, Bran's age, wearing a black cape and the Western-style ruff collar, leading thirty thousand blood-thirsty masterless samurai and peasants against the castles throughout Chinzei. All the horrors of a civil war were laid before him: bodies hacked to pieces and strewn over the battlefields; limbs torn away by bullets and cannon balls, cripples wading in the mud; babies taken from their mothers; priests tortured, monks hung and quartered; the beleaguered defenders starving to death behind the walls of Hara, forced to eat their horses, dogs and corpses. Death, destruction, suffering brought through actions of those worshipping the Warrior God on the pious Yamato and on themselves alike.

At last the vision changed. He saw another boy, green-eyed, on some black metal ship, sneaking up to a man crouched over a map, with a large wrench in his hand. With a deft stroke on the head, the boy knocked the Captain out. He then dropped the wrench and took a sword from under one of the bunk beds. At that moment Bran realised this was no longer a vision - this was reality.

He looked down. Shigemasa was gone; the tower was locked from inside.

In the middle of the vaulted hall a large feast was being prepared. Nagomi sat beside Satō, just before the altar, slightly uncomfortable on the reclining bench. Heishichi observed the proceedings from further at the back, making notes. With Bran and Captain Kawamura back at the ship, the other missing member of the party was Torishi. The bear-man had disappeared into the woods for the night.

One of the townspeople stood up, holding a heavy stringed instrument, beaten and ancient; to its plucking sounds, the rest of the gathering started a chant in a language unknown to Nagomi. It was more a recitation than singing, not unlike the official prayers of the High Priests in Yamato shrines, but faster and more rhythmical.

After the singing, *pater* Kukai stepped onto the altar, with a staff in one hand and a bronze sickle in another.

"Bring out the *haoma!*" he announced, stamping the staff on the floor.

Several girls in long, white, translucent flowing robes came out with clay pitchers. Nagomi presented a small cup she had been given at the beginning of the ceremony and one of the girls filled it with a milky liquid, smelling of pine needles.

"What do you think it is?" she asked Satō.

"Maybe some kind of saké? It's got a strong smell."

The wizardess quaffed the drink, but Nagomi hesitated. These, after all, were the *Sun Worshippers*. They may look benign now, but she was raised on the tales of their blood-thirst and cruelty. What if it was poison, or some strange drug? She looked around and poured the liquid on the floor. Just when she was about to ask Satō about the taste, the door burst open. Bran ran into the building, holding his sword in outstretched hands. The children and women screamed. A man rose from the back bench to stop him but Bran slashed his sword and the villager fell among the plates and pots with a cry, bleeding from his forehead. The rest of the townspeople rushed in panic towards the altar, leaving only Heishichi sitting on his bench, observing the scene with bemusement.

"Bran! What are you doing?" Nagomi stepped forward, but Satō held her back.

"Wait, that's not him."

The wizardess put her hand on the hilt and approached Bran, who now stood in the middle of the aisle, ready to strike. His eyes were deep dark and burning with hate.

"Itakura-*dono*," she said.

The spirit in Bran's body looked her straight in the eyes.

"Step aside, girl. I have no quarrel with thee. Or have they converted thou as well?"

"These are peaceful people, *Taishō-dono*. Not rebels from Shimabara."

"They are all enemies of the Divine *Mikado!* Step aside, I said!" The General tried to push his way past Satō, but the girl drew her own sword. The blades clashed.

"I *knew* thou wouldst be on their side. Thou art half-barbarian thyself."

Shigemasa pressed forward, but Satō was strong too. They were in a clinch. The General looked around. He was surrounded by the congregation, closing in on him from all sides. A few of them held walking sticks or fishing knives threateningly.

"Nngh!" The General pushed once again; Satō slid dangerously on the stone floor, but still had her sword raised. A few of the townsfolk leapt between her and the samurai.

At the back, Heishichi stood up with a half-frown, stretching his knuckles. Shigemasa cast him a furious glance, then turned back to Satō and the men before him.

"I'll get thee yet, traitor. I'll get all of you!" he cried, then spun around and ran towards the temple door, slashing his sword at one more worshipper who failed to get out of his way fast enough. Heishichi made no effort to stop him.

"Help the wounded," Satō told Nagomi, sheathing her sword. The priestess nodded and crouched beside the man lying on the floor bleeding onto the stone slabs from a deep cut across the chest. When she looked back, the wizardess was already gone. She focused on the healing ritual. She cleared her mind, took a deep breath and put her hands on the man's wound. But before she could start, she felt a heavy hand on her shoulder. She looked up.

"We do not wish assistance from your demons, priestess," *pater* Kukai said.

Demons?

"He is dying. I can heal him."

"He will die a warrior's death, then. It is better to die and join the ranks of the Sun Warrior's army than to live through a pact with the demon."

Nagomi raised herself uncertainly. A few townspeople picked up the two wounded men and carried them away.

"We take care of our own," said the *pater*, "and we will seek revenge on the one who harmed them. The *Taikun* spy will not get away far."

"Bran is not a *Taikun* spy! He... he wasn't himself."

"Go on," the *pater* said with a frown.

"He shares his soul with a Spirit, who – "

"A Spirit? You mean a *deva*, a demon! I'm not surprised," the *pater* interrupted in a solemn voice, "in the presence of the Divine the *deva* often become agitated and angry."

He turned to his congregation, and raised his arms in a calming gesture.

"Behold! *Mitorasu-sama* brings us another sign of his power!" he cried. "To show us the dangers of the outside world, he brings a *deva* into our midst."

The townspeople cowered as the preacher continued. Heishichi appeared beside Nagomi.

"Stay close," he said. She nodded.

"Yes, this is how playing with the demonic rituals always has to end. Do not think I am blind or foolish. I know some of you still cling to the old ways. I have seen the shrines and statues in the forest. But I have ignored them for too long, and now we have been reminded all too well what the consequences of worshipping those demons are. The sword of the Sun will fall on them all."

He climbed the altar and picked up the bronze sickle.

"Bring out the bull," said *pater* Kukai.

"The bull! The bull!" the gathered cried. Nagomi's hair stood on end as she felt the crowd's growing frenzy. A short, stocky man in a black *gi* jacket opened the door to what looked like a pantry and carried out a small, terrified calf. One of the young girls in translucent robes approached the animal. Only her eyes, bright and blue, were visible above the veil and Nagomi could see fear and fascination in them as she reached out and put a circlet of silver thread and bells between the animal's horns. The crowd fell quiet in patient anticipation.

"Is that a… *symbolic* sacrifice?" she asked Heishichi. "Bran said they don't kill the innocent…"

"I don't think so," the *Daisen* replied, half of his mouth twisted in a sneer.

Pater Kukai spoke again to the agitated crowd.

"As the beloved Mithras had slain the Bull sent from the Otherworld," the priest intoned, "and brought life to the barren world, so do we bring the life of this bull to its end, to renew our bond with the Sun. Blessed be the Bull."

"Blessed be the Bull," the others chanted in unison.

"Let its blood wash over us, like the blood of our enemies. Let it drown the demons at our door. Let it clean the souls of our visitors so that they, too, can see the light of Truth."

The townspeople howled, "*Ia! Ia! Ia!*", while the *pater* raised his sickle over the calf's neck. The animal mowed, trying to break free, but the blade fell in that instant with a mortifying swish.

Nagomi could watch no more. She turned around, passed Heishichi by and ran out of the temple.

CHAPTER XII

The guards bowed deeply, stepping aside and allowing Lord Shimazu Nariakira's entourage into the great tunnel, linking the Kumamoto Castle with the city below.

Katō Kiyomasa knew how to build, he thought, admiring the craftsmanship of the smoothly polished great blocks of granite lining the walls. The tunnel was a unique feature of the castle; not only was it the last ditch of defence in case of a siege, it also allowed complete control over any visitors in time of peace, even those as illustrious as the daimyo of Satsuma. Strong guards were posted at either end, and both gates could be closed instantly, trapping everyone inside.

Lord Hosokawa Narimori waited at the top entrance, twiddling his fingers with a nervous smile on his face.

"Shimazu-*dono.* To what do I owe this unexpected pleasure?"

Less than an hour earlier, Nariakira's ship had entered the Kumamoto harbour. The surprise was complete; there was nobody at the pier to welcome the great Lord, no porters or couriers ready to take the luggage and messages, no soldiers to guard – and control – the passage. This was exactly as Nariakira had wanted it; before anyone in the castle could even think of sending a welcoming party, he crossed the city surrounded only by his own faithful retainers.

Had Nariakira done so in any other domain, it may well have been construed as an act of war; but there were strong ties of friendship between Kumamoto and Satsuma, and Lord Narimori could do nothing but swallow his pride and prepare to welcome the visitors as well as he could.

"There are urgent matters we need to discuss, Hosokawa-*dono.*"

"Of course, of course. You must forgive me. I had no time to prepare accommodation for your men."

"There will be no need. I'm not planning to stay the night."

Only the slightest shadow of surprise marred Narimori's face. It was unusual enough for a fellow daimyo to come unannounced; for him to leave on the same day was unheard of.

He's trying desperately to guess what I want, thought Nariakira.

"You have a splendid castle," he said as they climbed out of the tunnel onto the main courtyard. A magnificent view spread from the topmost terrace over the mist-covered mountains towards the distant sea.

"You've seen it many times, Nariakira-*dono,*" Narimori replied, his smile twitching even more.

"Yes, and I am always impressed by the work of your ancestors. With a decent garrison, this place would be unassailable."

"Let us hope this needs never be tested."

"Of course, of course. Do you still have that quiet room on the top floor?"

"Always. Do you want to go there right now? I thought a feast might…"

"My men will enjoy the feast while we talk."

The lord of Kumamoto frowned. Nariakira's actions were now verging upon insult to the host.

"And what is this?" he changed the subject, pointing to a large, man-sized piece of luggage which several of Nariakira's porters hauled behind them.

"*Oku,*" the daimyo of Satsuma replied with a broad smile, "a gift."

"I gather you've been busy lately, Narimori-*dono.*"

The two daimyos were sitting alone in the Quiet Room, the most secret place in the castle hidden between the thick walls of the top floor, safe from the prying eyes or ears of any spies.

"I have, but how did you know?"

The eyes of the lord of Kumamoto darted constantly towards the corner of the room where, leaning against the thick supporting beam, stood the mysterious "gift" from Satsuma. There was the faintest of golden glints in these eyes, Nariakira noticed; Hosokawa's skin had an unhealthy, pale hue, and a fresh silken bandage was wrapped around his left forearm.

Did they promise you immortality? More power? My domain?

"It's the only explanation for you not informing me of the recent developments."

Narimori scowled. Lord Nariakira was deliberately pushing the boundaries of proper conduct; the daimyo of Kumamoto had no obligation to inform him of anything. Nevertheless, whenever he didn't, it roused suspicions.

"What… particular developments do you mean?"

"The Immortal Swordsman visited me as well, a few days ago. He told me about the Eight-headed Serpent and the return of the Shard of Fukuchiyama. I trust you are fully aware of the importance of these events."

The lord of Kumamoto was flustered.

"I… I was just going to write you a letter. But you understand, of course, with what happened in Kirishima – many of my retainers died in the fire, such a thing has not happened in two hundred – "

"Some of my men perished there too, Narimori-*dono,*" Nariakira said, nodding sagely. "Terrible tragedy. But let it not divert our attention from what is really important. Have you received any news from the Court lately? You're *closer* to Edo than I am."

Narimori's continuing grimace showed that the play on words did not go unnoticed.

"I know the *Taikun* demands troops from all loyal daimyo. But you were surely aware of that as well, Nariakira-*dono.*"

For the first time in the conversation, the lord of Satsuma was caught off guard.

"News travels slowly across the mountains. When did that happen?"

"I only got the summons a week ago."

"And how do you plan to respond?"

"The warriors of Kumamoto serve only the lord of this castle."

Of course. I wonder - how long did you think you could afford to ignore the Taikun's *orders? Perhaps that's what swayed you in the end: fear of Edo is still strong.*

"I wonder what prompted that demand."

"There's a war on in Qin again – and this time in the North. Perhaps the Court is wary of the Barbarians gathering in strength on our doorstep."

"That would be new. They've been ignoring the threat for decades."

"I…" Narimori's voice broke. "I'm sorry, Nariakira-*dono,* but what *is* that thing?"

Nariakira chuckled.

"Of course, no point in keeping you in the dark any longer."

He stood up, came up to the gift, and pulled down the cover. Narimori gasped aloud. The falling fabric revealed an incredibly life-like sculpture – of the lord of Kumamoto himself.

"I had one made of myself," said Nariakira. "It's almost a perfect replica."

"I still don't understand…"

"Oh, allow me to demonstrate."

He turned the key clock-wise and the automaton stirred to life. It looked around, blinked eerily and then opened its mouth.

"Honoured to meet you, Hosokawa-*dono.*" Even its voice was a good copy of Narimori's slightly high-pitched timbre.

Nariakira switched it off.

"The *kagemusha* doubles are unreliable and hard to come by. This machine will fool any assassin long enough for your bodyguards to arrive."

"Oh… Oh, I see! It is a great gift indeed, Nariakira-*dono.*"

"You don't want to take a closer look?"

Lord Narimori stood a step away from the automaton, cautious of the strange technology. The automatons known to most aristocrats in Yamato were mere toys; there were only a few people skilled enough to create something as immense as this doppelganger.

"Did Tanaka-*sensei* help you with its creation?" asked Narimori.

"I leave details to my wizards," replied Nariakira with a shrug, "but I wouldn't be surprised. Notice the craftsmanship. There are almost as many joints in the hand as in a real one."

While Lord Narimori leaned over to admire the artificial muscles, Nariakira reached again towards the key and turned it – this time counter-clockwise. The automaton came to life again; its hands shot forward, grabbing Narimori's shoulders in a tight grip. A hypodermic needle, hidden in one of the fingers, injected the concentrated venom of a *habu* snake into Narimori's arm. The daimyo struggled briefly but vainly with the onset of paralysis. When the toxin finished its work, the living lord of Kumamoto looked almost indistinguishable from his artificial doppelganger. Only his eyes were different, filled with pain and terror.

"I know you can hear me," said Nariakira. "The poison will not kill you – and the paralysis should pass in a few days. Of course, by then you will be safe in my castle."

He turned a hidden knob at the back of the automaton; the metal grip slackened, releasing the hapless lord into Nariakira's arms.

"I'm sure you'll agree this was a much more elegant solution than, say, sending an assassin. In a way, I'm glad your little bit of thievery prompted me to action. I let you do as you pleased for far too long."

With some effort, he leaned Narimori against the wall beside the machine.

"The automaton will announce your retirement and removal into a mountain monastery, where none shall disturb you but the men I trust. You know which ones I mean – I'm sure my brother supplied you with the list a long time ago... They will also make sure your son is a more... *reliable* ally. The warriors of Kumamoto are famous for their skill and bravery. I need to be sure they are on my side."

He covered the paralyzed daimyo with the cloth and turned the automaton back again.

"I'm sorry you didn't like my gift, Narimori-*dono*. I will order it taken back right away," he said, looking straight in the machine's eyes.

Shigemasa climbed up a narrow stone path in frenzy. The waning moon did little to illuminate the thick, almost jungle-like forest of cryptomeria and camphor trees covering the steep hill. With the two minds struggling for domination, a strange madness was overtaking the boy's body as he ventured upwards through the woods, across the vines and muddied boulders, using his sheathed sword as support.

A small spring seeped out of the rocks halfway up the slope. The stream trickled across the path, wetting the pebbles and boring a watery groove in the sand. Shigemasa tripped on the slippery stones and fell, cutting a deep gash in his head on a boulder. The pain and blood only added to his confusion, as the General trudged on, ever higher and further away from the accursed village.

He stumbled out onto a small, perfectly round glade in front of a dark, gloomy cave. A circle of white round stones stained brown surrounded the glade's edge. There was a dark, foreboding presence here, the air was dense, stuffy and smelled of old blood. Shigemasa took a weak step forward and then fell down, overpowered by the glade's energies.

When he came to, he discovered his hands had been tied up with string. He tried the knots – they were coarse, but strong. He was lying just outside the circle of stones by a small campfire. The Kumaso man was sitting opposite on a large, flat mossy boulder.

"What is the meaning of this?" Shigemasa flailed about. "Let me go this instant! I order thee, savage!"

The Kumaso man patted his beard and smiled softly.

"I always wanted to talk to you, old Spirit."

"Thou shalt die for this insolence." Shigemasa seethed and gnashed his – Bran's – teeth.

"I'm looking forward to seeing my family," the bear-man said, "but it's not yet my time. Neither is it yours."

Shigemasa grunted indignantly and sat up.

"The heretics must die," he said finally, as the silence prolonged.

"Why?"

"They are the greatest foe!" Shigemasa shouted, spittle flowing from Bran's lips.

"Now I know why my spirit could not ascend to the Heavens – and why Fate brought me to meet the boy. It is my duty to rid the Yamato of the last of the heretics!"

"All these people want is to be left in peace!"

"Thou art a fool, savage. They may seem meagre now, but they are cunning and wily. Like a weed, thou let one offshoot live and then one day they will grow over an entire garden."

"So you've met them before."

"I *died* fighting them. But the *Taikun* had prevailed in the end, and we wiped them out!"

The bear-man stopped smiling and stood up. His face twisted in pain and anger, and he swatted his head with his hand in some strange expression of emotion. He grabbed Shigemasa by the hair and snarled in his face, baring his teeth like an angry animal.

"Wipe out. It's all you valley people can do. Wipe out the Heretics. Wipe out the Kumaso. Wipe out the Yōkai. Wipe out anyone that is different… Until only you are left, with your metal swords, and your paper houses, and your *shrines* where the Spirits are imprisoned!"

"There would be no Spirits at all had the Heretics got their way!" the General said, spitting. "They will overthrow the order of things. They will bring the civil war back. I must stop them before it's too late. I have seen the coming Darkness."

Torishi stepped back and laughed.

"You think *they* are the Darkness? *They* are the reason you remain stuck in the mortal world?"

"What else? No demon brought so much foulness to this land as their Warrior God."

The bear-man's look changed from anger to pity.

"I know your kind. You're the hunter that boasts of killing the grey-haired, toothless and clawless old bear. But the *real* beast remains, still threatening the forest."

The General was silent for a while.

"What art thou saying?" he said at last.

"What is your duty, Spirit?"

"To serve and protect the Empire," the General answered without hesitation.

The bear-man ran his fingers through his beard.

"I was the greatest hunter in my village. I thought I was protecting my family, my people. But I failed to see the real danger before it was too late."

The Kumaso returned to his boulder, leaving the General alone. Shigemasa's eyes fell on the stone circle. Only now did he notice that one of the small white stones was roughly carved in the shape of *Jizō*, the bald guide into the Otherworld.

"What is this place?" he asked. "I sense... there was some great evil here."

"I sense it too," said the Kumaso, "but now it's gone."

Shigemasa's thoughts raced. It must have been a place where the heretics performed their darkest rituals; where they summoned their demon servants. But why did Fate bring him here to this circle of black magic so powerful even a remnant of it was making him, a ghost, shiver?

Twenty thousand souls had defended the Hara Castle, he remembered. *Men, women, children.*

The *Taikun* had ordered them all dead. At the end of the siege over a hundred thousand soldiers charged the walls of the heretic fortress. And now all that was left of them was this one little town with one little temple.

He noticed the bright red cloth around the *Jizō* statue, fresh flowers and a cup of saké. He smiled to himself. The Kumaso was right – the old bear was toothless and senile.

The General closed his eyes and prayed to the bald god for guidance. *Jizō* was the protector of lost souls, and who was he but a soul lost between this and another world?

The red dot pulsated in the distance.

He was in a dark place. By now, Bran was able to recognize the red dust plain by the smell of damp earth and the sound of distant, incessant winds.

But there was another light: a translucent flame shimmering with unnatural colours, ghostly blues and otherworldly purples. He started walking in its direction and soon began to make out silhouettes of people in hooded robes standing around the bonfire. They were also wraith-like, made of white and blue light and mists. The wind tore them like clouds.

The scene was surrounded by a circle of white stones and faint phantoms of trees, vanishing into darkness. The ghostly men did not seem to notice Bran as he stepped even closer, intrigued. One of them was wearing the Phrygian cap of a *pater*.

Mithraists. What is this? A vision, but of what... the future? The past?

The bonfire gave out no heat; on the contrary, the closer Bran got, the colder the air grew. Bran's breath became visible; an unpleasant, metallic scent lingered on his tongue.

Something was happening. A body was brought into the circle and thrown on the ground. It hovered eerily a few inches above the red dirt. Then, one by one, the gathered stood above it and cut their forearms deeply with phantom blades. Blood poured on the body like a stream of pale blue light. At last, the *pater* did the same, closing the circle. He raised a brightly glowing talisman showing the horned cross-in-circle, the symbol of the Mithraists. His lips moved in a silent incantation.

Somewhere in the distance, drums began to roll.

Two of the hooded men held the body by its arms and legs; it stirred, twitched and started thrashing about. The *pater* touched its head with the talisman and it quietened. He ordered the men to let go.

Slowly, staggering, the dead man rose from the ground. His body was black with a red tinge, only the eyes shone like golden nuggets. His teeth were long and sharp. He lunged at the priest, but covered his eyes before the talisman's light and bent his knees in a show of subservience.

The drums grew louder, more frantic.

A Fanged, Bran recognized the creature. *This is how a Fanged is created.*

The newly born Abomination looked around the circle, and raised its head, sniffing, hunting. Its glowing golden eyes met Bran's and its muscles tensed.

It sees me!

The creature leapt outside the vision, out of the circle of ghosts with terrifying speed, and suddenly appeared on the red dust plain in the flesh. It was no longer a wispy wraith; its naked skin was pale and bloodless, but its sinews and muscles were all too real, as were the claws and long fangs. Its face was twisted in agony and rage. Before Bran could react, it jumped at him, pinning him to the ground.

They wrestled; the Fanged's teeth tried to reach Bran's neck. He fought back with all his might, but the creature was strong, stronger than Bran, and the claws tearing at his wrists seemed to sap the boy's energy; he couldn't summon a shield or a lance. *Llambed Seal,* he thought in desperation. *Will it work here?*

The drums stopped abruptly and a shadow appeared over Bran and the Abomination: another man, wearing a mask lined with white heron feathers and a colourful kaftan, with both hands raised in the air, holding sharpened bits of steel. He struck at the Fanged between the shoulder blades and disappeared.

The creature howled, screeched, and jumped up, trying to reach the blades embedded in its back, but within seconds, a black rot spread from the twin wounds and engulfed its entire body. With an agonizing cry, the Fanged flailed its arms and then exploded in a cloud of grey ash. The blades fell on the red dust with a clunk, their ends twisted and melted.

What in Annwn just happened?

With an effort, Bran remembered the *Egungun* dancer's ritual in far away Ekó, and his father's anger at what he perceived as an assassination attempt.

Not the first time he was wrong, he thought.

He heard steps and turned around, Soul Lance in his hand, this time ready to fight. It was Shigemasa; he seemed weakened and dishevelled.

"Come, boy," the General said with a tired voice. "Time to go back to the others."

They touched hands and Bran woke upon an overgrown forest glade surrounded by polished white stones. The same metallic scent lingered in the air.

His hands were tied up with string; the light of a campfire flickered on the glistening leaves of the camphor trees. Torishi, sitting on one of the boulders, noticed him awake. He observed Bran for a moment, then nodded, stood up, drew his long dagger and slashed through the knots.

There was no trace of Bran, the path had ended long ago, and everywhere she looked, the wood looked exactly the same.

She was alone in the dark forest; she was tired and lost, her head ached and her stomach rumbled.

What was I thinking? I will have to wait until dawn to get back.

She felt a numb pain in the corners of her eyes and behind her ears. She felt hot.

It's that damn drug. Nagomi was right not to drink it.

She loosened her clothes and staggered on from tree to tree.

I need to walk down the slope... keep straight...

There were lights among the camphor trees, colourful wisps and flashes like the ones showing under closed eyelids. Satō shook her head and the lights disappeared, but not for long.

I'm being poisoned, she realised and giggled. *Why am I giggling? This is terrible.*

She laughed out loud.

Another, greater light appeared behind the trunk of a huge tree. When it moved towards her, she saw that it was the shape of a man.

Is that their God, the Sun? Is that what they see?

The shining man came closer with his hand stretched towards her; he was completely naked. She recognized him at last.

"Bran!" she cried. "I'm so glad I found you! Why are you – "

The boy put his finger on her mouth.

"What are you..."

He pulled her towards him and slid a hand underneath her kimono. When he kissed her, his lips were as hot as the Sun.

"I'm fine," Captain Kawamura replied to Nagomi's offer of help. He scratched the roughly bandaged bump on his head.

"I assume it was the boy who hit me, but I didn't see it"

"He wasn't being himself," Nagomi explained for the second time that day. "He has a Spirit within him."

"I wish you'd told me before he got mad," the Captain said, wincing, "we should have locked him in for the night."

He invited her to the cockpit for *cha* and they waited. Not an hour had passed before a quickly moving figure appeared on the pier. In the ship's storm light, Nagomi recognized the *Daisen*.

"Start the engine," ordered Heishichi as soon as he jumped on board.

"What about the others?" asked Kawamura.

"They're not here?" the wizard looked around in surprise. "Doesn't matter. We have to set sail."

"What happened?"

"See for yourself." The *Daisen* pointed at the town. A long, dense line of torches, like a festival procession, snaked along the sea shore silently, slowly moving towards the harbour.

"They're coming to conquer the demons," he said.

"We're not going anywhere!" protested Nagomi. "We have to go look for the others."

The Captain looked doubtfully at the pitch-black forest covering the steep slopes.

"We won't find anyone in the night."

"The ship is more important," the *Daisen* said. "You know your duty, Captain."

Kawamura nodded heavily and disappeared into the engine room. Soon the deck rumbled with the rhythmical beating of the pistons.

The crowd was getting nearer; the first torches were almost at the pier. Nagomi stared into the darkness, hoping – praying – to see anyone returning from the forest. She noticed the Captain untying the mooring ropes.

"No!" she said. "We have to wait!"

"I'm sorry, priestess-*sama*. I have my orders."

Before the last of the ropes unravelled, Nagomi grabbed Torishi's bow and arrows from the bench and leapt overboard onto the wooden pier. She ran towards the head of the procession, which was almost at the harbour.

"Stop! Please, we mean you no harm," she said, catching her breath. "Just let us wait for our friends."

The *pater* raised his hand. The congregation behind him slowed down and began to spread out in a half-circle around her.

"Behold, the servant of the *Deva!*" the priest bellowed, pointing his finger accusingly at Nagomi. "The Adversary takes many guises."

She stepped back, alarmed, and drew her bow with shaking arms, aiming at the *pater*.

"Let us sail away in peace, we won't – "

She screamed as the priest leapt towards her and pushed the bow away; the string twanged sadly and the arrow flew into darkness. He grabbed her by the arm with one hand and drew a long sacrificial knife from the folds of his robe with the other. His eyes gleamed madly. The crowd closed in on her.

"I am a star which goes with thee and shines out of the depths," he intoned. "I spy out my enemies, swoop down upon them, scatter and slaughter them. I – "

She tried to wriggle herself out of the iron grasp. She heard a wild roar and a heavy, earth-shaking thumping, followed by cries of panic. The priest let loose her arm and when she turned, she saw a great black bear charging towards her, sweeping the people aside with swipes of its huge paws.

The bear stood between her and the priest, and growled, baring its teeth, its sides heaving. The priest dropped the knife and backed away, joining his retreating attendants.

"Nagomi, quick!"

She turned and saw Bran standing on the pier beside the *Iroha Maru*, waving at her to follow. He was carrying a barely-conscious Satō on his back.

The bear roared once more and they both ran towards Bran and the ship.

"I was aware of everything," said Bran, drinking *cha* prepared by Kawamura, "but I couldn't reason with the *Taishō*. He would not listen; he went mad with rage. We struggled for control of the body on the mountain path and he was stronger in his rage."

"I wonder what finally made him give up," said Torishi.

The boy shook his head.

"He prayed to the *Jizō* for advice, but whatever happened then was between himself and the Gods. He is silent now. I can barely feel his presence."

"What about Sacchan?" worried Nagomi, wiping the wizardess's feverish forehead with cold, damp cloth. "What happened to her?"

"It's the potion," Heishichi spoke. Everyone turned towards him.

"You let her drink the *haoma*?" asked Bran.

"You know it?"

"I know *of* it. It's the sacred potion of the Sun Priests. They claim it allows them to unite with their Gods."

"Is it harmful?" asked Nagomi.

"It shouldn't be. But it may be a shock to the unprepared."

"I know the smell," said Heishichi. "It's the *maō* plant. They must be getting it from the same source as my supplier."

"What does it do?" asked Nagomi.

"In clear, concentrated form, we use it to keep alert and awake. But this concoction…" He shrugged. "It turned the townspeople to frenzy. They danced naked in the night."

Satō stirred and moaned. "*Bran…don't…*" she whispered.

Bran felt everyone's stare.

"I didn't…" he started, his face burning.

The wizardess woke up with a gasp. She looked around, bewildered.

"Where am I?"

"You're back on the ship," Nagomi said, holding the wizardess's hand.

Satō's wandering eyes found Bran, and the girl let out a stifled cry, covering herself with her hands.

"Whatever you think happened, it wasn't me," he said, trying to sound calming.

"It's true," added Torishi. "I was with him all the time."

The wizardess sighed and lay down again.

"It…it doesn't matter. When can we set off?"

"We are well on our way, Takashima-*sama*," said Kawamura. "Safe in the open sea."

It was their last evening out at sea, a dark, cold, unpleasant twilight. Sailing north, they had left the early Satsuma summer far behind. The wind howled down the funnels and vents, whistling ominously, shackles clanged on the rigging in alarm. The little ship rocked up and down on rolling waves as the paddles struggled to gain a grip on the water and keep the vessel on course.

Bran came out onto the deck to sharpen his Prydain sword. Sparks fluttered in the darkness with every grinding stroke of the blade on the damp whetting stone. Mindless work which allowed his thoughts to wander. He recognized the waters even in the night; the *Iroha Maru* was passing through the bay between Shimabara and Kumamoto.

This is where everything started.

Tokojiro's betrayal and the fight at Mogi, the first quarrel with Shigemasa, the wobbly ferry to Kuchinotsu…

It seems so long ago now.

He recalled the many times he could have died on the journey or become trapped within his mind. It was an odd thought. Before coming to Yamato, he never thought about dying or even coming to harm…

Even after the Ladon *I wasn't really worried,* he thought. *I have the Llambed Seal after all.*

Llambed… his thoughts now drifted back to Gwynedd.

They taught us how to kill and not get killed, he realized, recalling how much time and effort he had spent learning combat spells, summoning shields and falling safely off the back of the dragon. While wyverns and gryphons were good for transport and cargo, first and foremost the dragons were, after all, beasts of war. It seemed so obvious in hindsight.

They pretended we were all going to be wyrm lore scholars, he scoffed. *"Sanctity of life" – what a joke! Most of us would end up as soldiers in some dragoon regiment or other. Ready to die for The Dragon Throne. I wonder how many of my class are dead already?*

And that was why his father was so concerned about Emrys. Swamp dragons were perceived as useless in combat. Dylan wished his son to follow in his footsteps after all…

He stopped his work and checked the sword. The runes along the fuller glowed with dull blue. The Prydain blade would not get any sharper; it wasn't as well made as Satō's katana. The sword had drunk so much blood since his arrival in Kiyō...

Every highborn here carries a sword from youth, he thought. *They are all taught how to kill with it. I wonder if they realize what it does to them.*

He sheathed the weapon and looked around. He noticed a figure sitting on the bow in complete silence. It was the *Daisen*, Heishichi, clad in a thick brown coat that protected him from the cold wind.

"You don't carry a sword," said Bran.

"I'm a merchant's son."

"Not even a commoner's *kodachi?*"

"I have no need for crude weapons. I'm the *Daisen.*"

Bran leaned against the gunwale and faced the wind.

"What did your master need my dragon for?"

Heishichi smirked.

"Politics. What do you care?"

"His Excellency's assistance was very valuable. I wonder what he wants in exchange?"

"I am not privy to the daimyo's plans."

"Then can you at least tell me why *you* are here?"

"To observe and study," the *Daisen* said. "And to help Captain Kawamura with the ship."

Not to fight, then.

"You still hope you can bring the dragon back to your Master. I told you, it's attuned to *me* only. I won't let you have it."

"Then the beast is of no use to His Excellency."

Should I tell him?

"There may be others."

Heishichi looked up, for the first time genuinely interested.

"How do you know?"

"A skilled dragon rider can sense other dragons if they're close enough," Bran explained.

The wizard stood up.

"What do you sense?"

Bran smiled.

"If I tell you now, I have nothing left to bargain with."

Heishichi's fist lit on fire; his face remained calm, but his scarred cheek twitched.

"Don't play with me, boy. I can squeeze that information out of you."

Bran took a step back and summoned a *tarian*.

"You're welcome to try. You're not an *onmyōji*. Your magic is the same as mine and I grew up learning how to use it."

The Soul Lance shimmered in his open palm. Bran noticed it was at least a foot longer than it had been the last time he'd used it.

"What do you two think you're doing?" the voice belonging to Captain Kawamura boomed behind Bran. "Fighting on my ship? I'll throw you both overboard!"

Heishichi cast the Captain an irritated look and extinguished his flame. He went past Bran towards his cabin.

"It's not wise to make an enemy out of the *Daisen*," said Kawamura.

"I get the feeling we weren't going to be friends anyway," replied Bran.

Satō stepped out onto the jetty and looked around with dismay. The sky was monochromic grey. A flat field of dull-yellow reeds, combed by the breeze spread as far as she could see; the monotony was interrupted by a few decrepit willow trees and tall fishing net poles. The canal into which they had sailed in the morning was boringly straight, its waters murky and dim; the only thing of interest for miles was a lonely, seemingly abandoned, small white-washed teahouse standing beside the jetty. She had never seen a more desolate, empty place.

A long, flat-bottomed boat powered by a single man, standing straight and pushing on a long pole approached down the canal. There was something familiar in the oarsman's towering bulk; as he got closer, Satō noticed the unmistakable purple cloak on his shoulders.

"Dōraku-*sama*!"

The Swordsman pulled back the bamboo hat and grinned at her.

The white-washed teahouse was not abandoned after all. The inside was surprisingly clean and cosy; sitting beside the fireplace sunk in the middle of the floor, Satō almost forgot about the emptiness and bleakness outside.

The six people who came on the ship and Master Dōraku barely fitted into the small room. Satō had to sit close to Bran, conscious of not having taken a proper bath or washing her clothes in days. Every time their eyes met, she was reminded of the strange encounter in the forest. She knew it was just a vision sent by the *maō* plant, but it didn't make her any more comfortable.

Master Dōraku poured everyone saké from a rice straw-wrapped bottle he had brought from the boat and, after raising a toast to their successful arrival, said:

"We have little time to linger. I'll be taking you today to Yanagawa, and we'll pick up the chase from there."

"The chase?" asked Satō.

"I hunted the Crimson Robe for the last few days. They did capture your *dorako* after all," he said to Bran. The boy exchanged glances with Nagomi. "And while it means they're moving slowly, they are far ahead of us already."

"Did you see how the *dorako* was captured?" asked Heishichi.

The Swordsman shook his head.

"They had already left Aso-san when I got there."

"They are moving north," said Bran. "I sensed it last night. What's to the north?"

"The Crimson Robe's island fortress, Ganryūjima" the samurai replied. "If he manages to get there, we'll be in a much more difficult position."

Satō drank her saké in one gulp and put the cup on the floor.

"Then what are we waiting for? Let's go after them!"

CHAPTER XIII

In Satō's mind this was supposed to be a hot pursuit; but in reality, the flat-bottomed boat advanced lazily up the canal, pushed onwards by rhythmical prods of Dōraku's pole. Her only consolation was that they were still moving faster than they would have on foot through this bleak, inhospitable landscape of marsh, reclaimed land and submerged rice paddies.

Brown-shelled turtles lived in droves in the canal, huddling every boulder or floating log; snakes writhed their way along the boat's edge, and fish popped up curiously, hoping for a crumb. Once in a while the boat passed a village – a few straw-roofed huts, a storehouse raised on pillars and a tiny red-gate of a shrine. Several locals would come out to the bank to watch the boat pass, but they neither smiled nor waved, just stared with tired eyes.

"How long until we get to some civilization?" asked Satō.

"This is civilization!" replied Dōraku, chuckling. "These people are its pioneers. It's a hard life on reclaimed land. But I can see what you mean. Yanagawa is just beyond those hills."

He pointed to a grey, jagged shadow on the horizon. It seemed just as distant as it had when they started. She closed her eyes and sighed.

"Tell us how you defeated those wolves," she asked, hoping a diverting tale of swashbuckling and derring-do would take her mind off the overwhelming dullness.

"I didn't."

"*Eeh?*" She opened her eyes wide.

"There were far too many of them. They destroyed me; tore my body into pieces."

She looked into his eyes to see if he was joking.

"But you still survived?"

"Such is the power of the Curse."

"Then what chance do *we* stand against the Crimson Robe?" asked Bran.

"We can still be stopped," the Swordsman replied with a grin, "and defeated."

A large eel jumped away from under the pole. Satō thought long about what she just heard.

"You call it a Curse," she said at last, "but it seems a blessing to me."

For a moment, the oar in Master Dōraku's hands stopped.

"I would rather die ten times than have this Curse upon me," he said slowly.

"But why? What's so bad about it? You're immortal, powerful, fast –"

"All this and more, Takashima Satō." He stared at her with cold eyes. "But I am no longer *human*. The Curse replaced everything I ever was, turned me into a slave of my addiction and a slave of the man who had brought me to this sad imitation of life. I know you wizards play with blood magic and hope you can control it if used in moderation, but it's a fool's hope. Stay away from it, girl."

As the Swordsman spoke, his eyes turned black like coal, and a cold wind rose about the boat, carrying with it the stench of blood and death. Satō reeled back.

"That... that's not you," said Nagomi quietly, breaking the silence. The priestess was sitting at the bow, with her fingers in the cool water, keeping silent throughout most of the journey.

"That was me for the first ten years, young priestess-*sama*," said Master Dōraku, his voice kind once again. "I *was* a monster. I did things I can never repent of, never forget. My soul is corrupted forever."

"What happened after the ten years?" Nagomi asked.

"I met a *Butsu* priest... but it's a long story. He showed me the path, and taught me how to keep to it. It took me another ten years of meditation and wandering to release myself from the shackles the Curse had put upon me. But even then, the freedom was never complete."

"The wolf," said Bran. "That's why you said the spirits were after you."

The Swordsman smiled and nodded.

"What wolf?" asked Satō, disorientated. "What are you talking about?"

"Karasu-*sama* found me feeding on a wolf the night I met you in the forest. I thought I managed to lie my way out back then, but – "

"I always suspected something was wrong," said Bran. "Is that why Shimazu-*dono* called you a renegade? Because you broke your Curse?"

"There's more than that. There is... politics among our kind. I always stayed out of it."

"But you're familiar with the Crimson Robe."

"That's different. I knew him when we were both still alive."

"Can you tell us his name?" asked Satō. "We keep calling him Crimson Robe, but..."

"One of his names was Ganryū Kojirō." He paused; Satō guessed he was checking if anyone recognized the name. But there was no such man mentioned in any of the books and stories she knew.

"And now I must ask you all to bow your heads," the Swordsman said.

"What?"

"There's a low bridge coming," he added, crouching.

Wulfhere blinked repeatedly, trying to get the soot and smoke from his eyes. The wind was blowing the flames of the pyre in his direction.

The funeral was a symbolic one, of course. No search party ever found the Reeve's body – or discovered what happened to Commodore Dylan after he was forced to use the Seal. Banneret Edern was – officially – the last to see the two riders before they disappeared out of sight, pursued by the Qin dragons deep beyond the enemy lines.

Not the Banneret, Wulfhere corrected himself. *Commodore Edern.*

The ceremony over, the small crowd of soldiers began to disperse. Wulfhere limped towards his tent; after the victory at Chansu the camp grew, and petty officers like him now had separate quarters all to themselves. A guard of Qin volunteers stood before the entrance to protect their "hero".

Wulf spotted the familiar dark blue cap and jacket of Li, and slowed down, letting the interpreter catch up to him.

"A touching ceremony," the Qin man said, "and a great loss for all of us."

"Yes," said Wulf, not sure how to respond.

"If a loss it was," Li added.

The interpreter glanced left and right and asked the boy to step aside. They walked up to the sloping bank of a canal marking the southern edge of the Marines camp.

"I will tell you a secret, boy," Li started. "You see, we have some spies among the Rebels. Quite a lot, actually."

He knows.

Wulf decided not to tell Ardian Seton everything he had seen, sensing the information he had would prove more valuable as a well-kept secret.

"Listen," Li looked around once again and leaned over to whisper in Wulfhere's ear. "One of our spies saw a Silver dragon heading out to sea, south of Shanglin; it carried two people on its back."

"What are you saying...?"

"The Commodore and the Reeve, we can only guess. But why would they do that, I wonder?"

"A clandestine mission, no doubt," Wulf said, tearing blades of weak grass from the soft, damp ground.

"Oh, that's right!" Li clapped his hands. "But why fly out into the sea? There's nothing out there."

Should I tell him? What can I get in exchange, I wonder...

It was now Wulhere's time to turn conspiratorial. He lowered his voice.

"Banneret... Commodore Edern was not the last to see Commodore Dylan. I was."

A servant climbed down to the water beside Wulf with a mule in tow. The animal lowered its head and started drinking from the canal.

"This is not a good place," said Li. He stood up and wiped mud off his trousers. "Come to the landing glade in an hour."

Li stared at Wulfhere with eyes opened as wide as his arched eyebrows allowed.

"*Aiya!* You spied on your own commander? Why?"

He paced up and down the short landing glade, with his hands behind his back. His golden dragon, coiled on the grass, observed him through half-closed eyes.

"I'm just naturally curious," replied Wulf with a shrug.

He doesn't need to know everything. He had already made his decision; whatever Commodore Dylan was doing, it seemed the Qin would learn about it sooner or later. Wulf's information was valuable only for so long. If he wanted to get something out of what he knew, now was the time.

"My father taught me there is great power in knowing what others don't – and great profit."

Li stopped.

"Your father is a wise man," he said with a nod, "and you're a dangerous boy. But... *Yamato?* Are you sure?"

"You know what it is?" asked Wulfhere.

"Of course! A large island kingdom, east of Qin. Rich and powerful. We have an outpost in one of their cities, where we send one ship per year for some trade. Your Bataavians have a similar arrangement. Nobody else is allowed – few know of its existence."

Wulfhere's curiosity was immediately piqued.

A hidden land? One I've never heard anything about?

"And why is it so important that the Commodore went there?"

"If the Dracaland found a way to reach Yamato, this completely changes the balance of power!"

"How is it even possible we didn't find it earlier?"

"They hide behind an impenetrable sea barrier. They call it the 'Divine wind'."

Everyone here hides behind shields and barriers, noted Wulfhere. *People and nations alike.*

"If you already know the way to Yamato, why do you want to follow the Commodore?"

"The Qin ship is not scheduled for another six months. By that time it may be too late: the Dracaland will gain a foothold and will be impossible to remove."

Li tugged on his short, sharp beard.

"No, no. I can't just stand idly by. This war is yesterday's news," he said, more to himself, nodding at the army camp. He then turned east and looked towards the sky.

"I see it. What happens in Yamato now will decide the future. Not only of that kingdom, but also of Qin. Maybe the whole world. I must be there. I must prepare."

"Prepare for what? Are you thinking of another war? This one's not finished yet."

"That's how Empires are forged. Qin has grown complacent for too long. War rejuvenates states. Already the Rebellion is causing changes: we have Western weapons, Western training... But the Court at Ta Du is still reluctant to embrace the modern world. A new war may... I must go after them."

Wulfhere recognized in the Qin man the same cunning and ambition as his own, the same struggle against the odds and mishaps of Fate to prove his greatness.

A kindred spirit.

"You're not just an interpreter, are you?"

The Qin man smiled. Wulfhere ran his hand against the golden scales of Li's dragon, deep in thought. They were small, smooth and shimmering, like flakes of polished stone; the skin was colder to touch than that of a Western mount. The beast lowered its antlered head and purred. One of its long whiskers wriggled in the air as if it was a separate creature.

"I think she likes you."

"*She?*"

The Western mounts were almost exclusively stallions. Females were used only by civilians, or cooped up in hatcheries.

"Naturally. The mares make the best mounts – patient, gentle and hardy. Just what I need for a long journey. Now, about the Commodore… what else have you heard?"

"I will tell you all, if you take me with you," Wulf said, surprising himself as much as Li.

"*You?* You're a Dracalish soldier. Your place is in the army. Why would you want to go with me?"

"A Warwick doesn't study history," he replied, at last, with a family saying, "a Warwick *makes* history."

"Well said." Li replied. "I will send for you in the morning. We are not sneaking out like Commodore *Dí Lán*; it will be an official trip. I will present you to the court at Ta Du. The hero of Qiang River."

Wulf smiled.

I can't let Bran take all the glory.

"Are you alright?" asked Li. "I didn't know your race could turn that colour."

"I'm… fine," replied Wulf with great effort. He found it hard to get used to the way the Qin dragon moved in the air. When the weather was good, it swayed from side to side, like a snake on sand; when it had to pick up speed, or face strong currents, it undulated up and down, like a boat in a storm. Either way, the long, serpentine neck he was straddling behind Li, kept bobbing about, causing Wulf to suffer bouts of sea sickness for the first few hours of the flight.

Not seeing the wings flap on either side was disconcerting. Wulf knew all dragons relied on the magic of the Ninth Wind for flying, rather than their wings, but there was something reassuring in the thought that a Western dragon would have always enough lift to glide to safety if the magic failed. The Qin beast looked like it would topple to the ground like a stone – as Wulf had seen happen so many times during this war.

Like all Qin dragons, *long*, this one – "Yuyan" – was much longer than any Western beast; there was enough space on her neck for two comfortable saddles. The rider had little protection from the elements; Li used no *tarian*, and the dragon's breath was not as hot or dense as that of its Western cousins, so they couldn't cruise as high and fast as Wulf was used to.

The sea below them was a featureless expanse of grey, green and dark blue; Wulf had no idea where they were, and could only hope Li knew better. The position of the sun told him they were moving roughly east, but that was where his knowledge ended. In the morning they had passed a few small islets and reefs, but nothing since.

"There is a strong current running from the Tagalogs north-by-north-east," Li spoke, snapping Wulf from a lazy daydream. "No maps show where it ends, but it's the best way to reach Yamato, if one is in a hurry."

"Are we far from it?"

"I'm not sure. I was rather hoping we'd reach some islands by now."

"What?" Wulf sat up, awakened. "Are you telling me we're lost?"

"I'm just an interpreter, after all," Li replied. "Reading maps is not my forte. But judging by the sun's position..."

"*The sun?* Don't you have a compass?"

"We're too close to the Sea Maze," said Li, pointing north, where a thin line of dark, ominous clouds shrouded the horizon. "My compass is no good here."

"Oh, great." Wulf slumped in the saddle. "So much for making history: I'll be the first Western soldier to die on the back of a Qin dragon..."

"Hush, boy. Look sharp. We *must* be close. The sun is bright, the sea is calm; we are bound to spot something."

Wulfhere stared at the navy blue surface until his eyes watered. There was nothing but white ripples on the waves as far as he could see.

"We need to get higher," he said.

"We'll freeze."

"I can put a *tarian* up to shield both of us, though not for long."

Li nodded and pulled on the reins. The golden dragon gracefully coiled upwards and climbed smoothly on the current of the Ninth Wind. Three thousand feet later, Li levelled the flight.

"The dragon likes it here," said Wulf. "It's where she belongs."

"How do you know?"

"Can't you feel it? Through the Farlink?"

"What is *Fá-ling?*"

"Farlink! How do you steer your beast?"

"With these," Li replied, tightening the reins, "and these," he added, waving his legs. "How else?"

Wulf opened his mouth and then closed it. The idea of riding a dragon without a Farlink was preposterous – and terrifying.

She will throw us down any moment... why did I want us to fly so high?

Instinctively, he looked down towards the sea.

"Look," he said, grabbing Li's shoulder. "Over there. Straight ahead."

A column of thick black smoke rose in the middle of the ocean.

A ship on fire.

Chief Councillor Abe felt his knees weaken as he approached the camp of the Barbarians.

We were fools, he realized, *to think we could have done anything to stop them. No wonder Qin gave in so quickly.*

One of the grey-hooded invaders came up in quick, military steps, followed by a small Yamato man: the interpreter. Abe looked to his right, where his own interpreter stood, stiff and formal. Einosuke's nostrils flared and his eyes were unblinking, set forward.

He's fighting the dragon fear. Brave lad.

The man before him cast down the grey hood. He was shorter and older than the other Westerners, but had an unmistakable air of authority about him. He said a few words in his odd language. To Abe's ears it sounded like a mangled, barking version of Bataavian, but he could discern no understandable words. He looked at Einosuke. The interpreter cleared his throat.

"This… this is Komtur Mathiun Perai of the Western Navy of Tyr Gorllewin."

Gorllewin? I've never heard of them.

"I am Abe Masahiro, Chief *Rōju* Councillor to his Illustrious Excellency, *Taikun* Tokugawa Ieyoshi. Do you know what that means?"

"I was made aware of the ruling system of your country by that man," the Komtur replied, nodding at Hotta, who was standing further at the back. There wasn't anyone else in the Yamato delegation; it was crucial for the secret to be kept between as few men as possible.

"I bring a response from the Council," said Abe, handing the Komtur a scroll. Einosuke had spent two nights translating the edict into the language of the Westerners.

The Komtur reached into the inside pocket of his cloak and put on wire-framed spectacles to read the missive. The glasses made him look like a common clerk. It seemed almost impossible that this portly man commanded a squadron of dragons.

He finished reading and nodded.

"Not quite what we came for, but it's good enough," he said. "What is the place you wanted us to relocate to?"

"A small port of Shimoda, thirty *ri* south-west of here."

The Komtur thought about it for a while, then nodded again.

"Very well. But I will need something from you: proof of the *Taikun's* good intentions."

"What do you want?"

"There is a ship coming from our country. It brings supplies."

"We can supply you with everything you need. Food, medicine, meat for the *dorako…*"

The Komtur smiled.

"That's very generous, but there are things you have no way of providing. This ship must be allowed through the Sea Maze."

"Impossible!"

"This is the opening condition. No ship, no negotiations."

One of the beasts growled and raised its head. It licked the air with a long, greyish tongue.

"The dragons are growing hungry, Councillor," the Westerner added.

Let in even more Barbarians? Without the Council's consent... This would be the last decision I ever made.

"Give me a minute," he said and nodded at Hotta Naosuke. The two moved aside to discuss the new development.

"We have no choice," Naosuke said. "Our position is clear: the Council gave us the remit to open the negotiations. That means we have the right to accept or decline any propositions."

"But... that means I have to speak to the *Taikun* about it! Only he can open a passage through the Divine Winds."

"The Westerners can use the Dejima route and sail up the coast."

"And how do you propose to do that? We don't know the route."

"The Kiyō *bugyō* knows it. And he owes us a few favours after the bungling of the Takashima affair."

"That's too risky. The ship would have to go past Satsuma and Tosa!"

"We'll let them know how crucial it is not to be spotted. They seem willing to cooperate."

Abe pinched his lower lip in thought. He returned to the Westerner.

"Where is this ship of yours now?"

"It's stationed near the island you call Tamna. We can contact it swiftly, if need be."

How? That's beyond the Divine Winds!

"Then let them know. We have to make some preparations, but the route will be opened in two weeks. They need to be at least twenty *ri* south of Kiyō by then."

The Komtur mulled it over.

"All right. I accept that."

He turned to the rest of his men and shouted some orders. They started packing up the camp. The Westerner then turned to Abe and spoke briefly.

"He... he wants you to come with him, *tono*" explained Einosuke.

"Wha... what?"

"He wants you to show him the way to Shimoda."

"Give us a few days, and we will have the map ready."

"There's no time for that. My man will translate," the Komtur said, pointing to the small Yamato, who was standing quietly all this time, looking uncomfortable in the big grey cloak of the Westerners.

Abe looked helplessly around. The other Councillor shrugged, his eyes lowered again. *What did I get myself into...?*

"Send horses to Shimoda," Abe told Naosuke, with a sigh. "I will be at the Gyokusen Temple in the town – if I survive this at all..."

Once, in his youth, the Chief Councillor had climbed half-way up Mount Fuji; from there, he could see far across the land, over the forests, fields, towns and little villages, all the way down to the Ashi Lake, glittering like a shard of sapphire among the pine woods. He expected the view from the back of the dragon – when he finally dared to open his eyes – would be something similar.

It was nothing like that.

The earth beneath him moved at a great speed; the forests all blurred into one big green haze, interrupted by brighter spots of what he guessed were villages or open fields. To his left shimmered a brocade strip of the sea, and to his right – the unmistakable cone of the Fuji-san, the only recognizable feature in this fast changing landscape.

He remembered the freezing cold he had endured on the high mountain slope and was surprised at how comfortable and warm the flight was. He could breathe easily. He guessed some invisible barrier protected the dragon riders from the buffeting winds.

"Too fast..." he said.

The interpreter repeated his words to the Komtur. Their dragon was the only one carrying more than two people, but it didn't seem in the least burdened by the additional weight.

"What?"

"I can't tell where we are at this speed."

The Westerner pulled on the reins and the beast slowed. Abe looked down, fighting with the fear creeping into every pore in his skin. They were flying over a flat plain, with the mountains rising to the right, towards Fuji-san. From the height he couldn't even see the individual homes in the villages they passed, just spots of straw-yellow, or grey and blue where the tiled roofs outnumbered the thatches. He tried to remember the maps he had studied when he was still the young Councillor for Maintenance of the Imperial Highways.

We must be over Kanagawa, he thought. *Is this how the Gods see us?*

"Look for a large river and follow it to the sea," he said. "Then we just need to fly west along the shoreline and then due south."

We could govern this land so much better if we had these flying beasts...

Soon his administrator's mind took over the fear.

There's a canal that needs cleaning. And here, a good road – disappearing into nowhere. Who's the daimyo here? I need to send him a stern letter...

"Is that the river?" asked Komtur, pointing to a wide blue string running across the plain.

"I think so. That's the Sagami Bay, anyway," replied Abe. If his calculations were right, they had covered the distance of ten *ri* in less than half an hour. A fast courier needed half a day to reach that far.

Naosuke is right. We need these people on our side. No matter the cost.

CHAPTER XIV

Satō lowered her head as the boat passed under a water gate in a white-washed wall; beyond it lay a city of red brick storehouses and rich merchant mansions. The hydrangeas were in full bloom, cascading down the walls and bursting in bright blues and purples from under the weeping willows. The water was full of other boats. The oarsmen smiled at them as they passed, waving welcomingly at Master Dōraku, before disappearing into another branch of the criss-crossing network of waterways.

The canals seemed to replace the streets in this strange city. There were inns and teahouses serving the people on the boats; mansions and temples opening onto the water side. Each house had its own little boat. The closer Master Dōraku got them to the town centre, the denser the traffic grew on the main canal, until they had to wait in line before being able to pass under a narrow bridge.

The boat neared another bridge-gate, this time guarded by spearmen and archers. The Swordsman looked up at the Captain of the guards and nodded. The gate screeched open, letting the boat into the Yanagawa Castle.

"You will find lodgings over there," Master Dōraku said, pointing to a long building of grey stone. "Please follow me, Takashima-*sama*"

"Just me?"

"I have something to show you."

The samurai left her waiting in the main donjon's vast vestibule, and disappeared up the great wooden staircase. A minute or so later a grey-haired, white-bearded man climbed down the stairs, assisted by a young boy. It had taken Satō a while to remember where she had seen this face and that clan crest before.

"Tanaka-*sama*!"

The old mechanician patted her on the shoulders.

"My child, I'm so glad to see you well. We were so worried about you."

"We?"

"Many people tracked the progress of your quest. When we heard the dire news from Kirishima... but come, there's somebody waiting to see you."

She followed him up the grand staircase. The castle donjon was decorated sparingly, with a few scrolls and flower vases, except for the third floor, where the walls had been daubed with gold and silver paint.

"Did you ever get to use my glove?" the mechanician asked, as they turned into another corridor. There were very few people in the castle; a few hurrying courtsmen and ladies, and a couple of guards on every level. The daimyo of this province, she guessed, must have been spending the year in his Edo residence.

"Yes, Tanaka-*sama*. It worked perfectly."

"Bring it to me later; I may be able to do some more adjustments. Here we are."

He slid open the door to a small room, with cranes and turtles painted on the walls. In its middle, on a western-style chair sat a bent, shrivelled man, wrapped in blankets. He raised his head slowly.

"Father!"

She ran up to him and kneeled by his side, kissing his hand. He looked at her, but said nothing and there was no recognition in his eyes.

"This is your heir, Shūhan-*sama*," said Master Tanaka. "Satō is here."

"Sa-tō…" Shūhan's lips twitched in a feeble, forced smile.

Satō stood up, kissed her father on the forehead and wiped tears from her eyes. She turned to Master Tanaka.

"Did they torture him?"

"Not physically. The priests found nothing to cure."

"Then what happened?"

"I'm afraid he spent too long under the effect of blood magic; whoever held him captive, was an adept of the Forbidden Art. To make matters worse, Shūhan-*sama* used the Art to send us a signal. That's how we were able to find him, but it cost him dearly. His mind is…how to say it? Blood-addled."

Satō studied her father with terror.

Blood-addled? Is that how it ends?

She noticed his other hand was clutching a jagged piece of bronze metal. The edges were stained dark red.

"What's that he's holding?"

"It's a shard of a mirror. We found him with it, but he refuses to let go. I think it feeds his addiction."

"When will he get better?"

Master Tanaka did not reply; his silence told her enough. She held Shūhan's hand tightly, but dared not look into his crazed eyes again.

"I will avenge you, Father."

She took a slow wander through the castle grounds, under the weeping willows and wisteria waterfalls; the gardens were empty, save for an old gardener cutting the hedgerow into shape.

This is my world now, she thought. *Empty and lonely.*

She stumbled upon an old canal, overgrown with reeds and duck-weed. A single dead fish was floating on the surface. She sat down and wept.

She wept for her father and for herself, for the life she had lost and for the future she did not know. She was an orphan, an exile, and an outlaw, with no possessions other than what she carried with her. Her family name was tainted. If she was a man, she would become a *rōnin*, a masterless sellsword. But as a woman…

She looked at her reflection in the pond. Nagomi was right; even the bandages would not help long. She had been fooling herself, thinking she could play at being a boy forever. Even in Kiyō, her eccentricity was barely tolerated.

Now she was at the whim of other men. If she was lucky, she would be adopted by one of her father's remaining friends and sold off into an arranged marriage.

Marriage? She scoffed, bitterly.

And who would even want me, without a name and dowry?

She had always loathed the concept, but now even that seemed like an unattainable dream. Being a third or fourth concubine of some bored nobleman amused by her feistiness long enough to fill her belly with a bastard child was the best she could count on – if she was *lucky*...

The only other alternatives coming to her mind were a monastery or a house of entertainment. She imagined herself at the beck and call of drunken, red-faced lechers and revulsion rose in her throat.

There were no more tears left in her eyes; she stood up, her mind now clear.

None of this, she decided. *None of these things will happen to* me. *I am the heir of the Takashima School. As long as I have my sword and my magic, I will carve my own future. A* new *future.*

She went in search of the grey-stone building where the others were accommodated.

Bran welcomed her with a big grin on his face.

"Look what I got! A messenger arrived with orders from Satsuma… And he brought my ring!"

He showed her the jewel with pride; the blue stone was dim and dark.

"That's… great, Bran."

"What happened? You look like you've seen a ghost."

"A ghost?"

She raised up her anguished face to him. He put the ring away and became serious.

"It's just an expression. You didn't *really* see a ghost, did you?"

"Might as well," she said. "I've seen my Father."

"He's here? In the castle?"

She nodded. She was finding it hard to speak, with tears welling in her throat she was desperate not to show.

Be strong.

"Sit down." Bran took her by the arm and led into the common room. "I'll call for something to drink."

When she finished recounting her meeting with Shūhan, she noticed she had let him hold her hand all through the tale. The waitress brought *cha* and Satō withdrew her hand to grasp the teacup.

"But that's… good, isn't it?" Bran asked. "He's alive."

Is he serious?

"It would be *better* if he was dead. At least he would die like a samurai. What he's now reduced to, it's... ten times worse."

She hid her face in the cup.

"We will get the Crimson Robe... that Ganryū," said Bran. "And make him pay."

"Of course we will," she said.

She woke up with a start. Faint moonlight illuminated the silhouette of a man sitting in the corner of the room.

"Don't fear, child," a familiar voice spoke softly, "it's me."

Is this another vision?

Satō looked at Nagomi; the priestess slept soundly.

"Are you... are you real?"

"I am real. I snuck out of the castle"

"But... you were out of your mind. Blood-addled."

"Because I saw you...I was able to fight the Curse."

The Curse? He can't mean...

"What is happening to you? Wait, I'll light the lamp..."

"No! You can't see me like this. I came to tell you... you have to kill me, child."

"Father..."

"No, listen! You didn't think He allowed me to escape? It was a *ruse*. He's using me. He already knows you're here, and the boy... you should kill me before He... forces me to harm you."

"He... forces you to...?"

His shadow crept a little towards her.

"It now takes all my strength to oppose Him, but I don't know how much longer I can go on."

"I... we can't –" she said, but her hand reached for the dagger she kept under the *futon*.

"I'm already dead..." his voice turned hoarse. "Please... I can sense Him coming..."

His words were pleading, but his tone was unpleasant, slithering. Suddenly he jumped at her and pinned her to the floor; she dropped the dagger. His breath smelled of stale blood, his fingers clutched her arms like claws, fingernails tearing through the cotton of her night shirt. He brought his face near to hers. In the faint moonlight she saw the face she knew so well now contorted in a grimace of pain and fury, his teeth bared, sharp.

"*Where is he,*" he said in a hissing voice she didn't recognize. "*Where's the boy?*"

He was too strong; she couldn't resist his grasp. Her left shoulder – where the Crimson Robe's bronze dagger had hit her – pulsated with agonizing pain spreading all over her upper body. She wanted to scream for help, but the sound stifled in her throat. She felt herself forced to answer.

"In... the room... upstairs..."

"*You will take me to him.*"

"Yes…"

He raised her from the floor and pushed her forward, holding her tight. She felt something trickle down her arm where Shūhan's fingers dug into skin and flesh. Her eyes were full of tears.

The door slid open; a lanky man stood on the corridor, holding a lantern in one hand. His other fist was set on fire.

"Down," ordered Heishichi. She dropped to her knees, feeling the joints strain in her father's grip.

"*Brand!*" The *Daisen* cried and opened his fist; a tongue of flame burst above Satō's head, then another. The grip on her arm slackened and she scrambled into the corridor before looking back. When she finally did, the entire upper half of Shūhan's body was on fire; eerily, he neither flailed nor cried, just stood there, burning down. He reached out a flaming hand towards her; through the flame she could see his mouth move, trying to say something – *I'm sorry? I love you?* – but no voice came from the disintegrating lips.

Satō heard a scream from inside the room.

"Nagomi's still there!"

The *Daisen* threw another ball of flame at the half-burned body, but Shūhan – what was left of him – didn't fall down. He took a staggering step forward.

She heard heavy steps - Torishi came down the corridor towards them. He burst into the room, pushing Shūhan to the floor, leapt over the flames and, seconds later, emerged with Nagomi in his arms. On the way out, he grabbed Satō by the sleeve.

"We must go," he said.

"Wait," she said. "I need to finish this."

She approached cautiously, watching the remains of her father burn. She stretched out a trembling hand.

"*Bevries,*" she said. "*Bevries. Bevries.*"

She kept repeating the spell until Shūhan's body was covered in a thick icy tomb and all her power was spent.

The world around her turned black and she dropped to the floor, exhausted.

Satō played with the *teppō* gun she had received along with the adjusted glove from Master Tanaka after her father's funeral.

"You will need it more than I do," the teary-eyed old mechanician had said.

She unscrewed and screwed the hidden handle repeatedly, finding solace in the clicking sound. She looked around. Everyone in the boat was silent, grim-faced. The only glimpse of colour was the dull light shining off the blue stone on Bran's finger.

"Are you going to be wearing it now, then?" she asked.

"It's the only way to be sure it's not stolen again."

Torishi leaned over to study the ring with interest.

"What is it?" she asked.

"The Little People wore shards of such blue stone around their necks," the bear-man answered.

"The Little People?" asked Bran.

"The Ancients," said Nagomi. "His people knew them a long time ago. But why did they do that?"

"Not sure," the bear-man replied with an apologizing shrug, "it may have had something to do with the dragons."

Bran scratched his nose.

"The drawings in the tomb," he said. "So they *did* worship the dragons."

"Yes. The beasts were their Spirit animals, much like the bears were for us."

"What happened to those shards?"

"Gone, like the Little People… stolen, sold for food… there were many who dug up their tombs and looted them."

The bear-man leaned back. Nobody said anything more, only Bran raised his ring finger to the dim sun, letting the cold light play on the jagged facets.

The flat, muddy, reed-covered banks of the Chikugo River passed lazily on both sides. Satō was getting sick of the sight of those reeds, and the weeping willows.

"This is the worst part of our journey," she murmured. "And I thought being lost in the Takachiho forest was bad."

"Not long now, wizardess-*sama*," said Master Dōraku. He had given the oar to Torishi, who alone seemed to be enjoying himself on this mode of journey.

"We should soon reach Kurume, where we swap to horses."

Horses?

"I can't ride a horse," she said.

"Then you are welcome to join me in the saddle. The Kurume horses are exceptional creatures. Descended from the legendary Ikezuki. We're lucky the daimyo is a friend."

Bran moved closer; he and Nagomi were sitting at a bench closer to the bow; Heishichi sat alone in the last one.

"A friend, you say? A friend to whom?"

"Good question, Karasu-*sama*," the Swordsman said with a weak smile. "He is a long-time ally to Nariakira-*dono*'s cause. And since we're wearing Satsuma colours now…"

"Nariakira-*dono* seems to have friends everywhere."

"That's just because we choose our path wisely. To the East, West and North of here, all daimyos are loyal to the *Taikun*. Some even belong to his family. The Kurume is the last safe place until Nagato."

The name reminded Satō of something.

"I had a student from Nagato," she said. "I wonder what happened to him. Hadn't seen him since… since…"

Her voice broke as she remembered the last time she had seen her father alive and well, the morning before she went to Master Tanaka's lecture. Bran reached his hand to her, but she turned him down.

"I'm all right. What is the *cause* that you spoke of?" she asked the Swordsman. "My…" she choked and coughed, "my Honourable Father belonged to some conspiracy he never discussed with me. Was it part of the same cause?"

"It's not up to me to explain His Excellency's plans," Master Dōraku replied.

"We will bring the *Taikun* down. One way or another," said Heishichi from his lonely post, "and wake this land from its sleep."

Satō turned around in shock. This was the first time she had heard somebody speak so clearly and without hesitation on the matter.

"Bring the *Taikun*… that's insane!"

"The Prophecy…" whispered Nagomi. "*The mightiest will fall.* It's all coming true."

"Why is it insane?" asked Bran. "He is just a man, isn't he? How did his family come to such power, anyway?"

Satō looked up at Master Dōraku. As the witness of the beginnings of the *Taikun's* rule, he seemed the most suitable person to tell the story. But the Swordsman nodded at her with a smile.

"Three hundred years ago, a great Civil War ravaged Yamato," she started. "Daimyo against daimyo, local warlords, rebel monks, peasant armies and so on… until a mighty warlord defeated everyone else and united the nation under his rule."

"The first Tokugawa *Taikun*," guessed Bran. "Ieyasu, wasn't it?"

"No, the unifier's name was Oda. Ieyasu was just one of his lieutenants at the time."

"Then how…"

"Ieyasu wielded the greatest weapon of all: patience," said Master Dōraku. "He waited until the great Oda and all his heirs and successors died out or were killed, leaving only a child of five. He then announced himself a regent in the child's name."

"There was resistance, of course," continued Satō. "And an alliance of clans faced him at Sekigahara in the most terrible battle of all. But Ieyasu won against all the odds. After that, there was no one left to oppose him."

Bran turned to Heishichi. "I'm guessing the Shimazu were on the losing side."

"He bribed and cheated his way to victory," the wizard replied, his face contorted in anger. "He lured the clans with false promises and divided the allies. And the Tokugawas have been doing it ever since."

"What happened to the child? The five-year old?"

"Forced to suicide some years after the battle," replied Master Dōraku. "Along with the rest of the family."

"That's not strictly true," said Heishichi, looking strangely at the Swordsman.

"Oh, there are other threads of the story, of course," Master Dōraku agreed, "but I don't think there is any need to get into those details now."

Bran stared at the flowing river, mulling over all the new information, then looked at Satō.

"I thought you said civil wars and revolts like that don't happen in Yamato."

She shook her head.

"Not anymore. Not under the Tokugawas. The *Taikuns* have all the armies, all the money, all the key castles. They hold children of all the major clans as hostages in Edo. And nobody wants to repeat the bloodshed of the Civil War just to replace one tyrant with another."

"Satsuma seems to think otherwise," Bran replied, nodding at Heishichi.

"Foolish dreams," she barked. "They did nothing for two hundred years."

Heishichi snorted with indignation. "The time was not right," he said. "One day... soon."

"The clans will never support you. To them, a Shimazu is no better than a Tokugawa."

"I don't know much about these things, of course," Bran said with a patient nod. "And this is not my war to wage. But I remember what you've told me about your Father's beliefs. Some might say those were foolish dreams as well."

Satō wanted to scoff with another angry remark, but she held her tongue.

He's right. My Father believed a change for the better was possible in Yamato.

A sudden thought struck her. She turned to Heishichi and bowed before him. The *Daisen* raised an eyebrow.

"I'm sorry, my words were rash. If my Honourable Father thought it wise to ally himself with Satsuma, I am bound to honour his commitment. As soon as this is over, I will return with you to Kagoshima."

A shadow of a smile flickered across the *Daisen*'s face and he bowed back.

Dōraku's eyes narrowed as he steered the boat towards the harbour. Bran followed his gaze towards the castle towering on a low hilltop over the fork in the river.

"That's the *Taikun*'s hollyhock crest on the ramparts. What's going on?"

"It seems a friend is a friend no more," remarked Heishichi. "We should land somewhere else. Look, there are soldiers on the pier."

Dōraku turned the boat about and headed for another, smaller quay beside a tall garden wall. A vermillion *torii* gate on the far end of the pier marked the entrance to a shrine.

"I will wait here, with Torishi-*sama*," the Swordsman said. "You find out what's happening in the city."

"You really can't step onto a sacred ground, can you?" Bran asked. "Even after all you've gone through?"

"There is no redemption for me," the Swordsman said. "The Spirits are waiting behind that *torii* to tear my soul to shreds."

"Would *that* kill you?"

"I don't know. It might be the closest thing to death. Now go."

There's something he's not telling me, thought Bran. Dōraku's face was surprisingly easy to read, as if so near to a shrine his mask had shattered.

Or maybe I'm just getting better at it.

After all, he now knew the Fanged's deepest secret: his creation. He hadn't asked Dōraku about his vision from Amakusa yet; he had a feeling the samurai would not be eager to discuss his "birth" so openly. But he often thought about what it meant. While the men he saw in the vision were of Yamato birth, they were all Sun Worshippers; probably rebels from Shimabara, like Shigemasa had said. Did it mean the ritual had come here from the West? From... Rome?

They were using it to raise fallen soldiers at first, but soon discovered that by using blood magic curses they could imbue the walking dead with great power, and keep them under control.

Doctor Campion's words rang in his ears.

Of course – when the Vasconians first came here, the Wizardry Wars were still being fought.

Necromancy. Vanquished and long forgotten in the West – but here, in Yamato...

"Are you coming, Bran?" Satō called him from beyond the *torii* gate.

"Yes, there is a great deal of disturbance in Kurume," said the stocky, square-jawed, balding man. He wore an old, stained set of lamellar armour over his high priest robe. "For one, I'm being held under house arrest here."

It had quickly occurred to Bran that Dōraku had not chosen his mooring place by accident. The high priest of the shrine, introducing himself as Maki Izumi, welcomed them with open arms and led them straight to his study. Heishichi handed him a folded piece of paper marked with the Shimazu crest. Obviously, the man was one of the "friends" the Swordsman had mentioned.

"Edo is in turmoil," said Izumi. "They sent requests for additional troops to all the daimyos. It's almost as if they're preparing for war – or a revolt."

"Preposterous idea," said Heishichi.

"Of course."

"I thought Yorishige-*dono* could be trusted," Heishichi continued. As the official representative of Satsuma, he was the only one talking. Bran was soon lost in the exchange, anyway; the names of the lords and domains mentioned in the conversation meant little or nothing to him.

"He is. But he can't openly defy the *Taikun's* orders! Not with Saga and Kokura on our doorstep. We are but a small, poor domain, not like the mighty Satsuma."

"It's a test of loyalty," guessed Heishichi. Izumi nodded.

"That's why His Excellency keeps me away from the court. He knows my name is not popular in Edo. I'm telling you, *Daisen-sama*, something's stirred the pot. Satsuma must make its move soon, or it will be too late."

"Perhaps it has. Have you read the letter?"

"Ah, the letter, yes. Excuse me for a moment."

The High Priest unravelled the paper and put on a pair of horn-rimmed spectacles, similar to the ones Heishichi wore. His face brightened as he neared the bottom of the page. He finished and smacked a fist on the table.

"Good news?" asked Satō.

"The best news! Finally, matters are moving in the right direction. But, Nariakira-*dono* asks me to provide the bearer of this letter with any help they may require. What is it that you need of me?"

"We need horses," said Heishichi.

"You mean the Ikezuki breed, or you would have just bought some on the market."

"That's right."

The High Priest frowned.

"That may be difficult. All the horses have been requisitioned into the castle, for the army."

"If it was easy, we wouldn't need your help."

Izumi went over to the window overlooking the shrine garden. In this gesture, and in many small others, he reminded Bran of Lord Nariakira.

"I can help you – but under a condition. You must take me with you."

"I'm afraid our mission –"

"No, not on the mission. Just into the castle and out of the city. I need to get away from this backwater place, go to where something important is happening."

"I don't see how that will be a problem," said Satō, before Heishichi managed to open his mouth. Bran caught the *Daisen* give the wizardess an irritated glance.

The High Priest turned around and clapped his hands.

"Splendid. There's an old tunnel leading from here to the castle grounds. It's guarded on the other side, but nothing we shouldn't be able to deal with."

"*We?*" Heishichi said doubtfully. The High Priest smiled and opened a small, narrow cupboard. Inside, on a lacquered stand, rested a splendid sword in a glistening black-and-gold scabbard.

"History was not the only thing we were taught at Mito," he said with a mischievous grin.

Bran bowed before the main altar in the shrine's Offertory Hall, rang the bell and clapped twice, as he saw other visitors do.

The Suiten-gu Shrine was dedicated to the spirits of water and some long-forgotten *Mikado* unfortunate enough to drown in a battle centuries ago. But Bran wasn't here to pray; he wanted to talk to Shigemasa, and being in the presence of other Spirits while doing this made him feel somehow safer. He dared not yet return to the red dirt plain to meet the General face-to-face.

"Tell me, *Taishō,*" he said, "You have sworn loyalty to the *Taikun,* have you not?

There was silence at first, and then the familiar bubbling of Shigemasa's ever angry thoughts coming to the surface.

"*And what do you know about the* Taikun, *Barbarian? None of this concerns you.*"

"I know his officials would arrest me on sight, and then cut my head off."

Shigemasa snarled.

"*They wouldn't waste a sword on a Barbarian's head. You'd be hanged, crucified or boiled alive, depending on the judge's mood.*"

Bran could feel the General's anger burning. There was some deep, personal grievance buried within Shigemasa's thoughts.

"*I swore fealty to the first of the Tokugawas, yes. But he is long dead, like me,*" he said at last. "*The oaths do not carry into the afterlife.*"

"I need to know you are not going to denounce us. You are now in the company of rebels and traitors, after all."

"*It would achieve nothing. It wouldn't stop the Darkness.*"

Ah. The Darkness.

A pilgrim standing patiently behind Bran coughed. The boy stepped aside, letting the man get closer to the altar.

"I heard you talk about it with Torishi."

"*It's no secret. Even your little priestess knows about it.*"

"Nagomi?"

"*All soothsayers see it. The Darkness that gathers around Yamato. Not even the Spirits can peer through it.*"

"What do you think it means?"

"*Nothing good, I reckon. Maybe it's the limit of our prophecies. The Gift is not like your Barbarian science, with measures and numbers.*"

"Yes. Vague and mysterious – unless you *need* it to be precise."

A drop of rain fell on the pavement beside Bran. He looked up; the silver clouds lined with navy blue gathered above him.

"You never told me that place of red dust was the Otherworld," he said, heading for the grey-stone house.

"*You never asked.*"

"Does it all look like that? Featureless and dark…?"

"*That's only the place the living can access. A forecourt of the Otherworld, as it were. And your place is… a bit different to others.*"

"My place – you mean the tower."

"*I've seen castles… mansions… The red-headed priestess' mind is like a fortified temple. But never just a tall stone tower.*"

"You can see into other people's minds?"

"*I could never get past all the walls and wards. Only with you I am bonded enough to break through.*"

There must be a way to use it, thought Bran.

"Could I reach the place where the Spirits gather?"

"*Not without dying first.*"

"The Kumaso could."

"*Those… half-animals,*" Shigemasa scoffed with resentment. "*I don't know how it works for them. Turn into a bear, for all I know. Why would you want to go there?*"

"It's something Dōraku said… about the Spirits waiting to tear his soul apart."

"*You think you'd find a way to destroy the Crimson Robe.*"

"The Crimson Robe… yes, that's right."

Shigemasa chuckled.

"*Oh, I see! Hedging your bets. You're growing clever for your age, boy.*"

"My father is a diplomat," said Bran, "it must be in my blood too." He couldn't help smiling to himself.

"I like the game you're playing, boy."

The narrow, damp tunnel stretched for a good mile. The road was straight and well lit – two of Izumi's students illuminated the way with paper lanterns – and it didn't take long for Bran and the others to reach its end.

"So what's so special about these horses?" he asked Satō.

"Ikezuki was the horse of Yoritomo," she replied, "a warlord from the Genpei Wars, seven hundred years ago. A foal of a wild mountain mare and a *qilin*. It was said to be able to swim across the sea and run as fast as a flying *ryū*. His brother Yoshitsune used another horse of that breed to hunt dragons."

"And what are they doing *here?*"

"This shrine is dedicated to those fallen in the Genpei Wars," said Izumi, overhearing their conversation. "After the war, Yoritomo gave his horse to us as an offering, and we've been breeding its kin ever since."

A rotting ladder reached a trap door. Izumi approached it cautiously and tried out the first rung. It held.

"Ishi, Bashi, turn those lights down," he ordered his students. The inside of the tunnel turned pitch black.

"The door opens to a small courtyard in the southern corner of the castle grounds," the priest's voice rang in the darkness. "There're usually two or three soldiers immediately by the door, and more in the guardroom further on. But we'd do best not to be noticed by them. Remember, none of your fireworks; we're trying to be stealthy."

"Where are the horses?" asked Bran. His hand rested on the guard of his sword. He didn't like the plan; it was one thing to slay monsters and demons, or even men who were out to get them. But now they were considering killing some innocent soldiers, whose only fault was standing between them and some mounts. Why couldn't they just buy some horses from the market, like Izumi had suggested?

"The stables are on the right hand side, not far from the Eastern Gate. If your friends outside will do as planned," he added, meaning Dōraku and Torishi, "we should be out of the castle in no time."

"Go on, then," said Heishichi. "Open that door."

The door screeched and a narrow strip of dim light appeared in the blackness.

CHAPTER XV

Shakushain stood on the shore with his arms crossed, watching the dozen grey-clad men struggle to transport a great iron box from an oxcart platform onto the flat-bottomed ferry.

In the cold breeze, they sweated more than the effort required; the beast inside, though now sound asleep and separated by a sheet of rune-scratched steel, still exerted its terrifying influence on anyone who got close. Even from a distance, he felt the chill reaching into his mind, a palpable, primeval fear telling him to run and hide in some dark cave. He could almost see its dark feelers flowing from inside the box. No bear, wolf or wild boar had ever made him feel this way. He was impressed with the way Ganryū's men were managing to hold on to their sanity so close to the monster.

The fear was so strong that only Ganryū himself could board the boat. The others boarded another, smaller vessel, to follow the Fanged towards the small island in the middle of the straits.

Before boarding, Shakushain came up to Koro and crouched down, so that their faces were level.

"Do you remember how we used to race across the Ishikari River?" he asked.

Koro smiled at the memory.

"When we get close to the island, I want you to pretend you've fallen off the boat, dive and swim to the northern shore. It shouldn't be more than five *chō*. Can you make it?"

The little man nodded.

"Why?" he asked.

"I don't like the way Ganryū looks at your necklace. He wants it, I can feel it."

"He does," Koro agreed. "He wants to have a pair."

"A pair?" Shakushain frowned. "What do you mean?"

"The red one puts to sleep; the blue one wakes."

Shakushain looked sharply towards Ganryū; the Fanged was already on the ferry, pushing the vessel away with the long pole. "Do you think he knows?"

"He's not certain. The stone's power is hidden from strangers."

"Good." Shakushain nodded. "One day you'll have to tell me what it is," he added with a smile. He stood up.

"Hide somewhere for a couple of days. I don't think I'll be staying here for too long. And don't worry – I'll make sure nobody follows you."

Satō stepped over the body of the guard, wiping his blood off the blade. She tried not to look at his face; he wasn't much older than her.

He didn't even attack her, just threatened her with a brandished spear. The other guards had charged at the High Priest and his students; they died valiantly, in battle, before Satō even managed to climb out of the trap door. But this boy... he was too afraid to strike, and too dutiful to run away.

"Get him!" Master Heishichi had urged her. "Before he alarms the others!"

A sickening thought fluttered through her mind as her sword fell on the guard's chest.

Is this what civil war is like? Yamato killing Yamato in battle?

She felt herself pushed onwards. The *Daisen* dragged her out of the small courtyard into the open space. She heard shouting and saw dots of dancing light heading towards them from the direction of the donjon.

Soldiers with lanterns, she guessed.

It was too late for stealth – they had been detected.

"In here," cried Izumi. The gate to the long, low building of red brick was locked shut, but only for a moment: in one great burst of flame Master Heishichi released his irritation at being unable to use magic earlier. The smouldering remains of the gate swung open.

The horses inside started kicking and wheezing in panic. Satō stopped on the threshold, overcome by the all too familiar fear.

"Which are the ones we're looking for?" asked Bran. She noticed his sword was still sheathed and it made her feel even more guilty.

"The calm ones," said Izumi with a grin. "The big white ones. They should be already bridled. Each of you take one and lead it out. Hurry!"

"We need time to saddle," said Bran.

"Nobody saddles an Ikezuki!" Izumi said with a chuckle. "Don't worry, it'll be all right; you won't feel a thing. You too, boy –" To Satō's terror, he seemed to be talking to her. "Go help!"

She closed her eyes and stepped inside; her entire body wanting to run away. The smell and the noise overwhelmed her. She bumped into something big, soft and warm. She opened her eyes and found herself staring straight into another pair, dark brown and calm, belonging to a giant white horse. Fear took her over.

"Ah, good, take this one, I'll get another," one of Izumi's students said and pushed the bridle strap into her clammy hands.

The animal nudged her with its nose. Satō almost fell down.

What do I do now? Do I just... pull it?

She tugged on the leather strap gently and the animal took a step forward.

"Move, you're blocking the way!" Somebody shouted from behind. The girl shook her head.

Pull yourself together, Takashima Satō.

Every step towards the stable door felt like a mile, but at last she was outside. She saw a full-scale battle in the castle courtyard, with soldiers now running towards them from every direction. Torishi and Master Dōraku were already there, alongside Master Heishichi and the High Priest – the bear-man behind, shooting his bow, the Swordsman in front, whirling the twin blades; she cast a quick glance towards the Eastern Gate and saw it open wide, with several guards lying dead from arrow-shots. She felt sick.

"Right, that's the last one," said Bran, leading another of the white horses out of the stables. He gasped.

"By the Red Dragon's Beard, what's going on here?"

"Release the others," the High Priest commanded, "it will add to the confusion."

Ishi and Bashi ran inside. Moments later, a dozen terrified horses galloped past her, straight towards the soldiers.

"Now! Mount up! *Daisen-sama*, do as we planned."

Master Heishichi spread his hands apart and weaved a complex pattern, shouting a couple of Bataavian spell words in quick succession. A wall of flame rose between him and the castle guards.

Satō felt herself picked up and put onto the back of the horse nearest to her. Master Dōraku leapt in front of her.

"Hold tight!"

"To what?"

"To me!" the Swordsman replied, laughing. She clung to his back and shut her eyes tight as the horse underneath her bolted forward.

She had no idea how much time had passed. Everything was hazy and blurry; her backside and thighs ached with a thousand burns and tears. At last, the horse stopped and she slid to the ground.

They were on the outskirts of the city, just beyond the last line of houses, near the river. Satō saw Bran help Nagomi dismount carefully from the horse she shared with the boy; the wizardess felt a pang of irritation and looked away. She noted that Master Heishichi sat on his mount almost as precariously as she had. She guessed the merchant's son didn't have much practice in bareback riding, either.

Master Izumi and one of his students remained mounted, watching the road behind anxiously. The other boy was missing. There was one more member of the party she couldn't account for... Only then did she notice that Master Dōraku was carrying a bow and a quiver on his back.

"Where is Torishi?"

"He will meet us in two days near Kokura."

"I didn't see him take a horse."

Master Dōraku chuckled. "The Chief of the Kumaso doesn't need a horse."

"Will he know the way? He's never been in these parts."

"He will manage," the Swordsman replied. "And now we'd better go too," he added. "The chase will be upon us any minute. Izumi-*sama*?"

"We part here. I'm grateful for your help," said Master Izumi. "I hope we'll meet again, in Satsuma."

"Is that where you're going?"

"Where else! Oh, and have this; who knows, it may come in useful." He cast the Swordsman a small pouch of red embroidered cloth. "A *Dan-no-Ura* talisman. This one works," he added with a wink, then spurred his horse and galloped south, followed by the one remaining student; Satō couldn't tell whether it was Ishi or Bashi.

"Right. Allow me, please. " Master Dōraku grabbed Satō by the waist and lifted her back onto the horse.

"I hope you don't mind getting a bit wet."

"Why? Where are we going?"

"To the other side," he replied, pointing to the Chikugo River, flowing wide and wild this far from the sea. "Let's see if these horses are really as good swimmers as the legends say."

Bran stroked the horse's snow white neck. Its mane shimmered silver in the moonlight, and its eyes glinted like amber. The horse was silent and serious, just as it had been all night. It never so much as snorted.

He soon learned to appreciate the mount's value. After crossing the river as easily as if it was a garden pond, the horse had now been galloping for hours, without showing the least signs of tiredness. Moreover, the ride was smooth and mercifully gentle on his body, something Bran had been most worried about. He never liked horse-riding much, always preferring the dragon; but this ride, with the road beneath them zooming at incredible speed and the cold wind battering against his head, was as close to flying as he could have hoped. There was even, in the way the horse responded instantly and intuitively to his commands, something resembling a primitive Farlink, a faint buzz of connection. Bran could easily imagine riding a horse like this into battle against a dragon.

He still wasn't sure if getting the horses was worth risking their lives for, rousing the defences of an entire castle and sacrificing one of Izumi's students. As he rode away from the Eastern Gate, Bran had seen the boy fall off his mount with an arrow in the back. Something didn't feel right about it all…

"We've been had," he said to himself.

"I'm sorry?" asked Nagomi; the girl had been clinging desperately to his back at the beginning of their escape, but by now had managed to relax her grip a little, growing steadily used to the new mode of transport.

"We've been used," he said aloud. "This was never about the horses or us catching up with the Crimson Robe."

"Then why…?"

"Politics, I guess. We helped that High Priest escape – obviously he's important to somebody at Satsuma – and disrupted the war preparations by burning the stables and stealing the horses. Maybe even provoked some clash between the lords."

This sounds exactly like something my father would have done, he thought.

"*War?* There is a war coming?"

"Haven't you heard what Izumi-*sama* was saying? The *Taikun* mobilizes the troops throughout the country. Even I can tell this is bad."

"You're a soldier. You know how these things work."

I'm not a soldier. I was just raised by one.

"You're the one who foresaw all this," he replied. "You've seen the Darkness."

Nagomi fell silent. Without turning around, Bran imagined her frowning and mulling over what he just said.

"I didn't tell anyone…"

So Shigemasa was right.

"What is it? What did you see?"

"Dark clouds over Yamato. A storm of carrion crows. A bloody dawn."

"I don't know much about prophecies, but that can't be good."

"No, I don't think it is," said Nagomi. She sighed and leaned her head against his shoulders. "There is something else I keep seeing…"

She told him about the three men invading an old man's castle in her dream. Now he frowned.

Grey Hoods! The Rome or…the Gorllewin? They are in Qin... And the green-eyed man — is that…my father? Who's the bearded fellow, then?

"Have you told anyone about this dream?"

"No," she answered. "Not even Sacchan. I dream many dreams."

"And yet you remembered this one."

"This one was different… this one scared me."

Some half an hour later Dōraku's horse slowed down to a trot, allowing Bran to match its speed.

"That's enough for today," the Swordsman said. "These may be half-mythical horses, but they are not immortal — and I bet you are tired too."

Bran nodded, although he felt he could still ride for a few hours more. It was only after he dismounted to help with breaking camp that he felt the pain and numbness in his legs. The girls collected firewood, while he and Dōraku rubbed the horses dry with straw and led them to a small stream and a glade of fresh, moist grass.

"We've covered more ground than I hoped for," said Dōraku patting one horse on the neck. The animals neighed uneasily. "Can you tell where your *dorako* is now?"

Bran leaned against the pine tree and closed his eyes.

"It's closer, but still ahead of us," he said.

And so is the other dragon, he thought. *Far to the north… towards Edo! Did the Taikun get a beast of his own?*

The Swordsman frowned. "Ganryū might reach Kokura before us at this rate."

"Then shouldn't we be riding further?"

"No, no," Dōraku shook his head. "I can't risk you all being exhausted by the time we confront him."

Confront him?

"We don't even know how – or if – we can kill him," he said, but Dōraku said nothing.

Bran sat under the pine tree, focusing on the black spot inside the campfire flames.

"Taishō-sama."

He waited a while for the General to bubble up.

"I'm listening, boy."

"Have you learnt anything?"

"I saw your beast again, boy. It's looking rather forlorn."

"Forlorn?"

Bran closed his eyes and instantly transported his mind to the plain of red dust. Following Shigemasa's lead, he found the phantom jade dragon shuffling about, dragging its tail across the red sand with its head held low. His heart sank.

It looks sick.

He approached the beast slowly. The dragon raised its head and looked up at Bran, but there was no recognition in its eyes. Lowering its neck again, it trundled on.

We've been through this! What's wrong now? And I even have my ring now –

He looked at his hand: the ring was missing. He frowned.

Why is it gone?

Since his conversation with Torishi, Bran had been growing certain that the blue shard was the whole reason behind what, he had thought, was his natural affinity to the dragons.

There was nothing special about me, after all, he had reasoned. *My Farlink quotient, Emrys's obedience... it was all down to this little shard of crystal.*

Dylan had never shown an affinity for having a good contact with his mounts; *he had scars to prove it,* after all. So where would Bran's sudden talent had come from?

Did Ifor know about the stone's power? Did he learn it from that Yamato woman, Ōmon?

He opened his eyes, returning to the real world, and reached into his satchel. He took the medallion out; the sad, almond-eyed face appeared under his touch. Who was she anyway? She didn't seem exotic to him now; he could appreciate her mysterious beauty. She was older than and not as regal as Atsuko, but she was a beauty nonetheless. No wonder Ifor fell for her...

She faced the Crimson Robe too, he remembered.

He chased her all the way to Dejima – all for that little piece of blue stone?

Would Dōraku know...?

He put it back into the bag and noticed Satō approach him.

"Hullo."

"May I –?" she asked. He nodded. She sat down beside him, wrapping her arms around her knees.

"You didn't fight in Kurume," she said.

"I'm not going to kill anyone over some horses," he replied.

She looked at him with a curious expression. "You're always so reluctant to take life. Is this because of what the Western wizards teach about the *mogelijkheit*?"

"You know the theory of potentials?"

"Of course. What Rangaku scholar doesn't? But it's just a theory, and few believe it in Yamato."

"I thought that was it at first," Bran admitted, "but now I think it's something within me. Certainly, the wizards in the Dracalish army have no such qualms." He remembered the bloody history of the Empire, the destruction he had seen in Qin, and his father's personal accounts of war. Dylan must have lost the count of lives he had taken long ago. It did not seem to diminish his powers in the least, but what did he really know about his father?

Maybe that's it, he thought, looking at his hands and imagining the full power of dragon flame surging through his fingers. *Maybe I just don't want to become like him: a man who can kill with a thought.*

"You'll become a *Butsu* monk at this rate," the wizardess said and chuckled softly.

He looked back at her and noticed she was playing absent-mindedly with a small piece of polished bronze.

"What's that?" he asked.

She showed it to him. There was a strange rune scratched on the surface; the edges of the bronze were stained dark red.

"My Father had it on him when he... died. I don't know why."

Another man dead because of me, thought Bran.

"Tanaka-*sama* said the rune must have been copied from the Crimson Robe; the whole place where they found him was covered in runes of this design."

"Why did you keep it?"

"Wouldn't you? I thought he maybe... wanted me to have it."

The light of the campfire glinted red off the bronze; the colour of Nagomi's hair.

"So I hear you're not going back to Kiyō," Bran said.

"There's nothing for me to go back to," she replied.

"What about all the things you left behind? What about the Dragon Book?"

She smiled.

"I have *seen* a *dorako*, Bran. What more do I need? Besides, you've already taught me more than any scholar in Yamato will ever learn."

"I wish I paid more attention in school," he said. "I always thought being able to fly well was all that mattered."

"It would be all that matters to me."

"My grades were terrible, but they still offered me a baccalaureate," he said with a chuckle.

"What does it mean?"

"More years in school. Had I agreed to that, I would never have come here."

"You wouldn't have lost Emris."

"I wouldn't have met you," he said and looked at her; with her chin on her knees, the back of her neck showed pale in the campfire light. His previous fascination with her nude body now seemed vulgar and barbaric. In Kagoshima, he had learned to appreciate the true beauty of a woman. How much more sensuous was this pale triangle of skin, cut off neatly by the collar of the *kosode* and the black pony-tail. Bran felt the warmth spread from his loins to his stomach and the desire to hold her close. He reached out to touch her. She brushed her cheek against his fingers.

"Tomorrow, can I ride with you?" she asked. There was innocence in the question, belying anything that had ever happened – or could happen – between them.

"I would like that very much."

Bran took the bronze spyglass from his satchel. It screwed open with a screech.

I haven't used it in a while. I almost forgot I had it.

The lens fogged up and, as he waited for it to clear, he studied the view below.

"It's bigger than I remembered," said Dōraku.

The fir-covered hill on which Bran, Dōraku and Heishichi were standing overlooked a narrow, stormy strait, in the middle of which, lay a flat island stretching from north to south. It was shaped like a great ship, narrow at the ends, wide in the centre, a quarter of a mile long and about a hundred yards in breadth. On the southern side it was sheltered from the tides by a reef of jagged black rocks.

Looking further west, Bran spotted tall, white castles rising on hilltops on either side of the narrows, like twin watchtowers guarding the sea passage – Nagato domain's Chōfu in the North and Ogasawara's Kokura to the south, as Dōraku had explained earlier.

At last the spyglass was good for use and he could investigate the ship-shaped island more closely. The entire perimeter was surrounded by a tall earthen wall; most of the land was given to a green meadow, or pasture, with several clumps of wind-bent trees. A rectangular, two-storey mansion stood on a raised mound on the northern tip, with several long, low buildings of white stone scattered around it. The only obvious way onto the island was by a single pier jutting out in the direction of Kokura, surrounded by watchtowers and battlements.

Bran counted at least ten guards in grey uniforms he remembered from Kirishima, wandering around the precinct; he reported this to Dōraku.

"There are more in the watchtowers," the Swordsman said. "These are Ganryū's private troops. His students."

"Students?"

"Officially, this island is the headquarters of a fencing school, Ganryū *Dōjō*. Most of his followers recruit from its students."

"There is a flag up on the mansion," said Bran. "It looks like… an octopus?"

Dōraku chuckled. "An Eight-headed Serpent," he corrected Bran, before turning serious. "That means Ganryū's inside."

I guessed as much. I can sense Emrys down there.

"He flaunts the banner of the Serpent so openly?" asked Heishichi.

"You know what it is?"

"A secret order of assassins and troublemakers. Some say they were behind every failed rebellion against the *Taikun*."

"Not *every*," said Dōraku. "But they were more than just assassins. Each head of the Serpent is an ancient Fanged."

"That banner has not been seen in a century," murmured Heishichi. "Shimazu-*dono* must be informed."

"You've never mentioned it before." Bran turned to Dōraku with an accusing stare.

"Their power is all but spent," the Swordsman said with a shrug. "Ganryū is an arrogant fool to use this symbol for himself."

Once again it struck Bran how much Dōraku knew about the Crimson Robe's affairs.

They've known each other for hundreds of years.

"Were you one of the Serpent?" he asked, putting away the spyglass.

"Never," the Swordsman replied firmly. "I grew apart from the other Fanged long before the Eight gathered for the first time. I was one of the first, really. Me and Ganryū, died and Cursed at the same time. Of course, Chiyome was the eldest of us all, but…" his voice trailed off.

"How did you die?"

Dōraku's eyes narrowed.

"It's a strange moment to ask a question like that."

"I've long been curious – and we might not get another chance to talk about it."

The Swordsman scratched his beard.

"Betrayal. It was supposed to be just another duel; I've won many like it before. But my enemy's blade was poisoned. I smashed his ribs and killed him on the spot, but he managed to scratch me. I suffered in agony for days before finally succumbing to the toxin."

"Was it Ganryū who killed you?"

Dōraku didn't answer, confirming Bran's suspicions.

"We should go back to the others. It's getting late."

"A storm is coming," Bran pointed to the steel-coloured clouds gathering on the eastern sky.

Satō groaned.

"A contingent of skilled swordsmen inside a fortress? Shouldn't we just have asked Nariakira-*dono* for a hundred of his samurai?"

"This is still Ogasawara land," replied Dōraku. To her surprise he seemed to have taken her seriously. "Nariakira-*dono* would never agree to use his banners in what would be an open declaration of war."

"We need an *army* just to get inside. We've already faced the Crimson Robe once, and we've failed! With all the wizards of Satsuma and warriors of Kumamoto on our side."

"You didn't have me," the Fanged replied with a grin. "But what I'm most worried about is you, Karasu-*sama*."

"Me?" asked Bran.

"Can you guarantee your *dorako* can be controlled this time?"

Bran gazed in the direction of the island fortress, then shook his head.

"I can't. I don't know what kind of power the Crimson Robe has over my beast. What I *can* guarantee is that, if it does turn against us, I will stop it."

Dōraku tapped his fingers on the hilt of his sword.

"No matter now. Let's get down to the beach."

Satō followed him down the path, but noticed Nagomi didn't move from where she was standing.

"What is it?"

"I'd only be in the way…"

"Don't be ridiculous."

"She's right," said Bran. Satō grimaced at him. *Don't!*

"We can't risk her life again," the boy continued. "She'll be safe here until we come back."

Torishi sniffed. "There's death in the air tonight."

He had arrived in the morning, having run all the previous day.

Nagomi stood up straight.

"I'm not a coward. I want to help, but I don't know *how*."

"Against Ganryū you are as useful as anyone, if not more, princess-*sama*" Dōraku boomed over Satō's head. "You wield the power of the *kami*. That's the best weapon against the likes of us."

"Tell me then, Dōraku-*sama*, what should I do?"

Dōraku shook his head.

"This is not my domain. It must flow from within you – when the right time comes."

Nagomi nodded and passed Bran, who shook his head. The priestess turned.

"Well, what are you waiting for?"

By the time they reached the shingle beach, the wind had picked up, surging high waves billowing against the shoreline. The storm clouds covered the sky with a black shroud, and any minute it was going to start raining. The white horses pricked their ears nervously.

"We're too late," decided Master Dōraku. "Not even the Ikezuki can swim in that weather. Let's get back to the camp and wait it out."

"No." Satō stood up, defiant. Since Shūhan's death she had been pushing away the thoughts about her future and focused on destroying the Crimson Robe, that cursed *creature* that destroyed her father and her life along with him. The very thought made the blood run hot in her veins.

And there was something else, too… some force pulling her towards the island fortress, a deep yearning. She needed to heed its call.

She put on the glove and studied the blue-glowing dial. Just as she had guessed, the oncoming storm was filled with magical energies.

"We've delayed too long. We go tonight."

"Don't be foolish, girl. Look at the waves. The tide is rising."

"We go tonight." Her voice was sharp and strong, leaving no room for objection.

"I am heir to the Takashima *Dōjō*. I will not be held back by wind!"

Master Dōraku opened his mouth to oppose her, but seemed to change his mind. He looked at the horses, then at Torishi.

"Are you up to it, Last of the Kumaso?" asked Dōraku. "No man swam the Kannon Strait in the storm before."

Torishi smiled.

"What about a bear?"

The Swordsman laughed.

"Very well then! At least the guards will be less watchful in this foul weather."

CHAPTER XVI

The ship rolled gently on the waves of the Inner Sea. The weather outside was as fine as anyone could expect at this time of year – which wasn't good news for the boat's Captain trying to reach Chōfu, the capital city of Nagato, before the end of the month.

Shōin didn't mind. He had plenty of time. He was sitting cross-legged, alone, staring at the four cups of water before him. His cabin was a luxury he badly needed, but could barely afford, even after selling all but one of his books to the antiquarian in Kiyō. Each cup was marked with an elemental rune at the bottom. The cups were borrowed from the ship's cook. The runes he had scribbled himself.

He couldn't focus on the magic; as so often lately, he was wondering what had happened at the Takashima *Dōjō*. An accident with a magic artefact, was the official explanation for Master Takashima's death – but then, what happened to Takashima-*sensei*? Why didn't she return to the school after the incident? And what of the other boy in the class, that annoying Keinosuke? Shōin never learned the answer to any of the questions. With the closing of the *dōjō*, he had no reason to say in Kiyō any longer. The school's sudden bad reputation reflected on its students, and no other teacher of *Rangaku* wanted to take him in. It was time to return home and start preparing for the take-over of his father's business.

This did not mean, however, that Shōin was going to give up his studies. He knew he had talent; *sensei* had said so herself. It would have been improper to squander it. That's why he was now playing with the water cups, desperately trying to clear his mind enough to execute a spell – any spell.

He was trying to discover his affiliated element, just as *sensei* had taught him:

You will choose your element, eventually, or rather, it will choose you. You will find some of the transformations are easier to perform, some invocations don't require as much effort.

He stretched his palms over the four cups, imagining the flow of magical energies through his body and down to his fingers; he was summoning a raw power, without focus. If his calculations were right, one of the cups should react to the magic faster and stronger.

But it seemed his calculations were wrong. This wasn't the first time he had tried the experiment; time and again, the results were the same: the frost rune made the water freeze, the fire rune made it boil; the water in the air cup bubbled up and the earth cup's thin clay walls cracked. All at the same time and, as far as he could tell, with identical intensity.

There was only one logical explanation to what was happening, but Shōin refused to acknowledge it. *Perhaps I'm too young and inexperienced,* he thought. *Perhaps my affiliation did not yet fully manifest. Maybe the difference is there, but too small for me to see.*

He bit his lips and felt the familiar jolt of power run through his hands; with each try, it came quicker and more powerfully. The four cups under his fingers burst into pieces.

A gentle bump announced the ship's arrival at Chōfu, and jolted Shōin out of his meditation. He looked around; the shards of a dozen cups were strewn all over the cabin's floor, among the densely scribbled sheets of paper. The cook had refused to give him any more, so he had to try to mend the pieces together for his continuing experiments. The pieces broke into even more shards, until he had to forget trying to work with water altogether and start on just the broken bits of clay. He didn't need the water as a conduit anymore, anyway; the clay itself melted, froze, whirled in the air or dissipated into dust under his fingers.

He gathered his notes, picked up his only remaining book – the small handbook of basic spellwork from Takashima *Dōjō* – and the bundle of clothes, and stepped outside into the sun for the first time in over a week.

As he waited his turn to step down onto the pier, Shōin noticed the crew and other passengers giving him frightened glances. He leaned overboard and looked at his reflection in the water. He saw a famished boy, with sunken cheeks, unkempt hair and deep blue bags under his eyes.

That's strange, he thought, calmly. *No. That's not me. I just need to rest and eat a proper, dry-land dinner. It's the sea.*

And then he remembered the words of Satō-*sensei* and shook his head. *"Their life energy is spent too fast. They die young."*

The familiar yellow clay walls of the Chōfu castle town spread welcomingly before him, like mother's arms. It had been two years since he had last seen them; he was eager to reach home.

"You, boy!"

Shōin walked on, recognizing neither the voice, nor a reason why anyone should call him.

"Hey, you, with the book!"

He stopped, turned and saw a man in the drab overcoat, marked with a red pentacle – the uniform of a Kiyō policeman. He was accompanied by another, younger man, supporting himself on a bamboo stick; a nasty scar ran across the left side of his face underneath a black eye-patch.

They pursued me all the way here? Impossible...

"That's a Takashima book, isn't it? I recognize the crest."

Shōin dropped his bundle of clothes, clutched the handbook to his chest – and ran. The policeman behind him swore and launched in pursuit; but this was Shōin's home town. He knew every nook and alleyway. He zigzagged in the narrow streets, past the merchant's houses, over the canal bridge, up the temple hill. He hid behind the pine tree and looked down the street. The policeman was nowhere to be seen.

Who was this? What did he want?

"Kuso!"

Doshin Koyata returned to the harbour, swearing and panting. He found Tokojiro kneeling, rummaging through the boy's belongings.

"Leave it, we're not thieves."

"If we don't pick it up, somebody else will," replied the interpreter. "He will be looking for these things."

"It's just some spare clothes. He'll get new ones."

"These may not be easy to replace," said Tokojiro. He stood up with effort and handed Koyata several sheets of densely-written paper.

"Some notes."

The *doshin* browsed through them quickly.

"Magic." He shrugged. "I have no idea what any of this means."

"Neither do I, but I recognize this hand-writing," Tokojiro said, pointing to a comment scribbled on the margin in red ink next to a set of complex runes: *Good thinking, but the last line is all wrong. Check your equations.*

"That's the Takashima girl," said Tokojiro. "The same as in the dragon book."

"So I was right. It *was* a Takashima crest."

"Of course. The boy must have been one of the school's students."

Koyata scratched his nose, trying to remember his Kiyō investigation.

"There were two boys in the youngest class... one was a son of an aristocrat; that couldn't have been him. These are merchant clothes."

"Why does it matter who it is? Why do you care?"

Koyata looked at the bunch of papers in his hand.

"You're right, it probably doesn't matter. It's just... it feels somehow ominous to meet that boy here, of all places. So far from Kiyō and everything we've gone through."

"All the more reason to leave this wretched place," Tokojiro said with a grimace. "When does the Naniwa ship set off?"

"Tomorrow morning. You should go to the guesthouse, get some rest. I'll stick around, ask the locals. I may find somebody willing to deliver these things to the boy."

"You're not in Kiyō anymore, *doshin*. This isn't one of your *cases*."

Koyata smiled.

"I can't help it. A policeman is never off-duty."

Shōin followed the Mōri clan retainer nervously across the moat, up the sloping ramp, through the heavy wooden gate and up the stone stairs.

He had never been to the Chōfu Castle before. In fact, he had never been inside any castle. The only reason a member of the merchant class like him could be summoned to a daimyo's residence was to be punished or interrogated.

Which one was the case here, he wondered? *And why the secrecy?*

The retainer said nothing about the purpose of his visit when he had come to take Shōin away from his father's workshop.

He was led to a grand chamber at the third floor of the castle where he was told to wait for the lord of the castle to talk to him. Shōin lay prostrate on the straw mat floor, desperately trying to remember what he could have done that was of such importance to the daimyo.

He heard soft steps and the rustle of silk.

"Get up," he heard a calm, but firm, voice. He sat up. A young man, no more than thirty years old, was staring at Shōin from the podium at the other end of the room. His mouth drooped a little and his cheeks were sunken; there was a sadness and world-weariness in the man's eyes, surprising in one so young.

"But you are just a child!" the man said. He shouted to somebody hiding behind the paper wall: "Are you sure that's him?"

"Yes, *kakka,*" another voice replied.

This is the daimyo of Chōshu? This is Mōri Takachika?

"How old are you, boy?"

"I'm... fourteen, *kakka.*"

The daimyo shook his head. He stood up and came closer to Shōin. He was holding some pieces of paper in his hand.

"Are these yours?"

Shōin looked up. *My notes!*

"Yes, *kakka.*"

"I found myself in possession of these a few days ago. Somebody was asking around in Chōfu for the owner of these papers."

"I... lost them at the harbour."

"Did you *really* write all these yourself?"

"Yes, *kakka.* Some of it is just notes from school..."

"Where did you learn magic?"

"At the Takashima *Dōjō* in Kiyō."

"Why did you leave?"

"The school was disbanded. The headmaster died in an accident, and my teacher has gone... missing."

"Hmm."

The daimyo returned to his podium and browsed through the papers.

"It says here you think anyone can be taught *Rangaku.* What does it mean?"

"The scholars in Kiyō think you need to first show affinity to some of Yamato's old arts – fencing, *onmyōji,* archery, the way of *cha* – before attempting to learn the Western magic," explained Shōin. "Even the Takashima method, advanced as it is, involves weeks of unnecessary training with the sword, *kakka.*"

"So you don't believe that's the way."

"I think anyone with the tiniest bit of talent can start learning *Rangaku* straightaway. It is, in fact, much simpler than our ways. Even a commoner like me could grasp the basics in a matter of weeks. Of course, that's just a theory..."

Lord Mori nodded slowly.

"I have a school here in the castle. You may have heard of it – Meirinkan."

"Of course, *kakka*. One of the three finest in the country."

The daimyo smiled.

"That may be, but without a *Rangaku* faculty it's quickly becoming obsolete. All my wizards are old and useless – or spies for Edo and Satsuma. I had my court mage read these notes. He could barely follow the more complex theories. I need someone whom I can trust. Can I trust you, Yoshida-*kun*?"

"I am your servant, *kakka!*" Shōin cried out and beat his head against the straw mat in awe. To be spoken to in this manner by the daimyo of Chōshu himself was a privilege almost too great to bear.

"You will establish a faculty of Western learning at Meirinkan. All my resources are at your disposal. You cannot fail. The tide of war is rising – and I'm going to need an *army* of wizards soon."

The evening sky darkened quickly under the thickening cover of the storm clouds. The horses treaded carefully into the foamy surf of the rising tide, their manes flowing in the wind. Bran sensed his mount's hesitation. He caressed it on the neck, trying to calm it down. He lit up a faint flamespark and looked around to see how everyone else was doing; he noted that Heishichi did not yet move from the beach.

"What's he doing?" he shouted to Dōraku over the wind.

"Leave him. His orders are just to observe."

Bran wanted to add some nasty remark, but a sudden tall wave washed over him, almost throwing him and Satō off the horse. They were now out into the open waters of the strait, and the sea heaved and tumbled all around them.

This is insane. I should've known it's suicidal.

Another spray pummelled him. He felt Satō's hands slipping off his waist and caught her just before she fell into the water.

"We must go back!" he shouted to her, "before it's too late!"

"No!" She clung closer. "Hold my hand tight. Don't let go."

"I don't think that will…"

"Just do it."

He grasped her wrist with all his strength. He felt her wiggle about for a moment, and then heard her cry a spellword in Bataavian.

"*Hoor mij, zee! Hoor mij, elementen! Kalm jezelf!*"

He looked back – she was holding her sword aloft, pointing it into the waves. Her hand was clad in a leather glove, with several bits of metal sewn to it, gears and dials. She shouted the spell two more times; with her third cry, the waters around the horse calmed as if somebody had poured oil on them.

Bran saw Dōraku lead his horse behind them into the corridor formed in the wake of Satō's spell, followed by the bobbing black shape of Torishi's bear form.

It was an impressive feat, but Bran wondered how long Satō could sustain the spell, and in what fighting shape she'd be once they reach the island. Her jaws were clenched in determination; sweat mixed with rain on her face. The corridor was beginning to taper as the force of the sea battered against the magic barrier.

Half-way through, the horses began to struggle; they were now in the middle of the mighty current linking the inner sea in the south-west with the Great Ocean to the north-east.

A boat would have trouble crossing this strait, not just these poor animals.

But something else drew his attention among the waves. In the blue darkness he saw a white mist, whiffs of smoke and whirls of haze coming out of the billows.

"Can you see that?" he shouted back to Dōraku and Nagomi. The Swordsman looked up and nodded with a frown.

"There are faces in the water!" cried the priestess. The mists formed into human forms, masks twisted in anger, dying, agonized expressions.

"It's just like the Cave in Suwa," said Bran, "They must be spirits of the dead!"

"It's the wights of *Dan-no-ura*!" Dōraku shouted back. "Those who drowned in the battle!"

The commotion was beginning to break Satō's concentration. Her sword arm dropped and the corridor between the raging waters was now barely the width of a horse. Sea spray blew again in Bran's face, salt getting in his eyes.

"Why are they so angry?" he heard Nagomi ask. The spirit faces were twisted in fury. "Are they serving the Crimson Robe?"

"No," replied Dōraku, "these are forces more ancient and more powerful than any Fanged. They hate all the living. They must have been awoken by the storm."

"They're not attacking," said Bran, "maybe they're just trying to scare us away."

"It's the talisman from Suitengu," Dōraku said, reaching into his sleeve for the embroidered pouch. At the sight of the amulet, the wights pulled away. "But it won't hold them forever."

As if in response, the wights returned a moment later, and in greater numbers. A few flew past Bran, flashing bared teeth and staring with bulging eyes. A rogue wave broke through Satō's barrier and washed over the horse.

Bran put up a *tarian*, hoping to at least protect himself and the wizardess from the cold and waves; he couldn't do much for the others.

"What do we do? We can't go back, we're more than halfway through. Satō can't fight both the waves *and* the ghosts."

"*Let me out, boy*" a voice spoke in Bran's head.

"It's no time for your tricks."

"*Don't be a fool. If you drown, I'll be stuck here forever.*"

Bran thought fast. The wights were growing bolder and more aggressive with every minute, and Satō's safe passage corridor was beginning to waver, along with her strength and determination. Nobody else seemed to offer any solutions.

"What do you need?"

"The priestess's help. And the talisman."

Bran leaned back.

"Give that pouch to Nagomi, quickly," he shouted.

"Tell the girl to meditate as if she was at the Waters."

The priestess thought Bran's hasty explanation over and then nodded. "I understand."

She closed her eyes and started chanting. Her body then seemed to glow with a soft, fuzzy light, her copper hair rose in an unseen wind. Dōraku, sitting in front of her, stirred uneasily and his face tensed as if in great pain.

The light around Nagomi grew in all directions. When it reached Bran, he felt a jolt and a buzz, and then Shigemasa was no longer in his head.

We must be as visible as a lighthouse.

The boy's neck was beginning to hurt from looking over his shoulder. The light solidified, forming the semi-translucent shape of a samurai, imposing in full armour, holding a broad *naginata* halberd, blade down, ready to strike.

Shigemasa shouted an ancient challenge. The wights understood; they poured at the General in droves, drawn to the light like moths to a flame. The halberd slashed through their wispy bodies with ease. The *Taishō* laughed, elated, launching himself into battle.

Bran spurred his horse; the animal picked up the pace. By the time they reached the reefs and shallow waters nearer the island, it was foaming at the mouth and heaving. Bran let the horse climb the rising sea bottom until the water reached only up to its chest. Then he dismounted into the cold water with a splash.

Satō slumped and slid off the horse, half-conscious. He grabbed and held her until she could stand on her own again, then sat her on a flat, black rock.

"You were brilliant," he whispered in her ear and kissed her on the cheek. She waved him away, exhausted. The sea resumed its rage around them, and they were drenched to the bone, but they were now sheltered from the worst of the storm by the reefs and a spur of the island's shore.

Dōraku led his horse by the reins into the shallows, half-wading, half-swimming. Nagomi lay on the animal's back breathless, legs and arms hanging down its sides. The light around her dimmed into a faint aura. Shigemasa waved his *naginata* a few more times before fading away and Bran heard his thoughts again.

"Glorious battle! We must do it again some time, boy."

Glad somebody enjoyed it…

"*You* seem exhausted," Bran said to Dōraku. The Swordsman looked at him with heavy eyes and attempted a weak, shrug-off smile.

"The girl's power is… quite astonishing," he replied.

So Nagomi can hurt you so much even without trying to... Bran thought with surprising satisfaction.

A great black bear was the last to wade into the shallows away from the horses. Together, they strode up to the ochre-daubed wall surrounding the island. The water here reached only up to their knees and, at last, they could rest.

We're about to go into battle, and there's not one of us that doesn't look exhausted, Bran thought, taking stock of the company. He knocked on the wall; it was a solid, thick earthenware construction. Even at his best he couldn't hope to burn it through with magic.

"What now? I think I forgot to bring my battering ram."

"There's a secret entrance not far from here."

"How do you know?"

"I helped build it," Dōraku answered. "I told you, me and Ganryū go back a long time."

So you keep saying...

"Perhaps you could share some hints as to how to defeat him."

The Swordsman scratched his beard.

"He's got a penchant for theatrics. I've always told him it would be his doom, and I'd love to see this prediction come true."

"*Theatrics?* That's it? No weak spots, no secret spells or talismans?"

"Salt helps, if you've got some," Dōraku replied with a grin, "but you don't get to live for three centuries without taking care of all your weak spots."

With the flamespark's light reduced to that of a candle, Bran moved carefully along the ochre wall, touching his way.

"There's a depression here," he said, "a finger's breadth."

"That will be it," said Dōraku. "Torishi-*sama,* give me a hand with this one. It's bound to be a bit rusty." Torishi, now back in his human form, was grumpy and silent. Water trickled down his naked, scarred body in thick rivulets. The two strongmen pushed against the wall with all their strength. A narrow crack appeared at first, then the outline of a door. Sea water rushed in, helping the gate to swing open.

Bran's horse had to lower its head to cross the threshold. Beyond the wall lay a beach of white pebbles, now licked by the tide flowing in through the secret door, and a slipway with a single flat-bottomed boat tied to a mooring post. A thick line of trees and bramble separated the cove from the rest of the island.

"This isn't very secure for a fortress," remarked Bran, eyeing the wall with suspicion.

"It would only open for one of the Fanged," explained Dōraku. "Looks like Ganryū still uses it from time to time."

"Why would he need to sneak away? He's the lord and master on this island."

"He doesn't trust even his own students."

Bran helped Torishi close the gate and then followed the rest of the company onto the beach. The island was filled with magic – nasty, dark power which made his sensitive body sick. Satō lay down on the pebbles and closed her eyes, catching her breath. Dōraku helped Nagomi off the mount and laid her beside the resting wizardess.

Torishi unravelled a bundle of his belongings tied to one of the horses. He put on the loincloth, bark-spun tunic and the head-scarf and tied the long dagger to his waist. He strung the bow and checked if the arrows were loose enough in the quiver. He then knelt by Nagomi and caressed her copper hair.

"Little priestess." These were his first words on this side of the strait. He reached into a small wooden box he carried with him and took out several sprigs of some herb. Somehow, they had managed to remain dry throughout the ordeal. He crushed the herb under her nose.

Nagomi gasped and woke up. Torishi smiled and moved to Satō to repeat the procedure, but the wizardess pushed his hand away and sat up on her own.

"I'm fine. I just need a few minutes to catch my breath."

She twiddled a brass knob on her glove.

"Quite a performance, wizardess-*sama*," said Dōraku. "Your Honourable Father would have been proud."

She nodded.

"Are we safe here?" asked Nagomi.

"Ganryū wouldn't want his men to come here. But there will be guards just beyond those trees."

"I assume you have a plan," said Bran.

"Your *dorako* will be kept somewhere in Ganryū's residence; perhaps in the garden. All we need to do is charge the mansion's gates and break through."

"You make it sound easy. But there's a small *army* between us and the mansion, and two watch-towers overlooking the place."

"We'll try to sneak as far as possible. If stealth fails, I will lead the charge with Torishi-*sama*. That should keep most of Ganryū's men occupied."

"Are they just swordsmen? No mages, no *yamabushi*?"

"No. Ganryū is jealous of power. He's the only one allowed to use it on the island. I think he's afraid others would use it up," Dōraku added with a quiet chuckle.

Bran noticed Satō trying to stand up, and leapt to her aid. The wizardess held a hand to her forehead.

"Are you alright?"

"I... yes. This place... can you feel it? I smell blood," said Satō and shivered.

"At least we know it's definitely the right place," he said with a forced smile.

"Have you rested?" Dōraku asked. He had just finished tying up the horses to the mooring post. "We'd best be going."

Satō nodded. Like Torishi before her, she too readied her weapon. The sword slid in and out of the sheath with ease. Bran did the same; there was some resistance at first.

Eh…I forgot to oil it, he thought. *It will rust badly.*

He saw Nagomi pull out the remains of her paper-tasselled wand, ruined by sea water. She eyed it sadly and threw it away. Satō came up to the priestess and gave her a dagger.

"I don't really – "

"Just in case," said the wizardess. "I have my gun."

"I wouldn't even know how to use it."

"Press here," said Satō quietly, touching Nagomi's chest, "if it comes to the worst. It's a swift death."

Dōraku turned to the group and gave them a long, solemn look. His hands rested on the hilts of his twin blades. He hid his face in the shadow of the purple hood.

"We're ready," said Bran.

CHAPTER XVII

The trees provided them with shelter for about twenty yards, but the grove ended abruptly, opening onto a long and narrow courtyard running across the length of the island. At the far end, the white-washed walls of the two-storey mansion loomed in the faint light of the stone lanterns beyond a loose bamboo hedge.

The fortress was asleep but for the lone watchtower, its light directed outside the island at the sea; the other tower, Bran remembered, stood watch over the pier on the southern end of the island. The entire central courtyard was bathed in pitch black darkness. In the occasional distant flash of lightning Bran could make out some long, low buildings on the right-hand side.

"It looks so quiet…" he whispered.

"Make no mistake – they *will* be expecting us," said Dōraku. "Be prepared. I'll try to get us as close as possible without them noticing."

Bran tried to use True Sight and immediately regretted it; it was like looking into the heart of an explosion. The island was covered with dense energy flows, some ancient, some new; a rainbow of bright lights and colours too painful to bear. He shut his eyes and shook his head, waiting for the after-image to dissipate.

The Swordsman bid them all crouch and sneak along the western edge of the courtyard, past the hedgerow, along what looked like the training grounds. Bran walked carefully among the straw poles for practicing sword cuts, archery target boards, dummies of soft wood for spear and halberd training, empty weapon racks. The closer they got to the centre of the island, the darker it got, until they walked almost blind, touching their way.

The noise of the wind and storm drowned their footsteps. It started raining in earnest again, a fierce shower battered against Bran's face. The gravel beneath his feet turned to slushy mire.

They were almost half way across the courtyard when a lightning strike bathed the island in a bright white light. Five shadows were cast against the white gravel, five silhouettes cut out sharply by the flash, for just an instant, a blink of an eye.

Bran heard the rustle of the bush on his left, and the sound of many sandal-clad feet on the mud; Dōraku's blade swished in the darkness, and somebody fell down with a cry. Another lightning blasted even closer, and in its light he saw a dozen or so swordsmen in grey clothes, charging at him from all sides. He flashed a flamespark, reached for his sword, and felt a thud on the back of his head.

Satō drew her thunder gun and aimed it at the nearest group. The blinding-white lightning leapt from one man to another; three warriors fell at once. The wizardess herself almost fell, stunned by the recoil. She looked behind; she was being surrounded. Twenty, thirty swordsmen were heading towards her, pouring from the direction of the low stone buildings. She pulled the trigger again, but the charge was not yet full and the weapon's electrodes sizzled in vain. She thrust it back into her sash and drew the sword.

With mighty swipes of his fists, Torishi made his way through the enemy and reached Satō just as her frost-covered blade cut side-ways through the first of the spears, splitting it in two. Another warrior fell with an ice-lance embedded in his chest. The bear-man grabbed her at the waist and, despite her protests, dragged her behind, punching his way back towards Master Dōraku, who was fighting what seemed now like fifty men at once. Satō noticed Nagomi, cowering behind the Swordsman, clutching the Spirit Light in her hands.

Against all reason, he seemed to have the upper hand in this battle. There was a half-circle as wide as his two ruthless swords could reach where none of the attackers dared approach. At least a dozen bodies lay sprawled on the ground beneath his feet.

"This is like Ichijōji all over again!" Master Dōraku cried, and laughed.

Ichijōji! The story in Master Kawakami's book – the nameless swordsman…

Was that… him?

Seeing Master Dōraku now she could easily believe what she had once thought was an exaggeration. The attackers numbered less than a hundred this time, but it wouldn't have made any difference if there were twice as many. The Swordsman enjoyed himself immensely, taunting the warriors, threatening them with pretend attacks and licking the bloodied blades of his swords. When he stepped forward, the crowd rippled back in fear. He was like a bear cornered, not by a pack of hounds, but by a swarm of rats. In desperation the archers tried to pierce him with arrows but he simply sliced the missiles in half.

"Come on!" he goaded, laughing, "Is this the best the Ganryū *Dōjō* has to offer? Do I fight children or men?"

His blades whirled around the spears and halberds, and broke through steel chains. He jumped and rolled, slashed high and low, turned and twisted, dodged and parried. None of the enemies' blades even touched his clothes. The smell of blood mixed with rain and mud.

"If only I could fight like that…" said Satō, filled with profound awe, forgetting about the danger for a moment.

Torishi grunted. "He lost his humanity to gain this power."

"If that's what it takes," she whispered, shaking.

"Where's Bran?" asked Nagomi.

"They took him – towards the mansion!" said Satō.

"Go get him then!" Master Dōraku yelled. He moved forward, cleaving a corridor through the enemy as if he was cutting a path through the bamboo grove.

"Kumaso, lead the way." His eyes glinted gold for a moment, then turned black. His face contorted in a fierce, blood-thirsty grimace.

"They will stay here, with me," he seethed through bared teeth, glinting black and sharp in the light that shone from the watchtower.

Satō darted towards the residence, still a hundred yards away. Arrows twanged about her from the balcony of the watchtower. She saw Torishi draw his bow and, not even slowing his run, let two arrows lose one after another. Two archers fell to the ground.

They reached a small wicket gate in the bamboo fence. Torishi kicked it in with ease. A pair of guards appeared on the path beyond the bamboo fence, their spears lowered against the intruders. Torishi roared, grabbed the shaft of the nearest spear and pulled it. The helpless soldier stumbled forwards, his face meeting the bear-man's head with a bloody result. The other guard struck at Satō, but the wizardess deflected the spear's blade and cut him across the chest with ease. The guard fell back with his arms thrown apart.

The path climbed up the raised mound through an azalea thicket beyond which lay the door of the mansion; a thick slab of ancient, riveted bronze. Its frame was scribbled in odd runes. The markings glowed bright blue. The dial on her glove twitched when she ran her finger along them.

Torishi barged against the door with his shoulder, but it didn't budge.

"The runes," said Satō, pointing to the door frame. "Like on my father's shard."

She took the piece of bronze from her sleeve and put it up to the door.

"Hand me the dagger," she asked Nagomi.

With the tip of the blade she copied the rune onto the door's surface. Nothing happened. Satō cut her finger and pressed it to the scratch. A jolt ran from her hand, along the shoulder, to the place where the bronze dagger had hit her. The copper conduits on the glove buzzed and sparked. The rune drank her blood greedily; the markings on the frame glowed purple. The door swung wide open.

They ran out onto a small square garden surrounded by a shaded veranda. A tall, broad-shouldered figure awaited them, casting a huge black shadow in the light of a burning brazier.

Silently, the enemy approached. He had a beard almost as thick and bushy as that of Torishi, and long, black, braided hair; his clothes bore similar ornaments to those of the bear-man, but were more elaborate and colourful. Several bronze bracelets jangled on his wrists. He was unarmed, but poised to strike. She noticed beads of glass and polished stone tied into the man's beard and hair.

Satō raised her sword, but Torishi put his hand on the blade and pushed it down. He stepped forward, his face grave, his fists clenched. The two giants seemed like long lost brothers.

"*Irankarapte, nipa,*" said the bear-man.

"*Irangarapte na*," the other one replied, raising his fist to his chest.

"You know him?" Nagomi whispered. Torishi shook his head.

"He's my kin. Of those who departed north and lost their unity with the Bear."

The two hairy giants stared at each other for a long while.

"I cannot let you pass," the Northerner said.

Torishi grunted. "Then I will fight you."

He then turned to Satō and Nagomi.

"Go. I shall join you later."

Torishi had never told the young cubs of how he had wandered about the forest for days and months, slowly losing his human mind along with the will to live.

He wanted to forget about his wife dying a slow and painful death, her skin covered in bloody blisters; about his daughter, the last child buried in the burial pit. When the hunters finally found him, he had been resolved to die with no regrets. He let them trap him.

Since he first met the three youths, he had sensed a greatness inside them; courage and strength they themselves had not even begun to realize. The Spirits had confirmed his suspicions; *go with them,* they said. *Help them fulfil their destiny.* Once, he had resolved to die because he had no reason to live. Now he wanted to live, because they had given him a reason to die.

He met his opponent's gaze.

"Why are you with the *Shamo*?" the Northerner asked, not unkindly. "I know what they did to your people."

"I am not here with the *Shamo*," replied Torishi. "I am here with three young cubs that need help. Why are *you* here? Do you not know who lords over this island?"

"I know he is a demon that feeds on blood," the Northerner said, laughing. "How is that different from any other *Shamo*?"

"What will you gain in exchange for your service?"

"He promised me he would help unite the tribes of the North and drive away the *Shamo* from our mountains and forests."

"And you believed him?"

"Of course not. But he also promised me a great hunt, and a good fight. And on those he delivered."

He looked the bear-man over and nodded in appreciation.

"You seem strong. I hope you Southerners have not forgotten how to brawl."

"There are no more Southerners. I'm the last of the Kumaso."

"Pity. But don't think I'll go easy on you because of that."

"I might think that. The bear won't."

Torishi laid his weapons on the ground and raised his arms high with a roar. In a flash of lightning, the great black bear appeared, the glistening fur quickly soaking in the rain. He felt his reason slowly give way to bloody instinct.

The Northerner let out a joyous cackle.

"A worthy opponent, at last!"

He leapt forward and grappled with Torishi in a deadly embrace.

Satō crossed the courtyard and broke through the door in the northern wall. There was another corridor here, dark, narrow and winding.

The corridor seemed empty, but she stopped. They were in enemy territory, and there had to be traps and ambushes waiting if the Crimson Robe expected their arrival. She was not trained in True Sight, but her senses had grown sharper ever since she had first stepped on the island, as if she was somehow growing attuned to the energies of the place.

"Look out!" she cried and pulled Nagomi down to the ground just as a pair of darts zipped above their heads. The *shinobi* assassin in a tight black uniform leapt down noiselessly from the top-right corner. The chain-and-sickle weapon whizzed through the air inches from Satō's neck. The wizardess rolled aside and jumped to her feet, her sword in her hand.

Between the black facemask and the dark blue hood she could only see the eyes of the assassin, seething with fury, concentrated.

It's the kunoichi *woman from Kirishima.*

Satō accepted the unspoken challenge and stepped forward.

"I will give you a fair duel," she said. "But this one's just you and me."

The assassin narrowed her glinting eyes, looking at Nagomi as if she had only noticed her now.

"I killed you once already, priestess," she said. "Twice would be bad luck."

"I can't leave you alone," said Nagomi.

"You must," replied Satō. "Somebody has to save Bran."

"But I'm —"

"My patience is running out," the assassin seethed through her mask.

"Go!" Satō pushed Nagomi towards the darkness of the corridor. The assassin made no move to stop the priestess as she went past her.

When Satō had entered the hall, the *shinobi* had thrown *three* poisoned darts at her. Two she managed to avoid, the third embedded itself in her left thigh. The numbing poison was slowly spreading through the entire leg.

A sudden, unwanted memory came to her now. The master of one of Kiyō's best fencing schools, humiliating her in the test match, breaking her leg with the wooden sword. He had done it to teach her a lesson; Satō easily surpassed all other applicants, but she had to be shown her place. A girl could never be a swordsman.

It had been this contempt which forced her on the path to years of lonely, arduous training of both magic and swordsmanship; fighting against straw dummies, wooden boards, and her father's illusions, she pursued perfection. Had she been a boy, it would have been enough for her to be of average skill; but as a female, she had to be the best to be considered equal.

But that was all theory and mock fighting. Nobody in Kiyō wanted to spar with her. The men deemed it beneath them, the boys weren't skilful enough.

The month-old wound in her shoulder throbbed with heat, like a second heart.

All this knowledge and training would have been for nothing, she thought, *had I not met Bran and gone off on this quest...*

She had got a chance to try herself against the bandits, the *rōnin* and the hunters... She stood her own against Master Kawakami and that old annoying Spirit in Bran's head. She had gained more experience and confidence in the last month than in her entire life. At Kirishima, just for a second, the wizardess had glimpsed what it would have been like to achieve self-mastery, the unity of purpose and means which had been, until then, only a theory in Shūhan's writings.

And now, at long last, she faced an opponent of equal skill in a proper duel.

Another woman.

The assassin's dark, cold eyes studied Satō in silence, as they both circled each other slowly, looking for an opening. The sickle whooshed on the end of the chain rhythmically like a pendulum. The tight uniform clung to her taut, supple muscles, leaving no doubt as to her physical prowess. The wizardess wondered briefly if the *shinobi*'s life had been as difficult as hers.

Worse, probably, she thought. *She ended up here.*

"Who was the man in Kirishima? Your lover?"

The pendulum stopped.

"He was my everything."

"I'm sorry. It was the heat of the battle."

"Enough."

There was a barely noticeable flinch in the assassin's stance; she was ready to strike. Satō focused on the single point at the end of her sword. She felt the energies of the island go through her like freezing winter wind. The countless, ancient spirits of those who had died in the many battles fought over the Kanmon Strait; and the new, evil force brought on by the Crimson Robe's dark deeds. She knew now why he had banned anyone else from using magic here – and what power had been calling her to the island: his presence alone made it a miniature magical nexus, the *mogelijkheit* of the place almost as strong in its concentration as the Takachiho Mountain.

She no longer needed to speak out the spells. She didn't even need to use the needle in her glove: all the power of her blood, that trickling down her knee, the one making her left palm slippery or that running through her veins, was now at her disposal. In the darkness of the narrow corridor, she and the blade became one; a streamlined conduit of magic. Her senses sharpened, her movements magically enhanced.

For a brief moment, in a flash of concentration, the wizardess saw the world the way the Scryers saw it. She saw all the points in time, all the possible outcomes of the duel. At last, before what might have been her final battle, she became what Takashima Shūhan had wanted her to be; the samurai wizard.

And when the *shinobi*'s sickle blade struck for the first time – her sword was already there.

The winding corridor was eerily quiet. On one side there were rooms Nagomi dared not enter, on the other it ran along the back garden. Lightning flashes painted the shadows of the trees on the semi-translucent paper windows. The monotonous noise of the rain shrouded the faint sound of blades clashing back in the mansion where Satō fought her deadly duel. The smell of freshly blooming peonies lingered in the heavy air, seeping through the cracks in the wall.

Nagomi touched her way forward; the corridor turned left, then right, then split in two opposite directions. The wall in front of her was made of solid oaken planks, and there was nothing on either side that could help her choose.

She pulled the Spirit Light and studied the way the orange flame danced in the beaker. A sudden chilling gust of wind blew from the right-hand wing, bending the flame. She turned there and, after twenty paces, she reached a dead end; the same plain oaken wall. She was ready to turn back, but the cold wind made the orange light flicker again – and it seemed to be seeping *from the wall*.

She could hear steps running towards her from the other end of the corridor: guards, she guessed. She moved the dancing beaker up and down the wall, looking for the source of the draught. There was a narrow slit in one of the planks. She drew Satō's dagger and pushed it in. Something clicked, and the wall slid open, revealing a cold, narrow, stone staircase leading straight down, into even blacker darkness.

Hearing the guards approaching the place where the corridor split, Nagomi took a deep breath and stepped onto the first stair. The wall slid noiselessly behind her.

There were no more doors to pass. The staircase led her to a long hallway lined with flat slabs of white stone. A hundred or so paces later, she reached a large square room with walls and floor of the same material, made bright by a single flaming brazier.

A broad ramp led out of the room on the opposite side; between this puzzling gateway and Nagomi stood a huge, ornate, steel-walled box, with only a narrow opening at the top.

The priestess felt a paralyzing fear creeping over her, as if oozing from the box. Her knees buckled under her and her teeth chattered. She hugged the Spirit Light close and withdrew until her back touched the cold stone wall.

What monster is this…?

And then she remembered. She had seen this place before – in a dream, in Kagoshima.

Emris! I found Bran's dragon!

Gathering all her courage she stepped forward.

Maybe if I could open it... I could release it? Would that help?

She touched the steel wall. It was cold and vibrating slowly as the beast within breathed. It belonged to a Fanged – how would a demon like that make sure only he could open the container? She looked the box over, pressed and pushed the coiling, snake-shaped carvings, tugged and pulled on the runed walls, all to no avail.

What trickery or magic would he use?

Then she had an idea. She took a hairpin and pricked her finger. A large drop of blood appeared at the tip. She pressed it against the wall of the box. The metal glowed purple for a moment, absorbing the red liquid, but nothing else happened.

Not enough, she thought desperately. She took the dagger and slashed her left palm deeply. She cried out; it hurt and bled a lot more than she expected; a thick stream of red liquid trickled down her wrist and forearm.

Suddenly, she felt she had become the focus of somebody's attention. The torch light dimmed, the air grew cold and stale; Nagomi's breath quickened. The primeval fear she had felt before was replaced by the terror of the Otherworld. Drawn to the blood like hungry *koi* fish in the shrine pond, malevolent, tortured spirits were swirling all around her. She put her palms together and spoke a quick prayer with trembling lips. Her hands glowed with weak blue light, and the air nearest her cleared enough so she could breathe freely again.

In a hurry she smeared as much of the blood as she could onto the surface of the metal box. The wall glowed again in the shape of a magic rune, much brighter this time, and something inside clicked.

Clutching her bleeding hand, Nagomi opened the door. A wave of hot, stale air rushed from the inside, as if from a furnace. She saw the shadow of a massive, heavily breathing beast. This was the first time she had seen the *dorako* up close. She had never imagined anything so big could live on land, much less fly. The beast lay asleep, bound in thick steel chains.

Strangely, now that she could see the dragon, her fear lessened. The evil spirits perished, as if unable to withstand the monster's presence. The priestess approached the beast closer. Its scales were warm to touch and smelled of brimstone. She studied the chain and discovered it was all one length of metal links, wrapped around the beast's body, with no padlock or knot. She pulled on it with all her might, but it didn't budge. The sleeping dragon growled and shuddered. Its claws contracted, scratching the iron floor of the box. She jumped away.

A distant thunder rolled above, its rumble reaching the underground room magnified by the echo. The dragon stirred and the snake eyes flashed open. Fear was beginning to grip her in its cold grasp again; the dragon's jaws could easily snap her in half, its claws shred her to pieces...

But she didn't step back. She watched the monster stand up shakily. With a shrug of its massive shoulders and flap of muscular wings, it ripped both the chain and the steel box apart as if they were made of paper.

The priestess was resolved to die.

With dorako at Bran's side, the battle is as good as won.

She closed her eyes and felt the dragon come closer.

Seconds passed and nothing happened. Surprised, she opened her eyes; the dragon gazed at her patiently. It lowered its neck beside her.

"You... you want me to...?"

The dragon snorted. Nagomi clumsily mounted the beast's neck. Not sure what to hold on to, she grabbed one of the long, sharp horns protruding from the dragon's head. As soon as she did that, Emrys turned and shot through the ramp, into the stormy night outside.

CHAPTER XVIII

"Wake up, boy!"

A nagging voice prodded Bran slowly into consciousness. His first feeling was a strange, numbing pain, difficult to localize.

"Careful. Don't open your eyes yet."

"Why…?"

"I can sense He's near. Pretend you're still asleep."

"It hurts…"

Bran twitched his hands and felt thin blades piercing deep into the skin on his forearms and shoulders. Something sharp was stuck in his neck as well, pulsating in the rhythm of his heart.

He half-opened one eye. His head was spinning. He was sitting in a high metal chair in a small room, encircled by bright candles. Bronze needles and tubes of oiled canvas were sticking out of his arm. Spiked bracelets kept his wrists and ankles safely in place.

He couldn't see much else without opening his eyes fully; but he could sense a dark, cold presence in the room.

"This room feels exactly like that place above the heretics' town," observed Shigemasa.

"He's draining me…"

"He's changing you into one of his own!"

Bran strained to focus; with clenched fists and gritted teeth, he summoned a *bwcler* along his left arm. He gasped as the magic shield cut through the tubes and tore the needles out of his body. Blood spurted from the open vein.

"You're awake," a freezing voice spoke. Bran opened his eyes fully. The Crimson Robe was sitting cross-legged on the floor before him, outside the circle of candles, underneath a fresco of an eight-headed serpent outlined with black paint on the clay-daubed wall. He held the glowing orb of red crystal in his hand. The great two-handed sword lay by his right side – and Bran's Prydain blade at his left, along with the satchel and all the items from inside were laid out neatly, the blue ring among them. The Fanged was studying the medallion with great interest when he noticed Bran stir and gasp.

"Fascinating," he said. "I wonder just how much she told your grandfather."

How does he know?

The Crimson Robe gestured at somebody beyond Bran's field of view. Something moved, slithering and shuffling in the periphery of his vision, a bright orange robe on a dark, withered body; an odd smell of lacquers and essential oils licked his nostrils. A skeletal hand, covered with dried up skin, browned with age, picked up the needles and tubes from the floor and hovered over Bran's arm, still protected by the *bwcler*.

"You can't keep that shield forever," the Crimson Robe said. "How do you like my chair? It's an old Western design. Vasconian, I believe."

A Roman device! A remnant of the Wizardry Wars.

The Fanged was right – Bran could feel power flow from his veins along with the blood, and through the wounds inflicted by the bronze spikes on his hands and legs. Even a powerful wizard would not last long in this trap.

But I'm not a wizard, thought Bran. The Crimson Robe did not know everything. Bran was a dragon rider; the source of his power was his mount. And Emrys was somewhere near. He could feel it again, just as close as in Kirishima. And just like then, despite the same veil, the envelope of dark energy separating them, the dragon's life energy flowed towards him – a narrow trickle but enough to sustain whatever the chair drained from him.

There was something else, very faint under all the layers of spent energy, hunger, and fear; an undercurrent of longing, like a sad, wistful song hummed in the distance; the dragon was lonely and miserable. These weren't the feelings of a *feral* beast at all!

"Why are you smiling?" the Crimson Robe asked, irritation slipping into his voice. Bran became serious. The Fanged stood up, picking up Bran's sword and weighing it in his hand. The runes on the blade glowed a sickly pale blue.

Theatrics.

"Tell me, have you come here to *duel* me, boy? Sword against sword?" The Fanged raised his eyebrow in mocking surprise. "You would die in one second from my swallow-tail cut," he said with a sneer.

Bran recognized this sneer. It was the sneer of one who believes himself superior to all around him. Wulfhere and his bullies always sported this grimace on their pure-blood Seaxe faces; always stronger, faster and more self-confident than Bran. But this time, there would be no teachers coming to help, no roofs to leap from...

"What's the matter, boy? Fear got your tongue?" Crimson Robe said in the prolonged silence.

He dismissed the creature holding the tubes and needles and stepped forward. Bran said nothing. He was breathing heavily, his mind focused.

Just a little bit closer...

Ganryū leaned over to examine the contraption. Bran rejoiced quietly in his confusion – and what he was sensing from Emrys. The dragon finally noticed his rider's presence; the sad song turned into one of joy and welcome. The link wasn't yet strong enough to summon the Dragonform, but maybe...

The Crimson Robe straightened, his golden eyes studying the boy with annoyed curiosity.

"Why are you – "

"*Rhew!*"

A narrow, blade-like tongue of dragon flame burst from Bran's open palm. The Fanged covered his face with the wide sleeve of his robe. Fire enveloped him, as Bran continued to feed it with the dragon's energy. The bluish flame poured ceaselessly from the outstretched hand. At last, when he was certain that no thing, living or dead, could survive so much heat, the boy let go, exhausted.

The scorched remains of the robe fell to the floor. Ganryū's skin peeled off in burned patches, the ends of his black hair were singed white. The sickly-sweet stench of charred flesh and boiled blood filled the room. But the Fanged was still alive. He spat out bits of flesh and loose teeth.

"You ruined my robe, Barbarian. It will take a lot of blood to dye a new one."
At the flick of his fingers, the straps and bracelets snapped open. He dropped the sword with a clang and raised Bran from the chair by the neck.

His eyes turned black, his fangs glistened.

"I will drink you dry, and then move on to your friends. I will leave the priestess for last, so she can watch you *all* die."

The boy lifted his head and looked straight into the demon's jet-black eyes.

"Fooled you."

For a moment, Ganryū's eyes reverted to gold as he looked at the boy with confusion. Bran pressed his right palm against the Fanged's chest. The blade of the Soul Lance pierced the demon through.

"*Gwrthyrru!*"

The spell ran down the lance; the push threw Ganryū ten feet back against the wall. The red jewel dropped from his hand and rolled off into the corner of the room. Bran fell to the floor, his consciousness slipping away.

The Fanged shook his head, half-stunned, and jumped at the boy with a furious snarl.

"You'll pay for this!" he yowled and Bran felt a terrible, paralysing pain he didn't know existed as fangs tore his skin and hot blood gushed from a vein. Ganryū lapped it up and spat it out in Bran's face.

"Just as I thought, disgusting. Now I'll have to drink a Yamato girl to get rid of the taste."

He stood up.

My shirt's all wet, the boy thought, dying.

And then the roof exploded.

The dragon carried Nagomi high into the storm; she held on for dear life to his scaly neck, swathed in the beast's hot, brimstone-smelling breath, too scared to open her eyes. After a few seconds, however, the fear passed, replaced by a rush of excitement. She looked down at the mansion and the garden below her and laughed. She had never experienced anything more exhilarating than this.

"*Bran!*" she remembered. The dragon roared and banked sideways, almost dropping her; she grabbed the horns at the beast's neck.

"I'm sorry if it hurts," she said, but the dragon paid no attention. It swooped down towards a small square building in the middle of the garden, the size of a tea pavilion.

The dragon landed, crushing a wall and part of the roof with its weight, its wings spanning almost an entire length of the hut. It lowered its neck so that Nagomi could slide off it to the floor, trembling. She stepped over what looked like a pile of bones wrapped in skin, covered in a monk's robe, half-crushed by the rubble, and looked around.

It took her a few seconds to guess that the tall, half-burned, naked man standing over Bran's mangled body was the Crimson Robe himself. The demon cursed and looked around the room, barely noticing the dragon. A large round jewel, glowing weak red, lay in the corner. Nagomi recognized it in an instant.

What through blood stone can you see?

Emrys roared and spat a lash of flame, but failed to stop the Fanged from reaching the stone. The stench was sickening. The demon's hand was now little more than strips of fried meat hanging off the bones, but there were enough muscles and tendons still left for him to grab the jewel strongly. The jewel shone blood red.

The dragon flapped its wings and breathed fire again, but something was wrong. It swayed from side to side; for a moment the beast rose, towering over the Fanged, but then it dropped to the ground with a fleshy thud.

The Fanged stared at Nagomi with eyes black as night.

"*You.*" He drew and pointed his great sword at her. He seemed to have no difficulty wielding it with only one hand. The discarded scabbard clanged on the stone floor. "I know you. You saw me take the orb from Mekari."

She stepped back.

The Prophecy. It was him!

She thought about the glowing white light she had summoned during the sea crossing; the pain it had caused Master Dōraku…

But before she could even start the chant, the Crimson Robe leapt across the room with inhuman speed and landed several feet from her, raising his two-handed sword. She cowered before the falling blade.

Time slowed down to a crawl. A humming noise filled Bran's ears, and milky white mist shrouded the world around him.

He felt dirt under his feet. He stooped down and picked up a handful. It was the colour of iron ore; he was somewhere on the red-dirt plain again.

He wandered blindly through the mist until the ground beneath his feet started to rise. He found himself on a hill top. There were other peaks rising from the white mist, and an entire mountain range on the horizon.

A wind blew, parting a tunnel in the mist. Somebody was coming through.

"*Taishō!*" Bran shouted. The General picked up the pace, climbing up the hill the boy was standing on.

"You've made it here, boy," he said.

"Where is *here*?"

"This is the place you wanted to see. Where the Spirits dwell."

"You mean I'm... dead?"

"Not yet. Then you'd be beyond those mountains," the General said, pointing to the jagged peaks. "But you've not long to go."

"But I can't die... I need to save Emrys! And Nagomi... and Satō... everyone's relying on me!"

"Calm down, boy. I'm not looking forward to spending eternity on this island. The wights of *Dan-no-Ura* make for poor companions. I'm here to help you."

"Can you really do that? Can you bring me back from the dead?"

"I told you, you're not dead yet! First, we need to find your beast. Can you sense where it is?"

Bran closed his eyes and focused as he had done so many times before. Instantly, he picked up a faint buzz.

"Over there," he said, pointing towards a nearby hill, split in two by a dark gorge.

The phantom Emrys waited for Bran at the saddle of the gorge, sitting on hind legs bent like a sphinx, wings spread wide on the ground.

Its sage eyes followed the boy as he neared the beast cautiously. Bran reached out his hand, but the dragon flapped its wings and leapt aside.

"What's wrong, Emrys?"

He ran up to it again, and again the dragon raised its wings. Bran jumped and grabbed the horns on its neck; the beast whinnied and shook its head up, glaring at the rider with mad, bulging eyes, like a frightened horse.

"Ease!" cried Bran, sending soothing thoughts through Farlink. "Ease, Emrys!"

But the beast was in panic. It launched into the air with Bran clutching at the horns. Bran managed to hook a leg around its neck and gain a firmer grip. He could feel his signals reaching the dragon, but there was no response.

"Perhaps it doesn't want you to fly it," cried Shigemasa, observing the scene from a safe distance.

"What do you mean?"

The General shrugged. "It's your mount."

Bran clung to the dragon's green scales with his entire body and dug deep into the beast's mind, past all the barriers and past the dumb, beastly bewilderment.

Like a jewel hidden in the darkness, Bran found the dragon's true feelings. The connection was still there, faint and erratic; the beast had fought hunger, exhaustion and its feral nature, still loyal, still, amazingly, steadfast and obedient. Just as it had always been – ever since Bran had got the ring ...

The ring.

Bran looked at his hand. The blue stone was missing again.

What does that mean?

And then it dawned on him. The ring he got from Lord Shimazu was a fake; a forgery. That's why he wasn't able to use it anymore.

Of course. He's keeping the stone for himself. But that means…

He remembered the first time he had flown Emrys; it was just a brief flight over the Caer Wyddno; he'd flown above the town earlier, with Dylan, so he hadn't thought anything would surprise him. But the way the wind felt around him that day, the exhilaration of altitude and speed, the freedom, it was like nothing he had ever dreamt of before. It had taken Bran just a few flights like that to establish a strong, special bond with the jade green dragon.

Dylan had always dismissed his story as fanciful.

"You were just an impressionable child," he'd say. *"No rider your age had ever achieved a Farlink. You were imagining things."*

Did I have my ring then, on that first flight? He tried to remember. No, he wouldn't have got it for at least a year.

The beast flew on its own over hundreds of miles of featureless sea in search of Bran. It struggled to find his rider and remain in contact through weeks of entrapment and bondage. This connection was not the result of some magic stone. There was no other dragon like Emrys. And Bran wanted to repay this loyalty. He had crossed an unknown land, fought powerful enemies, all to find and free Emrys from its shackles.

"I will not give up yet," he whispered and closed his eyes.

He sensed an impulse coming now from the phantom dragon, almost a message; Emrys was *telling him what to do.*

"Dragon Form? Here? Now? But… Oh, I see. *Y Ddraig Ffurf!"*

He felt his body disappear, melt and fuse with that of the phantom jade dragon.

Bran saw Ganryū's blade fall on the priestess and shot his head forward; he wanted to bite the Fanged through, but miscalculated and instead punched him through the wall into the garden outside.

Bran leapt after him. Unused to having wings, and struggling to stay aloft, he swayed from side to side. His claws caught in the rubble and tumbled down. He shook his head, stunned, but picked himself up. He saw Ganryū stare at the gem in his hand in surprise and disgust, trying to comprehend why it didn't have any effect on the dragon.

"No matter," the Fanged decided. "I don't need *this* to kill you all."

He let go of the gem and grasped the sword in two hands, raising it flat above his head.

The boy spewed fire. The pure dragon flame was nothing like the poor imitation Bran had tried before. Hot like the Sun itself, it burned the rest of the skin and flesh off of Ganryū. What stood now in the garden was a blackened skeleton covered with patches of scorched muscles and tendons, staring at the dragon from empty eye sockets. But the Curse still powered the Fanged, and he still held the sword firmly with blazing hands.

"Is that all you've got?" the lipless mouth said and laughed. Bran heard in the voice the buzz of the Otherworld he had heard a long time ago in the roar of the skeleton dragon. Ganryū leapt high and struck. Bran dodged, but the sword grazed his neck, cutting through the celadon scales. The wound burned as if doused with acid.

A magic blade! I must be more careful.

He leapt into the air and flapped his wings a few times to stay aloft. The chaotic Ninth Wind of the island buffeted him about, like a paper toy. He swooped down and snapped his jaws, but Ganryū rolled safely aside and Bran's teeth only caught dirt. He flew back up but not before the magic blade struck again, leaving a deep, bleeding gash.

Ganryū could not reach him in the air, but Bran did not dare to get close to the great sword. His flame could not cause the Fanged any more harm. It was stalemate.

Nagomi lifted Bran's head; he was covered in his own blood and there was no heartbeat in his chest. A torn, gaping wound on his neck left no doubts to his fate. The dragon rider was dead.

She did not cry. All the despair and panic floated away, leaving just an empty shell behind. Her mind withdrew, fleeing from all the pain and suffering. The world around her turned hazy, distant.

A streak of white fur leapt out from the mist. A white fox coiled around her legs and nudged her sleeve with its long, slender nose. Nagomi stood up and pulled the Spirit Light from within the folds of her priestly robe. The orange flame burst brightly, clearing the darkness.

Bran heard a beautiful chant coming from the pavilion. He looked down and squinted, the dragon's eyes blinded by the bright white light. Nagomi's voice, clear, pure and strong, filled the garden. Her skin glowed with the sacred light, reflecting the one dancing in the clay beaker she was holding. Her body was ablaze; she was a naked pillar of light. The white flame surrounded her and spread in a spherical wave, her copper hair raised by the hot wind. The sphere grew, encompassing the entire pavilion and the garden around it, until it reached Ganryū. The Fanged cried out in pain, dropped his sword and covered his ears.

"The screech! Make it stop!"

He stepped back.

"It burns!"

But it was too late. His body froze as the divine whirlwind of light and fire tore into the bones, causing him to howl in agony. He reached out the skeletal hand at Bran.

"Make. It. Stop."

The smouldering knuckles clenched into a fist as the Fanged gathered all his remaining power and struck back. The holy flame withered, pushed away by the darkness of his cursed soul.

The chanting stopped; Bran heard her abrupt cry, the sound of shattering clay, and felt himself torn away from the dragon back into his own body.

The world was bathed in dazzling, warm light. The white haze receded only enough for him to see outlines of what was going on around him. His body was strangely weightless, wispy and... fragrant? There was no mistake, his skin – strangely pale, glowing white – smelled of cherry blossom and incense. The walls of the pavilion – what was still left of them – were shattered and half-melted, as if after some enormous explosion.

"Focus, boy. You have not won the fight yet," a familiar voice spoke beside Bran. The General's spirit hovered in the air the same way it did back at the straits.

"Pick up the sword," the old ghost ordered. "Kill Ganryū."

"But..."

"Trust me. Pierce him with your blade."

The boy picked up his weapon and stepped over a smouldering crossbeam into the garden. The Fanged turned his attention from fighting off Emrys and stared at Bran, nuggets of gold gleaming within the terrifying, scorched skull.

"You're only prolonging the inevitable, boy. You can't kill me. Nobody can kill me!"

He let another cone of dragon flame wash over his charred bones and raised his *nodachi* sword at the boy.

"Can't you see? You will all die here. You, your beast and your little priestess."

Bran grabbed the sword's hilt with two hands and, with a desperate cry, charged and thrust it straight into Ganryū's chest.

The blade wedged between the ribs where the creature's heart would have been if it hadn't already turned to ash, and Bran had to let it go to dodge the edge of the *nodachi* falling beside his head. Ganryū gloated, but the laughter died in his throat.

The General, a pale white waft of smoke, a phantom of mist and vapour clad in ghostly armour, appeared beside Ganryū, reached for the sword and wrapped his hands on the hilt.

"Your Curse, demon. I will take it upon myself. It's the only way."

"No! You can't..." cried the Fanged, but it was too late. The sword in his chest turned black. Ganryū fell to his knees.

"No!" he repeated defiantly.

He looked past Bran, towards the mansion gate where Dōraku stood, observing the scene in silence, his two swords dripping with blood.

"Shinmen..." Ganryū whispered, "...you are... late... again."

His skull cracked and shattered, and he crumbled to the floor in pile of ash and loose, old bones.

The General's spirit beamed with heavenly radiance, and his ghostly face was, at long last, content and fulfilled.

"Farewell Bran ap Dylan gan Cantre'r Gwaelod. You are a real samurai now. Take care of Yamato for me."

"Farewell, Itakura Shigemasa-*dono*."

The spirit vanished in a haze of wisps and a twirl of raindrops.

"Emrys," Bran commanded. "I know you can hear me now. Come to me."

The dragon landed before Bran. It was wounded in several places. Thick, dark red blood oozed where Ganryū's blade cut the deepest. Bran touched the dragon's warm scales. Emrys purred with joy. At long last, they were united.

Bran's world swirled and turned cold, empty and dark.

Drops of icy rain fell on his face. Bran was lying on the wet, muddy ground. When he opened his eyes, he saw Emrys leaning above him. The beast nudged him with its warm nose like a worried dog.

"It's all right. I'm all right," he croaked, reaching out to pat the beast's snout.

Somehow, Ganryū's crystal orb was in Bran's hand. Its surface, smooth like glass, was cooling rapidly, but still warm to touch. He hid it inside the sleeve.

He stood up slowly, achingly, and looked around. In front of him was the wicket gate where Dōraku had held back the entire army of Ganryū's students. There was blood and gore everywhere, slowly washed away into the gutters by the rain. Corpses, whole and hacked, entire body parts and bits and pieces, slashed away by the Fanged's blades.

Bile rose inside his throat as the morbid smell of death and flesh penetrated his nostrils, mixed with the heavy, damp scent of rain and salty sea air. He bent forward and retched. He felt sorry for the warriors. They were followers of his enemy, and as such, his enemies; but, in a way, they got involved in this battle where they stood no chance. So many of them had perished without even learning the name of a man who killed them.

Those who remained alive were now standing in a half-circle around Bran and his dragon, grim and defeated, rain trickling down their lowered heads, their weapons thrown down in hopeless surrender. The dragon rider could not look into their sullen eyes for long.

Turning around, he saw Dōraku standing beside Emrys, silent, his face a featureless mask, the rain washing away any signs of battle. The Fanged held unconscious Nagomi in his arms. She seemed as faint as after Kirishima, but her skin had a healthy glow and there were no visible injuries.

Torishi and Satō walked slowly from the direction of the mansion. The bear-man glanced at the boy, but if he was surprised to see his Prydain face, he didn't show it. The wizardess limped, supporting herself on Torishi's shoulder. Her *hakama* was soaked in blood, her face covered in bruises and cuts.

"You're alive!" shouted Bran. His heart felt suddenly lighter. "I thought _"

He stopped, seeing another man appearing from behind, a hairy giant similar in gait and posture to Torishi. His skin was slashed and torn, but he stood straight and looked the boy proudly in the eyes.

Bran rushed to help the wizardess down the path. She smiled at him weakly, absent-mindedly.

"Who's that?" He nodded at the giant.

"One of Ganryū's men," she replied.

"I have no reason to fight you anymore," the hairy giant said. "I will depart for the North tomorrow."

"Are we letting him go?" Bran asked Torishi.

"He fought honourably," replied the bear-man, "in defence of his Master. Why should I begrudge him?"

"How's Nagomi?" asked Satō.

"She seems fine. We won. And we're all alive."

"We're all alive," repeated Satō in disbelief.

CHAPTER XIX

Azumi parted the azalea bush and looked carefully around. A blue magpie screeched in the hydrangeas. It was dawning.

She had the right to feel angry, robbed of her right to avenge Ozun. But she knew she had been almost unbelievably lucky. Not only did she manage to survive meeting that terrible man with twin blades again and flee, the intruders succeeded in *destroying* the Crimson Robe!

She always sensed the plan was too complicated to succeed; she had been telling him that all the time.

"Why not just kill them all when they arrive?" she boggled.

"The boy is the prize," the Crimson Robe had explained. "I need him alive, and separated from Dōraku and the priestess. Without them, he'll be helpless."

She shook her head; *everything went wrong.* The dragon broke free. The priestess reached the boy in time. And then the unthinkable happened: the Curse had been reversed... it seemed these children were indeed favoured by the Gods.

And now she was free, released from the Fanged's dark grip. She could start her life anew...

Without Ozun.

The Master's death meant the *yamabushi* could no longer be brought to life. But –

There is another Fanged. The one with two blades, Dōraku. And where there were two, there could've been more.

What did Shō say before he died? "I serve one of the Eight Heads."

Ganryū's banner. Eight-headed Serpent. A faint hope quickened her breath.

They will send somebody here to investigate, she thought. *They will be looking for survivors...*

She picked up the basket containing Ozun's head, tied it onto her back and stepped onto the garden path. After a few steps she stumbled over something. A pile of blackened bones and the charred and twisted remains of a sword still smouldering with dark vapours and glowing a faint, ghostly light. Some remnant of the battle. She picked it up carefully through her sleeve; it pulsated with heat.

This is bound to attract their attention.

Azumi moved stealthily through the garden, around the mansion and onto the courtyard, hiding among the target dummies. She passed a group of grey-clad *rōnin* sitting on the wet ground in the rain. They weren't even tied up; the Swordsman's watchful eye was enough to keep them from running away.

The Fanged turned around and faced Azumi.

He can see me, she realized; her hair stood on end. There was no way she could hide from those golden eyes. Had he interrupted her duel with the wizard girl the night before only to feed on her now?

But the Swordsman made no move.

He's... letting me go!

She ran the rest of the way, across the courtyard and through the thicket separating the secret cove from the rest of the island. Through an opening in the ochre wall she saw five of Ganryū's students rowing the small boat out into the sea; there was no other way off the island. She picked up the pace. They spotted her, but did not stop. One of them turned towards the shore – she recognized Hajime by his broken nose, the leader of the Crimson Robe's assault squad, and his finest student. He stood up on the stern and watched her wade in the shallows after the boat. Salt water attacked her wounds with a thousand needles and clawed its way into her eyes. Blinded and in pain, she tripped; the weight of the basket on her back pushed her down and the sea closed over her head.

A strong hand grabbed her and pulled her, bubbling and struggling onto the boat.

"Stop making so much noise," the leader barked. "For an assassin, you're terribly clumsy."

Bran finished bandaging Satō's left forearm. It was one of the many wounds she had suffered in the duel. He wrapped the girl's hand in an herbal poultice, prepared by Torishi to draw out any poison, and tightened the linen wrappings. The girl hissed.

"Careful!"

"I'm sorry. I've always been clumsy with this sort of thing. How's the leg?"

"A little better, but it hurts when I walk. What about you? You're not looking so great yourself. Your neck…"

"I'll be fine," he said. "Just a little sore."

He rubbed the great, ugly torn scar running across his neck and collar-bone. Nagomi's light had brought him to life and healed the shattered muscles and tendons, but was not enough to restore the mutilated skin torn by the cursed claws and fangs.

"Dōraku says it may never heal," he added. "But I don't care. I'm just glad to be alive. Nagomi's not going to be sleeping for three days again, is she?"

"She woke up. What exactly happened up there?"

"I… I'm not sure. It was all like a dream. She channelled tremendous amounts of power. Brought me back to life, held Ganryū enthralled…"

"I can't believe she got to ride the *dorako*. Remember, you promised to take me too!"

"I know." Bran nodded. His head remained in the nod a little too long; a lump grew in his throat.

"Let's go see Nagomi," he said, standing up quickly.

They walked across the gravel courtyard arm in arm; Bran thought she was squeezing him a little bit tighter than was needed just to support herself – but couldn't tell for sure. Ganryū's students were digging graves for their slain comrades under Torishi's command. Bran remembered the dozens of hacked corpses lying on the dirt in a pool of blood.

I don't think I'll be able to forget it.

Satō stopped before the nearest set of graves and bowed.

"They fought bravely. They deserve respect," she said.

Bran bowed too, but out of pity he was feeling for every life lost during their quest.

Respect? They served a blood-thirsty demon and were willing to die for his sake. They were stupid or greedy. I have no respect for any of them.

"What happened to the *kunoichi* woman?" he asked.

Satō shrugged.

"She fled when Dōraku-*sama* arrived. She must have got off the island in one of the morning boats."

"You don't know? What if she's still hiding somewhere?"

Satō shook her head. "It's over, Bran. Don't worry."

They entered one of the low stone houses Dōraku had commandeered into an infirmary.

"How do you feel?" Bran asked, sitting down by the priestess's bed. She was wrapped in Satō's travel cloak and a thin blanket.

"I feel... strange. Weak. It's not a bad feeling though, more like... when you sit in a nice hot bath for too long and it wears you out. I'm all warm inside."

"What do you remember?"

"Not much... I was in a world of bright white fog..."

The Otherworld.

"You saved us all. You saved me," said Bran. "I... don't know how to thank you."

"It wasn't me... it was the power of the *kami* –" Nagomi gasped and reached her hand to touch Bran's face. Her hand was warm.

"You look –!"

Bran nodded.

"Itakura Shigemasa-*dono* is no more. Without him, I have no power to change the way I look."

"What are you going to do now?" asked Nagomi. "You will be arrested the moment we get off this island."

"Arrested?" Satō laughed. "He's got a *dragon* now – I don't think he has to worry about *Taikun's* men."

"I haven't thought of all that yet," Bran answered. "Everything's still... for now we all need to rest, bathe, eat," he added with a forced smile.

"A bath!" Satō clapped her hands. "Where do you think it is?"

"I'll go ask Dōraku. I needed to talk to him about something anyway."

He found the Fanged alone in a shack by the training grounds, sitting by a low table, smoking his long pipe and browsing through some papers.

Dōraku looked at Bran curiously.

"You can't change anymore," he said.

"No. That's gone with the *Taishō*."

"But you still speak our language."

"It seems I haven't forgotten anything."

The Swordsman nodded. "That's something, at least. How are the others?"

"They're all fine, I guess. They could use a bath, though. And some more food."

"There's a kitchen for the guards," Dōraku pointed to a small building, plastered white, "and a bathhouse attached to it. What about your *dorako*?"

"It's fine too. The wounds heal fast. It killed one of our horses, I'm afraid. I'm really sorry about that..."

The Fanged nodded.

"Sad, but understandable. The beast must not have eaten for days."

Bran scratched his cheek.

"I thought one of your kind cannot be killed."

Dōraku put the pipe away.

"Yes, who would've thought that would work? Another soul taking the Curse upon itself voluntarily..."

It must have given even you a fright.

"What will happen to Ganryū's men?" asked Bran.

"Left or preparing to leave. As soon as we finish the burials. I let them go, save for a few who will carry the wounded. There's a supply ship coming in today from Kokura, it should take the rest of them to the mainland."

"And the Ogasawara Clan? You said it's their land..."

"We'll be out of here before they get curious. Don't worry, boy, I'm sure the Ogasawaras will soon have more important things to lose sleep over. As will everyone else in Yamato. I read through some of these papers," Dōraku said, gesturing to a pile of documents before him. "I fear there may be no stopping the war after all."

"What are these?"

"Letters and documents from Ganryū's private chest. I hope they will give me some clues as to what the others are planning."

"The others – you mean the Eight-headed Serpent?"

"You remembered," said Dōraku with a smile and tapped his pipe on the table.

"So they are not a spent force after all."

"No, I suppose not. They must be hoping to gain something from the approaching chaos."

You knew all the time.

"Will this help?" Bran took the red gem from his sleeve. "I wish I knew what it really was."

Dōraku turned the jewel in his fingers, puffing the pipe.

"They call these the Tide Jewels. They are as old as Yamato, if not more. Each holds a different power; I don't know what this one did exactly, apart from apparently being able to influence your *dorako*. Heishichi-*sama* will know more."

The Swordsman handed the orb back to Bran, but the boy refused it.

"It's yours," said Dōraku. "Think of it as the spoils of war."

"I have no need for it. If you don't want it, give it to… Satō."

The Fanged put down the papers and stared at Bran in silence.

"I had hoped you would at least take some time to rest," he said at last.

"I've made my decision. The longer I stay, the more painful it will be for me to leave – and the more chance you have to convince me otherwise."

"Have you told the girls?"

Bran shook his head. "No. But I can't stay here. Do you understand?"

The Fanged nodded.

"This is not my home. This is not my world! And now I can't even disguise myself as one of you anymore. I have to go back."

"You don't have to explain. Are you leaving right now?"

"Yes. I have everything prepared."

"Do you know the way?"

"I know where West is."

The Fanged shook his head. "You'd soon get lost in the open sea. Here, take this," he said, giving Bran a rolled piece of paper.

"I found it in the chest along with the letters. It's a map drawn in Western style. I wish I knew how Ganryū came into its possession."

Bran unrolled the scroll.

"We are here." Dōraku pointed to a spot on the map between two of the largest islands. "You should go south-west along the coast – that way you'll have navigation points all along your route. Then when you get to Hirado turn due west, crossing the Divine Winds – hopefully – until you get to Tamna Island – that's Chosun land, but remote and sparsely populated. It's only a hundred *ri* from there to Qin."

"What's this?" Bran lifted a piece of paper which had fallen from the map as it was unrolled. The Fanged glanced at it.

"It's the copy of a missive from the *Taikun*'s High Council."

"And how did Ganryū get *that*?"

"Good question. The Serpent must have spies high in Edo. The letter is not a day old."

"Won't you need it?"

"I know what it says. But it might be of interest to your people."

Bran rolled the letter and the map and opened his satchel to put them in. This reminded him of something.

He took the medallion out and showed it to Dōraku.

"Did you know her?"

The Fanged studied the thaumaturgic image.

"Who's Ifor?"

"My grandfather."

"Your grandfather, eh? And he was…?"

"A sailor on MS Phaeton. They met in Kiyō."

"What strange fate."

It looked like Dōraku wanted to add something else, but he must have changed his mind for he just smiled wistfully.

"Then I guessed right – you knew her."

"I helped her flee Ganryū. Last I saw her she was safe at Dejima."

"So you didn't know the Crimson Robe found her eventually? That he attacked Dejima?"

Dōraku shook his head. "I was… otherwise occupied. What happened to her?"

Bran felt strange describing the events of the past to this being, so much older and wiser than himself.

You always seem to know everything.

"MS Phaeton arrived in Kiyō at the same time; she fled on board. I think she sailed to Prydain with my grandfather."

The Swordsman let out a short laugh.

"I wish I could have seen Ganryū's face."

"Why was he after her?" asked Bran.

"She was the last guardian of the Shard of Fukuchiyama."

"The Shard of – you mean my ring?"

Dōraku nodded.

"It was a part of some powerful artefact Ganryū was trying to collect. Another Tide Jewel, perhaps. He always chased after trinkets like these – and that was reason enough for me to try and stop him."

It's obviously more than just some trinket, Bran thought. *The daimyo of Kumamoto wanted it as well, and now…*

"Now Nariakira-*sama* has it."

"So the copy didn't fool you for long. We couldn't risk it falling into wrong hands, you understand…"

"I don't really care." Bran waved his hand.

This is not my war.

"The stone belongs here, in Yamato," he said. "To me it was just a memory of my grandfather. This will suffice," he added, shaking the medallion. "I must be going now."

Dōraku stood up and the boy bowed. The samurai bowed back and reached his hand out to Bran.

"I know this is how you Westerners bid farewell. Farewell, Bran-Karasu-*sama*."

The boy shook the Swordsman's hand.

"Farewell Dōraku-*sama*. Tell Nagomi and Satō, I..." Bran fought back tears welling up in his eyes. He shook his head. "No, don't tell them anything. I hope they will understand."

Shakushain stood among a dozen or so students of the Ganryū *Dōjō* on the pier, waiting for the supply ship to carry them back to the mainland.

They all seemed dejected and broken. They had been caught in the fight between demons, so there was neither shame in defeat, nor obligation to die or avenge the Crimson Robe. They were his students – but not his retainers after all; and now it was time for them to search other schools and other masters.

The ferry's Captain was surprised to see them, and even more surprised and disappointed about the news that there would be no more need for his services. Shakushain guessed he was already calculating how to recover his losses and where to move on with his business.

I wonder how Koro is faring. He remembered the last time he saw his small, dark face – under the waves of the Kanmon Strait as they waved at each other: Koro swimming away with strong beats of his short legs, Shakushain strangling one of the grey swordsmen who jumped into the sea with him.

"The currents of *Dan-no-ura* are deadly," he had explained then.

They were half-way to the shore when the wind and waves around the boat stopped. The sail fluttered and hung impotently. The Captain grunted and gave the few crewmembers an order to row across the flat surface of the Kanmon Straits. Shakushain volunteered for oar duty; at least it was something to keep his mind and body occupied. He hated being idle.

Several of the students noticed the odd silence and came up to the edge of the boat.

"Hey, look at this, what's going on?"

"The water is calm only around the boat. There's waves further out."

"That's not natural. Do you think it's the ghosts of *Dan-no-ura*?"

"They only ever come out on stormy nights..."

"Maybe the Master's death brought them out."

"What's this?"

One of them pointed to the sky. Shakushain looked up. A bright, blazing light appeared in the clouds and was falling towards the ship at great speed.

"It's going to hit!" somebody cried. "Jump out!"

But it was too late. The fiery missile struck the boat, shattering through the decks and hull. A ball of flame engulfed the ship and everyone on it, before dissipating in the cold water in a cloud of hot steam.

The waves and wind returned.

Torii Heishichi brushed the wooden boards of the pier with a sandal-clad foot, erasing the Falling Star character he had drawn in white chalk. He was breathing heavily, cursing his bad health. He adjusted his spectacles, wiped a trickle of blood from his nose and looked at the sea with satisfaction.

It was the first time he used it in the field: the first native Yamato spell; not copied and learned from *Rangaku* books, but created from scratch through the combined efforts of the wizards of Kagoshima. Written in Qin characters instead of Western runes, spoken in Yamato Spell Tongue instead of Bataavian. And it worked perfectly. Where mere moments ago a large supply ship was rowing towards the shore, there was now nothing but silence and emptiness. Only a few smouldering wooden boards bobbed up onto the surface.

Excellent.

"No witnesses," he repeated the daimyo's order to himself.

Bran buckled the saddle-bag packed with a little food for the journey, checked the reins, bridle and harness, tightened straps and buckles. He improvised the tack from bits and pieces he had found in Ganryū's stables. He patted Emrys tenderly on the snout. The dragon answered with a low, welcoming grunt.

"I bet *you* can't wait to leave this place."

The dragon snarled.

"I'm really sorry for everything you had to go through," said Bran, stroking the thick, scaly neck. He felt guilty for abandoning the dragon – and enraged at those who forced them to stay apart.

"I'll make it up to you somehow, I promise. And..." He put his arms around the neck and pressed his forehead against the scales. "I'm so proud of you, Emrys. I really am." The beast purred and puffed a little wisp of grey smoke.

Bran jumped on the dragon's back – no horse saddle was big enough to fit Emrys – put on the goggles, and lightly squeezed the beast's sides with his knees. It felt great to be able to fly again.

From the moment they departed the island, Bran noticed something was different. Emrys reacted to commands faster and more smoothly than ever; the sensory feedback was far stronger: Bran felt the wind on his arms as if they were wings; his eyesight grew sharper, and he could swear he started feeling the magical energies on his skin without the need for True Sight.

Could it be...?

He leaned down, touching the green scales just like he had in the Otherworld the night before, and closed his eyes. He whispered the spell words and felt his mind meld with that of Emrys in a soft flash of light.

He became aware of all the minute details of the land below: individual people on the roads and in the fishing boats, sharks and tuna in the ocean, black kites in the sky. He saw the currents of magic running through the air and sensed the flows of the Ninth Wind. He heard the buzz of a distant Farlink, the one he had been sensing for days, now far clearer and precise, coming from the North; *four riders,* he could tell with remarkable precision. Finally, he felt himself on his back, a light enough burden, clinging precariously to his neck.

The strain of trying to reconcile being in two places at once made him dizzy and Bran let go of the dragon's mind, returning to his own body.

Nobody's ever done anything like this before, he thought. At least, he'd never heard or read of a Farlink gone so far, or of such strange use of the Dragonform – and if there was any subject he knew about, it was the dragon lore. Something had happened to him and Emrys in Yamato's Otherworld, something unique; was this Shigemasa's parting gift?

He patted the dragon on the neck and breathed deeply.

CHAPTER XX

The lights of the city twinkled in the distance like a second Milky Way low over the horizon. In the darkness, these flickers and the dark shadows of tall hills above them outlined a wedge-shaped, narrow bay.

Samuel lowered the peculiar twin-lens spyglass he had borrowed from the Admiral and handed it back to him.

"How do you like the Porro glasses, *Doktor*?" asked Otterson.

"Curious invention," replied Samuel. "Not as good as a magical spyglass, of course, but impressive for a Roman device."

"This is the finest harbour I've seen in these waters," the Admiral said. "Such a waste."

"What happens now?"

"In the *morgoen* they will spot us."

Diana was not able to submerge since the accident, and with the damaged rudder was no longer as nimble as it once was.

"I hope they will send a pilot to guide us into the harbour."

"What if they attack?"

"The *spion* said the Yamato have no *kanoner* that would break through this hull," the Admiral said, patting the steel plate.

"He also said they have no mistfire ships."

Otterson frowned.

"With our two *kanoner* and a *torpeder* launcher we should be fine. But I'd rather avoid starting another war. Let's hope they'll be... how you say... *resonlig*?"

"Reasonable," offered Samuel.

"Yes. Let's hope the Yamato officials will be reasonable."

The Admiral knocked at the hatch with his staff. It screeched open.

"*Amiral...*" Samuel said quietly, "what is behind the door of bronze?"

Since his discovery, he had been dreaming of the hidden room – dark, heavy dreams of something, or someone, trying to break free.

Otterson looked sharply at Samuel, then back at the twinkling city in the distance.

"It's a weapon, *Doktor*. One that I hope never to have to use."

Satō left Nagomi in the infirmary and went outside; Bran and Dōraku were nowhere to be seen. The courtyard was eerily empty and quiet.

She passed the wicket gate and climbed the path through the azalea thicket before entering through the rune-covered door into Ganryū's abandoned mansion. She walked through the narrow, dark, silent corridors. Some of the rooms along the way were opened wide, or even broken into – by the staff of the mansion, trying to loot as much as they could before fleeing, she guessed. There was a fortune scattered on the tatami floors: gold, jewels, overthrown vases, ancient scrolls torn off the walls. An iron-bound chest, still locked. A collection of antique weapons. A cabinet of exotic wood, one of its doors hanging loose from the hinges, another stolen. Satō passed it all by, barely taking notice. She could sense Ganryū's Curse still lingering on all this treasure and she didn't want to have anything to do with it.

On the wooden boards where she had fought the assassin she noticed the stains of spattered blood; she crouched to touch it. There was more of it than she remembered. *It was a long fight. If Master Dōraku had not come, I wonder…*

She touched her left shoulder. The pain was still there, faint but distracting. The blade with which Ganryū had wounded her was not of his making, so there was no reason to believe the injury would disappear after his death. Still, she was a little disappointed.

The patterns of magic she could sense in the mansion had been dissipating since the Crimson Robe's demise, and were now barely noticeable. Though the wooden walls looked solid, she had a feeling the building will soon fall apart without the blood energy supporting it. Unless some other demon or wizard took the island for his abode, in time there would be nothing left to tell the tale of the Ganryū *Dōjō*.

In the garden, among the scorched trees and cratered ground, the remnants of the battle, a few hydrangeas valiantly sprouted blue and purple buds. Satō followed the path to the ruined pavilion. Rubble and ash were strewn everywhere, some still smouldering and crackling with the energy of the powerful magic.

She picked up one of the still sizzling pieces of rubble. She didn't need Nagomi's power of sightseeing to know that what happened last night had been just the first battle of a coming war. She tried to reconstruct what the fight may have looked like, based on what Bran had told her in the morning.

The Crimson Robe stood there, she imagined, *and Bran faced him here. Alone. And stood his ground.*

Bran may not have been a Yamato, and he may have been reluctant to kill, but he had fought as bravely as any samurai. He had proven his worth ten times over.

Why was I so hard on him?

Repeatedly spurning his advances must have hurt him.

Was it all just because he was a foreigner?

"A proper Yamato boy", she scoffed. "Is that really what I wanted?"

She wasn't sure herself why it was that way.

Was I afraid he'd disappear, like Nagomi's father?

The more Satō thought about it, the angrier she was at her former self. *I promised myself a new future,* she remembered. And what better chance for a new future could she have than with Bran? For a moment, she clung to the idea of getting help from daimyo of Satsuma. But how much assistance would Lord

Nariakira *really* offer, and how much would she have to bargain for it? She wasn't so naïve to think he would do anything for her out of good will. Once again she had to face the humiliating reality of being a woman in Yamato. What other man would appreciate her resolve and independence better than a foreigner, who came from a country ruled by a woman?

How could I have been so stupid?

She stood up from the rubble, resolved to seek the boy out and tell him what she had just decided. A cross-shaped shadow passed over the garden; she looked up, just in time to see the jade-green shape disappear into the clouds.

Bran flew along the coast, just as Dōraku had advised him, but far enough from the land not to be seen by anyone below. The rain clouds parted and the sun was shining at his back. He did not try the mind meld again – he resolved to try it when he was somewhere safe.

He tried not to think of his decision to leave Yamato. There would be plenty of time for regrets later.

It was the right thing, he kept telling himself. *What else was I supposed to do?*

He was going home, or at least in the direction of home. In a few days he would reach Huating, and then he'd try to find out what had happened to his father and the rest of the Marines. Some of them were bound to have survived… He hadn't thought about Qin in a long time. What state was the Empire in now? What happened to the rebellion?

Whatever was going on, he was certain Dylan – if he was still alive – was right in the middle of it.

By evening, Bran reached an archipelago of small islands around a narrow bay. He unrolled Dōraku's map to make sure he was in the right place. As he did so, a monogram in the corner of the cartouche caught his eye. Four Roman letters: P.F.V.S.

Nagomi's father.

He studied the map more carefully. It was drawn with a strong, yet precise hand. The shoreline was rendered in great detail but, inland, only certain geographical features were marked: roads, mountain passes, river crossings and local fortresses. Garrison sizes were noted in thin black ink.

This is a military map. He was *a spy after all!*

He couldn't read any more in the quickly falling twilight. It was time to look for a place to stay the night to rest up before next day's long flight across the Divine Winds. Bran chose to land on one of the uninhabited islets, far from the ship lanes and human settlements, and lay among the roots of a great cedar tree, covering himself with a cloak.

He quickly fell asleep, still tired after the night's events.

He wasn't sure how, or even *if,* he could fly across the Divine Winds. Emrys had done it, but the beast was rider-less and confused. The storm certainly *looked* imposing: an impenetrable wall of black clouds, torn through with howling, hurricane-speed winds. Thunder struck so densely that at times it formed webs of blue light encompassing the entire horizon. Through the holes in the clouds, Bran saw torrential rain and streams of hail. Flying closer, he noticed something else, a sight now almost familiar: the white light wisps of trapped Spirits, thrown every which way by the wind.

There must be thousands of them here, he thought. *Tens of thousands. Have they all drowned at sea?*

He took a deep breath and looked over his shoulder, towards Yamato. *This is it,* he thought. *Once past this, there will be no going back.*

What if I am never able to return? He swallowed hard. Never again see those cedar forests? Never walk on the cobbled streets? Taste the food? Smell the air?

He would be like Nagomi's real father, forever torn between two worlds, unable to see his loved ones again. He shook his head.

It's different now, he realized. *Sooner or later, Dracaland will move into Yamato. And when it does… I could become a diplomat. Not a spy, not a soldier like father, just a mediator and interpreter. I know the language; I understand how they think…*

Bran wondered what Dylan would say about his travels across the foreign and hostile land in pursuit of a dragon.

He would tell me to forget all about it and find an easier way to return home. Look, I will buy you a Highland Azure, he would say, now let's bribe the captain of this ship and have him sail us to Huating!

Bran chuckled. He thought he did rather well, all things considered. At least he managed to stay alive.

Emrys snorted and shook its head.

"All right, all right, we're going…"

He spurred Emrys higher, hoping to fly over the worst of the rumbling storm. At around five thousand feet, the clouds began to thin enough for the dragon to risk flying through. Enveloped by the cocoon of warm air – a by-product of the dragon's metabolism – and protected by a light *tarian,* Bran braced himself as he and his dragon braved the hurricane.

The Spirits from the storm below climbed towards him; their faces were white masks twisted with anguish and fury.

I could use Shigemasa and his halberd now, he thought. As they got closer, he started to recognize some of them. There was the bird-like *tengu* goblin; here, a reptilian *kappa* sprite. White foxes and raccoons, and other beings he had not yet heard about.

All the magical creatures, he realized with a shudder. *Yōkai! Is that what's happened to them?* Trapped in the Divine Wind, sentenced forever to harass those who would dare to sail to Yamato without the *Taikun's* permission?

He increased the power of the *tarian* and climbed another couple of hundred feet, out of the range of the damned Spirits swirling below like a shoal of frenzied sharks.

It took Bran half a day to cross the hundred or so miles of the Divine Winds and catch the first glimpse of the Tamna Island. Both he and Emrys were exhausted and eager to land somewhere, anywhere. The island on the horizon was welcomingly large, forty miles across at least, with a great volcano rising into the clouds right in the middle. As he got closer, Bran spotted a few more small islets to the north, looming through the haze – and a squadron of ships anchored in the open sea.

They were undoubtedly Western ships; one large, black mistfire ironclad, and a few auxiliary vessels around it. A couple of large dragons flew overhead. Bran's heart started beating fast. It could only be a Dracaland fleet! Home!

He wanted to fly straight towards the ships; but then the sun glimpsed through the clouds and reflected off the wings of the beasts.

They were onyx black.

Bran slowed Emrys down and had it hover in place high above the surface of the sea, at a distance – the dragon's light green scales made for a good camouflage against the clear sky. Black wings... there were no black dragons. Not in Dracaland, not in Midgard, not even in Varyaga...

A hooded man flying over the wall. Nagomi's prophetic dream. Were these the dragons he had felt before? No, the distant buzz had definitely been coming from within the Divine Winds barrier, somewhere in Yamato. But it was of a similar nature to what he sensed now; these riders must have been a scouting party – or reinforcements...

He studied the squadron through his spyglass. Only when he saw dots of people moving on deck did he realize how immense the flagship of the flotilla was. Half as big as *Ladon*, its deck was wide and flat, a typical dragon carrier. Bran was wondering how many dragons such a giant ship could accommodate, when one of the beasts landed on the wide deck. This gave him a size reference, as dots of the crew surrounded the dragon to take it to the stable.

Impossible. It must be a trick of perspective...

He pointed his spyglass to the other dragon still circling the fleet, looking for a rider on its back. At first he thought there was none, before noticing the tiny silhouette clinging between the massive shoulder blades. That dispelled any doubt.

Compared to these black winged monsters even Afreolus was small. A tiny dragon like Emrys was like a kittiwake next to a gannet. Only a secluded and secretive nation could have managed to breed such terrifying monsters in secret, a nation such as... He tried to spot the design on the ship's banner flapping in the wind; he couldn't see it clearly, but was almost certain it was the horned circle-and-cross sigil of the Gorllewin.

He remembered seeing the crest in Bharata, and later in Qin. *Scouts and spies, all over the Eastern Oceans. I wonder if father ever guessed what they were really after. But their dragons... How did they manage to hide these monsters?*

He turned the spyglass back to the ship; the lens blurred momentarily, as if a wisp of mist had obscured his vision. A second later the mist was gone, and Bran found himself looking at a snow-white, fat, squat beast sprawling on the deck: a *Snaellander,* just like the ones he had seen in Fan Yu.

Glamour, he realized. *Like the Shadowclouds. The four from Qin must be the ones I sensed in Yamato.*

Suddenly the white dragon launched again, turning back into the jet-black and sleek beast mid-flight. The other mount stopped circling around the squadron and turned towards Bran and Emrys.

They saw me.

The Tamna Island was not far, but the dragons approached at great speed. Bran dived down, towards the rocky shoreline; the surface of the island was pock-marked with ancient craters and lava streams, overgrown by thick jungle. There were plenty of places to hide.

Why would I hide? The Gorllewin are not the enemies of Dracaland.

Something inside him wanted to get as far away as possible from the enormous black beasts. Emrys lunged among the tall trees of the island with the two pursuers on his tail. Now Bran could really test the newly gained ability to control the dragon's body as well as his own. Zigzagging between the mighty tree trunks, avoiding the rocky outcrops, skirting past stone pillars and arches, he was getting steadily away from the black dragons, which were too big to follow him into the narrow crags and crevices.

But Emrys was getting tired; it had been an exhausting day already, and the small dragon could not keep flying for long. Bran swooped to the bottom of one such crevice, deep and tight, ending in a large cave with walls of smooth, glittering crystal. He landed Emrys in front of the cave and led it inside. His heart thumping, he pulled out the letter Dōraku had given him and read quickly through the brief note.

It was addressed to the commander of a ship stationed near the Tamna Island; a description of the opening of negotiations between the Great Council of Edo and the invading Western force. The proposals were surprisingly lenient: opening of ports, trade monopoly, full diplomatic liaisons. Bran tried to wrap his head around it; everything he had heard in Yamato pointed to the Edo government being ready to fight any foreigners to the death if need be, to keep them off the "Sacred Land". Was it all a façade? It seemed the *Taikun* was ready to sell his nation to the highest bidder. Bran knew now what the price of this purchase was.

He imagined the *Taikun's* samurai riding the mighty flying beasts into battle, supported by modern navy and army built with the help of the Grey Hoods. No rebellion against them would have a chance to succeed. Satsuma and its allies would not last a day, crushed and trampled under the claws of the black dragons.

And what are the Grey Hoods getting in the bargain? Trade opportunities? No, that can't be enough…

A vision from Amakusa, the dark, forgotten ritual of necromancy, flashed through his mind. Bran swore loudly and crushed the piece of paper in his hand. He felt manipulated. Dōraku knew what was in the letter when he had given it to him. He had planned the route for his return home as well, so that the boy would "chance" upon the Western fleet near Tamna. But what did he expect from Bran? Turn around, hand over his dragon to Satsuma? Die in a war he didn't care about?

Emrys snarled and growled. Bran heard the rush of wind from the enormous wings. One of the black dragons hovered over the crevice.

"This must be the place," the rider shouted. Bran was surprised at first to hear him speak in a mixture of Seaxe and Prydain, until he remembered the Gorllewin had started as the colony of Gwynedd several centuries ago. He heard the other dragon fly near, and they both landed almost on top of the cave.

"Come down and see if he's really here. Be careful."

One of the riders appeared in the cave's entrance brandishing a broad sword with an eagle-shaped hilt. He threw back the hood of his grey greatcloak; his hair was fair and cropped short, shorter even than the Dracaland military style. He saw Bran and Emrys and jumped back.

"By the Bull's Horns, who the hell are *you*?"

"What is it, Thorfinn?" the other rider cried.

"You'd better come down and see for yourself! *You* – " the rider waved his sword at Bran, "out!"

Easy, Bran ordered Emrys silently and stepped into the light. The other rider came down to take a good look at him.

"What are these funny clothes he's wearing?"

"I've no idea," replied the first one, Thorfinn. "But he's definitely not from around here."

"I thought we were supposed to be the only ones."

"Maybe the narrow-eyes are playing on several fronts."

"I don't like this whole endeavour. We should have just stayed in Huating."

"Have you not read the first squadron's reports yet? Huating is a goner! I'm sure the rebels have overcome it by now, and we never got anywhere with those Black Lotus guys. Yamato is more eager to cooperate."

Huating a goner? What about Dylan and the Second Regiment?

"I wouldn't trust any of the narrow-eyes. Qin, Yamato, Nam, they're all the same, lying heathen bastards. I'm sure they're plotting something against us even as they sign the treaties."

"That's not for us to discuss, ensign. What do we do with him?"

"Take him back to the ship. The Vice Komtur will want to have a word. You – " the rider turned back to Bran and pointed to one of the black dragons. "Dragon. Now. Understand?"

"I can fly on my own," the boy replied. This took them aback.

"You speak our language?"

"I speak *Prydain.*"

They exchanged looks.

"What are you doing here, boy?"

"I am a Dracalish soldier and I will speak to your Commander only," Bran said defiantly. He wasn't afraid of the two riders; he had already assessed them. Like all Old Faithers, they bore no magic weapons or shields. Thorfinn wielded a gunpowder pistol of complex design, but obviously did not deem the unarmed boy enough of a threat to draw it. Even if they knew how to draw upon their dragons' power – and something in their gait told Bran they weren't ready to do so – the boy was confident he could fight his way out, if need be. Would he be able to flee the black beasts? He looked at one of the dragons peering curiously over the crevice; its head alone was as big as half of Emrys's entire body. The beasts had already proved themselves resilient in pursuit.

I would need to kill the riders to be sure of escaping...

But now he was intrigued. He wanted to learn what possible reason had brought the Gorllewin to these seas.

And there was something else the riders had mentioned... *Black Lotus.* The tattoo on the saboteur's arm... Bran never forgot that image. Did the Grey Hoods know who caused the *Ladon*'s disaster?

The riders looked at each other again and shrugged.

"All right. Mount up," said Thorfinn. "But no tricks; you stand no chance against the Black Wings."

"And wherever you were heading to, you can forget about it now," added the other. "You're coming with us. All the way to Yamato."

CHAPTER XXI

Hotta Naosuke entered a vast underground chamber lit only by a few torches; the flickering light outlined six silhouettes in the shadows – four men and two women, all clad in long, flowing robes and wearing masks of demons; twisted faces painted in garish colours.

They stood in a circle in the middle of the cavern floor, waiting. One of them, wearing the white robe, stepped into the centre.

The Speaker guides the ceremony, but is not the leader, remembered Naosuke. *All Heads of the Serpent are equal, but one.*

There should have been seven of the celebrants; today one of them could not come. And there was only one reason why a Head would miss the Gathering.

"Today, our circle is broken," the Speaker boomed. "Today, the unthinkable has happened. One of us will never again grace us with his presence; never again grant us his wisdom and strength. Mars's Curse has been lifted!"

A murmur spread about the circle. They had already guessed what had happened.

"A war is upon us," the Speaker continued, "we are being attacked once again, and in our very heart. Ganryū was one of our finest and bravest. He will be remembered.'

"He will be remembered," the others repeated in unison.

"What about Mars's plans?" asked one of the Heads, wearing a golden robe and a black and yellow horned face of an *oni*. "Have they failed? It would be a major setback to our cause."

"Some have," the Speaker replied, "but not all. Some are still going strong."

"Who will replace him?" asked one of the women, her robe silver, and her mask a pale fox's head.

The Speaker clapped his hands.

"Initiate, come forth!"

Naosuke put on his mask – it was a blank, white, featureless surface with only holes for eyes and mouth – and stepped slowly out of the shadows.

"Show yourself."

He lifted his mask and bowed with pride. He had dreamed of joining the Eight-headed Serpent ever since his recruitment into the ranks of the Fanged twenty years before. He never actually imagined it would be possible, not before decades or centuries passed – a Head would have to be destroyed or retire before another took his place. And yet, here he was, the youngest, the least experienced of them all.

"Your name and position, Initiate."

"Councillor to His Illustrious Excellency, *Taikun* of Yamato. Hotta Naosuke."

The others murmured again.

"Who will vouch for the Initiate?" the Speaker asked.

"I will," said a tall, broad-shouldered man in the robe woven of metallic thread shimmering in the light of the torches like fire, and the mask of a leopard. When Hotta had first met him, in the library of the Mito school, the man had been using a common samurai name; here, in the Circle, he was known as Jupiter of the Bronze Robe, the master strategist of the Serpent.

"I confirm that Hotta Naosuke has passed his tests and is ready to join our ranks," said Jupiter.

The Speaker nodded and asked:

"Are there any here who would object?"

Hotta cast a quick glance around. None uttered a word.

"Then, as is our custom, Initiate, step into the circle in place of the one who has created you. You will take his name and position as yourself: Mars, of *the Crimson Robe.*"

Naosuke took his place in the half-circle, his hands nervously squeezing the ends of his fresh robe. It still smelled of the sacrificial blood with which it had been infused. At the Speaker's gesture, the remaining Heads began the ritual of Recognition. One by one, in a line, they approached Naosuke and showed him their faces without masks. That way the new Initiate was able to learn the identities of all of them.

"Yui Shōsetsu, Saturn of the White Robe," said the Speaker, the last in line. Naosuke recognized every name; they were all ancient, hidden in the shadows behind fallen plots and failed rebellions.

And me among them. Me, Hotta Naosuke, aged thirty-nine.

He knew he was lucky; had Ganryū succeeded in turning Takashima Shūhan before his demise, it would have been the old wizard standing in Naosuke's place.

Luck is also a talent.

After the entire procession passed, the six Fangeds stepped aside, letting Naosuke approach the wall of black, semi-opaque crystal. He stepped forward with a deep bow. Behind the crystal, in the flickering light, he saw the Armour: a cuirass of polished steel plate of old *Nanbando* Western style, topped with the pointy helmet and the long silver feather.

There was another man standing next to the Armour, behind the crystal; he was not a Fanged, but looked more like a demon in samurai clothes: seven feet tall, muscular, and... dark as night. His skin glistened like polished mahogany. He observed Naosuke with great white eyes in silence.

So it's true. Oda does have a black samurai for a servant.

Two flames lit up in the eye sockets of the Armour's metal mask.

"Hotta." A dark, chilling voice spoke. "*A clan of traitors.*"

"It... it's an old story, Master..."

"*Quiet. Your ancestor's betrayal brought me my first victory.*"

Naosuke felt the eyes study him all over.

"*Blood red is the colour of your clan.*"

"Yes. The Red Devils of Sekigahara."

"*How fitting. You may yet be of more use to me than Ganryū. His arrogance and recklessness were always troublesome, and his plans needlessly elaborate. And now it seems we may not require his trinkets after all. When you're done with the ritual, I want you to tell me all about your dealings with these... new Westerners.*"

The flaring eyes grew dim and then vanished. Naosuke turned around and stepped into his place in the complete circle. The Speaker then presented Naosuke with his new mask: a green and black *tengu*, a mountain goblin.

"The wheel rotates," the Speaker intoned, "the spoke is replaced. The ox cart rolls forward. Our journey continues."

"Our journey continues," the others repeated. Naosuke was a little late with the unison murmur. He noticed a scorning glance from one of the masked Eight.

No matter, he thought. *I am part of the Serpent now. Nothing can change it. Now all my plans can be set in motion.*

He remembered the last words of the Prophecy his Master, Jupiter of the Bronze Robe, had revealed to him, all those years ago:

The Eight-Headed Serpent rises,

But the Storm God's sword is sheathed.

At the breaking of the world

The Mightiest will fall

And his dying cry will break open

The Gates to the Other World.

-THE END-

APPENDICES

APPENDIX I:
GLOSSARY OF FOREIGN WORDS

(Bat.) — Bataavian
(Yam.) — Yamato
(Pryd.) — Prydain
(Seax.) — Seaxe

aardse nor *(Bat.)* spell word, "Earth Tomb"
amazake *(Yam.)* a traditional sweet drink from fermented rice
ardian *(Seax.)* the Commander of a Regiment in the Royal Marines
banneret *(Seax.)* the Commander of a Banner in the Royal Marines
bento *(Yam.)* a boxed lunch, usually made of rice, fish and pickled
vegetables
bevries *(Bat.)* spell word, "Freeze"
biwa *(Yam.)* fruit of loquat tree
blodeuyn *(Pryd.)* spell word, "Flowers"
bugyō *(Yam.)* chief magistrate of an autonomous city
bwcler *(Pryd.)* magical shield covering a fighter's arm, a buckler
cha *(Yam.)* green tea
chwalu *(Pryd.)* spell word, "Unravel"
Corianiaid *(Pryd.)* a race of red-haired dwarves from Rheged
cwrw *(Pryd.)* beer
dab *(Pryd.)* creature, thing or a person
daimyo *(Yam.)* feudal lord of a province
daisen *(Yam.)* chief wizard
dap *(Pryd.)* the same size and shape as something
dengaku *(Yam.)* a meal of grilled tofu or vegetables topped with sauce
denka, -denka *(Yam.)* honorific, referring to the member of the royal
family
derwydd *(Pryd.)* druid
deva *(Latin)* demon
dōjō *(Yam.)* school of martial arts or fencing
dono, -dono *(Yam.)* honorific, referring to a noble man of a higher
level
dorako *(Yam.)* Western dragon
doshin *(Yam.)* chief of Police
dōtanuki *(Yam.)* a type of katana, longer and heavier than usual
draca hiw *(Seax.)* spell word, "Dragon Form"
draigg *(Pryd.)* a dragon
duw *(Pryd.)* a swearword

dwt *(Pryd.)* a young child

egungun *(Yoruba)* a holy spirit, also a shaman dancer representing Egungun

enenra *(Yam.)* a spirit born of smoke

faeder *(Seax.)* father

fudai *(Yam.)* an "inner circle" clan; one of the vassals of the Tokugawa Taikun before the battle of Sekigahara

futon *(Yam.)* a roll-out mattress filled with rice husks

gaikokujin *(Yam.)* a foreigner, non-Yamato person

genoeg *(Bat.)* spell word, "Enough" (to mark the end of a continuous spell)

gornestau *(Pryd.)* magical duel

graddio *(Pryd.)* school graduation ceremony

gwrthyrru *(Pryd.)* spell word, "Repel"

hakama *(Yam.)* split trousers

hamon *(Yam.)* visual effect created on the blade through hardening process

haoma *(Latin)* ritual potion of the Mithraists

haori *(Yam.)* a type of outer jacket

hatamoto *(Yam.)* the Taikun's retainer, samurai in direct service to the Taikun

hime, -hime *(Yam.)* honorific, referring to women of high position

igo *(Yam.)* a board game for two players, using identical black and white tokens

ijslaag *(Bat.)* spell word, "Ice Layer"

inro *(Yam.)* a wooden container for holding small objects, hanging from a sash

inugami *(Yam.)* a dog spirit

jawch *(Pryd.)* a swearword

jutte *(Yam.)* police truncheon

kabuki *(Yam.)* a form of classical dance theater

kagura *(Yam.)* a type of theatrical dance with religious themes

kakka *(Yam.)* honorific, referring to lords of the province or heads of the clans

kambe *(Yam.)* a shrine servant taken from an adjacent village

kami *(Yam.)* God or Spirit in Yamato mythology

kanpai *(Yam.)* Cheers!

kappa *(Yam.)* a water sprite, reptilian humanoid

katana *(Yam.)* the main Yamato sword, over 60cm in length

kaya *(Yam.)* a bright yellow wood used for making igo boards

kekkai *(Yam.)* a magical shield, similar to tarian

kimono *(Yam.)* official layered robe of the noble class

kirin *(Yam.)* a chimerical creature of Qin, body of a deer and the head of a dragon with a large single horn

kodachi *(Yam.)* a short Yamato sword, less than 60cm in length

koenig *(Seax.)* the monarch of the Varyaga Khaganate

kosode *(Yam.)* basic, loose fitting robe for both men and women

kun, -kun *(Yam.)* honorific, referring to young persons of the same social status

kunoichi *(Yam.)* a female shinobi assassin

kuso *(Yam.)* a swearword

lloegr *(Pryd. arch.)* Dracaland east of the Dyke

llwch *(Pryd.)* spell word, "Dust"

long *(Qin)* Qin dragon

ma jiang *(Qin)* gambling board game

mam *(Pryd.)* mother

mamgu *(Pryd.)* grandmother

Matsubara *(Yam.)* the family of katana swordsmiths

metsuke *(Yam.)* inspector representative of the Taikun

mikado *(Yam.)* the divine Emperor of Yamato

mikan *(Yam.)* fruit of tangerine tree

mithraeum *(Latin)* temple of Mithras

mitorashita *(Yam.)* worshippers of Mithras

mochi *(Yam.)* a sweet made of rice gluten

mogelijkheid *(Bat.)* magical potential

monpe *(Yam.)* workman's trousers

nanbando *(Yam.)* "in the Western style"

naginata *(Yam.)* a polearm formed of a katana blade set in a bamboo shaft

nodachi *(Yam.)* a large, two-handed sword, over 120cm in length

noren *(Yam.)* a curtain hanging over the shop entrance, with the logo of the establishment

oba *(Yoruba)* chieftain

obi *(Yam.)* a silk sash wrapped around the waist

obidame *(Yam.)* a buckle for tying the obi sash

oden *(Yam.)* a type of stew

omikuji *(Yam.)* fortunes written on a strip of paper

onmyōji *(Yam.)* a practitioner of traditional Yamato magic

onmyōdō *(Yam.)* traditional Yamato magic

oppertovenaar *(Bat.)* overwizard of Dejima

pater *(Latin)* "father", priest

pilipala *(Pryd.)* spell word, "butterfly"

proost *(Bat.)* Cheers!

rangaku *(Yam.)* "Western Sciences", study of Western magic and technology

rangakusha *(Yam.)* a practitioner of Western magic

reeve *(Seax.)* the Staff Sergeant in the Royal Marines

rhew *(Pryd.)* spell word, "frost" (also used to summon dragon flame)

ri *(Yam.)* measure of distance, approx. 4 km

rōnin *(Yam.)* a masterless samurai

ryū *(Yam.)* a Yamato dragon

Saesneg *(Pryd.)* (slur) Seaxe

sakaki *(Yam.)* a flowering evergreen tree, used to produce sacred paraphernalia

sama, -sama *(Yam.)* honorific, referring to peers of the same social status

sencha *(Yam.)* popular kind of tea

sensei, -sensei *(Yam.)* honorific, referring to teachers and doctors

shamisen *(Yam.)* a three-stringed musical instrument

shamo *(Ezo)* people living in the islands of Yamato, south of Ezo

shinobi *(Yam.)* assassin

shōchū *(Yam.)* strong liquor (25-35% proof)

shōgi *(Yam.)* strategic board game similar to chess

shukubo *(Yam.)* accommodation for temple pilgrims

sokukamibutsu *(Yam.)* a self-mummified monk

stadtholder *(Bat.)* the ruler of Bataavia

swyfen *(Seax.)* a swearword

tabako *(Yam.)* tobacco

tadcu *(Pryd.)* grandfather

tafarn *(Pryd.)* tavern, inn

tafl *(Pryd.)* strategic board game, played on a checkered board

taid *(Pryd.)* grandfather

taikun *(Yam.)* military ruler of Yamato

taipan *(Qin)* leader of a trading company

Taishō *(Yam.)* field marshal, commander-in-chief of all the forces in the field

tarian *(Pryd.)* magical shield surrounding entire body

tengu *(Yam.)* a forest goblin

tenpura *(Yam.)* small fish and vegetables fried in batter

teppo *(Yam.)* a "thunder gun" - hand-held lightning thrower

terauke *(Yam.)* a passport produced by an affiliate temple

tono, -dono *(Yam.)* honorific, referring to a noble man of a higher level

torii *(Yam.)* wooden or stone gate to the shrine

tozama *(Yam.)* an "outer circle" clan that was forced to become the vassal of the Tokugawa Taikun after the battle of Sekigahara

tsuba *(Yam.)* a handguard of the katana

twinkelbal *(Bat.)* sparkleball; a stone used for thaumaturgy practice

twp *(Pryd.)* insult, "stupid, simple"

tylwyth teg *(Pryd.)* Faer Folk, a race of tall, silver- or golden-haired humanoids

waelisc *(Seax.)* (slur) Prydain

wakashu *(Yam.)* an "unbroken" youth, a virgin

wakizashi *(Yam.)* a short sword used as a side arm, 30-60cm in length

xiexie *(Qin)* "thank you"

y ddraig goch *(Pryd.)* Red Dragon

y ddraig ffurf *(Pryd.)* spell word, "Dragon Form"

yamabushi *(Yam.)* an ascetic mountain hermit

yōkai *(Yam.)* evil spirit, demon

ystlumod *(Pryd.)* spell word, "bats"

yukata *(Yam.)* casual summer clothing, simple light robe

APPENDIX II:
GLOSSARY OF CHARACTERS

GWYNEDD

CANTRE'R GWAELOD

IFOR AP MEURIG o Cantre'r Gwaelod

b. 2541 a.u.c. Midshipman on *Phaeton* under Captain Broughton Reynolds. Married to Branwen ferch Rhodri.

DYLAN AB IFOR o Cantre'r Gwaelod

b. 2566 a.u.c. Ardian of the Second Dragoons Regiment of the Royal Marines.

Mount: Highland Silver, Afreolus *(Unruly)*

BRAN AP DYLAN o Cantre'r Gwaelod

b. 2590 a.u.c. A graduate of Dracology at the Llambed Academy of Mystic Arts.

Mount: Rhos Jade, Emrys *(Ambrosius)*

RHIAN FERCH RHYS

b. 2569 a.u.c. Cunning-woman from southern Gwynedd.

LLAMBED ACADEMY

YWAIN MAB URIEN
b. ca. 1200 a.u.c. (assumed) Headmaster of the Llambed Academy. A
Corrie.
INGRID MAGNUSDOTTIR
Dean of Dracology
Mount: Highland Grey, Grima (*Shadow of the Night*)
NICOLAUS CAMPION
Head of Astrology
EITHNE MacALPIN
b. 2591 a.u.c. A student of Geomancy from Alba.
MADOC AB OWAIN o Llyn
b. 2590 a.u.c. A student of Dracology.
Mount: Eryni Ruby, Barfog (*Bearded*)

ROYAL MARINES

EDERN mab Gwyn

b. 2526 a.u.c. Banneret of the Second Dragoons Regiment of the Royal Marines. A Tylwyth Teg.

Mount: Highland Silver, Nodwydd (*Needle*)

GWENLLIAN ferch Harri

b. 2577 a.u.c. Reeve of the Second Dragoons Regiment of the Royal Marines.

Mount: Highland Silver, Tywyll (*Dark*)

SAMUEL ben Hagin

b. 2546 a.u.c. The ship's doctor.

AKINTOYE

Former *Oba* (ruler) of the city of Éko, reinstalled by the Dracalish Navy.

BROUGHTON REYNOLDS

b. 2542 a.u.c. Rear Admiral of East Bharata and Qin Station

ALEXANDER SETON

b. 2567 a.u.c. Ardian of the Twelfth Regiment of Light Dragoons

WULFHERE of WARWICK

b. 2589 a.u.c. Soldier of the Twelfth Regiment of Light Dragoons. Descendant of Richard Warwick the Kingmaker.

Mount: Highland Azure, Eolhsand (*Amber*)

HYWEL AP CADELL o Llyn

b. 2590 a.u.c. Soldier of the Twelfth Regiment of Light Dragoons.

Mount: Eryni Ruby, Taran Goch (*Red Thunder*)

KEYNA MARRAK

b. 2590 a.u.c. Soldier of the Twelfth Regiment of Light Dragoons

Mount: Kernow Crimson, Elvenn (*Spark*)

ISAMBARD D. BRUNEL

b. 2559 a.u.c. Arch-wizard of the Clistane Academy, designer of *Ladon*.

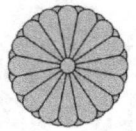

YAMATO

KIYŌ

MIZUNO TADANORI

b. 2563 a.u.c. *Bugyō* — Magistrate of Kiyō. *Hatamoto* retainer of the Taikun.

KOYATA JŪMONJI

b. 2570 a.u.c. *Doshin* — chief of police — of the Merchant's District in Kiyō

ISHIDA TAKUYA

b. 2566 a.u.c. Lieutenant of *Doshin* Koyata

HIRATA MITSUYU

b. 2574 a.u.c. Lieutenant of *Doshin* Koyata

NAMIKOSHI TOKOJIRO

b. 2581 a.u.c. An interpreter of Dracalish language.

TSUKINARI SHIGEZAEMON

b. 2578 a.u.c. Captain of the guards of Kiyō Magistrate

BLACK RAVEN SOMERLED

b. 2577 a.u.c. Cast-away, teacher of Dracalish

MORIYAMA EINOSUKE

b. 2573 a.u.c. Interpreter of Dracalish at Edo court, school friend of Tokojiro Namikoshi

HEIAN

MUTSUHITO
b. 2595 a.u.c. Crown Prince of Yamato
KŌMEI
b. 2576 a.u.c. 121st Divine Mikado (Emperor) of Yamato

DEJIMA

HENDRIK CURZIUS
b. 2566 a.u.c. *Oppertovenaar* (Overwizard) of the Bataavian outpost of Dejima.
GERHARDUS FABIUS
b. 2559 a.u.c. Captain of the *"Soembing"*

SAKUMA

SAKUMA ZŌZAN
b. 2564 a.u.c. A scholar of *Rangaku*.
SAKUMA KEINOSUKE
b. 2594 a.u.c. A student at the Takashima School of Wizardry.

ITŌ

ITŌ TAKI, neé Kusumoto

b. 2556 a.u.c. Wife of Itō Keisuke, a Western-style physician, owner of the Sōfukuji Infirmary.

ITŌ INE

b. 2580 a.u.c. A nurse and physician at the Sōfukuji Infirmary.

ITŌ NAGOMI

b. 2591 a.u.c. An apprentice at the Suwa shrine.

TANAKA

TANAKA HISASHIGE

b. 2552 a.u.c. A scholar of *Rangaku* magic, mechanician and thaumaturgist.

TANAKA DAIKICHI

b. 2598 a.u.c. Heir and apprentice of Hisashige Tanaka.

SUWA SHRINE

HOSOKI KAZUKO

b. 2567 a.u.c. High Priestess of Suwa Shrine.

IKŌ

A servant girl at the Suwa Shrine

TAKASHIMA

TAKASHIMA SHŪHAN
b. 2544 a.u.c. A *Rangaku* scholar, head of the Takashima School of Wizardry.
TAKASHIMA SATŌ
b. 2589 a.u.c. Heir of Takashima School of Wizardry.
YOSHIDA SHŌIN
b. 2594 a.u.c. A student at the Takashima School of Wizardry.

HOSOKAWA

HOSOKAWA NARIMORI
b. 2557 a.u.c. Daimyo of Kumamoto domain, lord of Kumamoto Castle.

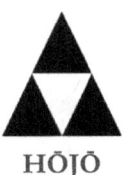

HŌJŌ

YOKOI SHŌNAN
b. 2562 a.u.c. A scholar and reformer at the Hosokawa's court in Kumamoto.
MOTODA NAGAZANE
b. 2571 a.u.c. A student of Yokoi Shonan.

SATSUMA

SHIMAZU NARIAKIRA
b.2562 a.u.c. Daimyō of the province of Satsuma, lord of Kagoshima Castle.

SHIMAZU HISAMITSU
b. 2570 a.u.c. Younger brother of Shimazu Nariakira

SHIMAZU ATSU
b. 2589 a.u.c. Adopted daughter of Shimazu Nariakira, princess of Satsuma.

KAWAMURA SUMIYOSHI
b. 2589 a.u.c. Mechanician, Captain of the Iroha Maru

TORII HEISHICHI
b. 2557 a.u.c. *Daisen,* Arch-wizard of Satsuma

KOMATSU KIYOKADO
b. 2588 a.u.c. A samurai of Satsuma.

ŌKUBO MINEKO
b. 2591 a.u.c. A court servant girl in the court of Satsuma.

SUGIMOTO YOSHIO
b. 2566 a.u.c. An earth-wizard from Satsuma, student of Torii Heishichi.

SUGIMOTO HACHIRO
b. 2547 a.u.c. A samurai of Hayato, retainer of Satsuma Domain.

YOKŌ
A servant girl at the Kirishima Shrine

KUMASO

TORISHI KAYA
b. 2569 a.u.c. Chieftain of the last village of the Kumaso People.

KUMAMOTO

MAGONOJO ITSUNEN
b. 2579 a.u.c. A monk at Honmyōji temple, host of *shukubo*.

MOTOMENOSUKE INGEN
b. 2570 a.u.c. A monk at Honmyōji temple, cook of *shukubo*.

IPPONIN
b. 2538 a.u.c., d. 2606 a.u.c. Previous abbot of Honmyōji temple

CHIZONIN
b. 2565 a.u.c. Current abbot of Honmyōji temple

SOZAEMON FURUHASHI
b. 2567 a.u.c. Fifteenth abbot of the Unganzenji Temple

KATŌ KIYOMASA (I)
b. 2315, d. 2364 Founder of Kumamoto Castle, general, one of the *Seven Spears of Shizugatake*

KATŌ KIYOMASA (II)
b. 2570 Captain of the Guards Regiment at Kumamoto Castle.

GENSAI KAWAKAMI
b. 2577 A retainer of the Kumamoto Domain. Master swordsman.

ITSUNEN SHOYU
b. 2579 a.u.c. A monk at Honmyōji temple, host of *shukubo*.

INGEN RYUKI
b. 2570 a.u.c. A monk at Honmyōji temple, cook of *shukubo*.

IPPONIN
b. 2538 a.u.c, d. 2606 a.u.c. Previous abbot of Honmyōji temple

CHIZONIN
b. 2565, Current abbot of Honmyōji temple

KŪKAI
b. 2555 a.u.c., *pater* (Mithraist priest) of the Sakitsu town on Amakusa Island

TOKUGAWA

TOKUGAWA IEYOSHI

b. 2546 a.u.c. Twelfth Taikun of Yamato

TOKUGAWA IESADA

b. 2577 a.u.c. Eldest son and heir of Tokugawa Ieyoshi

KAYAMA YEZAIMON

b. 2547 a.u.c. Daimyo of Uraga, commander of coastal defences of Edo Bay

MORIYAMA EINOSUKE

b. 2573 a.u.c. Interpreter of Dracalish at Edo court, school friend of Tokojiro Namikoshi

MASAHIRO ABE

b. 2572 a.u.c. Chief Senior Councillor in the Taikun's government

HOTTA NAOSUKE

b. 2568 a.u.c. Senior Councillor in the Taikun's government

MAKINO TADAMASA

b. 2552 a.u.c. Senior Councillor in the Taikun's government, chief of Edo defences.

KUZE HIROCHIKA

b. 2572 a.u.c. Senior Councillor in the Taikun's government.

MATSUDAIRA

MATSUDAIRA NOBUTSUNA
b. 2349 a.u.c. — d. 2415 Commander of the Taikun's forces in the final victory over the Shimabara Rebellion.

MATSUDAIRA TADAKATA
b. 2565 a.u.c. Senior Councillor in the Taikun's government.

MATSUDAIRA NORIYASU
b. 2548 a.u.c. Senior Councillor in the Taikun's government.

MITO

AIZAWA SEISHISAI
b. 2534 a.u.c. A scholar and a thinker of the Mito School.

NOBUMITSU AOYAMA
b. 2560 a.u.c. A student, later scholar at Mito School

TENKŌ TOYODA
b. 2558 a.u.c. A student, later scholar at Mito School

ITAKURA

ITAKURA SHIGEMASA
b. 2341, d. 2391 a.u.c. Daimyo of Fukōzu Han in Mikawa Province, commander of Taikun's forces during Shimabara Rebellion.

TOSA

TAKECHI HANPEITA
b. 2582 a.u.c. Samurai of Tosa Domain

ARIMA

ARIMA YORISHIGE
b. 2581 a.u.c. Eleventh daimyo of Kurume Domain
MAKI IZUMI
b. 2566 a.u.c. High Priest of the Suiten-gu Shrine, retainer of Arima clan, scholar and revolutionary

SAGA

NABESHIMA NAOMASA
b. 2568 a.u.c. *Daimyo* of the Saga Domain.
SHINPEI ETŌ
b. 2587 a.u.c. Retainer of the Saga Domain.

EIGHT-HEADED SERPENT

OZUN
b. 2581 a.u.c. A renegade *Yamabushi* priest

AZUMI
b. 2585 a.u.c. The last of the line of *shinobi* assassins of Koga

SHŌ IKU
b. 2566 a.u.c. Last heir of the royal family of Nansei Islands

SAITŌ HAJIME
b. 2587 a.u.c. Student of the Ganryu Dojo, commander of its 1st Squad.

SHAKUSHAIN
b. 2569 a.u.c. A native warrior from the northernmost island of Ezo

KORO
b. 2558 a.u.c. A man of the ancient native race of Ezo, friend of Shakushain

UNRYŪ KYŪKICHI
b. 2575 a.u.c. Sumo wrestler from Yonogawa. 10th Yokozuna

TYR GORLLEWIN

MATHIUN PERAI
b. 2547 a.u.c. Komtur of the Western Navy of Tyr Gorllewin.

VARYAGA KHAGANATE

FRIDRIK OTTERSON
b. 2568 a.u.c. Varyagan admiral, Captain of the *Diana*.
MAGNUS INGVARSSON
b. 2549 a.u.c. The ship's doctor on *Diana*.
HJALMAR NOBELIUS
b. 2554 a.u.c. Varyagan inventor and thaumaturgist, creator of the
Diana.

QIN

TSENG KUO-FAN "BOHAN"
b. 2564 a.u.c. An eminent Qin official, general and scholar, commander of the Eastern Army.
LI HUNG-CHANG
b. 2576 a.u.c. A scholar, officer and translator. Personal aide to Tseng Kuo-Fan.
BOU MAI
A Tanka fish merchant in Fan Yu.

APPENDIX III:
TIMELINE OF THE HISTORY OF THE WORLD

(all dates counted since the founding of Rome, 753 BC of our reckoning)

0 a.u.c. — Founding of Rome

704 — Gnaeus Pompeius destroys Julius Caesar at Dyrrhachium. Rome's expansion turns eastward. The Northern Gauls rebel and throw off the Roman yolk.

718 — Marcus Antonius defeats Sextus Pompeius at the Battle of Actium.

737 — Alexander Helios, son of Antony & Cleopatra, becomes a joint ruler of Egypt and Rome.

796 — Drusilla of Mauretania leads the first Roman Invasion of Prydain.

814 — Battle of Watling Street. Romans defeated by Queen Boudicca. Suetonius's army dispersed by the Derwydd of Mona. Romans retreat from Prydain.

831 — Imperator Sampsiceramus brings the worship of Mithras from the East.

859 — Roman General Traian defeats Dacian dragon riders with aid of a Great Dragon Ladon discovered under Mount Etna.

870 — Hadrian, son of Traian becomes the Imperator after Sampsiceramus and leads a second Invasion of Prydain.

873 — The Ninth Legion discovers the Brycheiniog Gate and is transported to the land of Faer Folk. The invasion is halted at Trachd Romra.

910—916 — Brigantes rebellion in northern Prydain. Romans retreat south of Trisantona River. The new province is called Britannia Cistrisantona.

950 — Battle of Lugdunum. Septimius Severus vanquishes a rebellion in northern Gaul and marches on to Prydain, extending Rome's dominion north of Trisantona.

995 — Shapur I of Persia converts to Mani's heresy.

1000 — Imperator Philip celebrates the first Millenium

ca. 1000 — The Horse Lords arrive in the West. They bring the Steppe Dragons with them. The dragons soon go feral in the foreign land.

1027 — Imperator Aurelian makes Sol Invictus and Mithras official cult of the Imperium.

1083 — Imperator Constantine builds Constantinopolis as the second capital of the Imperium.

1115 — Julian begins to rethink and reorganize Rome's State Religion in a Neoplatonic manner.

1117 — Julian captures Ctezifon and the ideas of Mani spread throughout the east of Imperium.

ca. 1130 — Feral Steppe Dragons start appearing across the Rhine and Danube.

1134 — Under Julian's guidance and in theological conflict with Mani, Mithraic priests forge monotheistic cult of Sol and its son, the Bull—Slayer. The Constantinople Creed is written. Most other Gods are delegated to serving as Aspects of the Sun God or demons to be defeated.

1158—1198 — A religious civil war erupts throughout the Imperium, between traditionalist Mithraists (mostly in the West) and Manicheans (mostly in the East).

1159 — The Crossing of the Rhine. With the Imperium weakened by war, a flock of Steppe Dragons crosses the Rhine and ravages the land. Abandoned by the Imperium, Armorican druids defend their land. The Armorican Kingdom established. Hispania and Mauretania are cut off from the Imperium as dragons settle in Pyrenees and along the coast. Local warlords take over the rule of many provinces.

1160 — Western legions abandon Prydain to face the growing threat of the dragons.

1198 — I War of Imperiums ends in face of the dragon threat.

1193 — Arthur the Faer becomes the chieftain of the Faer in Brycheiniog.

1202 — The Seaxe land in Dracaland and push the people of Prydain westwards. Many of them flee to the safety of the Faer Land. Arthur is hailed as the King of Prydain, but is forced to move even further West, to the fortress of Dinas Emrys in Eryri.

1204 — Battle of Catalaunian Fields. Armorican, Roman and Midgard armies defeat a flock of Great Dragons.

1218 — Red Dragon discovered under Dinas Emrys.

1204—1244 — The Great Cull. Nearly all dragons within the Imperium are destroyed.

1210—1244 — Imperator Majorian reconquers most of Southern Gaul, Hispania and Mauretania from the local warlords. His military and economic reforms strengthen the Imperium.

1217—1239 — A kingdom of Suessiones thrives in Northern Gaul.

1239 — Suessiones unite with Armorica. In a battle that ensues this year, the two Gallic kingdoms, with some help from Arthur, defeat invading king Clovis of Franks.

1243 — Battle of Mount Badon. Red Dragons of the Prydain defeat the White Dragons of the Seaxe. The latter are allowed to settle peacefully.

1243—1253 — Arthur conquers Eriu and the Picts, becomes the High King of All Islands

1244—1269 — Imperator Gundobad. His rule was focused on pushing the dragons out of southern Gaul and reducing their threat to Rome.

1250—1450 — Age of Unbridled Flame

1269—1271 — Sack of Rome. While the legions fight the wild dragons along the Rhine, Midgardians cross the Alps and invade Italia. Imperator Gundobad dies in retreat.

1271—1279 — Imperator Justin I moves the court permanently to Constantinople.

1294 — A plague erupts in the North, devastating the Barbarians.

1318 — Imperator Justinian begins a bloody campaign to recapture the West of the Empire.

1327—1329 — Justinian's chief general Lucius Tiberius fights Frollo of Armorica over the Alpine passes and access to southern Gaul. Defeated Frollo agrees to become a Roman governor.

1328 — Beowulf the Geat kills and is killed by a dragon. On his deathbed, he grants his kingdom to Arthur.

1329 — Arthur defeats Frollo and conquers the province he rules. Prydain settlers move into Armorica, calling the land Breizh, with a capital at Ker Ys.

1331 — Lucius Tiberius is chosen as the new Imperator.

1333 — With the help of the Geats, Arthur conquers the home land of the Varyaga clans. Their chieftains move east, where they will later establish cities along the trade route to Constantinople.

1335 — Imperator Lucius Tiberius defeated by Arthur. For two years, Rome is under Arthur's rule.

1337 — Arthur converts to Mithraism. Incited by this, Mordred the Heathen betrays him and destroys the gates to Faerie Kingdom in Brycheiniog. Arthur dies and is buried at Ynys Enlli. His Empire crumbles as the energies from the shattering gates awake the dragons once again. The Dragon Age begins.

1340—1453 — Rome manages to keep most of its possessions south of Alps—Danube line, but the rest of the West falls under the shadow of the

Dragon Age. The Mithraist religion spreads beyond the borders of the Empire as men flee to stone caves of the mithraeums to hide from dragons. All local Gods are turned into demons to be defeated by the Bull—Slayer. The faithful become dominated by a clergy hierarchy based in Rome.

1369 — With the death of Constantine, Arthur's son, the Prydain kingdom splits. The title of the king falls to the ruling house in Gwynedd.

1375 — A prophet in Central Persia revives the ancient cult of Azi Dahaka, Great Dragon. Azian Dragon Riders sweep through the Persia and northern Africa.

1392 — Rome loses Egypt to the Azi.

1403 — The Utigurs invade Dacia and Thracia.

1405 — Rome loses Carthage to the Azi.

1438 — Battle of Dun Nechtain halts the Seaxe advance north.

1400—2000 Age of Azian domination. The Azian magi bring Elemental Wizardry and Thaumaturgy — forgotten after the Mithraists' coming to power — back to the West.

Wars in Iberia, Sicilia, southern Gaul, Balkans. Vasconians defeat Azians with help of their mountain dragons.

Universities teaching Mystic Arts sprout in Italia and Breizh.

The organized Mithraic church in Rome sees it as heresy and an attempt to disrupt the Empire from within.

1500—1550 Offa's Dyke is built as eternal boundary between Seaxe and Prydain.

1521 — Karl Store, chieftain of the Franks, unites all the tribes of Midgard and is elected king.

1543 — Karl conquers vast territories to the North and East of his kingdom.

1561 — Karl enters Rome, marries Imperatrix Irene and crowns himself Imperator.

1581 — Rome under Karl extends back into Pannonia, and further towards Bohemia.

1597 — Rhodri Mawr reunites all of Prydain west of the Dyke.

1615 — Rodrig conquers Eastern Slavs establishing Khaganat of Varyaga, soon spreading from Sapmi in the north, through Nygard to Koenugard in the south.

1681 — With death of Imperator Ludovicus, Midgard and Breizh split from Rome. War of Four Kings (Midgard, Breizh, Rome and Constantinople).

1650—1700 — Kabar invasions. The Kabars are confined to the eastern part of Pannonia plain.

1681—1778 — Rome under Macedonian dynasty expands northwards across Carpathian Mountains. Mesco of Polania becomes a loyal vassal.

1750 — Norsemen sailors cross the Western Ocean and begin to colonize Helluland, Markland and Vinland.

1768 — Imperator Basil II. Vanquishes the Utigurs and regains control over Thracia and Dacia, and fights with the Khaganat of Varyaga over the Red Ruthenia. Imperium Romanum at its greatest extent since Constantin. Basil moves the capital back to Rome.

1774 — Boleslaus of Polania elected King of Midgard.

1788 — Chief Maslav defeats Rome—supported armies of King Lambert of Midgard and establishes a Pagan kingdom of Venedia, uniting Slavs and Prussians living around the Suebic Sea. After this defeat, the duchy of Polania is mostly incorporated into Midgard.

1796 — Maslav's daughter marries Harthacnut's son and allies with the Vikings of Jomsborg against Niflheimr. Their alliance expands west of Oder.

1819 — Harold Hardrada, king of Niflheimr and Venedia, invades the Seaxe kingdom of Dracaland.

1820—1830— Bleddyn ap Cynfyn fights the Norsemen.

1850—2150 — The Arab Wars: a series of campaigns in which Rome fights for the corridor along the Red Sea, to connect the Empire with the rich trade ports of Axum and an entrance to the Indian Ocean. Several Rome— dependent principalities established along the Red Sea.

1889 — Owain the Wyrmslayer destroys the Norse Dragons at Crug Mawr. The Seaxe cast off the Norse rule, with the Breizh soon following suit. The Norse nobles, however, continue to have influence in the Dracaland.

Venedia elects a prince of the Pomeranian family as its chieftain.

1895 — The School of Dragonslaying established near Llambed in Gwynedd.

1923 — Madoc ab Owain sails to the New World and establishes a Prydain colony of Tyr Gorllewin, south of Vinland. The colonists then mix with the locals and their dragons go feral.

1928 — In Yamato, a young warrior named Yoshitsune kills his first dragon in Kurama.

1938 — The Battle of Dan-no-Ura ends the bloody Genpei Wars, over the course of which most dragons in Yamato perish.

1984 — Mysterious Inquisition rampages throughout the Imperium. The wizards flee Iberia, Provincia and Italia to the north and into Azian lands.

2000 — Rome celebrates the Second Millenium.

2004 — The Horse Lords invade Varyaga and Pannonia, but are repelled at a great cost.

2000—2100 Wizards fleeing from persecution into the mountains of Vasconia, on the northern coast of Iberia, invent and develop Weather Magic.

2011 — Eadmund III's attempts to bring continental style of rule results in the rebellion of his earls.

2017 — Battle of Lewes. Llywelyn II unites with Norse—Seaxe earl Alexander Stronghill against king Eadmund III, last of the Wessex line. Eadmund III dies in battle. Alexander establishes the dynasty of Stronghills on Lundenburgh throne. His daughter marries Llywellyn. Eadweard flees to his northern domain of Loncastre.

2017 — 2214 — Kings of the Seaxe elected by Witan parliament.

2036 — Llywelyn II defeats Eadweard the Last's dragons in battles of Moel—y—Don and Conwy.

2045 — The Llambed College starts teaching Applied Dracology instead of Dragonslaying.

2048 — A brief civil war between Henry I Stronghill (who ascended to Gwynedd throne based on Llywelyn's will) and Madog ap Llywelyn.

2049 — Gwenlian I, daughter of Henry Stronghill, gains the Lundenburgh throne. First union of Gwynedd and Dracaland.

2049—2137 — Pictish Wars: Loncastrians intervene in a succession dispute in Alba and battle for supremacy of the North with Picts. Without dragons, eventually they and all their lands (from Cumbria to Jorvik) fall under Alba control.

2073 — Vasconian sailors begin the Age of Discovery by sailing to Tyr Gorllewin (Cantre'r Madoc) and Vinland — and back.

2137 — House Loncastre and Kings of Alba unite into one family, as Robert, son of Eadweard Lancaster and Marjorie Mar, conquers all the land north of Humber.

2150 — Kalmar Union. Niflheimr and Midgard thrones united, to prevent the claims to the Niflheimr throne by the kings of Alba.

2152 — The southern Dracaland kingdom is divided upon death of Llywelyn son of Gwenlian. Gwynedd remains with house Aberffraw (Owain Glyndwr) while Dracaland falls to Llywelyn's cousin, Henry II of Corieltauvi.

2152—2214 Sixty Years War: House Loncastre fights Norsemen over the claims to their ancestral lands in Niflheimr and Alba (claim of Alba kings). Breizh and Venedia join the war against Midgard.

2159 — Vlad III, ruler of the Marca Balcana, reawakens Dacian dragons and halts Azian march into Europe.

2206 — Constantinople falls to Azi Shahr. Imperator Constantine V killed in defence of his capital. Frederik III of Pannonia becomes the new Imperator of Rome. Most Balkans are conquered by Azians.

2214 — At the end of the Sixty Years War, Midgard becomes greatly diminished. Loncastrians gain monetary compensation and the Norse colony at Vinland, Venedia gains Sapmi and Silesia, Breizh expands eastwards to Rhine and Alps.

2214—2238 — The War of Three Thorns. Three kingdoms vie for succession: Picts (thistle), Saxons (rose) and Gwynedd (gorse)

2214 — Having secured his position in the North, Eadweard Loncastre invades the South with help of Richard Warwick and defeats the last of the Stronghills (Henry IV). He is elected king of all Seaxe, but his rule is unpopular.

2220—2326 — A Civil War erupts in Yamato.

2224 — Battle of Barnet. Richard Warwick defeats Eadweard, with help from the Prydain.

2235 — Warwick recaptures most of Loncashire and Jorvikshire from Alba.

2238 — Harri ap Edwrd Tudur, or Harri the Uniter, prince of Gwynedd, defeats Warwick on Bosworth Field. Second Act of Union between Gwynedd and Dracaland.

2245—2263 — Across the Ocean, Rome begins the conquest of the Carib Isles and northern shores of the newly discovered southern continent.

2258 — A wizard Lutherius conjures his ninety theses at Mythraeum in Nuremberg.

2263 — The Aztecs summon their Blood God who turns most of their Empire into a pool of blood. The Romans halt their advance.

2264 — The Vasconians capture the port of Goa in Bharata.

2277 — 2401 — The growing conflict between wizards and the Sun Priests erupts into the Wizardry Wars.

2286 — Arthur II Tudur separates Dracaland from the Sun Church.

2288 — The Vasconians capture the port of Haojing in Qin.

2296 — The Vasconians land in Yamato.

2310 — A Sun Priest known only as Pater Franc discovers ancient rites of Necromancy in Hellas and Marca Balcana. The secret knowledge is soon used in the wars against the Wizards and the Azi.

2313—2356 The Arch—wizard Dee co—rules Dracaland with Queen Eilwen I.

2317 — First mention of the Grey Hoods, inspired by Dee, who want to combine Mithraic orthodoxy with Dragon worship and wizardry.

2321 — Oda enters the Yamato capital of Heian and establishes a puppet Taikun under his command.

2323 — Vasconian outpost in Yokoseura is attacked by unknown assailants and burned down with all inhabitants. Western traders move to Kiyo.

2326 — Takeda Shingen is killed by his own personal assassin, Chiyome.

2328 — After victorious Battle of Nagashino, Oda conquers most of Yamato except Uesugi domain.

2331 — Uesugi dies in mysterious circumstances.

2335 — Oda is killed at Honnoji. His lieutenant Taiko gains power.

2338 — Dracalish colony of Roanoke established in Tyr Gorllewin.

2341 — Vasconian invasion fleet heading for Dracaland is destroyed by the magic of Witch Doideag.

2351 — Taiko dies. Tokugawa, another of Oda's lieutenants, bids for power.

2353 — Tokugawa wins the battle of Sekigahara and unites Yamato under his rule.

2356— Eilwen I Tudur dies without issue. Domnall VII, the king of Picts, ascends to the throne of Dracaland as Domnall I.

2357 — Dee is banished from court and sails to New World.

2360 — The colony of New Noviomagus established by the Bataavians in the New World.

2373—2393 — The Yokai War in Yamato results in destruction of all magical creatures.

2374 — The Mayflower journey brings Grey Hoods to Roanoke. They, and the other colonists, are never heard from again.

2382 — Dracaland intervenes in the Wizardry War in Breizh and relieves the siege of Ar'Rochel.

2391—2392 — The Shimabara Rebellion in Yamato.

2393 — Yamato is surrounded by the impenetrable Sea Maze.

2400 — A Wizard army captures Castle Aberteifi, the last stronghold of the Sun Priests in Gwynedd. Many monsters are released from its dungeons and disappear into the marshes.

2401 — Peace of Westfall. Under the terms of peace, all necromancy in Europe is to be destroyed and forgotten. Lands north of the Imperium retain freedom to study Wizardry, but it's subdued in the Imperium. Technological gap between North and South widens. Picts and Eriu remain anti—wizard, and Eogan I son of Domnall tries to introduce anti—wizardry laws.

2403 — Boym the Venedian reaches Qin, witnessing the fall of the ruling dynasty.

2406 — Cromwell abolishes Dracaland monarchy under Eogan I.

2414 — New Qin dynasty surrounds the country with the Haijin barrier, excluding the Vasconian outpost at Haojing.

2438 — Eogan II tries to win back his southern throne and dies.

2443 — Darien Scheme. Alba establishes a colony in the Isthmus of Darien, quickly becoming a new colonial power.

2465 — Lord Protector Richard Cromwell dies. War of Succession. With money from the Darien scheme Eithne I leads an invasion into Dracaland.

2467 — Monarchy is re—established with Act of Settlement under George I, a Midgardian duke of House Welf—Este. Distantly related to both Eithne I and Eilwen I, George I sits both on the Dragon Throne and the Stag Throne. The cousins of Eithne I retreat to the northern Highlands.

2480 — George II ascends to throne.

2493 — Vitus Bering establishes the city of Alexisborg in Avacha Bay on the coast of Yupi peninsula.

2498 — Eogan III, Duke of Arcaibh, tries to win back his southern throne.

2513 — George III ascends to throne.

2529 — Gorllewin begin their secret breeding programme, using feral dragons from Cantre'r Madoc and ancient Norse dragons from Vinland.

2539 — Dracaland buys a province of Tanbaek from Varyaga to establish industrial base in Tanais Basin.

2542 — Republican revolution in Breizh.

2548—2568 — What will later be known as the Kyrnosian War erupts when Rome invades Breizh, weakened by the recent revolution. The invading army is led by a general from Kyrnosia called Neapolion. The Dracaland sends a fleet into the Roman Sea.

2558 — Battle of Cape Spartel. Dracaland destroys the Roman navy.

2559 — Neapolion overthrows Habsburg dynasty and becomes the Imperator of Rome. Rome conquers most of Breizh, Batavia, Midgard and Venedia, marches against Varyaga and Dracaland.

2560 — Most Bataavian colonies given over to Rome.

2561 — *Phaeton* incident in Yamato.

2565—2583 — Anti—thaumaturgy rebellions in northern Dracaland and Brigstow.

2568 — Neapolion defeated and Rome retreats to old borders. Neapolion remains Imperator.

2571 — The Bharata Wars end with Dracaland victory and control of the northern part of the subcontinent.

2574 — Neapolion II crowned Imperator. His realm is largely uneventful.

2592 — The *Carnatic* incident sparks a Dracalish—Qin War, which ends with the total victory by Dracaland.

2594 — The colony of Fragrant Harbour and the Fan Yu trading factory are established.

2604 — Neapolion III crowned Imperator. He embarks on a new colonization effort, sending Vasconian ships out into the seas again.

2605 — Hjalmar Nobelius invents a submarine. Admiral Otterson sails from Alexisborg on a secret mission to Yamato.

2607 — War breaks out in the Scythian Sea between the Varyaga and Azi Shahr. The Heavenly Army captures Xijiang. MFS *Ladon* sails from Brigstow.

APPENDIX IV:
MITHRAIST LITURGIC CALENDAR

March 20-25: Spring Equinox/Nowruz. Mithras rises from the Otherworld, reborn through the rock. At that moment, the powers of the Bull and Mithras are equal (they are both in the world).

April 1: Veneralia/Yasna of Venus, Feast of Immortality, Love and Plants. The Nymph Degree Initiation.

May 1: Isis Bona Dea, Feast of Grain Sowing.

May 9-13: Lemuria, Festival of the Dead.

May 15: Mercuralia/Yasna of Mercury, Feast of Abundance, Riches, Spring rains and Water. The Crow Degree Initiation.

June 15: Vestalia, Festival of Isis Vesta celebrating her arrival to the birthing house in the Otherworld.

June 20-25: Summer Solstice/Tiregan. The most important feast of the year begins the Summer Cycle of festivals. Mithras shoots at the Bull, producing rain from the rock. He later chases the Bull into the cavern and kills it. Sol comes down to Earth to witness the fight and feasts with Mithras. It is also the day when Isis is the most powerful, as Mithras is tired after the fight and busy with the feast. This is when she gives birth to good spirits and minor Gods conceived during the previous year's wedding night. She blesses the Earth with the bull's blood to ensure good harvest.

August 15: Dianalia/Yasna of Luna, Feast of Devotion, Compassion, Harvest and Earth. The Persea Degree Initiation.

August 25: Vulcanalia, Feast of Burning Sun, celebrating Sol's arrival to feast with Mithras.

September 9: Ludi Romani/Yasna of Jupiter, Feast of Wisdom, Justice and Animals. The Lion Degree Initiation.

September 20-25: Autumn Equinox/Merhgan There is a great feast, where Isis and Mithras renew their wedding vows. This is the best day for weddings and love-making. During the wedding night, Mithras "dies" and descends into the Otherworld. Again, Bull and Mithras are equal (they are both not in the world).

October 15: Fontanalia/Abanagan, Feast of Autumn Rains.

November 13: Feroniae/Atargan, Feast of Holy Fire.

December 17: Saturnalia/Yasna of Saturn, Feast of Death, Passing of Time and Metals. The Pater Degree Initiation.

December 20-25: Winter Solstice/Yalda. The Bull is released into the world, along with many demons. But with it is released the hope of Mithras's return: his "birth". The veil of the Night is pierced where the Bull breaks out, and the first light from Mithras's underground abode promises his return.

February 14: Lupercalia, Feast of Faunus, Wolf and Erotic Love, celebrating Mithras and Isis last night in the Otherworld.

March 1: Faeria Marti/Yasna of Mars, Feast of Truth, Bravery, War and Fire. The Soldier Degree Initiation.

By James Calbraith

The Year of the Dragon

Other works

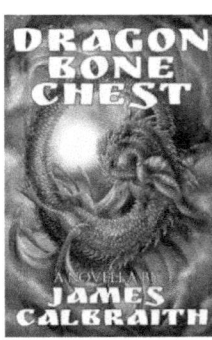 

For more information about the author and books please visit:

jamescalbraith.com

Or sign up for the newsletter at:

tinyletter.com/jcalbraith